William Fairfax

Handbook to Australasia

SALZWASSER
VERLAG

William Fairfax

Handbook to Australasia

Reprint of the original, first published in 1859.

1st Edition 2022 | ISBN: 978-3-37512-885-2

Verlag (Publisher): Salzwasser Verlag GmbH, Zeilweg 44, 60439 Frankfurt, Deutschland
Vertretungsberechtigt (Authorized to represent): E. Roepke, Zeilweg 44, 60439 Frankfurt, Deutschland
Druck (Print): Books on Demand GmbH, In de Tarpen 42, 22848 Norderstedt, Deutschland

HANDBOOK

TO

AUSTRALASIA;

BEING A BRIEF

Historical and Descriptive Account

OF

VICTORIA, TASMANIA, SOUTH AUSTRALIA, NEW SOUTH WALES,
WESTERN AUSTRALIA, AND NEW ZEALAND:

EDITED

BY WILLIAM FAIRFAX.

WITH A MAP OF THE AUSTRALASIAN COLONIES.

Melbourne:

PRINTED AND PUBLISHED BY WILLIAM FAIRFAX AND CO.,

NEXT "ARGUS" OFFICE, COLLINS STREET.

1859.

PREFACE.

The object of this work is to supply a narrative of facts. The design of the editor has been to furnish a supplement to *Bradshaw's Guide to Victoria*, which should contain as brief, but yet as comprehensive an account as possible, of the past history and present condition of the Australian Colonies.

It was originally intended that this *Handbook* should not exceed 200 pages. But when the project became known, it excited so warm an interest as to lead to many suggestions that came from various parts of the colonies—suggestions too valuable to be disregarded. But in the endeavour to embody them the work has increased to its present dimensions, necessitating the proprietors, very reluctantly, to raise the price.

Some apology may be deemed necessary for the delay in the publication. But the fact is, the information had to be obtained from diversified sources, depending on such a variety of contingencies, which the editor could not control, that the successive postponement, though very vexatious, has been unavoidable.

It will be readily perceived that a considerable prominence has been given, in the *Handbook*, to Victoria. This has arisen partly from the rapid progress it has made, especially since the discovery of the gold-fields, in the acquisition of all the materials of civilization and influence, perhaps unsurpassed in the annals of colonization, which rendered it needful that ampler and more specific data should be given, from which to form an accurate judgment; and partly from the fact that the editor, being a resident in Victoria, has had much readier access to the sources of intelligence than he could possibly realize in reference to the other colonies. He peremptorily, however, disclaims any predominant wish that it should have been so. In fact it was primarily designed that each colony should occupy an equal space in the work, but this was soon found to be impossible.

A large number of books has been written upon Australia.* The editor, however, has depended but little on these in preparing the present work, but has had recourse for the most part to the first sources of information. Some quotations, however, have been made, but this general acknowledgment must suffice where a more definite reference is not given.

Especial acknowledgments are due to His Excellency Sir Henry Barkly, for his courtesy in recommending the Heads of Departments to supply the various details given under the Government of Victoria. The recommendation was cheerfully responded to, and some very important new tables, &c., were prepared. The editor is also under obligations to many gentlemen and friends for valuable assistance afforded, to whom he takes this opportunity of expressing his sincere thanks. But he has been laid under an interdict by some of them from mentioning their names. In order therefore to avoid the appearance of invidiousness, he has been compelled to satisfy himself with this general expression of his gratitude.

---

* See catalogue as per contents.

It will be perceived by some of the contributors that the copy they kindly supplied has been in some instances altered, for reasons too numerous to mention, but principally that the character of the whole might be as similar as possible. Defects it is very likely will be observed, but the reader will notice these with candour, when he is reminded that the daily attention of the editor is absorbed by business and other claims, and that this work, for the most part, has been prepared during the hours of night. But his one object has been, whatever it might cost him, to give as faithful a view as possible of these colonies. How far he has succeeded others must judge. Some points of interest may, 'tis true, have been omitted, but if so, it is from accident and not from design.

This publication is an experiment. If successful, it may be issued yearly, as *Bradshaw's Guide to Victoria* is issued monthly, to which frequent reference is made in this volume in the chapter on Victoria. But if not issued yearly, it may appear after certain lapses of time, as changes in the different colonies may demand. It will afford the editor, therefore, peculiar gratification to be favored with letters expressive of opinions, containing additional intelligence, or suggesting improvements.

The expenses of getting up the work have been heavy, and a large sale must be effected before the proprietors can anticipate the least profit. But, whatever may be the fate of this *Handbook*, the editor will have the satisfaction of knowing, that no efforts have been spared to furnish as comprehensive and accurate a compendium as possible of the history and present condition of these splendid colonies of the British empire.

Melbourne, December 18, 1858.

NOTE.—It may be necessary to explain or apologise for the use of numeral characters in marking the first 140 pages of this work. The Tasmanian information having been completed first, it was printed; but it was afterwards found that the space originally allotted to Victoria was quite inadequate; this plan was therefore adopted in order to surmount the difficulty.

CONTENTS.

VICTORIA.

VICTORIA.—(*Continued.*)

VICTORIA.—(*Continued.*)

TASMANIA.

SOUTH AUSTRALIA.

NEW SOUTH WALES.

WESTERN AUSTRALIA.

NEW ZEALAND.

ERRATUM.

Page xliii, line sixteen from the bottom, *for* Sir R. Nickle *read* Mr. J. V. F. L. Foster.

CALENDAR FOR 1859.

Month																																
JAN.	Day of Month.	1	2	3	4	5	6	7	8	9	10	11	12	13	14	15	16	17	18	19	20	21	22	23	24	25	26	27	28	29	30	31
	Day of Week.	Sa	S	M	Tu	W	Th	F	Sa	S	M	Tu	W	Th	F	Sa	S	M	Tu	W	Th	F	Sa	S	M	Tu	W	Th	F	Sa	S	M
FEB.	Day of Month.	1	2	3	4	5	6	8	7	9	10	11	12	13	14	15	16	17	18	19	20	21	22	23	24	25	26	27	28			
	Day of Week.	Tu	W	Th	F	Sa	S	M	Tu	W	Th	F	Sa	S	M	Tu	W	Th	F	Sa	S	M	Tu	W	Th	F	Sa	S	M			
MAR.	Day of Month.	1	2	3	4	5	6	7	8	9	10	11	12	13	14	15	16	17	18	19	20	21	22	23	24	25	26	27	28	29	30	31
	Day of Week.	Tu	W	Th	F	Sa	S	M	Tu	W	Th	F	Sa	S	M	Tu	W	Th	F	Sa	S	M	Tu	W	Th	F	Sa	S	M	Tu	W	Th
APR.	Day of Month.	1	2	3	4	5	6	7	8	9	10	11	12	13	14	15	16	17	18	19	20	21	22	23	24	25	26	27	28	29	30	
	Day of Week.	F	Sa	S	M	Tu	W	Th	F	Sa	S	M	Tu	W	Th	F	Sa	S	M	Tu	W	Th	F	Sa	S	M	Tu	W	Th	F	Sa	
MAY.	Day of Month.	1	2	3	4	5	6	7	8	9	10	11	12	13	14	15	16	17	18	19	20	21	22	23	24	25	26	27	28	29	30	31
	Day of Week.	S	M	Tu	W	Th	F	Sa	S	M	Tu	W	Th	F	Sa	S	M	Tu	W	Th	F	Sa	S	M	Tu	W	Th	F	Sa	S	M	Tu
JUNE.	Day of Month.	1	2	3	4	5	6	7	8	9	10	11	12	13	14	15	16	17	18	19	20	21	22	23	24	25	26	27	28	29	30	
	Day of Week.	W	Th	F	Sa	S	M	Tu	W	Th	F	Sa	S	M	Tu	W	Th	F	Sa	S	M	Tu	W	Th	F	Sa	S	M	Tu	W	Th	
JULY.	Day of Month.	1	2	3	4	5	6	7	8	9	10	11	12	13	14	15	16	17	18	19	20	21	22	23	24	25	26	27	28	29	30	31
	Day of Week.	F	Sa	S	M	Tu	W	Th	F	Sa	S	M	Tu	W	Th	F	Sa	S	M	Tu	W	Th	F	Sa	S	M	Tu	W	Th	F	Sa	S
AUG.	Day of Month.	1	2	3	4	5	6	7	8	9	10	11	12	13	14	15	16	17	18	19	20	21	22	23	24	25	26	27	28	29	30	31
	Day of Week.	M	Tu	W	Th	F	Sa	S	M	Tu	W	Th	F	Sa	S	M	Tu	W	Th	F	Sa	S	M	Tu	W	Th	F	Sa	S	M	Tu	W
SEPT.	Day of Month.	1	2	3	4	5	6	7	8	9	10	11	12	13	14	15	16	17	18	19	20	21	22	23	24	25	26	27	28	29	30	
	Day of Week.	Th	F	Sa	S	M	Tu	W	Th	F	Sa	S	M	Tu	W	Th	F	Sa	S	M	Tu	W	Th	F	Sa	S	M	Tu	W	Th	F	
OCT.	Day of Month.	1	2	3	4	5	6	7	8	9	10	11	12	13	14	15	16	17	18	19	20	21	22	23	24	25	26	27	28	29	30	31
	Day of Week.	Sa	S	M	Tu	W	Th	F	Sa	S	M	Tu	W	Th	F	Sa	S	M	Tu	W	Th	F	Sa	S	M	Tu	W	Th	F	Sa	S	M
NOV.	Day of Month.	1	2	3	4	5	6	7	8	9	10	11	12	13	14	15	16	17	18	19	20	21	22	23	24	25	26	27	28	29	30	
	Day of Week.	Tu	W	Th	F	Sa	S	M	Tu	W	Th	F	Sa	S	M	Tu	W	Th	F	Sa	S	M	Tu	W	Th	F	S	S	M	Tu	W	
DEC.	Day of Month.	1	2	3	4	5	6	7	8	9	10	11	12	13	14	15	16	17	18	19	20	21	22	23	24	25	26	27	28	29	30	31
	Day of Week.	Th	F	Sa	S	M	Tu	W	Th	F	Sa	S	M	Tu	W	Th	F	Sa	S	M	Tu	W	Th	F	Sa	S	M	Tu	W	Th	F	Sa

VICTORIA (Port Phillip).

POSITION AND BOUNDARIES.

Victoria, the most southern settlement of Australia, is situate between the parallels of 141° and 150° east longitude, and 34° and 39° south latitude. Beginning at the extreme north-western point on the River Murray, 34° south latitude, and 141° east longitude, it is separated from South Australia by a divisional line which passes down to the sea-coast near the mouth of the River Glenelg, approaching 38° south latitude, so that its south-westernmost point is 38° south latitude, and 141° east longitude. Its southern boundary is traced by a very sinuous coast line, which separates it from Tasmania by Bass's Straits, its extreme southernmost point being Wilson's Promontory, in 39° 17′ south latitude, 146° 25′ east longitude. From Wilson's Promontory, the south-east side is bounded by the Southern Ocean as far as Cape Howe, 150° east longitude, 37° 30′ south latitude. On its northern side it is limited by a straight line drawn from Cape Howe to the head of the River Murray, near Mount Kosciusko, from which point that river constitutes its divisional line from New South Wales.

HISTORY.

Lieutenant Murray, R. N., of the brig *Lady Nelson*, in February 1802, first discovered the waters of Port Phillip, and after a cursory survey, named the point at the entrance "Nepean," and the hill seen from the Heads, "Arthur's Seat," names which they still bear. On the 27th of April, 1802, Lieut. Flinders, having entered Port Phillip Bay, and supposing he was the first to have discovered it, made an accurate survey of its waters. Visiting the hills near Geelong, he named them Station Peaks, and the peninsula, Indented Head. Early in 1803, the Lieut. Governor of New South Wales, Philip Gidleigh King, Capt. R.N., despatched the Surveyor-General, Mr. Grimes, to examine and report on the capabilities of the bay, when he found the river at its head, now called the Yarra. Thirty-two years afterwards, in 1835,

Mr. J. P. Fawkner found, near the falls, part of an iron pot, buried some eight inches in the soil, which had probably been left by the party of Flinders or Grimes. This splendid bay was first called Port Phillip in honor of the Governor, Capt. Philip G. King.

In 1802, Lord Hobart, Secretary for the Colonies, acting on the advice of Mr. Capper, one of the clerks in his office, projected the formation of a new settlement at Port Phillip, Bass's Straits, the chief town of which colony should transmit his name to posterity. In the latter part of the same year, the *Calcutta*, a vessel of war of 50 guns, was commissioned, and commenced taking in convicts at the Nore, from Woolwich, and after proceeding to Spithead completed her complement of about 360 male convicts from the Portsmouth hulks. The merchant ship *Ocean* of 600 tons, Capt. Mathews, was chartered to assist in the carriage of stores, settlers, and civil officers; the two vessels were to take out provisions to last three years, including the voyage. In addition to the convicts there were between forty and fifty marines, some few free settlers, and about twenty-five women, wives of the marines, settlers, or convicts, together with about ten children. These, with a few Government officers, were the first settlers of Port Phillip. The *Calcutta* arrived at Port Phillip Heads on the 9th or 10th of October, 1803, the *Ocean* a few days prior. The Governor, Lieut.-Col. Collins, R.M., commenced landing the people a few days after, having cleared a plot of ground for the camp, tents being erected to lodge all, whether free or bond. The landing was completed on the 19th of October. The site of the settlement was on Point Nepean, about five or six miles within the heads. There was no fresh water at that spot, but it was discovered under Arthur's Seat, when the *Calcutta* took in water there, and proceeded to Sydney. The River Yarra was discovered and reported to Governor Collins by a runaway convict, who returned almost starved to death. A number of the convicts took to the woods, and only one returned. On the 24th December, William Buckley and three others ran from the New Settlement; one of them, Charles Shore, a butcher, was shot at, wounded, and retaken; the others effected their escape. Buckley joined Batman's men on Indented Head in August, 1835, nearly thirty-two years after. He was of a stupid nature, and had not learned anything of the country except the mere coast line of the bay.

It was provided by Lord Hobart that if the Lieut. Governor was compelled to remove from his first landing place to any distance, he should receive five hundred guineas. This bait, and the absconding of some twenty convicts, determined the removal of the whole population to Van Diemen's Land. The Sydney Government, having previously surveyed the River Derwent, despatched, in August, 1803, Lieut. Bowen with some few marines, settlers, and convicts, to that port. On their recommendation, Governor Collins proceeded thither, but not approving of Risdon, the place selected by Lieut. Bowen, he fixed on Sullivan's Cove, where the landing of the people took place, February 16th, 1804. The *Ocean* transport was the vessel employed, in which the whole of the people, stores, &c., were removed in two trips, the last of which took place in June, 1804.

In 1824, Messrs. Hume and Hovell, squatters residing near Lake George, resolved to explore the southern part of New Holland. Pursuing their course, they kept on the western side, clear of the Australian Alps, discovered a fine river which they named the Hume, now called the Murray, crossed several smaller rivers, and eventually reached Port Phillip Bay, at the river Exe or Werribee, in December, 1824. Returning to Sydney, they reported having found a fine grazing country and an overland route to Western Port. An account of their discoveries was published in the "Sydney Gazette." Subsequently, however, it was discovered to be Port Phillip Bay, and not Western Port, they had touched upon. Their flattering account stimulated the Sydney Government to despatch Captain Wright with troops, convicts, &c., to form a settlement at Western Port; but as colonial governors and military men were not the best judges where to settle, or how to form a colony profitably in a new country, this also was given up, and the whole party removed to Sydney.

In 1834, the Messrs. Henty, of Launceston, sent over vessels, boats, and many able seamen, to form a whaling establishment at Portland Bay.* This was clearly the first permanent settlement of British subjects in this province. The Hentys have maintained their hold continuously from 1834 to the present day, their flocks and herds having increased surprisingly.

To Mr. John Batman, a gentleman who must rank with the Hentys as a pioneer, Victoria is exceedingly indebted. He had been for a long time endeavouring to obtain assistance to pass over and colonise Port Phillip, and in 1835 he succeeded in drawing the attention of persons in authority to his scheme. Governor Arthur suggested the organisation of a company to pass over and make some sort of bargain with the aborigines for the purchase of these lands, to form mighty squattages; and Mr. Joseph Tice Gellibrand, a barrister, ex-Attorney-General of Van Diemen's Land, one of the copartners, drew up a deed to be signed by the aborigines. The company, consisting of fourteen persons,†

---

* See particulars under heads of Portland, Warrnambool, and Belfast.

† The names of the shareholders of the company, whom Mr. Henry Batman was employed by and associated with, from Van Diemen's Land, were as follows:—1. Charles Swanston, Captain E.I.C.S., Member of Governor Arthur's Council. 2. T. Bannister, Sheriff. 3. James Simpson,

subscribed funds to fit out a small schooner of about 15 tons (*Rebecca*) in which to send over Mr. Henry Batman, some Sydney aborigines, and a few European servants, with looking glasses, beads, and a few bags of flour for barter. Fawkner and his party tried to obtain a passage over before Batman started, and failed. Captain Cain disappointed them, and they missed the *Sally Ann* which was chartered for Portland Bay by the Messrs. Henty, so that eventually Mr. Batman and his party left in the *Rebecca*, Captain Harwood, May the 12th, but were wind-bound at Port Sorell until the 26th or 28th May; then they ran over in thirty hours, and landed at Indented Head, near Queenscliffe. Batman selected a spot near that for the company's settlement, and sent the *Rebecca* to Hobson's Bay; thence he travelled overland by Geelong until he made the Saltwater river, crossed it, passed over the Moonee Ponds, and finally made the Merri Creek, near where the Yan Yean waterpipes are placed. At that place Batman fell in with the brothers Jagga Jagga and some more aborigines, where, about the 5th or 6th of June, 1835, he produced his deed, prepared by the ex-Attorney-General, J. T. Gellibrand, and induced the poor ignorant men to make some marks upon it as signatures. Batman stated that he had taken with him some Sydney blacks, whom he employed to read over and translate this document to the Port Phillip aborigines. The deed professed that the aborigines had marked in Batman's presence the whole boundaries set out therein, viz:—"All that tract of country situate and being at Port Phillip, running from the branch of the river at the top of the port, about seven miles from the mouth of the river, forty miles north-east, and from thence forty miles across Iramoo Downs or Plains, and from thence south-west across Mount Villamanata to Geelong Harbor at the head of the same, and containing 500,000 acres, more or less." This being all traversed over, the trees were marked, &c., in part of two days and one night, besides other forty miles from Geelong to the vessel at Gellibrand's Point. Mr. J. Batman was then laboring under the disease that cut

---

a Police Magistrate. 4. Joseph Tice Gellibrand, ex-Attorney-General Barrister.—5. Henry Arthur, Collector of Customs, nephew of Governor Arthur. 6. J. and W. Robertson, Drapers, one share. 7. John Hilder Wedge, Government Surveyor. 8. John Sinclair, Overseer of Convicts, Launceston. 9. John Thomas Collicott, Postmaster, Hobart Town. 10. Anthony Cottrell, Chief Constable, Launceston. 11. W. G. Sams, Sheriff, Launceston. 12. M. Connolly, a dealer. 13. George Mercer, an E. I. Officer, residing in Britain. 14. John Batman, Farmer, near Ben Lomond. And as the lands were divided into seventeen lots, it gave good color to the rumor that three lots were reserved as bribes to the British Ministers to allow the purchase from the aborigines to stand good. But notwithstanding all Governor Arthur's interest, backed up by Capt. Swanston and the arguments of Mr. Gellibrand, in an interview with Sir Richard Bourke, the deed was declared null. But £7000 worth of land was given to the company as expenses repaid.

short his career. He subsequently produced another deed signed by the Jagga Jagga brothers and others, selling to him and the co-partners the whole of Indented Head, called 100,000 acres. This deed, a copy of which is printed in "Arden's Port Phillip," states that the aborigines and Batman's men marked the trees due south from the head of Geelong Bay, a distance of ten miles, omitting to account for the Barwon river, which was subsequently found to cross this track, forming a wide sheet of water. Moreover, the Jagga Jagga brothers were men of the western hill tribes, and could have no pretensions to these lands, but would most likely have suffered death had they presumed to intrude thereon without previous notice and permission.

In July, 1835, a project to colonise Port Phillip entered the mind of Mr. J. P. Fawkner, who had been led to believe that fine grazing lands existed in the interior. He formed a party, consisting of Messrs. William and Samuel Jackson, Robert Hay Marr, George Evans, and Captain Lancy, who were willing to accompany him. He purchased the *Enterprize* from Mr. John Anderson Brown, and as soon as she could be got ready, embarked the party at Launceston. Fawkner and his party left Launceston about the middle of July. He was taken ill during the first few days of the voyage, and a foul wind driving the vessel back to George Town, he there landed with one of his horses, leaving two on board, having previously filled up a code of directions for the guidance of Captain Lancey, as his agent, in charge of his servants and goods, with full directions how to proceed with the survey, and on no account to settle except upon a permanent running stream of good water. The party searched the whole range of Western Port, and then commenced on the eastern side of Port Phillip, until they found the Yarra, where they fixed on what is now known as Batman's Hill, marking out ten acres for each of the party, and drew lots for the plots. Having pitched their tents, they proceeded to form a garden, and plant out a large quantity of fruit trees, &c., shipped by Mr. Fawkner, and within one week from the landing, August 29, 1835, a garden was formed, trees planted, seeds sown, and five acres of ground ploughed, harrowed, and sown with wheat. Subsequently, Mr. Fawkner removed his establishment, and fixed his tent at the rear of the site of the present Custom House (where he opened the first public house), in order to be near the fresh water, and contiguous to the place where he moored his vessel, exactly opposite the present Yarra Hotel, in William-street. Shortly after Messrs. Lancey, Marr, Evans, and Wm. Jackson had settled, as directed, on the Yarra, Mr. J. H. Wedge came to them from Batman's station at Indented Head, the Sydney Blacks having reported the arrival of the *Enterprize*. He went back to the station, and immediately, accompanied by Henry Batman with men and stores, returned to the new settlement, and ordered Fawkner's party off his land. The Messrs. Lancey and Co., would not acknowledge his right to interfere, and therefore treated the threat with contempt.

The first cattle and sheep were landed from the *Norval* on November 10th, 1835, consisting of fifty pure Hereford cows, belonging to Dr. Thomson, and five hundred sheep, the property of Mr. Connolly, of Belfast. Messrs. Cowie, Stead, Steiglitz, Estcourt, and Ferguson came by this trip.

About March, 1836, Major Mitchell proceeded in his exploration of the interior of the country, passing from Sydney out to Portland Bay. He named the interior Australia Felix. Mr. George Evans, now a farmer on the Deep Creek, and Mr. Samuel Jackson, a wealthy squatter in the Portland district, are cognisant of the facts related above.

When Mr. Fawkner and his family, with the Lancey party, arrived at Port Phillip on October, 9, 1835, thirty-two years after his first arrival, he found the herbage so rich, and the country altogether so attractive, that he determined upon making it his home. Birds abounded on the water; ducks, teal, geese, swans, &c., were in thousands. The new colonists lived on board the *Enterprize* for a month, whilst a wooden house was being erected, with the materials brought over from Launceston. Batman's people lived in sod huts or tents. In November, Mr. John Batman came over to examine his vast squattage, and repeated his order, through his brother Henry, to Mr. Fawkner to remove off his land, he laying claim to all the lands on the north side of the Yarra. Upon refusal, he sent one of the Sydney aborigines to inform Fawkner that if he did not leave instantly he would drive him off by force of arms. This threat was treated very lightly. Whilst, however, Fawkner was building his house, Buckley, who had joined Batman's party at Indented Head, and now resided with them, sent out messengers and collected some two or three hundred blacks—men, women, and children; and about the same time the Goulburn, Barrabool, and Western Port blacks laid a plan to murder all the white people. One of the Melbourne aborigines, who had been kindly treated by Fawkner's party, and had received presents from them, came privately and gave information. Recourse was had to Wm. Buckley to learn the real nature of this communication, and it was found that the men were all armed and painted for war. Fawkner and Batman, in this emergency, collected and armed, entered into a treaty with these foes, on the condition that they should all quit the township and cross to the south side of the Yarra. The boats of the colonists put them over the river, the rest of the men standing as guards with loaded firearms.

The *Enterprize* was the first vessel, larger than a whale boat, that ever reached the basin at Melbourne, and it took the crew and passengers some days to gather and fix tea tree stakes, as water or river marks, by which to keep clear of the shoals.

Very few settlers and not much stock came over to Port Phillip during the remainder of the year 1835. In March, 1836, Dr. Thomson (now Mayor of Geelong), arrived with his family, and acted as an arbitrator by general consent. His tent was, in fact, the first police office in Melbourne. On June 1st, 1836, a council of the people was held, to frame regulations for their guidance; and the proposal of Messrs. Gellibrand and Swanston, to the Port Phillipians, to submit their property and personal liberty to the control of members of the Batman co-partnery, was rejected, on the motion of Mr. Fawkner. Dr. Thomson contemplating a removal to Geelong, Mr. James Simpson was appointed general arbitrator, and was to call in two assistants if he thought proper. A Mr Stewart, a Sydney magistrate, was present at this time, and was authorised to report upon the conduct of the colonists. Advantage was taken of his presence, and a petition forwarded through him to Governor Bourke, asking for the appointment of magistrates and police to maintain order, pointing out that the cost could be defrayed by levying duties on imported goods. Settlers and stock poured over as soon as it became known that Governor Sir Richard Bourke had disallowed the scheme of wresting the lands from the aborigines for a few looking glasses. Batman and his family came over in June, a house having been built for him at the first landing place. Constant employment in bringing over sheep was found for the *Adelaide* schooner, the *Henry* brig, the *Champion*, the *Enterprize* and others; and huts rose on all parts of the present town. The sheep were generally landed at Gellibrand's point, and then driven to their destination. Early in that year, Mr. Franks, one of the first emigrants in 1803, and his shepherd, were killed by some of the Goulburn tribe of blacks. Their station was at Cotterill's Sugarloaf, near the River Exe or Werribee. They were both killed at one moment by two men, who, pretending friendship, smote them down by driving their tomahawks into the back of their heads. A party was soon sent out after them, led by four of the Melbourne blacks, who recovered part of the property stolen, and took vengeance on some of the tribe to which the murderers belonged. The Flagstaff Hill was selected for a burial ground. The child of a man of the name of Goodman was the first who was buried by the Europeans at Melbourne. Mr. Franks and his man were interred there, attended by all the residents. In September, 1836, Sir Richard Bourke sent Captain Lonsdale, as police magistrate, with a party of soldiers and convicts, and with them Messrs. Webb, customs officer; Mr. Craig, Commissariat; D'Arcey, Russell and Darke, surveyors. The settlement was thus placed under legal British rule.

The extraordinary progress of the settlement was evidenced in 1837, when it was estimated that there was a population of 500, with 140,000 sheep, 2,500 cattle and 150 horses. Sir Richard Bourke, therefore, resolved on a tour of inspection, and in April of that year entered the bay on board the *Rattlesnake*, commanded by Captain Hobson, whose name, as a mark of honor, was given to the inlet. His Excellency also gave the name Williamstown, in honor of the reigning sovereign, to the proposed township at Hobson's Bay. Melbourne, the proposed metropolis of the district, was named by him after Lord Melbourne; and Geelong, the proposed township at the head of Corio Bay. The settlers waited on His Excellency, and every possible mark of respect was exhibited. Arrangements were made to put up portions of the surveyed allotments to public sale; and after having seen something of the interior, the Governor returned to Sydney.

The first land sale was held on June 1st, 1837. and realised from £18 to £78 per allotment; the second was held on 1st November, as a matter of indulgence on the part of the Governor:—since the sales of town and suburban allotments that were held in Sydney, a year later, realised prices that quadrupled those obtained in Melbourne.

In this year the colony had to mourn the loss of Joseph Tice Gellibrand, an able lawyer of some notoriety in Van Diemen's Land, who had been amongst the most energetic of those that promoted the colonization of Port Phillip. In company with another lawyer, Mr. Hesse, under the guidance of a shepherd, he started from Geelong for the interior. The party lost their way, and these two gentlemen, separated from their guide, and having wandered in the bush, were never more seen; although from scattered items of information, long afterwards obtained from the aborigines, there appears but little doubt that the unfortunate gentlemen perished a short time after leaving their guide, in the neighborhood of Lake Corangamite, which, in consequence of its saltness, they are said to have mistaken for an inlet of the sea.

From the earliest period Port Phillip became noted for the lively and bustling spirit that characterised the colonists. This tone of enterprise and go-a-headism soon made it apparent to the Sydney authorities that a mere police establishment was insufficient for the requirements of the province, and measures were taken to establish a local administration. C. J. LaTrobe was gazetted on 30th July, 1839, as superintendent, and on the 30th September he initiated, by his own arrival in Port Phillip, the political history of the colony. On the 2nd October the first interview took place between the superintendent and the colonists in the Auction Company's rooms, Collins-street, and no small amount of congratulation was felt by all in the event. Captain Lonsdale, who had previously acted as police magistrate, was advanced to the post of sub-treasurer; Mr. James Simpson succeeded to the vacant office of stipendiary magistrate; and Mr. Croke was constituted chief legal adviser.

The next movement of importance was a public meeting held in the store of Mr. Isaac Hind, on the 30th December, 1840, to take measures for the separation of Port Phillip from the government of New South Wales. It was felt that the incorporation of the southern province with the older colony was an accident arising from the action of Sir Richard Bourke in promptly linking the new settlement with the dependency he ruled, and not from any expressed opinion of the Imperial Government as to the propriety of this step. Port Phillip, indeed, lay within the boundary of the New South Wales Government; and the home authorities did not contravene the act of Sir R. Bourke. In point of political justice, however, the morality of the Sydney powers became questionable by the mal-appropriation of the revenues of the southern dependency to the aggrandisement of the middle district. They strove, in opposition to a royal order to that effect, to prevent the commanded separation ot the two districts in matters pertaining to the sales of land, so that the land revenue might be poured into the coffers of the Sydney government, and be appropriated to their purposes. The governor, sustained by the nominees of the Crown, and by the expressed opinion of a public meeting of the colonists, refused to do justice to Port Phillip. The spoliation suffered by this province, therefore, may be estimated by a comparison of the revenue from all sources, and the expenditure up to 1842, when it appeared that the total revenue was £616,895 11s. 8d; total expenditure, 459,411 5s 0½d.; leaving a balance of £157,484 6s. 7½d.; which was appropriated by New South Wales to its own purposes, Port Phillip losing to that extent. At the unanimous and enthusiastic meeting alluded to above a petition was adopted requesting the Imperial Government that the orders in council appointing the territorial boundaries of Port Phillip might be maintained, and that at the earliest possible period the separation of Port Phillip as a distinct colony should be effected. On the 1st March, 1841, a second meeting on this topic was held, at which an instrument was prepared, to be placed in the hands of the members of Parliament, in which the principles and statements of the Sydney magnates were combated, and the necessity for the separation of Port Phillip was powerfully attested. Three colonists, who contemplated a visit to England, were charged with the circulation of this document, and the general support of its intent; but the result of their efforts proved that Sydney influence was paramount, for the time, in Downing street.

The discovery of Gipps Land, about this time, is another fact in the progress of the colony. The wreck of the steamer

Clonmel, at Corner Inlet, led to the commencement of a communication by water with this part of the province. The land communication was opened up by the exploring efforts of Mr. MacMillan. This part of the colony, with its fertile soil, its numerous rivers, and its salubrious climate, sheltered by the Australian Alps from the hot winds, and by ranges eastward of it from extremes of cold, is destined to take no mean position as the resort of colonists desirous to settle permanently with their families.

Among the more pressing exigencies of the rising colony was the necessity for a resident judge; and in this year Mr. John Walpole Willis, a puisne judge of the Supreme Court of New South Wales, received the appointment. He arrived in March, and the limits of his jurisdiction were declared to be co-extensive with that of the superintendency. His task was no easy one, owing to the license prevailing before the establishment of a Supreme Court; and this was further increased by the first monetary crisis, at that time fast hastening to its climax, which Port Phillip underwent. Mr. Willis was also eccentric, in many respects, and made many and powerful enemies, who eventually succeeded in inducing Mr. Latrobe, by an arbitrary act, to depose him from the exercise of his functions, in 1843.

In October of this year, His Excellency Sir George Gipps visited Port Phillip, and held a levee on the 25th of the month, receiving addresses, &c. He visited Geelong and the surrounding country the following day, was entertained at a public dinner on the 28th, and on the following day sailed for Sydney.

Amongst other circumstances having an influence on the progress of the colony, the sale of special surveys, in accordance with the system prevalent in South Australia, may be named. By the payment into the Treasury of £5,120, a requisitionist could obtain a section of eight square miles in any part of the unreserved territory. In June, three sections in Gipps Land, three in the neighbourhood of Melbourne, one at Kilmore, and one at Port Fairy, were applied for; and these have become centres of agricultural effort from that period.

While having to contend for territorial rights against the exactions of Sydney, the colony was further threatened with an aggression by the suggestion of the Land and Emigration Commissioners, recommending the severance of the Portland Bay district, and its annexation to the colony of South Australia, as a means of enabling the latter to refund its debt to the Imperial Government. This necessitated a meeting of the colonists, at which resolutions against the proposed alteration were carried.

The publication of Sir Thomas Mitchell's narrative of his expedition of Port Phillip had told with remarkable effect on the aspiring minds of multitudes in Britain, who, allured by the enticing prospects opened up in Australia Felix, as the distinguished explorer had denominated this rich country, commenced a tide of emigration in 1839, which continued to increase till 1842. The Port Phillip mania was also strongly felt in Van Diemen's Land. The superior pastures of Port Phillip afforded facilities in the management of stock, which the older colonies did not possess. Prices rapidly rose. Stock was purchased in New South Wales and Van Diemen's Land, and driven to the new settlement by hurrying competitors. Rumours of high profits awakened attention in Britain, and attracted immigrants. Many of them brought sums of money which were accounted considerable capital in those days.

The eager competition of the new colonists thus drawn from so many sources forced prices of stock and of all commodities to exorbitant rates. Land speculation ran high amongst the increasing multitudes, so that prices mounted from tens to thousands; and allotments that originally brought £40, were sold at £4,000. The interchanges of lands were rapid; the conveyance was slow, and the issue of Crown grants slower still. While the mania lasted, the factitious prosperity of the traders blinded them to the real condition of the purchasers, and consequently to their own; and, presuming on their fancied wealth, extravagance in business and in the style of living became the order of the day. Champagne breakfasts, suburban residences, and other similar ruinous modes of expending a fortune, prevailed. This order of things was at its height in 1840; and a universal crash was only delayed by the continued stream of immigration. The land fund, however, failed in 1841, and affected the inflocking of immigrants from the parent land; prices fell; depression and difficulties beame universal, and towards the close of 1842, the condition of the colony was one of wide-spread bankruptcy. The severe time of reckoning had come; and before the commercial atmosphere was cleared, nearly 1400 insolvencies in Sydney and 300 in Melbourne were recorded in the space of three years.

In the crisis of these depressions, new life was poured into the civic and political status of the colony by an Imperial Act, which provided for a partially representative government and for the incorporation of towns. In accordance with the provisions of this Act, Melbourne was, on the 1st of December, 1842, erected into a corporation; the town was divided into four wards; the election of councillors took place, and, on the 9th, the Town Council met, and chose Henry Condell, Esq , mayor; H. Condell and Andrew Russell, aldermen for six years; and H. W. Mortimer and W. Kerr, aldermen for three years. The Council, notwithstanding inevitable favoritism, greatly benefited the city, and still continues to increase the material prosperity and comfort of the inhabitants.

The legislative provisions of the abovenamed Act came into practical operation in June, 1843. Prior to this, the whole legislative and executive functions of the government were held by the governor, with a council of Crown nominees. Representation under such a system was out of the question. By the new Act, however, a legislative council of thirty-six members, of whom twelve were to be nominees of the Crown, and the remaining twenty-four to be elected by the colonists, was called into existence. The powers of this council were restricted to the making of laws not repugnant to those of England; but the Crown retained the absolute control of the lands and their revenue. The number of representatives allotted to Port Phillip was six. The representation thus obtained was unsatisfactory to the colonists. The members allotted were few in number, and the complaint became general that the interests of Port Phillip were swamped by those of New South Wales. At first, however, the sanguine colonists regarded the privilege as a boon of no small value, and indulged in the fallacious hope that at least political justice would, in such an assembly, be accorded to Port Phillip; but the earliest experience of its working proved that the revenues of the colony were to be appropriated to the older settlement, and that too with the apparent consent of our own representatives. The first election returned H. Condell, Esq., for the city, and Messrs. Ebden, Walker, Lang, Thomson, and Nicholson, for the district. Mr. Condell's election was contested by Mr. Curr; the contest assumed the form of Protestant and Catholic, and the triumph of Mr. Condell resulted in a riot. Some acts of violence were committed, the Riot Act was read and the military were called out before the mob was dispersed.

Coincident in time with this event, the suspension of Judge Willis by his Excellency the Governor added another element of rancour to the bitter feuds then raging. Numerous influential citizens considered themselves insulted and oppressed by his measures and demeanour, in which sentiment, as was supposed by some, his Honor the Superintendent participated; but among the people generally he was held in esteem, and numerous addresses were presented to him when leaving these shores for England. The act of the Governor was declared by the home authorities to be illegal, and Justice Willis received a satisfactory compensation.

In 1843, the first series of Australian Sketches, by Mr. Thomas McCombie (now the Hon. Thomas McCombie, M.L.C.),* of Melbourne, appeared in Tait's Edinburgh Magazine, and were the means of calling much attention to the colony; the work was republished in a separate form. In 1846, Mr. Westgarth's "Port Phillip" also issued from the Edinburgh press.

Throughout the whole of 1843 the aspect presented by the city and its inhabitants was most cheerless. The appearance of the town was scattered, the thoroughfares were unformed

* This gentleman has written a very elaborate history of Victoria, from which some of these facts are taken.

and studded with stumps of trees, and traversed by ravines, even in Collins-street, from which bullock drays had to be dug; and in one instance two children were drowned in the waters at the end of Elizabeth street. The faces of the citizens as they met in the streets seemed devoid of hope, a funereal gloom overspread them—no jolly, rollicking squatters now appeared among them; their sheep were worth at the most 4s. each; the stations did not pay expenses even to those who had not absolutely lost all title to them, of whom there were not a few. Wool was so low that it would hardly pay the expenses of shearing. Land and houses did not realise a tenth of their former value. Public confidence was destroyed. This lowest depth reached, the tide began to turn. Wool, the previous staple of the colony, was now to be supplemented by tallow as the next great article of colonial export. There had been a steady increase in the quantity of the former in each succeeding year. In the second year of the colony the export of wool was 175,000 lbs., in 1844 it amounted to 4,326,000 lbs. But in the incumbered condition of the squatters the resort to the "boiling down" system offered the prospect of immediate relief. There were at this time nearly two millions sheep in the district, so that whole flocks were driven to these establishments, where the carcases were, by a steam process, compelled to yield their tallow, and the skins, bones, hoofs and refuse were disposed of at the readiest markets. The cattle were in like manner boiled down; and some progress made in beef curing, of parts that would not yield tallow. In the early part of 1844 the quantity of tallow exported was 429 tons. In a short time the squatters and cattle-owners were able to meet their liabilities and to wipe off incumbrances. Hence in 1846 there was an advance in prices for live stock. This threatened the tallow trade, but it was found to be too remunerative to be abandoned, so that in 1850 it had increased to an export of 4,489 tons. The discovery of gold, however, has caused so large an immigration, that the squatters find abundant sale for their surplus stock without driving them to the old slaughter-houses.

Meantime the corporation was busy n their municipal duties; streets were formed and macadamized, pathways were kerbed, public buildings, churches and schools were erected, the city began to give notice that it intended to be A CITY. (See article on corporation).

Just as the squatters were emerging from their pecuniary embarrassments, as above described, and began to assume to be "a power in the State," Sir George Gipps published his "Squatting Regulations" of the 2nd April, 1844. Previously, each squatter could hold any quantity of land by the payment of £10 annually; so that for such a nominal rental the holdings of some equalled a principality. The government proposed to establish an equitable charge in proportion to the capabilities of the "runs," and that £2 10s. should be assessed on every additional 1000 sheep above 4000, which the minimum £10 fee allowed; and these regulations were published by His Excellency without the knowledge and consent of the legislature. This was offensive in two points; first, from its monetary pressure on men who had just emerged from overwhelming difficulties, and had still to struggle to maintain their position; and secondly, because, having obtained a partial representation, they were determined to uphold the liberties of the colony, and to subvert the oppressive government prerogative, so glaringly manifested in the mode of framing and publishing these "squatting regulations." The majority of the Legislative Assembly in Sydney were squatters themselves or intimately connected with squatters: and the uncontrolled administration of the Crown lands and their revenues by the executive, was considered by them as a political evil; they therefore asserted their claim to the land and revenues, while Sir George Gipps was equally firm in maintaining his prerogative. In June, 1844, a really public meeting was held outside the Mechanics Institution, Collins-street, which was called "The Squatters' Meeting." Hither these gentlemen in large numbers rode in procession, and on this occasion resolutions were triumphantly carried condemnatory of the famous "squatting regulations." In Sydney these resolutions took effect in the formation of "the Pastoral Association," which, while admitting the reasonableness of an additional fee, protested against the principle and action of irresponsible authority Hence, the defence of personal interests became mixed with the assertion of political rights, and the latter made it popular; and the association pursued its course till, in 1847, it issued in the celebrated "Orders in Council," of which hereafter.

Just about the commencement of these struggles in 1844 with the representatives of the Crown, Dr. Lang, one of the six Port Phillip members, moved in the Assembly—"That an address be presented to Her Majesty, praying that she will be graciously peased to direct that the requisite steps may be taken for the speedy and entire separation of the district of Port Phillip from the territory of New South Wales; and its erection into a separate and independent colony." Nineteen voted against the six. Hence these framed a petition in January 1845, which was presented to His Excellency, to be forwarded for presentation to Her Majesty. In answer, the Executive Council were instructed to examine these members and others on the subject, which having been done, they recommended the separation. As an expression of the colonists' appreciation of his labors, Dr. Lang was entertained at a public dinner in the Queen's Theatre, Queen-street, in February, 1846, on an occasion of his visit to this district.

Two remarkable occurrences happened during the year 1844.

A grand assembling of the aborigines was held to the north of the city in July. For days previous to this great event tribes came flocking from all quarters to this centre. The numbers were estimated at about 700. Some alarm was experienced by the timid; but the whole purport of the meeting was a corroboree. A strange and wild scene was presented the fires around the city, the females with their opossum or kangaroo rugs folded so as to serve the purpose of a drum, on which they beat time to the dancers, who from sunset till near dawn sustained their laborious antics, companies of warriors from the various tribes succeeding each other, and keeping up the fun.

The following October witnessed the overflow of the Yarra to an extent unknown to the aborigines. It was in a great measure owing to a south-westerly wind blowing strongly in at the Heads, and damming up the waters of the port; so that the heavy rains with which the river was charged could not escape. The city was insulated, the lower parts were flooded, and much damage inflicted on the surrounding country.

Immigration having ceased in consequence, as noted, of the failure of the land fund, and a considerable number of the laboring class having increased in wealth and possessions, assuming the position of masters, there was beginning to be felt a great dearth of servants; wages were rising in consequence, and still the requisite supply could not be obtained. In these circumstances the home Government formed the purpose of making the colony a place of secondary punishment for their convicts. These men, drafted from the penitentiaries of Britain, were to be landed as free men; free in every sense, except that they might not return to Britain. The *Royal George* imported the first cargo of these exiles to this colony in November, 1844. The transaction was a species of social smuggling, for it was kept in concealment that they were exiles until they were landed. Though there was an element of convictism, from the older colonies, in our midst, yet they were not recognised as such. The colony was free, and this attempt of the Government to reduce this happy position by any modification of their convict system, was deeply resented by all, except many of the squatters. Hence arose a contest between these and the general public. No doubt they did not desire such an addition to the population *per se*, but they were in urgent want of shepherds, agricultural laborers and servants; and, unless they accepted this boon offered by the government, where, and how were they to obtain them? The home Government had given a positive refusal to assist emigration; and the adjoining colonies could furnish only the more objectionable class of expirees. On the other hand the laboring class had no desire for a reduction in the rates of wages; and the other intelligent and respectable portion of the public felt that they might anticipate for themselves and their children the worst evils of a convict class from such an element poured into the population. A meeting of squatters was held, at which they carried a resolution to the effect that it would be beneficial to Port Phillip to receive the exiles A counter meeting was held immediately afterwards, numerously attended, chiefly by the working classes, at which resolutions in condemnation of the course pursued by the English Government were carried. Mr. LaTrobe, on his own responsibility and at the request of the citizens, orderet the next vessel freighted with these objectionable emigrands to proceed to Sydney, and after some more vessels being refused, the attempt was abandoned by the imperial powers. In the following year, when immigration of the right stamp was resumed, the wreck of the first vessel, the *Cataraqui*, involving a loss of 414 persons, served to check the tide of emigration, as well as being a most serious and immediate loss to the colony.

In furtherance of a scheme of emigration, the practical necessity for which was becoming daily more urgent, it had been proposed to pledge the Crown lands of New South Wales to raise a loan for this purpose. The rather expensive experience of Sydney politics as regarded this district, and of Sydney equity or iniquity respecting its interests, made it at once apparent that the Port Phillip territory would be alienated to raise funds for the supply of labor to the middle district; and would complicate the question of separation. A meeting was therefore held of the most influential colonists, in September, 1845, to petition the Queen against this unrighteous proposal. Resolutions also that a loan on its own lands, in aid of emigration, should be effected, were passed; and a delegate, A. Cunningham, Esq., was appointed to proceed to England to secure these purposes. The chairman was instructed to forward immediately a copy of the proceedings to the Secretary for the Colonies, and request him not to act on the opposed proposal till the arrival of the delegate.

Some of the surface movements in the social and political life of the colonists, already briefly noticed, will have indicated the conflicting views which result in the formation of parties in a state, as now concentrating themselves into definite spheres of action. It will be necessary, therefore, that a more distinct statement in relation to these be made towards a clear understanding of some subsequent movements. With many eminent and admirable qualities as a gentleman and lieutenant-governor, Mr. LaTrobe evidenced, both in his personal intercourse, and his official labors, that his predilections were not merely Conservative but Tory to an extreme. He regarded with alarm and disgust the republican sentiments that were being diffused and strengthened in the community; mistakenly fearing that they were incompatible with a firm loyalty. With such views, and thinking the colony was too immature for the possession and judicious use of free institutions, he was in heart opposed to the measures directed towards their attainment; and in conduct, without openly opposing men and measures, he availed himself of his official position to maintain his private views and to support prerogative. It accorded with these sentiments, and was promotive of his continuance in the office of superintendent, to be as sparing as possible of the moneys voted for public objects in Port Phillip, which though little more than a moiety of her revenue, were permitted to lapse year after year, as unexpended, into the coffers of Sydney. In short he played into the hands of Sydney, and may be considered as a party on her side.

The squatters, again, by the question of the exiles, appear as a party, who, in the protection and furtherance of their own interests, stand opposed to what may be regarded as those of the general public, and their rights subsequently brought them into conflict with the more general public on the land question.

The Catholic interest, as a politico-religious party, showed out in the first election and the riot then occurring. In these earlier times also an Orange Institution and anti-Catholic feeling amongst some citizens, called this into unhappy exercise, which became evident in 1846, when the foundation stone of Princes Bridge and of the Hospital was laid. It was a day of general rejoicing; a procession was formed of all the sectional ranks, trades, officials and orders. The Freemasons had the direction of the ceremony, Mr. LaTrobe laid the stone of Princes Bridge, and Dr. Palmer (now Sir J. Palmer) that of the Hospital. The Catholic clergy refused to take part in the scene on some sectarian ground; and there had like to have been a disturbance. But a few months afterwards, the smouldering discontent burst into a flame, when the Orange Society proposed to celebrate the Battle of the Boyne. An armed attack was made on their place of assembly, which was repelled. Several were severely wounded in the conflict. That night and the following day the city was kept in a state of alarm. The Catholic party assembled in arms on the Flagstaff-hill, and after the magistrates with the soldiers had stopped the assembling of the Orangemen, they succeeded in inducing the other party to disband. The building of the Protestant Hall, at the corner of Little Collins and Stephen-streets, for the holding of Orange festivals, was a result on the one side; while on the other, it called into existence St. Patrick's Hall, Bourke-street, west; which subsequently was hired by the Government as the first place of assembly for the Legislative Council. This element of party strife is still seen in operation in elections, and in matters of change of ministry.

"The Orders in Council" were issued by the Imperial Government, on 9th March, 1847, and were received by the squatting interest with enthusiasm. These were due to the exertions of the Pastoral Association, and had little influence on the position of the squatters of the middle district, but involved vast changes on the side of Port Phillip. These regulations divided the Crown lands into three sections, the settled, the intermediate and the unsettled districts. The first class comprised 25 miles around Melbourne, 15 miles around Geelong, and 10 miles around Portland and Alberton, with a few other reservations. The second comprised the three existing counties, Bourke, Grant and Normanby, surrounding Melbourne, Geelong and Portland, to which were added 21 new counties, then defined, which together comprised nearly half the territorial area of the district. The third division comprised the other half of the colony, containing lands of every quality. The regulations conferred on the squatter a pre-emptive right according to the following terms:—For the unsettled district, £2 10s. annually is the rent for the area required to depasture 1000 sheep; these lands are open to purchase by the occupant at £1 per acre, within the term of the 14 years' lease. At the expiration of the lease, the lands may be put up for sale, if the lessee declines his pre-emption. For the intermediate district, leases not exceeding 8 years, with pre-emptive right, but subject to sale at the close of each year after 60 days' notice. In the settled district leases of one year, with power to depasture on unsold land. These regulations have created a resistance that still exists, by conferring privileges on the squatters that conflict with the general interest of the people. The squatters are in actual possession: and by their pre-emptive rights might defy intruders, so that every onward movement becomes an encroachment on some of them. At the period when the "regulations" came into operation, the squatters had, by surmounting previous difficulties, become in regard to wealth an independent body, upon whom were conferred invidious distinctions and needless benefits, and who, by the changes ensuing on the gold discovery, are now placed in the position of an unpopular and grasping confederacy. Still, it must be borne in mind, that at the time of the gold discovery, the greater portion of the squatting stations had changed hands; and that the new occupants had given a money valuation for the lands over which their flocks depastured; besides which, their occupation formed the chief source, the mainspring of our colonial wealth, up to the time the mineral resources of the land were developed; then, there were 1000 licensees of Crown lands, employing 20,000 dependants, with a live stock of 30,000 horses, 400,000 cattle, and upwards of 6,000,000 sheep. That men in such a position had and have peculiar rights, who will dispute? That they should present claims for compensation is but reasonable, and that some equitable system, to meet their just demand should be devised, is most desirable. In the present and prospective position of the colony, where such immense tracts of land are available for agricultural purposes to our increasing population, the squatting system occupying so large a surface, is impracticable. The political and social inequality created by conferring long and exclusive leases on certain members of the community must be abolished; and the pre-emptive right must be suppressed, as an economic and a political injustice in the sale of lands immensely below their value.

The advent of the Rev. Charles Perry, D.D., in the commencement of 1848, and his installation as first Bishop of Melbourne, may be regarded as the first actual step in the separation of the colony from New South Wales. His diocese comprised the Episcopalian community throughout the southern district; and thereby the ecclesiastical relations of this denomination were transferred from the Bishop of Sydney to a local ecclesiastic. By this event also the "town" thenceforth became the "city" of Melbourne.

The great politico-ecclesiastical question of Voluntaryism, which has lately occupied so much of the labors of our senators on the 53rd clause of the Constitution Bill, was initiated as a subject of controversy, by the Rev. A. Morison, the only Independent minister in the colony, during the following month of May, preaching and publishing four lectures on the book of "Revelation," in which he handled the subject of "State-aid" unsparingly. As the lectures were delivered at a time when great quiet pervaded all circles, and no topic of public interest was being agitated, they furnished occasion of universal talk; and a most amusing degree of excitement was produced by so simple a matter, the rev. gentleman obtaining a limited measure of applause from some quarters, and an unmeasured store of condemnation from those in favor of State-aid. It was the first war-note, however, on a question which has become the motto of a political party still at work.

The political atmosphere meantime was gathering clouds, which menaced the position of the superintendent, Mr. LaTrobe. The Town Council had already placed themselves in an attitude of hostility towards him, in consequence of his endeavour, privately, to contravene their request to the Sydney Government, that the unused funds granted for Port Phillip should be entrusted to their care for purposes of public improvements. Mr. LaTrobe's correspondence, injuriously reflecting on the character and prudence of the Port Phillipians, was published; and as a consequence, in June, 1848, the Council, upon the motion of Mr. M'Combie, agreed to the following resolution:—"That the Legislative Committee be instructed to prepare an humble petition to Her Most Gracious Majesty the Queen, praying for the removal of His Honor Charles Joseph LaTrobe, Esq., from the office of Superintendent of the District of Port Phillip, on account of his systematic mismanagement of the money voted for the service of the province, his neglect of public works of paramount consequence, and his repeated breaches of faith in his official transactions with this Council, in matters of high public importance." In order to back up this resolution, a great public meeting was held opposite the Court House, attended by 3000 persons, and presided over by Mr. M'Combie, and a petition for the recal of the Superintendent carried by acclamation. The Secretary of State acknowledged both memorials, but refused to disturb Mr. LaTrobe in his government.

The period of five years, for which the Port Phillip representatives had been elected to serve in the Legislative Assembly at Sydney, having closed, the writ for another election was issued for July following. The bitter mockery of representation, by which our honorable six were haplessly compelled to countenance the spoliation of their province, had become so galling, that some of them refused to stand again for election. Mr. J. V. F. L. Foster was put in nomination for the district, but, there being no other *bonâ fide* candidates for the five seats, the electors present prevailed upon him to withdraw; no candidates were placed in nomination, and the writ was returned. At the nomination for the city of Melbourne, five days later, the Government had prevailed on Mr. Foster to come forward, in order that the yoke of servitude might be replaced on their unwilling shoulders. The Government placed Mr. Foster in nomination, and he would have been returned, had not Earl Grey been placed in nomination against him. This was done to show to the world that representation in Sydney was a farce. The return of Earl Grey was carried by a triumphant majority; a letter was sent to the Under Secretary of State for the Colonies by Mr. M'Combie, the proposer of Earl Grey, explaining the whole of the circumstances of the peculiar case. This act of the Melbournites found no sympathy at Geelong, where a meeting was held, that the electors might express publicly their condemnation of such a procedure. In order to understand this difference of opinion, it may be well, in this place, to offer some explanation of the causes leading to opposition between Geelong and Melbourne. Geelong was a sort of centre to the squatting interest. Its growth and prosperity depended wholly on the wool trade, and supplies to the stations; and it claimed thus early to be the "commercial pivot" of the colony. A pleasant rivalry, therefore had long subsisted between the governmental and squatting metropolises, which had its play on all kinds of occasions. The squatters' policy, as before suggested, differed widely from the general interests of the people; and the weight of their influence was ordinarily given to the Government side of all questions that did not immediately implicate their own interest. The Government found it necessary to have *bonâ fide* members returned for Port Phillip, since if two were deficient, they could not act. Geelong was therefore wheedled,—was made the place of nomination for a new writ of election. Five local candidates were put in nomination, and five British peers by the opposition, but the Geelongites triumphed.

The emigration and separation movements were the absorbing topics of the closing periods of this year (1848), and through the following two years. The inequality of the sexes in the colony, being in the ratio of three to one, had led to schemes for promoting female immigration. One means had been opened to the immigration agents in Britain whereby this want of the colony and a pressure on the surplus population of the home countries could at once be met, in sending to the colony the Irish female orphans, who were poured into the colony to the number of 2,219, during the eighteen months terminating 1st July, 1849. The colony, however, as usual, suffered a pecuniary wrong in this transaction. The whole of the expenses were defrayed from our immigration fund, and neither the Treasury nor parish funds in the home countries were laid under contributions to aid in furtherance of this project. These girls were uneducated and untrained, and universal complaints were heard in domestic circles of the uselessness of the imported article; it was unmarketable. The great majority were said to be Roman Catholics and a national and sectarian prejudice was called into action. The opponents to their introduction declared that they were likely to become the wives of a people of whom four-fifths were Protestant, and excited some clamor on the subject.

The Rev. J. D. Lang, D.D., the while was in Britain, making most strenuous efforts in a scheme of emigration that contemplated the rectification of this error, as well as the equally formidable one into which the squatters had fallen. He saw that in the present progress of population the squatters would form an aristocracy, and their dependants a kind of serfdom; and as the former were in a great measure indifferent whence they procured their laborers, be they convicts, Chinese, South Sea Islanders, or any other, so that they obtained cheap labor, his object was to promote an emigration of small capitalists, who should form a yeomanry in the land. He put in operation all agencies to arouse the attention of such persons in Britain and Ireland to the advantages offered by Port Phillip and Moreton Bay. By the newspapers, public lectures, and such means, he labored to further this scheme of immigration; and, to accomplish this object, he besieged the official authorities in England, but encountered only obstruction. Abandoning hope in this direction, he gave these authorities a scathing benediction, and set at work a scheme of emigration that should be self-paying. By means of these labors, the *Larpent* was sent out in 1849 with the right class of emigrants, which was followed by the *Travancore*, and finally he arrived himself in the early part of 1850, in the *Clifton*, having, among others, four ministers and twenty-two divinity students as emigrants. Dr. Lang experienced much difficulty in these labors, for being unable to meet some of the responsibilities he incurred in these patriotic efforts, he suffered an incarceration for debt in the Melbourne gaol during May, 1850.

Another element, which has strengthened the framework of society among us, was the German emigration. On 11th February, 1849, the first ship, the *Godeffroy*, followed in a short time by two others, the *Dockenhaden* and *Wappaus*, introduced about 1000 of these useful artizans and agriculturists to the colony. Committees of German emigration cared for them, both in Melbourne and Geelong.

A further addition to our immigrants was aided by the Society for the Promotion of Emigration, similar to Dr. Lang's in the class of persons to be aided, formed in 1848 by some members of Parliament and other influential persons, who were desirous of directing the tide of emigration from the United States to the Australian possessions. This society had in 1850 assisted 3000 emigrants to proceed to different settlements in Australia. The total of emigration to Port Phillip, by means of the various societies and agencies for 1849, was 9,728.

The transportation question still continued to be agitated. The view which the British Government were disposed to take of this was that the question was one which solely concerned themselves, and therefore one in which the colonists could not be allowed a voice. To the colonists, however, it was vital, as the real evils of the system pressed on them alone, by the continued stream of pollution thus flowing into society. The colonial minister intimated that the requests of the colonists should be so far respected, that transportation of criminals to New South Wales should be discontinued; and that Van Diemen's Land was to be made the chief receptacle of convicts for the future. In this purpose they found a ready accomplice in Sir W. Denison, the Governor of Van Diemen's Land, who supported the wishes of the Imperial Government in opposition to the earnest remonstrances of his people. By extensive issues of tickets-of-leave and other means, he facilitated the removal of the prisoners from Van Diemen's to Port Phillip, as the nearest and most exposed dependency, so that a constant influx of those obnoxious colonists was poured on our shores, with the intention of relieving the penal colony of its overwhelming criminal population. During 1849, the ships freighted with the exiles entered our ports, but were invariably ordered to proceed to Sydney by the superintendent, who deserved the best thanks of the public for his resolution on this point: though the colony is, perhaps, more deeply indebted to Sir Charles FitzRoy for saving it from pollution, who, being at this time in Melbourne on a visit, in reply to a deputation which waited on him, agreed to order the *Randolph*, then daily expected, to proceed to Sydney; for which he was severely censured in New South Wales. Some of the settlers at Portland Bay, however, resolved to have their wants supplied from this source, and addressed a petition to His Honor, requesting that the exiles should be sent to them instead of being furthered to Sydney, and received in answer a flat refusal, Mr. LaTrobe's moral sense agreeing with the general feeling of the people on this point. A monster anti-transportation meeting was held on the 18th July, to urge on the Government the necessity of taking measures against Sir W. Denison's policy in granting pardons on the condition that the pardoned immediately left that colony: and the deputation who waited on His Honor found him all readiness to co-operate with them to prevent the evils thus threatened. This was followed by a similar meeting at Geelong; and on the 20th August a second monster meeting was held, at which a petition to Her Majesty was adopted, reprobating Earl Grey's convict policy, and setting forth the intolerable evils inflicted on a free people by the Government persisting in this course against the strongly expressed views of the colonists.

In January, 1849, a public meeting was held in Melbourne, for the purpose of asserting the right of the squatters and tenant farmers to the elective franchise. The purpose of the meeting was effectively opposed by some, who, while admitting the equity of the principle asserted, denied its justice in the special case then sought to be supported. The defeated squatters fled to their stronghold, Geelong, and were successful at meetings held there on this subject.

His Excellency Sir C. FitzRoy paid the colony a visit in March of this year. The customary address and honours suitable to a vice-regal visit followed. His Excellency had a narrow escape from an alarming accident while being driven to Jolimont.

Reports reached the colony, at various times throughout the year, of the purpose of the Imperial Parliament to take into consideration the question of the government of the Australian colonies. These rumors took a settled form, when it became known that Mr. Roebuck had asked leave (on 24th May) to bring in a bill on this subject; but withdrew his motion when informed by Mr. Hawes, from his place, that after Whitsunday holidays he was prepared to introduce a bill to give local self-government to the colonies. It was known that the separation of Port Phillip would be an article of the proposed bill; and in anticipation of the event, Her Majesty had been pleased, the preceding year, to signify that she would confer the high distinction of her name, Victoria, on the youngest of her colonies. The hope thus excited of a speedy liberation from our thraldom was doomed to disappointment. In expectation of the event, however, Mr. Mackinnon called for documents, &c., in the Legislative Council, with a purpose to move for an adjustment of expenditure between Sydney and Port Phillip, so as to obtain a refunding of the vast sums of which the latter had been deprived. The spoliation had at that time reached the formidable amount of £358,163 2s. 6½d.; but an offset of £86,280 for the expenses of general government was made, leaving, nevertheless, the respectable balance of £268,882 2s. 6½d. as the claim of this province.

The golden opinions Mr. LaTrobe had earned for himself by his resolute action in the matter of convicts and exiles were suddenly dissipated, and a bitter animosity aroused against him, by a letter to the Secretary for the Colonies coming to hand, in which he expressed views unfavorable to free institutions being conferred on the colony. His sentiments may be gathered from the following extract – "That any form of constitution which may be proposed for the colony, for some years to come at least, which takes the government out of the hands of a governor, executive, and nominee council, and substitutes for the latter a representative body, will be ill-suited to its real state and position, and will render the administration of its government as a distinct colony, upon whom soever it may devolve, a task of exceedingly great difficulty and responsibility." This culminating offence destroyed the prestige of his personal virtues, and subjected him to suspicion and hostility throughout the whole of his subsequent administration. As the delay of separation was protracted, meetings were held in November and December to adopt measures to stimulate the Parliament in carrying on the bill more vigorously.

The discovery of gold in California in 1848, drew off many colonists from Australia. Port Phillip suffered the loss of only 466. But on the 31st of January, 1849, the first announcement of the discovery of gold in our province was made by a shepherd furnishing some specimens for assay to Mr. Brentani. The Pyrenees was spoken of as the locality, and exploring parties who visitedthe spot declared the highly promising auriferous quality of the region. The excitement consequent soon died away, as a report gained credit that the specimens produced in Melbourne were manufactured. But a project of greater promise was the mining of coal, which was resumed this year. It had been long known that this valuable article of commerce existed in the country; and exertions by associations and private individuals were directed to Western Port, where it was reported a workable seam had been found. The law-officer (Mr. Croke) had declared, however, that permission to mine could not be given; but, upon reference of the matter to Sydney, the permission was granted; and in June a company was formed at a public meeting, £700 subscribed to meet preliminary expenses, and a work initiated, which was stopped only by the discovery of the goldfields and the changes consequent thereon. Among the events of this year was the incorporation of Geelong, its promotion to the rank of a free warehousing port, and the establishment in it of a circuit court of justice. At first there was a proposal to make it an exceptional case, by giving the Government a power over its procedure, but it was finally incorporated on the same terms as the City of Melbourne.

In the month of November the heavy floods occasioned serious damage in and about Melbourne, and throughout the district.

Great improvements were being effected in the city through the operation of the building societies. The rental was estimated at £100,000. The population, including Richmond, was estimated at 25,000; that of the whole district 60,000, nearly double the number for 1846.

Social distinctions in the titles of prelates were a matter of controversy in the United Kingdom that extended its influence to the colony. The Roman Catholic prelates contended for the extension of the title of lordship, and equal status with the Anglican prelates. The titular rank of a bishop was derived from his seat among the peers in the House of Lords. A special clause was inserted in the (Irish) Act of Union, providing for the Irish bishops the possession of the honor which they previously enjoyed in the Irish House of Parliament. The Romish bishops were grieved that they should not enjoy the same titles. Hence the Imperial Parliament provided that in Ireland and the Colonies, the title as a courtesy should be extended alike to Anglican and Romish prelates; but the Government of New South Wales was instructed that the Roman archbishop in that colony should not take precedence of the English bishop, nor should any Roman bishop be recognised under any local title that had been bestowed in the Anglican Church. The year 1850, therefore, opened with the controversy between the Bishop of Melbourne and the Right Rev. A. Goold, Roman Catholic bishop, on this subject, which has not since been mooted in the colony.

In February, a monster meeting was held to express the sympathy of the colony with the Cape colonists in their resistance of convictism, that was attempted to be forced on them. This was a result, not only of admiration of the boldness of the colonists that expelled pollution from their shores, at the risk of apparent treason to the parent State, but was contemplated as a means of strongly impressing the home Government with the determination of the Colony to resist in like manner the convict policy pursued towards itself.

In March, a horticultural society was established, and its first exhibition was held in the Botanical Gardens.

The rapid extension of Melbourne by the formation of new streets, lanes, &c., while no adequate provision was made for sewerage, and these thoroughfares becoming quagmires by the constant traffic of the citizens, raised the question of the sanitary condition of the city into urgent importance. The Municipal Council held meetings, and on the 18th June a public meeting was held to receive the City Surveyor's (Mr. Blackburn) report. The estimated cost of works necessary was £100,000. The Council petitioned the Queen that a moiety of the territorial revenue should be placed at its disposal for these purposes, and in the meantime it was resolved to commence with the central portion of the city. Those who walk round the city at the present time could not form an idea of the alteration then commenced, by which ruts and gullies have given place to present order and safety.

In this month also, the foundation stone of the Benevolent Asylum was laid, amidst an assemblage of 10,000 persons. A procession was formed, and the customary holiday enjoyments were sought by the citizens. The harmony of the occasion was slightly disturbed by the opposition of the Roman Catholic clergy, some of whose prejudices were violated, and they threatened to withdraw the support of their communion from the institution.

A novel class of immigrants arrived in the *Culloden*, in July, "the distressed needle-women." These were the numerous class of destitute females accumulated in London, who being objects of sympathy and beneficent exertion, some under the humane project of the Hon. Sydney Herbert, were shipped off to Port Phillip, and were immediately engaged as domestic servants.

About this time, a very exciting event occurred on its becoming known that Mr. Henry Moor, one of our representatives in the Legislative Council and Registrar of the Diocese, had introduced two bills into the Assembly—one the Church Temporalities Bill, and the other the Church Discipline Bill. The excitement and opposition to these were universal. The clergy and members of the Church of England felt aggrieved, that instruments having such an important bearing on their own position, even if they had been advantageous, were attempted to be obtained without their previous knowledge and consent; while the members of other religious denominations complained of a clause in the Temporalities Bill, which enacted that a grant might be made toward the erection of any church out of the portion of the money appropriated by the State to the maintenance of religion which belonged to the Church of England, upon the sum of £100 being raised by voluntary contributions; whereas, as the law then stood, no grant could be made toward a place of worship of any religious denomination, until £300 had been subscribed. This clause merely regulated the distribution of Church of England moneys; but the people supposed that it would give that church an advantage over all others in the colony. Many were also very indignant at the provision of the Church

Discipline Bill, for erecting an episcopal ecclesiastical court, with power to summon witnesses and to administer oaths. Public meetings were held in Geelong; and in August, the Mayor presided over a public meeting in Melbourne, at which, while condemning the bills and all connected with the introduction of them, there was a very free ventilation of the question of the severance of the Church, in all its sections, from the State. The bills were withdrawn, on the proposal for a second reading being opposed.

Immediately after this excitement, the first draft of the Colonies Bill, having passed the Imperial Parliament in May, was published, and measures were talked of to celebrate the approaching event of separation in a manner suitable to its importance.

On the 28th August, the first public meeting for establishing gas works was held, at which it was affirmed that the time had now arrived when the introduction of gas was necessary, and a committee was organised The Rev. J. Allen had awakened an interest on the subject, and delivered lectures proving that we possessed all the facilities of supply, and that the project could be executed with advantage to all parties concerned. The company obtained land at the west end of Collins-street, but ultimately removed to the swamp; and after years of delay, and a large expenditure, have admirably succeeded.

The project of an universal exhibition in London had set the active spirits among us at work, and an industrial exhibition was erected, with a view of stimulating improvements and discoveries in developing the capabilities of the colony.

The act of the licensing bench, in limiting the number of licensed victuallers and suppressing disorderly houses of resort, occasioned a conflicting movement among this class of colonists; but the moral sense of the community was on the side of the magistrates, and they generally approved of the measures then introduced.

In September, a meeting of 2000 male adults was held opposite the Police Office, presided over by the Mayor. The object of the "monster meeting" was to petition the legislature against the importation of criminals of every class, and upon any terms whatever, into the colony; and to express public sympathy with Van Diemen's Land, and an opinion against the whole system of criminal transportation.

On November 12th, the announcement was made public that on the previous night the intelligence of the passing, by royal assent, of the Australian Colonies Bill had been brought by the *Lysander*. The rejoicings were universal, and extended over three days. Prince's Bridge was opened with a grand procession, the city was illuminated, public thanksgiving in the churches was offered, dinners, fancy balls, fireworks, balloons, and every possible mode of giving vent to the gladness of a people devised, and even the establishment of a commemorative annual fair proposed; and the year closed, after the lull of this excitement, in the calm anticipation of the practical working of the privileges conferred upon us.

In the commencement of 1851 the transportation question presented a formidable aspect in the formation of the Austrálian League. It had its origin in Van Diemen's Land, where the bitterest fruits were being gathered; and delegates were sent to Port Phillip and Sydney, to organise a moral force which should effectually influence the Imperial Government. The Rev. John West and W. Weston, Esq., arrived on 19th January, and an impressive meeting was held in the Queen's Theatre on the 1st of the following month, when the "League" was inaugurated, which tended to the ultimate settling of the question.

The 6th of the same month was a day of terror. Black Thursday will be memorable in the Colony for the desolations of fire that swept the country, destroying property and lives. The benevolent feeling of the colonists was stimulated for the sufferers, and at a meeting in Geelong £1,100, and at one in Melbourne £1,600 were raised to alleviate the distress thus caused.

The discovery of gold at Bathurst, New South Wales, had acted as a counteractive to the Californian emigration, but operated to the prejudice of Port Phillip, in drawing off a multitude to that locality. This stimulated the desire of finding a gold-field in the latter province, and in June the first reliable report of a discovery in the Plenty Ranges produced great excitement. But prospecting parties were abroad in various directions; and as the Plenty diggings were not very successful, a meeting was held in June, at which it was provided that 200 guineas should be awarded to the discoverer of a remunerative gold-field, and in the course of time reports came of such discoveries in various localities.

The 1st of July, being the day appointed by the Home Authorities for the Act of Separation to take effect, the Superintendent, Mr. LaTrobe, assumed the title of Lieutenant-Governor of Victoria; he and the official staff were sworn in, the first levée was held, and rejoicing was general for the separation and independence of Victoria. St. Patrick's Hall was rented as the Parliament House, and after the elections the house met for the first time, on 11th November, 1851, Speaker and Chairman of Committees appointed, days and hours of meeting arranged, and in an assemblage of the beauty and fashion of the city, the Governor delivered his first speech.

During the previous month the Ballaarat diggings had filled with astonishment and expectation the minds of all; Geelong and Melbourne were deserted of their male population—all handicraft had ceased, and in a few weeks 10,000 swarmed at Golden Point. While the Council was first assembling, Mount Alexander diggings were reported as far surpassing Ballaarat.

The report of these rich gold-fields spreading far and wide, immediately produced that vast immigration from all quarters, which may be estimated by the fact, that when at its height, 10,000 immigrants were actually, in one week, landed at Melbourne. The quinquennial census which had come off in March of this year shewed that the population of Port Phillip was 80,000, of which 23,000 were in Melbourne and 8,000 in Geelong; but a year sufficed to nearly double this number. The constitution of the new Assembly was at first composed of two-thirds elected members, and one-third of the nominees of the Crown; half of these nominees being office-holders, and half unofficial. The influx of population necessitated an increase of representatives, but its relative proportions were preserved. This form of representation in a single house, continued till November, 1856, when a new form of government by double chambers was brought into operation.

In the first session the subject of prayer in the House was contested, and lost by a majority of one. As the Executive had taken charge of the gold-fields, and appointed commissioners, regulated license fee, and established an escort, a considerable increase of the revenue followed. The Executive therefore were disposed to pay all the expenses arising from the gold-fields. But as salaries had to be increased, the representatives refused to authorise more than the sums placed on the estimates, demanding of the Executive the overplus payments from the gold revenue. This was the next great contest, and the representatives triumphed on the gold question. This was settled in the next session, by the transference of the funds and administration of the gold-fields to the Assembly. The customs also were placed under their control. The land revenues had heretofore been appropriated in half to emigration purposes, but the home Government now placed the retained moiety at the disposal of the Colonial Legislature, a sum of £300,000. As an ultimate boon, the Legislature was called to consider what alterations were considered necessary or desirable to be effected in the whole system for the utmost advantage of the colony. This was not owing to any special steps taken in the colony to bring about any change in its general constitution, but to the political phases of New South Wales which led to an organic reconstruction in both colonies. The Legislative Council in New South Wales, expiring in 1851 before the separation of Port Phillip, had adopted, on the motion of Mr. William C. Wentworth, a strongly worded remonstrance against the incomplete form of Representative Government, and the inadequate control of their financial affairs which had been hitherto conceded to the colonists. The remonstrance which had been the legacy of one Council, was entered upon as the heritage of its successor. Mr. Wentworth again moved and carried it. It was transmitted to England, presented and read at the table in the House of

Commons as a remarkable document. The attention excited by the colonies stimulated the effect which the political remonstrances of New South Wales had produced. The British Government acquiesced in the demands of that colony, and, unsolicited, proffered to the neighboring colonies the same form of government which was granted to New South Wales. The type proposed was a government through two houses of legislature; and the colonies were requested to deliberate upon the subject, and transmit the results to England. The form of government, selected by the Legislative Council for Victoria, was based on two houses, both elected by the people. For the purposes of forming the Legislative Council or Upper House, the colony was subdivided into six provinces, to each of which five members were allotted,—one member in each province to retire at the end of two years. The member lowest on the poll in each district to retire first, and his place to be supplied by election. The freehold qualification of an elector for the Council was to be property worth £1000, or worth annually £100. Retired officers, barristers, solicitors, clergymen, and leaseholders to the amount of £100 were also to have votes. The Legislative Assembly was to be composed of sixty members, elected bythirty seven districts. The duration of the Assembly was to be five years; the qualification of electors was to be freehold property worth £50 in the whole, or worth £5 a year; or leasehold of £10 annually; or salary of £100 annually; or the possession of a license to occupy Crown lands for the space of twelve months. The whole of the revenues of the colony were to form one fund, to be administered under Parliamentary sanction within the colony by a Governor acting on the advice of responsible officers; and all appointments to office within the colony (except those of the responsible officers themselves), were to be made by the Governor, with the advice of his Executive Council. The British Government acquiesced in the propositions of the colonists, and a short statute was enacted to enable the Queen to assent to the bills sent home. The announcement of the Queen's assent reached Victoria in the end of the year 1855, but more than a year was suffered to elapse before the provisions of the new form of government were brought into operation. On the 21st November, 1856, the two houses of legislature were convened by proclamation of the Acting Governor, General Edward Macarthur; and from that date, therefore, Responsible Government may be held to have been inaugurated.

Reverting to the second session of our first parliament, another topic of fierce debate was the State-aid question. £6,000 was the sum allotted at that time in aid of religion, for distribution among all who would accept it. The purport of the debate was to expunge this amount from the estimates, but it resulted in the amount being increased to £30,000, and when the new constitution was framed, the 53rd clause made the sum £50,000. A vigorous effort was made by the oppositionists in 1857, to expunge this clause, which was carried by a small majority in the Legislative Assembly, but ultimately rejected by the Upper House; so that it is still the law of the land.

A committee of enquiry sat during this session on the subject of education. The feeling prevailing in the house was in favor of the National Education system. But as the "Denominational" was in the ascendant, and dissatisfaction with both were expressed by the parties examined by the committee, they concluded to recommend assistance to be given to "public schools." There was a vote also of £50,000 to commence the Melbourne University.

The squatting question was one of great interest, and became one of strong partizanship, because the squatting interest, together with the nominees, could command a majority in the Council. The demands for the unlocking the lands were urgent, the difficulties of surveying were great, and the Orders in Council withstood the appropriation of the lands around the gold-fields. Hence the popular representatives requested the Government to issue leases under the Orders in Council for the intermediate districts, with a view to have them opened to public sale; but an amendment was carried which embraced the whole Orders in Council, and consequently the unsettled districts. Public meetings were held, and the Government and Council were condemned, so that the whole question had to be remitted to the home Government.

The total revenue for 1851 was £380,000, but when the year 1852 closed, the revenue had reached £1,577,000, consequently the succeeding year witnessed a lavish expenditure, as there seemed scarcely a possibility of exhausting the income. The resignation of Mr. LaTrobe and the appointment of a successor occurred, and in the interval between the departure of one and the arrival of the other, Sir R. Nickle administered the affairs as Acting-Governor. It was a high day on which Sir C. Hotham landed; the cordial and ostentatious reception that awaited him was in some measure due to the adverse feeling towards his predecessor, as well as to his own high repute. But Victoria had then attained the height of prosperity, and the tide had already turned. Speculation had been rampant, the old settlers, greatly disturbed by the altered state of things, had gone off in crowds, the enormous revenues derived by sales, rents, &c., of their fortunate early days enabling them to live luxuriantly as absentees. Sir C. Hotham set himself to the task of personally ascertaining the true state of public accounts, and in 1854 presented to the country and its government a deficiency of income to expenditure of £1,085,000. The budget for 1855 shewed the still more alarming deficiency of £2,836,000 to meet public engagements and wants. Much of this was caused by the engagements and public works undertaken prior to Sir Charles Hotham taking office, and the Colonial Secretary, Mr. J. V. F. L. Foster, to whose mismanagement it was in a great measure attributed, had to resign office. Mr. W. C. Haines was appointed his successor, and as the Council refused to increase the taxation, he had to reduce the estimates for 1855 from £4,101,293 to £2,388,816, and the colony soon began to rectify its mistakes.

The social changes wrought by the gold discovery were extensive and thorough, so much so that Port Phillip is a phase of society as widely different from Victoria as can be conceived. "*Bouleversement*" is the only word that will adequately describe the change. The employed were of greater importance than the employers. The excesses and extravagance of the diggers are indescribable. Life became a riot, and its courtesies were in a great measure, disregarded. The immense immigration swallowed up the old residents, the most respectable and wealthy of whom, as s ated, became absentees. The offscourings of the adjoining colonies were poured into our midst. In 1855 there were twelve gold-fields; four, viz., Anderson's Creek, Ballaarat, Mount Alexander, and Bendigo, were discovered in 1851; the Ovens in 1852; the M'Ivor and Goulburn in 1853; and the remainder in 1854: over these the immigrants spread. But the great evil was the influx of the Van Diemen's Land expirees, who were liberated by the policy of Sir W. Denison. Bushranging and every species of villany were resorted to by them, which was carried on in every part of the country, and even in the cities, where "sticking-up" became a common occurrence. Five of these desperadoes took possession of the St. Kilda road, within a few miles of the central part of the city, and within an hour captured and plundered twenty persons. A well concerted attack was made on the "Private Escort," by a gang near the Black forest, who succeeded in plundering that armed force. In consequence of these and other enormities proved to have been committed mainly by convicts, a bill called the "Convicts' Prevention Bill" passed the legislature, which, while reprobated by the other colonies, and especially Tasmania, was a means, in some slight degree, of repressing the intolerable nuisance. There were numerous diggers from almost all nations, Germans, French, Italians, Chinese, Americans, and old Californians, who brought their distinctive notions of rights and freedom to bear on their avocations of digging; and in the wretched condition of our social constitution in those days, the *emeute* at Ballaarat, December 3rd, 1854, seemed an inevitable consequence. The government arrangements were, that each digger paid a license fee of 30s. per month for a claim of 12 feet square. The commissioners were empowered to make daily visits accompanied by the police, and compel the diggers to shew their licenses. As disaffection to the Government was spreading among such a mixed population, the police force had to be increased, and to meet this additional expense the license fee was rigidly collected, and this impost was laid on every one connected with gold operations, whether digging or not. An additional law made it imperative on the diggers to act as special constables, under the penalty of being treated as rogues and vagabonds. Meetings were held on the various gold-fields, and the miners resolved to resist the fee altogether, and committees were formed to protect the interest of the miners. The vexatious "license hunting" followed, and the irritation became excessive towards the Government and its officials, the commissioners and police. The Eureka Hotel was the resort of the worst characters at Ballaarat, and its proprietor was generally detested, but the local authorities did not interfere for its suppression; a murder was committed in this house, and Bentley, the landlord, escaped justice on his first trial. The people, persuaded of the guilt of him and his mob, attacked and burnt down the hotel, in October, and would not permit the authorities to interfere. When Bentley and his accomplices were again tried, they were found guilty of manslaughter; but the effect of this on the public mind was to inflame the people against the Government, and stump orators urged them on to acts of rebellion, and commenced to enrol bands to resist the authorities by armed force. Sir C. Hotham finally ordered all the available force to Ballaarat to quell this formidable outbreak. Meantime, the ringleaders of the Eureka Hotel riot were captured, tried, condemned, and had lenient sentences passed on them, as the juries censured the Ballaarat authorities. The consequence was, that the diggers began to drill, and made all preparation for a struggle. On 28th November, 1854, the first attack was made on a detachment of the 12th regiment, and a second shortly after, on another detachment of the 40th regiment. On the 3rd December, an attack was made by the military on the entrenchment of the insurgents, in which a number were killed on both sides. The rebels were scattered, martial law proclaimed, and a Royal Commission appointed to proceed to the spot, and examine into the condition of the gold-field. These gentlemen found the grievances of the miners to be truly heavy, and recommended a complete change in the administration of their affairs, that a duty be laid upon gold instead of the license fee, a co-partnery system, franchise to the miner, and disputes to be arbitrated by a locally elected body, with an efficient chairman. These recommendations were adopted, and the mining districts were restored to quiet.

The Royal Commission was the first to call the attention of the Government to the serious considerations arising from the tide of Chinese immigration. It had set in about the commencement of 1854, and already there were 10,000 Chinamen on the various gold-fields. A social difficulty was thus originated, which continued to increase as the numbers were reported in succeeding years to be 30,000 and even 50,000, and some of these people asserted that their countrymen were "all coming." As a restrictive measure, a poll-tax of £10 was levied on every Chinamen entering the port, and the vessels were limited to one for every 10 tons of their register. But South Australia offered facilities by overland to evade the law; and the legislature, in consequence, removed the tonnage restriction, retaining the £10 fine. Protectors and interpreters were provided by the Government. There is great antipathy manifested to them on the gold-fields, and assaults and mal-treatment are frequent. At Ballaarat, a newspaper in Chinese was established in May, 1856, and in September they erected a Joss House on Emerald Hill, Melbourne. But few females accompany them; they, however, in some instances, succeed in obtaining wives, chiefly from among Irish girls. A mission has been established for their benefit, of which the Rev. Mr. Young and a few Chinese Christians are the agents. The success of this effort is not great, and the paucity of the funds for the mission does not attes· its popularity.

The railway projects started into being in 1852. The first line, from Melbourne to Sandridge, was commenced in January, 1853, and opened in September, 1854, a result of private enterprise; and, subsequently, a branch of this line was extended to St. Kilda. The Melbourne and Williamstown line was commenced shortly after, and was designed to be carried out to Mount Alexander and the Murray River, but was ultimately sold to the Government. The Geelong and Melbourne line was commenced in 1853, and was opened on 25th June, 1857. A line to Ballaarat from Geelong was projected, but abandoned, in consequence of the Government purposing to construct the trunk lines of the colony. To this end surveys have been made, and two lines are proposed: to Castlemaine and Sandhurst from Melbourne, and to Ballaarat from Geelong; the cost is estimated at about £6,000,000, to be raised by debentures, at 6 per cent *

The proclamation of the New Constitution by Sir Charles Hotham, in the house of legislature, on 23rd November, 1855, effected a great political change, by introducing a really responsible government. In this altered condition, the ministers were to be held responsible for the estimates; but those, who were ministers, in anticipation, now found that it was questionable whether the proposed estimates were their *own* or were the Governor's, which under the former system involved them in no responsibility. The law officers recommended that they should in the first instance resign, which accordingly they did; and the day following the Governor sent for Mr. Haines, the Colonial Secretary of yesterday, and invited him to form a ministry as now Chief Secretary. He accepted office and then

* For more definite information, see Railways.

Mr. Stawell, the Attorney-General, Mr. Childers, the Collector of Customs, and Captain Clarke, the Surveyor-General, accepted office under him. The announcement of the resignations took the House by surprise, but explanations were refused till next day, when, of course, the new ministry made its appearance. The Governor sent a message to the House intimating his views of his own relation to the ministry, to the effect that while these were responsible to the House, he held them accountable to himself as representing the powers of the Empire; and demanded that all measures to be introduced by them should first have his sanction. A resolution of censure on the ministers for taking office under such arbitrary and unconstitutional claims was lost by a majority of one; the gentlemen whose conduct was impugned not scrupling to vote in favor of their own conduct, although placed in the anomalous position of voting, as Sir Charles Hotham's nominees, on a question of responsibility to the people. A large majority of elected members was arrayed against them. On 18th December, the question of vote by ballot was introduced by the opposition. The ministry would not allow it to be an open question, as it deeply affected an electoral act which was then under consideration in the House; after two debates the motion was carried by a majority of eight, and next day the ministry resigned. Mr. W. Nicholson was sent for, and attempted the formation of a ministry; but as there was no desire to disturb the old ministry, these finally recalled their resignations. Writs were issued for the new elections, and the parliament was appointed to assemble on 21st November, 1855. In the crisis of these struggles, Sir C. Hotham died, on 31st December, 1855, the event being attributed partly to the mental anxiety occasioned by his position, but principally to the over-wrought condition to which he was reduced by continuous labor at his post, acting on a frame weakened by exposure in tropical climates.

The provisions of the New Constitution called forth great discussion at public meetings, and its defects excited the cry for reform in several points, as in the nominee system which was still a part of the new code, the inequality conferred on the squattocracy, and the property qualification of representatives. The new elections, in the middle of 1856, shewed the prevalence of democratic sentiments in the community. The tests of the candidates were, manhood suffrage, equal elections, anti-state aid to religion, and national education, telegraphs, railways, posts, &c. The whole of the former popular representatives were returned, and on the 25th November, Major-General Macarthur, the acting Lieutenant-Governor, gave what was in reality the ministerial speech, in opening the first free parliament. Major-General Macarthur had rather allowed matters to manage themselves than interfere in any way, and had, by his affability of demeanor, considerably ingratiated himself with those with whom he was brought into contact. The reforms promised in "the speech" were—appointments to the civil service by examination, a new arrangement in the Audit office, rescinding "the Orders in Council," railways, a national bank, extension of electric telegraphs, tariffs, education, no state-aid to religion, law reform, and immigration. The Government carried the property qualification by a majority of five against the equality scheme of the opposition on the manhood suffrage question. The property qualification of members was the next important point of debate, in which the Government was defeated. But on the immigration scheme, the sum placed on the estimates exceeded the sum contemplated to be expended by £150,000. This occasioned a vote of censure, which being carried, the ministry resigned; and Mr. John O'Shanassy was sent for to form a ministry; the following gentlemen accepted office under him:—Mr. J. V. F. L. Foster, Treasurer; Mr. A. F. A. Greeves, Commissioner of Customs; Mr. C. Gavan Duffy, Commissioner of Public Works; Mr. G. S. W. Horne, Commissioner of Crown Lands; Mr. H. S. Chapman, Attorney-General; and Mr. J. D. Wood, Solicitor-General.

Sir H. Barkly arrived by the *Oneida*, the first ship that arrived belonging to the European and Australian Steam Navigation Company, in December, 1856. He was received with the customary demonstrations and formalities. His policy is very much that of non-interference; while his patronage of the literary, scientific and philanthrophic institutions of the colony is wise and liberal.* The resignation of the Haines ministry, occurred three months after the arrival of His Excellency, on 3rd March, 1857. The new ministry held office for barely six weeks. The political programme of Mr. John O'Shanassy, taken with the strong antipathy felt towards some of his colleagues, issued on the 22nd April in a vote of "Want of Confidence," which was carried by 34 against 19. The new ministry consisted of—Mr. W. C. Haines, Chief Secretary; Mr. J. M'Culloch, Commissioner of Trade and Customs; Mr. C. H. Ebden, Treasurer; Mr. A. Michie, Attorney-General; Mr. D. Moore, President of Board of Land and Works; Mr. T. H. Fellows, Solicitor-General; Mr. W. H. F. Mitchell, Postmaster-General. There was a change effected in the officers of the ministry, by the consolidation of the heretofore separate offices of public lands and public works, which had had severally a commissioner. One commissioner now was placed in office over both, and the Postmaster-General was now first constituted a ministerial officer, and the appointment vested in the cabinet, from its importance to the commercial interests of the colony. The new cabinet held office for the greater part of a year, and on the 24th February, 1858, a resignation

* See article respecting His Excellency elsewhere.

was declared in consequence of a motion by Captain Clarke, on a question affecting the schedule of Electoral Districts as proposed by the ministry. After some manœuvering in the political circles, a coalition ministry was formed thus:—Chief Secretary, Mr. John O'Shanassy; Treasurer, Mr. G. Harker; Attorney-General, Mr. H. S. Chapman; Solicitor-General, Mr. R. D. Ireland; Postmaster-General, Dr. G. S. Evans; Commissioner of Land and Works, Mr. C. Gavan Duffy; Customs, Mr. Henry Miller.

Amidst these ministerial changes various bills passed into law, which had considerable influence on the progress of the country. The measures for facilitating internal communication by railways, which are in process of being realised. The consolidation of local self-government by erection of municipalities in localities willing to undertake the implied responsibilities. The Crown lands bill, which it is said was carried through the lower house by a compromise, was rejected by the upper by a large majority, and was the occasion of several popular representatives being cast with their constituencies. The state-aid question, on account of which, it is also said, these compromises were yielded, was rejected by the upper house by a majority of one.

The subject of prison dicipline became a very serious question, by reason of the number of criminals, the inadequate provision for their management, and the spirit of resistance exhibited by them. Gaol accommodation was scanty, so that stockades and hulks, as well as prisons, were crowded. In one road gang, four prisoners attempted an escape, when two were killed and two escaped. The next was a bold attempt under the criminal Captain Melville to capture a boat, by which they were being towed to the hulk; two of the boat's crew were murdered, and two of the convicts perished. The tragedy was consummated by a third attack, and the murder of Mr. Price, the superintendent of convicts. The treatment of criminals is a subject that admits of loud condemnation of the Government by those who do not consider that the authorities have not an Alladin lamp to cause the erection of a prison palace in one night. Yet as a committee of inquiry sat on this question so early as 1852, there is ground for censure that more has not been done to effect salutary changes, and the revelations of prison-life by the convict Melville were such as to shock our common humanity, in the exposure of a system of vengeance, and not of reform, as the recognised principle of gaol economy. Happily, since the installation of Mr. W. P. N. Champ, a great change has been effected in the convict department. (See page 60.)

The subject of immigration, on which the first ministr was ousted, has undergone great change, in the appointment of an immigration agent for the colony, whose work would be to promote immigration by partial payments, so as to balance the disadvantage of distance and cost of voyage between this colony and North America, and with a special view to favor female immigration as a means of equalizing the sexes in the colony.

The education bill proposed the consolidation of the present existing boards, by the adoption of a national system analogous to that of Canada; but the introduction of a clause excluding all religious teaching from the school, and forbidding the use of the school-houses for the purpose of religious instruction, aroused an opposition from nearly all the denominations, who petitioned that the measure might not become law. The question is still before the house

The rapid advance made by the city and colony generally is the wonder of all visitors. The noble structures that have been erected in Melbourne*—the Parliament Houses, the Treasury, the Public Library, the Hospital, the Benevolent Asylum, the City Court, the County Court, the Gaols and Police Barracks, the Military Barracks, the Exhibition Building, the richly ornamented Banks, the Custom House, the Churches, in a pure style of ecclesiastical architecture, the Chamber of Commerce, together with the massive stores and offices of our merchants, all fascinate the eyes of strangers, though from familiarity the resident passes them without notice. These attest the wealth and importance of the colony, while the townships rapidly progressing where there are centres of population, and the extension of the agricultural enterprise of the colony, begin to give a fixity to colonial life that for years past has been unknown. Improvements in the condition of society will result from settled habits; and such improvements become daily more visible. Some of our worst evils, we may hope, have passed away; and if the future of Victoria shall exhibit less of the hurry and excitement of the last few years the advantages thus conferred will be the means of a permanent and glorious onward progress.

ABORIGINES.

The aborigines of Australia belong to the Malay family of mankind, but differ in many essential points. They have no affinity whatever to the New Zealanders. They use no clothing of any description, except square rugs, made of opossum skins, which are neatly stitched together, and which are thrown loosely around the body. In the coldest winter nights, when ice is formed, and rain and hail is pouring down upon them in torrents, they will, for greater protection, prop up a few boughs and pieces of the bark of trees to protect them from the rain. The different tribes are, however, fast diminishing; one after another becoming extinct, in accordance with that universal

* See article on Melbourne.

law which removes the weak from the path of the strong. Diseases, arising from excesses in which their acquaintance with the lowest class of civilisation soon makes them adepts, either suddenly carry them off, or make them liable to attacks of fever, rheumatism, &c. Attempts have been made to convert them to Christianity, but they have been generally unsuccessful, except under such fortunate circumstances as have enabled their friends to keep them absolutely estranged from their tribe and their habits. These instances of success, although pressed forward by lay colonists as giving grounds for hope if imitated on a large scale, have in one instance only been seized upon as the foundation of a comprehensive experiment in South Australia, where the Venerable Archdeacon Hale has seen his exertions blessed far beyond the expectations which the result of other missionary labors would have justified. With this exception the missions amongst the aborigines may be regarded as a series of experiments which have signally failed from first to last; and although from the first the settlers acquainted with the habits of the natives have pointed out that one failure would be followed by another, unless a system of isolation of converts from their tribes could be ensured, the missionaries of various persuasions have persisted with a zeal worthy of their object, but with a blindness which could secure no result but failure, in forming station after station just sufficiently remote from civilisation to afford slight hopes of success at the outset, but so close to its borders, that the onward march of the tide has soon engulphed the feeble results attained; and drunkenness and vice have made a moral havoc in the tribes, which disease has quickly consummated in death.

In 1838 a chief protector and four assistants were appointed for the tribes in Port Phillip. In the same year the Wesleyans formed a mission at Buntingdale, and in 1840 had four additional reserves in different quarters of the district, and homesteads established, to facilitate intercourse with the natives. In 1841 a corps of native police was embodied from among the Melbourne and Western Port tribes. In 1846 an aboriginal school for children of both sexes was established by labors of private individuals. In 1851 two Moravian missionaries established themselves at Lake Boga near the River Murray, to ascertain what their peculiar system could effect in the habits of the natives, and finally in 1853 the Episcopalians commenced a mission which is now in operation.

Up to 1848 the Government was at an outlay on behalf of the Wesleyan mission of about £6,700; of the aboriginal school, £800; for the protectorate, £42,200; native police, £11,000; a total of £61,000 for thirteen years, and no results of any value followed.

PHYSICAL GEOGRAPHY.*

The area of the colony was estimated, in a return laid before the Legislature nearly three years ago by the Surveyor-General, at 55,571,840 acres, or 86,831 square miles; that is, Victoria is nearly as large as England, Scotland, and Wales united; England having 50,922 miles, Scotland 81,324 miles, and Wales 7,898 miles; or in all 89,644 square miles. The acreage of England and Wales is computed by Major Dawson, R.E., at about thirty-eight millions, and that of Scotland at twenty millions; total, fifty-eight millions of acres, or two millions and a half more than the computed acreage of Victoria.

The country is generally low and level. There are extensive plains broken by ranges of inconsiderable height. The great range, which divides the waters flowing northward to the Murray from those running southward to the sea, extends from the Australian Alps to Wilson's Promontory, east of Western Port. The highest peaks are from 2,500 to 8,000 feet above the sea level. A great spur extends from the sources of the River Goulburn westward, to the sources of the Rivers Campaspe and Loddon, and a second extends thence westward to the Grampians. The Watershed, formed by these ranges, is nearly parallel to the coast, and its mean distance therefrom is about seventy miles. Extensive plains are found in the Wimmera district, in the north-western parts of the colony, and those, broken by ranges running north and south, extend thence to the county of Rodney and beyond the Goulburn. Plains of moderate extent, interrupted by chains of hills, stretch from the River Plenty to the Hopkins. The following table shows the approximate heights of some of the most elevated points in Victoria :—

Chain.	Name of hill or locality.	Feet.
First chain. Australian Alps, North-east to South-west.	The Cobboras	5,000 to 7,000
	Mount Pinnabar	4,100
	Plain of Omeo	3,100
	Mount Bullock, near Gibbo	2,160
	The Bogong Ranges	5,000 to 7,000
	May Day Hills, Beechworth	1,700 to 2,500
	Mount Valentia..	8,000 to 4,000
	Corranworabul	2,500
Second Chain. East to west.	Mount Leonard..	5,000 to 6,000
	Mount Disappointment	2,000
	Jayjerk, Mount Ida	1,500 to 2,000
	Mount Macedon	8,400
	Mount Alexander	8,298

* See article on Geology. Remarks on Agriculture, Land, &c., will be found in other parts of the work.

Chain.		Name of hill or locality.	Feet.
3rd Chain.	East to west.	Mount Buninyong	2,500
		Bullarook	2,400
		Mount Franklyn	1,700

Pyrenees, and other mounts to the Eastward.	Feet	Grampians and other mountains to the westward.	Feet.
Mt. Kosciusko (Strzelecki)	6,510	Mt. William (Mitchell)	5,400
„ Karribogong (Kosciusko?)	6,563	„ Sturgeon	1,957
„ Buller, between 5,000 and	6,000	„ Abrupt	2,621
„ Wellington and Gisborne	5,269	„ Napier	1,444
Castle Hill or Mt. Macmillan	4,860	„ Rouse	1,269
Tomboritka	5,865	„ Dundas	1,288
Bald Hill	4,668	„ Pierrepoint	891
Bo-Bo, or Baw Baw	5,062	„ Bainbugge	942
Notch Hill	4,625	Richmond Hill	720
Ben Cruachan	2,912	Mt. Eckersby	515
Taylor	1,463	„ Clay	657
Omeo Plains (Strzelecki)	3,100	„ Kincaird	736
Wilson's Promontory.		„ Elles	614
Mt. Wilson	2,500		
„ Hunter	1,138		
„ Singapore	451		

A great extent of country is occupied by palæozoic Rocks and masses of Granite.* The older and newer silurian are fossiliferous, and *trilobites graptolites*, *terebratulæ*, and many specimens of the *orthidiform brachiopoda* have been discovered in the neighborhood of Melbourne, on the Yarra, near Gisborne, at Heathcote, and at Sandhurst. In the neighborhood of the gold-fields, the palæozoic rocks are covered by thin deposits of the newer Tertiaries, composed of the detritus of quartz veins, and the surrounding rocks are often highly auriferous. The quartz veins are found principally in the vicinity of the granite, and they run generally north and south. A large extent of country south of the dividing range, extending from the River Plenty westward to the River Hopkins, is occupied by basalt and volcanic rocks. Some of the volcanoes are comparatively recent; but there are no evidences at present to shew that any have been active during the historical period. Some of the most remarkable volcanic hills are Mount Warrenheip, Mount Buninyong, Mount Warrion, Mount Gellibrand, Mount Hesse, Mount Moriac, Mount Leura, Mount Myrtown, Mount Franklyn, Mount Elephant, and Tower Hill.

Coal is found at Cape Patterson and near Cape Otway. Durable sandstone, suitable for building purposes, has not yet been discovered; but a useful limestone is found in many places. The basaltic rocks and granite, though difficult to work, are of excellent quality, and from the nature of their composition are durable. Thin beds of tertiary rocks, highly

* These notes are principally from Archer's *Facts and Figures.*

fossiliferous, extend from the coast a considerable distance inland, in many parts of the colony. They afford rough building stones, and in some localities limestone and a rich hematite.

The Rivers south of the main dividing ranges, flowing southward to the sea, are the Genoa and Snowy rivers, the Tambo, the Nicholson, the Mitchell, the Avon, the Thomson, the M'Alister, the Tarra, the Albert, the La Trobe, the Bass, the Yarra Yarra, with its tributary the Plenty, the Saltwater river, the Werribee, the Moorabool, Barwon, and Yarrowee, the Gellibrand, the Hopkins, the Eumeralla and the Glenelg. Thence, flowing northward to the Murray, are the Mitta Mitta, the Goulburn, the Campaspe and Coliban, the Loddon, the Avoca, and the Wimmera. The most important, the Murray, has several sources. The most south-eastern is the Indi, or Limestone, from Forest Hill, though the largest stream comes from near Mount Kosciusko. After a short northern course it turns to the westward, and reaches the sea, through Lake Victoria, into Encounter Bay. Its length is 2,400 miles, of which 2,000 are navigable. One-third of its course is in South Australia. (See page 135.)

Cape Otway is 60 miles south-west of Port Phillip Heads, and Volney 15 miles west of Otway. Point Flinders is 6 miles west of Port Phillip. The Heads of Port Phillip are, Lonsdale Point on the west, and Point Nepean on the east side. Shortland's Bluff is within the entrance on the west side, and Point Henry off Geelong Harbor. Cape Schanck is between Western Port and Port Phillip.

Lawrence and Lady Percy's Islands are in Portland Bay; French and Phillip are in Western Port. French, the inner one, is 15 miles long by 10 broad; Phillip is 20 by 7. Glennie and Cleft are west of Wilson's Promontory; Seal Isles and Rabbit are to the east, and Rodonto Rock is to the south. Snake or Latrobe Island, 12 miles long, is at the entrance of Corner Inlet. Sunday, 5 miles long, is north of it, at the entrance of Port Albert. Lance is between Lake Reeve and the sea, and Raymond between Lake King and Lake Victoria. Gabo, having a lighthouse, is near Cape Howe.

The lakes of Victoria are very numerous, but, in general, are shallow. The most extensive are Lakes Wellington, King, Victoria, and Reeve, in the Gipps Land District; Lakes Colac, Korangamite, Gnarpurt, Colongulac, Timboon, Pormbeet, Terang, and Tower Hill Lake, in the Western District; and Lakes Hindmarsh, Albacuytea, and Tyrrell, in the Wimmera District. Permanent springs are rare, and the country is not well watered. In wet seasons, the river basins are full, the plains become swampy, and marshes expand into lakes; but in dry seasons, the rivers dwindle into thin small streams, and many of the lakes become dry or salt.

Much of the basaltic soil is good, eminently suitable for horticultural purposes, and the plains, during a considerable portion of the year, afford good grass. Some of the palæozoic ranges would, it is believed, grow the finest description of grasses, and a vast extent of land is suited to the growth of cereals. Roughly dividing the country, we have tracts which are pastoral only to the extent of about 40,700 square miles; both pastoral and agricultural, about 26,000 ditto; auriferous, about 583 ditto; unavailable (i.e., land not explored, scrubby, or ill-watered, of which, perhaps, much may prove auriferous), about 19,548 ditto; making a total of 86,831 ditto, or 55,571,840 acres. Of the auriferous land about 180 square miles, or 115,200 acres, have been actually tested, and are at present being worked more or less. Of course the above figures are but vaguely approximate, but they will, however, serve to give a pretty accurate idea of the natural resources of the country.

The harbors are not very numerous, the principal one being Port Phillip Bay, which is 40 miles long, and nearly as broad, having an area of 900 square miles. The entrance between the Heads is two miles across. This bay contains two large and excellent harbors, viz., Hobson's Bay and Corio Bay, the ports respectively of Melbourne and Geelong. Portland Bay is a tolerably good harbor, but is exposed to the south-east wind and the swell of the Southern Ocean. Port Fairy, the harbor of Belfast, is inferior, in point of safety and convenience, to Portland. Lady Bay, the harbor of Warrnambool, is also exposed, and is shoal near the shore. Western Port contains a good harbor, but the entrance is not deep. In Gipps Land are also Port Albert and Welshpool, two excellent harbors. (See page 85.)

CLIMATE.

The Meteorology of Australia has scarcely, as yet, been investigated. It is true that observations have been taken at some stations for a considerable period, but until the results of a long series of ol servations, under an uniform system, at numerous stations, are available, it will be impossible to draw conclusions either useful to the colonist or valuable to science. Perhaps no portion of the globe is more interesting in all that relates to the phenomena of climate than Australia. A vast island-continent, stretching through more than 28 degrees from north to south, and with a breadth of 2,400 miles—on the east having the Pacific, and on the west the Indian Ocean —it presents climates almost as varied, and influences as numerous as any of the great continental divisions. Of these, however, it would be impossible, at present, to give any general or comprehensive description. The utmost that can be done with the few data available, is to give the results, meagre as they are, which have been deduced from observations taken during the last few years.

In Victoria the barometer and thermometer were observed at Melbourne from 1846 to 1851, inclusive, and the means deduced from these are given in *Archer's Statistical Register of Victoria*. They are as follow :—

	Mean Barometer. in.	Mean Thermometer. °
January	30·065	67·94
February	29·909	67·31
March	30·099	63·92
April	29·991	60·56
May	29.962	54·91
June	29·960	51·00
July	29·983	49·34
August	29·942	50·66
September	29·964	55·08
October	29·968	58·97
November	29·835	62·25
December	29·846	66·29
Means ..	29·960	59·02

Observations were commenced at Melbourne, in 1855, at the Surveyor-General's office, and the means of the barometer and thermometer are as follow :—

	1855-6		1856-7		1857-8	
	Mean Bar. in.	Mean Ther. °	Mean Bar. in.	Mean Ther. °	Mean Bar. in.	Mean Ther. °
February ..	,,	,,	29·964	68·7	29·956	72·3
March ..	,,	,,	30·187	70·4	29·966	65.0
April	,,	,,	30·050	61·4	30·176	62·2
May	,,	,,	30·121	53·8	30·272	52·3
June	30·249	50·3	29·915	50·7	29·916	49·7
July	30·093	48·3	30·044	46·8	30·075	49·4
August ..	30·010	50·7	29·917	51·8	30·144	51·5
September ..	29·997	54·3	29·958	54·7	30·081	53·2
October ..	30·042	58·5	29·949	57·3	29·906	68·7
November ..	29·920	61·9	29·904	59·6	29·977	60·4
December ..	29·968	64·7	29·899	61·4	29 935	57·1
January ..	30·031	67 9	29·874	66·4	29·875	72.1
Means	,,	,,	29·977	58·5	30·019	59·5

The highest temperature in shade recorded since the above series was commenced, was 109·2 on the 23rd December, 1857, and the lowest, 29·7, on the 12th July, 1855.

The mean temperature of the dewpoint is approximately 49·0, and the mean dryness is therefore 10·.

Rain.—The rain-fall at Melbourne, in 1855, was as follows:—June, 1·84 in.; July, 1·74 in.; August, 0·84 in.; September, 4·14 in.; October, 2·65 in.; November, 1·63 in.; and December, 3·98 in. In 1856 :—January, 2·38 in.; February, 0·97 in.; March, 2.81 in.; April, 4·76 in.; May, 2·96 in.; June, 2·79 in.; July, 2·35 in.; August, 1·22 in.; September, 3·49 in.; October, 2·78 in. ; November, 1·39 in.; and December, 1·84 in. In 1857 :—January, 1·23 in.; February, 3·98 in.; March, 3·80 in.

April, 0·99 in.; May, 2·00 in.; June, 1·99 in.; July, 1·16 in.; August, 1·69 in.; September, 3·83 in.; October, 5·28 in.; November, 2·12 in.; and December, 0·83 in. Total for the year 1856, 29·74 in. Total for the year 1857, 28·90 in.

Some districts in Victoria are occasionally visited by floods, but it does not appear that they are frequent, or that they extend over a considerable area. In New South Wales they are sometimes of a most serious character; and at such times the rivers, when stemmed by a gale from the eastward, overflow their banks, and the destruction in consequence is very great.

Droughts of long continuance are said to be not infrequent in some parts of Australia. Unfortunately, we have no very clear accounts of any that have occurred in Victoria, and, therefore, any speculations as to their cause are out of the question.

WIND.—The number of days on which the wind blows from each point throughout the year, at Melbourne, may be stated, approximately, as follows:—N., 70 days; N.E., 35 days; E., 15 days; S.E., 30 days; S., 75 days; S.W., 45 days; W., 35 days; N.W., 30 days; and calm, 30 days. In autumn and winter the northerly winds exceed the southerly, and in spring and summer the southerly winds exceed the northerly. Hot winds are frequent in summer, and they occasionally blow in spring and autumn. They are exceedingly dry, and invariably their approach is indicated by a sudden and often considerable depression of the barometer. They do not appear to be injurious to health, except, perhaps, in towns where there is much dust. They are supposed to be notably deficient in ozone. The westerly and south-westerly (cold winds), on the contrary, are sometimes saturated with ozone; and are seldom deficient.

The following table shews the mean temperature for each season; and for the year at twenty-five places. The temperatures for many of the stations have been computed from the tables given in Kaemtz's Meteorology, and others are derived from Daniell's Meteorology, and the Meteorological Report for 1853-4, by Lieut.-Colonel James, Royal Engineers:—

TOWN OR PLACE.	MEAN TEMPERATURE FOR THE Year.	Winter.	Spring.	Sum.	Autm.
	°	°	°	°	°
Melbourne (approx.)	59·0	50·0	57·0	69·0	61·0
Geelong (approx.)	58·1	49·5	58·6	67·1	57·5
Heathcote (approx.)	57·1	45·6	53·9	72·5	56·5
Rome	59·8	46·8	57·8	73·1	62·0
Montpellier	59·5(?)	44·4	56·8	75·9	60·9
Florence	59·6	44·3	58·5	75·3	60·3
Madrid	57·5	42·0	57·5	74·1	56·6
Naples (near)	61·5	49·6	59·3	74·8	62·2
Lisbon	61·5	52·3	59·9	71·0	62·6
Laguna (Teneriffe)	62·6	56·4	59·7	68·3	65·2
Paris	51·4	38·0	50·8	64·8	52·0
London	49·9	38·6	4[illegible]·6	62·2	50·1

Town or Place.	Mean Temperature for the Year.	Winter.	Spring.	Sum.	Autm.
Dublin	49·2	40·1	47·0	59·9	49·9
Cape of Good Hope	66·2	58·6	65·4	74·1	66·9
Sevastopol	52·7	35·2	50·3	71·0	54·6
Washington	54·8	36·1	50·3(?)	71·0	56·1
Rio Janiero	73·6	68·5	72·5	78·9	74·4
Calcutta	78·3	67·8	82·5	83·4	79·0
Bombay	78·8	73·7(?)	80·9	82·5	81·1
Madras	82·0	76·6	83·4	86·3	81·5
Brussels	50·3	36·5	50·1	64·7	50·3
Funchal	65·6	61·3	63·5	69·9	67·6
Freemantle, W. Australia ..	62·6	56·0	63·0	70·0	61·5
Parramatta. New South Wales	64·5	54·5	66·5	73·9	64·5
Hobart Town	52·4	42·0	52·8	63·1	51·6

An examination of the above table places our climate in a favorable point of view. Compare the climates of Melbourne and Madrid, and it will be seen what erroneous impressions would be given by merely quoting the mean temperature of each place. Even the temperatures of the seasons are not sufficient when we seek to know whether one climate is more salubrious than another. We must inquire as to the daily and monthly range of temperature, the mean humidity, and the range of humidity, the force of the wind, and the solar and terrestrial radiation.

Such tables would be of inestimable value to us at a time when foreign animals and plants are to be introduced to this country and domesticated. Constantly we hear of proposals to expend large sums for the procuring of animals which one scorching summer would either destroy or seriously deteriorate; and the cultivation of many plants is talked of, which would neither brave our winters nor survive the summers. And again, there are, undoubtedly, numerous animals and many fruits which might be introduced with advantage, and to which the climate would be favorable.

Meteorological Observatories, under the direction of Mr. R. Brough Smyth, F.G.S.L., are established in Victoria at Melbourne, Geelong, Heathcote, Sandhurst, Beechworth, Ballaarat, Camperdown, Portland, Castlemaine, Kooyoora, Mount Warrenheip, Ararat, Green Hills, Mount Ararat, Winter's Swamp, Port Albert, Welshpool, Mount Egerton, Tyntynderr (Swan Hill), Yan Yean, Gabo Island. Others are about to be established at a point on the Lower Murray, at Echuca, and on the coast. The names, &c., of the observers are inserted in *Bradshaw's Monthly Guide to Victoria.*

Observations are taken every day at 9½ a.m., 3½ p.m., and 9½ p.m. At the stations supplied with a complete set of standard instruments, a rigid uniformity of system is maintained. The barometers have all been compared with the standard in Melbourne. The dry and wet bulb thermometers are Kew standards, and the maximum and minimum are by Casella and Co., and Negretti and Zambra, and they have been compared with Kew standards. The rain gauges are nearly fourteen inches in diameter, and are on the construction adopted by the corps of Royal Engineers. A modification of Lawson's thermometer stand has been tested and approved: and several, exactly alike in every respect, have been sent to the observatories. The amount of ozone in the atmosphere is recorded at 9½ a.m., and at 9½ p.m. Moffatt's ozonometer is used. Complete sets of instruments have not yet been supplied to all the observatories; but such as are recorded have. in nearly every case, been compared with the standards,

Weekly reports of the state of the weather, signed by the observer, are, in most cases, sent to the local newspapers. A monthly report of the observations, in full, is published at the observatory, Melbourne; and a quarterly abstract, and an annual report embracing all the observations during the year, are regularly printed

NOTE.—Meteorological observatories are established in New South Wales under the direction of the Rev. W. Scott, Colonial Astronomer; in South Australia under the direction of Mr. Charles Todd, Superintendent of Magnetic Telegraphs, and in Tasmania under the direction of the Royal Society. In 1855, in consequence of the exertions of the Hon. Andrew Clarke, then Surveyor-General, the systems of observation in use in the various colonies were as far as possible assimilated. In New South Wales and Victoria they are nearly alike, the Colonial Astronomer, on his arrival in New South Wales, having adopted the system for his observatories which had been established in Victoria by the director, Mr. Smyth.

GEOLOGY.

Previous to the year 1850, the only published information relative to the geological structure of Victoria (then known as the Port Phillip district, or Australia Felix) was to be found in the works of Sir Thomas Mitchell and Count Strzelecki In 1845, Mr. J. Bute Jukes visited Port Phillip, as naturalist to the surveying expedition of H.M.S. *Fly*, Captain Blackwood, and in a small work entitled "Sketch of the Physical Structure of Australia," published in 1850, after his return to England, he gives a brief description of his own observations—made during a stay of only twelve days—on the structure of the country in the immediate vicinity of Melbourne and Geelong; he also recapitulates the previously published observations of Sir Thomas Mitchell on the Port Phillip district, which with those of Count Strzelecki and his own, may be said to include all that was known of the geological structure of Victoria up to the commencement of 1851.

In October, 1851, or shortly after the first discovery of gold in Victoria, Mr. Latrobe wrote to the Secretary of State for the Colonies as follows:—

No. 40.

Melbourne, Oct. 20th, 1851.

My Lord,—Referring to the late discovery of widely-extended and exceedingly valuable deposits of gold in this colony, and of the possibility that from this time forward the precious metal may be looked upon as one of the sources of revenue derivable from the Crown Lands, I would urge upon Her Majesty's Government the propriety of selecting and appointing as mineral surveyor for this colony, a gentleman possessed of the requisite qualifications, and acquaintance with geological science and phenomena.

2. I find myself greatly embarrassed at this time for want of the services of a competent agent of this class.

3. Should it be considered expedient to adopt my suggestion, I would venture to recommend that the salary allowed to the officer selected should not be under five hundred pounds per annum, with allowance for travelling expenses.

I have, &c.,
(Signed,) C. J. La TROBE.

To the Right Hon. Earl Grey, &c.

In consequence of this application, a geologist was appointed to proceed to Victoria who had been employed nearly seven years on the staff of the Geological Survey of Great Britain, under the direction of the late Sir Henry De la Bèche. The appointment was made in May, 1852, and in November, 1853, Mr. A. R. C. Selwyn arrived in the colony. After about two months, occupied in making a cursory examination of the principal gold-fields then known, it was considered advisable, as being the only way in which permanently valuable results could be obtained, at once to commence a survey which should form the basis for the construction of a detailed and connected geological map of the colony, and to conduct the work, so far as the nature of the country and the available means permitted, exactly on the model of the British Geological Survey.

The Geological Survey of Victoria was accordingly commenced at Mount Alexander, in April, 1853, and was carried on as expeditiously as the very limited means granted for the purpose would allow, until the 30th June, 1855, when it was stopped for a time, by order of the Government, on grounds of economy.

Up to the above date, the total area surveyed was about 3,402 square miles. The observations made were recorded with as much accuracy of detail as was practicable on the only topographical map then available for the purpose, a very imperfect one, on a scale of half an inch to one mile. This map, though of scientific interest, was far too small to be of any practical value in directing the operations of the miner. Short geological notes or reports on the structure of the areas embraced in these surveys have been printed as Parliamentary papers.

At the commencement of 1856 (probably due in a great measure to the liberal spirit in which the matter was then taken up by the Hon. Capt. A. Clarke, the late Surveyor-General), the survey was recommenced, and has since been carried on, on a scale more commensurate with the object in view; and which, if continued, will enable it to be made a work which will prove not only an interesting and valuable contribution to science, but also permanently and practically useful.

Since the above date an area of 1,512 square miles, extending from Hobson's Bay, north to Kilmore, and north-west to Tarradale, has been surveyed. The observations made have been laid down most minutely on maps, on a scale of two inches to one mile. These are being engraved, and will shortly be published in a consecutive series of quarter sheets, each embracing fifty-four square miles. Considering that the geological survey of Great Britain has now been in progress for upwards of twenty-three years, with the aid of numberless advantages favorable to its rapid progress, which do not exist in a new country, including a numerous staff of highly competent observers, and topographical maps of the most perfect description; and notwithstanding these combined advantages, it is only quite recently that the structure of some of the more complicated districts has been correctly worked out and explained, while many others still remain to be examined; it becomes almost unnecessary to say, that at present, it is impossible to give any sketch of the geology of this colony, embracing as it does an area nearly equal to that of Great Britain, which could be regarded as more than a very imperfect outline. Any such sketch must be founded almost entirely upon the observations of the geological survey staff, made over only a limited portion of the colony, during a period of little more than three years; it would, therefore, require much modification, and perhaps, in some instances entire reconstruction, from the result of future observations over more extended areas.

Though, up to the present time only 4,914 square miles have been actually surveyed, very much more extended areas have been traversed and cursorily examined. The observations made prove that by far the greater portion of Victoria is occupied by formations which belong to only two of the great geologic epochs, viz.:—"primary" or "palæozoic," and "tertiary" or "cainozoic."

Many of the well-known European groups, or subdivisions of the above epochs, have been recognised. Others are apparently missing, but those that do exist contain a fossil fauna, of which many species and more genera are identical with those found in the equivalent European group.* They also occupy the same relative geological position, and exhibit a most striking similarity in general lithological character.

---

* A lower silurian bivalve shell has been found in great abundance in the "spoil heaps" from the Bendigo quartz reefs, which is also characteristic of the lower or cambro silurian rocks, associated with gold quartz veins in North Wales.

I.—LOWER PALÆOZOIC ROCKS.

The rocks from which the whole of the gold has been originally derived are of the primary or palæozoic epoch, including the cambrian, cambro silurian, and upper silurian groups. They consist, in their lower members, as in Britain, chiefly of schistose and slaty rocks, with numerous beds of hard, gritty quartoze, and also, soft and fine grained micaceous sandstones. The latter often afford good freestone for building purposes; and the former, occasionally, flags and roofing slates. Freestones from these beds are much used at Castlemaine and Sandhurst. In the upper portions, which apparently do not extend anywhere to the westward of the meridian of Keilor, shaly "mudstones," inter-stratified with beds of hard and soft grits and fine grained micaceous sandstones, are most prevalent.

Wherever any of these palæozoic rocks appear on the surface, but more particularly in their lower or older portions, they are intersected by innumerable veins of white quartz, from the smallest thread to many feet in thickness, and all apparently more or less auriferous. With respect to the origin of these veins, there appears no reason whatever to suppose that they are due to any causes different from those which have operated in the formation and filling up of all other mineral veins, whether of tin, copper, or any other crystalline mineral; and any explanation which satisfactorily accounts for all the effects produced in one case will probably be equally applicable to the other. Besides gold, many metallic minerals exist in the quartz veins of Victoria; but, with the exception of tin and antimony, none have as yet been discovered in workable quantity.

At intervals throughout the palæozoic strata, large areas occur exclusively occupied by granitic and other "plutonic" rocks. These have invariably hardened and metamorphosed, for a short distance from the point of junction, the stratified rocks amongst which they have been intruded, and are, therefore, of more recent origin; but in no instance do they appear to have exercised the smallest influence in determining the general strike, dips or contortions of the latter, or their present often nearly vertical position; and so far as is at present known, the granitic areas contain little or no gold, either in veins or in older drifts, at a distance from their junction with the palæozoic rocks.

The area occupied by these older palæozoic and plutonic rocks, exclusive of Gipps Land, either on the surface or overlaid by newer tertiary deposits immediately derived from them, and where they do not exceed, with their contemporaneous and overlying sheets of basaltic lava, 800 feet in thickness, could not be estimated at less than 30,000 square miles; and if from this we deduct 10,000 square miles, occupied by the plutonic rocks above noticed, and others which are not auriferous, we have 20,000 square miles, over which there is every probability of gold being found in remunerative quantities, either in quartz veins, traversing cambrian, cambro silurian and upper siluriau rocks, or in overlying tertiary sands and gravels, many of the older and richest portions of which are now concealed under the widely extended sheets of basaltic lava, by which they have been preserved from denudation.

II.—UPPER PALÆOZOIC OR MESOZOIC ROCKS.

The coal bearing rocks of Australia are largely developed in certain districts in Victoria. The Barrabool Hills, Cape Otway, Western Port, part of Gipps Land, aud probably in the Grampians. Outliers or detached patches of these rocks also occur near Bacchus Marsh and at Kyneton, proving their former extension over wide areas, from which they must have been removed by denudation. They afford the best freestone for building which has yet been obtained in the colony, but do not contain any mineral veins or auriferous deposits. No fossil fauna has yet been discovered in them. The flora they contain is of an oolitic type, and they are, therefore, considered by Professor McCoy to belong to the mesozoic or secondary epoch. They have, however, as yet, been very little examined in Victoria; and no very satisfactory or conclusive evidence exists at present as to their exact position in the geologic series. Beds of the same age and relative geological position rest in Tasmania, conformably on, and gradually pass downwards into calcareous beds of true carbonife ous age, which overlie quite unconformal ly the upturned and denuded edges of lower silurian or cambrian rocks, and the entire group has, generally, if we except the oolitic character of its fossil flora, more resemblance to the carboniferous than the oolitic rocks of Europe. In all probability, however, it will eventually be found that in Australia, as in America and India, carboniferous rocks occur, of both palæozoic and mesozoic age

At Western Port, near Cape Patterson, a few seams of coal of good quality occur. Only two have yet been discovered which are sufficiently thick to be profitably worked; but, from their general character, as also from that of the beds with which they are associated, it might be inferred that they are permanent only over very limited areas. A shaft recently sunk by the Government, to test the extension of the Cape Patterson seams, fully confirms this inference, as the seam, which is upwards of three feet thick, where cropping on the beach, contains only twenty inches of coal, in three bands, in the shaft, about 30 yards distant.

Whether any thicker and more permanent seams exist in lower portions of the formation, is at present uncertain. A shaft and bore, 300 feet deep, has been contract d for, for the purpose of testing this, and is now being executed at the cost of the Government.

In previous years considerable sums, which might have been saved by a very small amount of geological knowledge and investigation, have been injudiciously and fruitlessly expended, both in the Cape Patterson, Cape Otway, and Barrabool Hills districts, in searching for workable seams of coal.

III.—TERTIARY OR CAINOZOIC ROCKS.

Rocks referable to one or other of the groups of this epoch, occupy, probably, fully two thirds, or 60,000 square miles of the surface of Victoria. They rest nearly horizontally on all the older formations, and over large areas are interstratified, especially in their upper portions, with extensive sheets of basaltic lava, and other recent volcanic products. They extend from the sea level to elevations of 1,500 or 2,000 feet.

In many parts of the colony, more particularly the seaboard and the Murray basin, they include beds which, from their organic contents and relative geological position, are evidently representatives of the eocene, miocene, pliocence, and pleistocene deposits of Europe.

The precise position of the gold drifts in the above series is at present exceedingly doubtful. No beds are yet known in Victoria associated with or forming a portion of these drifts, in which fossil marine fauna exist; neither has any gold been obtained from underneath the known fossiliferous tertiary formations above mentioned; the only means there is, therefore, at present, of deciding this question, is an examination of the geological position of the gold bearing tertiaries and the fossiliferous tertiaries relatively to the contemporaneous and overlying volcanic products; and it is then found that the miocene tertiary sands, clays, and limestones of the seaboard, occupy the same geological position as the older gold drifts or sands, clays, and quartz gravels of the gold-fields. This would lead to the inference that the older gold drifts are of miocene age; the evidence, however, is by no means satisfactory, and the question must remain to be decided by more extended investigation. That there are gold drifts indicating at least three distinct deposits, the result of successive upheavals and depressions, is quite certain, at the same time they may possibly be only subdivisions of an extended pleistocene period.

These three auriferous deposits sometimes occur in the same locality: and in this fact lies the explanation of the first, second, and sometimes third bottom discovered by the miner, the last being always on the solid or unmoved palæozoic rock.

This question of the true age of the gold drifts is of very great practical importance, inasmuch as if they really extend to the age of the miocene tertiaries, several thousand square miles might be added to the auriferous area of Victoria. In any case, however, there can be no doubt that the gold mines of Victoria, if worked with the requisite combination of skill, labor, capital, and efficient machinery, will prove as permanently profitable as the tin, copper, and lead mines of Great Britain.

Government Geologist, Alfred R. C. Selwyn; Palæontologist, Professor McCoy. There are four field-assistants, two draftsmen, eight laborers, and one engraver, employed in connexion with the geological survey.

GOLD.

The following table, showing the quantity and value of the gold exported from Victoria up to the present time, will place in the clearest and most compendious point of view the progress of this interesting branch of industry, so far as the results can be ascertained from the official returns of exports from Victoria. The figures, however, are exclusive of the large amount carried away by private hand, and which is known to have been very considerable previous to the legislative enactment imposing an export duty and providing the penalty of forfeiture in case of non-entry at the Customs :—

Year.	Quantity.	Value.
	Oz.	£
1851	145,137	438,777
1852	1,988,526	6,135,728
1853	2,497,723	8,644,529
1854	2,144,699	8,255,550
1855	2,751,535	10,904,150
1856	2,985,991	11,943,458
1857	2,762,460	10,987,591
1858, to 30th June	1,279,767	5,119,069
Total	16,555,838	62,428,852

Having before us the country and the population, the next question naturally arising is, what have the latter been doing, and what have they accomplished? The principal occupation of the people, as is well known, has been gold-seeking, and the Registrar-General supplies us with information of the results. The first operations were of a very primitive nature. The tin basin and the cradle were the principal implements. The gold was sought for only in alluvial flats, and there was a prospect of these being speedily worked out. The condition of the digger was that of a gambler. It was uncertain and frequently miserable. To show the change that has taken place, it is only necessary to give the following statement of mechanical appliances now in use, which have succeeded the old system of digging by mere isolated exertions, extracted from official returns of the machinery employed on the gold-fields in the month of May last:—282 steam-engines, 4,256 puddling-machines, 133 quartz-crushing machines, 908 toms, sluices, and dams, 508 whims and whips, 66 horse machines, 200 water-wheels, 13 boring machines, 1 smelting machine.

Although the average quantity of gold produced has not increased during the last two years, the circumstance is more than compensated by the unquestionable permanence of the future supply, arising from the highly auriferous character of the quartz formations which so extensively pervade the country. While gold was only obtainable by workings on and near the surface, it was fairly a question whether the produce, for any long series of years, could be maintained at anything approaching to the rich yields of the early discoveries. So great, however, have been the results of quartz crushing, that the exhaustion of our gold mines has now become a contingency too remote for present speculation. So great is the produce of the quartz reefs becoming, that it is estimated that 60 per cent. of the gold brought from the Bendigo district alone, one of the oldest and most celebrated of the gold-fields, is at present obtained by the quartz miners. This field, which at one time had exhibited signs of comparative exhaustion, is now in consequence rapidly regaining its original eminent position as a valuable gold yielding district.

A TABLE showing the average melting loss and fineness of Alluvial Gold of the several Victorian Gold-Fields.*

	Melting loss per cent..	Fineness of the resulting bar gold. c. gr.	c. gr.	c. gr.
Amherst ..	2 to 3 6-10 ..	23 2	to 23 2 6-8	average 23 2 4-8
Anderson's Ck.	.. ..	23 1 4-8		
Ararat	1¾ to 2¾ ..	23 0 5-8	to 23 1 5-8	
Avoca	2	23 1 6-8	to 23 2 5-8	
Ballaarat ..	¼ to 3. Average of good samples 1 per cent.	23 2 5-8	to 23 2 7-8 (Mixed samples lower.)	
Blackwood ..	.. ..	23 0		
Buckland ..	.. ..	22 3 6-8		
Caledonia ..	.. ..	23 1 5-8		
Castlemaine ..	1⅓ to 3 3-10 (average 2¼).	22 3 3-8	to 23 0 1-8	average 22 3 7-8
Chinaman's Flat	.. ..	23 2 7-8		
Coliban ..	.. ..	22 2 2-8		
Creswick ..	1½ to 2½ ..	23 1 7-8	to 23 2 5-8	
Do., Spring Hill	2 to 2½ ..	22 2 7-8		
Dunolly ..	1½ to 2½ ..	23 1 3-8	to 23 2 4-8	
Gipps Land District†—				
Shean's Point	2¾	20 3 5-8		
Dry Gully ..	3½	20 3 2-8		
Lower Creek	2¾	21 4-8		
Swift Creek ..	2	21 2 4-8		
Boggy Creek	1	23 1 6-8		
Gibb's C. near Mitta Mitta	2¾	21 0 4-8		
Goulburn ..	.. ..	23 0 2-8		
Do., new rush	.. ..	22 0 7-8		
Do., Frenchman's Gully	.. ..	23 0 5-8		
Hell's Hole, Goulburn River ..	.. ..	22 0 5-8	to 22 0 7-8	
Jones' Creek ..	2	23 0 3-8	to 23 0 6-8	average 23 0 4-8
Kilmore ..	2¼	23 0	to 23 0 6-8	
Kingower ..	.. ..	22 3 4-8	to 22 3 6-8	
Korong ..	1¼ to 1½, and much higher in cases.	23 1 2-8	to 23 2 6-8	

* From calculations made by Mr. George Foord, Assayer, Melbourne.

	Melting loss per cent.	Fineness of the resulting bar gold. c. gr.	c. gr.	c. gr.
Linton's (Sm. C.)	2¼	22 3		
Do. (Armstrong's)	1¾	23 1		
Maryborough..	2	23 2 1-8	to 23 2 7-8	average 23 2 4-8
Do. White Hills	.. ..	23 2 6-8		
M'Ivor** ..	1 7-8 to 3 6-10 (average 2½).	23 0 5-8	to 23 2 7-8	average 23 2 4-8 (good samples).
Mt. Franklyn..	2¼	22 2 6-8		
New Bendigo..	.. ..	23 1 2-8		
Ovens* ..	2½ to 3½ ..	23 2 6-8	Lower when admixed with Goulburn or Omeo.	
Woolshed, fused	1¼ to 2 6-10	23 2 1-8	to 23 3	average 23 2 7-8
Spring Creek	.. ..	23 2 2-8		
9-Mile Creek	.. ..	23 2 6-8		
3-Mile Creek	3½	23 2 6-8		
Running Ck.	6 or less ..	23 2 3-8		
Pleasant Creek	.. ..	22 2 4-8	to 22 3 4-8	
Raglan ..	.. ..	23 1 3-8	to 23 2	
Sandhurst ..	1¾ to 2¼ ..	22 3 6-8	to 23 0 2-8	average 22 3 7-8
White Hills..	2¾	23 2		
Epsom dust..	1	23 0 4-8		
Tarradale ..	.. ..	23 0		
Tarrangower ..	.. ..	23 0 3-8		

NOTE.—In genuine samples of alluvial gold, although the amount of melting loss will very much depend upon the care in cleaning exercised by the buyer, the fineness is pretty constant for each field, and will seldom deviate from the average mark more than a few eighths of a carat grain. With matrix gold, however, the case is very different, and samples from the same reef—even from the same claim—will often differ widely as to melting loss and fineness, according to the treatment in roasting and crushing. Matrix gold is usually lower than alluvial gold from the same locality; there are, however, exceptional cases.

As examples of the fineness of amalgam gold, the following may be quoted:—

	c. gr.	c. gr.	c. gr.
Mariner's Reef, Maryborough ..	23 2 7-8	to 23 3 2-8‡	
White Horse Reef ,, ..	22 3 7-8‖		
Simmons' Reef, Mt. Blackwood ..	23 0 2-8	to 23 1 2-8§	
Mount Gold, Castlemaine ..	23 0 3-8		
Tarrangower, Eagle Hawk ..	23 1		
,, Bee-hive Reef ..	23 0 4-8		
,, Nuggety Reef ..	23 0 3-8		
Ballaarat, amalgam gold ..	22 2 3-8	to 23 0 1-8	
Avoca, ,, ..	22 3 3-8	to 23 0 7-8	
Mt. Franklyn ,, ..	20 1 3-8	to 23 2 1-8	
,, the fineness usually ranging between	22 2 2-8	to 22 3 5-8	
Sandhurst, quartz gold	21 2 7-8	to 23 0	average 22 3 5-8
Coliban, amalgamated	22 3 3-8		
Amherst, amalgam gold ..	22 3 3-8	to 23 2 6-8	
,, usual fineness from ..	23 1 2-8	to 23 2 4-8	
Steiglitz, amalgam gold ..	17 2 1-8	to 22 2 5-8	average 21 2
Goulburn, amalgam	17 0 1-8	to 23 1 5-8	
,, usual from	21 2 2-8	to 23 1 4-8	
Korong, amalgam	22 2 4-8	to 23 1 5-8	

The melting loss of amalgam gold varies between ½ and 15 per cent.

** Quality of M'Ivor gold gradually lowering.

* High melting loss due to tin oxide.

† Gipps Land gold gets finer as the locality approaches seaboard.

‡ The highest known matrix gold higher than Maryborough alluvial.

‖ Lower than Maryborough alluvial.

§ Higher than Blackwood alluvial.

SEWERAGE AND WATER COMMISSION.

The Yan Yean Reservoir, from which Melbourne derives its abundant supply of water, takes rank as one of the largest artificial sheets of water in the world. It is situated about nineteen miles north of Melbourne at the foot of the Plenty Ranges, in the parish of Yan Yean, from whence it derives its name; it was formerly a valley amongst the hills, known as Rider's swamp, and is nearly surrounded by the natural elevation of the ground, but is enclosed at the outlet of the valley by a gigantic embankment 3159 feet in length, 31 feet high at its highest point, 20 feet wide at the top, 170 feet wide at the bottom, with slopes of 3 to 1 towards the water and 2 to 1 towards the land. In the centre of this embankment is a solid wall of puddle founded 10 feet below the natural surface of the ground, 30 feet thick at the bottom, and 10 feet thick at the top. This embankment, by stopping the drainage from the hills, has turned the valley into a lake covering an area of about 1300 acres, 2½ miles across at its widest point, 9 miles in circumference, of a maximum depth of 25 feet 6 inches, and having a capacity of nearly 6,500,000,000 gallons, or rather more than three years' supply for a population of 200,000 persons, allowing for each person thirty gallons per day for all purposes. This immense body of water is the accumulated drainage, 1st, from the rain fall over a water-shed of 4,650 acres, exclusive of the area of the reservoir itself; 2nd, of about 600 acres drained by the watercourse connecting the River Plenty with the reservoir; and, 3rd, of the valley of the Plenty, embracing an area of about 40,000 acres; the Plenty River, which serves as a vehicle to convey this drainage into the reservoir, having been connected with it partly by an open cut and partly by a tunnel 440 yards in length, driven through one of the hills surrounding the reservoir. In case, however, of the water rising to within 5 feet of the top of the embankment, a bye-wash has been constructed, by means of which the surplus water escapes and is returned through a channel into the River Plenty. The water in the Yan Yean, which stands at its highest level about 600 feet above high-tide in the River Yarra, is conveyed to Melbourne by 19 miles of iron piping, the pressure in which is reduced by several valves of original construction, the water is distributed through the streets by about 55 miles of mains, besides which upwards of 30 miles of mains have been provided, and are now being laid down, for conveying the water to the suburbs. Considerable discussion has taken place respecting the quality of the water from the Yan Yean, and in the face of conflicting statements it would be inadvisable for us to express an opinion. The idea of supplying Melbourne with water from the Yan Yean originated with the late Mr. James Blackburn, the City Surveyor of Melbourne, who made the preliminary survey in 1850, and laid his plan before the City Council on August 9th, 1851. After the incorporation of the Commission of Sewers and Water Supply the scheme, with some modifications, was finally adopted, and Mr. Blackburn was appointed consulting engineer, and Mr. Matthew Bullock Jackson, engineer to the commission. Mr. Blackburn did not, however, live to see more than the commencement of his great work, which was carried out by Mr. Jackson, by whom all the details were designed, and the work conducted to a successful issue. The works were four years in progress, the first sod of the embankment having been turned by Mr. Latrobe on the 20th December, 1853, and Melbourne was supplied with the water towards the latter end of the year 1857; the official ceremony of turning on the water was performed by the Hon. Major-General Macarthur on the 31st December, 1857. The cost of the works, including all contingencies, has been £664,452. A sum of £90,606 was expended on works for temporary supply; likewise £38,317 has been incurred in preparatory measures towards the future sewerage of the city of Melbourne. The Commission was established under the Act 16 Victoria, No. 39 (assented to on 8th February, 1853), intituled, "An Act to establish a Board of Commissioners for the better sewerage and drainage of the City of Melbourne, and for supplying water thereto, and to the suburbs thereof." By this Act the Board is to consist of four members, three to be nominated by the Governor, with the advice of the Executive Council, and the other to be the Mayor of the City of Melbourne for the time being, who shall be an *ex officio* member of the Board. The said Act constitutes the Board a body politic and corporate, and as such it is able and capable to sue and be sued, and to prosecute and inform in all courts of law, as well criminal as civil, and in courts of equity, and to have and execute all the powers and duties vested in it by the said Act. The present management is in the hands of a Commission, consisting of the Hon. G. S. W. Horne (President), Messrs. F. A. Powlett, R. H. Horne, and the Mayor of Melbourne. Secretary: F. J. Bury.

ELECTRIC TELEGRAPH.

The works in connexion with this system of rapid intercommunication were commenced in November, 1853, by Samuel W. McGowan, the present General Superintendent of Telegraphs. First line opened to Williamstown in February, 1854; to Geelong in November of the same year; and to Queenscliff in January, 1855.

The business in 1854 amounted to 3,869 messages; in 1855, to 12,241; in 1856, to 13,741; total, 29,851.

During the same period the revenue derived amounted to

£6,611 9s. 11d., and the value of dispatches in the public service amounted to £6,583 14s. 4d.

In December, 1856, communication was opened with Ballaarat; and in January, 1857, with Sandhurst, embracing *en route* Gisborne, Kyneton, and Castlemaine.

In 1857, the number of messages transmitted reached 26,480; the revenue, £4,662 1s. 5d.; and the value of messages on the public service, £1,352 3s. 6d. Arrangements were also concluded between the respective Governments of New South Wales, Victoria, South Australia, and Tasmania for a mutual extension of lines to points at the boundaries of the several colonies where the communication might be joined, and a continuous connection formed between Adelaide, Melbourne, Sydney, and Hobart Town, embracing all places of importance *en route*.

The lines within Victoria, for carrying out the general scheme have been completed and in successful working order for several months past. The line from Melbourne to Adelaide was opened on July 19, 1858, but it is not expected that the entire line will be opened between Adelaide and Sydney before the latter part of the present year, and between Victoria and Tasmania in the early part of 1859.

Offices are established and communication now open, at Melbourne, Kilmore, Longwood, Benalla, Wangaratta, Beechworth, Belvoir, Albury, Sandhurst, Castlemaine, Kyneton, Gisborne, Sandridge, Williamstown, Geelong, Queenscliff, Ballaarat, Fiery Creek (Raglan), Streatham, Hexham, Warrnambool, Belfast, Portland.

Lines are at present under contract and in course of construction, which, when completed, will bring Melbourne into telegraphic connection with Maldon, Dunolly, Carisbrook, Maryborough, Avoca, Daylesford, Creswick, and Echuca.

The line connecting with Tasmania will proceed from Geelong to Cape Otway, *via* Apollo Bay, thence by submarine cable to King Island, thence to Three Hummock Island, thence to a point on the north coast of Tasmania. Communication will be maintained with Cape Otway and King Island.

THE BOTANICAL GARDENS.

The Botanical Gardens at Melbourne are situated on the left bank of the River Yarra, and are within half-a-mile of the city. Improvements have been made, of late, to a considerable extent, under the direction of Dr. Ferdinand Mueller, the Government Botanist, who also in various ways has promoted the science of botany in this colony.

Among the recent additions to the Melbourne Botanical Gardens are the following:—A palmhouse has been erected on one of the rises, a tasteful edifice, which, when filled with plants, cannot fail to become very attractive to the friends of horticulture. The orchestra pavilion, built in a prominent part of the gardens, may be regarded as quite an ornament in the landscape, and numerous have been the visitors who have assembled around it in the afternoons, when, by the kindness of the officers of the 40th regiment, the military band was permitted to attend.

An aviary, constructed of wood and wire, partially covered with climbers, and including some shrubs and small trees, has been erected in a gully below the rustic bridge; thus the sight and song of the birds may be fully enjoyed without disturbing them. Hitherto nightingales, thrushes, blackbirds, goldfinches, linnets, and a considerable number of canary birds have been contributed by the liberality of the Philosophical Institute of Victoria and of various donors. Our expectation of adding from this place many European song-birds to the Fauna of Australia, by giving freedom to the young broods, will at least, in regard to canary birds be fully realised.

A small menagerie has been formed, chiefly of marsupial animals and of water birds; for the latter, islands will be formed in the rather extensive lagoon, as soon as means permit.

The footbridge built across the Yarra, by facilitating so much the access to the gardens, has greatly augmented the number of visitors; on an average more than 3000 enjoy, on Sundays alone, the recreation and instruction which the picturesque site of the garden, the manifold delightful views from its rises, and the variety of plants now under cultivation, afford. Many new walks have been formed through the lawns; some of them have lately been lined with young trees of the Moreton Bay grevillea, with the Illawarra flame-tree, and the poplar sterculia, all highly recommendable for avenues, as combining evergreen umbrageous foliage with beauty in habit and flower. A portion of the garden, recently laid out, exhibits a number of plants arranged according to systematic classification, principally intended for demonstrating to students the mutual affinities of plants. A medicinal and economical garden is under progress, which, it is hoped, will become of some importance when the Botanical Museum and Lecture Room shall be built in this establishment, so that living plants, their preparations, and their productions, as well as collections of dried plants, woods, fruits, &c., may be simultaneously studied under the aid of lectures, books, diagrams, &c. Meanwhile a collection of botanical specimens, from various parts of Australia, has been deposited in the University Museum, and another herbarium, restricted to Victorian plants, has been prepared for the Public Library.

It is the intention to erect, in the centre of the garden, a spacious ornamental pavilion for horticultural exhibitions, occasional bazaars for benevolent purposes, &c.

The contemplated extension of the Yan Yean pipes to this

establishment, will greatly tend to the improvement of the plantations in the elevated parts of the garden.

The Pinetum, commenced on the abrupt declivities towards the lagoon, has latterly been extended by rows of araucarias and groups of other pines. All those parts of the garden which stood particularly in need of it, have within the last few months, been drained by under-ground pipes.

The number of different kinds of plants has been nearly doubled since last year, about 8,000 species being now under cultivation, of which it would be beyond the limits of these pages to specify all those of peculiar interest. But in the open grounds may be noticed the Paraguay and the Chinese tea, the cotton plant (producing occasionally, without protection, its cotton), the sugar maple, the cork oaks, the Chinese tallow tree, the liquorice, the New Zealand flax, the manna ash, the Chinese grass-cloth plant, the different Kauri pines of East Australia, New Zealand, and the South Sea Islands, the famous Wellingtonia (the so-called "big tree" of California), the argan tree, the quandang, the Australian sassafras, the American sarsaparilla, the Mediterranean caper, the banya banya tree of Moreton Bay, the oak chesnut, Spanish chesnut, red cedar, sumach, corob tree, &c.

In the greenhouses may be noticed the cochineal cactus, the cherimoyer, the staghorn ferns, the ginger, cardamon, cinnamon, and other spice plants, the monkey bread tree, several palms and screw pines, the anetto plant, the logwood tree, &c.

The director of the gardens is particularly anxious to augment the number of useful plants in this establishment, and will endeavor to see them gradually distributed over the country. Public gardens, reserves, and ground for plantations, in various parts of the colony, are generally supplied with young plants from this establishment.

Although an extensive correspondence has been opened with the administrators of public and private gardens of many countries, and although a regular system of interchange commenced, it will be highly gratifying to the director of our gardens to be aided by the friendly co-operation of his patriotic fellow-colonists in introducing plants, chiefly of ornament or utility, from abroad. The requirements of a young and struggling establishment like this are numerous, but attention is directed to a paper on a general introduction of useful plants into Victoria, published this year in the second part of Vol. II. of the Transactions of the Philosophical Institute of Melbourne, containing a brief summary of some of the principal plants desirable either for our gardens or for distribution over the country. As an instance of how much remains to be accomplished in this direction, we may adduce, that of several hundred distinct kinds of South African heaths, not more than one dozen have been hitherto introduced into the gardens of Victoria, whilst most of them would thrive in our climate. The minute seeds of these and numerous other equally handsome plants might readily be conveyed in letters. Other large genera of the Cape flora, such as mesembryanthemums, pelargoniums, &c., are in an equally scanty proportion, represented in our gardens.

It may be finally stated that the establishment would always be in a position to offer an equivalent for any contributions received. And whilst it is particularly desired that the vessels of our merchants will favor us occasionally with importations of living plants from foreign ports, the Government Botanist will always be extremely glad to afford information on the best method of packing plants, bulbs, seeds, &c., and will gladly assist by all means within his reach to promote the important object of rendering the vegetable treasures of other countries available to the colony.

The Zoological Gardens are in course of formation on the opposite bank of the river.

RELIGION.

The names of the ministers of the various churches, and the places at which they severally reside, are inserted in *Bradshaw's Monthly Guide to Victoria*,

The following table shows the number of persons and places of worship belonging to the principal religious denominations, in the years 1851 and 1857 respectively, according to the census returns:—

	1851.		1857	
	Persons.	Churches.	Persons.	Churches.
Church of England, &c. ..	37,433	7	175,418	99
Presbyterians	11,608	8	65,935	55
Wesleyan Methodists ..	4,988	5	28,305	192
Other Protestants	4,313	2	27,521	59
Roman Catholics	18,014	5	77,351	64
Jews	364	1	2,208	4
Mahomedans and Pagans ..	201	..	27,254	
Residue	424	..	6,774	
TOTALS	77,345	28	410,766	473

NOTE.—In the column for 1857 the numbers entered under the head of "Church of England, &c.," include 15,520 persons simply styling themselves "Protestants," and 221 of the Free Church; and under the head of "Other Protestants" are included 10,858 Independents, 6,484 Baptists, 6,574 Lutherans, 1,480 Unitarians, besides 2,125 belonging to minor sects. This arrangement is necessitated by the very limited nature of the Census Returns for 1851, with which comparison is made.

We have endeavoured to secure information respecting the progress of the various denominations, and feel gratified in giving the following statements, supplied from authentic sources:—

CHURCH OF ENGLAND.

The Episcopalian Church in Victoria, as regards assistance or countenance from the State, is on precisely the same footing as other denominations of professing Christians. Her proportion of the grant of £50,000 allowed by the present Constitution of the colony for religious purposes, is £23,000, one-half of which goes to assist in the building of churches and parsonages, and the other towards the maintenance of the clergy; so that in a great measure for building, and almost entirely for the latter object, the church is dependent on her members for support. And those, having in their native islands been accustomed to an establishment which required nothing of this kind from them, are, with a few striking exceptions, slow to perceive the full extent of their responsibilities, and consequently the progress of this Church been by no means in proportion to that made by smaller bodies, whose members have been early trained to know that whatever is done by their community must be done by their own liberality, and their own exertions.

The Church of England in this colony is under the episcopate of the Right Rev. Charles Perry, D.D., formerly Fellow and Tutor of Trinity College, Cambridge, consecrated Bishop of Melbourne on St. Peter's Day, 1847, when the see of Melbourne was created, embracing within it the whole district of Port Phillip, now the colony of Victoria. Before that date the Church of England in Australia had but one bishop (the late Bishop Broughton), but in the year 1847 three new sees were created, viz., Adelaide, Newcastle and Melbourne. The Bishop of Melbourne arrived by the ship *Stag*, on the 24th January, 1848, accompanied by the Rev. H. B. Macartney, D.D., now Dean and Archdeacon of Melbourne, the Rev. Francis Hales, now Chaplain of Trinity Church, Launceston, and the Rev. D. Newham, formerly Incumbent of St. Peter's, who died in the year 1851. On the bishop's landing he proceeded at once to the Episcopal church in Melbourne, which was not only unconsecrated but unfinished, and was received by the only clergyman there, the Rev. A. C. Thomson. At the time of the bishop's arrival, Melbourne contained a population of 12,000 persons, but there was but one clergyman of the Church of England ministering in it, and but two others in the whole district of Port Phillip; the two being the Rev. E. Collins, located at Geelong, and the Rev. J. Y. Wilson, at Portland, where he still officiates. There were then but two churches in Melbourne, St. James's and St. Peter's, and neither of these were completed.

The site on which St. James's Cathedral, Melbourne, now stands had been granted by the Government of Sir Richard Bourke, and service was conducted in the absence of a clergyman, for a time, by James Smith, Esq., in a small wooden building erected on that ground. In April, 1837, the first baptism was performed by the Rev. J. B. Naylor, and in the following April, Melbourne was visited by the Lord Bishop of Sydney. In October, 1838, the late Rev. J. C. Grylls was appointed to the chaplaincy of St. James, and was succeeded by the Rev. J. Y. Wilson, now of Portland, and the Rev. A. C. Thomson, who, as stated, held the chaplaincy at the time of the bishop's arrival.

On the 25th June, 1848, the bishop held his first ordination, and on the 31st of October, his first confirmation, when he administered the rite to eighty-seven persons.

The first church consecrated by the bishop was St. Peter's, Melbourne, on the 29th of March, 1853: and the following churches have since been consecrated:—St. James's Cathedral, Melbourne; Trinity Church, Williamstown; and St. Stephen's, Richmond. None of the other churches throughout the diocese have as yet been consecrated, as this ceremony is not performed until the building stands altogether free from debt. In the mean time divine service is performed in them under the bishop's license.

The progress of the Church of England since the arrival of the bishop has been so far satisfactory, that it has gained upon a population increasing with almost unparalleled rapidity. The proportion in 1848 was about one clergyman to 13,000 of the whole people, now it is about one to 17,400, exclusive of lay-readers. There are three archdeaconries; Melbourne, Geelong, and Portland; including Bourke, and the countries west and south of it. The other parts of the diocese are under no subordinate superintendence. At the present time there are sixty-three duly licensed clergymen officiating in different parts of the diocese, assisted by a number of lay-readers; and, exclusive of tents and buildings belonging to private individuals, there are one hundred and thirty-eight places of worship, of which upwards of thirty are large, and generally handsome churches. The number of the members of the Church of England in the diocese is about 160,000, the population of the whole colony being about 470,000.

In connexion with the church, and assisted by the Denominational Board, there are 169 schools, conducted by 250 teachers, with an average attendance of 8,489 children, and about 13,141 on the books. A few of the schools, particularly on the new gold-fields, are held in tents capable of removal from place to place; and some are in buildings hired or lent, while there are several substantial buildings of brick, iron, or wood.

Two very handsome grammar schools have also been erected, one in Melbourne, the other in Geelong (see particulars elsewhere). They have been built partly by subscription and partly by grants from the Colonial Government. About 200 youths are now receiving a liberal education in them, and there is accommodation for a much larger number.

A mission to the Aborigines has been established on the south bank of the Murray River, opposite to its junction with the Darling River, on a piece of land granted for that purpose by the Government. Its missionaries have been successful in gaining the confidence of the natives, who freely resort to them, and leave their children to their care; but the migratory habits of the people present a hitherto insuperable barrier to the progress of the work.

The great wants of the Church of England in this diocese are, first, a mission to the Chinese—(a Chinese mission has been in operation in Victoria for some years, connected with various churches)—and secondly, a mission to the scattered European population, whether pastoral or engaged upon the new and changeable gold fields. If men suitable to the work could be obtained, there is little doubt but that they would be supported by the people.

A very important act was passed by the Colonial Legislature in the year 1854, authorising the bishop, clergy and laity of the Church of England to assemble periodically and legislate for its own government. So much importance did the bishop attach to this act, that, it having been reserved for the Royal assent, he went to England for the express purpose of representing its necessity before the question of the giving or withholding the Royal assent should be decided; and there is every reason to believe that had not this step been taken, the Act of the Colonial Legislature would not have been ratified.

The Assembly is a representative body. It held its first sitting on the 11th October, 1856, and has had since then three sittings, having passed some very important acts, among which may be mentioned those relating to the constitution of parishes, and to church patronage (which is now very much in the hands of the laity), the trial of ecclesiastical offences, and the management of the temporal affairs of the church; they have also considered very attentively its financial position, and have agreed to suggestions for raising one general church fund, with a parochial fund in every parish, which it is believed if acted upon, will be found most valuable in providing for the temporal wants of the diocese. On the whole, although the progress of the Church of England in Victoria has been far from what it ought to have been, considering the number of its members, and though many parts of the diocese are still in a state of religious destitution, it has certainly gained rather than lost ground within the last eleven years, and has been enabled to adapt itself to the altered position of the colony, so as still to present its ordinances unchanged and unmutilated to a constantly changing population, and to hold on its way under circumstances as new to its bishop and ministers as to its people.

ROMAN CATHOLIC CHURCH.

The Very Rev. P. B. Geoghegan, the senior Vicar-General of the Diocese, and present Pastor of Williamstown, may be termed the Pioneer of the Roman Catholic Mission in Victoria, for he was the first priest who set foot on her shores, and celebrated his first Mass on Pentecost Sunday, 19th May, 1839, in an unroofed store at the corner of Elizabeth and Little Collins streets, where the Colonial Bank of Australasia now stands. In a short time the Government granted a site for a church at the intersection of Elizabeth and Lonsdale streets; a temporary wooden building was put up, and on this spot was founded on the 4th October, 1841, the Church of St. Francis, which was formally opened for Divine service, October 23rd, 1845, and is one of the neatest ecclesiastical structures in the Metropolis. For several years "Father Geoghegan" had devolving upon him the spiritual responsibility of a rapidly increasing Catholic population, and the number of ministers coming to his aid was very limited, until the consecration of the Right Rev. Dr. Goold as first bishop, who arrived overland from Sydney, on the 4th October, 1848, the anniversary of the foundation of St. Francis. By this time several churches were erected throughout the country, and the efforts of the bishop to propagate the faith and extend the mission were powerfully assisted by the establishment of the Catholic Association, which was inaugurated by the bishop, Dr Geoghegan, and the clergy and laity, at a public meeting held in St. Francis' Hall, on the fourth Sunday of January, 1849. One of the primary objects of this institution was the organization of a fund for procuring clergymen from home, and in effecting this it was eminently successful, for large sums were subscribed and economically and judiciously applied to the designed purpose. By such means the bishop was enabled to meet the frequent demands upon him for more pastors, and the subjoined facts will best show the present state of the mission. At the date we write the Roman Catholic population may be estimated at between 70,000 and 80,000; and exclusive of the bishop, there are two vicars-general, 30 priests, 64 churches, 1 college, and 1 convent. There are 91 Catholic schools in connexion with the Denominational System, and these were attended (as per recent returns) by 5,369 pupils, viz., 2,708 boys, and 2,666 girls. They are superintended by 84 teachers and 45 assistant teachers; but in considering the educational progress made, a large number of private Catholic schools must not be overlooked, though there is no reliable data at the moment available for ascertaining their extent. In addition to these should be mentioned the St. Patrick's Diocesan College, East Melbourne, presided over by the Very Rev. L. B. Shiel, assisted by a professorial staff. This establishment prepares students for the Church and the liberal learned professions. The convent school, under the management of the Sisters of Mercy, imparts a superior education to a number of young ladies, and in a few months the building additions in course of erection will enable accommodation to be made for the reception of boarders. Amongst the Catholic charitable institutions, the most prominent is the St Vincent de Paul's Orphanage, Emerald Hill. It is a becoming memento of the zealous labors of its founder, the late Rev. G. A. Ward, is sustained by voluntary contributions, and can receive at least one hundred children. The foundation stone of St. Augustine's Orphanage, Geelong, was laid by the Bishop, on the 3rd Sunday of Lent, 1857, and was opened August 28th, 1858. A House of Refuge is about to be opened by the Sisters of Mercy; its object is to provide an asylum for the many unprotected young women who are occasionally passengers in immigrant ships from Europe. The building is being vigorously proceeded with.

WESLEYAN METHODIST CHURCH.

The first sermon preached in Melbourne by a Christian minister was delivered by the late Rev. Joseph Orton, Wesleyan minister, who, in 1837, visited Port Phillip from Hobart Town, with reference to the establishment of a mission to the Aborigines, and also to ascertain the probabilities of commencing a cause among the few Europeans and others who had begun to settle on the land. The late Rev. B. Hurst and the Rev. F. Tuckfield were the first ministers of the Wesleyan Church who were appointed to Port Phillip. They came from England early in 1838, and commenced a mission to the Aborigines at Bunting Dale, near Lake Colac. This mission was abandoned in 1848, the results having been most unsatisfactory. The Rev. S. Wilkinson was appointed to Melbourne in 1840, before which period a society had been formed, and services regularly conducted by local preachers, who were visited and assisted occasionally by Messrs. Hurst and Tuckfield, from Bunting Dale. The first chapel was erected in Collins-street, in 1840 and 1841. About the same time chapels were erected at Williamstown and Geelong. In 1850, ten years after the appointment of the first minister, the number of ministers had increased to five, the Rev. Wm. Butters having charge; whilst in and around Melbourne, Geelong, and Portland, there were nearly 600 church members. The number of chapels had also considerably increased.

Since 1850, the Wesleyan Church has, to a considerable extent, kept pace with the rapid growth of the institutions of the colony. The more settled state of the population, and the improved organization of the societies in consequence of the appointment of ministers to nearly all parts of the interior, render it easy to obtain statistics. At the conference of the Australasian Wesleyan Methodist Church, held in Hobart Town in January, 1858, the following statistics were officially recorded as those of the Victoria district:—Ministers, 30; local preachers, 259; Sunday school teachers, 895; chapels, 96; other preaching places, including school houses, 41; church members,

3,194; on trial for membership, 324; number of children in the Sabbath schools, 6,819; number of Sabbath schools, 98; number of persons regularly attending the Wesleyan ministry, about 26,300. There were also 65 day schools, in which about 4,500 children were receiving instruction, and in which 125 teachers were employed. Several large and respectable places of worship are now being erected in various parts of the colony, among which may be particularly named the elegant church in Lonsdale-street, the substantial and handsome chapels in St. Kilda and Ballaarat, and a neat and suitable building just commenced at the corner of Bourke and William streets. Applications have been received for the appointment of additional ministers in various parts of the gold-fields, and the staff will be considerably increased in a short time. The Rev. D. J. Draper is chairman of the district.

CONGREGATIONALISTS OR INDEPENDENTS.

These two designations are indifferently applied to the same body of Christians. The doctrines held and preached by them accord generally with those found in the standards of the Established Churches of England and Scotland. The Independents and Baptists are identical in every respect in their sentiments and usages, except on the point of baptism, the former practising pædo-baptism, the latter confining themselves to the baptism of adults.

The commencement of Congregationalism in Victoria dates as far back as 1837, and was owing to the zeal of Henry Hopkins, Esq., of Hobart Town, who, on visiting Port Phillip, and seeing the opening a young colony presented for useful labor, wrote to the Congregational Colonial Missionary Society in England to send out a minister for the new settlement of Melbourne. The Rev. W. Waterfield accordingly came in the year 1838. Worship was for a time carried on in a temporary place, but on September 3, 1838, the foundation stone of the first permanent building in Victoria for ecclesiastical purposes, was laid on the Eastern-hill, Collins-street, then untouched bush; and the church was opened for public use on January 1st, 1841. The Hon. J. P. Fawkner, M.L.C., one of the founders of the colony, took an active part in these proceedings. In March, 1843, Mr. Waterfield removed to Van Diemen's Land, where he still labors at Green Ponds, and was succeeded in the course of the same year by the Rev. Alexander Morison, who was sent over by the Home Missionary Society of that colony, and who still continues to be the pastor of this parent church. The Rev. B. Cuzens, the minister next arriving, took charge, in 1849, of the church then seeking establishment in Geelong. The following year, 1850, when the Rev. T. Odell arrived, a second church at the west end of Melbourne commenced, with the cordial concurrence and co-operation of the first church, Mr. Odell being chosen pastor; ultimately the excellent Gothic chapel in Lonsdale-street, in which he now officiates, was erected. The arrival, in 1853, of the Rev. W. B. Landells, who left England on account of his health, led to the formation of a third church, at Collingwood, and the building of a handsome Grecian chapel in Oxford-street. As openings presented themselves, and as ministers arrived, initial steps were taken to organize congregations in various localities, and by 1853 churches were formed and ministers settled at Prahran, Richmond, Brighton, St. Kilda, Geelong, and Kyneton; these were the Rev. W. Moss, Prahran; Rev. J. Simper, succeeded by Rev. J. P. Sunderland, Richmond; Rev. J. Apperly and Rev. A. Scales, at Geelong. The Colonial Missionary Society in England deeming it desirable, from the great influx of population arising from the gold discovery, to furnish an additional supply of ministers for Victoria, sent out the Revds. R. Fletcher, J. L. Poore, and E. Day, who arrived in March, 1854; and in due course there arrived, under the auspices of the same society, the Revds. H. Thomas, B.A., G. C. Morrison, M.A. (deceased), and W. R. Fletcher, M.A., W. C. Robinson, W. R. Lewis, J. Summers, J. Sleigh, J. H. Jackson, R. Bowman, J. Firth, J. G. Reed, B.A. (deceased). The Rev. W. A. Lind, late of the London Missionary Society, is settled at Ballaarat. Immediately on the arrival of Messrs. Fletcher and Poore, a Home Missionary Society was formed to further the work of evangelization, and a large sum of money was subscribed,—but the commercial crisis which followed soon after brought it to a close in about two years. A second society was established in January, 1857, and is now in active operation. A fund was raised for bringing out additional ministers for this and the neighbouring colonies, which amounted to near £2,400, of which £1,200 was furnished by Victoria, and Mr. Poore was sent to England to endeavour to augment this fund by subscriptions, and to look out and send men suitable for the work. The result of this effort has been the arrival in Australia of sixteen ministers.

The statistics of the body, as nearly as can be ascertained, are as follow:—About 27 congregations worshipping every Sabbath; 21 churches regularly formed, the remaining six congregations being recently gathered and not yet fully organized. Of the 27 places of worship, about 13 are permanent structures, *i.e.* built of brick or stone, and 14 are temporary, built of wood or iron. There are about 23 ministers settled over congregations, and 5 or 6 without pastoral charges. In several cases a manse is provided for the minister's use.

A Congregational Union for Victoria was formed, the last meeting of which was held in May, 1856. This has been succeeded by another, which was established in October, 1857, and of which the Rev. W. B. Landells is chairman for the present year.

Free Conferences of ministers and laymen, delegated from he unions of the four colonies of Australia, have been held; the first in Melbourne, in February, 1855; the second in Sydney, in February, 1857; and the last in Hobart Town, in February, 1858, when various resolutions were passed affecting the interests of the denomination at large. Under the auspices of these conferences a monthly periodical for the use of the four colonies has been established, the *Southern Spectator*, edited by the Rev. R. Fletcher, of St. Kilda. An organization was formed for providing education for ministerial candidates, but only one or two students have as yet presented themselves.

The denomination cannot show imposing figures in relation to day-school education. They have but few schools in connexion with the Denominational Board as they have not generally supported that system, but for the most part have thrown in their influence to support the National schools. A Sunday school is attached to nearly every chapel.

BAPTISTS.

The first organisation of Baptists in the Colony of Victoria was effected in the year 1841, by Mr. J. J. Mouritz of Collingwood. About the close of 1842, the Rev. John Ham, of Birmingham, having on his way to Sydney touched at the Port of Melbourne, was induced by the prospects of usefulness presented to him to remain at Melbourne for a time, no regularly ordained Baptist minister having arrived previously. Mr. Ham preached for some time in the Hall of the Mechanics' Institution and was so successful that he felt it his duty, at the earnest solicitation of the friends who had rallied round him, to settle permanently among them. Accordingly a church was formed on the 20th July, 1843, and the foundation stone of the Collins-street chapel was laid by the Rev. John Saunders, of Sydney, in June, 1845.

The Rev. John Ham continued his pastoral care of the Collins-street church till the close of 1847, when the state of his health compelled him to remove to a milder climate, and he accepted the pastorate of the Baptist Church at Sydney, vacated by the Rev. John Saunders, on account of ill-health.

During the residence of Mr. Ham in Melbourne, a mission to the Aborigines was organised and sustained for several years by the Collins-street church. This mission was confined to the young, and for some time gave indications of success. The children of the Yarra tribe, with a few others were located at the junction of the Merri Creek with the Yarra, where commodious buildings were erected, and where the boys were taught gardening and the girls needlework, in addition to the usual religious and secular education. It had, however, to be abandoned, partly owing to the evil influence of the white population, and partly to the proximity of the parents of the pupils, who generally induced their children to leave the establishment as they grew up, and to adopt the roving habits of their ancestors.

From 1847 to 1856 no organised effort was made by the denomination to obtain ministerial services; and during that period the churches in Melbourne were supplied by the Rev. W. P. Scott, Mr. John Lush, and other lay members. Mr. Lush preached very acceptably in the Collins-street chapel for several years; and during this period churches were formed and chapels erected at Geelong, Brighton, Prahran, Kew, &c.

The prospects of this body of Christians is at present very cheering. The arrival of the Rev. James Taylor and the Rev. Isaac New, both from Birmingham, has been hailed with delight, and there is every reason to believe that the labors of these gentlemen will be greatly blessed. Churches are being organised in many parts of the country and more ministers for this colony, are on their way from England. The present number of Baptists in Victoria is about 6,000, so that the wants of the people cannot be met for some time to come. The Collins-street chapel has lately been much enlarged to accommodate the increasing congregation, under the ministry of the Rev. James Taylor, while the church at Albert-street are compelled to erect a much larger building than that they have occupied, under the ministry of the Rev. I. New.

Early in the present year (1858) the "Baptist Association of Victoria" was formed, having in view among other objects the formation of a fund to aid in the outfit and passage of ministers for the colony, as well as their temporary support after their arrival. Already there are ten churches enrolled in this association; and under its auspices a denominational magazine has appeared, entitled "*The Australasian Baptist Magazine*," edited by the Revs. New and Taylor. This effort to do good is likely to be successful, judging from the character of the two numbers which have been published.

PRESBYTERIANS.

The Presbyterians of Victoria are chiefly natives of Scotland and the north of Ireland. By the last census (March 1857), it appears that the number of Presbyterians in this colony at that date was 65,935, being more than a sixth of the whole population, and the influence of the denomination may be estimated by the fact that of the thirty gentlemen who compose the Legislative Council of Victoria, more than one-third are Presbyterians.

The first Presbyterian minister who preached the Gospel in the district, then known as Port Phillip, was the Rev. James Clow, a retired Indian Chaplain, who came to Australia for his health, upwards of twenty one years ago; and who still lives to benefit the Church by his long experience and mature wisdom.

The first Presbyterian minister settled in Melbourne, was the late Rev. James Forbes, who departed this life in 1851, greatly lamented. The Rev. Andrew Love arrived soon after Mr. Forbes, and settled at Geelong.

As the Presbyterian Church of Australia was an offshoot of the Church of Scotland, and as immigrants from Scotland were continually arriving with Scotch feelings and sympathies, the Church here soon felt the influence of the disruption of 1843. Mr. Forbes, of Melbourne, went with the Free Church movement, and he was soon joined by the Rev. John Tait, Geelong; and the Rev. Thomas Hastie, Buninyong. The Free Church Synod was strengthened subsequently by the Revds. Adam Cairns, D.D., and Macintosh Mackay, LL.D., as well as by several younger brethren. Mr. Forbes was succeeded in the Scots Church by the Rev. Irving Hetherington; and the Synod of Victoria (Mr. Hetherington's) has received supplies of ministers both from Scotland and Ireland.

The Presbyterianism of Victoria is divided into three branches: viz., the Synod of Victoria, Free Church, and United Presbyterians. The church courts and ministers of these sections profess amicable relations with each other, but the evils of division are felt, and a general union has been long contemplated; articles of union are under consideration, embracing adherence to the Westminster Standards, and the independence of the proposed United Church, which is to be called the Presbyterian Church of Victoria. There are six Presbyterian congregations in the city of Melbourne proper, and nine more in the immediate suburbs, including St. Kilda. The churches in which some of these congregations worship, such as Chalmers' Church, St. Andrew's Church, and the Scots' Church, are very handsome and commodious buildings. The number of ordained Presbyterian ministers now (October 1858) in Victoria, is fifty-seven. These are located all over th colony, and the are several probationers about to be ordained.

The Church of Scotland has always been famous for the interest she has taken in education, and the Presbyterians of Victoria are in this respect proving themselves worthy of the parent church. Many of the congregations have efficient week-day schools and Sabbath schools; and there is, besides the Central Institute in Melbourne, the Scotch College (see another page), which holds a high place as a school of learning.

UNITED METHODIST FREE CHURCHES.

This body of Christians has for some years been known in the colony under the name of the Wesleyan Methodist Association; but in consequence of the amalgamation in

England of the Wesleyan Reformers with the Wesleyan Methodist Association, in 1857, the new designation of the "United Methodist Free Churches" has been adopted, thus effecting a similar combination in Australasia. This union of two very considerable secessions from the original conference body of Methodists has been effected by the acceptance of certain principles laid down as "the basis of union," the principal features of which are, that "the will of God, as revealed in the Holy Scriptures, is the only and sufficient rule of Christian faith, practice, church organization and government; and that as every Church has a scriptural right to determine all questions affecting its own officers, members, religious ordinances, or other local affairs, no conference, annual assembly, or other meeting, however constituted, has any scriptural right to make any law or rule relative thereto, or to alter or annul the decisions of any church or circuit." The annual assembly of this denomination is constituted of the freely chosen representatives of the churches in circuit, and its general purposes are to provide and station itinerant preachers, and to manage the funds raised for the promulgation of the Gospel at home and abroad, or to effect the union of any other churches that may be desirous of joining the connexion.

In the year 1851 the Rev. Joseph Townend arrived from England as a missionary belonging to the Wesleyan Methodist Association, and preached his first sermon in a small room or preaching place in Collingwood, to a company consisting of about 40 persons. Amid many difficulties and discouragements he succeeded in raising and enlarging a church upon the principles of Christian liberty advocated by the Association in England. A chapel was erected in Albert-street, Collingwood, which was afterwards purchased by the corporation, and the present neat structure raised in George-street. Chapels have lately been erected also in Hoddle-street, Collingwood; at Pentridge, Kew, Richmond, and Tullamarine. At Windsor one is in course of erection, and preaching places are established in Brunswick and Quarries. The number of itinerant preachers is increased to four, two for Melbourne, one for Geelong, and one for Ballaarat. At the annual assembly held in Geelong, January, 1858, the following statistics were recorded:—Number of circuits 4, viz., Melbourne, Geelong, Hobart Town, and Adelaide. Total number of members, 244; chapels and preaching places, 15; local preachers, 29; average number of the congregation, 988; Sabbath schools, 12 (scholars, 669; teachers, 66); day schools, 3 (scholars, 150; teachers, 4). During the year there has been an increase of circuits, chapels, and schools. Application has also been made to England for at least six additional missionaries to meet the various openings which have been presented to the United Methodist Free churches.

GERMAN LUTHERAN CHURCH.

The first body of German immigrants, chiefly Lutherans, arrived in Melbourne in 1849. These were followed by similar bodies in 1850. Having no ordained minister able to speak their tongue, they met for prayer and the reading of the word of God in the Rev. A. Morison's chapel in the afternoon of every Lord's day. Twice an attempt was made to form a Lutheran church and congregation in Melbourne, in 1850, by the Rev. M. Rupprecht, and two years later by the Rev. A. Kappler, but both attempts failed. The number of Germans, however, having considerably increased through the gold discovery, the Rev M. Goethe succeeded in forming congregations at Melbourne, and Germantown, near Geelong, towards the close of 1852. The first church was erected on the Eastern Hill, Melbourne, in 1853 and 1854. About the same time a school-room was erected at Germantown. At the time of the first Lutheran Synod, held in Melbourne in May, 1856, the number of ordained ministers in Victoria was three, and that of teachers three. Since that time the number of ministers has increased to five, that of teachers to seven, and that of churches and chapels to six.

UNITARIANS.

The first steps to organize this body in Melbourne, were taken at a meeting of its members (ten in number), at Mr. Dueidin's residence, 29th November, 1852. The Unitarians celebrated public worship for the first time in the colony at the Mechanics' Institution, on Sunday, 30th January, 1853, the Rev. Maxwell Davidson officiating as minister. A subscription was at the same time started towards erecting a church, and the present edifice on the Eastern-hill was opened on the 16th April, 1854. This building (which is even now in a very unfinished state) cost upwards of £4,000. In October, 1857, Mr. Davidson relinquished office as minister, and was succeeded by the Rev. Henry Higginson, brother-in-law of the well-known James Martineau, an Unitarian Minister in England.

The number of avowed Unitarians in the colony, according to the last census, is 1,500. The Unitarians have recently opened a temporary place of worship at St. Kilda, under the ministration of the Rev. William Bowen, M.A. A church belonging to this denomination has also been lately built at Ballaarat.

JEWISH RELIGION.

The first public meeting of the Jews for divine service was held at the stores of Messrs. Benjamin, Collins-street, in 1840, at which about ten persons assembled. In 1841, about twenty-five persons commenced holding services on the "Rowsh Harshono" (new year) at the building known as the Port Phillip Club Hotel, Flinders-street, service being performed on this and previous occasions by lay members of the community. The first congregation was then established under the designation of the Sheirith Yisrael Melbourne Hebrew Congregation, and subsequent services were regularly held in a room belonging to Messrs. Benjamin, devoted by them exclusively for this purpose, Mr. A. H. Hart acting as hon. reader.

In 1844 a grant of land was obtained from the Government for building a synagogue, on the site where it is at present situated in Bourke-street west, Melbourne, and also a portion of land for their use as a cemetery. In 1847 the small synagogue was opened at the rear of the present building. In 1848 the Jewish Philanthropic Society was established, and the following year the Rev. Moses Rintel was appointed minister of the community.

In 1854, in consequence of the increased number of Jewish residents, the present large synagogue was erected, at a cost of £7000, and is now decorated and completed. The Rev. E M. Myers was elected minister of the congregation in May, 1857, in place of the Rev. Moses Rintel, resigned.

In 1856 "The United Friends Jewish Benefit Society" was established, and the Rev. Moses Rintel was elected its first President.

In March, 1857, a numerous meeting of the Jewish community residing in the east end of the city was held, for the purpose of founding a local synagogue, which from its desirability was at once established, under the title of the "Mickva Yisrael Melbourne Synagogue." Solomon Solomons, Esq., was elected president, and M. Nelson, Esq , treasurer. The Rev. M. Rintel consenting to officiate as minister, they at once proceeded to and obtained the necessary registrations, and secured their right to the use of the burial ground and mortuary chapel. The first service was held in Spring-street (in the premises formerly used as the Melbourne Grammar School), and in consequence of the increase of its members more extensive premises were leased in Great Lonsdale-street, east. The residents in that part of the city availing themselves of its proximity, the synagogue is regularly opened for divine service on Mondays and Thursdays, the four times on every Sabbath and festivals, and oftener when required. As soon as a site shall have been secured, it is the intention to erect a synagogue in that part of the city.

In 1858 the Jewish ladies of Melbourne established a society, supported by voluntary contributions, for the purpose of supplying medical assistance, clothing, and nourishments to poor married Jewish women during their accouchement.

EDUCATION.

THE UNIVERSITY OF MELBOURNE.

Is a corporation established by an Act of Council, 16 Vict., c. 34, to which the Royal Assent was given by His Excellency C. J. LaTrobe, Esq., on the 22nd January, 1853.

Constitution.—The University at present consists of a council only, to which a senate consisting of all masters of arts doctors of law medicine and music will be added so soon as the number of such graduates has reached one hundred. All executive power is now, and will then remain in the hands of the council, but all alterations in statutes and regulations and all additions to them will ultimately be subject to the veto of the senate. At present they require only the approbation of His Excellency the Governor.

The council, in which the whole management of the affairs of the University is vested, consists, according to the Act, of twenty members, sixteen of whom must be laymen. The council was originally appointed and vacancies therein are still filled up by the Governor. After the constitution of the senate, vacancie will be filled up by that body.

The chancellor and the vice-chancellor are appointed by the council out of its own members. Hitherto the elections have been annual. The former office has been filled since the establishment of the University by His Honor Mr. Justice Barry, the latter is held at present by A. C. Brownless, Esq., M.D.

There are four professors of the following subjects:—1. Philology and Logic; 2. Mathematics; 3. Natural Science; 4. History and Political Economy; and two Lecturers in Law. The professors are not members of the council, but form a board, of which the chancellor and vice-chancellor are *ex officio* members, to superintend the studies of the University under the statutes, and to furnish to the council such information as that body may require.

No religious test is required from any member officer or student of the University.

The University has an annual endowment of £9000.

Degrees.—The University may confer the following degrees: bachelor of arts, master of arts, bachelor of medicine, doctor of medicine, bachelor of laws, doctor of laws, bachelor of music, doctor of music, after examination; or without examination on graduates of other universities.

Course of Study.—This is at present prescribed in one faculty only, that of arts. The student, after passing the matriculation examination is required to attend lectures in the University during three years;* at the end of the first to pass an examination in five of the courses of lectures of that

---

* These regulations, so far as regards *attendance on lectures*, are now altered. See last paragraph p. lxxxix.

year; at the end of the second, in five of the courses of the second, together with the subjects of the first; at the end of the third, in five of the courses of the third, and the subjects of the second. Passing this last examination will entitle to the degree of B.A., if the candidate has attended lectures and passed examinations on Greek and Latin each for two years, and on Geometry and Natural Philosophy each for one year.

The higher degree of M.A. is attainable at the close of two years after the B.A., on passing a further examination and attending two courses of lectures during that period.

It will be seen that none can attain a degree in the University of Melbourne, save those who are able to master to some extent both classics and mathematics.

Exhibitions, Scholarships and Honors.—At matriculation there are two exhibitions of £50 each, one for classics and one for mathematics. At the close of the first year, the names of all who pass with credit are arranged in classes, and two exhibitions of £50 each are awarded, one for classics and English, one for mathematics. At the end of the second year, the names are arranged in the same way, and four exhibitions of the same value are given for classics and English, mathematics, natural science, history and logic. Those who have passed the ordinary B.A. examination can obtain honors in either or all of four schools, language and logic, mathematics and physics, natural science, social science; and two scholarships of £100 a year, tenable for two years, are annually awarded.

Buildings.—The foundation stone of the University was laid on the 3rd July, 1854, by His Excellency Sir Charles Hotham. The portion already erected forms three sides of a quadrangle in the late perpendicular style, the south side which will be the front towards Melbourne being unbuilt. On the east and the west sides are the professors' lodgings, two lecture rooms, the registry, &c. The north side contains on the ground floor the natural philosophy apparatus room with a lecture theatre adjoining, also the natural science apparatus room, laboratory and lecture theatre. In the centre is the staircase leading to

The Museum.—Here are placed the University and the National Collection, which well merit a visit; but though great pains have been taken to economise space in the four large rooms in which the collections are contained, still they do not afford sufficient accommodation for the proper display of the specimens. (See other page.)

The Library consists of about 3000 volumes, which are at present placed in the registry. The books are mainly illustrative of the four departments of study on which lectures are given in the University. The collection of books should be more numerous in a University library, but the available surplus of the annual endowment has of late been mainly devoted to the improvement of the grounds.

THE GROUNDS surrounding the University contain forty acres, which are being gradually laid out, part as pleasure grounds, part as an elaborate botanical garden; but a considerable time must necessarily elapse before they can be brought thoroughly into order. The museum, the library and the grounds are open to the public.

PRESENT POSITION AND FUTURE PROSPECTS OF THE UNIVERSITY.—An elaborate machinery for educational purposes has been described: the question naturally remaining is, how has it worked? Those who judge only from what meets the eye may pronounce it to have failed, since the matriculated students at present attending the University lectures amount to thirteen only: and the annual entry which was 16 in 1855, and 7 in each of the following years, was in 1858, only 2. But in forming a judgment, the special circumstances of the case must be borne in mind: In 1855, at the opening of the University, no examination was held, any who presented themselves were allowed to enter. The want of all previous training soon became evident students gradually found that they could not come up to the standard of the annual examinations, till finally only four out of the sixteen remained to present themselves for the degree of B.A. at the end of three years. From the opening of the University till now the want of good large training schools has been felt, schools which the honors of the University should incite to emulation, and which should supply the University with well-prepared students. The institution of such schools as are presently to be described will meet this want; but we may fairly assume that but for the existence of the University, shewing the deficiencies in education, they would never have been established.

But it will not be enough to have our National University only occupying the place of Oxford or of Cambridge, a great seat of upper and middle class education. Not the pupils of Victorian Etons or Harrows alone should look to the University as their goal, but education generally should be placed in such relation to the University, that the poorest lad in the primary school may hope, if his talents warrant it, to enter this the highest seat of education.

The conferring of degrees by examination only, on a system somewhat resembling that of Dublin, which the council has recently announced its intention of doing, and for which arrangements are now in progress, will do much to increase the usefulness, and therefore the popularity of the University: and will also hasten the establishment of the senate. The number of graduates, all admitted *ad eundem gradum* from other Universites, who are entitled to belong to the senate, is now twenty-three, or not quite a quarter of the the number required.

The number of students attending the Lectures in Law is now thirty-two, from which fact it may fairly be presumed that other courses of special education, as for example, Medicine and Engineering, would, if provided by the University, draw many more *Alumni* to her walls.

DENOMINATIONAL SCHOOLS.

On the 11th February, 1848, the Denominational School Board was appointed to superintend the temporal regulation and inspection of the respective Denominational Schools in the colony, then the district of Port Phillip, supported either wholly or in part from the public funds, it being clearly laid down, according to the minute of their instructions, that all that related to the religious teaching would be exclusively entrusted to and regulated by the resident clergyman of the denomination to which the school belonged.

At that early period, the Board had under its direction only 27 schools, containing in the aggregate 2,596 children under education, whilst the total population of the colony was 60,390. At the present time (Oct. 1858), with a population of about 480,000, the Board has under its supervision 460 schools, with an attendance of about 30,000 children, the proportion of children attending Denominational schools to the total population at each period being respectively 1 in 23 and 1 in 16.

The progress of Denominational Schools since the commencement of the operations of the Board in 1849, may be shown as follows:—

At the end of	Schools.	Scholars.	Population.	At Denominational schools.
1849	27	2,596	60,390	1 in 23
1850	54	3,870	69,739	1 " 18
1851	74	4,999	83,350	1 " 17
1852	89	6 836	148,627	1 " 22
1853	125	9,517	198,496	1 " 21
1854	218	14,364	273,865	1 " 19
1855	300	17,711	319,379	1 " 18
1856	368	21,267	348,460	1 " 16
1857	423	27,314	449,207	1 " 18

The instruction given in Denominational Schools (besides the moral and religious training carried on under the direction of clergymen of different denominations) comprises reading, writing, grammar, arithmetic, geography, natural science, music, and drawing. In many schools, however, in addition to the above, algebra and geometry are taught, while in a fe there are classes for French and Latin.

The children frequenting the schools range in age between four and sixteen. The majority of the children attending the schools lies between the age of eight and eleven, and after twelve their numbers sensibly decrease.

The teachers in the Denominational Schools are, for the most part, as efficient as could be expected in so young a colony, unassisted by complete normal or training establishments. The salaries received by them vary from about £120 per annum, to about £400. Some of them receive about £300, although the average throughout the whole colony of masters' salaries, does not exceed £200 per annum. The salaries of mistresses average £150 per annum, so that mistresses appear on the whole to be better remunerated, in proportion, than masters. All teachers and assistants appointed must submit to an examination under the Inspector of the district in which the school may be situated. There are at present employed under the Board about 900 teachers.

The officers of the Board for carrying out the superintendence of the schools and examination of teachers, &c., are five inspectors, each superintending a separate and well defined district. There is also a Normal Inspector, who, in addition to the ordinary duties of a District Inspector, directs the Church of England training establishment at St. James's. The Secretary transacts the general business of the office.

The colony is divided, for inspectoral purposes, into the following divisions:—Central Southern district, Mr. R. H. Budd; Central Western district, Mr. Sasse; Central Eastern district, Mr. Geary; Ballaarat district, Mr. Bonwick; Sandhurst and Castlemaine, Mr. Parker; Geelong district, Mr. Miller.

STATEMENT of Schools in operation, shewing number on the Roll and average attendance for 31st December, 1857.

	Schools in operation.	On the Roll.			Average Attendance		
		Boys.	Girls.	Total.	Boys.	Girls.	Total.
Church of England ..	189	6,242	5,705	11,947	4,098	3,478	7,576
Scots' Church	17	596	494	1,090	428	340	768
Free Church	35	1,249	1,071	2,320	876	711	1,587
Wesleyan	69	2,577	2,249	4,826	1,688	1,330	3,018
Wesleyan Association..	2	81	95	176	51	50	101
Independent	9	249	209	458	192	156	348
Baptist	1	12	51	63	8	32	40
Lutheran	3	77	64	141	61	44	105
Bible Christian	1	31	66	97	19	35	54
Roman Catholic . ..	91	2,703	2,666	5,369	1,842	1,855	3,697
Combined	1	24	32	56	..	..	..
Congregational	1	56	56	112	37	30	67
Primitive Methodists..	1	37	13	50	22	7	29
Totals	420	13,934	12,771	26,705	9,317	8,068	17,385

NATIONAL SCHOOLS.

The sum contributed by the State in 1851 towards Education was £3,470; the amount voted in 1857 by the Legislature for primary schools was £125,000, which, under the management of the two educational boards, the Denominational and the National, provided schooling for 31,086 children. The most recent statistics of schools are given in the subjoined table:—

	Number of Schools.		Number of Scholars.	
	1851.	1857	1851.	1857.
Denominational Schools ...	74	399	5,208	24,973
National Schools	6	101	261	6,113
Private Schools	49	138	1,601	3,437
TOTALS	129	638	7,070	34,523

In 1851, the number of schools was 129, or one school for every 600 persons, and 7,070 scholars, or one in 11 of the population. In 1857, the number of schools was 638, or one in 600, and the scholars were 34,323, or one in 11. With reference to practical results, we find that in 1851 the number of the population who could read and write was 44,631, or more than 58 per cent.; while in 1857, the number who could read and write was 249,386, or upwards of 60 per cent.

The Board of Commissioners for National Education was incorporated during the first session of the Legislative Council in Victoria, in 1851, shortly after the separation of the colony from New South Wales, for the object, as expressed in the Act of Incorporation, of "superintending the formation and management of schools, to be conducted under Lord Stanley's national system of education."

The Board commenced its operations in the early part of 1852. The following table shows the progressive increase in the number of schools and scholars, up to the present time:—

Year.	No. of Schools.	On the Rolls.	Average Attendance.
1851	6	342	
1852	9	552	362
1853	27	1783	908
1854	42	2969	1772
1855	58	3532	2509
1856	85	4804	3553
1857	101	6113	4462

This increase would have been much greater, had not the Board, during the past three years, been most seriously hampered from want of funds.

In connexion with the Board, a Model School and Training Establishment has been formed. In the former, it is intended that the best modes of instruction shall be exhibited; and in the latter, persons desirous of qualifying themselves for the office of teachers are instructed and trained, while they receive practical lessons in the art of teaching in the model schools.

Of the number of children on the rolls in 1857 :—

2439	or 40	per cent.	were	Church of England.
1481	or 24	,,	,,	Presbyterian
705	or 12	,,	,,	Wesleyan.
392	or 6	,,	,,	Independent.
781	or 13	,,	,,	Roman Catholic.
315	or 5	,,	,,	Other Denominations.

The building is situated at the corner of Spring and Lonsdale Streets, Melbourne.

CHURCH OF ENGLAND GRAMMAR SCHOOL, MELBOURNE.

This handsome and capacious edifice, situated on the St. Kilda road, was constructed for the purpose of meeting a want that had long been felt previous to its erection,—the want of a superior school for the education of boys in this colony. It has been built by members of the Church of England, assisted by a liberal grant from the Government. The sum of £50,000 was, in the year 1853, voted by the legislature in aid of grammar schools in connexion with the various Christian denominations; the proportion falling to the Church of England being £20,788 14s. In addition to this, grants of land were made, and thus aided several very superior educational establishments have been formed in various parts of the colony, one of which is that under consideration.

The commencement of the building was for a long time delayed in consequence of the difficulty found in obtaining a suitable site; the one originally proposed was near the University, but this could not be procured, and after a great deal of negotiation, Sir Charles Hotham, with the advice of his Executive Council, was induced to grant the present site, consisting of about fifteen acres of land, it having been made a condition that the building to be erected upon it should be subject to the approval of the Government. This condition greatly delayed the work, as the plan originally selected was not acceptable to the Government officials. At length the design for the present building was produced and approved of. It was the result of competition, Messrs. Webb and Taylor being the architects. The school, when completed, will have a much more striking appearance than it now presents. The principal front will face the Gardiner's Creek Road, and have in the centre a very handsome tower. It will require, to carry out fully the design, an additional expenditure of near £10,000.

The portion of the work already executed has cost nearly £20,000, of which £13,783 14s. has been contributed from the Government grant of £20,788 14s.; the remainder of this grant having been expended upon the Church of England Grammar

School at Geelong. The £13,783 14s. has been supplemented by private contributions to the extent of several thousand pounds, made up by a comparatively small number of persons, between thirty and forty individuals having each contributed one hundred pounds.

The school was opened in April, 1858, under the superintendence of the Rev. Dr. Bromby, who had been appointed in England by gentlemen specially entrusted with the responsibility of selecting the head master. On the first day of the opening, nearly one hundred pupils were admitted, and the numbers have since gone on increasing. The school is calculated to receive about three hundred boys, including about sixty boarders, and there is every reason to believe that all the accommodation it can afford will be required.

The school is watched over by a council, but its scholastic management is confided to the head master; a certain proportion of the school fees being paid over to the council for the purpose of keeping the building in repair, completing the design of the architect, and the formation of a reserve fund. Contributors of £50 and upwards are entitled to be governors, and to a remission of one third of the school fees for boys nominated by them; a contribution of £50 giving a right to one, and of £150 to two nominations. The school although carried on in connexion with the Church of England, is open to all denominations. There are some special privileges given to the children of clergymen which it is not here necessary to particularise.

GEELONG GRAMMAR SCHOOL.

This institution, of a similar character to the preceding, being in connexion with the Church of England, was established in 1855, transferred to the present building on the 15th April, 1858, and publicly opened on 21st June. The new structure cost about £12,500, is large and remarkably elegant. There are 120 scholars, forty of whom are boarders; five resident masters, four of whom are graduates of the English universities, the principal being the Rev. George Oakley Vance, M.A. The school is under the control of seven trustees, who have decided that the formularies of the Church of England shall not be used in the religious instruction of those in whose case any objection may be made. There is a scholarship connected with the school, tenable at the Melbourne University.

SCOTCH COLLEGE, MELBOURNE.

This building is situated on the Eastern-hill, having a large number of scholars, the actual daily attendance being about 170, including day pupils, day boarders, and residents. The principal is Mr. Alexander Morrison, A.M.; and the teachers, including Dr. Macadam, comprise gentlemen who have taken high degrees in the mother country. The object of the institution is to furnish an education of the highest order to prepare young gentlemen for the University, learned professions, or mercantile pursuits, and generally to afford to the youth of the Australian Colonies all the advantages which could be derived from the best educational and boarding establishments in the mother country. The institution was established in 1851.

MISCELLANEOUS INSTITUTIONS.

MELBOURNE HOSPITAL.

The first attempt to provide hospital accommodation for the early settlers on the site of Melbourne was very inadequate, being a rude log hut of two rooms, used for the treble purpose of post-office, police-office, and hospital; but at last becoming uninhabitable, a house in Little Collins-street, near the site of the present Temple Court, was taken for the purposes of the hospital alone. A meeting was held on the 24th September, 1844, when it was directed that an application should be made to Sir George Gipps, the then Governor of New South Wales, for a site of land, and for a sum of £500 in aid of the fund for erecting an hospital and attaching buildings. The money was granted on condition that the recipients should raise a similar sum among themselves. This point was important, as had the building been erected wholly out of Government funds, its management would not have vested in the public. With an energy and liberality commendable in the highest degree, the then scanty population speedily raised the required amount, and on the 5th of March, 1845, a meeting was held at the Royal Hotel (upon the site of the present Criterion), when resolutions were passed expressive of the importance and immediate necessity of erecting an hospital for Port Phillip, and it was resolved that an hospital be established under the name of the Melbourne Hospital. On the following day a requisition was forwarded to James Montgomery, Esq., requesting him to convene a meeting of the governors and subscribers on the 19th of March, to appoint a committee to prepare rules for the Institution. Among the persons signing the requisition were Dr. Geoghegan, R. W. Pohlman, Esq., Dr. O'Mullane, Dr. E. Barker, and many other old and respected colonists. At this meeting a committee was also formed for the purpose of obtaining a grant of land, and the governors were empowered to enter into contracts for the erection of an hospital on a site to be approved of. The foundation stone was laid early in 1846, with masonic ceremonies befitting the importance of the occasion. A meeting was held on the 15th July, 1847, when Drs. Hobson, O'Mullane, and Howitt, were elected physicians; and Messrs. Greeves, Thomas, and Campbell, surgeons to the institution. The Hospital was then opened for the reception of patients.

The following is a statement for each year since that period:—

Year.		In-Patients.		Out-Patients.
1848	..	89	..	98
1849	..	197	..	123
1850	..	222	..	134
1851	..	260	..	159
1852	..	636	..	170
1853	..	1,561	..	325
1854	..	1,605	..	1,704
1855	..	1,559	..	2,700
1856	..	1,725	..	3,393
1857	..	1,870	..	3,903
	Total..	9,724	..	12,709

The whole number of in-patients, and those receiving medical advice and medicines not residing in the Hospital, amounts to 22,433. The noble building is situated in Lonsdale-street, and contains 333 beds, independent of accommodation for offices, secretary's apartments, stores, servants' rooms, &c. The last addition made cost £11,000, providing 140 beds. The institution is under the management of a committee, elected annually from the subscribers, and is supported by Government aid and voluntary contributions. Life governors subscribing £20, and annual governors of £2, have the privilege of having one in and one out-patient at all times on the books of the institution, subject to the approval of the committee of management.

The Honorary Medical Staff consists of four physicians and four surgeons; there are also resident in the institution a house-surgeon and assistant, resident secretary, matron and two dispensers.

BENEVOLENT ASYLUM.

The declared objects of this Institution are "To relieve the aged and infirm, disabled or destitute, of all creeds or nations, and to minister to them the comforts of religion."

The first public meeting in connexion with the establishment of an Asylum, was held in the Mechanics' Institute, on 12th October, 1849, the Mayor in the chair. A committee was appointed to take initiatory steps, and at a second public meeting, held on the 8th November in the same year, the necessity for a General Asylum, into which the destitute could be received, was fully recognised. The object of the meeting was to provide proper lodgings for the destitute objects of their care, and exercising such control as to make the relief afforded really beneficial. Nearly one-half of the applicants for admission into the Hospital were fitter subjects for an Asylum owing to the incurable nature of their diseases and the completely shattered state of their constitutions.

With the concurrence of His Honor C. J. La Trobe, after wards Governor, the Government agreed to give an eligible site of ten acres for buildings and grounds, to be vested in Trustees to be named by the subscribers, and also promised a grant of £1,000, subsequently supplemented by £500, towards the erection of suitable buildings, on condition of the public contributing an equal amount, and a prospect of an annual grant towards the maintenance of the Institution.

The foundation stone was laid by His Honor C. J. La Trobe, on 24th June, 1850, assisted by the Masonic Fraternity, and all the Constituted Authorities, a large concourse of the inhabitants of the city and district being present, the occasion having been observed as a general holiday in Melbourne. The original building was calculated to afford accommodation for 71 males and 71 females, and cost £3,427, towards defraying which, Government, as already said, contributed £1,500, the public raising by subscription and collections £2,254, leaving in the treasurer's hands a surplus of £326.

The Asylum was opened for the reception of inmates on 27th November, 1851, the number received up to the end of the year being 32. In the following year 78 additional inmates were admitted. During the year 1853, 274 inmates were received, and on the 31st December of that year, there were 126 inmates in the Asylum, exclusive of officials and servants. During the past year, 1857, there were 536 applications for admission, of these 113 were refused for want of room, 63 referred to other institutions, 16 assisted to the interior or other colonies, 152 received out-door relief, and 192 were admitted into the Asylum.

Since the Institution was first opened various improvements and additions have been made to the buildings, and during the past year a new wing has been added, giving accommodation for 74 additional inmates, and adding much to the internal comfort of the Institution, and very materially improving the appearance of the building, which is now one of the finest in Melbourne. The total cost of the old building was about £9,000, and of the new wing and improvements £13,000. The building is now capable of containing 224 inmates, and is at present full, with a demand for more accommodation.

The Institution is supported partly by Government partly by voluntary contributions, it being necessary in order to secure any Government grant that the voluntary contributions shall amount to one third of that grant.

The office-bearers consist of a president, two vice-presidents, honorary treasurer, and a general committee not exceeding eighteen governors (exclusive of *ex officio* members) elected at the annual general meeting, by and from among the governors.

The president, vice-president, the Chief Secretary, the Mayor of Melbourne, the honorary Medical Officers, the resident principal Ministers of each Congregation making a collection for the funds, and the honorary treasurer, are the *ex officio* members of the committee of management.

Every donor of £20 and upwards is a life governor, and every person raising by one or more collections £20, and the executor first named in any will bequeathing £50 and upwards to the Institution have the rights and privileges of life governors. Every subscriber of one guinea and upwards is an annual governor, having the privilege of voting at the election of office-bearers, and those paying two guineas have the privilege of recommending cases of distress for relief.

The medical staff consists of two honorary physicians, two honorary surgeons, and a resident medical officer.

The internal control and management is entrusted to a superintendent and matron, and the efficient manner in which the Institution has been conducted by the committee of management, combining care for the comfort and well being of the inmates with economy in the expenditure of the public money, has fully realised the expectations of the original promoters.

MELBOURNE LYING-IN HOSPITAL AND INFIRMARY FOR DISEASES OF WOMEN AND CHILDREN.

In the month of August, 1856, some benevolent ladies became impressed with the want of such an Institution as the above. A meeting was convened at the Deanery to discuss the subject, and during inquiry it became known to some of the ladies that Dr. J. Maund and Dr. R. T. Tracy having long felt the need that existed of a Lying-in Hospital, were then actually in treaty for leasing a suitable house in Albert-street, Melbourne, and had determined to set the Institution on foot, trusting to the support of the public to maintain it when its benefits were proved.

The ladies resolved to co-operate with these gentlemen, and formed a committee and liberally subscribed to start the Hospital. Since then the charity has gone on increasing. A site for a permanent building was obtained from Government in an excellent situation in Madeline-street. A splendid building has just been completed. Towards the building fund over £2,000 was obtained by voluntary subscriptions, and £4,000 granted by Parliament.

During the last two years 250 women have been accouched in the Hospital, happily without a death, and 990 women and children have received advice and medicines as out-patients.

IMMIGRANTS' AID SOCIETY.

This institution was established in 1858, its object being to afford advice and temporary shelter to newly arrived persons in need thereof, irrespective of creed or country, but not being "Government" assisted immigrants.

The management of the establishment is vested in the hands of an executive committee comprised of seven gentlemen, elected annually from various religious denominations, and meeting weekly for the reception of applications and for finance; also a general committee consisting of clergymen of every denomination resident in Melbourne, meeting periodically to receive the reports of the executive committee and for general business; likewise an honorary secretary and treasurer, with a resident secretary as superintendent.

The operations of this society have proved eminently useful to newly arrived immigrants, and a most essential auxiliary to all other institutions. Upwards of 16,500 "relief grants" have been issued since the establishment of the society, at an outlay of nearly £18,000. The project originated through the emergency arising from the great and sudden influx of immigrants in 1852-3, by which, in the undeveloped resources of the colony, much temporary distress was induced. A public subscription, throughout Melbourne and vicinity, was raised to the amount of nearly £9000, upon the express arrangement with the Government of the time that the society should receive a grant to the extent of four times the amount so contributed. This promise, however, was not fulfilled, but in lieu thereof a moderate annual grant has been voted by the Legislature (as provided by the "Emigrants' Fund" arising from the Poll Tax, levied under the Passenger Act, 18 Victoria, Cap. 15 and 16, which fund is provided expressly for relief of destitute immigrants); also with the use of buildings on the south side of the Yarra River, Melbourne, now known as the Immigrants' Home, Princes Bridge.

These buildings were formerly appropriated by the immigration department as a temporary asylum for about forty married couples and families, upon payment of a weekly rental for each room. Since their possession by this society the accommodation has been much extended and varied in character.

So far as practicable, measures are adopted to overtake such exigencies of immigrants, for the time being, not otherwise provided for—thus, previous to the enlargement of the Melbourne hospital, sick wards were provided, with medical aid, attendance, &c; also, a lying-in ward until the establishment of a lying-in hospital for such cases.

The institution at the present date embraces lodging for single male and female inmates; separate rooms for a few families, and (as one pressing emergency yet unprovided for) a home for destitute children not eligible for the orphan asylums, for whom the necessary sleeping and dining rooms are set apart, with play-ground. There is also a school-room attached, and a teacher (provided by the National School board).

Of the adult inmates, when the house is not occupied by new arrivals, the majority are either out-door patients of the hospital, convalescents therefrom, too weak to undertake immediate employment—and, those of the "unemployed" males unequal to ordinary manual labor, for whom temporary employment sufficient for procuring food is provided.

The society insists as the principle of all its operations, that the aid rendered shall be only temporary, and that all inmates of the home shall be required to employ themselves to the extent of their ability; every means being taken to induce and promote self-reliance, and to discountenance dependence upon eleemosynary aid, which neither the funds nor objects of the society, nor the interests of the inmates themselves will permit.

For those sickly necessitous persons, not being newly arrived immigrants, relief tickets are issued, which the benevolent public purchase at a cost of 2s. 6d. each; for which sum full two days food and lodging is given, the plan being intended to obviate the objectionable and much abused practice of indiscriminate money relief.

A record is kept of the cases relieved, by which objects unworthy of further aid are denounced and habitual mendicancy prevented.

This society may be truly termed the Victorian strangers' friend, as it takes cognizance, so far as its extremely moderate income permits, of those cases ineligible or unprovided for by other institutions.

Besides the foregoing, immigrants' luggage is also stored upon the premises at a small weekly charge.

The usefulness of this society has been greatly promoted by the resident secretary, Dr. Earley, under whose superintendence the entire operations are conducted. For six years past this gentleman has devoted his attention to the systematic amelioration of the difficulties and wants of immigrants on the one hand, and the checking of imposition or idleness on the other.

MUSEUM OF NATURAL HISTORY, GEOLOGY, MINING AND AGRICULTURE.

The Public Museum of Natural History in Victoria was commenced by His Excellency Mr. LaTrobe and Capt. Clarke, when surveyor-general; and in the first instance a considerable collection of the birds, with a less perfect series of the quadrupeds, and a few specimens of the other divisions of the animal kingdom were got together. The best of these were, however, sent to the Paris Exhibition, and the specimens which remained formed a small museum, rarely visited, displayed in the upper rooms of the old assay office, by Mr. Blandowski, who was employed to collect specimens and information illustrative of the natural history of the country, for the "Museum of Natural History" branch of the survey department.

Shortly after Sir Charles Hotham arrived, it seemed to him that the museum establishment was an expense that should be done away with, in the then existing state of the country; and having directed that the collections should be removed to make way for the present survey offices, and refusing to sanction any expenditure for a new museum, an arrangement was suggested by Professor M'Coy for the preservation and extension of the collection, by which the Government offered to place the colonial specimens in the custody of the University, on condition of that body erecting a suitable museum building to contain them. The specimens were to be freely open to the public and were to remain the property of the Government, so that the corporation of the University could have no power at any time of excluding the public from them, or disposing of them in any way. The University accepted the trust, and parliament having contributed, on the above conditions, £10,000 towards the erection of the museum, the northern wing of the University was built at a cost of upwards of £26,000, having the entire length of the upper floor formed into an admirably suited museum of four fine rooms. In these museums every precaution has been taken to ensure the most abundant light, with entire absence of that great destroyer of natural history specimens, dust. This is kept from the specimens not only by the large enclosed and planted grounds surrounding the building, which could not have been had in town, but by fastening the glass of the windows into the stone without sashes, and by well made glass cases.

The museums, both of the state and the University, are alike freely open to the public; the latter being confined to the eastern room (principally mineralogical and geological collections), and the former occupying the other three. The geological and palæontological collections of the University are very complete, and have been stratigraphically arranged by the professor of natural science, and carefully labelled so as to give a complete view of modern geology. Professor M'Coy has also arranged the fine collection of minerals in such a way that the crystalline system and chemical constitution of each is seen at a glance.

The next large room is devoted exclusively to the natural products of the colony of Victoria; there we find the quadrupeds, birds, fishes, &c. of the country, classified in zoological order, the class marked over each case, the order, genus and species, locality and common name being given on the printed forms adopted for the labels. When the naming is finished and the collection nearly complete, it is intended to publish cheap illustrated volumes descriptive of all the classes, so that the public may become familiar with the objects by name, and thus render it possible for observers in various parts of the country to record their observations in such a form as will lay the foundation for a true natural history of the colony. In this "Victorian room" is also a series of the woods of the colony, contributed by Dr. Müller, and the palæontological specimens collected by Mr. Selwyn's staff for the illustration of the geological survey.

The first room on the right of the staircase is devoted to general zoology; and here the main groupings are illustrative of the great geographical divisions of the earth's surface, as marked by the distribution of animals; bringing the theories of "specific centres of creation," "representative forms," and other interesting points in the philosophy of zoology strikingly before the eye. Each of the geographical groups is, of course, zoologically classified, and the labelling of the specimens is far advanced, with the order, family, genus, species, locality and common name of each. Owing to the intercession of Professor M'Coy with the scientific men at home, this part of the collection has received, and is receiving many large and valuable additions, and in some departments will soon rival some of the great public collections of Britain, and many specimens already exhibited are so rare as to be found in very few even of these.

The west room contains the first commencement of an Agricultural Museum, comprising a fine collection of seeds by Mr. Macmillan, and a few models. But by the kindness of Professor Henslow it is expected to be enriched before the end of the year with copies of the agricultural objects in his Museum of Agricultural Botany at Kew, models of the best machines, &c., &c., so as to be as useful and instructive as the other more advanced sections. This room also contains one of the most practically useful and interesting sections (commenced by Professor M'Coy last year) of the whole—viz., the "Mining Museum." Here may be seen all the tools and machines used in both alluvial gold-washing and mining in Victoria, all the larger machinery being illustrated by beautifully accurate working models, shewing every detail of construction. Here also are models of the mines of Ballaarat, Buninyong, &c., formed of the actual materials, showing all the underground strata, the shafts, drives, timbering, &c., exactly to scale. Here also may be seen various foreign machines for boring for water and coal; the Russian gold-washing machinery employed in the Ural mountains, and various drawings of machinery, and physical and geological maps of the gold-fields.

There are daily expected for this division of the museum consignments, from Professor M'Coy's correspondents, of the tools used in the famous mines of Europe, and models of mining machines as well as metallurgical specimens from the various British and Continental Mining-Schools. This room is much frequented by the miners.

The proximity of the museums to the University lecture rooms and laboratory, renders them doubly useful for instruction, and renders the establishment of schools of mining, agriculture and engineering, such as exist in many of the European and American Universities, an easy matter.

The number of visitors for August of this year was 1,747, and for July, 1,888.

The public have free admission daily (Sunday excepted) from 9 a.m. to 5 p.m. Professor M'Coy is head of the department, as Director of Museums.

PHILOSOPHICAL INSTITUTE.

During the winter of 1854 the attention of many scientific gentlemen in Victoria was directed to the necessity of having some general means of communication one with another; and Mr. William Sydney Gibbons, the Microscopist, proposed that a society should be established under the title of the Victorian Institute. This gentleman communicated with many persons of known scientific reputation, and the Institute was founded under his management. His Honor Mr. Justice Barry was elected President; and Dr. Maund, Frederick Sinnett, Esq., George Higinbotham, Esq., and others of scientific eminence, held office in the council.

At nearly the same time, and with similar views, the Philosophical Society was established.—President, the Honorable Andrew Clarke, Capt., R.E.; Members of Council, Godfrey Howitt, Esq., M.D., the Rev. A. Morison, A. R. C. Selwyn, Esq., Dr. Müller, S. Iffla, Esq., M.D., Dr. Eades, Dr. Wilkie and others. The first general meeting of the Philosophical Society was held at the Assay Office (the present Public Lands Office) on the 12th August, 1854, and subsequently the meetings were held monthly. The society progressed very rapidly after its inauguration, and numerous papers were read, the principal contributors being Clement Hodgskinson, Esq., C.E., Dr. Wilkie, Dr. Müller, R. Brough Smyth, Esq., William Blansdowski, Esq., and Dr. Davy.

In course of time it was found that an amalgamation of the Victorian Institute and the Philosophical Society was desirable, and several conferences were held of committees of the respective societies. After some delays the two societies were amalgamated, under the title of the Philosophical Institute of Victoria, and the first general meeting was held on the 10th July, 1855.

In 1855 the transactions and proceedings of the Philosophical Society and the Victorian Institute were published, the colony derived much benefit from the dissemination of the papers amongst the various learned societies throughout the world. At that time the members of the societies were not numerous, and none came forward for election unless they were in some manner directly or indirectly connected with scientific investigations, and it was expected that every member would contribute either original papers or specimens of natural history for exhibition at the meetings. Of late candidates for election have been more numerous, and the principle of the British Association has been adopted, where every respectable man is considered eligible who takes sufficient interest in science to induce him to subscribe to its funds.

His Excellency Sir Henry Barkly, with his characteristic regard for every institution in any manner connected with the welfare of the colony, has largely extended his patronage to the Philosophical Institute, and very frequently honors the meetings with his presence.

ASTRONOMY.

The Astronomical Observatory of the Colony, situated in Williamstown, is in Longitude 9 h. 39 m. 54″ 4‴ east, and 37° 52′ 7″ 7‴ south, and was established in the year 1853, for the immediate purposes of commercial astronomy. Time balls at Williamstown and Melbourne have been erected, by which signals of Greenwich time are given to enable masters of vessels lying in Hobson's Bay to obtain errors and rates for their chronometers, and for general public convenience. In addition to the time balls, night signals are made from the lighthouse, which is in telegraphic communication with the Observatory.

The establishment was at first very limited, possessing only a small transit instrument, an astronomical clock, and a few minor instruments, the whole of the duties being carried on by the superintendent, Mr. R. L. J. Ellery. Within the last few years considerable improvements and additions have been made, and the Observatory is now in as an efficient a state as its compass allows.

The establishment consists at present of two wooden buildings erected within the telegraph reserve at Gellibrand's point, Williamstown; one of them containing meridian and computing rooms, and the other a small equatorial room.

The instruments consist of a transit instrument by Troughton and Simms of London; 3 feet six inches focal length, with 3 inches effective aperture; a sidereal transit clock by Frodsham, a mean time clock, an eighteen inch altazimuth circle by Troughton, with chronometers, sextants and other minor adjuncts of an astronomical observatory. The transit instrument is mounted on stone piers, the foundations of which are solid masonry for a considerable depth below the surface. The sidereal clock has for its support a massive stone pillar standing upon the same foundations as the transit piers. The altazimuth is placed upon a solid circular pier also of stone in the equatorial room. There is in addition to these a staff of meteorological instruments.

The work of the observatory consists in the observations necessary for maintaining true time, and for latitude and longitude, especially the latter, the accurate determination of which forms one of the most difficult problems in practical astronomy. Eclipses, occultations, and all occasional astronomical phenomena are carefully observed and recorded, and a catalogue of south circum polar stars is in course of formation. The Observatory being in electric communication with all the telegraph stations in the colony, time signals are sent to them daily at one o'clock, p.m. Observatory time, when the time balls at Melbourne and Williamstown are simultaneously dropped. It is intended eventually to supply all the seaport and some of the principal inland towns with time signals in order that uniform mean time may be obtained throughout the colony.

The available horizon on the meridian is from about 48° north declination to 30° polar distance below the pole south. The south pole star (σ) *sigma octantis* is within 48′ of the celestial pole, but being only of the 6th magnitude is very difficult to find without fixed instruments.

The zodiacal light is frequently very bright in the evening, generally most visible on those nights immediately preceding or following conjunction of the moon.

The climate of Victoria, from the clearness of its atmosphere, affords extraordinary advantages for the prosecution of astronomical research of thé highest class, and it is to be hoped that the Government may be induced to provide instruments of a superior class, in order that the observatory may not only be sufficiently effective for all the commercial purposes of the colony, but may be enabled to contribute something to astronomical knowledge generally.

FREEMASONRY IN VICTORIA.*

Freemasonry has been defined a Moral order, instituted with the praiseworthy design of recalling to our remembrance the most sublime truths in the midst of the most innocent and social pleasures, founded on brotherly love and charity. Its branches now extend to every part of the civilized world. It has identified itself with the people of Victoria, become a cherished institution, and exercises a potent influence amongst them.

---

* Prepared by an eminent member of the Craft.

There are in Victoria (in 1858) twenty-eight lodges and four Royal Arch Chapters under the English, nine lodges under the Irish, and three under the Scottish Grand Lodges, and one Royal Arch Chapter under the Scottish Supreme Grand Chapter, the aggregate number of members of which lodges and chapters is about 3,500, exclusive of a similar number of Freemasons who, from various causes, have not yet affiliated with any of these lodges.

The brief space allotted for our subject precludes the introduction into our *résumé* of little more than an enumeration of events in the annals of Freemasonry in the colony. The constitution of the first lodge, the Australia Felix, under the English Grand Lodge, took place at Melbourne on the 25th March, 1840. The first W. Master was Br. George B. Smyth, who was installed by Br. John Stephen, P.M., who invested the officers and performed the several ceremonies upon the occasion.

The next lodge formed in the colony was the Australia Felix Lodge of Hiram, at Melbourne, under the Irish Grand Lodge, on the 24th June, 1843, Br. John Thomas Smith, then the R. W. the Mayor of Melbourne, the first initiate in the English Lodge, was elected W. Master, Br. John Stephen. P.M., also performed the same ceremonies upon this occasion, as previously described in relation to the Australia Felix Lodge.

The first lodge in the colony under the Scottish Grand Lodge, though steps for its formation were taken in November, 1841, was not constituted until the 13th May, 1844. The ceremony of constitution and the installation of the R.W. Deputy Master, Br. Wm. Kerr, and investment of his officers being severally performed by Br. John Thomas Smith.

Sometime thereafter the United Tradesmen's Lodge, under the Scottish Grand Lodge, was constituted at Geelong, and Br. George Coppin, late of dramatic celebrity, who had obtained the warrant of constitution, was installed the first R.W. Master of the lodge.

During the interval between the constitution of these several lodges and the discovery of gold, the progress of Freemasonry, though subject to the usual vicissitudes, was considerable. Contrary, however, to prescriptive right, to take a secondary part in such ceremonies, the brethren assisted Charles J. LaTrobe, Esq., Superintendent of Port Phillip, and in his subsequent position as Lieutenant Governor of Victoria, to lay the foundation stones of several public structures, namely, the Supreme Court in July, 1842; Prince's Bridge and the Hospital in March, 1846; and the Benevolent Asylum in June, 1850. The R.W. Master of the Australasian Kilwinning Lodge, with the Masters of the other lodges, laid the foundation-stone of the Temperance Hall, Russell-street, in December, 1846.

The first Royal Arch Chapter in the colony, designated

the Australasian, affiliated with the Australia Felix Lodge, was constituted on the 7th May, 1844.

After the discovery of gold in 1851, an immense influx of Europeans arrived in the colony, and amongst them several brethren of great masonic experience, fully conversant with the various rituals and qualified to carry on the work of Freemasonry according to the ancient usages, customs, and landmarks of the order. Some of these brethren greatly accelerated the progress of Freemasonry in Victoria, and still continue to exercise a marked influence over it. Amongst these may be mentioned Br. J. J. Moody, a Past Provincial Junior Grand Warden for Cheshire, a Royal Arch Past Z., a Knight Templar, and Prince Grand Rose Croix; Br. E. T. Bradshaw, a P.M., a R.A., a Knight Templar and Knight of the 30th degree, H.R.D.M.; Br. Edward Sydes, P. Prov. G. Secretary for Somersetshire, a R.A. and Knight Templar; and Br. Robert Levick, a P.M. and R.A. past Z. These severally commenced their masonic labors in 1853. The latter brother established in 1854, and has successfully continued to the present a lodge of instruction, which has been of inestimable advantage to the craft. About two years thereafter Br. H. W. Lowry, a P.M., a R. A., and Knight Templar; Br. Professor Wilson, a R.A., and K.T.; and several other influential brethren from Britain, increased this phalanx of devoted Freemasons.

During the years 1853-4-5 the lodges increased rapidly in number, and warrants of dispensation were obtained to hold them at the principal gold-fields. During this period the foundation-stone of the Melbourne Gas Works and of the Western Market were respectively laid by Br. John Thomas Smith, then R.W. Mayor of Melbourne, assisted by the masters, officers, and brethren of the several lodges. Upon the former occasion a beautiful silver trowel, and upon the latter a massive one of pure Victorian gold, each with suitable inscriptions, were presented to Br. John T. Smith.

The great increase in lodges led to a desire for their united government by the formation of Provincial Grand Lodges, wherein each lodge, under its respective constitution, would be fully represented.

On the memorial of the Australasian Kilwinning Lodge, the Grand Lodge of Scotland appointed Br. James Hunter Ross, R.W.P.G. Master, but after appointing his officers and he and they being respectively installed and invested in July, 1847, he never summoned them to meet thereafter, and did not resign office until 1854. From the loss of his commission a successor was not appointed until the present year, Br. W. C. Haines, M.L.A., being recommended to the Duke of Athol for such appointment, one which, from the high character of Br. Haines, cannot fail to be generally approved.

In 1856 Br. John Thomas Smith, M.L.A., was appointed R.W.P.G. Master, under the Irish Constitution, for Victoria, by the Duke of Leinster, and the following year Lord Zetland appointed Captain Andrew Clarke, R.E., M.L.A., R.W.P.G. Master, under the English Constitution, for Victoria; there being then twelve lodges to be placed under his jurisdiction. Each of the Provincial Grand Lodges and Provincial Grand Masters were respectively constituted and installed, according to ancient usage, by Br. J. J. Moody, Past Provincial Junior Grand J. Warden for Cheshire, assisted by numerous Masters, Past Masters, and Brethren. Captain Clarke laid the foundation-stone of Collingwood bridge in 1856, with great *eclat*, in the presence of many thousands of spectators. The members of the Municipal Council of East Collingwood purchased and presented to him for the occasion a beautiful silver trowel suitably inscribed.

Prior to the departure of Br. Smith for Europe in July of the present year, and the departure of Br. Captain Clarke for Europe in August of the present year (1858), the brethren gave them sumptuous farewell banquets; the former was held at the Café de Paris, F. T. Gell, Esq., W.D.P.G.M., for Victoria (English Constitution) in the chair, and the latter at the Prince of Wales Hotel, Br. Professor Wilson, P.M. (Scottish Constitution) in the chair. Appropriate speeches were made on these respective occasions, and the Brethren testified their regard for the P.G. Masters in a manner so marked and fraternal as to inspire them with the most grateful feelings for such demonstrations of brotherly courtesy and attention.

An interesting event took place, during the present year, at Sandhurst—the consecration of the beautiful lodge, recently built therein, to Royal Arch Freemasonry. This ceremony, the installation of the Principals, the investment of the Officers, and exaltation of Candidates, were severally performed by Companion J. J. Moody, Past Z., who visited Sandhurst for the purpose. The ceremony of consecrating a Royal Arch Chapter was thus performed for the first time in Victoria.

A desire having been manifested for the introduction of the Chivalrous Degrees and the Ancient and Accepted Rite into Victoria, Benjamin Archer Kent, Esq., M.D., R.W.P.G.M. for South Australia, having been appointed Provincial Grand Commander of Knights Templar and of Prince Masons for the Australian Colonies, soon after his arrival from, and before his return again to, England, carried out this desire. In April he constituted the Pembroke Encampment of Knights Templar, at Melbourne, and installed Sir Knight E. T. Bradshaw Eminent Commander, and Sir Knights J. J. Moody and H. W. Lowry, respectively, First and Second Captains thereof.

On the same day he constituted the Sovereign Chapter of Knights of the Eagle and Pelican and Perfect Puissant Princes Grand Rose Croix of Victoria, under the supreme council of Sovereign Grand Inspectors General for England and Wales and the dependencies of Great Britain, and installed and inducted the following Sir Knights into office:—Most Wise Sovereign, J. J. Moody, Knight, 18th, and, under Scottish jurisdiction a Knight of the 33rd Degree of the O.M. First General, E. T. Bradshaw, Knight, K H., 30th; Second General, A. J. Gibb, Knight, K.H., 30th.

Such is a brief outline of the introduction into and progress of the several branches of Freemasonry in Victoria.

MILITARY DEPARTMENT.

(For Naval, see page 71.)

Sydney, New South Wales, was formerly the head quarters of the General Officer commanding the troops in the Australian colonies. In the year 1854, however, the British Government, consequent on the rapidly increasing importance of the Colony of Victoria, and regarding Melbourne as the most central military point in the command, added to which its postal proximity to England, directed the removal of the head quarters of the army thence. Accordingly, in August, 1854, the late Sir Robert Nickle, K.H., then Commander in Chief in these colonies, arrived at Melbourne with his staff, and established his head quarters in Victoria.

In May, 1855, Sir Robert Nickle died in Melbourne, when the command of the troops devolved on Colonel E. Macarthur, Deputy Adjutant-General. This officer was, in September of that year, appointed Commander of the Forces in the Australian colonies with the rank of Major-General, being succeeded as Deputy-Adjutant-General by Lieutenant-Colonel J. M. B. Neill

In January, 1856, Major-General Macarthur succeeded to the temporary Government of Victoria, by the death of His Excellency Sir C. Hotham, K.C.B., and administered the same until the arrival of His Excellency Sir Henry Barkly, K.C.B., the present Governor.

On the 17th July, 1857, Major-General Macarthur was nominated a C.B.

The present head quarters and military staff of the Australian command is composed as follows:—Major-General E. Macarthur, C.B., Commanding the Forces; Lieutenant-Colonel J. M. B. Neill, H.P., Deputy Adjutant-General; Captain Pitt, 80th Regiment, Assistant Military Secretary; Captain H. T. F. White, 40th Regim nt, Aide-de-Camp; Captain R. Hare, 40th Regiment, Major of Brigade. Capain G. Dean Pitt, District Inspector of Musketry. *Medical Staff*:—W. Lucas, Staff Surgeon, 1st Class, Principal Medical Officer; G. M. Webster, M.D., Staff Surgeon, 2nd Class; T. A. Corlet, Purveyor of the Forces. *Commissariat Staff*:—F. T. Coxworthy, Deputy Commissary-General.

Consequent on the discovery of gold in Victoria, and the vast increase of the population, it was deemed advisable to augment the military force in the colony, and, in June, 1852, the head quarters of the 40th Regiment, under command of Colonel Valiant, embarked at Cork, in Her Majesty's Troop Ship *Vulcan*, Commander H. Von Donop, and arrived at Melbourne on the 5th November of the same year.

The military force in Victoria had previously consisted of only a small detachment, generally from the regiment stationed in Sydney.

At a subsequent period a still greater amount of military force being thought desirable in the colony, the 1st battalion, 12th Regiment, under the command of Major Kempt, was directed to proceed from Cork to Melbourne, where it arrived on the 18th October, 1854.

This regiment remained at Melbourne until the close of 1855, when an augmentation to the 40th Regiment of four companies, under command of Major (now Lieutenant-Colonel) Neill arrived at Melbourne.

The 40th Regiment is the first corp the head quarters of which has been stationed in Melbourne, and it is now the only *regular* corps in the colony of Victoria; at one time it furnished detachments of one company each at the gold-fields of Ballaarat, Castlemaine, and Bendigo, and at the town of Geelong. All these have now been withdrawn, and the whole strength of the corps, with the exception of one company stationed at Adelaide, South Australia, has been concentrated in Melbourne.

Shortly after the arrival of the 40th, one company was mounted and equipped as light cavalry, with the view of being employed against bushrangers. The increasing numbers and efficiency of the police force, enabling it to compete with these robbers, the mounted company of the 40th was employed in the escort of gold and treasure from the different gold-fields to the Treasury at Melbourne. This arduous and highly responsible service was most successfully performed by the officers and men of the company, in acknowledgment of which a most deservedly complimentary General Order* was issued,

* GENERAL ORDER.—"Head Quarters, Melbourne, January 7th, 1857. In consequence of a representation from the Civil Power, deeming it expedient to undertake the custody and transmission of gold from the several offices in the interior to the Treasury at Melbourne, the Major-General directs, that the mounted company of the 40th Regiment, which has for a considerable period been charged with this important service, return to its legitimate duties at Head Quarters. The public records show that it has faithfully performed this duty for three years and eight months, dating from May, 1853, to the present time, during which period it escorted and delivered into the public Treasury no less than six millions (6,000,000) ounces of gold, valued at twenty-four millions (24,000,000) pounds sterling, and conveyed to and from the interior, in cash, £17,500,000, making a total of £41,500,000. At the representation of the administrative Government of Victoria, His Excellency Sir Henry Barkly

on the occasion of the Government dispensing with their services on the same footing as they had previously been entertained.

In order, however, to afford every facility to Government in the escort of the gold, the Major-General commanding allowed one sergeant and fifty rank and file of the 40th Regiment from those who had formerly belonged to the mounted company to continue their services, for the purpose of escorting gold and treasure, but under the direction of the Chief Commissioner of Police. In this duty they were employed until arrangements having been made by Government for the police to do the whole duty of the gold escort the military were directed to rejoin their corps.

A most gratifying report of the steadiness and efficiency of these soldiers, while they were attached to the police, was made by the the Chief Commissioner of that force.

A letter expressive of the satisfactory manner in which the mounted company, 40th Regiment, had conducted them selves while in civil employ, was also received from the Military Secretary to His Royal Highness The General Commanding in Chief.

The expense of the military has been defrayed as follows:—That for the mainte ance of the Head Quarter Staff, with the exception of the colonial allowance granted to each officer, is, and always has been, disbursed from the Imperial chest. Until the 31st December, 1857, the Imperial pay, and also the Colonial allowances of the Regiments stationed in Victoria, were defrayed by the colony. Since then, however, the Home Government have been requested by that of this colony to disburse the Imperial pay of the troops.

Ever since the arrival of the military here, the barrack accommodation has been, not only of a temporary character, but bad and inconvenient in every possible respect. There are, however, new barracks in the course of erection, near Princes Bridge.

VOLUNTEERS.

Consequent on the war with Russia, the attention of the colonists was directed to the expediency and necessity of organizing a military force, to co-operate with Her Majesty's troops in case of emergency, and in the year 1854, an Act was passed, authorising the raising of Volunteer corps.

---

has been pleased to express his sense of the admirable manner in which this detached force has conducted itself, in the discharge of the very responsible and peculiar duty assigned to it. Major-General Macarthur will have much pleasure in soliciting the especial notice of the General Commanding in Chief to the meritorious services of the officers, non-commissioned officers, and privates of this portion of the 40th Regiment, and in reporting for the satisfaction of His Royal Highness their at all times true and soldierlike bearing. By command (signed) J. M. B. NEILL, Lieut.-Col., Dep. Adjutant-General."

The Volunteer force of Victoria is as follows:—The Victoria Volunteer Artillery Corps, commanded by Lieutenant-Colonel Anderson. The Victorian Yoemanry Corps, commanded by Lieutenant-Colonel Ross. The Geelong Volunteer Rifle Corps, commanded by Lieutenant-Colonel Rede.

These corps were hurriedly raised during a time of considerable excitement. The system by which they are regulated is susceptible of much modification and very great improvement. The re-establishment of peace withdrew from them much of the interest with which they had been regarded by, and the encouragement they at first received from, the public. Notwithstanding this, however, the members of the corps have persevered in their voluntarily adopted calling, and have made a progress in it, which has been regarded, and reported on, by the military authorities as most creditable, and which, moreover, is the best proof of the zeal, aptitude, and cheerfulness of the officers and members of the several corps

One very great desideratum connected with the Volunteers is, that they should have better arms, and to this point, it is desirable and to be hoped, that Government will speedily direct their special and earnest attention.

The Volunteers of Victoria deserve every encouragement, and merit no small amount of praise; their services are unpaid, and, in the case of the Yeomanry, the expense of their costly uniforms and equipments is borne by the members themselves.

The following is the present strength of the regular and Volunteer forces in the colony, exclusive of the general staff.

Distribution.	Field-Officers.	Captains.	Subalterns.	Staff.	Sergeants.	Corporals.	Drummers.	Privates.
H.M. Troops, 40th Regiment	1	3	14	5	43	36	20	631
Victoria Vol. Artillery Corps	3	8	16	4	13	9	—	131
Vic. Vol. Yeoy. Cavalry Corps	2	1	4	2	6	6	1	81
Geelong Vol. Rifle Corps	1	1	2	1	3	4	1	59
Total	7	13	36	12	65	55	22	902

HOUSES OF PARLIAMENT, MELBOURNE.

The building of the Houses of Parliament was commenced in January, 1856.

The Legislative Chambers were opened for the despatch of business on the 21st of November, 1856. The formal opening by the Acting Governor Major General M'Arthur, took place on Tuesday the 25th of November, 1856.

The order of architecture employed in the Assembly is Roman Ionic, that of the Council is Corinthian. The Chambers are each 76 feet long, 40 feet wide and 36 feet high. The division lobbies are each 58 feet long and 15 feet wide, they are at present used for committee rooms. The whole of the ground floor is vaulted and for the present used for clerk's offices, store and record rooms. The Chambers form the centre or inside block, and are intended to be surrounded by a complete suite of buildings, comprising official residences, members' rooms, committee and reading rooms, library, refreshment rooms, &c. The inside block as it now appears measures 171 feet in length, 105 feet in width, and 60 feet in height. The entire building when completed will measure about 424 feet by 240 feet. The outer elevations are designed to have a colonnade, all round them, which will give a terrace for promenade 15 feet wide, the columns above the terrace will be 32 feet high. The order employed is Roman Doric. The tower fronting Bourke street will be 250 feet in height.

The cost of the work up to the present time is about £100,000. It will propably take 10 or 12 years to complete, and as the cost of future works will necessarily depend on the current rates of labor and material, no correct estimate can be made of what such value may be in years to come.

The portion now being proceeded with is for the Library and reading-rooms, which forms the centre of the east elevation, and measures 124 feet by 70 feet.

A model of the building to a scale of a quarter of an inch to the foot has been prepared, and can be inspected by all who desire to form an idea of the ultimate appearance of the edifice. The architects are Messrs. Knight and Kerr.

The Library, under the superintendence of Mr. Ridgway, was established in 1852, and now contains about 9,000 volumes of every description of literature. Nearly 6,000 volumes are shortly expected from England. The library is specially for the benefit and general use of the members of the Legislature, but every facility is given to the public by the librarian in all searches and inquiries strictly parliamentary and legislative.

BANKS.

The history of banking in this country has been one of uninterrupted prosperity. Its development will be seen by the following comparative statement:—

	1851.	1858.
No. of banks and branches in Victoria ..	6	56
No. of towns wherein banks are established	3	20

The extent to which banking business is carried on in some of the larger towns will be readily conceived from the fact that six of the banks have established branches in Geelong, seven in

Ballaarat, five in Sandhurst, four in Castlemaine, four in Beechworth, and three in Ararat; six towns have each two branch banks, and six others a banking establishment each.

The transactions of these banks will be most conveniently shown in a tabular form.

Table showing the average amount of the liabilities and assets of all the banks within Victoria in the year 1858, as compared with 1851:—

	1858. First Quarter.			1851. Fourth Quarter.		
Liabilities.	£	s.	d.	£	s.	d.
Notes in circulation	2,121,588	18	4	180,058	6	1
Bills in circulation	79,902	11	5	10,497	15	8
Deposits	6,017,446	15	10	822,253	19	7
Total Liabilities*	8,218,938	5	7	1,012,810	1	4
Assets.						
Coin	2,065,176	9	0	321,824	2	3
Bullion	533,139	5	8	..		
Landed Property	351,444	2	3	19,982	13	7
Government Securities..	286,865	0	0	..		
Debts due to Banks, including Notes, Bills of Exchange, and all Stock and Funded Debts	7,562,428	10	4	745,955	6	1
Total Assets†	10,799,053	7	3	1,087,726	1	11
Capital Account.						
Paid-up Capital	5,423,694	0	0	1,862,280	0	0
Amount of last Dividends	354,333	6	8	65,320	1	7
Reserved Profits after declaring such Dividends	1,228,347	7	11	158,051	3	6

Without attempting to enter into any minute analysis of this table, it will suffice to remark that although some of these banks have only been recently established, the aggregate sum last divided amounts to 13 per cent. per annum on the paid-up capital, besides reserved profits amounting to more than one-fifth of the subscribed capital.

Comparing the progress of population with these statistics of currency, we perceive that while the population has increased sixfold within the period under review, the notes in circulation have increased nearly twelve fold ; the coin and bullion more than eight-fold ; and the deposits between seven and eight-fold. The most remarkable feature presented by the bank returns is the enormous proportion which the deposits bear to the number of inhabitants ; being £12 16s. 3d. per head of the whole population.

The year 1854 appears to have been the climax of banking prosperity in this colony. The circulation in the end of 1853 was £1,919,086. In the first nine months of 1854 it

* Exclusive of liabilities of the banks and branches to one another.
† Exclusive of the debts due from the banks and branches to one another.

BANKS (JOINT-STOCK) IN AUSTRALIA.

Name of Bank.	When Established.	No. of Partners.	Paid-up Capital.	Reserve Fund.	Paid up per share.	Rate of Dividend.	No. of Branches.
* 1. Bank of Australasia	1834	938	£900,000	£401,778‡	£40	20 per cent.	17
† 2. Bank of New South Wales... ...	1817	345	£500,000	£150,000	£20	20 per cent.	17
†* 3. Eng., Scot. & Aus. Char. Bank...	1852	488	£500,000	£10,311	£20	6 per cent.	2
* 4. London Chartered Bank	1852	843	£700,000	£12,673	£20	6 per cent.	8
* 5. Oriental Bank Corporation... ...	1851	950	£1,256,325	£252,000	All	10 per cent.	11
* 6. Union Bank of Australia	1837	1,200	£820,000	£286,763	£25	20 per cent.	22
† 7. Bank of Victoria	1852	400	£500,000	£52,500	£5	10 per cent.	13
† 8. Colonial Bank of Australasia ...	1856	800	£312,500	£30,000	£5	10 per cent.	7
† 9. National Bank of Australasia ...	1858						

Those marked thus * have Offices in London. Those marked thus † are Colonial Institutions.

‡ Also Guarantee Fund.

The Bank of New South Wales is a Colonial Institution, but has an office in London.

NOTE.—The Branches of each Bank are inserted in *Bradshaw's Guide to Victoria.*

rose to £2,386,760. The deposits in the same year amounted to upwards of six millions sterling; coin and bullion, from three to four millions; and their advances to the colonists rose from £3,905,944 in the end of 1853, to £6,791,336 in the third quarter of 1854. In the latter year, the average population was 250,000. In order to understand clearly these facts, it will be necessary to compare the amounts with those of the present year, when the population is very nearly doubled. In the quarter ended 30th September last, the note circulation was £1,993,274, being £393,486 less than in the third quarter of 1854. The deposits in 1858 are £5,672,246, being considerably under the average amount in 1854. The specie is at present about a million less, and the advances to the colonists are about two millions more than in the former period. It cannot be denied that the banks are all the better for their former experience. It would be impossible to improve much upon their policy, which is firm and consistent, without being oppressive. There is no doubt that the bulk of our community is perfectly sound and stable, and if the reckless speculators of the mother country could only be taught a little caution, we doubt not that our mercantile and financial affairs would be speedily re-established.

SAVINGS' BANKS.

The returns of the Savings' Banks, an institution the working of which forms so sure an index to the material prosperity of the laboring classes, present results of a most gratifying character, manifesting as they do beyond all question the steadily increasing comfort of the people, and what is, perhaps, of more genuine importance, their perseverance in habits of economy and of careful provision for the future. It is understood that much of the deposits withdrawn in the course of the year have been applied to the purchase of land; and thus the Savings' Banks, by providing a secure place of deposit, and allowing a reasonable rate of interest, 4 per cent. per annum, for the savings of the working people, lend their aid towards the permanent settlement of the country.

It appears that on 31st December, 1851, the total amount lodged by the 1,208 depositors was £46,444. At the last annual balance period, viz., at 1st July, 1858, the total number of depositors was 7,242, and the total amount of balances at their credit, £432,243 8s. 8d. Average amount of balances, £59 13s. 9d.

The Savings' Banks in Victoria are separate institutions, under the management of local trustees appointed by the Commissioners of Savings' Banks, who are appointed by the Governor in Council, and have the general control of their administration and the investment of the funds, in accordance with the provisions of the Act of the Lieutenant-Governor and Legislative Council, 16 Victoria, No. 37, commonly called "The Savings' Bank Act, 1853." They are now established in Melbourne, Geelong, Castlemaine, Sandhurst, Ballaarat, Portland, and Belfast, and it is understood that the Commissioners intend shortly to establish banks at Beechworth and Maryborough.

INSURANCE COMPANIES IN AUSTRALIA.

Name of Company.	When Esta-blishd.	Liability of Share-holders.	Paid-up Capital.	Reserve Fund.	Investd. in the Colonies	Paid up per Share.	Rate of Dividend.	No. of Branches.	No. of Agencies.
			£	£	£				
COLONIAL COMPANIES.									
Australasian Fire and Life Assurance Co.	1857	Lim. dle.s.	62,500	5,084	26,700	£1		1	16
Colonial Insurance Company ..	1854	Unlimited	40,900	18,883	62,475	£1	10 per cent.	24	24
Derwent and Tamar Marine Insurance Co.	1841	Unlimited	5,000	18,716	118,023	£1	50 per cent.	4	4
Melbourne Fire Insurance Company ..	1858	500,000	12,580	5,855		10s.			
Victoria Fire and Marine Insurance Co.	1849		100,000	50,000	150,000	£25	£4 per share	21	21
ENGLISH COMPANIES.									
Liverpool and London Fire and Life Assurance Company	1836	Unlimited	188,422	899,596	180,000	£2	30 per cent.	9	
Northern Assurance Company ..	1836		62,988	350,000		£1	7½ per cent.	6	
People's Provident Life and Guarantee Assurance Society	1854	500,000	50,000	80,000 (income)		10s.	5 per c. & 20 p. c. of bonus	10	10
Professional Life Assurance Company ..	1847		250,000	12,500		10s.	15 per cent.	11	
Waterloo Life Assurance Company ..	1851		400,000				6 per cent.	4	

The Monarch Fire and Life Assurance Company has been incorporated with the Liverpool and London Fire and Life Assurance Co.

NOTE.—The Branches of each Insurance Company are inserted in *Bradshaw's Guide to Victoria*.

Among the Insurance Companies established in Melbourne are the following, who have not supplied us with figures:—Australian Mutual Provident Society; Cornwall Fire and Marine Insurance Co.; Hobart Town and Launceston Marine Insurance Company; Launceston Fire and Marine Insurance Co.; Melbourne Underwriters' Association; Tasmanian Fire Insurance Company. English Insurance Companies, the following:—Canton Marine Insurance Company; Church of England Fire and Life Assurance Company; Imperial Fire Insurance Company; Royal Fire and Life Assurance Company; Travellers' and Marine Insurance Co.; Unity Fire Insurance Association.

MISCELLANEOUS COMPANIES.

Capital of Melbourne and Hobson's Bay Railway Company, £350,000; St. Kilda and Brighton, £125,000; Geelong and Melbourne, £350,000; Melbourne and Suburban, £300,000. (See particulars of Railways, as per contents.)

Capital of Melbourne Exchange Company, £50,000; Melbourne Gas and Coke Company, £150,000; Ballaarat Gas Company, £50,000; Geelong Gas Company, £30,000; St. Kilda and Prahran Gas Company, £30,000; Melbourne Guarantee Company, £100,000; Studley Park Bridge Company, £12,000; St. Kilda Sea Bathing Company, £3,500; South Yarra Waterworks, £20,000; Bendigo Waterworks, £60,000.

AGRICULTURAL PRODUCE.

By the latest statistical returns, prepared in March, 1858, the quantity of land under crop amounted to 237,729 acres. The produce of the last harvest was: Wheat, 1,808,438 bushels; maize, 6,558 bushels; barley, 156,458 bushels; oats, 1,249,800 bushels; and of potatoes, 51,115 tons, besides other crops; while 401 acres were planted as vineyards, which yielded 5,761 gallons of wine, and supplied the markets with 518,463 lbs. of grapes.

Pre-eminent as Victoria is for its mineral wealth, it is scarcely less remarkable for its corn producing qualities in comparison with those of several other countries. The following table, showing the average produce per acre according to recent official documents, speaks for itself:—

Countries.	Bushels per Acre. Wheat.	Barley.	Oats.
Victoria, average of the years 1855-6-7 ..	23·1	30·3	29·3
Tasmania, 1850	16·5	24·2	23·7
South Australia, 1857	12·0	22·0	25·0
New South Wales, average of three years	15·4	16·7	16·7
State of New York	14·0	16·0	26·0
State of California, 1855	20·0	31·5	20·2

How closely the cultivator of the soil is treading on the foot-prints of the surveyor will be perceived from the following table, showing the increase in the number of occupiers of purchased land during the last few years in those inland districts in which the gold-fields are for the most part situated, and which until recently were closed against the farmers by the operation of the survey system:—

County or District.	No. of Occupiers of Land. 1856.	1857.	1858.
Dalhousie	325	588	622
Talbot	162	427	902
Ripon	25	130	201
Grenvile	50	180	274
East Loddon	115	269	581
The Murray	103	164	397
Total	780	1758	2982

The increase, therefore, in these districts, as compared with the year 1856, has been 125 per cent. in 1857, and in 1858, 282 per cent., showing an application of labor and capital to tillage probably unparalleled for rapidity, but fully warranted by the richness of the soil and the suitableness of the climate to agricultural pursuits.

The subjoined table is illustrative of the progress of tillage in the principal agricultural districts:—

District.	No. of Holders.	Total Acres in Cultivation.	Acres under Grain Crops.	Produce of Grain Crops in Bushels.
Bourke	2,874	74,145	31,948	713,446
Grant	2,107	48,461	33,838	705,115
Villiers	739	21,513	17,278	448,446
Talbot	902	20,446	11,282	338,253
Dalhousie	627	17,320	9,672	302,867
Loddon	634	10,982	2,438	52,259
Ripo	201	9,252	4,206	162,640
Murray	397	6,698	3,327	63,272
Evelyn	184	4,342	3,193	54,471
Mornington	229	4,173	3,423	74,181
Normanby	287	3,984	2,735	60,591

The extent of the land under crop in the years ending respectively in March, 1852, and 1858, is exhibited in the following table. Since the year 1854 the progress of agriculture has been much greater than that of population. The increase in 1857 as compared with 1854 was more than 400 per cent., while the increase in the number of inhabitants, according to the censuses of those years was 73 per cent. If agriculture continues to progress in this ratio, the country will not merely supply its own wants, but produce a large quantity in excess.

Year.	Total No. of Acres Cultivated.	Acres under Wheat.	Acres under Barley.	Acres under Oats.	Acres under Potatoes.	Other crops. Acres.
1852	57,298	29,623	1,327	6,426	2,375	17,547
1858	237,729	87,230	5,409	40,222	20,697	84,281

The value of the crops raised in the latter year, if estimated according to the market prices ruling in Melbourne at the present date, would be:—Wheat, £798,741; barley, £64,535; oats, £531,428; potatoes, £690,039; hay, £140,516; total, £3,025,254.

LIVE STOCK.

Two or three years ago some alarm was excited in this country, even among intelligent men, that there was likely to be a deficiency in live stock beyond even the power of the neighbouring colonies to supply, and prophecies were hazarded that the price of butchers' meat would ere long reach the famine rate of 2s. 6d. per lb. These fears are now dissipated. The numbers of sheep have diminished, but the deficiency in sheep is amply compensated by the increase in cattle and pigs. In 1851 the stock of the colony was as follows:—Horses,

21,219; cattle, 378,806; sheep, 6,032,783. By the aid of the staff which has been so carefully organised during the last two years for the annual collection of agricultural statistics, it has been ascertained that the stock in March, 1858, was—horses, 55,683; cattle, 614,537; sheep, 4,766,022; and at the commencement of this year there was an increase of 80,424 horned cattle, 22,946 pigs, 188,150 sheep, and 22,253 horses, over the numbers returned in 1856.

The quantity of cattle slaughtered during the year 1857-8 was—horned cattle, 176,947; sheep, 998,824; pigs, 25,249.

GAS.

The Gas and Coke Company was originated, and the Provisional Committee formed at Melbourne on the 28th August, 1850. The sum of money already expended on buildings and apparatus, and street mains, amounts to £150,000. The number of shares of £5 each issued has been 18,000, equal to £90,000; and 6,000 shares of £10 each, equal to £60,000; the total being £150,000. At 31st August, 1855, debentures bearing ten per cent. interest were issued to the extent of £50,000, since when £20,900 has been paid off, leaving £29,100 still unsettled. The total of shares and debentures amounts to £179,100. Dividends are paid on the capital at the rate of twelve per cent. per annum. About fifty miles of mains are laid; and forty miles of mains are now being received for the purpose of supplying Richmond, Prahran, St. Kilda, Emerald Hill, Sandridge and North Melbourne. The quantity of gas consumed is about 45,000,000 cubic feet per annum, the charge being 22s. 6d. per 1,000 cubic feet. The works are very extensive, situated on the north side of the Yarra Yarra River, adjacent to the city.

EUROPEAN MAILS.

The "European and Australian Royal Mail Company" have had the contract for conveying H.M. mails between Europe and Australia since the year 1856 The route is from Southampton to Malta (where the mail *viâ* Marseilles is received) and Alexandria; thence overland to Suez, where the mails are re-shipped, the steamers touching at Aden, Point de Galle, King George's Sound, Melbourne, and Sydney. This arrangement terminates in February, 1859.

The "Peninsular and Oriental Company" have the new contract for seven years, with some modifications in the route. The vessels are to call at Mauritius instead of Point de Galle, and to touch at Kangaroo Island to tranship the Adelaide mail. The new service will commence on the 12th March from Southampton (mail *viâ* Marseilles on the 16th), and the first vessel will be due at Melbourne on May 5th. The first homeward mail will leave Sydney on the 15th February. The contract time is 55 days, *viâ* Marseilles 50 days.

RAILWAYS.

Two lines have been constructed by private companies. The first, from Melbourne to Hobson's Bay, with a branch to St. Kilda, including a pier running 582 yards into the Bay at Sandridge, has cost £865,240. The average number of passengers weekly has been 10,240 to Sandridge and 17,800 to St. Kilda. The profits for the last half-year amounted to £29,972. The second is from Geelong to within eight miles of Melbourne. Its total cost has been £590,576. Two other private companies have recently been formed for the purpose of connecting the more populous suburban towns with the metropolis. For portions of the lines, contracts amounting to £820,000 have been entered into, and the works have been commenced. Finally, the Government, by authority of an Act of Parliament, has undertaken to construct upwards of two hundred miles of railway, including lines from Williamstown to Melbourne, from Melbourne to the Murray *viâ* Castlemaine and Bendigo, and from Geelong to Ballaarat, the lines to be completed in about four years. Contracts have been taken for the Sandhurst line, 94½ miles, amounting to £3,356,937, and for the Ballaarat line, 53 miles, to the amount of £1,271,841. It is expected that the line from Sandhurst to the Murray, being over a level country (57½ miles), will be constructed for about £500,000.

GEELONG AND MELBOURNE RAILWAY.

Capital in 17,500 shares of £20 each, £350,000. Mortgage debt £262,500.

This Company was incorporated on the 8th February, 1853, for the construction of a line of railway between Geelong and Melbourne; capital, £350,000. The portion of the line between Williamstown and Batman's Hill was subsequently ceded to the Melbourne, Mount Alexander, and Murray River Railway Company, on the understanding that the two lines should be carried on contemporaneously; but the Mount Alexander Company having failed to raise the necessary capital, transferred their rights and liabilities to the Government, by whom the branch line to Melbourne is now in course of construction.

The Government originally guaranteed interest at five per cent. on £200,000, which was extended on the accession of Sir Charles Hotham to the remainder of the capital; and in the latter part of the year 1854 an agency was established in London for the sale of shares, in which object the Company was entirely successful, and the line was completed to the proposed junction with the Government line, in length about forty miles, and opened for passenger traffic on the 25th of June, 1857.

But one line of rails has been as yet laid down; but the earth works and bridges are constructed for a double track; and the expense has consequently exceeded the estimated capital, the cost being about £600,000, or £15,000 per mile. A power is reserved to the Government, by the Company's Act, to purchase the undertaking after the year 1863, at the rate of £250 for every £100 capital subscribed, or sixteen years' purchase of the annual divisible profits of the three years then next preceding.

The passenger traffic, to which the operations of the Company have been so far confined, has yielded an average of about £800 per week, which leaves a surplus after the payment of all working expenses; and it is estimated that, when through to Melbourne, the receipts from goods and passengers will not be less than £2000 per week.

This railway forms a junction with the Williamstown branch line, at a distance of about two miles and a quarter from the Railway Pier, and an agreement exists under which the Geelong Company pay a toll to the Government for the use of the branch line. The greater portion of the land outside the town boundary is held by the Company under free grant from the Crown, as also about eleven acres of valuable land, upon which the station is erected. The railway is continued to the waters of Corio Bay by a curved pier, 1000 feet long, running into a depth of twenty-two feet water.

The Ballaarat railway now in progress branches from this line at a distance of about two miles from Geelong, and forty-two from Melbourne.

The accounts of the Company are made up to the 30th May and 30th of November, and the general meetings of shareholders are held at Geelong in January and July.

The traffic receipts being insufficient to pay the annual debenture interest amounting to £18,725 in consequence of the non-completion of the through line, the shareholders resolved at their last half-yearly meeting, to apply the guaranteed interest of five per cent to the payment of the mortgage interest. Directors qualification 20 shares. Shareholders liability limited to double the amount of his shares. Number of hares held in England, 15,872; in the colonies, 2,128

MELBOURNE AND HOBSON'S BAY RAILWAY.

This railway, which was commenced in January, 1853, and completed in September, 1854, has obviated the necessity that formerly existed of transporting goods from vessels in the Bay to Melbourne by small craft up the river Yarra Yarra for nine miles, by taking them from the ship's side on to a pier, and sending them into the heart of Melbourne, along a line of railway little more than two miles in length. Great doubts were at one time entertained as to the undertaking proving a remunerative one in a money point of view, and the shares were at one time at a very heavy discount. The working of the line has, however, shown a very large profit, the dividends having gradually increased, and have now reached fourteen per cent. on the paid up capital; a large surplus as a reserve fund being carried over after payment of the dividend.

This result is mainly attributable to the fact, that the largest ships are found to lie in perfect safety at the Pier, which at one time was thought too much exposed to admit of their being moored alongside in rough weather. This prejudice, however, has so entirely vanished that captains of large vessels, who before the experiment was tried viewed such an undertaking with great doubt as to safety, now gladly lay their ships alongside, and discharge cargo upon the Railway Pier.

In 1856, this Company undertook the construction of a branch line to St. Kilda, which is now in full operation for passenger traffic to the mutual benefit of the Company and the public. The returns upon this short line are it is believed larger than upon any line of equal length that has ever been constructed.

The accompanying statement shows the extent of the present traffic, and the general increase since the opening of the line.

Date.	No. of Passengers.		Merchandise.	Total Receipts.		
	Sandridge.	St. Kilda.				
Half-year ending—			Tons.	£	s.	d.
April 30, 1855........	151,036	—	9,513	16,810	14	3
Oct. 31, 1855........	119,372	—	18,622	15,424	18	5
April 30, 1856........	202,037	—	34,852	21,305	19	8
Oct. 31, 1856........	190,744	—	36,015	22,443	16	9
April 30, 1857........	232,973	—	48,173	28,273	12	4
Oct. 31, 1857........	228,919	382,464	64,148	39,039	12	1
April 30, 1858........	305,369	512,933	69,249	44,525	0	6
Total.	1,430.450	895 397	275,545	187,823	14	0

The Company are adding largely to their shed accommodation for goods, and have just completed a new line by carrying another bridge across the river Yarra, which gives a double line of rails to Sandridge, and will greatly facilitate the transmission of goods to and from the ships discharging at the Pier, which is in course of further extension, and has already been carried out to a length of 1,871 feet, by a uniform width of 60 feet, and a depth at low water of 23 feet, and giving pier accommodation for vessels of the following tonnage, viz.:—2 vessels under 500 tons register, 4 do. from 500 to 1,000 do., 6 do. of the largest tonnage of any ship that has ever entered Hobson's Bay.

MELBOURNE AND SUBURBAN RAILWAY.

This line was projected in 1856, but was not brought prominently before the public until the commencement of 1857.

The line at first proposed was to connect the City with the districts of Richmond, South Melbourne, Prahran, Windsor, St. Kilda, Elsternwick, Ellwood, Little Brighton, and Brighton proper, on the one hand; and Hawthorne and Kew, on the other.

A Provisional Committee was formed and received a sufficient amount of public support to warrant them in asking the Legislature to grant an Act of Incorporation.

At this period a distinct company was formed for the purpose of connecting the Hobson's Bay Terminus at St. Kilda with Brighton, and resulted in the Legislature allowing the rival company to construct that portion of the line lying between St. Kilda and Brighton; therefore, the route of the Melbourne and Suburban Railway is confined to that portion of the suburbs situated between Melbourne and Wellington-street, Prahran; and its branch, as originally laid out, to Hawthorne; with power conferred by the Act to use the Brighton and St. Kilda Railway to its terminus at Brighton.

The use of the other company's line has been reserved upon the usual traffic arrangements.

By this decision of the Legislature a great saving of outlay will be secured to the company, and although the original capital of £300,000 is not altered, it is estimated that the expenditure for the construction of the line from Melbourne to Windsor, with a branch from Richmond to Hawthorne, will not exceed £200,000.

The works were commenced on the 1st July last, and are progressing rapidly; and it is confidently hoped that the first section will be opened for traffic early in the present year.

The company are now serving the notices on the owners and occupiers of the land required for the road, and it is their intention to push forward the works with all possible dispatch to the river Yarra, both on the Brighton line and Hawthorne branch, and prepare for a commencement of the works on the south side of the river before the close of the year.

The advantages to be derived from connecting these districts with Melbourne, in a commercial point of view, as well as giving those localities facilities of rapid communication, can scarcely be exaggerated in importance.

The projectors believe that this Railway will be highly remunerative to the shareholders, and will realise the most sanguine expectations.

The liability is limited to the amount of the share.

MELBOURNE AND RIVER MURRAY RAILWAY.

A contract was signed on 7th June, 1858, between the President and Members of the Board of Land and Works and Messrs. Cornish and Bruce, for the formation and completion of the portion of this line of Railway, commencing at the junction with the Melbourne and Williamstown Railway, near Footscray, and extending to Sandhurst. The whole distance is about 79 miles. The contract price is £3,356,937 2s. 2d., and the whole works are to be completed by the 1st January, 1862.

It was intended to hold a grand inauguration and banquet at the turning of the first sod of the Victorian Railways, but it has been from time to time postponed in consequence of the indisposition of the Hon. the President of the Board of Lands and Works, and is now postponed till January, 1859, by which time it is understood the contractors will have completed the first twenty miles of the line.

The works on the Keilor Plains and Sunbury sections are being pushed forward with great vigour. Operations have also been begun on the Gisborne and Big Hill sections, and at Castlemaine and Elphinstone the works are being laid out with a view to their immediate commencement.

Some dissatisfaction at one time prevailed by the men requiring to be all paid the same wages, but the contractors remaining firm, the men able to work soon resumed operations and were followed by the others. The greatest quiet has since existed over the whole line.

The line in course of construction by Messrs. Evans, Merry and Co., from Geelong to Ballaarat, is mentioned in page cxxi., but full particulars have not been forwarded.

A line of railway is being made by the St. Kilda and Brighton Railway Company, to form a junction at St. Kilda. The contract has been taken by Mr. W. Randle.

MILLS AND MANUFACTORIES.

Mills, breweries, foundries, gas-works, together with agricultural implement and other manufactories, have been extensively introduced into many parts of the country. The statistical returns are not yet sufficiently completed to afford any accurate account of the numbers and description of these important evidences of industrial progress. The establishment of flour-mills in the interior has been so general as to have an important influence on the flour trade; and in place of being dependent on the seaboard towns, several of the principal gold-fields are, in a great measure, supplied with flour from wheat grown and ground in their immediate neighborhood.

POPULATION.

By the Census Act, 20 Vict., No. 2, it was provided the Registrar-General should receive all the schedules from the enumerators, and proceed to compile the tables of population from them.

The census was taken on the 29th March, 1857; and an approximate estimate of the population has been periodically kept up by means of the official quarterly returns of births, deaths and immigration, which are deposited in this department. In the year 1851, it was ascertained by census that the population was 77,345 persons, of whom 23,143 were congregated in the city of Melbourne, 18,348 in the surrounding county of Bourke, and 12,784 in the county of Grant, which includes the town of Geelong. By the 29th March, 1857, the population numbered 410,766, of whom 99,354 were located in Melbourne and its suburbs, 23,838 in Geelong; 121,520 being distributed over the rural districts, whilst the gold-fields alone, with their rapidly increasing townships, absorbed a total of no less than 166,550 souls. By the census, and from official returns of immigration and emigration, and of births and deaths, it was ascertained that on 30th June, 1858, the population was 477,345. It may be safely estimated that the number is now close upon 480,000; so that in seven years no fewer than 400,000 souls have been added to the population of Victoria. The rapidity with which this country has become peopled is almost unexampled in the history of any nation, ancient or modern. During the last three years, while the population has rapidly increased, the deaths have remained stationary. The births have increased in the same period nearly in proportion to the increase of population. The numbers are—deaths in 1855, 6,603; in 1856, 5,782; and in 1857, 7,455; and births, 11,941, 14,406 and 17,490 respectively. The influx of Chinese, numbering 34,874 persons, consisting almost entirely of males, has been the subject of much acrimonious discussion, and the Legislature has sought to discourage it by special taxes. A similar course of proceeding having been adopted in South Australia and New South Wales, it seems that Australian opinion is adverse to this description of immigration.

In the three years which elapsed between the censuses taken in 1851 and 1854, the number of inhabitants had trebled; and in the course of the four succeeding years even that population had doubled. The increase altogether has been sixfold within seven years. The manner in which this population has spread itself over the country may be gathered from the circumstance that while the census of 1854 showed but 114 townships and villages, the returns of the census of 1857 detail the number of inhabitants in no less than 204 of such settlements.

BIRTHS.—The number of births, marriages and deaths, and total population in Victoria on the 31st of December of each year from 1851–7, are given in the following summary:—

	Births.	Deaths.	Marriages.	Population.
1851	3,049	1,165	1,023	83,350
1852	3,756	2,105	1,958	148,627
1853	5,000	5,000	——	198,496
1854	7,542	6,261	3,765	273,865
1855	11,941	6,603	3,846	319,379
1856	14,406	5,732	4,116	348,460
1857	17,490	7,455	4,524	463,135

MELBOURNE.

The City of Melbourne and metropolis of Victoria is in the county of Bourke. It returns five members to the Legislative Assembly, and as it is situate within the Central Province has a voice in the election of five members for the Legislative Council. The population is about 50,000.

In the year 1835 the site was chosen for encampment by Messrs. J. P. Fawkner and John Batman, and so rapid was the progress of the settlement, that in 1837, Sir Richard Bourke, then Governor of New South Wales, determined upon paying an official visit to the prosperous and rising community. He named the town Melbourne, in honor of Lord Melbourne, then English Premier. It is the seat of government, and is situate on the banks of the river Yarra Yarra, about two and a half miles from Hobson's Bay, with which it is connected by a short line of railway (see Railways). By the course of the Yarra the distance is about eight miles. The position of the Meteorological Observatory, at the Crown Lands Office, is in latitude 37° 49′ 28″ S., longitude 144° 58′ 35″ E.

Melbourne has been described as the Southern City of the Seven Hills. There the likeness to Ancient Rome ceases; for it is but the growth of a single generation, and therefore possesses no monuments of antiquity, or works of ancient art of which it can boast. The seven hills alluded to, are the Melbourne Eastern and Western Hills, Batman's Hill, Emerald Hill, St. Kilda Hill, South Yarra Hill, and Richmond Hill. But some of these belong to what would be more correctly described as the suburbs of Melbourne. Three of them already are distinct municipalities, namely Emerald Hill, St. Kilda, and Richmond.

The town was incorporated in August, 1842, by an Act of the Legislative Council of New South Wales (6 Vict. No. 7), and mayor, aldermen, and councillors were thenceforward annually chosen. In 1848 it was erected into an episcopal see, and therefore became entitled to the dignity of "City." Originally it was divided into four, and subsequently into eight wards; one of which, Fitzroy Ward, was constituted a distinct municipality by proclamation dated 9th September, 1858. The seven wards into which it is now divided are Lonsdale, Bourke, Gipps, LaTrobe, Hotham, Smith, and Macarthur, each of which is represented by three councillors, and an alderman. The area of the corporation jurisdiction contains about 9,000 acres. Its boundaries are—on the north, a line two and a half miles, extending from Moonee Ponds to Northcote, thence by the Merri Creek to Heidelberg-bridge, thence along the Heidelberg-road, Reilly-street, Nicholson street, Victoria-parade, Hoddle-street to St. Kilda; thence along the St. Kilda-road to Princes-bridge, the river Yarra to the end of the Tea-tree scrub; thence by a straight line north to the Moonee Ponds, which completes the circuit, irrespective of Macarthur Ward lying between the south bank of the Yarra and Hobson's Bay.

The portion of the city known as Melbourne Proper is in Lonsdale, Bourke, Gipps, and LaTrobe wards. It was originally laid out in a rectangular block, and no provision was made for public squares or gardens, either for ornament or health. The five principal streets are 99 feet wide, and about a mile in length, running nearly east and west, named severally, Flinders, Collins, Bourke, Lonsdale and LaTrobe Streets; with smaller ones of 33 feet wide between each, of the same names, but with the addition of the adjective Little; except in the case of Flinders, the diminutive of which is Lane. These are crossed by nine others 99 feet wide, running north and south, namely, Spring, Stephen, Russell, Swanston, Elizabeth, Queen, William, King and Spencer Streets. The town is divided into east and west by Elizabeth-street, which is at the foot of the two principal hills upon which the city is built, and forms its main artery. This street is only about 22 feet above the level of the sea, and is often during heavy rains impassable to pedestrians, in consequence of the the great flow of water from the high ground. Several proposals to provide a remedy have been made, but nothing has yet been effectually done. In the immediate vicinity of the city proper, however, on either side, are large park-like reserves, which are included in the other wards, or separate the town from the suburbs.

Up to the year 1851, the year of the gold discovery

Melbourne was but an inconsiderable place, not much larger than an English small market town, but since that period its progress has been marked and substantial. The streets are now well metalled or macadamised, and the footpaths, which in the principal streets are twelve feet wide, are being rapidly paved with flag-stones, so that it may be hoped the notorious "Melbourne mud" will soon be only a matter of history. The town is well supplied with light, it having been lit with gas since January 1856. That prime necessary of life, water, is now no longer supplied to the inhabitants from the carrier's cart, but a plentiful supply from the Yan Yean reservoir (see page lxviii) now circulates through the greater portion of the metropolis, and is also being rapidly extended to the surrounding suburbs. The desirability of erecting ornamental fountains is engaging public attention, and doubtless these grateful and refreshing auxiliaries to health will soon occupy a conspicuous place amongst the improvements that are in progress.

The principal approach to the city from the south is by Princes-bridge, across the Yarra, which it spans by an arch of 150 feet. The foundation stone was laid with great *eclát* on the 20th March, 1846, a general holiday being observed on the occasion, and it was opened to the public November 12, 1850. Its cost was about £15,000. The bridge is a substantial structure of bluestone, but has only space for two lines of vehicles, and the footways are inconveniently narrow, so that it is quite inadequate to the traffic of the present day. A proposal has been made to remedy the defect by erecting a pathway on either side for the accommodation of pedestrians. Another bridge is contemplated, across the Falls, which will connect the city with Emerald Hill. There are also several other bridges across the river in its course round the suburbs. A light structure for foot passengers connects Richmond-park with the Botanical Gardens; an iron tubular bridge unites Richmond and Prahran; a frail wooden structure crosses the river at Hawthorne, which will shortly be replaced by a substantial bridge, now in course of erection; and the Johnston-street and Studley Park bridges connect Collingwood with Kew and Boroondara.

The number of houses, in 1843, according to the assessment made in the first quarter of that year, had reached to 1,095. These were variously constructed of brick and stone, iron and wood, zinc or canvas, and the styles of architecture were as multiform. The tide of immigration steadily increased, and in a proportionate ratio the number of habitations, and in the space of ten years they had reached to 4,980. By this time the news of the gold discoveries had given such a stimulus to immigration, that to provide for the wants of the inflowing stream of humanity, upwards of 4,000 additional buildings were erected in one year, so that in 1854 the number of houses had reached to 9,175. Year by year the character of the buildings has steadily advanced, and the frail tenements that were at first put up, having served their purpose, are now rapidly giving place to substantial stone and brick dwellings. By the terms of the Building Act now in operation, no wooden structures can be erected within the boundaries of the city, unless at a sufficient distance from other buildings to ensure isolation.

The style of the better class of shops in the principal streets may be compared with those of the City of London, but they would scarcely rank with those of the first-class west-end depôts. The goods, however, with which they are supplied are from the best markets of the world; and the rich and varied display of wearing apparel for the fair sex, or for supplying the wants of Young Australia, cannot fail to attract the attention of all new arrivals.

The massive bluestone stores along the line of wharves, as well as in other parts of the city, are conspicuous objects of attention, and bespeak the extent and importance of the commerce of Victoria.

Melbourne is already comparatively rich in stately public buildings, and many more are in course of erection. It will be sufficient for our present purpose to enumerate some of the principal. The new Houses of Legislature (see page cxii), the Treasury, and the Government Printing Offices, on the Eastern Hill, not only occupy a splended site, but will be conspicuous for their architectural grandeur.

Besides these, there are the old Government offices in William-street, the Gold Escort Office and Treasury, the Custom House, the Public Lands Office fitted up for the Survey, Railway, Geological, and Meteorological Department, and the old Post Office, in Bourke-street; the latter is soon to give place to a building that will be an ornament to the city. The legal buildings are, the Supreme Court, the County Court, Prothonotary's office, and Police courts. The lawyers have suites of chambers in a Temple Court, Collins-street west, so named in consequence of being built for the legal profession. The Vice-regal residence is situate at Toorak, about four miles from town.

The principal public commercial buildings are the Melbourne Exchange, the Hall of Commerce and Electric Telegraph Office, and the banks and offices of the different insurance companies. The market buildings are not yet completed.

The Town Hall, Swanston-street, is a large stone building, where the business of the corporation is transacted. In cases of fire, an alarm is given by the Town Hall bell, which summons a well-organised fire brigade, who, by means of the now plentiful supply of water from the Yan Yean, soon have the mastery of the devouring element.

Amongst the edifices consecrated to benevolence, are the

Melbourne Hospital, in Lonsdale-street; the Lying-in Hospital, at Carlton; the Benevolent Asylum, at North Melbourne, for the reception of the destitute; and the Yarra Bend Asylum for the insane. Besides these there are two Orphan Asylums, Immigrants and Female Homes, a Refuge for females; and several philanthropic societies in active operation.

A few years since the banks and hotels occupied the first rank amongst the public buildings. They still retain a prominent position, and the recent erections of some of the former far surpass in architectural splendour most of the structures of a like nature in the old country. The new buildings of the Bank of New South Wales; the English, Scottish, and Australian Chartered Bank; the Oriental Bank; and the Melbourne Savings' Bank, are illustrations of the fact. New structures for the London Chartered Bank and the Bank of Victoria are in progress. Many of the new hotels are of palatial appearance and proportions, fitted up with all the appliances of modern science, and decorated by the aid of the fine arts.

The principal educational establishments are the following:—The Melbourne University, founded in 1854, and opened to the public in 1856, is to the north of the city, about a mile from the Post Office, and is supported by an annual grant of £9,000. The Museum of Natural History is at the University. The Roman Catholic and Scotch Colleges, on the Eastern Hill, and the Church of England Grammar School, on the Domain-road, South Yarra. The Model Training School, in connexion with the National Board of Education, is on the Eastern Hill, and though not distinguished for its architectural beauties, is a commodious building, and doing good service in the cause of education. There are several minor schools, in connexion with either the National or Denominational Boards.

The ecclesiastical edifices are numerous, and many of them noble specimens of architecture. Belonging to the Church of England are—St. James's Cathedral, on the Western-hill; St. John's, Elizabeth-street; St. Mary's, North Melbourne; St. Paul's, Swanston-street; St. Peter's, Eastern-hill; and St. Mark's, Collingwood. The Presbyterians have the Scotch Church, Collins-street, east; Chalmers' Church, Eastern-hill; St. Andrew's, Carlton; beside several minor buildings. The Roman Catholics, have St. Francis' Cathedral, Lonsdale-street; St. Patrick's, Eastern Hill; St. George's, Carlton; St. Mary's, North Melbourne; St. Augustine's, and a Convent in Nicholson-street, Carlton.

The Wesleyans, Independents, and Baptists have some excellent chapels. The new "Wesley Church" in Lonsdale-street, equals, if it does not surpass, any building of a like nature in the city. The Independent chapel in Collins-street, the oldest in the Colony, is a very plain building, but it is in contemplation to erect a new one on its splendid site. The chapel in Lonsdale-street is an elegant structure. The other Congregational chapels are but temporary buildings with the exception of those in the suburbs, namely, Oxford-street, Collingwood, St. Kilda, and Richmond chapels, which are ornamental and commodious edifices. The Baptist chapels are in Collins-street and Albert-street; the former has been greatly enlarged, and the latter has been just built, both of which when completed will be fit to rank with any other chapels in the city. There are in addition some smaller ones in the city and suburbs. There are also a Lutheran church, a Unitarian Chapel, and a Chinese Chapel, together with Jewish synagogues. The Bethel or Floating Church is moored between Sandridge and Williamstown.

Of the Literary Institutions, the most conspicuous are the Public Library, in Swanston-street; and the Mechanics' Institute, Collins-street east. The Philosophical Institute, the Microscopical Society, the Horticultural Society, Fine Arts Society, Industrial Society, &c., hold their meetings either at the latter or other offices.

Amongst the miscellaneous public buildings must be noted the Exhibition Building, on the Western-hill, built after the style of the Great Exhibition Building in London, and erected for the purpose of receiving the Australian contributions to the Paris Exhibition in 1855. It is now used for the purpose of levées, concerts, balls, bazaars, &c., in connexion with charitable objects, and the subscription and other concerts of the Philharmonic Society. Also, the Protestant Hall, St. Patrick's Hall, the Melbourne Club, the Victorian Club, and others of a like nature.

There are three Theatres, the Royal, the Princesses, the Olympic, a Circus, besides several Concert Halls attached to some hotels. Cricket is very popular, as well as other out-door exercises, such as archery, boating, racing, &c. The race-course reserve is at Flemington.

In literary matters, there are three daily papers, published in Melbourne; eighteen newspapers or other periodicals weekly; eight monthly journals, besides three Prices Current, on the despatch of the European mail; one quarterly; and several annuals. In addition to these there are many pamphlets on the passing topics of the day constantly issuing from the press, but of larger literary efforts in the shape of good sized volumes, there is a comparative dearth, with the exception of the imported supply. All the principal works, however, issued from the British press soon find their way to the Australian metropolis.

The means of ready transit abound. All kinds of passenger vehicles are plentiful. The light car, the omnibus, and the dray, beside numerous private carriages, keep up constant traffic in its streets; and communication with the suburbs is constantly carried on at trifling rates. Steam boats and wherries also ply on the Yarra, at very moderate fares. Communication with the various gold-fields is by means of four and six-horse coaches, of a somewhat peculiar build, but adapted to the Australian roads. Heavy goods are carried by waggon or dray. The railways in existence, and in progress, are described elsewhere. (See page cxxi.)

As before remarked, there are several extensive reserves around the city, appropriated to public recreation. The most interesting and beautiful is that of the Botanical Gardens, on the south side of the Yarra, about a mile above Princes bridge, (see page lxx.). Adjoining the gardens is a beautiful reserve called the Military Hill, from which may be obtained a splendid view of the city and the surrounding country. On the west of the St. Kilda road, lies the South Park, which extends from Emerald Hill to St. Kilda. Opposite the Botanical Gardens, and connected by a foot-bridge, is the Richmond Paddock, a most beautiful locality and a delightful retreat from the dust and bustle of the city. The Melbourne Cricket Club Ground is situate in this park, and upon occasions of intercolonial and other matches, the paddock presents a most animated appearance, the company generally consisting of the *elite* of Melbourne, graced by a large concourse of ladies. On the Eastern Hill, and within the town boundaries, is a smaller reserve, called Fitzroy-square, which has been recently reclaimed, and being on undulating ground will one day become a most ornamental park. To the north-east is situated a large enclosure, termed Carlton Gardens; at present only in name—the gardens are now being formed. The beautiful gardens attached to the University are also open to the public.

The new Melbourne Cemetery is a spacious enclosure about a mile and a half from the Post-office. The use of the old one, near the Flagstaff Hill, has been discontinued since 1853, it having been found too small for the increasing population. The new City of the Dead is tastefully laid out, and adorned with many interesting and beautiful monuments, whose inscriptions tell of blighted hopes or record the virtues of those who rest there. It is divided into different portions, appropriated to the various denominational sections of the community, so that the religious differences of the living are perpetuated at the grave.

Melbourne is nearly encircled by populous and thriving suburban districts, which are connected by well-made macadamized roads. On the north are the more recently formed townships of Carlton and Brunswick. On the north-east is situated Collingwood, which rivals the city in population. On the east, Richmond, now celebrated for its Cremorne Gardens, where at night, during the summer months, entertainments are given similar in character to those of its Chelsea namesake. On the south-east, Toorak, Prahran, Windsor, and the favorite resort of all classes, St. Kilda and Brighton, situate on the shores of

Hobson's Bay. On the south the Emerald Hill: on the south-west, the landing port, Sandridge; and on the west and north-west, the rising districts of Flemington and Footscray, near which will be the junction of the new lines of Railway.

Beyond the suburbs are the pretty hamlets of Moonee Ponds, Northcote, Heidelberg, Kew, Boroondara, Caulfield, &c., which partake of a rural character, and where many of the more wealthy citizens have erected their country villas.

Beside the railways in course of formation, there are four principal thoroughfares out of Melbourne: the northern road, to Sandhurst and the River Murray; north-east, to Sydney; north-west *viâ* Ballaarat, to the Pyrenees Ranges; and south-east, to Gipps Land and Western Port.

MUNICIPALITIES AND THEIR PROGRESS.

There are twenty-six municipalities, as follow:—Ararat, Brunswick, Belfast, Ballaarat, Ballaarat East, Beechworth, Castlemaine, Carisbrook, Dunolly, Emerald Hill, East Collingwood, Fitzroy, Geelong, Kyneton, Kilmore, Melbourne, Maryborough, Maldon, Newtown and Chilwell, Prahran, Portland, Richmond, St. Kilda, Sandhurst, Williamstown, and Warrnambool.

The undermentioned are petitioning the Executive Council to be proclaimed municipalities:—Amherst, Brighton, Creswick, Hotham Ward, and Pentridge.

The extension of the municipal system is one of the most remarkable and pleasing features of this colony. Prior to 1855, there were only two corporate towns in Victoria. In 1858 the number had increased to twenty-one, which latter comprehended, according to the last census, a population of 88,815. The following is the summary of returns given by the Registrar-General: Number of houses erected, 37,213; number of miles of streets formed, 196; number of miles of streets metalled, 135; number of miles of streets channelled and kerbed, 60; expenditure on streets, £1,191,734; annual value of rateable property, £2,115,136.; revenue for the year 1857, £239,579; total expenditure for 1857, £316,969.

BRUNSWICK.

The Council of Brunswick was incorporated 20th October, 1857, since which time it has expended on the streets of the municipality £2,279 4s. The income during this period amounted to £5,586, of which £991 were collected by rates. There are 30 streets in the district measuring about 33 miles. The number of rateable properties is 1,200; the assessed value of which is £82,000. A blue-stone court-house is in course of erection at a cost of £1000.

EAST COLLINGWOOD.

East Collingwood was incorporated, its first Municipal Council elected on the 9th October, 1855. It compasses an area of about 1,100 acres; the Yarra Yarra river forming one of its boundaries, about 2½ miles in length. Its population, since greatly increased, was, in March 1857, when the census was taken, 10,775. The municipality contains upwards of 20 miles of streets, nearly all of which and their foot-ways are formed; about 15 miles of these streets are metalled; and part of this length channelled and kerbed.

The income of the Municipal Council from municipal rates, legislative grants, police fines, binding and license fees, from the time of its formation to the 9th April 1858, £25,615; expenditure on public works for the same period, £22,148. The total number of assessments for 1858, is 3,482, including upwards of 1000 allotments of vacant land.

The net valuation of the property of the municipality for 1858, amounted to £84,578, upon which a rate of one shilling was imposed producing £4,228 18s.

East Collingwood contains a handsome police court, at which Petty Sessions are held twice a week, and two excellent bridges connecting it across the Yarra with Kew, Hawthorne, Boroondara, and the Anderson gold-fields.

EMERALD HILL.

Emerald Hill was the first district in Victoria that availed itself of the privilege of local self-government, under Captain Clarke's Municipal Act, and was proclaimed a Municipality on 26th May, 1855. The total approximate area (exclusive of the south bank of the River Yarra, subsequently annexed), amounts to 1875 acres, from which has to be deducted about 990 acres, for the space taken up by the South Park, St. Kilda Railway, Government and other reserves, roads, streets, &c. The population is estimated at 7000 souls. The valuation of property for assessment for the Municipal year 1857-8, amounted to £52,606 10s.; the number of assessments 1903. There are 49 streets in the township, of these (exclusive of the works at present in progress) 4 miles 13 chains have been formed, 2 miles 77 chains metalled, 3 miles 4½ chains of channelling, 4 miles 29 chains of kerbing, and 24 chains of flagging have been laid down; the whole at a cost of £25,400.

PRAHRAN.

Proclaimed a municipal district, 23rd April, 1855. The income from all sources, up to 21st August, 1858, amounted to £29,462 8s. 2d., of which sum £29,064 17s. has been expended on public works; of this amount £22,059 10s. 1d. has been received from Government and £7,402 18s. 1d. from rates; there is still to be received from Government £2,473 6s. and over £4000 on rates, before the close of the municipal year in February next, all of which will be expended on public works. There are 125 streets in the municipality, measuring nearly thirty-one miles, 14 miles of streets all one chain in width. Two miles of road (Gardiner's Creek Road) was formed and metalled before the municipality was established, and 7 miles 33 chains have since been formed and metalled, and 5 miles formed on the permanent level. Nine miles 20 chains of footpath have been kerbed with blue gum planking, the entrance to 71 streets pitched with blue stone and the corners kerbed also with blue stone. 170 chains of channelling pitched. The valuation or assessment for 1856 amounted to £66,233 10s.; 1857, £83,648; 1858, £105,054 5s., upon which a rate of 17d. in the pound has been laid. Population on the 1st April, 1857, males 4,118, females, 4,054, total 8,172. Houses 1,954.

RICHMOND.

Date of first election, 22nd April, 1856. Valuation in 1856, £57,531; 1857, £72,465; 1858, £79,257. A rate of one shilling in the pound struck in each year. Population 10,000. Number of rateable properties, 3,120. 46 streets are now in the hands of contractors for the proper maintenance and repairs.

ST. KILDA.

The Municipal Council of St. Kilda was incorporated on the 11th March, 1857, since which time it has expended on public works £13,719 3s. The income during the same period (1½ years) has been £18,741 12s. 5d., of which £5,525 2s. 10d. was collected from rates. There are 23 miles of street in the municipality, and of these 15 miles 23 chains are formed, 8 miles metalled, 2 miles 20 chains kerbed, 5 miles 1 chain gravelled footpaths and 2 miles channelled; 3 bridges have been built and a great many pitched crossings. The annual rateable value of property within the municipality is £107,683 8s.

WILLIAMSTOWN.

The Council of Williamstown was incorporated on the 12th of March, 1856; since which time it has expended on public-works, £26,528 17s. 6d. The income during the same period has been, £26,644 1s. 9d., £5,321 19s. 6d. of which was collected from rates. There are fifty-two streets in the township, measuring 15 miles 40 chains, and of these 4 miles 15 chains have been formed and mettled. The length of paths formed and mettled is 15½ miles. The valuation of the town property for assessment is £69,366 10s., and the number of rateable properties 1,542.

GEELONG.

The earliest mention of "Geelong" occurs in the account of a journey overland made by Messrs. Hume and Hovell into the then unknown Southern country. In the year 1824, these explorers penetrated from Sydney to the shores of Port Phillip Bay, and learned from the blacks that the water before them was named Geelong.

The origin of the Town of Geelong was almost coeval with the arrival of the first settlers in Port Phillip. In the month of March, 1837, Sir Richard Bourke, the Governor, arrived at Port Phillip, from Sydney, and after making arrangements for local superintendence at Melbourne, visited Geelong. After consulting with Captain Fyans, the police magistrate, he gave instructions to the Surveyor-General to lay out the present township, or rather to lay out two townships, North Geelong on the bay, and South Geelong on the river. Since that period, the two have become merged, and a number of smaller villages been absorbed in the incorporated town of Geelong, embracing an area of thirty-six square miles.

Geelong is the capital town of the county of Grant, is remarkably picturesque, well laid out on ground sloping towards the Bay, and overlooking the anchorage. Its situation is adapted for the emporium of trade for the western district of the colony, and the outlet for all its export products, having a populous agricultural district around it. The distance from Melbourne by water is about 45, and 41 miles by Geelong and Melbourne Railway. Steamers run daily to and from Melbourne.

About a mile and a quarter from the bay, the river Barwon passes Geelong in its tortuous course to the ocean. After passing Geelong, the Barwon pursues a south-easterly course, for about nine or ten miles, when it spreads out into a series of lakes called Connewarre, and ultimately flows into the Great Southern Ocean. The river is crossed by a pontoon bridge, but there is in course of erection an iron bridge of two arches at a cost of £70,000.

On the western bank of the Barwon, there is much fine land and beautifully picturesque scenery, called the Barrabool hills, consisting of decomposed trap-rock, and presenting the most fertile soil to their very summits, covered with large farms and extensive vineyards.

The Harbor is a beautiful cove, running nearly east and west, and contains, like the outer bay, an admirable anchorage close up to the township on the northern shore, and well sheltered from the prevailing winds. It is to be regretted that a bar extends across the entrance to the harbor, which is now being cleared by a dredging machine, to a depth sufficient to admit a clipper fleet, a work which is expected to be completed in about eighteen months.

The present population is about 25,000 souls, a much smaller number than it contained prior to the establishment of the townships of Buninyong and Ballaarat, the consolidation of these gold-fields having permanently absorbed a large proportion of the inhabitants of Geelong, and temporarily checked its progress. When the bar is removed, so as to admit of vessels of heavy tonnage lying alongside the wharves, there is no doubt that direct consigning will be much increased, and trade generally improved.

The streets are laid out at right angles, evidently upon the same plan as those of Melbourne, the principal ones named after the rivers Moorabool and Yarra, are of ample width and adorned with a variety of handsome and substantial shops and buildings, but the same error which has deformed Melbourne, that of alternating the wide streets by mere lanes has prevailed here, notwithstanding which, in point of salubrity of air, and superiority of position, Geelong stands pre-eminent in the colony of Victoria.

The town of Geelong was incorporated by an Act passed by the Legislative Council of New South Wales, in the 13th year of Her present Majesty's reign, and assented to 12th October, 1849.

The public and private buildings are of a most substantial and ornamental character, comprising the Custom House, Post Office, Telegraph, Supreme Court, Police Office, Mechanics' Institute, Town Hall, Hall of Commerce; several Churches of English, Episcopalian, Presbyterian, Roman Catholic, Wesleyan, Independent, Baptist, and other denominations, and a corresponding number of schools, including two Grammar schools. (See another page.) The Theatre Royal has a plain unpretending exterior, but good internal arrangements.

The steady increase of the port of Geelong, may be gathered from the following return of the value of Imports and Revenue collected during the years mentioned :—

Years.	Value of Imports.	Revenue. £	s.	d.
1848	13,051	1,441	16	6
1849	33,532	10,708	12	3
1850	60,423	13,987	9	7
1851	122,318	20,588	10	7
1852	504,738	49,785	10	6
1853	1,705,522	116,307	5	1
1854	2,044,694	152,111	8	2
1855	1,207,838	161,643	18	0
1856	997,272	218,311	15	7
1857	1,177,843	242,992	7	9
	7,867,231	987,878	14	2

The completion of the Ballaarat Railway will make Geelong a place of great importance, as the sea-port of the western gold fields. (Particulars of the Railways, *vide* contents.)

The Corporation of Geelong has already formed 20 miles and 56 chains of metalled streets; 4 miles and 59 chains are kerbed and channelled; the total expenditure, up to 19th July 1858, being £277,184 10s. 6d. The number of houses in the municipality is 5,796. From May 1, 1850, to May 1, 1854, the sum of £41,199 was expended in the different wards, namely, Barwon, Bellerine, Villamanta, and Kardinia.

The following is a statement of the Receipts and Disbursements of the Geelong Corporation, for years ending 31st August:—

Year.	Revenue. £ s. d.	Expenditure. £ s. d.	Balance in Hand. £ s. d.
1853	17,638 1 1	17,619 3 4	18 17 9
1854	235,503 17 10	64,531 9 1	170,991 6 6
1855	29,486 14 9	198,800 7 0	1,677 14 3
			Due to Bank.
1856	29,276 15 8	34,511 0 1	3,556 10 2
1857	23,582 9 11	26,279 18 10	2,697 8 11

Municipalities have been lately formed in or near Geelong, called South Barwon, Newtown and Chilwell.

A tastefully laid out Botanical Garden has been constructed at the east end of Geelong, and already possesses a varied and extensive collection of shrubs, trees, and plants, which occupies an area of from 6 to 700 acres, well fenced in, and forming a most agreeable promenade and pleasure ground overlooking the Bay; the expenses of its maintenance being defrayed by an annual grant from Parliament.

There are two fine bathing establishments, the larger one of which is situate on the eastern beach; the other, more recently erected, and somewhat smaller, on the western.

A very delightful pleasure garden has been recently opened, at a short distance from Geelong, on the highest point of the Barrabool Hills; the beauty of its situation fully justifying its appellation of "Montpellier," and one of the most attractive spots for parties visiting the locality.

Geelong returns four representatives to the House of Assembly, and is included in the South-western Province, which sends five members to the Legislative Council.

COUNTRY DISTRICTS.

*** Names of official and other public men, the local institutions, the ministers of the various churches, &c., are published monthly in *Bradshaw's Guide to Victoria.*

AMHERST, or OLD DAISY HILL, is a very neat little township. It is situate about 12 miles south-west from Carisbrook, 12 south-east from Avoca, and 10 south from Maryborough. The country about Amherst is highly picturesque, and the soil is well suited for agricultural and horticultural purposes. There are three excellent hotels in the town. It has many of the features of a neat, well-built hamlet in England. The Daisy Hill gold-fields are well known. The locality is highly auriferous. The country from Amherst to Carisbrook is very beautiful, and has the advantage of a fair creek, which renders property in the neighbourhood desirable and valuable. Amherst has several banks and well-built churches, school-houses, &c.

ANDERSON'S CREEK.—WARRANDYTE.—On the south bank of the Yarra Yarra, about 14 miles from Melbourne, where there is a punt. The road lies through Hawthorne, Kew, Boroondara, and Doncaster, or through Heidelberg, across the punt at that place, and so through Templestowe to the Creek. Warrandyte, on Anderson's Creek on the Yarra Yarra, is a Government township, at which place is now erected the Local Court or Court of Mines for the St. Andrew's District, of which Caledonia and Anderson's Creek are component parts. There is also a police station, post-office, warden's offices, Government camp, and several stores. There are three quartz crushing machines, and one smelting machine. There is a postal communication twice a week. Anderson's Creek is a polling place for the county of Evelyn. On crossing the Yarra Yarra the northern bank at this place is very precipitous, but practicable for bullock drays. The ascent is short and the road from thence to Caledonia very fair. Population of Anderson's Creek and Caledonia, 1,450.

ARARAT is an inland mining township, in the county of Ripon. Was surveyed and sold in July, 1858. Is situated 134 miles from Melbourne, 60 from Ballaarat, 30 from Fiery Creek, and 25 from Pleasant Creek. Population of the district, 21,050. The land in the vicinity of Ararat is auriferous, and is at present being extensively worked. The air is clear and invigorating; good water is scarce. The town at present comprises one street, which contains many extensive stores and hotels, besides three banks. The *Ararat Advertiser* is published twice a week, and the *Ararat Times* once a week. Ararat is the centre and principal town of the Western Gold Fields.

AVOCA.—The town of Avoca was laid out in 1854, and is beautifully situated on the Avoca River, about twelve miles from its source in the Pyrenees. It is distant about 117 miles from Melbourne. The population of Avoca and its neighborhood is at present estimated at 4,450 persons, of whom 1,250 are Chinese. There are three public schools in the place, and one bank. Public worship is held in the Episcopalian and Wesleyan school-houses. Avoca is about 12 miles from Amherst, 16 miles from Maryborough, 25 miles from Dunolly, and 40 miles from Pleasant Creek, Ararat, Ballaarat, and Castlemaine, to which places there are coaches every other day. Criminal Sessions are held at Carisbrook, 3 miles from Maryborough. The telegraph is being extended to Avoca from Castlemaine, by way of Tarrengower, Dunolly, and Maryborough.

BACCHUS MARSH.—A township on the road to Ballaarat, about 34 miles from Melbourne. The population, including that of Pentland Hills, is about 1,500. There are a police office, mechanics' institute, road board office, and several churches. Fine agricultural land exists around the township.

BALLAARAT is the centre of the most extensive gold-field, and the capital of the counties of North Grant and North Grenville. It is distant from Melbourne 78 miles, from Geelong 53, Ararat 65, Pleasant Creek 85, Maryborough 45, Castlemaine 47, and Bendigo 75 miles. Ballaarat consists of two townships, West and East; the former was erected into a municipality on the 23rd of January, 1856; and the latter in June, 1857. Population of the Ballaarat district is over 40,000, half of which live in the two townships. Ballaarat West is well laid out on elevated ground, and is separated from Ballaarat East by the Yarrowee Creek. The town contains many handsome stone and brick buildings, several churches and chapels, five banks, and a hospital. The latter building is the finest on Ballaarat, and can accommodate over 200 patients. Ballaarat East is situate on a flat, and stretches from N.W. to S.E. about 2 miles. The main road, which is the principal street, contains several fine stores and shops, which are lit with gas, as also all the banks and hotels in both municipalities. The country in and about Ballaarat is composed of bold ranges, and extensive gullies and flats; most of the gullies run towards the large flat on which Ballaarat East is situate, and which is between 2 and 3 miles wide. Nearly all the gullies contain leads of gold, which are termed alluvial diggings, most of which run towards the flat, where several connect together and take their course in a westerly direction, thence followed up through Ballaarat West. At first the sinkings were shallow, but are now often over 250 feet deep, and are worked by steam machinery. The shallow ground, as well as those leads which were formerly worked by manual labor, have been worked over again by horse and steam power. Sluicing is extensively introduced in the district. In some of the deep leads blasting through rock of from 10 to 100 feet in thickness has to be resorted to. Some shafts have taken six to nine months to sink, and years will be necessary to work out the larger claims. Rich quartz mines are also opened in the district, and a large number of quartz crushing machines have been erected. The largest natural piece of gold in the world was found on Bakery Hill, Ballaarat, 180 feet from the surface, weighing 1,217 ozs., called the "Welcome Nugget." The ground about Ballaarat is suited for agricultural purposes, and extensive farms are in the process of cultivation. Ballaarat sustains two steam flour mills and several steam saw mills. There are three theatres and five concert halls, besides about 100 hotels; a new theatre is in course of erection.

BALLAN.—A township in the county of South Grant, situate on an eminence on the banks of the Werribee River, on the main road from Melbourne to Ballaarat, distant from the former 46 miles, from the latter 25 miles. It is surrounded by an agricultural district. The new Gordon gold-fields and Kerrit Barrett are 7 miles, and Mount Blackwood 14 miles distant. The climate is salubrious, but in the winter season, on account of its elevated position, very cold. During the dry season an extensive traffic is carried on between the Western gold-fields and Melbourne. There are a steam flour mill, post-office, and four stores.

BELVOIR, or WODONGA.—On the Wodonga Creek, on the Victoria side of the River Murray, opposite to the town of Albury. Population about 400.

BEECHWORTH.—The capital of the Murray district, and of the Ovens gold-fields, distant from Melbourne 166, and from the Murray river, 25 miles. It is situate on an eminence 1,725 feet above the level of the sea; was first surveyed in May, 1853; and, from its continued and rapid increase, was proclaimed a municipality in August, 1856; its population is about 2,500. Extensive stores and many private dwellings have been erected, an Athenæum and Chamber of Commerce established; and its public buildings, the banks of Australasia, New South Wales, and Victoria; the court-house, town-hall, hospital, churches, telegraph-office, and post-office, would do credit to the majority of the country towns in England. The town embraces a reserve of 945, and the municipality of 1,347 acres; the climate is remarkably healthy, the air being very pure and dry: average temperature, in winter, 47·8°, in summer, 68·7°. There is very little agricultural land within a radius of ten miles: the town principally depends for success on the prosperity of the surrounding diggings, and there is every indication of progress and prosperity. The *Ovens and Murray Advertiser*, and *Constitution* newspapers are published daily, and the *Mining Journal*, at Snake Valley, within five miles of Beechworth, weekly.

BELFAST, PORT FAIRY.—A seaport on the western coast, between Warrnambool and Portland, about 186 miles from Melbourne. The town is built on the banks of the River Moyne, at its confluence with the sea. It is laid out in the form of a quadrangle. The custom house is at the south end of Gipps-street. There are the usual public offices, such as court-house, police quarters, sub-treasury, road-board offices, municipal council chambers, and several large stores and wharves. The banks of Australasia and Victoria, the Wesleyan, Episcopal, and Presbyterian churches are fine buildings. There are also some good hotels. The *Belfast Gazette* and *Belfast Banner* are published weekly.

BENALLA.—On the Broken River, *en route* to Beechworth, Albury, and Sydney, about 119 miles from Melbourne. The village was laid out about the year 1846; it contained in 1853 about 250 nhabitants, and in 1858 numbers about 700, who are principally employed in agricultural pursuits, the land in the neighborhood being well adapted for the growth of grain. There are two excellent hotels, six stores, a steam flour mill, a brewery in course of erection, a National and Roman Catholic school, a Roman Catholic chapel, a court house, post office, and an electric telegraph office. Divine service in connexion with the Episcopalian, Roman Catholic, and Presbyterian churches is regularly held. Benalla is the head quarters of the police district of Wangaratta, Mansfield, Shepparton, Mulwaley, Violet Town, and Euroa. In winter the climate is delightful, but in summer the heat is excessive. The fruits of the temperate zone are grown in abundance, especially grapes, to which both climate and soil seem peculiarly adapted. The Strathbogie gold-field is 40 miles from Benalla.

BENDIGO.—Sandhurst is the centre of the Bendigo gold-field, county unnamed; it is distant from Melbourne 97 miles, Murray River 60, Campaspe 15, and Loddon 25 miles. The township of Sandhurst was erected into a municipality on the 10th January, 1856, beginning, south, at Golden Square, and running north, below the Wellington Hotel, White Hills. Population, over 12,000; average annual assessment, £150,000; actual value of buildings for municipal rate, between £900,000 and £1,000,000 sterling. There are many handsome stone and brick buildings, with showy plate glass fronts. The country in and about Sandhurst is composed of a number of bold ranges and extensive gullies; situated in many of these ranges are the rich quartz reefs, which have given a world-wide renown to the Bendigo gold-fields. The gullies are what are termed alluvial, and many of these have been turned over by the tub and cradle miner, and are now undergoing the process of puddling by horse-power. The estimated number of machines is 2050, each employing on an average, four men and two horses; the rough estimate of capital thus employed is half-a-million sterling. Pall Mall, the central business street, has some handsome structures. There is a well organised Mechanics' Institute, a handsome Theatre that cost £3,000, and the Shamrock Free Concert Hall. The Episcopalians, the Roman Catholics and the Wesleyans have handsome places of worship; and the Presbyterians and Independents are about erecting substantial buildings. Local manufactures are being established; there are an excellent pottery, a soap and candle manufactory, a steam flour and a steam saw mill and a tannery.

BLACKWOOD (MOUNT), situated in county of West Bourke, and distant about 54 miles to the north-west of Melbourne. A township at Golden Point has been surveyed and set out, but no land has as yet been sold. There are no buildings with the exception of wooden erections, and the generality of them are of a very temporary nature. There is a camp reserve, with court of petty sessions, police-barracks, and a gaol. Upwards of twenty stores are scattered up and down, and there are several licensed publicans. Also a post-office. Two Denominational schools in connexion with the Church of England. A Roman Catholic church is erected. There is no direct coach communication; the coach running between Melbourne and Ballaarat is the nearest conveyance, passengers from either of those places are set down at the Pentland Inn or Blows' Station, about 12 miles from Golden Point, both places being about equi-distant from the latter. A few stage waggons ply regularly to and from Melbourne. These diggings, which are principally alluvial, reach from Frenchman's Point to Simmons' Reef, running east and west, a distance of about eight miles along the Lerderderg River, and extend over numerous tributary gullies, covering an area of nearly eight square miles. At Simmons' Reef, quartz mining and crushing are carried on to a considerable extent. The machinery is nearly all driven by water power. Sluicing operations are carried on upon an extensive scale, and a few aqueducts of some pretensions have been constructed in connexion with the races, some of which are over six miles in length. There are a few puddling machines also, and a few small water wheels in use for pumping. The Blackwood diggings were discovered in 1854, and at one time the population was estimated at nearly 25,000. There has been a great falling off, however, in this respect, for the present population is supposed not to exceed 1,200. The declension took place almost immediately after the rush, and the population since has not fluctuated much over 1,000. The district lies high, the mean vertical height above the level of the sea being about 1,600 feet. It possesses in consequence of its altitude a highly bracing and healthy climate. Mountain forests, thickly scrubbed, surround it on all sides. Beautiful specimens of native heaths abound.

BUCKLAND.—The Buckland gold-field was discovered in October, 1853. The district includes Buckland River, Ovens River, Happy Billey Creek, and their tributaries, commencing on the Ovens River at the junction of the Happy Valley Creek. The Government camp on the Buckland is distant from Melbourne, by the Wangaratta-road, about 230 miles, but in a direct line only 175. Near the camp there are three public houses, a branch of the Oriental Bank Corporation, a denominational school, and seven or eight stores. The population of the district, according to the last census, was, males, 733; females, 192; children, 148; total other than Chinese, 1,073. The view from all parts of the Buckland River is very confined, but rather romantic, the ranges being very high and close. In winter the sun is only seen above the horizon six to seven hours during the day. Hitherto Buckland has been famed for the richness of the gold deposits found in alluvial matter. Several quartz reefs have recently been discovered. An abundant supply of water has been provided, and turned to advantage by the construction of dams and water races, the latter in some instances conveying water 10 to 16 miles. Considerable expense has been incurred in supplying this great desideratum to mining enterprise. A new gold-field has been discovered within the boundaries of the Buckland, on the Ovens River; the gold is coarse and heavy. The lead of the present workings on the Buckland are distant about 13 miles from its source, and is only separated from Livingstone Creek and Lake Omeo gold-fields by about half a degree of east longitude; but the snowy ranges of the Australian Alps form the impassible barrier. No land has been sold in the district, and consequently, as yet, there is hardly any sign of agriculture. The absence of the agriculturalist is partially remedied by most of the miners having small gardens attached to their huts. The site of a township has been surveyed on the Ovens crossing, distant on the Melbourne road about 15 miles from the camp; it is surrounded by fertile land; the scenery is very agreeable, embracing the valley along the banks of the Ovens River and the lofty ranges with which it is surrounded; the peaks of the Buffalo rising to an altitude of 5000 feet, and covered with snow during six months in the year.

BUNINYONG, an inland township in the county of Grant, is pleasantly situate 1 mile west from Mount Buninyong, in 36° 20′ S. lat., and 143° 55′ E. long., and is distant from Melbourne 89 miles, from Geelong 47 miles, and from Ballaarat 6 miles; the Geelong and Ballaarat road running through its centre. The volcanic soil here is of the richest and most productive nature, generally thickly timbered. From the high altitude of Buninyong and its neighborhood the air is bracing, and from the numerous fresh water springs with which this locality abounds the township is plentifully supplied with the best of water. The principal street is on the Ballaarat and Geelong Main Road, which is macadamised; there are several substantial buildings; one large stone hotel, a stone court of petty sessions and a warden's office, two large brick school-rooms, Episcopalian and Roman Catholic, and a large brick parsonage (Episcopalian), together with some handsome private residences. The *Telegraph* newspaper is published twice a week. Buninyong on the south and west is bounded by the famous Buninyong and Ballaarat Gold Fields, and within 3 miles of it, the first discovery of gold in Victoria was said to be made by Hiscock in a quartz-reef named after him. The population within the town boundary is about 4,000. One member of the Assembly represents the district of North Grant, of which Buninyong and the adjacent country form a division, and this division has a share in the representation of the South-Western Province in the Council.

CALEDONIA.—The St. Andrew diggings are 23 miles from Melbourne. The route is through Eltham and Kangaroo grounds.

CARISBROOK.—A municipal township, situate at the junction of Tallaroop and McCullum's Creeks, distant from Melbourne 99 miles, and from Castlemaine 25 miles. The surrounding country is fine agricultural land, and it is cultivated to a considerable extent. The streets are well planned and metalled, buildings mostly of brick, shops good, and an abundant supply of water. Coaches pass to and from Melbourne daily. Carisbrook is a magnificent site for a large town. The circuit court of the Avoca district is held here.

CASTLEMAINE, in the county of Talbot, Loddon district, is situate at the junction of Forest and Barker's Creeks, forming Campbell's Creek which flows into the Loddon. It is the central point of the gold-fields and of the colony, being nearly equi-distant from Port Phillip and the Murray River. It lies 77 miles north-west from Melbourne, with Sandhurst or Bendigo 28 miles to the north, and Maryborough or Simpson's diggings 30 miles to the west. Gold was discovered on Forest Creek in the latter part of 1851. In 1852 the site of the township was surveyed and part of it laid out in blocks of five acres, intersected by five streets running N. and S., and fifteen streets running E. and W., all 99 feet wide, and about 600 building allotments of one rood each have been sold, the town boundary extending to an area of two miles in length, by one mile wide. The Camp was established in 1852, and removed to its present site in 1854. It is adorned with some neat villas and public offices of wood, iron, and brick, together with barracks and stabling, and a few pretty garden plots. The first municipal council was elected in January, 1856. There are two newspapers, the *Mount Alexander Mail* and *Miner's Right*, published on alternate days. The hospital was established in 1853; it is a handsome stone building of two stories, with two wings built of brick, and affords accommodation for 60 patients. The first permanent place of worship was erected in 1855, and there are now seven substantial edifices of brick and stone—the Church of England, the Church of Rome, the Presbyterian, the Congregational, the Wesleyan, the Methodist, and the Bible Christians. The Free Church of Scotland use the Mechanics' Hall. There are also several smaller places of worship and school-houses in connexion with most of the above. The Town Hall is a neat brick building, and near it are the Post-office, Electric Telegraph, Sub-Treasury, and Gold Offices, Savings' Bank, Police Court, and Supreme Court House, all substantial stone edifices; the Mechanics' Institute is a commodious brick building, occupying a site near the Survey and Land Office. There are two flour mills, a large iron foundry, two smelting and assay offices for gold, a pottery, manufactories of soap and candles, and tanneries. A market is established and a weighbridge erected near the market houses. The Gaol is an extensive stone building, and the Powder Magazine, also of stone, is erected on a hill on the western town boundary. There are about eighteen hotels and two concert rooms in the town, and a theatre is in course ef erection. Cobb's coaches run three times a day to and from Melbourne, daily to Sandhurst and Maryborough, and other conveyances ply between the villages of Forest and Campbell's Creeks. There are four banks, beside a branch of the Provident Institute of Victoria and Deposit Bank. Extensive wholesale and retail trade is carried on with an extensive surrounding district.

CLUNES is about 12 miles in a north-westerly direction from Creswick, and is notable as being the place where an early discovery of gold was made; also at a more recent period for the prosperity of a co-operative company. The extensive operations of the Port Phillip and Colonial Gold Mining Company are carried on there. The working of the quartz reefs are systematically conducted. This is one of the best conducted mines in the colony, and reflects great credit on the leaseholders.

CRESWICK.—A township in the county of Talbot, situated about 12 miles north from Ballaarat, near the summit of the great dividing range. The distance from Melbourne is about 106 miles, and Geelong 64. It was surveyed and laid out in 1854, and will shortly be proclaimed a municipality. The land in the vicinity of Creswick is alluvial, of the most fertile description, and is well watered by numerous creeks. The Creswick Creek diggings have a high reputation, the government escort averaging about 1,000 ozs. per week. The population of the town is estimated at about 1,000, that of the surrounding gold-field at about 2,500; besides which there is a large and flourishing agricultural population, the parishes of Glendarnal, Ascot, and Spring Hill being within a circuit of 6 miles. The township contains one National, and three Denominational schools, and two banks, besides the usual government offices. A court of mines, and county court are held once every two months. The *Creswick Advertiser* is published once a week.

DAYLESFORD—Known as Jim Crow diggings, about 12 miles from Castlemaine.

DROMANNA.—In the Western Port district, twelve miles south of Schnapper Point, on the eastern coast of Port Phillip bay, at the foot of the eminence called Arthur's Seat. It was surveyed and laid out for a township in 1856. There is a trigonometrical tower of about 40 feet crowning Arthur's Seat, about 900 feet above the level of the sea.

DUNOLLY (Mount Moliagul), termed the key to the north-western gold-fields is situated about 125 miles from Melbourne; population 1,500. It contains several large wholesale stores, and many fine retail shops; five large hotels and four smaller public houses; a Church of England school house, used also as a church; a denominational school, Wesleyan chapel and school; four banks, and a mechanics' institute. A daily mail from Melbourne, and one conveyance daily to and from Maryborough. Dunolly was proclaimed a municipality in 1857. There is plenty of land adjoining the town well adapted for agriculture, unsold and unsurveyed. Several hundred acres are under cultivation in the neighborhood. Many of the neighboring gold-fields draw their supplies from Dunolly. The following are the distances from this township:—Burnt Creek 3 miles, Jones' Creek 7, Sandy Creek 11, Moliagul 8, Cochrane's 10, Kingower 20, McIntyre 15, Jordan's 25, Korong 40, Bet Bet 5. The quartz reefs are very rich, more particularly in the neighborhood of Sandy Creek. There is an abundance of excellent building stone near the town, and also a large brick-field.

ECHUCA.—An inland port, situate on the south bank of the River Murray, about a mile from Moama (Maiden's punt), and distant from Melbourne 135 miles. The sudden rise of this township is an illustration of individual enterprise successfully carried out. It is only four years since that Mr. Henry Hopwood settled there with a punt of superior construction, and as he anticipated an increased importation of live stock from New South Wales, prepared every facility for aiding that trade; the result has equalled his expectations. The site was well selected, being situated on a peninsula formed by the approximation of the two rivers Murray, and Campaspe, whose waters join immediately below the township. Echuca was surveyed in 1855, and most of it sold. The trunk line of the railway survey afterwards terminated there, as affording the most eligible locality for its extension at some future period into New South Wales. The consequence has been that as the Government will offer no more land for sale in the township nor suburbs until the line be completed, town lots are now exchanging hands at very high prices The trade of the town is chiefly supported by the overland stock traffic, and which in the year 1856–7 amounted to above £1,250,000 sterling. During the first years' operations of the South Australian Steam Navigation Company on the Murray, an attempt was made to connect the river trade at Echuca with the Bendigo gold district, but after a feeble trial, it was obliged to give way to the effects arising from the good road afterwards completed from the metropolis to Sandhurst; however, it still remains an entrepôt for that trade for the surrounding districts. Since the settlement of the locality, Mr. Hopwood has built a pontoon bridge across the Murray, 354 feet in length, and also, a span bridge across the Campaspe, 120 feet in length, with built approaches 170 feet in addition, with a clear inside width of 11 feet. This bridge, for the erection of which an Act of the Legislature had to be obtained, is of a novel construction, and before its being finally placed in its present position, was temporarily built and subjected to the test of a body of 204 soldiers marching across. The electric telegraph has been extended to the township, therefore connecting it with Melbourne and Adelaide. A fine hotel has been erected there, and a large wool and produce store. This is one of the most flourishing and advancing towns in the interior, is possessed of a large trade, and surrounded by some of the best pastoral country in the colony. The climate approaches that of the tropics, and attempts are now being made to cultivate the orange and other tropical productions.

FRANKSTON.—In the Western Port district, 29 miles from Melbourne, on the eastern coast of Port Phillip bay. Was surveyed and laid out for a township in the year 1853, having one roadside inn, a school-house, post-office and store. It is a police station.

GAP (THE).—On the Mount Alexander road, about 24 miles from Melbourne. It was laid out and proclaimed in 1854. There are twelve streets, intersected by the main road. It is 2 miles from Sunbury on the east, and 15 from Bacchus Marsh on the west; it is watered by the Coroit Creek, and contains three commodious hotels, five stores, post-office, and Denominational school, in which Divine Service is performed every Sabbath. The township is situated between two hills, and is 3000 feet above the level of the sea, commanding a view of the northern shore of Port Phillip Bay, from

Williamstown to Geelong. The air is most salubrious, and the scenery in the immediate neighborhood is very beautiful. The line of the Melbourne and Murray River Railway is about a mile from the township.

GIPPS LAND.—The principal towns are Tarraville, Port Albert. Sale, and Alberton. Tarraville is distant from Port Albert 3¼ miles, Alberton and Victoria 4 miles from Port Albert. Port Albert is situate about 112 miles from Melbourne, eastward of Port Phillip Heads. Cape Liptrap is 81 miles from Melbourne, forming the boundary of Gipps Land; the distance from Cape Liptrap to Wilson's Promontory being 30 miles. Port Albert was discovered by Mr. A. McMillan, of Bushy Park, on the 14th February, 1841. Several attempts were made by him at intervals, to open up the country, which ultimately proved successful. His efforts were furthered by Count Strzelecki, Capt. Ross, R.N., Dr. Arbuckle, Messrs. Cameron, McAlister, Bath, and others. The attacks made upon the exploring parties by the aborigines impeded their work, but in the year 1844 numerous lakes, rivers, and mountains were discovered, which were duly recorded in despatches forwarded to His Honor C. J. LaTrobe, by Mr. McMillan and Mr. C. J. Tyers. Providence Ponds, Lake Wellington, the Avon, McAlister, and Thomson rivers were discovered the first trip. The whole of the district was called Caledonia Australis. The large plains were discovered the first trip, and were called Mc Arthur Plains, after the late John McArthur, Esq., of Camden, New South Wales; the McAlister River was named after L. McAlister, Esq., of Clifton, New South Wales; the Thomson River after E. Deas Thomson, Esq., Sydney, then Colonial Secretary. The climate is very salubrious and the soil remarkably fertile. The large number of squatting stations in this part of Victoria indicate its advantages for stock, &c. Banks, societies, churches, schools, hotels, &c., are numerous in the principal districts. The *Gipps Land Guardian* is published in Port Albert every Friday. Weekly steam communication with Melbourne.

GISBORNE.—This township is 31 miles from Melbourne, on the Castlemaine-road. Several churches, schools, and societies, with good hotels. Coaches pass from Melbourne three times a day.

GOULBURN RIVER—(See article on Seymour).—Among the very few rivers in the colony of Victoria, having the slightest pretensions to never failing streams, the Goulburn should be classed the first. Little is really known of the capabilities of this fine river. Rising on the north side of the Australian Alps, or Great Dividing Range (within a few miles of the source of the Yarra, which falls from the south side), it waters an extensive tract of diversified country. Several important streams, the Howqua, Big River, Delatite, Acheron, and numerous other creeks join it in its northerly course, until it falls into the Murray a few miles east of Maiden's Punt. The upper part of the Goulburn, down to the township of Seymour, the crossing place of the Sydney-road, is a tortuous course of several hundred miles. Its numerous rocky falls and other obstructions in the shape of sandy bars and large fallen trees, render it impracticable to navigation; but from Seymour the entire length of this river to its junction with the Murray is about 350 miles. The Goulburn and Murray are navigable at the same period of the year, commercial operations being completely in the hands of traders in South Australia, who can absolutely come a distance of upwards of 2000 miles by water, deliver their goods in Victoria, and derive a profitable speculation from the result. They are thus enabled to discharge their cargoes and receive their return freights of wool, &c., at the very threshold of the north-eastern gold-fields of Victoria. The upper part of the Goulburn, above Seymour, is in many places extremely picturesque, interspersed with rocky falls, varied by overhanging trees of the gum tribes, with occasionally long vistas of the mimosa lining its banks. The prevailing character of the land through which it flows is good for most agricultural purposes, while the extensive rich alluvial flats, from their being frequently flooded by the rain, are better adapted for grazing purposes. The whole river teems with fish; the largest and best is the Murray cod, which is frequently caught weighing from 70 to 90 lbs.; but the finest flavored and most delicate eating, weigh from 15 to 25 lbs.; they are easily caught with a live frog or the small fish of almost any of the varieties found in the river. There are also the lobster, weighing as much as 3 lbs. or even more, and the pawn, which is found as large and as fine flavored as can be had in any part of the world. Wild fowl abound in the river, and every creek and lagoon in its route; the black duck, wood duck,; musk duck, teal, wild goose, and, occasionally the black swan and the shag, with an almost infinite variety of waders and other land birds, whose food is more plentifully found on the banks of rivers. That extraordinary amphibious animal, the platypus, is very numerous, also a large kind of water rat is frequently met with. The land animals are, perhaps, more numerous on the banks of this river than anywhere else in the colony; the opossum and native cat may be seen almost on every tree during the moonlight nights, and the footprints of the kangaroo may be seen in every secluded nook bordering the stream. The poor aboriginal is fast disappearing from the district of the Goulburn; a very few scattered remnants of their tribes are now to be met with, for wherever the white man plants his foot, the signal is sounded for the unfortunate black to retire before the progressive strides of civilization and improvement.

HAMILTON.—A post town, situated 60 miles inland, equi-distant from the sea-ports of Portland and Port Fairy, and about 184 miles from Melbourne. The Grange Burn runs through the site allotted for the town, and forms the boundary between the two counties of Normanby and Dundas. The principal mail roads from the capital run though Hamilton and branch off in all directions, to the westward, to Adelaide and the northern settlements. The land being of first-rate quality, it is surrounded on all sides by agricultural farms and a busy and thriving population, numbering about 3000. A large quantity of grain and hay is raised in the district, which finds a ready market at the Ararat diggings (65 miles distant). A steam flour mill is in operation, and a second is in course of erection. The town contains an Episcopalian, a Presbyterian, and a Roman Catholic chapel; the two former are of stone; the Presbyterian is just completed, and has a steeple intended to contain a town clock and bell. There are a National and a Denominational school; there is also a Public Library with a large collection of useful books; a Pastoral and an Agricultural

Society which hold periodical shows of stock and farm produce. The Road Board for the district hold their meetings in the township, and a municipal chamber will soon be added to its local institutions. There are six stores. The town is very well situated, and has a fine view of Mount Abrupt, one of the peaks of the Grampians. The country around is undulating and slightly wooded, principally with the blackwood tree. A few miles from the township are the Wannon Falls, at two points on the Wannon River. It is in the electoral district of Dundas and Follett.

HEATHCOTE.—About 66 miles from Melbourne. A rising township, the population being about 2,500. Several churches, hotels, &c. Gold escort leaves every fortnight.

KILMORE.—An inland town, about 36 miles from Melbourne, the capital of the counties of Dalhousie and Anglesey. Eight square miles of the land in and around Kilmore were purchased as a special survey by the Messrs. Rutledge, who afterwards sold it to Messrs. Lamb, Rogers and Co., of Sydney, by whom it was leased to farmers who have since become purchasers of their respective farms. About six years since the Government surveyed and laid out a township adjoining, now called the new town of Kilmore, all of which is now private property. Both towns united were proclaimed a municipality in July, 1856. The soil of Kilmore and surrounding district is of volcanic origin. The whole, or nearly so, of the lands between Kilmore and the Saltwater River in one direction, and Kilmore and Kyneton in another, are becoming rapidly settled upon, as are also the lands between Kilmore and the McIvor gold-fields. Kilmore being situated on the main Sydney-road, is the direct route to the Ovens, McIvor, and Goulburn gold-fields. Seymour, the proposed head of the navigation of the Goulburn River, is distant 23 miles. The Goulburn runs through rich and as yet unalienated land, and then unites with the Murray. The former can, it is supposed, be rendered navigable at a very trifling cost; the Government have promised that it shall be surveyed. Kilmore has a post-office and a daily mail, a court-house and gaol, a police station, a public hospital, a mechanics' institute and news room, telegraph station, road engineers' office, municipal office and flour mills, saw mills, &c., four churches and schools. *Kilmore Examiner*, published weekly.

KYNETON.—A thriving town, about 51 miles from Melbourne, on the Castlemaine-road. A municipality has been formed, and the churches, institutions. &c., are numerous. *Kyneton Observer* and *Kyneton Chronicle* published weekly.

LINTONS.—Lintons diggings commenced in the winter of 1855, and were, until lately (when a deep lead was found), shallow sinking. It is in the police district of Carngham, from which place it is distant about six miles, and eight miles from Smythe's Creek. It has a post-office, public house, and one or two stores. There are a few farms in the neighborhood. The nearest sea-port is Geelong *viâ* Pitfield; it is distant from Geelong about 64 miles.

LOCKWOOD.—An agricultural township and district, situated on Bullock Creek, about 10 miles south-west of Sandhurst, on the main roads connecting the various gold-fields. It is the largest agricultural district near Bendigo; its creek, in the summer a never-failing succession of large water-holes, is in the winter a running stream. The land is generally fertile, the water always good, and the climate healthy. The township itself is small, and its buildings are of wood. The farmers, however, along the creek for a distance of 10 miles, most of whom are freeholders, have neat houses and comfortable farms. The hotels are substantial and commodious. There is one Denominational school in connexion with the Wesleyan Church.

MALDON.—An inland town, about 11 miles from Castlemaine and 84 from Melbourne, at the base of Mount Tarrengower. It was proclaimed a municipality on August 6, 1858. The population of the district is about 7,000. From its contiguity to the valley of the Loddon and Muckleford, it is well supplied with vegetables, hay, country produce, &c. Its principle support is from the reefs around, which are very rich, but of late a large amount of gold has been obtained from the alluvial diggings. Of the two principal streets in the town, one is the route to Avoca, and the other to the Eagle Hawk Reef. The Episcopalians had a very neat edifice, used as church and school-house, but a severe storm in December, 1857, destroyed it, and it has not yet been rebuilt. The Wesleyans have a substantial building, capable of containing about 200 persons. A Presbyterian Church has been commenced. The view from Mount Tarrengower is one of the most extensive in the colony; from its heights can be seen Mount Macedon, Mount Alexander, Mount Blackwood, Jim Crow Valley of the Loddon, the Bald Hill at Carisbrook, Forest Creek, &c. The town contains a Denominational school, a court house, a post office, seven steam crushing machines, branches of the banks New South Wales and Victoria. *Tarrengower Times* and *Maldon Advertiser* are published twice a week. The quantity of gold forwarded by escort from Maldon during the months of May, June, July and August, 1858, amounted to 23,290 ozs., in very nearly equal proportions of alluvial and amalgamated gold, showing an average of 1370 ozs. per week. In September, 1858, the yield largely increased.

MARYBOROUGH.—The chief town of the trans-Loddon or North-Western gold-fields, in the county of Talbot. Distant from Melbourne 103 miles, on the Castlemaine road, from Castlemaine 30, from Tarrengower 20, from Dunolly 13, from Avoca 16, from Amherst 10, from Ballaarat 45, from Ararat 60. It was surveyed and laid out for a township in 1854, and was proclaimed a municipality in March, 1857. The land in the immediate vicinity of Maryborough is not of a fertile nature, and there is at present very little under cultivation. The air is remarkably dry and healthy; the heat excessive in summer, and water very scarce. The town is improving, and substantial and neat stone buildings are rapidly taking the place of wood and iron. Several public buildings are in course of construction, viz., supreme court, police court, post-office, council chambers, survey-office, sub-treasury and gold-office, gaol, and four handsome banks. The *Maryborough and Dunolly Advertiser* is published twice a week. The traffic, to and from Melbourne and all parts of the district, is great, as this is the centre of the district for coaching, postal branches and arrangements, and for gold buying and banking business. The population of Maryborough is about 3,000, but there is a large population scattered on all sides of the township that cannot correctly be enumerated in its population. Two members represent the county of Talbot, of which Maryborough is the north-western metropolis.

MURCHISON.—A township on the west bank of the Goulburn, between Seymour and the Murray. It is very prettily situate, and its contiguity (about ten or twelve miles) to the Goulburn or Waranga gold-fields, together with its being in the direct road from Bendigo to the Ovens, will no doubt raise it to an im ortant inland township. A large quantity of farm land is bought and cultivated in the neighborhood, the produce from which finds a ready sale at the adjoining diggings. Murchison, like Seymour, has its stores, post-office (post days three times a week), police barracks, blacksmiths' shops, cemetery, and race-course; it also has two hotels, and a good punt to connect the traffic across the river.

OMEO.—Omeo, the most eastern of the Victorian gold-fields, takes its name from Lake Omeo (now dry), from which the principal diggings, situated on Livingstone Creek (a tributary of the Mitta Mitta River), are distant 12 miles. Although properly belonging to Gipps Land, this gold-field is at present included in the mining district of Beechworth, from which town it is distant 150 miles. It is in the electoral district of Mitta Mitta, Murray. The nucleus of a town, including four hotels and several stores, has been formed on Livingstone Creek, where there are a resident magistrate and warden, a police-station and post-office. There is no agricultural land in the immediate vicinity, the country being mountainous, but at Tongio, in the valley of the River Tambo, about 12 miles from Livingstone Creek, and at the foot of the dividing range, some good agricultural land is now in course of survey. A series of townships have been laid out along the main post road through Gipps Land from Sale (the principal town of the upper district) to Bruthen, a township within 60 miles of Livingstone Creek, and whence the main road forks northward to Omeo, and eastward to the great grazing district of Maneroo, N.S.W. The distance from Port Albert, Gipps Land, is 175 miles; from Melbourne by the post road (*viâ* Dandenong, the Moe, and Sale) 305 miles. There are several diggings at various points within a radius of 40 miles from Omeo, both in the direction of Beechworth and in Gipps Land, the latter gold bearing a much higher value than that of Omeo. Hitherto the Omeo gold-field has been but imperfectly prospected, principally owing to its mountainous character and the consequent difficulty of access. A steamboat has now, however, been launched on the river Thompson, for the purpose of running between Sale and Bruthen, and it is anticipated that when it shall have commenced running there will be a considerable access to the population of the district. The population of the Warden's district of Omeo is, males, 413; females, 61; and children of both sexes, 74; total, 548. Omeo is about 3000 feet above the level of the sea, and the climate is remarkably healthy.

OSBORNE.—In the Western Port district, three miles south of Schnapper Point. Was surveyed and laid out for a township in the year 1856. Three miles below Osborne, at the southern extremity of Mount Martha, is a reserve, chosen for a marine residence of the Viceroy.

PLEASANT CREEK.—This district is 159 miles from Melbourne, on the Ballaarat line. There are branch banks, and six hotels. *Pleasant Creek Times*, published weekly. Coaches to and from Melbourne and Ararat daily.

PORTLAND.—The township of Portland is situated in latitude 38° 20′ S., and 141° 40′ E. longitude, at the head of the bay of the same name, about midway between Melbourne and Adelaide, being distant from the former 234, and from the latter 300 miles. It is the oldest settlement in the colony, having been occupied as a whaling station in 1833, although as a township it does not date earlier than 1842. A person named Dutton, in the employment of Mr. J. Sinclair, of Launceston, in 1832, first settled at Portland; but the influence and enterprise of the family of Henty, which arrived in 1834, has been one of the main causes of raising Portland to its present position. At a distance of twenty miles stands the Julia Percy Island, a mass of precipitous rock, about two miles in length from north to south by one in width, and rising to a height of from two to three hundred feet. At a distance of about five miles from the town and one from the main land, stand the Lawrence Rocks, also precipitous. These give the entrance to the bay a most picturesque appearance. There are two jetties. The old one is 600 feet long, and has a depth of water of eleven feet; the new one, just completed, was built by Messrs. Baillie; it is 910 feet long, and has a depth of water of seventeen feet. The anchorage is good; and with a breakwater to turn off the force of the sea during storms from the south-east, the harbor would be one of the finest and safest on the coast. The town rises from the bay on a gentle slope. The streets extend east and west, and north and south; many of the former open immediately towards the sea. To the south of the old jetty stand the custom house, the post office, the electric telegraph office, the court house, the gaol and the immigration depôt, all stone structures, excepting the last. In the same direction, on a lofty headland, from which it is proposed to construct a breakwater, stands the flagstaff; and opposite, is another lofty headland called the Whalers' Bluff; near these is the cricket ground. The extreme northern extension of the bay proper is shut in. In the neighborhood of the latter portion of the town, to the south, stands the benevolent asylum. There are five edifices in the town devoted to religious purposes; the English Church, situated at the junction of Julia and Percy streets; the Roman Catholic, Bentinck-street; the Presbyterian, in Tyers-street; the Free Presbyterian, in Palmer-street; the Methodist, in Percy-street; and the Congregational, in Tyers-street. There is also a building in Henty-street used by the Baptists. Two only of these buildings can lay claim to notice on architectural grounds, the English and the Roman Catholic churches; the former is of bluestone and in the modern Gothic style; the latter, not yet completed, is of freestone and in similar style, and promises to be a very handsome building. The cemetery is at the double corner, about a mile and a half north from the town. There are nine inns in the town. The stores are numerous, and some of them large and handsome. The Union Bank and the Bank of Australasia both have elegant stone structures. There are a mechanics' institute and a national school, both plain, substantial stone edifices. The steam flour mill in Glenelg-street is the property of E. Henty. There are town wells which yield a perpetual supply of excellent water. The neighborhood is thickly wooded.

Northward stands the Nine mile Forest, through which a tramway has been commenced. By this it is intended to connect the Grange with the port; £20,000 have already been granted by the Government for the completion of the first eight miles, about one-seventh of the distance. The suburbs, north and south, are divided from the town by a swamp and lagoon. The latter supplies an abundance of fresh water at all seasons, and is rendered exceedingly picturesque by the wild fowl frequenting it, and the boats skimming its surface. In the vicinity there are several fine residences. The climate is excellent, which, coupled with the pleasantness of its situation, renders it a desirable resort for invalids. Two newspapers are published in the town; the *Guardian*, three times a week, and the *Chronicle* twice a week. It returns two members to Parliament. Population 4000.

RYE.—In the Western Port district, 18 miles south of Schnapper Point, was surveyed in the year 1856. Lime stone abounds and several kilns are in operation. There is a Church of England school and a post-office. The well-known White Cliff is at the south-western corner of the town reserve.

SCHNAPPER POINT.—In the Western Port district, 38 miles from Melbourne on the Eastern coast of Port Phillip bay. It was surveyed in 1854. There are three hotels, several stores, Church of England schools, post-office, police station, &c., and a stone pier, which runs into twenty-two feet water, and completely shuts in and shelters the harbor. Schnapper Point is a most desirable place for marine residences. The scenery is picturesque; and the view from the top of Mount Martha, about six miles distant, which embraces the whole of Port Phillip Bay, and part of Bass's Straits, Arthur's Seat, the Plenty Ranges, Mount Macedon, Mount Buninyong, Station Peak, Point Nepean on both sides, and the coast line as far as Cape Otway, is perhaps unrivalled in this colony.

SEYMOUR.—Seymour is the principal township on the Goulburn, and is on the main line of road from Melbourne to Beechworth. It is one of the Murray Boroughs, and in conjunction with them returns one member to the Legislative Assembly; is situate in the Eastern Province, an extensive district which sends five representatives to the Upper House. The river divides the township into two parts; the population is small, principally engaged in agricultural pursuits. The land is generally good, though swampy in winter, being occasionally subject to floods. There are several good stores, post-office, blacksmith's shops, police station, a compact substantial steam flour-mill, a public cemetery, a race-course, and two good hotels, one on each side of the river. There are two punts for the convenience of the public—the government punt is about a mile above Seymour; the other, private property, plies close to the township: they are the best managed punts on the Goulburn, are very commodious and capable of conveying, with perfect safety, the heaviest laden drays across the river, the average breadth of which, under ordinary circumstances, is about 250 feet, but frequently much broader in the winter season. The river can readily be made navigable to a point some distance above Seymour; but it appears probable that Seymour or some place near it will be the head of the navigation, as it can more readily be connected with Melbourne by means of the tramway already constructed to Yan Yean, than can other parts of the river. The opening up of the Goulburn will bring Melbourne into communication with the Murray, Murrumbidgee, Darling, Edward, and a vast extent of country, the produce of which is now sent down the Murray to South Australasia. There is a daily post from Melbourne, the Beechworth mail passing, under present arrangements, every evening about six p.m.

STEIGLITZ.—An inland township, situated about 25 miles north of Geelong, on the eastern side of the Moorabool River, and about three miles from that river on a small creek. The land on which the township is built belongs to the Crown. The quartz-reefs, which are extensively worked, pass through the township from north to south, at the rear of a street called Regent-street. The land in the vicinity is barren and dry, and good water is scarce in summer. The air is salubrious and invigorating. Steiglitz contains three schools, an Episcopalian Denominational school, a Wesleyan, one at New Chum Reef, chiefly supported by Presbyterians,also a post-office and a court-house. The population on the gold-field itself is about 800, in the district about 1,300.

TARADALE.—An inland township, distant from Melbourne 62 miles, from Castlemaine 10 miles. The land around Taradale is of a fine agricultural description, about 2000 acres are under cultivation; good water abounds; the air is most invigorating. There are twelve streets in the township, but the buildings at present are confined to the main road. There are a court-house and police quarters, Episcopalian and Roman Catholic chapels, and a district survey office. Taradale is rapidly rising in importance; several rich quartz-reefs have been discovered, and one is now being worked by the Phœnix Gold Mining Company, the yield from which is very large. The other reefs have also yielded large quantities of gold. A viaduct, on the Melbourne and Murray River line, is to be erected at Taradale. Population about 1,430.

WANGARATTA.—An inland town, situate on the Ovens River, 144 miles from Melbourne, on the Sydney Road. It is the centre of a large agricultural and pastoral district. The town contains about 600 inhabitants, and is connected by a handsome single arch bridge, of timber, thrown over the Ovens River, a fine river which runs through the town, and is believed to be navigable as far as Wangaratta. The principal buildings are an English church, a Roman Catholic church, a large steam flour mill, a National school, and a telegraph station. There are six hotels. A new court house is about to be erected, also a bridge over the King River at Wangaratta, to connect the Oxley Plains with the town. It is one of the Murray Boroughs, returning one member to the Assembly. The land in the vicinity of Wangaratta is for the most part very rich, and well adapted for the growth of cereals, of which large quantities are produced at Tarrawingee, bordering on the town. The vine flourishes luxuriantly, as do most fruit trees, especially peaches and other stone fruit. The average price of land fit for cultivation is about 27s. 6d. per acre.

WARRNAMBOOL.—A seaport town, and capital of the counties of Villiers and Heytesbury, is situated on an eminence rising from Lady

Bay, in latitude 38° 24′ 5″ S., and longtitude 142° 32′ E.; bounded by the River Hopkins on the east, and the River Merri on the west. It was surveyed and laid out for a township, in August, 1847, and from its rapid progress was proclaimed a municipality on the 6th December, 1855. Warrnambool is the nearest port to Melbourne on the western coast, being 170 miles from the metropolis. Its bay affords good anchorage and shelter for vessels in all weather. There are excellent moorings laid down, and a new jetty has just been completed, from which there is a tramway into the town a distance of about three-quarters of a mile. The land in the vicinity of Warrnambool is alluvial and of the most fertile description. There are at present 13,450 acres under cultivation. The air is most salubrious and invigorating, and good water abounds. The town is composed of fourteen streets, a market square, with several public buildings. The Episcopalian church is a neat specimen of modern architecture, as are also the Catholic, Wesleyan, and Presbyterian churches, each having schools in connexion with them. The town contains National and Denominational schools, a court house, gaol, post-office, council chambers, telegraph station, custom house, immigration depôt, and benevolent asylum; one bonded store, four steam flour mills, and about twenty-five stores. There are also two banks, five hotels, and a mechanics' institute. *The Warrnambool Examiner* newspaper is published twice a week. The distance from the Great Western gold-fields is about 70 miles, and a good macadamised road is being made. The traffic already between them and Warrnambool is very great, as they afford an excellent outlet for the produce of the district. The population at the last census was—males, 801; females, 738: total, 1,539. One member represents the town, and two the counties, in Parliament.

WILLIAMSTOWN is situated on a peninsula, forming the southern side of Hobson's Bay, and affording to the shipping protection from the prevailing south-westerly winds. The works now in progress, consisting of two stone piers and two wooden wharves, one of which, forming the terminus of the Geelong and Melbourne railway, cannot fail to attract the eye of a stranger, combining as it does strength, security, and good workmanship, being 1,200 feet in length, by 58 feet in breadth, will bear favorable comparison with constructions of a similar character in the mother country; they are capable of securely berthing ships as large as the *Great Britain*, giving ample accommodation for discharging cargo. The old wharf is still used for passengers landing from steamboats, &c., and for goods. The distance from Melbourne by the railway, now nearly completed, is nine miles, but in a direct line across the Bay it is only four miles. The latter, at present, is the usual mode of access to the metropolis, and is accomplished by means of the *Comet* steamer to Sandridge, and thence by railway to Melbourne, within a period of thirty minutes, and at the rate of 1s. 6d. per passenger. It is anticipated, however, that before the close of the year, the bridge now being erected across the Saltwater River will be finished and the line completed direct from Williamstown to Melbourne, thus saving time and avoiding the inconvenience of the steamboat. Scarcely seven years ago, Williamstown was little more than a depôt for Government officers, whose avocations rendered it their necessary place of abode, and then its houses could be counted from the ships in the Bay; but now there are numerous stores, spacious hotels, churches and chapels, villas, and town residences. The town has now its resident magistrate, with a staff of well disciplined police, its municipal council, &c. Court houses have recently been erected of bluestone, of which many quarries exist in this locality. The other public buildings of note consist of a watch-house, two branch banks, harbor, pilot, and immigration offices; custom house, or rather cottage, and post-office, the latter being only a rented building. The greater number of these offices are situated in or near Thompson-street, the principal thoroughfare of the town, at the head of which is erected a handsome stone bridge, forming a communication across the railway to the southern part of the town. From this bridge, outlines of Mount Macedon, the Dandenong Ranges, with the adjacent country can be seen; while to seaward Mount Eliza, Arthur's Seat, Indented Head, and Station Peak, complete the circle whose shores mark the boundaries of Port Phillip Bay. Melbourne, Brighton, St. Kilda, and Sandridge, as well as the winding Yarra Yarra, may be viewed from several parts of Williamstown. There is a well-built fort at Gellibrand's Point, capable of mounting twelve of the heaviest description of guns. Williamstown claims the honor of having had the first electric telegraph communication established in Australia, which was opened to Melbourne in 1854. The telegraph office is a neat substantial stone building, surmounted by a square tower, on which stands the time ball staff. Adjoining and in connexion with this office, stands the observatory, a plain unpretending wooden building, well stocked with astronomical clocks, transit and other instruments. Mean time is noted by the drop of the time ball at noon, and also by the eclipse at two minutes to eight o'clock, and re-appearance of the light upon Gellibrand's Point at eight precisely every night. This latter plan, as a mode of furnishing the mean time to ships, was first introduced here, and is by nautical men, from its simplicity and accuracy, considered worthy of imitation in other ports. Until very lately all vessels over six or seven hundred tons when damaged under water either had to resort to the expensive and precarious mode of heaving down first one side and then the other, or had to leave the port and proceed to Sydney or India for the purpose of having these repairs effected. This state of things, however, is now altered, as the Government patent slip, erected at an expense of £75,000, is able to haul up all descriptions of vessels that frequent this port, except, perhaps, the very largest, and for these it is contemplated to construct a large graving dock. There is also another smaller patent slip by private enterprise in course of erection, calculated to haul up vessels of a thousand tons and under. The only floating dock in Victoria is moored off Williamstown, and is capable of taking in vessels of seven hundred tons. These maritime works, where the sound of the shipwright's mallet is ever heard, give to Williamstown the thorough characteristics of a seaport. The Government marine yard is situated between Ann-street wharf and the old pier. It covers two acres of ground, substantially fenced in with corrugated iron, within which are several commodious workshops for boat-builders, blacksmiths, and lamp-makers; also sheds where all boats, buoys, and beacons required for the Government service throughout the colony are built and repaired. Repairs to the lighting apparatus of the various lighthouses and lightships throughout the colony are effected there, and all marine stores are deposited by the different contractors, tested, assorted, and shipped from hence as required, to the various harbors, lighthouses, and marine stations throughout Victoria. Since the death of Mr. John Price, who was murdered on 26th March, 1856, by the prisoners, convict labor has been dispensed with, and the convicts are stationed in hulks on the north side of Hobson's Bay. The places of public worship consist of two substantial stone edifices belonging to the Wesleyans and Roman Catholics, two iron buildings, the property of the Episcopalians and Congregationalists, and a wooden building, temporarily used by the Presbyterians. The Episcopalians and Roman Catholics have erected ministers' residences contiguous to their respective churches, and the Presbyterians have built a stone manse on the Government site, where they contemplate erecting a substantial church. There are Denominational day schools attached to the Presbyterian, Roman Catholic, and Episcopalian churches. A National school has recently been opened, and there are various private schools for the youth of both sexes. The Bank of Australasia and English and Scottish Bank, and four insurance companies, have branch offices in the town. The only place of public amusement is the Mechanics' Institution, where lectures, concerts, and theatrical representations by amateurs take place. A Ladies' Benevolent Society, supported by voluntary subscriptions and grants from Government, has, for the last three years, liberally administered help to the destitute sick. Williamstown was proclaimed a municipality in April, 1856, and returns one member to the Legislative Assembly, and is now represented by Captain Charles James Perry. The richness of its soil renders all gardening operations peculiarly productive, and experience has shewn it to be a most healthy locality. The upper stratum of the whole locality is generally composed of either clay, garden earth, black mould, or shelly sand. At present but a limited extent of land is under cultivation, chiefly as market gardens, but there are also one or two farms. The town covers an area of four square miles, consisting of three divisions—Williamstown Proper, South Williamstown, and New Town or North Williamstown; and generally speaking the town is well laid out, and the streets broad. Sixteen acres of land have already been fenced in for public gardens, and a committee are making arrangements for the planting and laying out of the grounds. Some acres for a cemetery have also recently been fenced in, at a convenient central distance from the three branches of the town. Most of the inhabitants, including many of the working classes, live on their own freeholds, a fact which says much for the respectability and advancement of Williamstown.

WOOLSHED.—A division of the mining district of Beechworth, situate about 170 miles from Melbourne, and having for its boundaries the rivers Murray and Ovens, Indigo and Hodgson's Creek, includes the auriferous creek known as Reid's Creek, Woolshed, Sebastopol, El Dorado, Mooragee, and Sheep Station. Gold has been also discovered on the Indigo Creek, and several quartz-reefs, which promise to prove remunerative, have been recently discovered in that locality. The workings in this division consist of creek bed, bank and surface or hill workings. The first have been once worked, and are now being a second time occupied by the miners, who receive grants of extensive claims, and are engaged with the aid of machinery, in washing the alluvial deposits from the surface to the bed rock. The hill workings are at present but partially developed from the insufficient supply of water for ground sluicing, a want which will be removed on the plans of the Ovens Gold-fields Water Company being carried out. Reid's Creek was first worked in the years 1852-3, and at that time supported a population of some 8,000 persons. The Woolshed Creek was taken up by the miners in 1854, who then after many reverses, finally succeeded in combating, by the aid of water wheels and steam engines, the heavy underground drainage of water. The present population engaged in mining pursuits is estimated at 3,420, including 400 Chinese. Land of fertile description has been sold at Mooragee, 5 miles, Tarawagee, 8 miles, Indigo Creek, 10 miles, and Barnawartha, 14 miles from the Woolshed. Wheat of excellent quality is grown, and oaten hay for horse forage. Townships are laid out at Chiltern, Black Dog, and Barnawartha. Wahgunyah, a port on the River Murray, at which the Adelaide steamers stop, has large stores and steam flour mill, and is distant 25 miles from Woolshed. No land has yet been sold on the Woolshed, owing to its generally auriferous character. A warden, police magistrate and Chinese protector are stationed at Upper Woolshed, distance 6 miles from Beechworth, and Courts of Petty Sessions are daily held in a neat court house. The Court of Mines is held once a month. There are denominational schools in connexion with the Church of England and Roman Catholic Church, at Upper Woolshed and Reid's Creek.

YACKANDANDAH.—A township, between Beechworth and the Murray River, on the most direct route to the Snowy Creek, Mitta Mitta, and Omeo, from which latter place it is distant about 130 miles. The Yackandandah Creek, with the Kiewa or Little River, Sandy Creek and other tributaries of the Murray, form one of the divisions of the mining district of Beechworth. The town was surveyed and sold on February, 1857, and now contains several substantial stone and brick buildings. There are twelve or fourteen general stores, a court house, Denominational school-house, with Roman Catholic and Presbyterian places of worship, and two banks. The population is principally engaged in mining pursuits, but the land in the vicinity is considered suitable for agriculture, and adapted to the growth of the vine. Yackandandah is about 177 miles distant from Melbourne, 16 from Beechworth, and 22 from Albury on the River Murray.

POST TOWNS IN VICTORIA.

The following is a complete list of the Post Towns in Victoria, including the preceding districts, the figures prefixed denoting the number of miles distant from Melbourne:—

108 Alberton
Alphington
129 Amherst
271 Apsley
134 Ararat
40 Avenel
117 Avoca
34 Bacchus Marsh
46 Ballan
78 Ballaarat
130 Balmoral
80 Barringhup
67 Batesford
166 Beechworth
186 Belfast
49 Bellarine
184 Belvior
119 Benalla
30 Berwick
190 Branxholme
7 Brighton
45 Broadford
10 Broadmeadows
80 Brown Hills

16 Bulla
2¼ Brunswick
175 Buckland
89 Buninyong
89 Burrambeet
125 Campaspe
9 Campbellfield
65 Campbell's Creek
66 Camperdown
167 Caramut
99 Carisbrook
46 Carlsrhue
94 Carngham
71 Castlemaine
215 Casterton
198 Cavendish
72 Ceres
12 Cheltenham
67 Chewton
83 Clarendon
115 Clunes
127 Cochranes
206 Colac
180 Coleraine
1 Collingwood
26 Cranbourne
94 Cressy
106 Creswick's Creek
131 Crowlands
19 Dandenong
103 Daylesford
270 Digby
20 Donnybrook
50 Dromanna
35 Duck Ponds
46 Duneed
150 Dunkeld
140 Durham Ox
101 Eagle Hawk
130 Echuca
130 Elephant Bridge
64 Elphinstone
12 Eltham
1 Emerald Hill
14 Epping
7 Essendon
92 Euroa
Eversley
2 Flemington
4 Footscray
29 Frankston
76 Fryerstown
24 Gap
44 Geelong
31 Gisborne
107 Glenlyon
162 Glenorchy
96 Gnarwarre
116 Goldborough
55 Gordon's
Greensborough
130 Gt. Western Diggings (Ararat)

184 Hamilton
76 Harcourt
231 Harrow
3¼ Hawthorne
66 Heathcote
8 Heidelberg (see Warringal)
98 Hepburn
160 Hexham
219 Heywood
195 Horsham
71 Inverleigh
7 Janefield
119 Jones's Creek
Kangaroo Flat
19 Kangaroo Ground
10 Keilor
3 Kensington
165 Kerang (Lower Loddon)
3 Kew
36 Kilmore
140 Kingower
Koroit
51 Kyneton
95 Lake Learmonth
37 Lancefield
62 Lethbridge
105 Lexton
90 Lintons
28 Little River
89 Lockwood
85 Longwood
157 Lucknow
130 McIntyre's
Maidstone
84 Maldon
57 Malmsbury
85 Mansfield
103 Maryborough
24 Melton
71 Meredith
275 Merino
75 Merton
89 Miner's Rest
Mount Bolton
54 Mt. Blackwood
53 Mt. Egerton
76 Muckleford
106 Murchison
68 Myrtle Creek
141 Navarre
136 Newbridge
80 Newstead
171 Nine-Mile Creek (Ovens)
4 Northcote
9¼ Oakleigh
225 Omeo
195 Penshurst
36 Pentland Hills
5¼ Pentridge
Peter's Diggings

94 Pitfield
156 Pleasant Creek
112 Port Albert
234 Portland
3 Prahran
9 Preston
59 Queenscliff
110 Raglan
2 Richmond
81 Rokewood
98 Rushworth
120 Sale
97 Sandhurst
2¼ Sandridge
121 Sandy Creek
3¼ St. Kilda
149 St. Arnaud
23 St. Andrew's
77 Sebastopol (Bal.)
120 Serpentine Creek
38 Seymour
67 Shelford
157 Shepparton
107 Skipton
86 Smythe's Creek
38 Schnapper Point
14 Somerton
77 Steiglitz
129 Stratford
65 Strathloddon
125 Streatham
26 Sunbury
210 Swan Hill
2 South Yarra
62 Tarradale
111 Tarraville
185 Tarrawingee
3 Toorak
46 Tootgarook
170 Wahgunyah
30 Wallan Wallan
144 Wangaratta
170 Warrnambool
14 Warrandyte
8 Warringal
146 Wedderburn
23 Wittlesea
110 Whipstick
99 White Hills
95 Whroo
143 Wickliffe
4 Williamstown
64 Winchelsea
42 Woodend
Woodstock
166 Woodford
170 Woolshed Creek
18 Wyndham
177 Yackandandah
Yea
178 Yowen Hill

ACTS OF COUNCIL AND OF PARLIAMENT OF VICTORIA

Passed up to the end of Second Session, 1857—8.

INDEX to general subjects of all Acts passed by the Legislature of Victoria since the establishment of the Colony.

Those Acts which have been since repealed are marked R; those which have expired by effluxion of time without being continued by subsequent enactments are marked E.

GOVERNMENT OF VICTORIA.

On the separation of this colony from New South Wales, on the 1st July, 1851, Charles Joseph La Trobe Esq., was appointed Lieutenant-Governor, he having acted as Superintendent from the 30th September, 1839. Upon his departure for Europe, in May 1854, the then Colonial-Secretary, J. V. F. L. Foster, Esq, administered the affairs of Government till the arrival of Sir Charles Hotham, K.C.B., on 21st June, 1854. After his death, which took place on the 31st December, 1856, Major-General Macarthur, Commander of H.M. Forces, was, by the provisions of Her Majesty's Commission, Acting-Governor, and exercised the functions of both offices till the arrival of the present Viceroy, on the 23rd of December, 1856.

His Excellency Sir Henry Barkly, K.C.B., is the son of Æneas Barkly, Esq., merchant, London, and was born in 1815. He was educated at Bruce Castle, Tottenham, and entered Parliament, in 1845, as member for Leominster. He retained his seat until 1849, when he was appointed Governor of British Guiana, which office he continued to hold, with credit to himself and advantage to that colony, until 1853, when he was created a Knight Commander of the Bath, and appointed Governor of Jamaica. He retained this office for three years, gaining the good will of all classes of the colonists, and at the end of that period the high position which he now holds was offered to him. The dates of Sir Henry Barkly's appointments by the Queen are as follows:—Governor and Commander-in-Chief in and over British Guiana, 12th December, 1848. Captain-General and Governor-in-Chief in and over the Island of Jamaica and Dependencies, 9th August, 1853. Captain-General and Governor-in-Chief in and over the Colony of Victoria, 26th September, 1856. These appointments were successively offered to Sir Henry Barkly, by Her Majesty's Ministers for the time being. In 1840, Sir Henry was married to Elizabeth Helen, daughter of J. F. Timins, Esq., of Hilfield, Aldenham, Hertfordshire, and has issue, three sons and one daughter. The lamented death of Lady Barkly, at Toorak, on 17th April, 1857, just when her noble example and virtuous conduct began to exercise a great social influence in the community, caused a deep sorrow among all classes. The career of Sir Henry Barkly, in Victoria, has confirmed the high opinion previously entertained, and won for him the esteem of the whole community.

PARLIAMENT OF VICTORIA.

At the time of the separation of Port Phillip from New South Wales, in 1851, the Legislative Council, comprising representatives of the two districts, adopted, on the motion of

Mr. W. C. Wentworth, a remonstrance against the incomplete form of government accorded to the colonies. The local legislatures were invited by the English Government to suggest such constitutions as were most acceptable to each colony. New South Wales, Victoria, South Australia, and Tasmania, at different periods availed themselves of the offer thus made, and in each of them the chosen constitution is now undergoing trial. The Constitution Bill passed in Victoria was embodied as a schedule to a short statute, 18 and 19 Victoria, cap. 55, enabling Her Majesty to assent to the bill, slightly amended.

The *bicameral* form was adopted. Both houses are elected. Twelve months cannot elapse without a session of the Parliament. For names of members, &c., see pages 91 and 92.

THE EXECUTIVE COUNCIL.

The Executive Council is composed of such persons as the Governor may call upon to advise him. Before the inauguration of Responsible Government certain specified chief officers were, in accordance with Royal Instructions under Letters Patent, necessarily summoned by the Governor as Executive Councillors: but in Victoria, as in other colonies in which Responsible Government is established, the Governor has unfettered power to appoint Executive Councillors, it being understood that when they cease to command confidence and support as a ministry, they will resign their seats in the Executive Council (see book of Colonial Regulations emanating from Downing-street). Practically, therefore, the Executive Council consists of those who, for any time being, are members of the Government, and whose advice in the Executive Council is sought by their colleagues, subject to the condition that the Governor only can appoint Executive Councillors.

THE LEGISLATIVE COUNCIL.

The number of members of the Legislative Council in Victoria is thirty. They represent six provinces; viz., the central, the south, the south-western, the western, the north-western and the eastern. At the first general election in 1856, five members were chosen for each province. Of these the one who received the lowest number of votes in each district vacates his seat after the lapse of two years; and each other seat is vacated in rotation, so that the member highest on the poll has a term of office of ten years. The member succeeding at each periodic vacation in like manner is elected for ten years. Occasional vacancies by resignation or death are supplied by the election of a member, who is entitled to a seat for the same term which could have been enjoyed by the member who has vacated the seat. The seat of a member accepting office of profit in the public service becomes *ipso facto* vacant, but such member may be re-elected. Public contractors cannot be members of council. A member can resign his seat by a letter addressed to the

Governor. Absence for a session without leave of the council; the making of any declaration or taking of any oath of foreign allegiance or obedience; bankruptcy; becoming a public defaulter; being attainted of treason or convicted of felony, or becoming *non compos mentis*, are declared by the Constitution Act to be *ipso facto* causes of vacation of the seat of a member.

The Council cannot be dissolved, but by its periodical reconstruction six-tenths of its members are changed in each period of six years.

Bills for the appropriation of the revenue cannot originate in the Council.

The privileges of the House are equal to those of the House of Commons; the Constitution Act having made it lawful for the Legislature of Victoria to define its privileges so as not to exceed those of the House of Commons, and the first act passed in the first session of the Legislative Council and Legislative Assembly having defined the privileges of the two houses to be those which appertained to the House of Commons when the Constitution Act was passed.

The Council elects its own President, but it is in the power of the Governor to disallow the choice made.

A member of the Council is required to be thirty years of age and a natural born subject of the Queen, to have held or been entitled to for a period of twelve months before his election, a freehold in the colony of the value of five thousand pounds, or of the annual value of five hundred pounds above all charges affecting the same respectively. No judge of any Court in the colony, nor minister of any religious denomination can be a member of Council, and no person attainted of treason or convicted of felony within any part of Her Majesty's dominions is capable of being elected a member. An elector in a province which returns a member of Council must be seised (within that province), at law or in equity of lands or tenements of the clear value of one thousand pounds, or of the clear yearly value of one hundred pounds, or must be entitled as lessee or assignee for any unexpired period of any term originally created for a period of not less than five years. Occupiers as tenants liable to a yearly rent of not less than one hundred pounds are also entitled to vote. Graduates of any University in the British dominions, barristers, solicitors, legally qualified medical practitioners, ministers of any religious denomination, schoolmasters producing testimonials of qualification to teach under the Commissioners of Education of Great Britain and Ireland, or testimonials of some competent Board appointed by the Government of Victoria; officers or retired officers of Her Majesty's forces, or of the East India Company's service, except on actual service, are also entitled to vote. No person attaining the age of twenty-one years after the 23rd November, 1857 is entitled to be registered as a voter unless he can read and write. All voters must be duly registered on the Electoral

Roll of the province. A general list is annually made of all who claim to vote up to the 14th January. Special claims are received and special lists made out of claims sent in before the 14th days of April, July and October in each year. The Act under which registration must be effected is the Act 21 Victoria, No. 33, passed in the first session of the "Parliament of Victoria," as by the Privileges Act, 21 Victoria, No. 1, the Legislative Council and Legislative Assembly of Victoria are entitled to be styled.

All elections for the Council where a poll is demanded are conducted by ballot, under the provision of the Act 19 Victoria, No. 12.

Unless bills which alter the Constitution of the colony are passed at the second and third readings by an absolute majority of the whole number of the members of the Council and Assembly respectively, they cannot be presented for the Royal Assent, and such bills when so passed are to be reserved for the signification of Her Majesty's pleasure thereon. This limitation is withdrawn from bills relating to qualifications of electors, establishment of new electoral provinces or districts, increasing the number of members, &c., as set out in the 61st clause of the schedule to the Statute 18 and 19 Victoria, cap. 55.

The members of the Council are entitled to the prefix of "Honorable," during the period of their being members.

THE LEGISLATIVE ASSEMBLY.

The Legislative Assembly is composed of sixty members, who are returned by thirty-seven electoral districts. Two important changes in the constitution of the Legislative Assembly have since become law.

The property qualification required by members has been abolished, and the right of voting at elections for members of the Assembly has been conferred on all male subjects of Her Majesty of the age of twenty-one years, not subject to any legal incapacity.

The privileges of the Assembly are equivalent to those of the House of Commons, the Constitution Act having enabled the Local Parliament to define its own privileges (not in excess of those of the House of Commons), and the first act of the Parliament of Victoria defined those privileges to be the same as at the time of the passing of the Constitution Act were held by the Commons House of Parliament.

The Speaker (entitled to the prefix of "Honorable") is elected by the Assembly. A member can resign his seat by a letter addressed to the Speaker.

The seat of a member of Assembly is necessarily vacated by reason of the same causes as are already enumerated with regard to the Council, and the same restriction exists in both chambers with regard to ineligibility of contractors.

The qualification of electors in an electoral district returning members to the Assembly has undergone considerable revision since the promulgation of the existing Constitution. By the Act 21 Victoria, No. 33, the suffrage is extended to all male natural born subjects of Her Majesty residing in any district, and to all who have been naturalised or made denizens in Victoria three years previous to the day on which they may claim to be registered. Only two months residence in any district is required before registration. Possession of a freehold of the value of fifty pounds, or of the annual value of five pounds, also gives a claim to vote in the district in which the freehold is situate, whether the owner be resident therein or not. No voter can vote twice at any election though he be registered under the "manhood suffrage" title as well as under the title of "freeholder." No person can be registered as a voter who has attained the age of 21 years subsequently to the 23rd November, 1857, unless he can read and write. A general list of electors is made up to the 14th January in each year, and special lists are also made of claims sent to the registrars of a district before the 14th of April, July and October respectively. The claims made are published, and may be objected to in the manner prescribed in the Act. The lists are revised by the Magistrates in Petty Sessions.

Elections are conducted by ballot. The Legislative Assembly originates all bills for the appropriation of the revenue and for imposing taxes, but may not do so for any purpose which shall not have been first recommended by a message from the Governor during the current session. No differential duties can be imposed by the Legislature on the same class of goods imported from different countries.

The Assembly may be prorogued or dissolved by the Governor, but twelve months cannot intervene between the last day of one session and the first day of the next.

GOVERNMENT DEPARTMENTS.

The following account of the various departments of the Government has been gathered from the most reliable and authentic sources. The various tables of statistics tell their own tale, and the arrangement of the varied particulars under their respective heads, will be found useful for ready reference, and at the same time furnish the means of forming an accurate judgment of the progress already made by this infant colony.

Had the arrangement of the various departments been adopted according to rank, it would have been as follows:— Chief Secretary, Law, Treasury, Public Works, Customs, and Post-office. The difficulty, however, in obtaining the details of the required information necessitated our printing off several sheets before the whole of the copy was prepared We think this apology may be necessary for an apparent error of arrangement.

LAW DEPARTMENT.*

The Attorney and the Solicitor General, who are at the head of this department, have duties of an important nature to perform. As the Law Officers of the Crown, they are the Grand Jurors and Crown Prosecutors for the colony, and have not only the power to file an information and conduct the prosecution, in those cases when a previous investigation has taken place, and a committal for trial has been directed by a bench of Magistrates; but possess, also, the power of filing an information against, and procuring, upon such information, the arrest of any individual whom they may suspect to be guilty of any crime, without any previous investigation before a Justice as to the merits of the case.

Connected with this power the Attorney General is, under the Act 7 Vic. No. 5, enabled to procure the discharge of any person committed for trial, if on reading the depositions he is of opinion that the evidence is insufficient to support a conviction.

The Law officers have the responsibility of advising the Crown, the heads of Departments, and Benches of Magistrates in all matters of a legal nature, or in cases where the law is doubtful, or open to misconstruction.

The preparation of bills of Parliament introduced by the Government also falls within their province.

The Attorney and Solicitor General have, moreover, the direction and general supervision of the branch of the Civil Service connected with the administration of justice, including the departments of the Crown Solicitor, the Prothonotary, the Master in Equity, the Sheriffs, the County Courts, Courts of Mines, General Sessions and Courts of Insolvency, the Courts of Petty Sessions, and Coroners.

CROWN SOLICITOR.

The Crown Solicitor, being at present absent on leave, the department is divided into two branches, one of which is managed by the Acting Criminal Crown Solicitor, and the other by the Acting Civil Crown Solicitor.

The duties of the Criminal branch are to draw all informations against prisoners committed from the different Police Courts for trial before the Supreme Court of Melbourne, and the various Circuit Courts throughout the colony; to prepare briefs for Prosecuting Counsel; to get up the cases on behalf of the Crown; and to attend the Courts for the purpose of instructing the Prosecuting Counsel, and generally to conduct

---

* The Staff of the Supreme Court, with names of Barristers, Attorneys, &c., are published under head of Law Department, in *Bradshaw's Guide*.

the criminal business of the Country appertaining to the Supreme Court.

The duties of the Civil Branch are to conduct all Railway Business, Conveyances, Feoffments. To conduct all actions and suits instituted or defended by the Government, and generally to act as the Attorney for the Government in all matters relating to civil business.

SHERIFF'S DEPARTMENT.

The duties of the Department are to enforce all the judgments of the Supreme Court whether the same be against persons or property; to summon jurors for the Supreme and Circuit Courts, and jurors and assessors for the County Courts and Courts of General Sessions; to control and regulate the gaols, and generally to take charge of the court houses and see that proper order and decorum are observed within their precincts.

When the office of Sheriff was undertaken by Claud Farie, in November, 1852, the duties were of a very light nature as compared with what they have now become. The annexed Return of the number of writs issued for execution during the last six years, with amounts recovered under them, and also of the correspondence of the office will best shew the increase in the business of the department. All the expenditure of the department throughout the whole colony, and all correspondence connected therewith (as well as the general correspondence with the Government and other departments of the Public Service), is controlled and conducted in the Sheriff's Office in Melbourne. The return of writs, &c., appended hereto applies only to the Melbourne office, and there are many others addressed to the Sheriff at Geelong and to the Deputy-Sheriffs direct (without passing through the Central office), on which large sums are collected. A statement is also appended of the strength of the department, shewing also the number of goals in the colony and the number of prisoners received into each during the years 1856 and 1857. The gaols mentioned are those only under the control of the Sheriff, but besides these gaols proper, there are a number of watchhouses throughout the country, under the control of the Police Department, which have been proclaimed as gaols where prisoners committed for trial at the courts of General Sessions are detained for trial, and some few short sentenced prisoners perform their sentences; as at Warrnambool, Belfast, Ararat, Dunolly, Carisbrook, Alberton, and Kilmore. There were three gaols in Melbourne until the beginning of the year 1858, now there are only two, namely, the Central Gaol, George Wintle, Governor; and the Western Gaol.

The Eastern Gaol is now abolished. The number of prisoners received into it in 1856 was 485, and in 1857, 397.

The Western Gaol is for female prisoners committed for trial, and sentenced to short periods of incarceration; and is also used for the reception of such male lunatics as cannot be taken in at the Asylum, and a number of sick and destitute vagrants. Long sentenced females are now kept on board the hulk Lysander, in Hobson's Bay, in charge of the Penal Department. The number of prisoners received into this gaol (Western), in 1856, were 964; and in 1858, 906.

The Central Gaol receives all male offenders convicted in the Supreme Court and in the respective courts throughout the colony, except short sentenced prisoners (sentenced at Circuit Courts) who perform their sentences in the country gaols. It is also a gaol for general purposes for prisoners of all grades. The number of prisoners received in 1856, was 2,103; in 1857, 2,544.

GEELONG.—The North Geelong Gaol is a receptacle for male prisoners. The South Geelong for females. The number of prisoners received into these gaols was, in 1856, 959; and in 1857, 1,158. Sheriff, Robert Rede.

SANDHURST.—A gaol for the reception of male and female prisoners. The number of prisoners received, in 1856, 547; in 1857, 829. Deputy-Sheriff, Richard Colles. This gentleman is Deputy-Sheriff for the Northern Circuit District, both Sandhurst and Castlemaine being within it.

BEECHWORTH.—A gaol for the reception of male and female prisoners. The number of prisoners received was, in 1856, 489; in 1857, 600. Deputy-Sheriff, William Gore Brett.

Number of prisoners confined in all the gaols:—In 1856, 6,459; in 1857, 8,490.

The following gentlemen are Stipendiary Magistrates at the places named and act also as Deputy-Sheriffs, but merely for summoning juries:—Kilmore, Andrew McCrae; Hamilton, Cuthbert Fetherstonhaugh; Alberton, C. J. Tyers; Warrnambool, Lewis Gilles; Belfast, George Stewart; Carisbrook, Frederick Call; Kyneton, William Lavender.

A RETURN of the number of writs executed by the Sheriff, with the amounts recovered under them; and of the correspondence connected with the business of the department from 1st January 1852 to 15th June 1858. Also of the number of insolvencies registered from 1st January 1854 to 15th June 1858.

Years.	Number of writs.	Amount recovered			Insolvencies.	Letters sent out.
		£	s.	d.		
1852	134	3,784	10	7	—	158
1853	865	28,545	7	1	—	590
1854	1,680	86,429	6	2	232	1,243
1855	2,304	45,667	1	10	394	1,916
1856	1,820	48,170	9	1	233	2,192
1857	1,349	36,359	17	9	276	2,338
To 15th June, 1858	676	11,916	8	3	244	1,144

SUPREME COURT.

The first Court in the district of Port Phillip, now the Colony of Victoria, was held in the year 1841, in a small brick building at the corner of King and Bourke-streets, west. The Hon. John Walpole Willis, previously one of the Judges of the Supreme Court at Sydney, being the then Resident-Judge. In 1843, Mr. Willis was removed, and Mr. Jeffcott arrived from Sydney as his successor. In 1845, Mr. Justice Jeffcott resigned, and was succeeded by Mr. Roger Therry, now on the Sydney Bench, who remained in office until the beginning of 1846, when he was succeeded by Mr. Justice A'Beckett, now Sir William A'Beckett.

On the 1st July, 1851, Port Phillip was separated from New South Wales, and in January, 1852, Mr. Justice A'Beckett became Chief Justice of the Supreme Court of the Colony of Victoria, under the Act 15 Vic., No. 10, which created the said Court. In the same month Mr. Justice Barry was raised to the Bench. In July of the same year, Mr. Justice Williams, who previously filled the post of Solicitor-General, was appointed third Judge, and in June, 1856, Mr. Justice Molesworth, Solicitor-General, was made fourth Judge. Sir William A'Beckett having proceeded to England on leave of absence, His Honor Mr. Justice Barry became acting Chief Justice, which office he held until Sir William's arrival, in 1854.

In 1857, Sir William A'Beckett retired on a pension, and William Foster Stawell, Esq., now Sir William Foster Stawell, the first Attorney-General of Victoria, which appointment he held up to that year, was appointed Chief Justice.

EQUITY AND INSOLVENCY BRANCHES.

The Insolvent Court was first established in 1842, under the Act of Council 5 Vic. No. 17, and the appointment of Chief Commissioner of Insolvent Estates conferred on William Verner, Esq., who opened an office in the immediate neighborhood of the Supreme Court. In 1843 the business was removed to the present Court House, being the chambers now occupied by His Honor Mr. Justice Molesworth. Up to the end of 1843 the Commissioner received the whole of the Court fees, and carried on the office without expense to the Government. In 1844 he and his officers were placed on fixed salaries, and the fees paid into the Treasury. In 1845 the system of payment was altered, fees being substituted for fixed salaries, which continued to the 1st January, 1847. In April, 1846, Mr. Verner resigned, and Robert Williams Pohlman, Esq. was appointed Chief Commissioner of Insolvent Estates. On 15th July, 1851, Mr. Pohlman was also made Master in Equity, which combined offices he continued to hold until April, 1852, when he was appointed Judge of the County Court. On the 19th April, 1852, Frederick Wilkinson, Esq. was appointed Master in Equity and Chief Commissioner of Insolvent Estates (which offices he now holds); and in 1854 the Ecclesiastical business was added to the Master's office, and the Ecclesiastical Records handed over to him.

Under the Act 5 Vic. No. 17, the creditors of an estate were empowered to elect trustees, of their own choice, but the 7 Vic. No. 19 substituted official assignees instead, which appointment is made by the Chief Justice. The creditors can still appoint a trade assignee if necessary, to act with the Official Assignee.

The present Official Assignees are:—Edward Courtney, appointed 10th September, 1850; Robert Elwall Jacomb, appointed 22nd October, 1853; Alexander Laing, appointed 2nd February, 1855; Henry Steel Shaw, appointed 11th June, 1856.

MASTER IN EQUITY.

The sealing of bills, issuing subpœnas, in fact all the machinery of the Supreme Court in its Equity and Ecclesiastical Jurisdictions, take place and are carried on in the office of the Master in Equity.

He has to draw up all decrees, orders, and rules pronounced and granted by the Court, and before any such decrees and orders, and before any letters of administration or probates can be issued, has to read through the whole of the papers filed by the solicitors, in order to make himself thoroughly acquainted with the whole case.

It is his duty to prosecute inquiries as to facts, take accounts, appoint receivers and guardians, take bonds of administrators and their sureties, examine titles, settle and approve of recognizances, and to superintend and carry out many other matters of detail of the most various description, referred to him by the Court. Such inquiries and references involving, not unfrequently, the consideration of questions of great nicety and difficulty.

Another duty attached to the office of Master, is that of taxing bills of costs in Equity, Ecclesiastical, and Conveyancing. The Master also fulfils the responsible duty of Accountant-General. All moneys ordered to be paid into Court being paid by him to the Receiver of Revenue (hitherto paid into one of the banks in his name to the credit of the particular cause or matter).

In this the Master is assisted by the Chief Clerk who taxes bills of costs, draws up decrees and orders of the Court, when time permits, takes the bonds of administrators and their sureties, keeps the accounts of all moneys paid into and out of court; and superintends, generally, the arrangements of the offices.

EQUITY.

Year.	Suits commenced by bill.	Suits by rule nisi	Answers filed.	Replications filed.	Rolls filed.	Ex parte Applications Petition filed.	Decrees issued and orders.	Writs of injunctions.	Writs of Ne exeat Coloniâ issued.
1841	8	—	1		—		2	1	—
1842	17	—	5	4	—	2	45	6	—
1843	7	—	10	7	—	1	15	1	—
1844	6	—	5	2	—	10	21	3	—
1845	11	—	7	3	—	9	44	2	—
1846	1	—	2	1	—	—	13	—	—
1847	5	—	4	1	—	3	10	1	—
1848	4	—	1	1	—	2	4	0	—
1849	18	—	6	3	—	1	49	3	1
1850	5	—	2	2	—	3	32	2	1
1851	5	4	5	3	—	1	28	3	2
1852	9	15	4	3	—	1	36	1	—
1853	10	93	7	3	—	6	111	11	5
1854	106	—	—	—	53	9	181	21	5
1855	161	4	—	—	87	26	256	42	—
1856	120	—	—	—	55	11	74	48	2
1857	119	—	—	—	65	11	231	16	—
1858 Jan. to Sep.	91	—	—	—	40	15	160	11	—

INSOLVENCY.

Year.	No. of Insolvents.			Liabilities as shown in the Insolvents' Schedules.			Assets as shown in Insolvents' Schedules.			Deficiency.			Meetings held before Chief Com.
	Voluntary	Compulsory.	Total.	£	s.	d.	£	s.	d.	£	s.	d.	
1842	104	10	114	212,805	1	9	143,862	0	0	68,943	1	9	
1843	119	4	123	468,467	8	0	215,410	7	5	253,057	0	7	
1844	43	3	46	94,097	0	4	76,884	1	8	17,212	18	8	
1845	11	0	11	37,405	16	9	12,117	9	9	25,288	7	0	
1846	24	2	26	127,024	15	8	5,098	3	5	121,926	12	3	
1847	11	2	13	2,106	18	11	1,001	5	2	1,105	13	9	
1848	21	3	24	17,452	3	8	4,068	18	2	13,383	5	6	
1849	29	1	30	35,721	18	8	6,089	6	1	29,632	12	7	
1850	27	9	36	32,323	18	4	17,154	9	6	15,169	8	10	
1851	18	3	21	16,060	2	2	10,703	5	2	5,356	17	0	
1852	6	2	8	12,856	9	4	4,274	18	4	8,881	11	0	
1853	17	6	23	38,430	9	6	23,364	14	7	15,065	14	11	
1854	175	29	204	974,955	9	9	758,178	9	11	216,776	19	10	
1855	175	53	228	827,701	17	2	680,795	17	3	146,905	14	11	1147
1856	65	46	111	863,008	1	4	211,337	13	5	152,265	7	10¾	760
1857	164	46	210	846,394	10	8	447,843	8	11½	398,551	1	9	810
1858 to 30 Sep.	399	35	434	582,799	0	0	376,518	2	2	212,281	16	11	937

ECCLESIASTICAL.

Year taken out.	Administration with the will annexed.	Administrations to next of kin.	Administrations to widows.	Administrations to creditors.	To Executors of next of kin of deceased.	To Attorneys of next of Kin.			Total amount of properties sworn under the various classes of administration.			Total in Probates.
	£	£	£	£	£	£	s.	d.	£			£
	10	38	64	15								88
1854	17370	22751	67030	10336		1000	0	0	126837	0	0	291083
	9	35	42	8	1	8			98			64
1855	18430	16635	37472	3030	3000	6908	17	1	69257	17	1	219585
		27	36	4	1	5						
1856		42278	25988	1450	35000	1820	0	0	106236	0	0	149799
	8	59	33	6		24						
1857	8010	57295	41493	2000		5304	0	0	114894	0	0	250739
		32	52	11		14						75
1858 to 30th Sep.		10459	30009	4340		2982	0	0	58890	0	0	158895

Return of the Business heard and disposed of by the Supreme Court in its Equity, Insolvency, and Ecclesiastical Jurisdictions, from 25th October 1853 to the 31st December 1857.

EQUITY.	From Oct 25, 1853.	1854.	1855.	1856.	1857.
Rules Nisi and Orders Nisi granted ..	32	28	21	14	10
Rules and Orders Nisi made absolute ..	4	10	16	8	8
Rules and Orders discharged	8	13	6	4	1
Bills dismissed on motion	—	3	17	16	20
Bills dismissed at the hearing	—	2	4	9	2
Decrees in suits commenced by Rule Nisi	11	20	1	—	—
Decrees in suits commenced by Bill ..	—	7	25	41	34
Decrees on further directions	—	1	1	7	10
Issues directed	1	1	1	1	3
Demurrers allowed	—	1	8	1	4
Demurrers overruled	—	2	3	5	2
Motions granted	14	40	52	63	55
Motions refused	2	11	23	26	17
Injunctions granted on motion	—	7	12	6	11
Injunction motions refused	—	12	10	10	5
Ne Exeats granted	—	1	1	2	—
Cases Struck out	—	6	4	10	5
Judgments reserved	4	—	5	11	18
Postponements	9	2	7	16	8
Pleas allowed	—	—	1	—	—
Pleas overruled	—	—	1	1	—
Rehearings Granted	—	—	3	1	—
Vesting orders granted	—	—	—	5	13
Appeals in Equity	—	—	—	3	7
Attachments granted	—	3	8	5	2
ECCLESIASTICAL.					
Motions for Probates and Administrations granted	—	270	223	203	250
Number of times the Court sat	21	75	84	104	154

PROTHONOTARY'S DEPARTMENT.

The Prothonotary is required to attend the Supreme Court at its sittings in banco, to take notes of the applications made on motion and the decision of the Court thereon; when ordered by the Court or a Judge, he has to examine witnesses, and to report thereon; and when an amount claimed is a matter of calculation, he has to ascertain and decide in the same manner as before a jury, upon inquiry, the amount of the damages. These proceedings are generally attended by Counsel, and the examination of the witnesses is sometimes very voluminous. He is required to settle bonds for security for costs, to settle commissions, to issue exemplifications and memorials of judgments when required to ground proceedings upon in the Courts of the neighbouring colonies.

In the absence of the Prothonotary from his office, all acts which he is required to do may be done by the Chief Clerk. The Prothonotary and Chief Clerk tax bills of costs, both between party and party, and between attorney and client, from ten o'clock to three every day, both in term and vacation. In the progress of this busines, nice questions arise upon what are called cross issues, requiring a careful analysis, and examination of the case, and of the evidence; and, under the act regulating the taxation of Attorneys' Bills of Costs, they have very often to investigate and decide upon long and complicated accounts.

The Prothonotary is also charged with the responsible duty of receiving and paying into the Treasury moneys paid into Court by suitors, and of paying the same out of Court, to those parties entitled to receive them, also of collecting and accounting for the fee fund, such moneys amounting to a large sum annually.

The following is a summary of the general duties performed in the Prothonotary's office :—To keep a roll of barristers and attorneys admitted to practice; to keep a record of all commissioners appointed; to keep a book containing the names and residences of attorneys and of parties sueing and defending in person; to file and record all criminal informations, indictments, and convictions; to prepare abstracts and to pay the expenses of witnesses attending criminal trials; to seal, enter, index, and issue all writs of summons, capias, replevin, all writs of execution and subpœnas; to file and enter all appearances; to record and index all judgments signed, warrants of attorney, cognovit actionem, and writs and orders of attachment; to receive all records and prepare lists of causes for trial; to prepare and issue all jury precepts; to file all affidavits used before the Court or the Judges, at chambers, or upon taxation of costs; to furnish office copies of all documents when demanded, to attend to office searches, and to produce documents when required before the Judges or Court; to make entries of all proceedings in causes; to file memorandum alleging error in fact, and to deliver note of receipt thereof; to receive and file all appeals and special cases, and, after hearing, to draw and issue the order of the Court thereon; to issue and record all rules of Court.

CRIMINAL BUSINESS.

Year.	Indictments Filed.	Prisoners Tried.	Prisoners Convicted. — Felonies. — Offences against the Person	Prisoners Convicted. — Felonies. — Offences against property	Prisoners Convicted. — Felonies. — Total	Prisoners Convicted. — Misdemeanors	Capital Convictions.
1851	242	233	20	132	152	18	1
1852	482	605	147	221	368	103	4
1853	920	781	187	312	499	63	20
1854	608	538	85	223	308	62	9
1855	468	489	41	96	137	84	10
1856	420	494	70	167	237	85	11
1857	552	704	120	254	374	51	20
1858 to June 30	358	429	33	199	232	54	6

CIVIL BUSINESS.

Year.	Writs of Summons Issued.	Causes entered for Trial or Inquiry.	Judgments signed.	Executions issued.	Rules of Court.	Bills taxed.	Money paid into Court. £	s.	d.	Money paid out of Court. £	s.	d.	Fee Fund. £	s.	d.
1851	440	90	102	78			698	15	7	706	9	7	2871	9	1
1852	767	136	100	79	334		3857	19	4	3854	14	4	4028	4	3
1853	1755	449	328	168	547	517	14898	9	3	12548	7	5	3404	18	1
1854	3155	1304	1543	1294	546	1813	30265	0	6	22104	11	9	9889	0	2
1855	5671	1107	2461	2090	631	2639	17101	5	11	24390	6	6	12087	13	8
1856	3246	625	1417	1298	528	1230	13512	0	7	11828	8	10	7377	7	6
1857	4260	654	1846	1454	574	1259	17213	14	1	20181	2	3	8395	1	4
1858 to 30 June	2646	370	1103	909	211	784	8334	14	8	7685	3	1	4352	14	0

SUPREME AND CIRCUIT COURTS.

The Criminal Sessions of the Supreme Court are held at Melbourne every Month, except January. Circuit Courts are held at Geelong, Ballaarat, Castlemaine, Sandhurst, Beechworth, and Portland.

COUNTY COURTS, COURTS OF MINES, AND COURTS OF GENERAL SESSIONS

Are held at the places indicated in page 16 of *Bradshaw's Guide.*

The following TABLE shows the number of cases tried annually in the various County Courts and Courts of General Sessions throughout the Colony, from 1853 to 1857, inclusive.

	1853.		1854.		1855.		1856.		1857.	
	General Sessions.	County Court.	General Sessions.	County Court.	General Sessions.	County Court.	General Sessions.	County Court.	General Sessions.	County Court.
Alberton					2		6	49	4	104
Ararat										202
Ballaarat	41	14	80	495	215	1259	209	1656	146	1674
Beechworth			70	22	83	230	126	298	124	666
Belfast	9	118	14	171	6	145	1	145	5	143
Carisbrook					67	269	47	283	72	301
Castlemaine	86	183	13	406	24	527	26	613	11	956*
Geelong	59	231	83	666	29	815	85	511	84	550
Hamilton			2	5		20		14		22
Kilmore	13	37	21	154	26	418	15	192	19	181
Kyneton				60		165		152	6	165
Melbourne	106	1184	178	5852	67	7857	28†	5615	33†	5498
Portland			3	36	11	96	5	57	5	154
Sandhurst			59	195	105	522	78	740	69	1251
Warrnambool					2	84	6	187	7	252

PETTY SESSIONS.

The number of places where Petty Sessions are held is eighty-one; of these, forty-four are attended by Resident paid Magistrates, twenty-two are visited by paid Magistrates, and at the remaining eighteen branches the Magisterial business is conducted altogether by the unpaid Justices of the Peace.

CORONERS.

The necessary information may be obtained from *Bradshaw's Guide*, page 19.

CITY POLICE COURT.

This court may be considered as divided into two branches, one for criminal and the other for civil prosecutions. The criminal court sits daily, presided over by Charles P. Hackett, Esq., Police Magistrate, in the absence on leave of E. P. Sturt, Esq., Resident Magistrate.

The duties of the criminal branch are to dispose of all cases

* During 1854-5-6-7, prisoners were not tried at Castlemaine General Sessions, and the numbers stated are appeal cases.

† Since the beginning of 1856 criminal cases have not been tried by Melbourne General Sessions.

appearing on the daily charge sheet of persons arrested for felony, misdemeanours and other offences. The following is a summary of the general detail of duties performed :—Taking depositions and forwarding same to the Attorney-General in cases of commitment for trial, binding over witnesses to appear and prosecute, preparing warrants of commitment, information in cases of felony, orders and convictions in cases summarily disposed of, preparation of weekly returns of all cases disposed of, time and place of arrest, by whom arrested, nature of the offence, before whom tried, money or other property found on the person of the prisoner, how disposed of, &c.

In this court, the hearing and consideration of applications are held for auctioneers', publicans', hawkers' and pedlars', and pawnbrokers' licenses, (see pages 76 and 77), within the city, preparation of accounts of all forms, penalties, fees, &c., received and paid into the Treasury weekly, courts of revision quarterly of electoral lists for the Legislative Council and Assembly. The total number of cases disposed of at this branch of the City Court from 1st January to 30th September, 1858, was 7,006.

The civil business of the City Court is presided over by Septimus Martin Esq., J.P., acting for Charles P. Hackett, Esq., Police Magistrate. The court sits daily in the hearing of cases of assault, disputes between masters and servants, offences under the Management of Towns Act, orders of maintenance, &c. The number of cases disposed of in this court, from 1st January 1858 to 30th September 1858, amounts to 6,010.

LAND AND WORKS.

The Board of Land and Works is formed of the President, Vice-President, Commissioner of Public Works, Surveyor-General, Commissioner of Roads and Bridges, and Commissioner of Railways. The department under the control of the President, and in his absence the Vice-President, are the Crown lands, including survey, sale and management of lands of the colony, roads and bridges, public works, railways, Aborigines, sewerage and water supply. The duties connected with the various branches of the department are defined by the Board of Land and Works Act, 21 Vic., cap. xxxi. ; ditto amendment, 22 Vic., cap. lviii. Crown Lands Acts (see Adamson). Her Majesty's Orders in Council of various dates. Thistle Prevention Act, 19 Vic., cap. xiv. Road Act, 16 Vic., cap. xl. and 17 Vic., cap xxix. Police (town and country) Act, 18 Vic., cap. xiv. Sewerage, 16 Vic., No. 38, and Amendment Act of last session, &c., &c.

The duties of the President and Vice-President are clearly defined by the Acts.

CROWN LANDS.

Of the facilities afforded for the permanent settlement of this increasing population, it may be stated that there had been sold, in 1851, 99,769 acres to 77,345 persons, being little more than an acre and a quarter to each, while the number alienated up to the end of 1857 was 2,748,415 acres, sold to 450,000 persons, at the rate of six acres to each. The computed area of Victoria is about 55,644,160 acres, of which, so far as the survey returns at present extend, it is known there remain 35,352,486 acres fitted for agricultural and grazing purposes.

During the four years ending 31st December, 1857, 1,781,847 acres of land realised the sum of £3,994,524, being at an average price of £2 4s. 10d. per acre. This apparently high average has been caused by the limited quantity brought into market, as compared with the demand; and also includes the prices, necessarily high, realised for town and suburban lands.

Gradually, however, the price of country lands is being reduced, and may, ere long, be obtained at the Government price of £1 an acre.

One great advantage with regard to the unsold agricultural lands of this country is, that, for the greater part, they lie within the area of settlement, and close to markets. This is in the main attributable to the manner in which the population has distributed itself in masses over the whole extent of the country, in consequence of the general diffusion of its metallic wealth; and it forms a striking contrast in this respect with the case of most other new countries, where much of the agricultural land is to be found only in places remote from the present or probable early settlement of a dense population.

The following table has been forwarded by the Hon. the Commissioner of Public Works and Lands, as an authentic statement taken from the books in Crown Lands Office, Melbourne:—

Area of land in the colony, acres ..	55,644,160
No. of holders of purchased land ...	10,260
Acres of purchased land in occupation ..	2,113,134
Acres in crop ..	237,729
Occupied acres of purchased land not cultivated	1,875,405
Quantity of land sold by the Crown during the last ten years	2,541,913
Quantity of land unsold ..	52,882,544
Amount realised by land sales during the last ten years ..	£6,636,555
Average price per acre for the last ten years ...	£2 12s. 2d.
Average price per acre for the year 1857 ..	£2 2s. 7d.

The Occupation Branch of the Survey Department has the general superintendence of the occupation of Crown Lands, for both pastoral and other purposes throughout the colony of Victoria, excepting on the gold-fields.

All information as to squatting stations, districts, and particulars regarding licenses and assessments on stock, and occupation generally, can be obtained at the Crown Lands Office. The revenue from pastoral licenses, assessment and occupation licenses, in the year 1858, amounted to over £250,000.

ROADS AND BRIDGES.

The subjoined facts relate solely to the works accomplished under supervision of the Government. In 1851, not a single mile of macadamised road had been made beyond the towns of Melbourne and Geelong. At the close of 1857, 450 miles of road had been formed, of which 270 are macadamised; 300 bridges had been erected, and some miles of viaduct had been constructed. The expenditure upon these main roads, and upon bridges, wharves, piers, and public buildings, from the 1st January, 1851, to 31st December, 1857, was £4,821,848. Besides this amount, the Department of Public Works has entered into liabilities, by contracts and otherwise, to the extent of £500,000, which sum has been provided from the General Revenue, for the formation and repairs of roads and bridges for the year 1858.

These public roads and the expenditure upon them are quite irrespective of the great number of improvements which have been affected in various parts of Victoria through the instrumentality of district road boards (statistics of which we hope to give in our next volume), supplied by funds raised by local taxation, supplemented by grants from the general revenue, and disbursed under the direct control and supervision of these popularly elected local authorities. The number of these appears to be constantly on the increase.

The following is a list of road districts in the colony of Victoria that have been proclaimed up to the 20th October, 1858:—Alberton, Bacchus Marsh, Ballaarat, Barrabool, Belfast, Broadmeadows, Brighton, Buninyong, Caulfield, Connewarre, Dandenong (there is no Board for this district), Dundas, Eltham, Epping, Gardiner, Hampden and Heytesbury, Hawthorne, Heidleberg (road trust), Lanniston and Edgecombe (Kyneton), Nunawading, Oakleigh and Mulgrave (there is no Board for this district), Portarlington, Portland, Templestowe, Warrnambool, Willoromaoin (Kilmore), Woodend and Tylden, (there is no Board for this district), Woodstock, Upper Yarra, (there is no Board for this district). Applications have been received at this office for the proclamation of road districts at Carlsruhe, Colac, Creswick, Greensborough and Upper Plenty.

New maps, indicating the roads, bridges and public buildings in Victoria are in course of preparation by the Government, but no correct document has been issued at present which would enable us to give the particulars.

POST OFFICE.

Prior to July, 1851, the Post Office at Melbourne was a branch of the Post Office Department in Sydney, and of the extent of its transactions no accurate details can at present be supplied.

Upon the separation of the province of Port Phillip from New South Wales, the Post Office was placed under the charge of Captain McCrae, under the title of Chief Postmaster, and subsequently, under the designation of Postmaster-General.

Almost simultaneously with the separation of the colonies, the discovery of gold in Victoria induced a rapid influx of population, and the business of the Post Office was suddenly augmented to an almost unprecedented extent, as exemplified by the following

Statistics shewing the number of letters and newspapers which passed through the General Post Office, the number of Post Offices, the revenue and expenditure of the department, and the number of persons on the Melbourne staff for the years 1851 to 1857 inclusive:—

Year.	No of Letters passed through General Post Office.	No. of Newspapers passed through General Post Office.	No. of Post Offices.	Revenue.	Expenditure.	No. of Persons on Melbourne staff.
1851	504,425	456,741	44	£7,929 9 1	£11,483 7 5	14
1852	972,126	709,837	46	12,458 12 9	25,812 0 0	35
1853	2,038,999	1,618,789	62	25,733 12 11	78,086 1 0	77
1854	2,674,384	2,394,941	95	66,949 4 7	143,462 14 4	86
1855	2,990,992	2,349,656	89	80,108 19 9	106,118 6 9	64
1856	3,220,614	2,906,141	125	34,951 0 11½	98,681 18 0	72
1857	3,899,981	2,981,970	152	77,662 12 1	96,242 11 9	77

In the year 1857, the number of letters delivered inland was, 2,415,938; and despatched to other countries, 1,484,048. The newspapers delivered inland were, 1,333,489; and despatched to other countries, 1,648,581.

Previously to the inauguration of Responsible Government in Victoria the Post Office was under the control of the Colonial Secretary, and at the period stated, it was transferred to the charge of the Treasurer, who became its responsible head, and this arrangement continued until April, 1857, when the Post Office became a separate department, and, together with the Electric Telegraph Department, was placed under the control of a Responsible Minister, the details and general superintendence being confided to a Secretary, whose appointment is a permanent one.

The Rules and Regulations under which the business of the Post Office Department is conducted, are comprised in Acts 17 and 18 Victoria, Nos. 30 and 31.

The Rates of Postage chargeable in Victoria will be found in a comprehensive table published by the Post Office authorities, and inserted monthly in *Bradshaw's Guide to Victoria*, also regulations in reference to the postage of Newspapers; transmission of gold in letters; soldiers' and sailors' letters; exemptions; books and packets; unpaid, insufficiently paid, and irregularly posted letters; unclaimed letters; list of post towns, with closing of mails, and distances from Melbourne, &c.

In the month of July, 1858, a bill was introduced into the Legislative Assembly by the Hon. Dr. Evans, postmaster-general, and is now in force, for legalizing the issue and payment of Post Office Money Orders under certain regulations which will be found inserted in the monthly manual mentioned above.

The rapidly increasing business of the General Post Office, Melbourne, and the insufficient accommodation afforded in the old building, which had been enlarged so often as to render it unsightly, and unsuitable for the prompt performance of the work required, has necessitated the erection of a new edifice that shall serve for a Metropolitan Post Office for many years to come, and provide ample space for the public and the employés. The Legislature voted £25,000 for this purpose on the estimates of 1858, and a further sum of £30,000 is provided on the estimates of 1859. The Government advertised for plans, offering three premiums,—one for £300, one for £200, one for £100, for the best architectural designs, and similar premiums for the internal arrangements. Thes prizes were awarded, as follows:—.

	Architectural design.		
1st prize,	Messrs. Crouch & Wilson	...	£300.
2nd „	Mr. A. E. Johnson ...	...	£200.
3rd „	Mr. William Elsdon ...	...	£100.
	Internal arrangement.		
1st „	Mr. E. Romanis ...	..	£300.
2nd „	Mr. A. E. Johnson ...	...	£200.
3rd „	Messrs. Weaver & Kemp	...	£100.

It is understood to be the intention of Government to call for tenders forthwith, for the erection of the new structure, and it is probable that the centre of the City of Melbourne will shortly be adorned by a Post Office building worthy of Victoria.

CHIEF SECRETARY.

The departments of the Public Service under the control of the Hon. the Chief Secretary, are the Police, Penal Establishments, Gaols, Gold fields, Registration, and Statistics, Agriculture, Science, Electoral and Registration of Voters, Medical, Sanatory, Lunatic Asylum, Patents, and the Registration of Friendly Societies.

In the office of the Chief Secretary is transacted all government business relating to Municipalities (28 in number), and various local institutions. Certificates of Naturalization are prepared in this office, and also all Commissions, Patents, Writs and other documents under the Great Seal of the colony. The *Government Gazette* is compiled in this office.

Correspondence with the Governments of the other Australian colonies and New Zealand and with the Colonial Agent-General, as well as the ordinary miscellaneous correspondence with the public, is conducted in this office.

REGISTRAR-GENERAL'S DEPARTMENT.*

The Registrar-General's department was formed in the year 1853, in accordance with the provisions of the Act of Council 16 Vic., No. 26, commonly known as the "Registration Act." This measure enjoined—

1st. The division of the colony into registration districts, of which there are at the present time one hundred and twenty-three. And

2ndly. The appointment of one or more Registrars to each.

3rdly. The obligation on the part of the Registrars to record in the manner prescribed, and to make returns in the months of January, April, July and October to the chief office, Melbourne, of all cases of birth and death, without charge to the public individually.

4thly. That ministers of all denominations should in like manner register and make returns of all marriages solemnised by them.

When a birth, or death or marriage is registered, the particulars are entered on two different sheets, and the Registrar and the party or parties interested sign both sheets. One of these sheets is retained by the clergyman or Registrar, and the other one, literally agreeing with the former, is sent to the

* An account of the organization of this department by Mr. W. H. Archer, A.R.G., is given in pages 112, 113, and 114, of his *Statistical Register of Victoria*, 1854.

Registrar-General's office at the close of every quarter, and after careful examination as to errors or discrepancies is preserved there as a public record.

All children should be registered within sixty days after birth. The Registration Act requires (under a penalty for neglect) that the parents of a child born, or the occupier of the house wherein any birth or death may happen, shall give notice of such birth or death to the Deputy Registrar of the district.

Every person dying should be registered before the funeral takes place, so that the Deputy Registrar may give a certificate of registration to the undertaker, who after the body is buried, is required to attest place and date of interment. The importance of this proceeding may be estimated by sec. xxv. of the Act, where it is enacted that certified copies of registers or entries of registers, shall be received as *primâ facie* evidence in any Court of Justice,—" provided that no entry of the register of any death shall be received as evidence of the fact of such death, unless there shall also be an entry of the register of the burial."

As every inhabitant of the colony may, at some time or other be interested in knowing the precise time of some birth or death, and, as a complete system of registration will prevent much litigation in future years, and otherwise protect individual rights of property, besides throwing light on many social questions as to duration of life among children and the upgrown population, to the increase of statistical science, and the general advantage of the inhabitants of Victoria, it is of the utmost importance that the public should cordially co-operate in carrying out the registration system to its fullest extent.

All letters or packets on registration business to the Registrar General, or any of the Deputy Registrars, provided the sides are open, pass through the Post Office free of charge.

The number of names registered in the Birth, Death, and Marriage Index Books, numbered in July, 1858, about 112,000, and may be said to relate in some way or other to almost every family in the colony. The public has access to these carefully and methodically kept records from ten till four o'clock daily. The fee required for a search is 2s. 6d., and for a certificate 5s., in accordance with a proclamation made in the *Government Gazette* on the 28th day of April, 1854.

VACCINATION.

Under the provisions of the Act, 18 Vic., No. 4, commonly known as the " Vaccination Act," the colony has also been divided into districts, and public vaccinators have been appointed in each, who respectively attend on certain days of the week to vaccinate such children as may be brought to them for that purpose. A notice on such occasions is given by the vaccinator to the parents or guardians to take the children again for inspection on the eighth day following, under a penalty. After the successful vaccination of any child, the vaccinator gives a certificate to that effect to the parent or guardian, and forwards a duplicate to the Deputy Registrar of Births and Deaths for the district.

The Deputy Registrar on his part is required within twenty days after the registration of any birth, to give notice (on a printed form), to the parent or guardian to have the child vaccinated, and of the days and hours in each week that the Government vaccinator attends for that purpose, and on the certificates of successful vaccination being forwarded to him, to keep a register in duplicate of all such cases, one to be forwarded to the Registrar-General's office quarterly, and the other to be retained by himself. Such registers are open for public inspection gratis, and copies of entries are furnished on payment of the fee of 1s.

The fee to vaccinators paid by Government is 2s. 6d. for each successful case, and to Deputy Registrars 1s., for each entry of successful vaccination. The number of vaccinators is about ninety.

The public Vaccinators are also empowered to give certificates to the parents of the child not being in a fit state to be vaccinated, or being insusceptible of the vaccine disease: but the successful cases are the only ones of which any record is kept by the Deputy Registrar.

Any legally qualified medical practitioner, not being a public vaccinator, may vaccinate, but must give a certificate of each successful case to the parent or guardian and forward a duplicate to the Deputy Registrar of the district to be entered in his register.

Parents or guardians refusing to have their children vaccinated after having received a proper notice from the Deputy Registrar, or neglecting to appear before the vaccinator on the eighth day following, are liable to a penalty of 40s., which may be increased to £5.

PATENTS.

20 Vic., No. 3.

All letters patent granted by the Colonial Government are registered in the Chief Secretary's Office, and become operative from the day on which the specification is left at the office of the Chief Secretary.

The original specifications and drawings, and model (if any) are transferred by the Chief Secretary to the custody of the Registrar-General at the expiration of the six months' protection allowed by the act. The specifications are open to the inspection of the public during the usual office hours. Fee, one shilling.

No assignment of any patent, whether in whole or part, is legally valid without having been recorded in the Registrar-General's office.

AGRICULTURAL AND OTHER STATISTICS.

By a well-organised agency an account of live stock, agricultural produce, and other important particulars connected with the material prosperity of the colony, are taken annually by this department.

REGISTERED IMPORTED LIVE STOCK.

Quarterly returns of Registered Imported Live Stock are likewise received, and are published in the *Gazette*, in accordance with Act of Council 19 Vic., No. 21

FRIENDLY SOCIETIES.

Yearly abstracts of the experience of sickness and mortality occurring in Friendly Societies, as well as returns of their income and expenditure, are deposited there in accordance with Act 18 Vic., No. 41.

RAILWAYS.

A yearly return of shareholders of the Melbourne and Hobson's Bay Railway is open for inspection on the payment of 1s. for each inspection, in accordance with 16 Vic. (private Act), sec. 7.

INQUESTS.

All the depositions of inquests, from the year 1839 to the present time, have been transferred from the Attorney-General's department to this office, and the public can have access to the alphabetical indexes daily, without charge.

ELECTORAL ACT.

Under the Electoral Act, the Election Auditors are required to forward all election accounts to this office, where they are always open to inspection; and copies may be had on payment of a fee of 2s. 6d. for first 100 words, and 1s. for every 200 words over the first 100 words, in accordance with 21st section of 19th Vict., No. 11.

DEED BRANCH.

All grants from the Crown issued by the Government are copied, enrolled and examined here. A general index of the same is also kept for the use of the legal profession. Certified copies of Crown grants are made for proof of title &c., and likewise, certified copies of memorials, and of certificates to naturalize.

SUPREME COURT REGISTRY.

This office having been removed, now forms a branch of the Registrar-General's Department, and the public have access thereto during the usual office hours, for the purpose of registration of deeds of conveyance, mortgages on real property, liens on wool, mortgages on stock, &c. In the searching room, Crown grants, memorials of all deeds of conveyance, mortgages, &c., are kept with indexes for the convenience of parties searching for incumbrances. The fees of this branch are regulated by Act of Council.

GOLD-FIELDS OF VICTORIA.

For purposes of administration, the gold-fields are divided into six mining districts, which are again formed into sub-divisions. In each mining district there is a Mining Board, a staff of Wardens, Chinese Protectors, &c., and a Court of Mines.

The Mining Boards each consist of twelve members, who are elected for a term of twelve months by the miners residing in the several divisions; and these Boards are empowered to make bye-laws for regulating mining operations throughout their respective districts.

Disputes arising out of mining operations are adjudicated upon either by the Warden in charge of the division (with or without assessors, at the option of the disputants), or by the Court of Mines, which is presided over by a Judge, and is held periodically in various parts of the district. An appeal from the decision of a Warden, or Warden and assessors, to the Court of Mines is allowed, under certain restrictions. (Act 21 Vict. 32, sec. 84.

With reference to the following tables, it is to be observed that, independently of the effects produced by the opening of new ground, the population of the gold-fields fluctuates considerably at different periods of the year, being limited in various localities by the supply of water necessary for mining operations, as well as for the consumption of the population. The returns are furnished to the Government fortnightly, and being made up from minute details sent in from the local government officers, are found to be very close approximations —sufficiently so for all practical purposes. The general correctness of them may be gathered from the trifling difference between the estimated population on the 1st January, 1857. and the enumerated population according to the census taken on the 31st March following. Thus, for the Ballaarat district, the estimate was 49,000, and the enumeration 47,728; for the Castlemaine district the estimate and enumeration were respectively 28,500 and 31,331; for the Sandhurst district the Warden's estimate was 32,221, and the census returns showed the population to be 32,417.

Hitherto the pursuit of mining has not partaken, to any considerable extent, of a scientific character, and doubtless much labor has been uselessly expended, yet the nett results have been so astounding, that the gold-fields may justly occupy the first rank. The subjoined tables present at one view the rise, progress, and yield of the several auriferous districts.

Attention has been already called to the necessity of collecting and concentrating the engineering skill now within reach, and steps are in progress for the prosecution of the mining interest upon a more extended scale.

GOLD FIELDS OF VICTORIA.

RETURN OF THE ESTIMATED POPULATION OF THE VARIOUS MINING DISTRICTS IN JANUARY OF EACH YEAR.

District.			Other than Chinese.				Chinese.				Total.			
			Men.	Women.	Childrn.	Total.	Men.	Wom.	Child.	Total.	Men.	Women.	Childrn.	Total.
Ballaarat ..	January,	1852	180	25	50	255	..	..	..	..	180	25	50	255
,,	,,	1853	5,900	900	850	7,650	..	..	..	..	5,900	900	850	7,650
,,	,,	1854	15,550	3,050	3,600	22,200	..	..	..	..	15,550	3,050	3,600	22,200
,,	,,	1855	20,270	4,965	6,265	31,500	..	..	..	..	20,270	4,965	6,265	31,500
,,	,,	1856	40,300	2,500	4,430	47,230	3,296	2	2	3,300	43,596	2,502	4,432	50,530
,,	,,	1857	25,005	7,000	12,000	44,005	4,990	2	3	4,995	29,995	7,002	12,003	49,000
,,	,,	1858	29,485	7,130	11,405	48,020	5,694	..	6	5,700	35,179	7,130	11,411	53,720
Castlemaine	,,	1852	19,000	3,150	2,850	25,000	..	..	..	..	19,000	3,150	2,850	25,000
,,	,,	1853	19,000	3,700	3,300	26,000	..	..	..	..	19,000	3,700	3,300	26,000
,,	,,	1854	17,110	3,270	4,550	24,930	..	..	..	..	17,110	3,270	4,550	24,930
,,	,,	1855	12,080	2,994	3,896	18,970	..	..	..	..	12,080	2,994	3,896	18,970
,,	,,	1856	18,600	4,650	5,500	28,750	7,000	2	5	7,007	25,600	4,652	5,505	35,757
,,	,,	1857	14,600	3,950	5,150	23,700	4,800	..	..	4,800	19,400	3,950	5,150	28,500
,,	,,	1858	15,201	4,653	6,116	25,970	7,400	..	..	7,400	22,601	4,653	6,116	33,370
Avoca ..	,,	1852	..	..	..	..	..	..	..	..	..	..	..	..
,,	,,	1853	..	..	..	..	..	..	..	..	..	..	..	..
,,	,,	1854	..	..	..	..	..	..	..	..	..	..	..	..
,,	,,	1855	11,425	1,683	1,918	15,026	..	..	..	..	11,425	1,683	1,918	15,026
,,	,,	1856	17,600	3,600	5,600	26,800	3,200	..	..	3,200	20,800	3,600	5,600	30,000
,,	,,	1857	30,970	6,000	9,930	46,900	1,750	..	..	1,750	32,720	6,000	9,930	48,650
,,	,,	1858	33,907	5,766	11,387	51,060	5,140	..	..	5,140	39,047	5,766	11,387	56,200
Sandhurst ..	,,	1852	..	..	..	..	..	..	..	..	..	..	..	..
,,	,,	1853	15,000	1,500	500	17,000	..	..	..	..	15,000	1,500	500	17,000

,,	,,	1854	15,950	5,600	3,600	25,150	..	..	..	..	15,950	5,600	3,600	25,150
,,	,,	1855	15,525	3,895	3,480	22,900	..	..	..	..	15,525	3,895	3,480	22,900
,,	,,	1856	7,000	4,000	2,479	13,479	5,021	..	..	5,021	12,021	4,000	2,479	18,500
,,	,,	1857	11,000	8,000	9,000	28,000	4,221	..	..	4,221	15,221	8,000	9,000	32,221
,,	,,	1858	10,760	4,930	5,630	21,320	4,180	..	..	4,180	14,940	4,930	5,630	25,500
Beechworth	,,	1852	..	..	..	..	..	..	..	..	..	..	..	..
,,	,,	1853	4,000	800	200	5,000	..	..	..	..	4,000	800	200	5,000
,,	,,	1854	6,750	1,045	380	8,175	..	..	..	..	6,750	1,045	380	8,175
,,	,,	1855	3,730	445	670	4,845	..	..	..	..	3,730	445	670	4,845
,,	,,	1856	4,355	881	1,020	6,256	36	..	..	36	4,391	881	1,020	6,292
,,	,,	1857	9,620	1,997	1,969	13,586	2,850	..	..	2,850	12,470	1,997	1,969	16,436
,,	,,	1858	13,385	3,376	2,477	19,238	4,180	..	..	4,180	17,565	3,376	2,477	23,418
Anderson's Ck.	,,	1852	..	..	..	..	..	..	..	..	..	..	..	..
,,	,,	1853	..	..	..	..	..	..	..	..	..	..	..	..
,,	,,	1854	..	..	..	..	..	..	..	..	..	..	..	..
,,	,,	1855	..	..	..	..	..	..	..	..	..	..	..	..
,,	,,	1856	1,300	30	70	1,400	..	..	..	..	1,300	30	70	1,400
,,	,,	1857	1,080	60	110	1,250	..	..	..	..	1,080	60	110	1,250
,,	,,	1858	1,200	100	150	1,450	..	..	..	..	1,200	100	150	1,450
Total	,,	1852	19,180	3,175	2,900	25,255	..	..	..	..	19,180	3,175	2,900	25,255
,,	,,	1853	43,900	6,900	4,850	55,650	..	..	..	..	43,900	6,900	4,850	55,650
,,	,,	1854	55,360	12,965	12,130	80,455	..	..	..	..	55,360	12,965	12,130	80,455
,,	,,	1855	63,030	13,982	16,229	93,241	..	..	..	..	63,030	13,982	16,229	93,241
,,	,,	1856	89,155	15,661	19,099	123,915	18,553	4	7	18,564	107,708	15,665	19,106	142,479
,,	,,	1857	92,275	27,007	38,159	157,441	18,611	2	3	18,616	110,886	27,009	38,162	176,057
,,	,,	1858	103,938	25,955	37,165	167,058	26,594	..	6	26,600	130,532	25,955	37,171	193,658

Note.—Previous to the gold-fields of Sandhurst and Avoca becoming of such extent and importance as to render their formation into separate districts necessary, the population was included in the Castlemaine returns.

The above return gives the population of the several districts as bounded prior to the commencement of the present year. Since that date, considerable alterations have been made, as will be seen on reference to the return of the distribution on 24th April.

Return of the distribution of the Population of the various Gold-fields in the month of January of each year.

Locality.	Total in January of each Year.						
	1852	1853	1854	1855	1856	1857	1858
Ballaarat—							
Ballaarat	..	5,800	18,700	15,715	26,500	14,000	19,000
Buninyong	255					12,900	12,000
Creswick	..	1,850	3,500	15,785	13,300	7,450	6,000
Smyth's Creek ..	..					7,700	13,000
Steiglits & Mount Egerton ..	..	..	..	..	700	1,850	1,800
Fiery Creek ..	..	..	..	..	10,030	5,100	1,920
Total ..	255	7,650	22,200	31,500	50,530	49,000	53,720
Castlemaine—							
Castlemaine	..	..	..	..	..	2,500	2,850
Barker's Creek	..	..	..	..	..	700	800
Campbell's Crk.	25,000	26,000	15,330	10,770	14,457	2,000	3,600
Forest Creek	..	..	..	..	..	6,000	7,850
Maldon or Targr.	..	..	..	1,200	..	2,150	5,670
Fryer's Creek ..	..	..	4,000	5,200	10,800	7,500	5,150
Tarradale ..	..	..	..	..		2,000	1,850
Hepburn or Mt. Franklin ..	..	..	5,600	1,800	3,000	4,050	4,650
Mount Blackwood	..	..	..	..	7,500	1,600	950
Total ..	25,000	26,000	24,930	18,970	35,757	28,500	33,370
Avoca—							
Avoca	..	..	..	4,500	6,000	2,200	3,250
Maryborough ..	..	..	..	8,000	9,000	17,000	9,000
Amherst ..	..	..	..	1,400	7,400	2,800	5,250
Dunolly, Moliagul and Korong ..	..	..	..	1,126	7,600	24,200	11,130
Ararat ..	..	..	..	..	..	2,450	21,050
Pleasant Creek ..	..	..	..	..	..	..	6,520
Total ..	..	..	..	15,026	30,000	48,650	56,200
Sandhurst—							
Sandhurst ..	..	17,000	20,950	22,000	17,400	29,951	21,310
Heathcote ..	..	..	3,500	900	1,100	1,750	2,190
Waranga ..	..	..	700			520	2,000
Total ..	..	17,000	25,150	22,900	18,500	32,221	25,500
Beechworth—							
Beechwth., 3-Mile & Snake Valley	..	5,000	1,845	2,570	2,200	8,005	13,237
Woolshed ..	..	..	330	325	2,040	4,960	4,111
Yackandandah ..	..	..	..	1,300	1,700	2,571	3,243
Buckland ..	..	..	6,000	650	352	900	2,216
Omeo ..	..	..	..	..	..	..	611
Total ..	..	5,000	8,175	4,845	6,292	16,436	23,418
Anderson's Ck.—							
Anderson's Creek and Caledonia	..	..	..	..	1,400	1,250	1,450

See notes attached to return of population, p. 51.

Return of the distribution of the Population of the various Gold-fields on the 24th April, 1858.

Locality.	Popn.	District.
Avoca ..	2,775	Maryboro'
Amherst ..	4,200	do.
Ararat ..	10,650	Ararat.
Armstrong's and G.W. Diggings	5,000	do.
Anderson's Crk. and Caledonia	1,450	Castlemaine
Ballaarat North	17,000	Ballaarat
Buninyong ..	11,500	do.
Brown's ..	4,000	do.
Barker's Creek. See Castlemne.	..	Castlemaine
Beechworth and Spring Creek..	8,629	Beechworth
Buckland ..	1,818	do.
Creswick ..	8,500	Ballaarat
Carngham ..	4,000	do.
Castlemaine, Barker's, Campbell's & Forest Creeks ..	15,130	Castlemaine
Caledonia. See Anderson's Ck.	..	do.
Campbell's Crk. See Castlem.	..	do.
Cochrane's ..	1,500	Maryboro'
Dunolly and Sandy Creek..	5,030	do.
Fryer's Creek ..	11,442	Castlemaine
Forest Crk. See Castlemaine.	..	do.
Fiery Creek. See Raglan. ..	..	Ararat
G. W. Diggings. See Armstrg's.	..	do.
Heathcote ..	3,500	Sandhurst
Hepburn or Mt. Franklin ..	5,200	Castlemaine
Korong ..	1,450	Maryboro'
Kilmore ..	155	Sandhurst
Linton's ..	4,000	Ballarat
Mount Egerton	200	do.
Mt. Misery. See Woady Yallock	..	do.
Mt. Blackwood	1,000	do.
Maldon or Tarrg.	4,720	Castlemaine
Mount Franklin. See Hepburn	..	do.
Maryborough ..	12,500	Maryboro'
McCallum's ..	2,500	do.
Omeo ..	587	Beechworth
Pleasant Creek..	20,000	Ararat
Raglan or Fiery Creek ..	1,820	do.
Steiglitz ..	1,300	Ballarat
Smyth's Creek .	4,550	do.
St. Arnaud ..	650	Maryboro'
Sandy Crk. See Dunolly ..	..	do.
Sandhurst ..	20,645	Sandhurst
Spring Crk. See Beechworth ..	..	Beechworth
Snake Valley ..	2,928	do.
Tarradale ..	1,000	Castlemaine
Tarrangower. See Maldon ..	..	do.
Three-Mile Crk.	1,767	Beechworth
Woady Yallock & Mount Misery	1,100	Ballaarat
Waranga ..	1,200	Sandhurst
Woolshed ..	3,293	Beechworth
Yackandandah..	2,772	do.

Return of the Population of the various Mining Districts on 24th April, 1858.

District.	Other than Chinese.				Chinese.	Total.			
	Men.	Wom.	Chil.	Total.		Men.	Wom.	Chil.	Total.
Ballaarat ..	29,550	7,600	12,000	49,150	8,000	37,544	7,600	12,006	57,150
Castlemaine	21,433	3,922	5,460	30,815	8,127	29,560	3,922	5,460	38,942
Maryboro'	18,070	3,013	6,022	27,105	3,500	21,570	3,013	6,022	30,605
Ararat ..	23,880	4,350	5,570	33,800	3,070	26,950	4,350	5,570	36,870
Sandhurst ..	12,070	5,030	5,740	22,840	2,660	14,730	5,030	5,740	25,500
Beechworth	12,927	3,430	2,277	18,634	3,160	16,087	3,430	2,277	21,794
Total ..	117930	27,345	37.069	182344	28,517	146441	27,345	37,075	210,861

RETURN shewing the quantity of Gold received by Government Escort from the various Gold-fields of the Colony, from September, 1851, to 30th April, 1858.

Year.	Castlemaine and Out-Stations.		Sandhurst and Out-Stations.		Maryborough and Out-Stations.		Ballaarat and Out-Stations.		Beechworth and Out-Stations.		Year.	Total.	
	ozs.	dwts.	ozs.	dwts.	ozs.	dwts.	ozs.	dwts.	ozs.	dwts.		ozs.	dwts.
1855	536,708	7	372,737	10	287,195	4	736,777	5	198,979	13	1855	2,182,397	19
1856	372,864	10	599,066	10	327,238	10	992,241	15	334,557	10	1856	2,625,968	15
1857	315,777	0	525,017	17	348,547	0	946,329	10	345,349	0	1857	2,481,020	7
Apr. 30, 1858	129,494	5	155,623	0	92,517	15	309,327	15	89,182	0	Apr. 30, 1858	776,144	15
											1851	104,154	0
											1852	1,145,829	0
											1853	1,491,436	0
											1854	1,476,666	7
Total	1,354,844	2	1,652,444	17	1,055,498	9	2,984,676	5	968,068	3	..	12,233,617	3

For the first three months in 1855, the gold received from Sandhurst and Maryborough is included under the head of Castlemaine, the first mentioned places, previous to 1855, having been considered in the Castlemaine district.

Previous to 1855, the present subdivision of districts did not exist; the total quantity received from the gold-fields collectively is therefore only given. Castlemaine district includes Maldon and Blackwood;* Sandhurst district includes Heathcote* and Rushworth;* Maryborough district includes Avoca,* Amherst,* and Dunolly;* Ballaarat district includes Creswick,* Fiery Creek,* Ararat,* and Pleasant Creek;* Beechworth district includes Buckland* and Yackandandah.*

The Escorts from the places marked thus (*) are fortnightly, the rest weekly.

Return of the amount of gold forwarded by other than the Government Escorts, from the various gold-fields.

Name of Escort.		1852 ozs.	1853 ozs.	1854 ozs.
South Australian	.	230,256	94,276	...
Melbourne (Private)	...	900,941	395,846*	...
New South Wales	...	...	84,346	21,066
Total ...	...	1,131,197	574,468	21,066

Note.—Particulars of Gold and Mining will be found in other parts of the work—*vide* contents.

MEDICAL DEPARTMENT.

The Chief Medical Officer has the general control and superintendence of the lunatic asylum at Yarra Bend; the sanitary station at Point Nepean; the health officers' establishment at Queenscliffe; the immigration hospital at Batman's-hill; the provision of medical attendance, medicines, and medical comforts for the Government immigrants and the prisoners at the gaols and lockups throughout the colony; the payment of medical witnesses, in cases where persons are charged with lunacy; the execution of the provisions of the Compulsory Vaccination Act; the Central Board of Health; and the Medical Board of Victoria. The Chief Medical Officer is also chairman of the board appointed to administer the police reward fund; chairman of the board of visitors to the lunatic asylum; and a member of the board appointed to inspect newly-arrived immigrant vessels.

The Chief Medical Officer attends the prisoners, wardens, &c., in the stockades at Pentridge and Collingwood, and the gaols and watchhouses in Melbourne; and the Government immigrants in depôt or hospital at Melbourne. The prisoners confined in the penal hulks, Hobson's Bay, and watchhouses in Williamstown, are attended by the District Surgeon, Williamstown; and at Geelong, the District Surgeon attends the prisoners in the gaols and watchhouses, the Government immigrants, and the military. At Castlemaine, Sandhurst, Ballaarat, Beechworth, Kyneton, Ararat, Portland, Belfast, Warrnambool, and Port Albert, yearly contracts are made with resident practitioners for providing medical attendance and medicine for Government immigrants and prisoners. At other places, medical men attending prisoners are paid according to the following scale of fees, viz.:—For medical or surgical attendance, inclusive of all necessary medicines, within any city or township, 10s. 6d. per visit. At night double this fee. Travelling expenses, 10s. 6d. per mile, for each mile after the first. For minor surgical operations, £2 2s. The scale of payment

* Of this amount 2,823½ ounces were taken from the escort by armed bushrangers.

for capital operations to be submitted to the Chief Medical Officer. For examination of insane persons, and giving the necessary evidence and certificates, one guinea for each case; mileage at 2s. per mile.

Vaccination.—Under the Act 18 Vict., No. 4, which makes compulsory the vaccination of all children within three months after birth, public vaccinators are appointed for the vaccination of the children of those persons who are unable to pay, and applications for such appointments are made to the Chief Medical Officer. The fees allowed to public vaccinators by the Government are 2s. 6d. for each successful case of vaccination. The parents or guardians of children neglecting to have them vaccinated within the time stated are liable to a penalty of from two to five pounds. By the Act 21 Vict., No. 37, occupiers of houses where any case of small-pox occurs, and medical practitioners, to whose knowledge any case may come, are to report the same within twenty-four hours to the Local or Central Board of Health, under a penalty of twenty pounds.

YARRA BEND LUNATIC ASYLUM.

The Asylum is situated on one of the bends of the river Yarra, about four miles from Melbourne; and contained, on the 26th June, 1858, 433 patients—257 male and 176 female. The staff consists of the surgeon superintendent, a house steward and storekeeper, a dispenser, a matron, two cooks, a gardener, a carpenter, a carter, three laundresses, twenty-six male and fourteen female attendants. The Asylum was first opened in October, 1848, and at the end of that year contained only twenty patients. Since then, the number of patients has rapidly increased, the admissions during 1857 being 139. The original stone buildings were only constructed to accommodate sixty-four lunatics, but considerable additions have since been made; these additions being of a temporary nature, in consequence of the proposed construction of a new Asylum, on a site better adapted for the purpose than the present one.

The patients are provided with many means of amusement, such as cricket, skittles, football, and other out-door games; a library; billiards, bagatelle, cards, draughts, music, &c.; and a concert is got up once a week, concluding with a dance, at which a considerable number of the patients amuse themselves. Those who are able and willing to work are also employed in various useful ways about the Asylum.

The establishment is inspected each week by one of the official Visitors, and once in each month by the Board of Visitors. The Asylum is open to visitors from 10 till half-past 11 a.m. on Sundays, and from 10 to half-past 12 a.m., and from 2 to 4 p.m., on other days, subject to certain regulations. Not more than three visitors are permitted to inspect the Asylum at one time, and all visitors are to enter their names in the visitors' book. Visitors are not to enter into conversation with any of the patients without the sanction of the superintendent.

The following are the regulations necessary to be observed in procuring the admission of patients, with the scale of charges for such as enter as pay-patients, viz.:—A petition is to be signed by some relative or friend of the lunatic, and appended to a certificate of insanity, signed by two *legally qualified medical practitioners*. The papers are then to be submitted for the approval of one of the Judges of the Supreme Court, and, when thus completed, forwarded to the Chief Medical Officer, Melbourne, from whom information can be obtained as to when the patient can be admitted into the Asylum. In the case of pay-patients, the charges for maintenance are—1st class, £2 per week; 2nd class, 25s. per week; payable quarterly to the surgeon superintendent of the Lunatic Asylum, and a bond for the regular payment of whichever amount may be agreed upon is to be entered into by two responsible persons, and deposited with the superintendent. In the case of those patients whose friends are unable to pay for their maintenance in the Asylum, a certificate to that effect, signed by some respectable person acquainted with the circumstances of the lunatic, is to be annexed to the petition. The forms of petition, certificate, and bond can be obtained from the Chief Medical Officer, or the Surgeon Superintendent of the Asylum.

HEALTH OFFICER, QUEENSCLIFFE.

This officer is provided with a boat's crew of six men, and his duties are to board all vessels not intercolonial traders, arriving at the Port Phillip Heads, in order to ascertain whether any infectious disease exists on board, or whether there is any necessity for placing the vessel in quarantine. Masters of vessels passing through the Port Phillip Heads without being first cleared by the Health Officer are liable to severe penalties under the quarantine laws. The average detention of each vessel whilst being "hove-to" for the Health Officer is only about thirteen minutes.

SANITARY STATION, POINT NEPEAN.

This station is situated at the entrance of the Port Phillip Heads,and when the new buildings, which are now in progress, are completed, will consist of five separate hospitals, each capable of accommodating one hundred patients, with the officers' quarters, &c. The staff consists of a surgeon superintendent, a clerk and storekeeper, a nurse, and three laborers.

Vessels placed in quarantine by the Health Officer are taken within the limits of the quarantine anchorage, and have all the sick landed on the sanitary station; and, after performing the quarantine directed by the Governor in Council, and being thoroughly cleansed and fumigated, are allowed to proceed to their destination without having to wait in quarantine for the convalescence of the sick, who are detained in hospital till their recovery, and then forwarded to their destination. During the year 1857, eleven vessels were placed in quarantine: three from small-pox, four from typhus fever, two from scarlet fever, and two to perform quarantine of observation. Three hundred and ninety-six persons were landed on the station during the year, and the average detention of each vessel was about six days. The establishment has been found very efficacious in extinguishing and preventing the spread of the diseases for which the vessels were detained.

CENTRAL BOARD OF HEALTH.

The Central Board of Health is constituted to superintend the administration of the Public Health Act, 18 Vict., No. 13. The execution of the Act in the various districts to which its provisions are extended devolves upon local Boards of Health, which are invested with powers for the management of sewers and drains, the removal of nuisances, regulation of offensive trades, and generally for the promotion of the sanitary interests of the districts under their respective control.

The Corporations of Melbourne and Geelong, and the Council of any Municipal district to which the Act is extended, are, *ex officio*, the Local Boards of Health within their respective limits; but if the Act is extended to any other town or district without such limits, the Local Board of Health is appointed by His Excellency the Governor.

The provisions of the Public Health Act have been extended to the following towns, viz.:—Melbourne, Geelong, Williamstown, Emerald Hill, East Collingwood, Castlemaine, Prahran, Richmond, Sandhurst, Ballaarat, Warrnambool, Portland, St. Kilda, Ballaarat East, Queenscliffe, and Beechworth; in all these the Municipal Councils are the Local Boards of Health.

Local Boards are required by the Public Health Act to report the appearance of any infectious or contagious diseases to the Central Board, who are empowered to make and cause to be enforced such regulations as they may deem necessary for the prevention or mitigation of such diseases. The Central Board are also empowered to regulate the building or opening of hospitals, and to receive and determine appeals which may be made by any person against any order or regulation of any Local Board of Health, and generally to provide for the conservation of the public health, and the advancement of the sanitary interests of the colony.

MEDICAL BOARD.

The Medical Board of Victoria is established under an Act of the Governor and Legislative Council of New South Wales

(8 Vict., No. 8.), for the registration and publication of the names of legally qualified medical practitioners.

The qualifications necessary to registration as a legally qualified medical practitioner are defined in the Acts of Council, 2 Vict., No. 22, 8 Vict. No. 8, 9 Vict. No. 12, and 17 Vict. No. 14 (Adamson, fol. 1057—61), by which it is enacted that no person shall be deemed a legally qualified medical practitioner unless he shall have proved to the satisfaction of the Medical Board that he is a doctor or bachelor of medicine of some university, or a physician or surgeon licensed and admitted as such by some college of physicians or surgeons of Great Britain or Ireland, or a member or licentiate of the company of apothecaries in London or Dublin; or is or has been a medical officer, duly appointed and confirmed, of Her Majesty's sea or land service; and that any person desirous of being declared a legally qualified medical practitioner as aforesaid, shall submit his degree, diploma, or proof of his being so duly qualified, for the examination and approval of the said Medical Board, by whom a certificate of qualification will be granted.

Graduates of foreign universities are admitted as legally qualified medical practitioners, on complying with the requirements of the Act, 17 Vict No. 14, as follows:—The applicant must produce proof, satisfactory to the Medical Board, that he has followed a regular course of professional study in some medical or surgical school, college, or university, for at least four years, and must submit to the Board a diploma testifying to his being a graduate in medicine or surgery of some university which requires a residence of at least one year previous to graduation. The applicant must also have obtained the certificate and taken the oath required to be taken by the law relating to aliens in this colony. (Adamson, fol. 1075., 11 Vict., No. 39.)

Persons desirous of registration as legally qualified medical practitioners must, if residing within twenty-five miles of Melbourne, attend *personally* at the monthly meeting of the Medical Board, which is held on the first Monday in every month, at the Medical Department in Melbourne, submitting for inspection and approval of the Board their proofs of qualification, as above.

Medical practitioners residing at a distance of more than twenty-five miles from Melbourne, can obtain registration by making personal application to the President of the Board in Melbourne, at any period during the usual hours of business, on producing the necessary proofs of qualification, and making a declaration before a magistrate, a form of which can be obtained on application to the secretary.

A list of the names of legally qualified practitioners is published at the commencement of each year, and supplementary lists are published immediately after each meeting of the Board.

PENAL ESTABLISHMENTS.

The penal department in Victoria was formed by Mr. Samuel Barrow, in July, 1850, in anticipation of the separation of the district of Port Phillip from New South Wales, prior to which all prisoners convicted in this district were forwarded to Sydney.

Only one establishment (the Pentridge Stockade) was then required, of which Mr. Barrow was appointed Superintendent, but the number of prisoners so greatly increased, after the discovery of gold in Victoria, that several new establishments were formed, and Mr. Barrow was, on the 1st July, 1853, appointed Inspector-General of Penal Establishments in Victoria, which office he held until the 24th of January, 1854, when he was appointed Immigration Agent, and was succeeded by Mr. John Price, for many years previously commandant of Norfolk Island; this gentleman continued at the head of the department until the 26th of March, 1857, when he was murdered by a gang of convicts, on the works at Gellibrand's Point, and was succeeded by the present Inspector-General, Mr. William Thomas Napier Champ, formerly Chief Secretary of Van Diemen's Land, whose appointment dates from the 3rd of June, 1857.

The following return, "A," shews the number of prisoners on the 30th June and 31st December in each year, together with their cost and earnings.

Return "B" is a copy of one recently furnished to the Government, and shews the classification and condition of the prisoners in confinement, on the 31st of March last, who were then distributed as follows:—Pentridge Stockade, 606 males; Collingwood, 342 do.; Hulk "President," 78 do.; Hulk "Success," 90 do.; Hulk "Lysander," 19 do.; Hulk "Sacramento," 76 Females. Total, 1211.

There were also 17 children on board the "Sacramento," belonging to the female prisoners.

The prisoners have been employed as follows:—at Pentridge, in the first instance, in making the Sydney Road, between Melbourne and Pentridge, and subsequently in erecting buildings for their own accommodation, making clothing, boots, tools, and other mechanical work. At Collingwood, in quarrying stone and breaking metal. At Richmond, in making the road from Melbourne to the Bridge, near the Yarra at Hawthorne. At the Marine Stockade, in forming the streets of Williamstown. At the hulk "Sacramento," for a short period on the Geelong and Melbourne Railway, and subsequently, in conjunction with the prisoners from the hulk "Deborah," "Success," and "Lysander," at Gellibrand's Point, in quarrying stone, building the jetty, battery, and other works at that place. On board the hulk "President" the prisoners have never been sent to labor, having been retained in separate confinement, as have likewise those on board the "Success" since July 1857.

All the penal prisoners whom it was deemed safe to keep at labor were transferred from the Hulks to Pentridge and Collingwood Stockades during the latter part of 1857, so that the only male prisoners now confined on board the hulks are those penal prisoners whom it is deemed unsafe to work, and the seamen committed for offences on board their vessels.

At the latter end of December last, female prisoners, who had previously been confined in a most unsuitable building in Melbourne, were transferred, as a temporary arrangement, to the hulk "Sacramento," which had been previously vacated by the transfer of the men to Pentridge Stockade; the average number on board during the year has been 75 women and 16 children.

Several serious attempts to escape have been made, none of which, however, have been successful. In September, 1853, the gang at Gellibrand's Point attempted to rush upon the guard, but were fired upon and several of them wounded, three having to submit to amputation of the leg. Again in October, 1856, a daring attempt was made by a party of ten convicts, who seized the boat in which they were being towed from the works to the hulks, and murdered two boatmen, who resisted them; three of them were subsequently convicted of the murder, but were respited in consequence of some legal informality. Then in March, 1857, the gang from the "Success" hulk set upon and murdered the Inspector-General, Mr. Price, while on the works, having forced him down a declivity where they were sheltered from the fire of the guards, they then broke their irons with the intention of escaping, but were deterred and reduced to subordination by the steadiness of the guards and police who came to their assistance: fifteen of the ringleaders in this outrage were committed for trial, of whom seven were subsequently hung.

By the regulations now in force, prisoners under sentences of less than three years are restored to freedom, if they are attentive and industrious at work, and their general conduct in confinement is irreproachable, when they have completed two thirds of their sentences; prisoners under longer sentences receive tickets of leave, if well conducted, when they have served one half of their sentences; these tickets of leave enable them to reside and work for their own advantage in any district in the colony they may select; but places them under the surveillance of the police, to whom they are required to report their residences. If they continue to conduct themselves properly, they are restored to freedom when they have served for a period equal to one-third of the time they originally served in the gang.

B.—Numerical Return of Prisoners confined in Penal Establishments in the Colony of Victoria on March 31, 1858, showing their Offences, Sentences, Conduct, and Previous Condition.

Offence.	Periods of Sentences.										Conduct.					Before convicted in Colony.				Known to have been convicted before arriv. in Col.
	Life	15 yrs. and up.	12 yrs. and u. 15	10 yrs. and u. 12	7 yrs. and u. 10	5 yrs. and u. 7	3 yrs. and u. 5	1 year and u. 3	un. 1 year	Total.	Good.	Generally Good.	Unsatisfactory.	Bad.	Total	Once.	Twice.	3 Times and up.	Total.	
Males.																				
Murder..	1	6	..	..	..	..	..	..	..	7	4	3	..	..	7	..	..	..	..	2
Assault with Intent to Murder ..	..	4	2	..	2	..	..	1	..	9	3	5	1	..	9	..	..	..	..	7
Manslaughter	..	1	1	7	14	3	3	1	..	30	15	14	1	..	30	2	..	..	2	16
Shooting or Wounding with Intent	..	3	..	10	10	2	4	4	..	33	17	14	2	..	33	5	..	..	5	17
Cutting and Wounding	..	1	..	..	..	..	3	1	1	6	6	..	..	..	6	..	..	..	..	3
Stabbing	..	..	..	2	1	..	..	1	..	4	..	4	..	..	4	1	..	..	1	..
Rape	1	6	..	2	..	..	..	..	..	9	4	3	1	1	9	..	..	..	..	2
Assault with Intent to commit Rape	..	..	..	3	1	1	2	2	..	9	5	4	..	..	9	..	..	..	..	3
Assault on a Child	..	1	..	2	2	..	4	..	..	9	5	4	..	..	9	..	..	..	..	2
Unnatural Offence	..	6	..	1	..	..	..	..	..	7	..	5	1	1	7	2	..	..	2	4
Attempting an Unnatural Offence	..	..	..	1	..	..	2	..	..	3	2	1	..	..	3	..	..	..	..	..
Highway Robbery	..	9	8	9	3	5	1	..	..	35	4	20	6	5	35	4	..	..	4	28
Robbery in Company	..	16	8	31	16	5	1	1	..	78	21	40	13	4	78	10	1	..	11	42
Assault and Robbery	..	8	11	9	18	6	2	1	..	55	18	21	13	3	55	7	1	..	8	28
Robbery	..	9	13	16	7	8	4	11	1	69	20	30	11	8	69	6	..	..	6	32
Assault with Intent to Rob ..	..	4	1	3	2	1	1	2	..	14	2	3	7	2	14	3	..	..	3	9
Assault with Intent to do Grievous Bodily Harm	..	..	..	..	1	2	3	3	..	9	7	2	..	..	9	..	..	..	..	1
Burglary	..	1	..	7	12	13	8	..	..	41	19	17	4	1	41	10	3	..	13	18
Arson	..	..	..	1	..	1	..	3	..	5	3	2	..	..	5	..	..	..	..	1
Perjury	..	..	..	..	..	..	1	2	..	3	2	1	..	..	3	..	..	..	..	1
Horse Stealing	..	8	9	48	113	60	6	..	..	244	70	129	34	11	244	17	1	..	18	87
Unlawful Possession of Horses ..	..	..	..	..	3	2	3	3	2	13	6	6	1	..	13	..	1	1	2	7
Cattle Stealing	..	..	..	3	6	15	1	..	..	25	19	6	..	..	25	2	..	..	2	7
Stealing in or from a Dwelling ..	..	..	..	2	6	26	22	17	2	75	34	30	6	5	75	14	3	1	18	20

Stealing from the Person	..	..	2	1	1	17	9	9	1	40	20	17	2	1	40	6	..	1	7	14
Stealing	..	..	3	4	4	7	7	19	9	53	24	21	6	2	53	18	5	..	18	16
Receiving Stolen Goods	..	1	1	1	4	4	4	6	3	24	11	9	4	..	24	4	2	..	6	9
Feloniously Entering a Dwelling	..	..	..	..	6	..	..	..	1	7	3	4	..	..	7	..	..	..	..	..
Aiding and Abetting	..	..	..	1	..	..	..	..	..	1	..	1	..	..	1	..	..	..	..	1
Forgery	..	..	1	1	3	2	3	3	..	18	10	3	..	..	18	..	1	..	1	3
Uttering	..	..	4	1	1	2	7	4	..	19	8	8	3	..	19	4	..	..	4	7
Fraud	..	..	..	1	1	..	1	..	..	3	1	1	..	1	3	..	..	..	..	1
Embezzlement	..	..	..	..	..	..	1	4	..	5	5	..	..	..	5	..	..	..	..	..
Obtaining Goods or Money by False Pretences	..	..	..	..	..	2	1	6	..	9	7	2	..	..	9	2	1	..	3	1
Larceny	..	..	..	..	1	6	11	52	24	94	58	29	4	3	94	18	7	4	29	34
Assault	..	..	..	..	..	..	..	2	2	4	3	1	..	..	4	2	..	..	2	1
Misdemeanor	..	..	..	..	..	..	..	3	2	5	3	2	..	..	5	3	..	..	3	3
Vagrancy	..	..	..	..	..	..	..	21	22	43	28	11	4	..	43	14	3	3	25	16
Insubordination in the Army	..	..	..	..	..	1	4	..	..	5	3	2	..	..	5	..	..	..	..	..
Offences against the Mercantile, Marine, and Police Acts	..	..	..	..	..	..	..	..	17	17	17	..	..	..	17	..	..	..	..	..
Total	2	84	64	167	238	191	119	182	87	1184	487	475	124	48	1184	149	34	10	198	452
Females.																				
Murder	..	..	..	..	1	..	..	..	..	1	1	..	..	..	1	..	..	..	..	..
Attempting to Murder	..	..	..	..	..	..	1	..	..	1	..	1	..	..	1	..	..	..	..	..
Robbery	..	..	..	..	..	..	..	1	..	1	1	..	..	..	1	..	..	..	..	..
Uttering	..	..	..	..	..	..	..	1	..	1	1	..	..	..	1	..	..	..	..	..
Stealing from the Person	..	..	..	..	..	..	..	13	2	15	13	2	..	..	15	1	2	4	7	9
Obtaining Goods or Money by False Pretences	..	..	..	..	..	..	..	..	1	1	1	..	..	..	1	..	..	..	..	..
Stealing in a Dwelling	..	..	..	..	..	..	..	..	1	1	1	..	..	..	1	..	..	1	1	..
Larceny	..	..	..	..	..	..	1	1	13	15	15	..	..	..	15	1	..	3	4	3
Vagrancy	..	..	..	..	..	..	..	5	34	39	32	3	..	4	39	..	6	21	27	20
Assault	..	..	..	..	..	..	..	..	1	1	..	..	..	1	1	..	..	..	..	..
Total	..	..	..	..	1	..	2	21	52	76	65	6	..	5	76	2	8	29	39	32
Grand Total	2	84	64	167	239	191	121	203	139	1210	552	481	124	53	1210	151	42	39	232	482

A.—Return of Penal Establishments in Victoria.

Establishment.	Date of Opening of each Establishment.	1850. Prisrs. confined.		1851. Prisrs. confined.		1852. Prisrs. confined.		1853. Prisrs. confined.		1854. Prisrs. confined.		1855. Prisrs. confined.		1856. Prisrs. confined.		1857. Prisoners confined.		
		Jun 30	Dec. 31	Jun 30	Dec. 31	Jun 30	Dec. 31	Jun 30	Dec. 31	Jun 30	Dec. 31	Jun 30	Dec. 30	Jun 30	Dec. 31	Jun 30	Decem. 31	
		M.	M.	M.	M.	M.	M.	M.	M.	M.	M.	M.	M.	M.	M.	M.	M.	F.
Pentridge Stockade ..	5th Dec., 1850 ..	..	60	67	29	98	145	229	260	278	368	398	430	448	435	359	600	..
Collingwood Stockade..	3rd Feb., 1853 ..	..	..	..	..	..	..	90	102	118	237	307	297	287	353	345	364	..
Richmond Stockade ..	1st August, 1852 ..	..	..	..	..	..	51	53	45	51	49	..†	..	..	..	..	..	..
Marine Stockade ..	9th Sept., 1853 ..	..	..	..	..	..	..	..	95	140	138	..†	..	..	..	..	..	..
Hulk "President" ..	15th Dec., 1852 ..	..	..	..	..	..	85	89	96	79	78	80	80	78	45	78	79	..
Hulk "Deborah" ..	20th January, 1853..	..	..	..	..	..	..	92	166	139	163	..†	..	..	..	..	..	..
Hulk "Success" ..	1st July, 1853 ..	..	..	..	..	..	..	99	126	129	130	129	127	136	109	114	80	..
Hulk "Sacramento" ..	31st October, 1853 ..	..	..	..	..	..	..	..	79	118	127	126	122	106	121	123	..	58
Hulk "Lysander" ..	24th March, 1855 ..	..	..	..	..	..	..	..	..	..	..	243	290	267	283	202	84	..
Totals	.. ..	..	60	67	29*	98	281	652	969	1052	1290	1283	1346	1322	1346	1221	1207	58

	1851. £ s. d.	1852. £ s. d.	1853. £ s. d.	1854. £ s. d.	1855. £ s. d.	1856. £ s. d.	1857. £ s. d.
Cost of the Penal Establishments ..	3,172 7 4	17,583 8 0	74,281 16 6	117,198 10 1	90,288 1 5	90,399 13 8	73,413 1 10
Value of labor performed by prisoners	2,380 4 0	7,046 4 7	45,882 7 4	59,490 8 4	55,644 7 2	61,423 0 10	‡47,710 1 10½

* At the close of the year 1851, nearly all the prisoners were returned to Her Majesty's Gaol, in consequence of the difficulty experienced in procuring officers and guards, caused by the rush to the gold-fields.

† In the month of March, 1855, the Richmond and Marine Stockades and the hulk "Deborah" were abandoned, and on the 30th September, 1857, the hulk "Sacramento" was vacated by male prisoners, and occupied by female prisoners at close of same year.

‡ The reduction in the value of labor performed by prisoners in 1857, compared with 1856, was in consequence of their not being lowed to labor as usual after the murder of the late Inspector-Gen., in March, they being in a very excited state for some weeks after.

Under the heading of "Good" (p. 62) are included all prisoners against whom no offence has been recorded while in confinement. Under that of "Generally Good," such as have committed one or two trifling offences against discipline, but have otherwise conducted themselves with propriety. Under that of "Unsatisfactory" are those who have committed several offences, and whose general conduct has not been good. Under that of "Bad" are those men who have exhibited no disposition to conform to discipline, or who have committed serious crimes since their original conviction.

POLICE FORCE.

This force is organised under the provisions of the 16 Vict., No. 24, and the 17 Vict., No. 25. It consists of a Chief Commissioner, appointed by virtue of clause 2 of 16 Vict., No. 24, who has the entire management of the establishment, and the following grades:—Paymaster and Commissioner, Inspecting Superintendent, Superintendents, Inspectors, Sub-Inspectors, Sergeants, and Constables; also 1st, 2nd, and 3rd class detectives.

All vacancies in the grades above that of Constable, and up to and including that of Superintendent, are filled by promotion from the next inferior grade.

The advantages resulting from the whole force, throughout the colony, being under the control of one Superintending authority, whether that authority be an officer holding the position of Chief Commissioner or a Board of Commissioners, are obvious. Prompt circulation of reports of crime and descriptions of offenders, is thereby secured, and criminals are prevented from evading justice by removing from one locality to another. It is also advantageous that the whole of the Constabulary should be subject to the same regulations as regards appointments, promotions, rewards and punishments, drill, arms, &c. Statistical information can be more easily obtained by the Police, without materially interfering with their legitimate duties. A cordial and zealous co-operation is ensured between the police throughout the colony, and the extra duties devolving upon the department, such as escorting treasure and prisoners, carrying despatches that may be of importance to the Government, &c., &c., are easily and economically combined with the regular duties. Further, members of the force otherwise adapted for the service, but who, from local causes, may not be in a position to carry out their duties efficiently, at a particular station, can be readily transferred to other localities, and as every member of it is furnished with a complete equipment, including arms of the most improved description, the police force is rendered easily available, in case of need, as a disciplined and armed body.

The force is divided into Mounted and Foot, the latter

being sub-divided into ordinary foot police, water police, and detectives.

The territory of Victoria, for police purposes, is divided into a certain number of police districts, and each district into sub-districts or stations, which are further divided into beats or patrols. This division it must be observed, is one introduced simply for the purpose of facilitating the internal administration of the force, and although the divisions are called police districts, they differ from those proclaimed, from time to time in the *Gazette*, as police districts. The latter would be more correctly termed petty sessions districts.

Each district is under the charge of a Superintendent (who, as a rule, is in the Commission of the Peace), or an Inspector, acting as Superintendent. The officers in charge communicate direct with the Chief Commissioner, to whom they look for instructions.

The arrangement of police districts, and sub-districts or stations, with the strength of police at each, on the 1st June, 1858, is shewn in the following table:—

Station.	Officers.	Mount.		Foot.	
		Sergnt.	Cnstbl.	Sergnt.	Cnstbl.
Melbourne District—					
City proper	4	..	..	17	157
E. Collingwood	..	..	..	1	12
Emerald Hill	..	..	..	1	10
Sandridge	..	..	..	1	8
Bourke District—					
Richmond	1	..	8	1	2
Hawthorne	..	..	..	..	8
Kew	..	..	..	..	1
Boroondara	..	..	..	..	1
Brighton	..	..	2	1	3
Dandenong	..	..	1	1	..
Frankston	..	..	1	..	..
Point Nepean	..	..	2	..	..
Richmond Twnp.	..	..	..	2	9
Heidelberg	..	..	2	1	1
Caledonia	..	..	1	..	1
Yan Yean	..	..	2	1	..
Footscray	..	..	..	..	8
Williamstown	..	..	..	2	15
Flemington	..	..	..	..	8
Kellor	..	..	2	..	4
Sunbury	..	..	1	..	..
Deep Creek	..	..	1	..	..
Aitkin's Gap	..	..	2	..	1
Wyndham	..	..	1	..	1
Brunswick	..	..	..	1	2
Northcote	..	..	..	1	2
Oakleigh	..	..	1	..	..
St. Kilda	..	..	..	1	9
Prahran	..	..	..	1	6
South Yarra	..	..	..	..	2
Broadmeadows	..	..	1	..	1

Station.	Officers.	Mount.		Foot.	
		Sergnt.	Cnstbl.	Sergnt.	Cnstbl.
Bourke District—continued.					
Anderson's Creek	..	..	1	..	1
Eltham	..	..	1	..	1
Essendon	..	..	..	..	1
Pentridge	..	..	..	..	1
Preston	..	..	..	..	1
Geelong District—					
Geelong	3	1	10	6	26
Do. Water Police	..	..	..	1	5
Kildare	..	..	..	1	9
Batesford	..	..	1	..	1
Inverleigh	..	..	1	..	..
Shelford	..	..	2	..	..
Steiglitz	..	..	1	1	1
Queenscliffe	..	..	1	..	..
Meredith	..	..	1	..	2
Colac	..	..	1	..	1
Lethbridge	..	..	1	..	1
South Barwon	..	..	..	..	3
Ballaarat District—					
Ballaarat	2	..	8	2	22
Do. E. Munpalty.	..	..	..	1	10
Do. W. do.	..	..	..	1	6
Junction	..	..	..	..	2
Smyth's Creek	..	..	2	..	2
Buninyong	..	..	2	1	2
Burnt Bridge	..	..	..	..	1
Burrumbeet	..	..	1	..	..
Black Lead	..	..	..	..	2
Clunes	..	..	..	..	2
Carngham	..	..	2	..	3
Mount Egerton	..	..	1	..	..
Creswick	..	..	3	1	5

Station.	Officers.	Mount. Sergnt.	Mount. Cnstbl.	Foot. Sergnt.	Foot. Cnstbl.
Carlsruhe District—					
Carlsruhe	1	..	2	1	3
Gisborne	..	..	2	1	3
Bacchus Marsh	..	..	2	1	..
Black Forest	..	..	2	..	..
Lancefield	..	..	2	..	..
Woodend	..	..	1	..	1
Malmsbury	..	..	1	..	1
Ballan	..	..	2	..	1
Blackwood	..	..	2	..	1
Kyneton	1	..	2	1	3
Castlemaine District—					
Castlemaine	3	1	11	1	12
Do. Municipity	..	..	..	2	15
Mount Franklyn	1	..	2	..	3
Porcupine	..	..	1	..	1
Elphinstone	..	..	1	..	1
Golden Point	..	..	..	..	2
Pennyweight Hill, Vaughan	..	..	..	..	3
Maldon	..	..	2	1	3
Fryer's Creek	..	..	1	..	3
Forest Creek	..	..	..	..	3
Harcourt	..	..	1	..	1
Tarradale	..	..	1	1	2
Sandhurst District—					
Sandhurst	3	1	12	2	18
Do. Municipity	..	..	..	2	17
Robinson Crusoe	..	..	2	1	2
Golden Square	..	..	..	..	3
Eagle Hawk	..	..	2	1	4
Axedale	..	..	2	..	..
Epsom	..	..	..	..	3
White Hills	..	..	..	..	6
Serpentine Creek	..	..	2	..	..
Lockwood	..	..	2	..	..
Bullock Creek	..	..	2	..	..
Myers's Flat	..	..	2	..	2
Avoca District—					
Avoca	1	..	3	1	7
Lexton	..	..	2	..	1
New Bendigo	..	..	2	..	1
Navarre	..	..	2	..	..
Carisbrook District—					
Carisbrook	1	..	3	..	10
Maryboro'	1	..	2	..	12
Dunolly	..	..	3	1	5
Havelock	..	..	..	..	4
Amherst	..	..	2	1	4
Burnt Creek	..	..	..	..	2
The Springs	..	..	1	..	1
Wedderburne	..	..	1	..	1
Goldboro'	..	..	..	..	2
Wimmera District—					
Canton Lead	1	..	11	2	14
Pleasant Creek	..	..	2	1	13
Glenorchy	..	..	2	..	..

Station.	Officers.	Mount. Sergnt.	Mount. Cnstbl.	Foot. Sergnt.	Foot. Cnstbl.
Wimmera District—continued.					
Raglan	1	..	2	..	3
Horsham	..	1	2	..	..
Bwanga	..	..	1	..	..
Crowlands	..	..	2	..	1
Rose's Gap	..	..	1	..	..
Cathcart	1	1	5	..	2
Great Western	..	..	..	..	2
Swanhill District—					
Swanhill	1	..	2	..	1
Narung	..	..	1	..	..
Carwarp	..	..	1	..	..
Mildura, Cowana Bend	1	..	2	..	..
Kerang	..	..	1	..	..
Lake Boga	..	..	1	..	..
Toulibuck, T.Pnt.	..	..	1	..	..
McIvor District—					
Heathcote	1	..	3	1	9
McGuire's Punt	..	..	2	..	..
Murchison	..	..	2	..	..
Whroo	..	..	..	..	1
Rushworth	1	..	3	..	2
Runneymede	..	..	2	..	..
Echuca	..	..	2	1	..
Kilmore District—					
Kilmore	2	1	7	1	10
Avenal	..	..	1	..	1
Benalla	..	..	1	1	3
Euroa	..	..	1	..	..
Longwood	..	..	1	..	2
Seymour	..	..	1	..	1
Violet Town	..	..	1	..	1
Mansfield	..	..	2	..	..
Pyaleng	..	..	1	..	..
Yea	..	..	1	..	..
Kalkallo	..	..	2	..	1
Ovens District—					
Beechworth	2	..	9	4	21
Belvior	..	..	1	1	1
Wangaratta	..	..	2	1	2
Eldorado	..	..	..	..	1
Woolshed	..	..	1	..	3
Mulwala	..	..	1	..	1
Yackandandah	..	..	2	1	2
Sebastopol	..	..	..	..	2
Buckland	..	1	2	..	3
Do. Junction	..	..	..	..	2
Snake Valley	..	..	..	..	4
Allen's Flat	..	..	..	..	2
Quartz Reef	..	..	1	..	1
Hurdle Flat	..	..	..	..	2
Three Mile	..	..	..	..	2
Reid's Creek	..	..	..	..	2
Belfast District—					
Belfast	1	..	3	2	5
Dunkeld	..	..	2	..	..

tation.	Officers.	Mount. Sergnt.	Mount. Cnstbl.	Foot. Sergnt.	Foot. Cnstbl.	Station.	Officers.	Mount. Sergnt.	Mount. Cnstbl.	Foot. Sergnt.	Foot. Cnstbl.
Belfast District—continued.						*Gipps Land District—continued.*					
Warrnambool	..	..	2	1	5	Port Albert	..	..	1	..	1
Hexham	..	..	2	..	..	Mitchell	..	..	2	..	..
Hamilton	..	..	2	1	1	Stratford	..	..	2	..	..
Woodford	..	..	2	..	..	Livingstone Creek, Omeo	..	..	1	1	..
Caramut	..	..	2	..	..	*Water Police—*					
Portland District—						Victoria Block Ship	4	..	..	4	49
Portland	1	..	2	1	6	*Richmond Depôt—*					
Casterton	..	1	1	..	..	Depôt	4	2	12	4	25
Balmoral	..	..	2	..	..	Do. on sick leave	2	..	..	..	..
Harrow	..	..	2	..	..	*Detective Police*	1	..	..	..	33
Mount Eckersley	..	..	1	..	..						
Gipps Land District—											
Alberton	1	..	3	..	4						
Sale	1	..	2	1	1						
Tarraville	..	..	1	..	1	TOTAL	48	10	289	95	785

This arrangement is liable to constant change; for, as the population in the mining districts migrates from one locality to another, it becomes necessary to break up old stations and form new ones.

The entire force, as at present constituted, consists of 439 married, and 788 single men. Quarters are not provided by the Government for the families of constables, except at remote stations, where it would be too expensive, and in many cases impossible, for the constables to procure the necessary accommodation.

The following table will shew the religion and countries of the constabulary :—

Religion.	Countries.					
Protestants, 706	Englnd.	Irlnd.	Sctlnd.	Wals.	O. B. Dom.	Foreign.
R. Catholics, 521	256	871	73	5	14	8

The whole of the escort service of the Government is conducted by the police. The treasure is for the most part conveyed in wagons manufactured for the purpose at the police depôt, Richmond. These conveyances are drawn, on the principal lines of road, by four horses; and on the branch lines, light wagons, spring carts, and, in some cases, pack-horses, are used, according to the amount of treasure to be conveyed. The draught horses, conveyances, drivers, &c., as well as the guard, are supplied by the police department; and the following table will give an idea of the extent of the service :—

UP ESCORTS. | DOWN ESCORTS.

Dpt. fr	Arrive at						Depart from						Arr. at
Melbourne	Castlemaine.	Sandhurst.	Maryborough.	Avoca.	Dunolly.	Blackwood.	Blackwood.	Dunolly.	Avoca.	Maryborough.	Sandhurst.	Castlemaine.	Melbourne
Every Tusdy. 9 a.m.	Every Thursday 4 p.m.	Every Friday 4 p.m.	Every Friday 4 p.m.	Alternate Saturday 3 p.m.	Alternate Saturday 2 p.m.	Alternate Tuesdays 4 p.m.	Alternate Wedndy. 9 a.m.	Alternate Mondays 9 a.m.	Alternate Mondays 9 a.m.	Every Tuesday 9 a.m.	Every Tuesday 9 a.m.	Every Wedndy 9 a.m.	Every Friday. 2 p.m.

Depart from	Arrive at					Depart from					Arrive at
Melbourne.	Heathcote	Rushworth.	Beechworth.	Yackandandah.	Buckland	Buckland.	Yackandandah.	Beechworth.	Rushworth.	Heathcote	Melbourne.
Alternate Tuesdays 9 a.m.	Alternate Fridays 3 p.m.	Alternate Mondays 4 p.m.	Alternate Tuesdays 1 p.m.	Alternate Thursdays 4 p.m.	Alternate Saturdays 4 p.m.	Alternate Tuesdays 9 a.m.	Alternate Wednsdy. 9 a.m.	Alternate Fridays 9 a.m.	Alternate Saturdays 9 a.m.	Alternate Tuesdays 9 a.m.	Alternate Fridays 2 p.m.

Depart from	Arrive at					Depart from					Arrive at
Melbourne.	Ballaarat.	Creswick.	Raglan.	Ararat.	Pleasant Creek.	Pleasant Creek.	Ararat.	Raglan.	Creswick.	Ballaarat.	Melbourne.
Every Saturday 1 p.m.	Every Tuesday 4 p.m.	Alternate Tuesdays noon.	Alternate Thursdays 3 p.m.	Alternate Saturdays 2 p.m.	Alternate Tuesdays 4 p.m.	Alternate Wednsdy. 9 a.m.	Alternate Fridays 9 a.m.	Alternate Mondays 9 a.m.	Alternate Tuesdays noon.	Every Wednesdy. 9 a.m.	Every Friday 2 p.m.

N.B. The hours of arrival must of course vary with the state of the roads, &c.

The water police branch of the service consists of a number of officers, sergeants, and constables, under the charge of a superintendent, who is also commander of H. M. steam sloop *Victoria*, stationed in Hobson's Bay. The members of this branch are not only amenable to the same rules for the maintenance of discipline, and have the same powers as the other branches of the service, but have also special powers in regard to shipping, as laid down in 16 Vict., No. 33. An officer and a detachment of water police are stationed on the blockship, another detachment being stationed at Point Henry, Geelong.

The detectives, although subject to the same discipline, are, to a certain extent, a distinct body of the police force; their duty being to *detect* crime, that of the ordinary police to *prevent* it. Not being in uniform, each member of the detective police is furnished with a "warrant card," signed by the head of the department, to produce when necessary as a proof of the authority under which he is acting. Detectives are stationed in each of the more important districts, and the whole body is under the control of a superintendent, whose office is in Melbourne. Appointments to this branch of the service are, for the most part, made by selecting from the "preventive" police such men as are considered best suited for detective duty; but candidates for employment, who may be found to possess the peculiar qualifications considered necessary in a detective, are occasionally appointed.

Each member of the police force is furnished with a manual of instructions for his guidance, and further instructions are issued from time to time as the exigencies of the service require them. In addition to this, a small volume of extracts from such Acts of Council as confer powers upon or relate to the police, has been compiled, and a copy supplied to each member of the establishment.

A Police Gazette is published every Thursday, for the purpose of circulating to every member of the force all information of interest to the constabulary, and is issued from the Chief Commissioner's office. It contains notices of offences committed, warrants issued, horses and cattle stolen, &c., &c. All communications relating to matters of police interest are inserted gratuitously, on being addressed to the *Police Gazette Office*, Melbourne.

A Fund designated the *Police Reward Fund* has accumulated under the provisions of the 18 Vict., No 32, and the 30th section of the 16 Vict., No. 24. It is, at present, administered in accordance with the regulations of the 29th March, 1855, published in the *Government Gazette*, of the 5th April following; but a scheme has been prepared for its appropriation to a pension fund, so far as the police are concerned, which scheme is under the consideration of the Government.

Applicants for employment in the force are required to present themselves at the Police Depôt, Richmond. If after an examination, they are pronounced to be adapted for the performance of police duties, their names are placed on the list of "candidates," and, as vacancies occur, the applicants, after having been examined by the surgeon to the force, and declared by him to be physically qualified, are employed in turn, the preference being given to such as have had previous police experience. Candidates must be able to produce certificates of good character, and must be able to read and write well. After being engaged, they are retained a few days at the depôt, at Richmond, without pay. At the termination of this period, if reported suitable for the service, they are sworn in as "constables" and remain at the depôt a further period, to be drilled, and instructed in the rules of the service, until they are required to fill vacancies that occur in the various districts. Until so transferred, they do not receive the full pay of constables.

Note.—For Law and Police, *vide* contents.

NAVAL.

Her Majesty's Colonial Steam Sloop *Victoria*, 587 tons, 150 horse power, stationed in Hobson's Bay, Melbourne.

Present armament on board.—One long 56 cwt. 32 pounder, pivot gun, forward; two long 25 cwt. 32 pounders, broadside guns; with small arms complete in proportion to the above complement.

Is pierced and fitted for, in addition to the above.—One long 56 cwt. 32 pounder, pivot, aft; four more broadside 32 pounders of 25 cwt; having a shell room and magazine complete.

Officers.—Commander, W. H. Norman; 1st officer, G. A. Woods; 2nd officer, D. D. Chambers; chief engineer, Rd. Griffiths; assistant engineer, Alfred Arnold.

Warrant Officers.—Three.

Crew.—Petty officers, six; able seamen, twenty-one; firemen, eight; boys, seven; total, fifty.

The vessel was built by order of His late Excellency Sir Charles Hotham, by Messrs. Young, Son, Magnay and Co., of Limehouse, London, in 1855; and the engines by Messrs. George Rennie and Sons, under the immediate supervision of Commander Lockyer, R.N., assisted by her present commander, and by whom she was brought to this colony on 31st May, 1856; since which time her duties have been those of an armed despatch vessel, under the orders of the hon. the Chief Secretary, for the protection of the interests of the public, and is always kept ready for sea on telegraphic notice.

Since January, 1858, in addition to continuing the above duties, the Water Police of the port having been reduced from forty-two to ten men, the remainder were transferred to the books of the *Victoria*, and the duties of the bay and port continued by her officers and crew, under the orders and supervision of the Chief Commissioner of Police; and when the *Victoria* has to leave port, on any special service, the above ten men, with one sub-Inspector and two Serjeants, are left to continue the same on board the blockship, until her return; this number being in addition to her crew of fifty, as already stated above, does not in any way interfere with her efficiency. —For Military, *see* contents.

PUBLIC LIBRARY, MELBOURNE.

TRUSTEES:—The Chief Justice, Sir W. F. Stawell, Knight; the President of the Legislative Council, Sir F. Palmer, Knight; His Honor Mr. Justice Barry; H. C. E. Childers; and D. C. Macarthur. Librarian—Augustus Tulk.

The Library was opened to the public on February 11th, 1856. The amount of money expended upon the buildings and grounds has been £19,400.

BOOKS:—Number of volumes, 8,500; cost of ditto, £7,500; donations of books, 500 volumes; donations of coins, 320; autograph letters, 10. The books are distributed into the following classes:—British History, 950; British Literature, 1,000; General History, 775; Greek and Latin Literature, 400; French and Italian, 325; Science and Physiology, 1,200; Art and Architecture, 250; Polity and Political Economy and Law, 850; Philosophy and Theology, 600; Voyages, Travels, Atlases, &c., 500; Lexicography and Education, 400; Encyclopœdias and Serials, 750; Newspapers, 150; German Literature, 350; Total 8,500. (A list of works on Australasia is inserted elsewhere).

VISITORS:—Number of visitors, 1856:—morning, 16,000; evening, 7,769; Total, 23,769. Number of visitors, 1857:—morning, 25,325; evening, 23,901; Total, 49,226. During these two years the hours of admission were from 10 A.M. to 4 P.M., and from 6 P.M. to 9 P.M. The number of visitors from January 1st to May the 31st, 1858, has been:—morning, 15,128; evening, 13,173; Total, 28,301. On the 1st of January, 1858, the hours of admission were altered by order of the Trustees, and the public are now admitted from 10 A.M. to 9 P.M.

Six thousand volumes are shortly expected from England, to be added to the Library. The general character of these works will be scientific, although no branch of mental development has been entirely overlooked by the Trustees in their last year's order.

As the number of visitors has increased in a far greater proportion than the books, more room has been required; and to meet this demand, tenders for an extension of the building have been accepted, and the south wing will be completed shortly, under the superintendence of the architect, Mr. Joseph Reed.

The respect for public order and the good conduct of the visitors have been patent from the very opening of the institution. And the very slight loss of books, either by mutilation or abstraction, amounting in all to but seven volumes, in a period of two years and a-half, has not tended to throw any slur upon the absolutely free system of admission adopted by the Trustees. The public of Victoria may congratulate itself that even the exclusive ticket system of the British and other public libraries has not suceeeded so well as theirs.

The only holidays are Christmas Day and Good Friday, and the days appointed for quarterly cleaning.

Great credit is due to the Trustees for the zealous supervision which has evidently been exercised in regard to the character of the editions. The appearance of the books and the superior character of their bindings are equally creditable to the London bookseller, Mr. J. J. Guillaume, of Chester-square, by whom they have been supplied. A list of works on Australasia will be found in another part of this book.

THE TREASURY.

It may be as well to explain, previous to describing the duties of the Treasury Department, that after the revenue of the year has been appropriated by the Legislature for certain specific objects (by the Appropriation Act), that expenditure can, nevertheless, not take place without the authority of the Governor, which authority is issued as regards the expenditure upon each ministerial division of the service, upon the recommendation of the minister in charge of that division.

The division of the Government Service of which the Treasury is the head consists of,—first, the Treasury; second, the offices of the several Receivers and Paymasters (at present twelve in number); third, the Gold office, Melbourne, and the offices of the several Gold Receivers throughout the country (sixteen in number), many of which, however, are held jointly with the office of Receiver and Paymaster; fourth, the Store and Transport Department; fifth, the Government Printing Office.

The department of the Military (see other page), also including the several Volunteer Corps, is so far in the Treasurer's division of the service, that all applications for authority to incur expenditure out of colonial funds on account of this Department, or for the payment of the colonial allowance to Her Majesty's troops in the colony, are made to the Treasurer; and that all necessary business connected with it, requiring to be transacted through the office of a Responsible Minister is transacted through the Treasury.

The Audit office is so far connected with the Treasury, that authorities for the payment of the salaries and for the appointment of the officers, proceed from the Treasury; the Commissioners of Audit themselves holding office by the same terms as the judges of the Supreme Court, viz., during good behaviour.

The authority of the Governor also, for all payments of grants in aid of charitable institutions and of municipalities, of sums appropriated for special purposes by Acts other than the annual Appropriation Act (*e. g.* for payment of the grant in aid of public worship, of pensions, &c.), is obtained by the Treasurer, to whom, therefore, all applications for such payments should be addressed.

The Treasury Department, previous to the introduction of Responsible Government in November, 1855, was the same in fact, or very nearly so, as that of the Melbourne Receiver and Paymaster at present. The only essential difference arose from the number of Sub-Treasurers being at that time limited to three (Geelong, Portland and Belfast), and also from the fact that accounts for payment at a Sub-Treasury were then not forwarded through the Melbourne office.

Again, previously to 1856, the accounts of the colony were kept in the office of the Auditor-general, to which office all accounts for payment had to be transmitted in the first instance, for examination; if found correct, they were then forwarded by the Auditor-general to the Treasury for payment, the Governor's warrant to the Treasurer authorizing payment being first obtained by the Auditor-general.

Previous to the year 1856, the Governor's authority for all expenditure, for all appointments, or changes in appointments, &c., had to be obtained from the Governor through the office of the Chief Secretary, which formed, moreover, in other respects the channel of communication between the Governor and the several Departments, and also between the Governor and the public, respecting the general business of the Government.

On the introduction of Responsible Government, however, the supervision previously directly exercised by the Governor through the office of the Chief Secretary over the several Departments forming the Civil Service was transferred to the six ministerial officers (the Law Officers being considered as one), and the business formerly transacted through the Chief Secretary's office was therefore divided between the six ministerial Departments, to each of which a number of the other Departments was therefore attached with a view to this division.

In the division thus made, the Post-office, at that time without a separate ministerial head, was placed under the Treasurer; the Military, and the Audit Departments, on the other hand, remained attached to the Chief Secretary's Department.

In the commencement of 1856, a new system of keeping the public accounts was introduced (on the recommendation of a commission which had been appointed by Sir C. Hotham, to inquire into and report upon the financial administration of the colony), under which the keeping of the public "books" was transferred from the Audit Office to the Treasury, and the present mode of making payment of accounts previous to final audit was introduced. A large portion of the duties which had hitherto devolved on the Audit office was by this means transferred to the Treasury. The Treasurer, however, during this year continued to perform the duties of receiving and disbursing the public moneys as before, assisted by the establishment of, in April, 1856, six Sub-Treasuries at the several gold fields.

In the early part of 1857, a further change in the constitution of the Treasury (proper) was effected by transferring the duties of the receipt of revenue and the payment of accounts to a separate office, called that of "Receiver and Paymaster of the Treasury."

In this year also, the Post office Department was placed under a separate ministerial head, while the Audit Department towards the end of the year was reconstituted and placed upon its present footing.

The constitution of the ministerial office of the Treasurer has not been since altered, although the mode of payment of accounts, and of accounting for the receipt and payment of accounts (established on the report of Sir C. Hotham's finance committee), has been this year considerably modified, and the system, as amended, very stringently prescribed by the Audit Act.

The Treasury is now divided into three branches, viz.: — the Accountant's branch, where the books of the colony are kept; the Examination branch, in which accounts against the Government are examined previous to payment; and the Correspondence or Record branch, the duties of which involve not only correspondence and the record of correspondence, but the record of parliamentary documents, the preparation and record of authorities for expenditure issued by the Treasurer as a ministerial officer; the compilation of returns, and in part, the transaction of such business as falls to the Treasurer in his capacity of ministerial officer in charge of the Treasury Division, apart from that which belongs to his office of General Accountant.

The whole is presided over by an officer called the Under-Treasurer, who acts as the permanent head of the Treasury division, and as such carries on the routine of the office, subject to the supervision of the ministerial head, the Treasurer.

The object of this work being the guidance and information of the public in general, and not that of the Government staff, it is not necessary to explain the present system of accounts or the business of the office, except in so far as the public are affected in their transactions with the Treasury.

It will be sufficient, therefore, to explain that under this system the Treasurer has no power to pay or receive any portion of the public moneys himself. All he can do is to obtain orders upon the Banks, where the public receipts are lodged, to honor the cheques of the Receivers and Paymasters, for such and such particular accounts forwarded to them from the Treasury for payment. These orders the Banks cannot honor unless they are countersigned by the Commissioners of Audit, and the Commissioners of Audit cannot countersign them unless the accounts specified therein are within, or not in excess, of the sums voted by the Legislature; and unless the expenditure to be defrayed is legally incurred, that is, has been approved by the Legislature.

On an account reaching the Treasury it is examined, with a view to ascertaining, first, that the expenditure has been duly authorised; second, that it has been duly certified by the officer by whom, or for whose Department the expenditure was incurred.

Should the account be correct in these points, and no inaccuracy or imperfection be otherwise observed, it is then forwarded to the proper pay-office, the requisite steps being at the same time taken, as above mentioned, to cause the Paymaster's cheque in payment to be honored by the Bank. Should the account be correct it will, in ordinary cases, be forwarded to the pay-office for payment, within twenty-four hours of its reaching the Treasury. If the account be incorrect in any important particular it is impossible to state what consequent delay may be produced in obtaining payment; but the delay will not in that case be attributable to the Treasurer; and it is therefore well for claimants on the Government to bear in mind that the officer by whom any expense is incurred, is responsible for the proper obtaining of authority to incur that expense previously to incurring it, and for the proper completion in every respect, of the account for its payment. Claimants should, therefore, in all cases of delay, address themselves on the subject to the officer by whom the expenditure has been incurred, or to his ministerial head.

Accounts are forwarded for payment at the Melbourne pay-office unless directions are given on the face of the account for payment to be made at some other pay-office. Claimants, therefore, wishing to receive payments at any other pay-office, should write the words "payable at (naming the place)," distinctly on the face of their accounts. An account once passed to a particular pay-office cannot be transferred to any other. Accounts are payable either to the claimant himself, or to any one producing from the claimant an order for payment to be made to him; such order should be in either of the two printed forms, one being for payment to be made to the agent only, and the other payment either to the agent or to any one to whom he may transfer the order. In either case the amount to be paid must be written in words, not in figures, and the signature of the agent must be written previous to the presentation of the order to the Receiver and Paymaster.

LICENSES, &c.

The descriptions of licenses undermentioned are obtainable at the several receipt and pay-offices as explained in each case:—

Publican's General License.—This licence is obtainable under Act 13 Vict. No. 29, upon production of a certificate from the licensing Bench of the district authorising the issue, and the payment of £25; applications for certificates can be entertained by the Benches of Magistrates on the annual licensing day, viz:—the third Tuesday in April, or on the first Tuesday in September, December, and March. The licenses must be taken out previous to 30th June, if the certificate has been obtained upon the general licensing day in April, or within a month of the date of the certificate, should it have been obtained on one of the other days above mentioned. The Governor has power, however, to direct a license to be issued in any case, notwithstanding the prescribed period shall have elapsed on payment of a fine (in addition to the regular fee) not exceeding £10 in amount, and provided that the fee and additional fine be paid within a further period of twenty-eight days. Memorials to His Excellency for this purpose should be forwarded to the Treasury under cover to the Treasurer. The Governor can in cases of emergency issue a renewed publican's license without a certificate from the licensing bench; memorials for this purpose must also be forwarded to the Treasury under cover to the Treasurer.

Confectioners' Licenses.—The fee is £1. A certificate from the Bench must be produced, and the license is subject otherwise to the conditions above stated.

Packet Licenses are issuable by Receivers and Paymasters, under the Act 13 Vict., No. 29, and are for the sale of liquors on board vessels, a certificate from a Bench of Magistrates must be presented when applying for a license, and the conditions as to time of payment are the same as in the case of a publican's general license; the fee is £2.

Distillers' Licenses.—The following distillers' licenses are obtainable at the offices of the Receivers and Paymasters under the Act 13., Vic. No. 27. An apothecary's license for keeping a still of not more than eight gallons, contents for medicinal purposes, fee £2 ; a scientific license for scientific purposes, or for the distillation of perfumes, content not to exceed eight gallons, the fee £2 ; and a license for the distillation of brandy, for the manufacture of wine from the produce of a vineyard belonging to the licensee, the still not to exceed 50 gallons in content, nor to be less than 25 gallons, the fee is £1. Previous to obtaining one of either of the above descriptions of licenses, a recognizance must be entered into by the applicant, with two sureties in the sum of two hundred pounds, conditional that he will not make use of his still for other purposes than that for which the license is granted.

District Publicans' License.—This license is only obtainable in districts which have been specially proclaimed as subject to the Act 16 Vic., No. 35. The license will be issued by the Receiver and Paymaster of the district, upon payment of a fee o :£25, and the presentation *within* 14 *days of its date*, of the certificate of the Bench authorising the issue.

Refreshment Licenses are issuable also under the same Act, and are subject to the same conditions as the publicans' license; the fee is £1. They can be issued also by the Clerks of Petty Sessions.

Auctioneers' Licenses.—These are issuable by Receivers and Paymasters on payment of a fee of £25, and the presentation of a certificate from the Bench.—See Act 18 Vic. No. 23. The annual meeting for the issue of these certificates is held in November, but the Governor has power to direct a special meeting of the magistrates of any court of Petty Sessions to be held at any time. Applications for such authority must be made to His Excellency, under cover to the Treasurer. The licenses issuable under the Act are of two descriptions, general and district. The general are applicable to the whole colony, but the district to the police district for which the certificate is issued only. The fee in either case is £25, but at the annual meeting the Benches of Melbourne and Geelong only are empowered to grant certificates for general licenses, although the Governor can specially empower any Bench to entertain an application for a general license.

Wholesale Spirit Merchants' and Brewers' Licenses.—These are issuable by Receivers and Paymasters on presentation of a certificate from the Clerk to the Bench of the district for which the license is sought, that the applicant has registered himself as a wholesale spirit merchant (or brewer as the case may be). The fee is £25 for a wholesale spirit merchant's license, and £10 for a brewer's for the whole year, or a proportionate sum in either case, for the rest of the year after the date of registration. Vendors of imported malt liquor or wines are included in or under the designation of "wholesale spirit merchants," and vendors of colonial malt liquor or wines under that of "brewers." The same license will serve for more than one place of business in the same town or district, but not for one in one town or district and another in another.

Deeds of Crown Lands are forwarded from the Survey Office when prepared, direct to the Receiver and Paymaster of the district in which the land has been sold; they will, however, upon application to the Treasurer, be transferred to any other receipt and pay-office for issue, which the grantee may desire. The fees chargeable on the issue of deeds are as follows:—For land not exceeding 50 acres, £1; more than 50 and not exceeding 300, £1 5s.; 300 and upwards, £1 10s. Double fees are chargeable when the deed has been above a year in the office of a Receiver and Paymaster unissued.

Naturalization Certificates are prepared in the office of the Chief Secretary, to whom application should be made for any information which may be required concerning them. They are issued by Receivers and Paymasters on payment of a fee of £1 1s.

Purchase of Land.—A deposit of not less than 10 per cent. on the purchase money must be paid at the sale, to the officer conducting it, the balance must be paid to the Receiver and Paymaster of the district, (unless arrangements have been made for payment, within the prescribed time, to the officer conducting the sale) within one month of the sale, on penalty of the land and the deposit being forfeited.

Selection of Lands.—Lands advertised as open for purchase by selection, may be purchased at the office of a Receiver and Paymaster. Payment of the full price advertised must be made when applying to be permitted to purchase, but the amount will only be received conditionally on the selection being ultimately allowed by the Governor in Council. Should the selection be disallowed the money will, on application, be returned to the person paying.

Depasture Licenses.—The fees due from the occupants of Crown lands are advertised at the commencement of each year, and must be paid (at the office of any Receiver and Paymaster, before the termination of the month of March. If payment be not made, a fine of 25 per cent. upon the original amount is charged, and if payment be further delayed beyond a period of sixty days, the Crown can enter upon possession of the runs. Applications relative to the amount of the fee must be addressed to the President of the Board of Land and Works, the Treasury being concerned in the collection only.

Assessment on Stock.—This tax is payable also to any Receiver and Paymaster, the amount payable by each occupant of Crown lands being gazetted. One moiety must be paid by the end of May, the other by the end of November. Should payment not be tendered till after the above dates, an additional payment of one-ninth the original amount must be made. Should more than one month have elapsed, two-ninths become payable. In the event of payment being delayed more than two months the Act empowers the Governor in Council to direct that the amount already due, with a further sum equal to one-ninth the original amount, be levied upon the stock.

Trust and Suitors' Fund.—Under the Audit Act, moneys held in trust by Public Officers (by virtue of their offices) for others, and moneys paid into court are paid into the Treasury (*i.e.* to the Receiver and Paymaster). Receivers and Paymasters, however, are furnished with advances to enable them to make immediate repayment of all such sums upon application, and the officer by whom the money has been paid in is required to prepare and certify to an account for the claimant to present at the pay-office.

Paymasters and Receivers cannot make payment of any accounts with the exception of the above, unless such accounts shall have been transmitted to them for the purpose from the Treasury.

The duties of the Receivers and Paymasters of the Treasury are explained above; there are at present twelve of these officers.

At the gold-fields, the Receivers and Paymasters also hold the office of Gold-Receiver.

GOLD-OFFICE, MELBOURNE.

The business of the Gold-office, Melbourne, consists in the receipt of gold transmitted to Melbourne from the several gold-fields, and the issue thereof to the several owners; also in the receipt of cash and bank notes, &c., for despatch per escort to the several gold-fields (see *Bradshaw's Guide*, page 12) No charge is made for the transmission of gold to Melbourne if the export duty be paid upon it, otherwise a charge of one shilling per ounce from Beechworth and six-pence per ounce from the other gold-fields is made. The hours for obtaining gold from the gold-office, are 10 a.m. to 3 p.m., except on Saturday,

NOTE.—Particulars of Gold and Mining will be found in other parts of this work, *vide* Contents.

The duties of gold receivers at the gold-fields, include also that of the charge of gold on deposit, *i.e.* not for transmission to Melbourne, but deposited in the gold-office for safe custody. In some of the minor offices, however, gold is received for transmission by escort only.

when the hours are from 10 to 12. The Export Duty is payable at the Custom House.

POUNDS.

The form of notice respecting the payment of claims for the proceeds of impounded cattle was issued from the Treasury on 24th April, 1857, and will furnish the public with all necessary information on the subject. The account, when prepared as therein directed, must be forwarded to the Treasury.

AUDIT DEPARTMENT.

The Audit department has little connexion with the public. The duties of the office may be stated briefly to consist in the auditing of all accounts for expenditure after payment, and in auditing the accounts of the several Collectors and Receivers of revenue or public moneys. The Commissioners make periodic tours of inspection and report annually to the Legislature. The issue of the public stores is also audited by them.

There are three Commissioners, viz.—Messrs. C. H. Symonds, F. Jones, and A. J. Agg, whose term of office is secured by the Audit Act, on the same footing as that of the judges—viz., during good behaviour.

The business of the office is conducted by a staff, consisting, besides the commissioners, of a secretary and several clerks. As stated previously, the duties of this office formerly included many of those which are now performed by the Treasurer; new duties having devolved upon the Audit office.

Statement shewing the receipts and disbursements at the Public Treasury during the years from 1st July, 1851, to 30th June, 1858 inclusive. Treasury receipts—1851, £316,532 8s. 10d.; 1852, £1,634,447 11s. 2d.; 1853, £3,235,546 4s. 0d.; 1854, £3,088,063 19s. 4d.; 1855, £2,700,888 7s. 10d.; 1856, £2,973,472 15s. 5d.; 1857, £3,308,589 16s. 9d.; to 30th June, 1858, £1,841,046 17s. 7d. Treasury disbursements—1851, £211,425 10s. 8d.; 1852, £978.237 11s. 1d.; 1853, £3,213,580 0s. 6d.; 1854, £4,147,001 1s. 8d.; 1855, £2,637,053 16s. 10d.; 1856, £2,664,843 4s. 6d.; 1857, 2,596,689 15s. 5d.; to 30th June, 1858, £1,805,865 10s. 0d. A few liabilities amounting to about £1,200 are still outstanding on account of 1856. Further receipts to the amount of, say £28,000, may be expected on account of 1857,and the liabilities still outstanding on account of the ame year, may be taken at £567,000.

GOVERNMENT STORES.

In 1851 the business of this department was conducted in the Audit office, under the supervision of the Auditor General. In 1852, a distinct office was established in the old Supreme Court building, in King-street, at the corner of Bourke-street west; in the same year, Mr. L. Gilles was appointed the first Colonial Storekeeper, and on being removed to the office of Chief Clerk in the Colonial Secretary's office, he was succeeded by Mr. Charles Holmer, who held the office until the organisation of the Civil Commissariat, in October, 1853, by Mr. L. A. Moody; branches of which establishment were formed at Geelong, Portland, Belfast, and each of the principal gold-fields. In 1854 the old offices were destroyed by fire, the Civil Commissariat was abolished by the late Sir Charles Hotham, and the department re-constructed by Mr. Alfred J. Agg, in February, 1855, who was afterwards removed to the office of Under Treasurer in February, 1857; and succeeded by the present Government Storekeeper, Mr. R. Nash. The offices are held on the site where the department was first established, in a very substantial, convenient, and elegant stone building. It is the business of the Government Storekeeper to enter into contracts for the supply of stores, provisions, forage, and transport for the Government service, and make supplies to all departments in accordance with a very satisfactory code of regulations promulgated by an Order in Council for the management of this branch of the public service. Payments are made (as the case may be) through the Treasury, Melbourne, the Government Storekeeper, or the sub-Treasurer of the district where the expenditure may have been incurred. The office is placed under the ministerial direction of the Hon. the Treasurer.

Statement of the expenditure for supplies through the store and transport department during the undermentioned periods:—

1851, £7,975 19s. 5d., from the separation of New South Wales, 1st. July; 1852, £58,071 17s.; 1853, £266,749 10s.; 1854, £592,525 7s.; 1855, £187,138 4s.; 1856, £151,016 11s. 1d.; 1857, £149,647 4s. 5d.; 1858, £90,149 10s. 6d, to 30th June. Total, £1,510,274 4s. 3d.*

GOVERNMENT PRINTING OFFICE.

This department was formed for the purpose of enabling the Government to print the whole of the numerous documents required for the legislature, and by the various branches of the Public Service, and was founded in the month of November, 1851. Operations were at first commenced in a portion of the Audit office, in Lonsdale-st. west, but from the confined nature of the building, further accommodation soon became indispensable. In February, 1853, the office was removed to more extensive premises, being those at present occupied as the offices of the Central Road Board, but these also were shortly found to be inadequate to the increasing requirements of the service.

In May, 1853, a large wooden building was erected, adjoining the Government offices in William-street, for the purposes of a ball to be given by Lieutenant Governor LaTrobe in honor of Her Majesty's birth-day. Immediately after the ball, Mr. John Ferres, the Government Printer, applied to the Government to allow the building to

* The cost of the establishment in the year 1854, for salaries and allowances was £30,512 14s. 6d.; whilst it is estimated that £6,050 will cover the expenses of the present year.

remain, and to have it fitted up, and the whole appropriated to the Printing Department. The application was acceded to; instructions were given to proceed with alterations, and the compositors and pressmen commenced working in the new building on 14th July, 1853.

In 1854 it was deemed necessary, by the Government, to establish a book-binding branch in connection with the printing office, and under the control of the Government Printer. To accommodate this branch, a building was erected adjoining the printing office, in which the binding was executed, until the erection of the present offices.

The wooden building in William-street (since demolished) having become very dilapidated, and not being of sufficient extent to meet the still increasing demands upon the department, the present spacious building was commenced in November, 1856, and taken possession of by the Government Printer and his staff, at the latter end of May, 1858. It is situated in the reserve in which it is intended to erect the whole of the Government offices, and in the vicinity of the Houses of Parliament, Spring-street, Melbourne.

On the formation of the office in 1851, the amount of material was very limited, consisting of a small fount of long primer type and two inferior presses; the number of hands employed being only six. In 1853 large additions were made to the number of workmen employed. The material was also considerably increased and included one of Napier's perfecting printing machines, capable of throwing off from 1,000 to 1,200 copies per hour. This machine was driven by a fly-wheel worked by two men. In 1855 two additional machines were obtained, steam-power being applied to the three. Another machine has since been added, and the whole are now worked by a four-horse power table engine. There are also nine hand-presses in the office. The number of hands employed during the present year has averaged 86 in the printing department, and 24 in the binding branch, the whole being under the control of the Government Printer, assisted by three clerks and four overseers. The Treasurer is the official head of the establishment.

TRADE, CUSTOMS, SHIPPING, &c.

The various departments over which the Commissioner of Trade and Customs has control are as follow:—Customs, Immigration, Ports and Harbors, Lighthouses, Steam Navigation Board, Pilot Board, Distilleries, Powder Magazines, Shipping Masters, and Registrar of Shipping; and it is with subjects connected with the administration of these departments that he has to deal.

The duties of the Customs Department are defined by "the Customs Act, 1857," 21 Victoria, No. 13; and it is entrusted with the responsibility of collecting all the duties imposed under the following Acts:—Tariff, 18 Vic., No. 9; Gold, 18 Vic., No. 27; Tonnage, 17 Vic. No. 18; Pilotage, 17 Vic., No. 28; Passenger Rate, 16 Vic. No. 5; and Opium, 21 Vic., No. 7. The amounts collected during the past six years are set forth in the accompanying table:—

RETURN SHOWING THE AMOUNT OF DUTIES AND REVENUE COLLECTED DURING THE YEARS 1852, 3, 4, 5, 6 & 7.

	1852 £ s. d.	1853 £ s. d.	1854 £ s. d.	1855 s. d.	1856 £ s. d.	1857 £ s. d.
Spirits	193,172 13 9	555,836 4 1	513,171 0 6	617,054 19 10	759,691 10 9	759,235 19 3
Tobacco	70,000 11 3	88,583 2 5	95,460 9 6	112,448 9 6	122,676 6 0	101,070 15 6
Cigars	..	29,263 12 3	29,891 19 3	20,851 11 0	27,001 14 1	26,675 10 9
Snuff	..	757 2 4	1,079 15 7	192 10 0	534 11 11	508 8 6
Sugar	3,353 17 3	..	1,118 12 10	67,529 7 7	89,053 5 0	103,401 19 8
Flour and Grain	9,171 3 9	..	..	..	..	..
Molasses and Treacle	..	..	9 15 2	418 19 10	755 5 0	635 1 8
Tea	14,606 13 0	38,472 18 3	44,462 11 8	72,813 8 0	105,154 5 3	78,359 5 8
Coffee and Chicory	1,907 16 1	13,397 6 2	11,296 19 1	9,656 13 10	17,603 8 9	19,651 19 2
Opium	..	..	..	..	..	2,638 9 4
Wine	15,364 19 3	39,420 4 6	80,447 10 7	44,744 18 7	73,536 0 9	64,554 1 5
Beer	..	..	75,911 1 11	57,606 3 4	78,007 15 6	9,107 2 8
Cider	..	..	735 8 6	450 18 5	201 12 6	117 10 1
Other articles	20,437 10 1	..	..	..	..	..
Entrance and Clearance Fees	1,562 10 0	..	..	..	..	..
Lighthouse Dues	2,089 8 6	..	..	..	..	..
Pilotage	5,649 17 1	14,764 17 9	52,994 16 2	36,164 3 5	24,059 1 1	31,515 1 1
				Pass. Rates.	Pass. Rates.	Pass. Rates.
Wharfage	2,745 13 8	..	..	13,606 10 0	19,129 17 6	19,661 12 6
Tonnage	2,596 2 9	376 2 0	18,178 5	20,792 10 0	18,995 14 0	24,706 7 0
Other moneys	..	683 12 0	9,359 0	7,710 9 4	11,150 1 6	11,681 15 4
	342,708 16 5	781,555 1 9	934,147 5 9	1,082,041 12 8	1,347,550 9 7	1,343,515 19 7
Gold Export Duty	..	..	..	233,225 10 5	374,900 7 8	344,495 6 4
				1,315,267 3 1	1,722,450 17 8	1,688,011 5 11

These are all sources of public revenue of Victoria, with the exception of the pilot dues, which are distributed by the Pilot Board appointed under the 17 Vic., No. 28, to the various pilots according to their earnings. Of the whole revenues of the colony, upwards of one half is collected by this department, the cost of collection being a little over four per cent.

A return of the value of imports during the period from 1852 to 1857 is given below, together with the exports, specifying the two principal articles:—

Years.	Total Imports.	Total Exports. Wool.	Gold.	Other Articles.	Total Exports.
	£	£	£	£	£
1852	4,069,742	1,062,787	6,135,728	253,034	7,451,549
1853	15,842,637	1,651,871	8,644,529	765,143	11,061,543
1854	17,742,998	1,629,934	8,255,550	1,901,742	11,787,226
1855	11,568,904	1,390,621	10,903,645	1,174,928	13,469,194
1856	14,962,269	1,506,613	11 943,458	2,039,689	15,489,760
1857	17,256,209	1,335,642	10,987,591	2,756,279	15,079,512

These several returns will illustrate the immense progress made by this colony during the past six years, a growth which is unprecedented in any other quarter of the globe. Gold forms the chief article of export, being about two-thirds of the whole. The principal articles of import are the following:—Apparel and slops, beer and cider, flour and bread, grain, haberdashery, hardware, leather, timber, spirits and wine.

The following will shew the comparative declared value of the imports into Victoria in the years 1851 and 1857, from all parts of the world:—

Year.	From British Colonies. From Unitd Kingdom.	North America	Other British Possessns.	From United States.	From Foreign States.	TOTAL.
	£	£	£	£	£	£
1851	748,984	..	239,344	122	67,987	1,056,437
1857	10,122,201	13,111	5,588,780	782,846	749,321	17,256,209

The total amount of the imports during the seven years was £82,499,196. It is to be observed that a considerable difference prevails between the statement of the declared or estimated value of the exports from the mother country in the official returns printed in England and in Victoria: in the latter they are estimated at their value on the spot, after the cost of transmission and all other charges have been added; in the former only at their value at the time of shipment.

In the year 1853, the imports were from the respective

countries as follows:—From Great Britain, £8,288,226; from the West Indies, £14,973; from North America, £13,560; from other British Possessions, £5,036,311; from the United States of America, £1,668,606; from foreign States, £820,961; total, £15,842,637. In 1857, the imports were as follows:—from Great Britain, £10,122,201; from the British West Indies, *nil;* from British North America, £13,111; from other British Possessions, £5,588,730; from the United States of America, £784,643; from foreign States, £747,524: total, £17,256,209.

We now direct the readers attention to particular articles, and shall commence with flour. In 1853, the values of our imports of flour and other bread stuffs were in the following proportions:—From Great Britain, £162,159; from the West Indies and British North America, £1,006; from other British Possessions, almost wholly, of course, from the neighbouring colonies, £421,171; from the United States, £319,419; from foreign States, £42,346: total, £946,101. In 1857, the amounts were: from Great Britain, £23,837; from West Indies and British North America, *nil;* from other British Possessions, £812,402; from the United States, £68,178; from foreign States, £43,444; total, £937,861. In 1857, of the total quantity of breadstuffs, valued at about £2,000,000, consumed by this population, the amount imported from beyond the Australian colonies, was only to the value of £125,459.

For the purposes of the Department there are only six ports of "entry and clearance" at which customs duties are collected, viz.:—Melbourne, Geelong, Portland, Port Fairy, Port Albert, and Warrnambool; but duties are collected by the South Australian Government at Goolwa (situated at the mouth of the River Murray) on goods imported into Victoria *viâ* the river Murray, the tariff which has been adopted by special arrangement between the three Governments concerned, New South Wales, Victoria, and South Australia, being that of the first mentioned. The arrangements are carried out under legal enactments of these colonies, and the amount of duties so collected is at present divided equally between the colonies of New South Wales and Victoria, irrespective of the quantities of goods landed in either colony.

Every port has its "Collector of Customs," each of whom is responsible at his own port to carry out the Customs Laws, subordinate, however, to the Commissioner of Trade and Customs. It may be stated, however, that of the total amount of duties, about 82 per cent. is collected at Melbourne, 14 per cent. at Geelong, the remainder being collected at the other ports before enumerated.

The Customs Department was up to the year 1852 under the control of the Lords of the Treasury in London, but though the officers were accountable to the Treasury, the revenue collected formed a portion of that of the colony.

In addition to the local Acts, this department is entrusted

with the administration of the Imperial "Merchant Shipping Act, 1854"; and Imperial "Passengers' Act, 1855."

SHIPPING.

The following is a return showing the number of vessels and their tonnage, which have arrived in and departed from Victoria, during the period 1852-7, distinguishing their respective countries :—

VESSELS INWARDS.

	Great. Britain No.	Great. Britain Tons.	Brit. Poss. No.	Brit. Poss. Tons.	Untd. States. No.	Untd. States. Tons.	For. States. No.	For. States. Tons.	Total. No.	Total. Tons.
1852	251	168,919	1364	225,446	13	5,820	29	8,031	1657	408,216
1853	630	284,719	1740	351,066	119	53,988	105	31,700	2594	721,473
1854	650	349,342	1715	353,410	78	40,206	153	51,646	2596	794,604
1855	274	207,800	1443	274,180	50	27,173	13[illegible]	39,223	1897	548,376
1856	214	197,033	1552	274,794	55	35,328	99	31,454	1920	538,609
1857	307	290,680	1758	330,594	50	36,841	75	36,449	2190	694,564

VESSELS OUTWARDS.

	Great. Britain No.	Great. Britain Tons.	Brit. Poss. No.	Brit. Poss. Tons.	Untd. States. No.	Untd. States. Tons.	For. States. No.	For. States. Tons.	Total. No.	Total. Tons.
1852	68	36,936	1365	286,163	1*	222	41	26,975	1475	350,296
1853	94	61,321	1922	471,817	3	2,105	249	129,624	2268	664,867
1854	86	66,876	2082	582,133	12	4,137	427	195,691	2607	798,837
1855	81	66,711	1637	371,820	9	2,439	265	140,208	1992	581,178
1856	65	57,037	1705	384,489	4	1,049	185	95,787	1959	538,362
1857	64	64 717	1879	426,854	3	1,224	261	191,731	2207	684,526

* South Sea Islands.

The number of ships and vessels entered inwards at the Custom House in Victoria in 1851 was 710; in 1857 it was 2,190. The tonnage in 1851 was 128,959 tons; in 1857, 694,564 tons. The number of men in 1851 was 7,735; in 1857, 34,777. The increase in the number of vessels has consequently been 208 per cent., of tonnage 438 per cent., and of hands employed 349 per cent. The departures in 1851 comprised 657 vessels of all classes, having a total tonnage of 110,659 tons. In the year 1857 the number cleared outwards at the various custom houses in Victoria was 2,207, with a tonnage of 684,826, manned by 33,928 hands.

PORTS AND HARBORS.

The seaboard of Victoria embraces a range of about six hundred miles, the ports, harbors, rivers, bays, inlets and anchorages within which are under the care of the officers attached to the above department; the principal (the Chief Harbor Master) being stationed at Williamstown, from whence, by means of the electric telegraph, communication is now held with all the Western Ports; and in the event of wreck on the coast, or neighbourhood (now happily of rare occurrence), arrangements are made to send assistance either by despatching a Government or other vessel, as the case may demand.

To the Harbor Department is entrusted the supervision of the movements, berthing at wharves, moorings and safety of all vessels; the removal of sunken wrecks and other obstructions likely to impede free navigation; the enforcement of the harbor regulations within the limits of the various ports; also the charge, maintenance and supervision of all lighthouses, lightships and signal stations; the construction and placing of all beacons, buoys and moorings.

The officers and men immediately attached to the Harbor Department consist of one chief and six harbor masters, four clerks, four principal and ten assistant lighthouse keepers, three masters, three mates, and twelve seamen on board the lightships; one master, one mate, and seven seamen on board the buoy and lighthouse tender "Empire;" one superintendent and ten mechanics engaged in the marine yard, making and repairing buoys, beacons, boats, Government vessels, lighthouse apparatus, &c.

The expense of the Department is borne out of the general revenue, by an annual vote of the Legislature.

The waters of Port Phillip Bay spread over a surface of upwards of eight hundred square miles, three-fourths of which are available for anchorage, the depth nowhere inside the lighthouses exceeding fifteen fathoms.

Hobson's Bay is capable of affording shelter to upwards of eight hundred sail. The holding ground is excellent: the depth from three to four fathoms, over a bottom of stiff clay and mud.

The Harbor Dues consist of a tonnage rate of one shilling per ton levied upon all vessels arriving in any port. No vessel pays this duty more than once in six months; these dues are collected at the respective Custom Houses, and paid into the general revenue.

The appointment of pilots for Port Phillip, establishment of rates of pilotage, and general management of the pilot service, is entrusted by Act of Council to a Board, consisting of five members; the head office is at Williamstown. The expenses of the Pilot Department up to 1st September, 1854, was borne out of the general revenue by a vote of the Legislature, but since that period it has been self-supporting, and has now a reserve fund for sick and superannuation purposes. The staff consists of a secretary, thirty-seven pilots, all men of tried skill, who have safely piloted thousands of British and foreign vessels, comprising in their numbers the most noted and far-famed ships, both steam and sailing, afloat. Three excellent well appointed vessels cruise at all times, and in all weathers, outside Port Phillip Heads. Pilots are also appointed at all other ports within the colony. In addition to the regular licensed pilots, the Pilot Board grant licenses to skilled ship masters to pilot their own vessels when engaged in the colonial and coasting trades free of pilotage; these now number 510.

The rates of Pilotage for the ports are collected at the Custom House, and transmitted monthly to the Pilot Board, for distribution. A new code of rates was issued on 10th of August, 1858; and will be found in *Bradshaw's Guide to Victoria.*

Sailing directions for the various ports have been prepared by the Harbor Department and transmitted to all maritime countries, the Governments of which have, in many instances, republished them in their own language.

Flagstaffs are erected at all ports and lighthouses in Victoria; and as the electric telegraph is in full operation between Melbourne and all the Western Ports, namely, Portland Bay, Belfast, and Warrnambool, vessels detained on the coast, by light or contrary winds, might, when standing in shore, be reported by shewing their numbers, &c.

The Steam Navigation Board consists of five members, to whom are entrusted the licensing and supervision of all steam-vessels plying to and from the colony: those now under their control, number fifty-two.

The Board's Officers, namely, one inspector and one engineer, are constantly employed examining the machinery, hulls, lights, life-boats, life-buoys, and other appointments required by the Act of Council, No. 16 Vic., No. 25; and to the vigilant supervision so exercised may safely be attributed the few casualties that have been experienced from defective machinery within the colony.

As before remarked, Melbourne being the port where the greatest portion of the trade of Victoria concentrates, the amount of shipping arriving there is correspondingly large.

At Geelong, some few ships arrive direct from England, but owing to the existence of a bar which prevents vessels of any great tonnage coming up to the town, this port has not progressed in the same proportion as Melbourne. This bar is now, however, being removed, so that it may be expected that the importance of Geelong will increase. The trade of the other ports is confined to the coasting vessels, which convey supplies from, and wool and agricultural produce to, Melbourne.

At Melbourne, a Government Shipping Master is appointed to see that all seamen are properly engaged and discharged; that the wages due to them are paid; to inquire into and adjust differences between masters of vessels and their crews; to take care that proper medical treatment is administered to sick seamen; and to take charge of the effects of deceased seamen. In Geelong, the harbor master, and at the other ports the collector of customs, performs these duties. At Melbourne, during the year ending 31st May, 1858, the number of sailors engaged was 6,965; discharged, 4,284. Wages paid, £63,168; advances, £30,240.

About eighty beds are appropriated for sick sailors in the Melbourne Hospital. The Bethel or Seamen's Floating Church is anchored in Hobson's Bay. A Sailors' Home, for seamen of all nations, is about to be established at the port of Melbourne.

LIGHTHOUSES AND HARBOR LIGHTS.

Cape Otway Light, on extreme S.W. point of Cape Otway, Revolving, White. Flinders Light, on centre of Gabo Island, five miles and a half to the S.W. of Cape Howe, Fixed, White. Shortland's Bluff High Light, on Shortland's Bluff, Fixed, White. Shortland's Bluff Low Light, on Shortland's Bluff, Fixed, Red. Gellibrand's Point Light, on Gellibrand's Point, Fixed, Red. Upper Lightship, north end of west channel, Fixed (two lights), White. Swan Spit Lightship, on S.W. end of Swan Spit, Fixed (one light,) Red. Geelong Lightship, at eastern entrance of ship-channel near the Bird Rock, Fixed, White. Portland Pier-head Light, on end of old jetty, Fixed, Red. Geelong Pier-head Light, on end of steam-boat jetty, Fixed, White. Sandridge Jetty Light, on end of Sandridge jetty, Fixed, Red. Sandridge Railway Pier Light, on end of Sandridge Railway Pier, Fixed, Green. Williamstown Jetty Light, on end of old jetty, Fixed, Red.

New Lighthouses now building will be lighted sometime in November.—Cape Schank, on highest point of Cape Schank, Bass's Straits, Flashing, White. Wilson's Promontory, on extreme southern point of Wilson's Promontory, Bass's Straits, Fixed White.

BEACONS, at Nepean Rock, Point Nepean, Point Lonsdale, Swan Point High, Swan Point Low, Williamsand, Anonyma Rock.

BUOYS.

Port Phillip Bay.—Two between Symond's and west channels; eight south side of west channel; five north side of west channel: five south side of east channel; seven north side of east channel; five inner west channel; nine in Port Phillip Bay; three in Geelong Harbor, with several dolphins. Ships entering any port from sea, white buoys to be left on the starboard hand, black buoys on the port hand.

There are eight buoys and moorings at Port Fairy; two at Portland; six at Port Albert; and two at Warrnambool.

Life-Boat Stations, at Port Phillip Heads, Portland Bay, Belfast, Warrnambool, and Port Albert.

Tide tables to show time of High-water at Gellibrand's Point, Williamstown, and all ports within the colony, were published in the *Government Gazette* of June 22, 1858.

TIDAL SIGNALS.

Tidal Signals for River Yarra, Gellibrand's Point.—Black ball, yard-arm 8 ft. Ball over blue flag, 8½ ft. Red flag, 9 ft. Ball under blue flag, 9½ ft. Blue flag, yard arm, 10 ft. Blue flag, half-mast, 10½ ft. Red flag at mast-head, 11 ft. The number of vessels coming up the Bay is denoted by Marryatt's signals hoisted at the mast head. Overland Mail, red ensign at the mast-head. Steamers, red flag; if more than one, the number hoisted underneath. Tidal signals, hoisted at western yard-arm. Communications to ships, eastern yard-arm.

Tidal Signals, Geelong Bar.—One blue flag, 10 ft. One ball, 10½ ft. One ball, with blue flag over, 11 ft. One ball, blue flag under, 11½ ft. Two balls, 12 ft. Two balls, with blue flag under, 12½ ft. Two balls, with blue flag over, 13 ft. Two balls, red flag under, 13½ ft. Two balls, red flag over, 14 ft. Two balls, red flag between, 14½ ft. One red flag, 15 ft.

Tidal Signals, Point Lonsdale.—Blue flag, half-mast, flood, 1st quarter. Blue flag, mast-head, flood, 2nd quarter. Red flag, half-mast, flood, 3rd quarter. Red flag, mast-head, flood, last quarter. Blue flag, half-mast, with ball under, ebb, 1st quarter. Blue flag, mast head, ball under, ebb, 2nd quarter. Red flag, half-mast, with ball under, ebb, 3rd quarter. Red flag, mast-head, with ball under, ebb, last quarter.

Tidal Signals, Port Albert.—One black ball, 8 ft. One red flag, 9 ft. One white flag, 10 ft. One ball, with white flag over, 11 ft. Two balls, 12 feet. Two balls, with white flag under, 13 ft.

The new commercial code of signals for the use of all nations is (in addition to Marryatt's signals) in use at all the signal-stations within Victoria.

IMMIGRATION DEPARTMENT.

The business of the Immigration Department comprises:—

(1.) The introduction and distribution of Government Immigrants.

(2.) The protection of passengers arriving at, and departing from, the Colony by sea.

There are no records existing in the country which throw any light on the subject of Immigration prior to 1844, in which year the total number of arrivals was 2,648, while in the fourteen months ending 2nd March, 1851, the number had increased to 10,760. Subsequent returns show the arrivals in each year to have been as follows:—In 1852, 94,664 persons; 1853, 92,312; 1854, 83,410; 1855, 66,571; 1856, 41,594; 1857, 63,260.

Many of these arrivals, however, having by their industry acquired an independence, or a sufficiency of means to enable them to return to their native lands, or having been induced by various considerations to remove to other parts of Australia, a deduction must be made for the loss, which amounted in the year 1851 to 2,962 persons; 1852, to 31,038; 1853, to 42,443; and in the four years ending December, 1857, to 102,974 persons.

Government Immigration was, until 1857, maintained by funds appropriated under an Act of the Imperial Parliament, which provided that half the proceeds of the sales of land should be expended in the introduction of labor. Since the commencement of 1857, the amount to be expended in the importation of Government Immigrants has been voted by the Legislative Assembly.

The number of Government Immigrants introduced, from the separation of the Colony from New South Wales on 1st July 1851 to the 31st December 1857, is as follows:—

Period.		*Male.*	*Females.*	*Total.*
July to December,	1851	1,082	905	1,987
During	1852	7,762	7,715	15,477
"	1853	5,236	9,342	14,578
"	1854	5,456	10,862	16,318
"	1855	3,149	6,096	9,245
"	1856	1,763	2,916	4 679
"	1857	5,429	8,940	14,369
Totals.		29,877	46,776	76,653

The Department has branches at Williamstown, Geelong, Portland, Belfast, Warrnambool, and Port Albert.

At the Immigration Office, in Melbourne, a general record of all persons arriving at, and departing from, the Colony is kept, and information respecting them is given to persons applying by letter or otherwise. Instructions to immigrants, on their arrival at Melbourne, will be found under the head of "Immigrants' Aid Society," *vide* Contents.

Government Immigrants, on arrival, are received into the Depôts, where they are open to the public for engagement.

The single women are lodged in a separate Depôt, no access to which is allowed without a written permission which may be obtained at the Immigration Office. An introduction is required from all employers who may be unknown to the Immigration Agent, and no hotel or boarding house keeper is permitted on any account to hire single females.

Persons resident in Victoria, wishing to bring their relatives and friends from the United Kingdom, can secure passages for them in vessels chartered by Her Majesty's Land and Immigration Commissioners. The regulations vary from time to time, according to the circumstances of the colony; but the object of them is to promote the union of families which, without Government aid, might be separated. The principle in this system is, that upon a certain deposit being made, the Government undertakes to bring nominees to the colony, paying the remainder of the expenses incurred from funds voted from time to time for the encouragement of immigration, by the Colonial Legislature. The amount required to be deposited varies according to the age and sex of the nominee; but the average may be estimated at about one-third of the whole cost of the passage.

These regulations are published, when issued, in the *Government Gazette.*

The number of unassisted immigrants who have arrived in the Colony of Victoria by sea, from the 1st July 1851 to 31st December 1857, is shown by the subjoined table:—

Period.		*Males.*	*Females.*	*Total.*
July to December,	1851	7,512	1,517	9,029
During	1852	67,110	12,077	79,187
"	1853	60,796	16,938	77,734
"	1854	51,913	15,179	69,092
"	1855	44,740	12,586	57,326
"	1856	26,572	10,343	36,915
"	1857	35,461	13,400	48,861
Totals.		294,104	82,040	376,144

The number of departures from the colony by sea during the above period was about 178,455.

The official passenger lists of all vessels arriving at, and departing from, the Colony of Victoria, are preserved in the Immigration Office at Melbourne.

The duty of protecting passengers inwards and outwards, by sea, is imposed upon the Emigration Officers under the Imperial, and Colonial, Passengers' Acts. Emigration officers are stationed at each of the Ports of the Colony, and all ships conveying passengers are boarded and inspected by these officers, whose duty it is to see that the provisions of these Acts are duly complied with, and to render every assistance to passengers in the redress of their grievances. No passenger is allowed to leave a vessel until cleared by the Immigration Officer.

A charge of five shillings for each statute adult landed in the Colony is lev ed on the masters of vessels under the Act of Council, 18 Victoria, No. 5. An additional sum of ten pounds is required under the Act, 18 Victoria, No. 39, for every "male adult native of China, or its dependencies, or of any island in the Chinese Seas, or of any person born of Chinese parents," who may be landed in the colony.

GOVERNMENT, LAW, &c.

[A full and complete list of Names of Officials, with various particulars in reference to Railways, Institutions, Companies, Societies, Churches, Country Districts, &c., is corrected monthly in *Bradshaw's Guide to Victoria*, which is published as a companion to this annual *Handbook.*]

GOVERNMENT.—Captain-General and Governor-in-Chief and Vice-Admiral of Victoria: His Excellency Sir Henry Barkly, K.C.B. Private Secretary: Captain O. F. Timins. Military Secretary and Aide-de-Camp: Captain W. C. Bancroft. Clerk: R. Wadsworth.

EXECUTIVE COUNCIL.—Commander of Her Majesty's Forces in the Australian Colonies: Major-General Edward Macarthur. Chief Secretary: Hon. John O'Shanassy. Attorney-General: Hon. Henry Samuel Chapman. Solicitor-General: Hon. Richard Davies Ireland. Treasurer: Hon. George Harker. President of the Board of Land and Works: Hon. Charles Gavan Duffy. Commissioner of Trade and Customs: Hon. Henry Miller. Postmaster-General: Hon. George Samuel Evans. Clerk: J. H. Kay, R.N.

PARLIAMENT.—Legislative Council.—Composed of thirty Members for six Provinces. President: Hon. Sir James Frederick Palmer, Knight.

Chairman of Committees: Hon. John Hodgson. Members: Central Province (5), Hons. John Pascoe Fawkner, Thomas Howard Fellows, Nehemiah Guthridge, John Hodgson, John Hood; Eastern Province (5), Matthew Hervey, William Highett, James Stewart, Robert Thomson, Benjamin Williams; North-Western Province (5), John Allen, Dennis Patrick Keogh, W. H. Fancourt Mitchell, John Hunter Patterson, George Urquhart; Southern Province (5), John Barter Bennett, W. J. Turner Clarke, Donald Kennedy, Thomas M'Combie, Thomas Herbert Power; South-Western (5), James Cowie, James Henty, Robert Culbertson Hope, William Roope, James Ford Strachan; Western Province (5), Stephen George Henty, Henry Miller, James Frederick Palmer, Daniel Joseph Tierney, Charles Vaughan. Clerk: G. W. Rusden. Usher: Col. H. H. Farquharson.

LEGISLATIVE ASSEMBLY.—Composed of sixty Members for thirty-eight Districts. Speaker: Hon. Francis Murphy. Chairman of Committees: B. C. Aspinall. Members: Alberton (1), James Davis; Anglesey (1), Peter Snodgrass; Belfast (1), Francis E. Beaver; Brighton (1), Charles Hotson Ebden; Castlemaine (2), Richard D. Ireland, R. S. W. Sitwell; Colac (1), Theodore Hancock; Collingwood (2), Thomas Embling, George Harker; Dundas and Follet (1), William Thomas Mollison; East Bourke (2), A. F. A. Greeves, Richard Heales; Evelyn and Mornington (1), W. A. D. Anderson; Geelong (4), George Board, John Henry Brooke, Charles Sladen, Alexander Thomson; Gipps Land (1), John Johnson; Kilmore (1), John O'Shanassy; Kyneton Boroughs (1), George Walker Johnson; Loddon (2), John Downes Owens, Ebenezer Syme; Melbourne (5), Henry Langlands, Archd. Michie, David Moore, James Service, John Thomas Smith; Murray Boroughs (1), Francis Murphy; Normanby (1), Edward Henty; North Grenville (1), Peter Lalor; North Grant (1), John Basson Humffray; Ovens (1), John Dennistoun Wood; Polwarth, &c. (2), Colin Campbell, Jeremiah George Ware; Portland (2), John Findlay, D. A. Hughes; Richmond (2), Daniel Stodhart Campbell, George Samuel Evans; Rodney (1), John Everard; Sandhurst Boroughs (1), James M. Grant; South Bourke (2), Patrick O'Brien, Sidney Ricardo; South Grant (3), William Clark Haines, John Myles, Horatio Spencer Wills; South Melbourne (1), Andrew Clarke; St. Kilda (2), H. S. Chapman, J. B. Crews; Talbot (2), Butler C. Aspinall, David Blair; The Murray (2), Travers Adamson, Wm. Furlonge; Villiers, &c. (2), Charles Gavan Duffy, William Rutledge; Warrnambool (1), George Samuel Wegg Horne; West Bourke (2), Patrick Phelan, Joseph Wilkie; Williamstown (1), C. J. Perry; Wimmera (2). James McCulloch, John Quarterman. Clerk: John Barker. Clerk Assistant: A. G. Dumas. Sergeant-at-Arms: W. G. Palmer.

LAW.—Chief Justice: His Honor Sir W. Foster Stawell, Knt. Puisne Judges: His Honor Redmond Barry, His Honor Edward Eyre Williams, His Honor Robert Molesworth. Attorney-General: Hon. H. S. Chapman. Solicitor-General: Hon. R. D. Ireland. Crown Solicitor: Henry F. Gurner. Master in Equity and Chief Commissioner of Insolvent Estates: Frederick Wilkinson, Curator of Intestate Estates: George Shovelbottom. Prothonotary: John Alfred Porter. Sheriff: Claud Farie. [For lists of Commissioners for Taking Affidavits, Official Assignees, Deputy-Sheriffs, Chairmen and Judges of County Courts, Crown Prosecutors, Resident Magistrates, Clerks of Petty Sessions, Barristers, Attorneys, &c., &c., see *Bradshaw's Monthly Guide to Victoria.*]

MILITARY.—A detachment of the 40th Regiment, located in two barracks. Commander of the Forces: Hon. Edward Macarthur. Assistant Military Secretary: Lieut. J. T. J. Boyd. Deputy Adjutant-General: Lieut.-Colonel J. M. Bladen Neill. Major of Brigade: Captain Hare. Barrack Master: Lieut. Buckle. Volunteer Artillery Corps.—Lieutenant-Colonel: W. A. D. Anderson. Yeomanry Corps.—Lieutenant-Colonel: James H. Ross. (See particulars, per Index.)

NAVAL.—H. M. Colonial Steam Sloop *Victoria*, 3 guns. Commander: W. H. Norman. (See particulars, per Index.)

GOVERNMENT DEPARTMENTS.—Under Secretary, J. Moore. Co missioners of Audit: C. H. Symonds, F. Jones, A. J. Agg. Registrar-General: Norman Campbell. Assistant Registrar-General: W. H. Archer.

Gold Receiver: John Wilkinson. Chief Medical Officer and President of the Central Board of Health and Medical Board of Victoria: Wm. M'Crea, M.D. Surveyor-General: Charles Whybrow Ligar. Commissioner of Public Works: Hon. Captain Pasley. Commissioner of Roads and Bridges: John Steavenson. Engineer-in-Chief of Victorian Railways: G. C. Darbyshire. President of the Pilot Board, Chief Harbor Master, and Chairman of the Steam Navigation Board: Charles Ferguson. Superintendent of Electric Telegraphs: S. W. M'Gowan. Inspector-General of Penal Establishments: W. T. N. Champ. Chief Commissioner of Police: — Standish. Geological Surveyor: A. R. C. Selwyn. Director of Meteorological Observatories and Secretary to Board of Science: R. Brough Smyth. Government Botanist: Dr. Mueller. Chairman of Denominational School Board: Judge Pohlman. Chairman of National School Board: Hon. Sir James Palmer. Governor of Melbourne Gaol: George Wintle. Surgeon Superintendent at Sanitary Station: James Reed. Surgeon Superintendent of Yarra Bend Lunatic Asylum: R. Bowie. Librarian of Public Library: Augustus Tulk. Chief Inspector of Distilleries: W. R. Belcher. Government Printer: John Ferres. Government Storekeeper: Richard Nash. Director of Museum: Professor McCoy. Certifying Barrister of Friendly Societies: B. F. Bunny. Director of Model Farm: Thomas Skilling. Marine Surveyor for Victoria: M. G. H. W. Ross. Shipping Master and Registrar of Seamen: John J. Shillinglaw. Immigration Agent: J. D. Pinnock.

ECCLESIASTICAL.

[For particulars of History and Progress of Churches, see Contents.]

CHURCH OF ENGLAND.—Bishop of Melbourne: Right Rev. Charles Perry, D.D. Dean and Archdeacon of Melbourne: Very Rev. Hussey Burgh Macartney, D.D. Archdeacon of Geelong: Ven. Theodore Carlos Benoni Stretch, A.M. Archdeacon of Portland: Ven. Thomas Henry Braim, D.D. Revs. S. L. Chase, G. Goodman, J. Freeman, J. Darling, R. B. Barlow, J. Linskea, H. H. P. Handfield, C. Booth, W. Byrnes, G. Studdert, G. Pollard, P. Homan, W. McJennett, R. Stephens, J. T. Schleicher, J. Potter, C. Searle, J. Sullivan, W. R. L. Bennett, E. B. Clarke, T. B. Garlick, G. J. Russell, S. Taylor, J. B. Stair, C. P. M. Bardin, J. Barlow, R. B. Dickinson, E. Puckle, J. S. Low, H. E. Windle, J. C. T. Stretch, R. T. Cummins, T. Heron, W. Wood, T. Budd, J. Lynar, W. Singleton, F. G. Barton, H. W. W. Liddiard, W. Carter, J. Y. Wilson, J. H. Gregory, A. Crawford, J. D. Brennan, P. K. Simmons, J. Stone, W. N. Guinness, D. Seddon, J. Cheyne, W. Bean, L. A. Baker, A. J. M'Causland, F. T. C. Russell, P. T. Beamish, W. Copeland, J. G. Medland, E. Tanner, F. Smith, T. Dowell. Chancellor of the Diocese: C. J. Griffith, A.M. Registrar of the Diocese: T. T. a'Beckett.

ROMAN CATHOLIC CHURCH.—Right Rev. the Bishop, J. A. Goold, D.D.; Very Rev. the Vicar-General, J. Fitzpatrick, D.D.; Very Rev. the Vicar-General, P. B. Geoghegan, D.D.; Revs. L. Shiel, D. M'Evey, J. Bleasdale, J. Barry, J. Lane, B. Power, J. O'Connell, P. Niall, C. O'Hea, J. Madden, J. Hoyne, M. Downing, E. O'Connell, H. Geoghegan, P. Smyth, — Backhaus, T. O'Rorke, J. Kennedy, F. Kums, P. Verling, J. B. Hayes, M. O'Brien, W. Shinnick, E. M'Carthy, R. Rankin, M. Farrelly, — Slattery, J. Maloney, E. M'Carthy, R. Downing, P. Madden, — McGirr, R. Fennelly, P. Birch, M. Stack.

WESLEYAN CHURCHES.—Revs. D. J. Draper, W. L. Binks, T. Williams, W. P. Wells, J. S. Waugh, S. W. Worth, W. Hopkins, S. Knight, R. Hart, E. King, J. Atkin, W. Hill, G. Daniel, J. Dodgson, S. Waterhouse, W. C. Currey, G. B. Richards, W. Lightbody, J. Beckford, C. Lane, T. Taylor, J. W. Crisp, J. Albiston, W. Woodal, T. Raston, H. Chester, W. L. Blamires, J. Dare, C. Dubourg, J. Catterall, J. Mewton, J. C. Symons.

INDEPENDENT or CONGREGATIONAL CHURCHES.—Revs. A. Morison, R. Fletcher, W. B. Landells, R. Bowman, T. Odell, W. Moss, J. P. Sunderland, W. R. Lewis, H. Thomas, W. C. Robinson, J. Mirams, W. R. Fletcher, J. Apperly, J. H. Jackson, J. Brien, E. Day, J. Summers, H. Kidgell, J. Pitman, B. Couzins, — Moorish, J. Sleigh.

BAPTIST CHAPELS.—Revs. J. Taylor, Isaac New, J. Turner, B. Lemon, J. Collins, S. Hewlet, J. Moody, J. Slade, T. Sutton.

SYNOD OF VICTORIA.—Revs. I. Hethrington, G. M. Reed, J. Clow, T. Craig, P. Gunn, D. Boyd, A. Love, J. Gow, H. Blair, J. Low, J. Parker, W. Taggart, R. Hogg, A. Graham, S. Corrie, A. Duff.

FREE PRESBYTERIAN CHURCH OF VICTORIA.—Revs. A. Cairns, D.D., W. Fraser, G. Divorty, J. Clark, D. McDonald, J. Leigh, W. Simpson, A. Adams, T. Hastie, W. Henderson, A. Proudfoot, J. Storie, J. Moir, J. Mackie, D, McCalman.—The following Ministers have formed themselves into a separate Synod: Revs. W. Miller, A. Paul, A. McVean, A. Maxwell, J. Macdougall, A. W. Sinclair.

UNITED PRESBYTERIAN CHURCH.—Revs. A. M. Ramsay, R. Hamilton, A. McNicol, W. Ridley, D. H. Ballantyne, A. Scales. Clerk of Melbourne Presbytery: Rev. R. Hamilton.

UNITED PRESBYTERIAN SYNOD OF AUSTRALIA.—Revs. James Ballantyne, John Ballantyne, J. Cooper, W. Jarrett.

UNITED PRESBYTERIAN CHURCH OF SCOTLAND.—Revs. A. D. Kininmont, D. Chapman.

PRIMITIVE METHODISTS.—Revs. M. Clarke, W. Calvert, G. Watts, G. T. Hall, J. Gates, L. Dobinson.

UNITED METHODIST FREE CHURCHES.—Revs. J. Sayer, W. Middleton, J. Townend, M. W. Bradney.

There is also a Unitarian Church, Jews' Synagogue, Hebrew Congregation, Welsh Calvinistic Methodist Church, Plymouth Brethren, a body of Christians called Disciples of Christ, German Lutheran Church, Society of Friends' Meeting House, a religious body called the New Church, and a Chinese-Christian Meeting House in Melbourne.

COMPANIES, INSTITUTIONS, SOCIETIES, &c.*

COMPANIES.—Melbourne Exchange Company, Gas Company, Melbourne and Hobson's Bay Railway Company, Melbourne and Suburban Railway Company, Geelong and Melbourne Railway Company, St. Kilda and Brighton Railway Company, Studley Park Bridge Company, St. Kilda Sea Bathing Company, South Yarra Water Works Company, Bendigo Water Works Company. [Lists of Banks and Insurance Companies, with their respective amounts of subscribed capital, reserve fund, &c., are given elsewhere.]

INSTITUTIONS.—University of Melbourne, Philosophical Institute, Mechanics' Institutions, Mining Institute of Victoria, Victorian Institute of Architects, Public Library. *Benevolent Institutions*—Benevolent Asylum, Female Home, Female Refuge, Lunatic Asylum, Lying-in Hospital, Melbourne Hospital.

SOCIETIES.—*Religious Societies*—Bible Society, Bethel Union, Evangelical Alliance, Congregational Home Mission, Ladies' City Mission, London Missionary Society, Chinese Mission, Aborigines Mission, Sabbath Observance Society, Suppression of Vice Society, Tract Society. *Benevolent Societies*—Ladies' Benevolent Society, Humane Society, Immigrants' Aid Society, City Court Mission, Juvenile Traders' Association, Jewish Philanthropic Society, Ladies' Melbourne Visiting Society, Ladies' North Melbourne District Visiting Society, St. Mark's District Visiting Society, Sandridge District Visiting Society, Widow and Orphan Institution of the Colony of Victoria. *Temperance Societies*—Temperance League of Victoria, Band of Hope, Temperance and General Debating Society; and a Total Abstinence Society at nearly every large township. *Building Societies*—Atlas Building and Investment Society, City of Melbourne Suburban and Agricultural Freehold Home Society, Collingwood Equitable Mutual

* Names of New Companies, Societies, &c., on being established should be sent to the Editor, *Bradshaw's Guide* office, Melbourne.

Building Association, Colonial Freehold Land Society, Richmond Building and Investment Society, Second Collingwood Building and Investment Society, Second Union Benefit Building and Investment Society, Second Victoria Building and Investment Society. *Miscellaneous*—Chamber of Commerce, Melbourne Brokers' Association, Victorian Association of Marine Surveyors, Medical Society of Victoria, Microscopic Society, Pharmaceutical Society of Victoria, Philharmonic Society, Horticultural Society of Victoria, Zoological Society, Early Closing Association, Agricultural Club, Port Phillip Farmers' Society, German Association, German Liedertafel Harmonia, Victorian Society of Fine Arts, Melbourne Young Men's Mutual Improvement Association, Literary Association of the Companions of St. Augustine, St. Patrick's Society, Victorian Convention, Industrial Society, Licensed Victuallers' Association, Builders and Contractors' Association. Mutual Progressive Society of Operative Carpenters and Joiners, United Insurance Company's Fire Brigade, &c.

CLUBS.—Melbourne Club, Victorian Club, Melbourne Garrick Club, Melbourne Hunt Club, Victoria Jockey Club, Victoria Turf Club, Victoria Archery Club, Hawthorne Archery Club. *Cricket Clubs*—Coast, Collingwood, Emerald Hill, Hawthorne, I Zingari, Melbourne, Olympic, Phœnix, Richmond, South Park, South Yarra, Starlight, St. Kilda, St. Kilda Park, Twilight, University, Victoria, Williamstown, Williamstown Pioneer, Yarra Yarra, Corio, Moorabool, Ballaarat, Tarradale, Barker's Creek, Castlemaine, Maryborough, &c.

MASONIC LODGES.—English.—Provincial Grand Lodge of the District of Victoria, Lodge of Australia Felix, Lodge of Australasia, Unity and Prudence, Portland Lodge of Victoria, St. Kilda Lodge, Hobson's Bay Lodge, Golden Lodge of Bendigo, Victoria Lodge, Mount Alexander Lodge, Yarrowee Lodge, Yarra Yarra Lodge, Mt. Franklyn Lodge of Hiram, Ballaarat Lodge, Boroondara Lodge, Collingwood Lodge, Beechworth Lodge of St. John, Meridian Lodge of St. John, United Tradesmen's Lodge of Ballaarat East, Mackenzie Lodge, Lodge of Industry, Mariner's Lodge, Lodge of Mount Macedon, Lodge of Concord, Maryborough Lodge, Corinthian Lodge, Sandridge Marine Lodge, Richmond Lodge. *Lodges of Instruction:* Australia Felix, Collingwood Lodge, Lodge of Industry, Combermere Lodge, the Victoria General Lodge of Instruction. *Royal Arch Chapters:* Australasian Chapter, Bendigo Chapter, Collingwood Chapter, Meridian Chapter. *Knights Templar:* Pembroke Encampment of Victoria. *Ancient and Accepted Rite:* Sovereign Chapter of Knights of the Eagle and Pelican, and P. P. Princes Rose Croix. Irish.—Prov. Grand Lodge of Victoria, Australian Felix Lodge of Hiram, Washington Lodge, Victoria Lodge of East Collingwood, St. John's Tradesmen's Lodge, Buninyong Lodge, Moonee Ponds Rural Lodge, Rose, Thistle, and Shamrock Lodge, Carlton Lodge, Royal Park Lodge, King Solomon's Lodge. Scotch.—Provincial Grand Lodge of Victoria, Australasia Kilwinning Lodge, United Tradesmen's Lodge, Lodge of Judah. *Royal Arch Chapter:* United Tradesmen's Chapter, (For article on Freemasonry, *vide* Contents, and list of Lodges, in *Bradshaw's Guide.*)

ODD FELLOWS' LODGES.—Manchester Unity: Australia Felix, Melbourne, Victoria, Rose of England, Britannia, Hope of Richmond, Collingwood, Good Intent, Good Samaritan, Castlemaine, Olive Branch, Rose of Brunswick, Williamstown, Emerald Hill, Alliance, Geelong, Southern Star, Buninyong, Ballaarat, Prince of Wales, Bendigo, Gold Miners' Pride, James Roe, Strangers' Refuge. Ancient and Independent Order: Duke of York, Loyal Fitzroy, Prince Albert, Australian, Loyal Brothers, Loyal Ashby. Grand United Order: Felix, Prince of Wales, Victoria, Britannia, President, Brighton Union, Prince Albert, Rose, Napier, Eltham Union.

There are also Societies of Foresters, Rechabites, &c.

MISCELLANEOUS.

NATIONAL AND DENOMINATIONAL SCHOOLS.—(See Contents.)
GOLD OFFICES.—(See Contents.)
CORPORATIONS AND MUNICIPALITIES.—(See Contents.)
LAW, POLICE, AND PENAL.—(See Contents.)

IMMIGRATION REGULATIONS AND IMMIGRANTS' AID SOCIETY.—(See Contents.)

ELECTRIC TELEGRAPH.—(See Contents.)

LABOR MARKETS AND REGISTRY OFFICES are established in Melbourne and suburbs, where respectable male and female servants are engaged. Arrangements have been made for temporary accommodation for persons whose pecuniary circumstances are not able to provide shelter.

POST OFFICE, MELBOURNE.—Postmaster-General: Hon. G. S. Evans. Secretary: W. Turner. TOWN LETTERS—Under half oz., 2d.; exceeding half oz. and not exceeding 1 oz., 4d.; exceeding 1 oz. and not exceeding 2 oz., 8d.; exceeding 2 oz. and not exceeding 3 oz., 1s.; and every ounce or fraction of an ounce, 4d. additional. COUNTRY LETTERS—Under half zo., 4d.; exceeding half oz. and not exceeding 1 oz., 8d.; exceeding 1 oz. and not exceeding 2 oz., 1s. 4d.; exceeding 2 oz. and not exceeding 3 oz., 2s.; and every ounce or fraction of an ounce, 8d. additional. NEWSPAPERS—For delivery within Victoria, or for transmission from Victoria beyond seas, to be charged 1d. each; but newspapers for transmission to foreign countries and British colonies, *viâ* the United Kingdom, to be charged the additional rates in Scale B, issued at the General Post Office. BOOKS AND PACKETS—In and for Victoria and other Australian colonies: not exceeding 4 oz., 6d.; every additional 2 oz. or fraction of 2 oz., 3d. (weight not to exceed 1 lb.); in addition to which there shall be charged for transmission by ship one shilling as sea postage. Between Victoria and United Kingdom and India: for every weight not exceeding 4 oz., 6d.; for every additional 2 oz. or portion thereof up to any weight not exceeding 3 lbs., 3d.; in addition to which there shall be charged for sea postage on each packet. REGISTERED LETTERS are received daily from 9 a.m. to 4 p.m., but must be posted one hour prior to the closing of mails. NEWSPAPERS are cleared for despatch at 8.30 and 11 a.m., and at 1 p.m. and 4 p.m. CLOSING OF MAILS.—Notices of time of closing mails to all parts of the world are posted up in front of the Post Office. For Post Office statistics, *vide* contents.

RAILWAYS.—Details in reference to those lines in operation and in progress will be found elsewhere.

STEAMERS to Adelaide, Sydney, Hobart Town, Launceston, Geelong, Port Albert, Portland, Belfast, Warrnambool, Queenscliffe, St. Leonards-on-the-Bay, Schnapper Point, The Murray, New Zealand, &c.; also tug-boats and river steamers. See *Bradshaw's Guide* or daily papers. Information respecting the Royal Mail Line of Steamers in another part of this work.

SHIPS.—Liverpool and London lines of vessels, also to various parts of the world. Coasters to the different colonies.

BOATMENS' RATES AND FARES, with instructions, are published.

OMNIBUSES, CABS, DRAYS, AND OTHER CONVEYANCES.—Full particulars in *Bradshaw's Guide.*

NEWSPAPERS, &c.—A complete list of names, with time of publishing, in *Bradshaw's Guide.*

TARIFF.—Ale, porter, spruce, and other beer, cider, and perry, 6d. per gallon. Cigars, 8s. per lb. Coffee and chicory, 2d. per lb. Spirits, or strong waters, of any strength not exceeding the strength of proof by Syke's hydrometer, and so on in proportion for any greater or less strength than the strength of proof, 10s. per gallon. Spirits, cordials, liqueurs, or strong waters, sweetened or mixed with any article so that the degree of strength cannot be ascertained by Syke's hydrometer, 10s. per gallon. Spirits, perfumed, 10s. per gallon. Sugar, raw and refined, and sugar candy, 6s. per cwt. Molasses and treacle, 3s. per cwt. Opium, and all preparations thereof, 10s. per lb. Tea, 6d. per lb. Tobacco and snuff, 2s. per lb. Wine, 2s. per gallon. All other goods, wares, and merchandise free. Spirits in bulk under 14 gallons cannot be imported, of tobacco or cigars under 60 lbs., nor of opium under 45 lbs.

TASMANIA (VAN DIEMEN'S LAND).

PRELIMINARY.

On 1st December, 1642, Abel Jansen Tasman discovered this island, which he called Van Diemen in honor of the East Indian Governor-General. Captain Marion, in the Mascarin and Castries, seeking for a southern continent, entered Frederick Henry Bay on 4th March, 1772. On 9th March, 1773, Captain Furneaux, in the Adventure, a ship belonging to Captain Cook's fleet, anchored in Adventure Bay. On 25th January, 1777, Captain Cook, then on his third voyage, visited the same spot. On 20th April, 1792, Admiral Brune D'Entrecasteaux. in the Research, accompanied by Captain Huon Kermandee, in the Esperance, in search of La Perouse, brought up in Recherche Bay, and returned in January, next year. Their names are perpetuated by a channel, an island, and a river. Dr. Bass, in February, 1798, made the discovery that Tasmania was an island, and the straits separating it from New Holland still bear his name.

HISTORICAL.

Amongst the records of the early attempts to form the settlement of Port Phillip, there is preserved a document which throws some light upon the combination of circumstances which led the way to the foundation of the Colony of Tasmania. Colonel Collins, under date Port Phillip, 31st Dec., 1803, wrote in a general order, "It has never been my wish to make the Sabbath day other than a day of devotion and rest, but circumstances compel me to employ it in labor. In this the whole are concerned, since the sooner we are enabled to leave this unpromising and unproductive country, the sooner shall we be able to reap the advantage and enjoy the comforts of a more fertile spot." Thus the settlement of Victoria was postponed, and the colonization of Tasmania hastened by some thirty years. In due time the ship Ocean, with Captain Collins on board, entered Storm Bay, 16th February, 1804, sailed up the Derwent,—and on the 19th the Governor landed at Sullivan's Cove, the future harbor of Hobart Town. Lieut. Bowen, in the brig Lady Nelson, with a party from Port Jackson, had taken possession of the island, and settled on the east bank of the Derwent at Restdown, now Risdon, on 10th August, 1803. Colonel Patterson also sailed from Sydney to form a new settlement and take command at Port Dalrymple. York Town was first selected; then George Town; and Launceston was finally fixed on as the site of the northern capital. For several years had a desperate struggle for existence. Kangaroo were purchased by the Commissariat at 8d. per lb., and flour was £112 per ton. The rations were reduced in 1805-6 to a very low scale. Sometimes there was no sugar, at other times no beef or pork in the island. The wheat crop failed in 1807, and the price of that article rose to £4 a bushel, which would make flour about £200 a ton. In 1809 the settlers were allowed to pay their debts to the crown in wheat at 15s. a bushel. On 24th March, 1810, Governor Collins died, and it is asserted that two gentlemen the same night destroyed all his official documents by fire. It is a fact that the garrison order book is the only record of 1809 among the archives of the colony. An interregnum occurred, during which Lieutenant E. Lord, Captain Murray, and Lieutenant-Colonel Geils successively assumed the government. The population was estimated at 1500, and there was the same number of acres under wheat. Population began to stretch across to Launceston, the vicinity of which was more favorable for cultivation than the neighborhood of Hobart Town, and in 1812 Major Gordon was appointed commandant at Port Dalrymple. Governor Davey arrived on 4th February, 1813. On 19th June the two ports were first opened to commerce. In 1816 a census was taken, which showed a total of 1461,—211 being in Cornwall and 1250 in Buckingham, the two counties into which the whole island was then divided. That year there were 964 acres of wheat, 44 of barley, 5 of peas, and 41 of potatoes, also 34 horses, 1956 cattle, and 20,501 sheep, in Cornwall. On 9th April, 1817, Governor Sorrell arrived and Davey sailed. Regular roads began now to be formed. The stock in Buckingham consisted of 188 horses, 9868 cattle, 76,991 sheep, and 1552 pigs; the acres in cultivation in the same county were—wheat, 2767; barley, 138; peas and beans, 94, and potatoes, 196. Successful industry evoked commerce; 26 vessels arrived and 20 sailed; 20,000 bushels of wheat were exported to Sydney: and a weekly post was established between Launceston and Hobart Town. In 1819 the population, according to the muster roll, amounted to 4411. There were 7292 acres wheat, 316 barley, 263 peas and beans, 459 potatoes,—total, 8330 acres under cultivation. There were 363 horses, 23,124 head of horned cattle, and 172,128 sheep; 26 vessels arrived and the same number sailed: there were 164 children at public schools; the Supreme Court was first held at Hobart Town; and a Civil Court with jurisdiction up to £50, without appeal, was established; wheat to the value of £4000, beside meat, was exported. Next year 48,917 lbs. of salted meat were supplied to Sydney. Two churches were built in 1822. The population had increased in 1823 to 10,009 souls; 57 vessels of an aggregate tonnage of 17,988 entered inwards and 52 vessels, and tonnage 16,730, sailed. The imports were valued at £15,740, the exports at £24,734, and consisted of 55,522 bushels wheat, 49 bushels barley, 50 tons potatos, 226 casks oil, 52 packages whalebone, 24 casks seal skins, 20 dry ditto, 600 kangaroo skins, 50 logs pine, 50 logs cedar, 794 bales, 17,160 lbs. wool, 300 lbs. tallow. The customs duties amounted to £20,389. The ordinary and fixed expenses of government were £24,434. On 14th May, 1823, Colonel Arthur, the fourth Lieutenant-Governor, arrived. From that date the records of the progress of the colony are formal and authentic. He introduced a new system; and order and subordination were the watchwords of that administrative chief. Originally a convict settlement, Tasmania continued to be the receptacle of criminals, till the urgent remonstrances of the free settlers compelled the Home Government in 1853 to abandon transportation to its shores.

PHYSICAL FEATURES.

Tasmania is a mountainous country. Two chains run through it longitudinally, nearly due north and south, known as the Eastern and Western Tiers. The intermediate space can only be said to be partially occupied. While patches to the east are located, little to the west is appropriated, unless in close proximity to the northern shore. The conformation of many of the mountains rising from the principal chains or branching off as spurs, is singularly picturesque. Most of them have names. In the Eastern Tier, Ben Lomond rises to a height of 5002 feet above sea level, Ben Nevis, 3910; and in the Western Tier, Mount Humboldt is 5520 feet high, Dry's Bluff 4590, Mount Arrowsmith 4075, and Valentine Peak 6000, which can be seen 60 miles off.

The island is well watered, and abounds in rivers, rivulets, and creeks. The Derwent is a noble stream, flowing by Hobart Town. The Huon is also navigable and runs through a fertile country. The junction of the two Esks constitute the navigable Tamar and the town of Launceston is situated in the cleft or fork. The Mersey is a considerable stream, and its sea mouth is practicable for vessels drawing fourteen feet. Coasters can enter the Don, the Forth, the Leven, and some others on the northern coast. The south of the island is studded with safe bays or harbors; there are a few also on the eastern side. The west coast is bold, rocky, and inhospitable, but there are at least three accessible ports—Port Davey, Macquarie Harbor, and Pieman's River. If steam vessels were employed, a trade might be safely carried on at all seasons, and there is said to be abundance of good soil and fine timber awaiting the enterprise of man. There are numerous and extensive lakes on the elevated table lands, as Great Lake, Arthur's, Sorell, St. Clair, Echo and Crescent. The extreme length of Tasmania is 250 miles, and its extreme breadth 200, but the configuration is very irregular. It is nearly as large as Ireland, and contains an area of 24,000 square miles or 15,000,000 acres. This colony is, beyond the others, more English in its aspect. The proportion of appropriated soil, however, is small compared with the superficial area yet unsold. No climate could be more salubrious or favorable to the constitution of English men and women. All the fruits and flowers grown at home when transplanted only thrive more luxuriantly in Tasmania. The sheep land is the settled districts in nearly all occupied, but soil of surprising fertility for agricultural purposes, covered by valuable timber, will be available for a century. [Additional particulars respecting the features of the island will be found further on].

We have said this country is more English in its character than its neighbours. This remark applies to its natural as well as its social features—of course, we mean in the districts which have been longest settled. The surface of the island is uneven, and it presents every variety of scenery—the snow-capped mountain, the wild shore, the barren tract, the green valley, watered by never-failing rivers - the extensive sheep-land, and the wide expanse of agricultural country, studded with neat, or splendid homesteads, and made pleasant to the English eye by the subdivision into fields and highly-cultivated gardens, fenced by hedges such as adorn the landscapes of Britain. Tasmania has, from the commencement of the colony, been resorted to by settlers of unquestionable respectability, numbers of whom have been long settled on the land they occupy. Their possessions are of various extent, from perhaps 70,000 acres, downwards.

SEASONS, CLIMATE, AND NATURAL SCENERY.

Tasmania is situated between the parallels of 40° 43′ and 43° 33′ south latitude. The climate, as may be imagined from the geographical position of the colony is removed from the extremes of either heat or cold. The summers are not unpleasantly warm, and woollen clothes are worn throughout the year. The winters are never so cold, even in the more elevated tableland, as to put a stop to the operations of the agriculturist. The colonist, who forgets not at the winter season the hospitality and the good old fare of fatherland, takes his dinner with open windows, through which he looks on waving fields of corn almost ready for the sickle. The scientific labors of Count Strzelecki have established some facts in connection with the climatology of Tasmania which place the island in a very favorable light. Some parts of the Northern Coast of the island possess the climate of Cheltenham and parts of Switzerland, in summer, and a winter similar to that of Algiers, Sicily, or New Orleans; Launceston, in its summer, resembles La Rochelle and Toulouse, and in its winter, Lisbon. The climate of the South resembles that of Augsburg or Dantzic in summer, and that of Smyrna in winter. The climatic condition of the island may be estimated by its rich *flora*, and by the healthy condition of its indigenous animals.

SCENERY.—In order to convey to the reader an idea of the scenery to be met with in Tasmania, we cannot do better than quote from the work of Count Strzelecki. He says:—"On examining the indigenous organic forms of Van Diemen's Land, we find they exhibit, in common with the rest of New Holland, a general physiognomy which is exceptive with respect to the rest of the globe; and that this general aspect or physiognomy is especially remarkable in the peculiar vegetation which pervades the whole of Terra Australis. The course of the seasons, which in extra-tropical countries causes the leaves to fall, and diversifies the foliage with the fresh bright verdure of spring, or the gorgeous and variegated tints of autumn, has no influence upon the unvaried mantle of olive green which clothes the forests of Tasmania. On a nearer examination, however, this vegetation is discovered to possess much gracefulness in the form both of species and of individual trees, and many delicate or minute shades in its verdure, which, combined with the ever-changing ash grey color of the shedding bark of the *Eucalyptæ*, the undulating and often broken surface upon which it thrives, and the resplendent sky above, present a world of interest and attraction. Frequently it is so grouped as to exhibit contrasts of surpassing beauty, the more striking because they are abrupt and little expected. Amid the apparent sameness of the forest may be often found spots teeming with a gigantic and luxurious vegetation, sometimes laid out in stately groves, free from thicket or underwood, sometimes opening on glades and slopes, intersected with rivulets, carpeted with the softest turf, and which lack only the thatched and gabled cottage, with its blue smoke curling amid the trees, to realize a purely European picture. Sometimes, again, the forest skirts an open country of hill and plain, gracefully sprinkled with isolated clumps of trees, covered with the richest tufted herbage, and enamelled with flowers of varied form and colour; or it is lost in immense thickets, where innumerable flowering shrubs and elegant interwoven creepers, form bowers as impenetrable and as picturesque as those seen in the forests of Brazil."

NATURAL PRODUCTIONS.

The chief productions of the island consist of wheat, oats, and all kinds of agricultural produce, butter, wool, bark, hops, fruit, oil, whalebone, timber, and stone. The soil generally is remarkable for its fertility. After many years of production without the aid of manure it still continues to yield fair crops, and single acres of virgin soil have yielded 60 bushels of wheat, 100 bushels of oats, or 10 tons of potatoes. A bushel of wheat has been produced, weighing 71 pounds. Without pretending to particularise minutely the various descriptions of timber which this island produces, it may be proper to mention the gum and stringy-bark amongst the hardwoods chiefly used for house and shipbuilding purposes. It is very strong and durable, and the trees attain an immense growth: six feet in diameter is a common size. The blackwood and myrtle are in high esteem for cabinet-work; and there is also a very valuable description of pine. Wild flowers and heaths of great delicacy and beauty abound everywhere. Coal has been found in several parts of the colony, and mines are now worked at the Mersey, on the north side of the island, Douglas River and Schouten Island, on the east; and New Town and Port Arthur on the south; the mineral is known to exist in the neighborhood of Macquarie Harbor, and in the mountain ranges near Fingal there is a very extensive deposit of capital coal, which presents a very thick seam at the surface, and might be worked by adit with great profit if a rail or tramroad were constructed for carrying it to a shipping place. Limestone abounds in every part of the island; marble and slate are also obtained. There are inexhaustible beds of clay, adapted for both brickwork and pottery. Gold has been found in several localities, and some persons have prosecuted its search in the district of Fingal with considerable success; when contrasted with the yield of the Victorian diggings, however, our resources are insignificant. Iron, silver, lead, copper and tin are known to exist, but no considerable attempt has yet been made to develop the mineral resources. Freestone is obtained in the north, the centre, and the south of the island. A stone, commonly called "Ironstone," a species of trap, and admirably adapted for road-making, exists everywhere in vast quantities. The wheat of Tasmania is equal to any in the world—a fact established at the Great Exhibition of Industry—and the wool holds a high place in the home market. At Hobart Town, oil and whalebone form very important articles of export.

Twenty-seven vessels belonging to the port are engaged in the fisheries.

ZOOLOGY AND ENTOMOLOGY.

Of the wild animals of Tasmania little need be said. Of the carnivora the largest is an animal known as the hyæna, or, native tiger, which grows to the size of a large dog. There is another quadruped held in great horror by the flockmaster; much smaller than the hyæna, it is far more ferocious, and this peculiarity of character has obtained for it the name of "devil." The only other carnivorous animal is a species of cat, not unlike the polecat, either in its size or habits. The kangaroo feeds on grass, and is a timid, inoffensive creature. Opossums abound in prodigious numbers, sleeping in holes of trees during the day, and emerging at night to feed on the young foliage or grass. The wombat, or badger, which bears a kind of resemblance to both a pig and a bear, burrows in the earth, and feeds on roots; its flesh is said to resemble pork. Rats and mice are very numerous.

BIRDS.—There is a great variety, many being of fine plumage, and most of them fit for food. Of the rapacious order there are several species, the largest of which exceeds in size and strength the Golden Eagle of northern Europe, and is very destructive to lambs. There are at least six varieties of hawk, besides three or four species of owl. Cockatoos, both white and black, are common, and parrots, wood pigeons, snipe and quail, wild ducks and teal, are abundant. Black swans, formerly very common, have now retreated to the unsettled districts, where they are undisturbed by man. Pelicans, cormorants, penguins, gulls and cranes, line the sea-shore and margins of lakes and rivers.

FISH.—Freshwater fish are limited to very few species; of these the most in favor is the so-called herring, a small fish weighing four or five ounces, which appears to be migratory. Eels of an immense size, a sort of bream, barracouta, flatheads, king-fish, trumpeter, flounders, gurnet, cod, salmon-trout, mullet, garfish, plaice, perch, silver-fish, pike, blue-heads, and skates, are the principal at present known and eaten. Large sharks, porpoises, whales, &c., abound in all the Australian waters. Of shell-fish may be mentioned—oysters, muscles, cockles, periwinkles, wilks, mutton-fish, crabs, prawns, and cray-fish. Corals and sponges are also abundant.

INSECTS.—Amongst insects are—moths (some as large as a wren), bottle flies, gnats, musquitoes, great variety of beetles, ants (some very large—a purple sort an inch long), grasshoppers, tree locusts, crickets, tarantula, spider, mantis, common flies, and other insects well-known in England. The bee has been introduced with great success, and a considerable quantity of wild honey is now obtained in all parts of the country, produced by bees that originally escaped and are now rapidly increasing in numbers.

REPTILES.—There are several species of snake,—the black

whip, and diamond being the most common; they measure from eighteen inches to four feet, but specimens of the black snake are often met measuring over five feet long. All are armed with poison fangs, and the bite is speedily fatal unless the wounded part be instantly excised. If the part bitten is a finger or thumb, the safest plan is to cut off the member immediately; but if that cannot be done, a ligature should be tied as tightly as possible above the wound to prevent the poisoned blood from flowing back into the system, and the affected part should then be cut out, and every method employed to encourage profuse bleeding from the wound. Guannas, lizards, frogs, scorpions, and centipedes, are by no means uncommon, but though there is much venom in the sting of the two latter, casualties seldom occur from that cause.

POLITICAL.

From the foundation of the colony to 1823, it might be said to have been governed by garrison orders. A *carte blanche* could not have conveyed fuller powers than the local rulers exercised. How justice or injustice was administered in those days some records yet remain to tell. Acts of tyranny beyond the ordinary excesses of arbitrary government were perpetrated with impunity, and all classes were confounded in a regimen of despotism. They legislated without warrant; detained in custody and flogged English freemen; levied illegal duties; imposed unconstitutional restrictions; and inflicted cruel punishments for offences invented by themselves. Judge Advocate Wyld declared the legislative authority of the Governor equally binding with Acts of Parliament. Torture to extract confession was not uncommon. On 19th July, 1823, the British legislature passed "An Act for the better administration of justice in New South Wales and Van Diemen's Land, and for the better government thereof." The old courts were superseded, a Supreme Court erected, with criminal, civil, and ecclesiastical jurisdiction, and the Judges invested with the powers enjoyed by King's Bench, Common Pleas, and Exchequer. A military jury of seven officers on full pay was retained for criminal cases; and for civil issues a Judge and two Justices—the latter named by the Governor,—but plaintiff or defendant might apply for a jury of twelve freeholders. Courts of Quarter Session and Request for sums under £10 were at the same time constituted. The semblance of a legislature was also conferred. The Governor, with the advice of a nominated council or the major part of them, was empowered to enact ordinances not repugnant to the law of England. The then-existing duties were made perpetual, and no fresh taxes were to be imposed except for local purposes. The Governor, with the assent of one member, could pass any law, even, in case of rebellion, though all might dissent; and the Sovereign could enact a law rejected by the Councils. Colonel Arthur was a strict disciplinarian—a man of method, and estimable in private life. But he was an officer, and had no sympathy with popular liberty. He dealt with the colonists as with soldiers: disobedience was always followed by punishment. During his long tenure of office and vigilant superintendence, the resources of the colony were rapidly developed, extensive public works executed, and vice in every form discountenanced. He did what he believed to be best for all, and he could not understand how people should wish to interfere either by advice or authority. A portion of that apathy and absence of self-reliance, which still characterise some of the old settlers, is to be traced to Col. Arthur, who was never tired of accomplishing material improvements for the benefit of all. The roads made, the bridges built, the buildings erected, are the best monuments of his reign; and the systematic order into which he brought the affairs of every department has not been materially improved upon. He was a benevolent autocrat, and misused the tyrant power he possessed, as little perhaps, as any man placed in similar circumstances. General Darling proclaimed the independence of the colony on 3rd December, 1825, and sailed for Sydney. Arthur thus became "Excellency" instead of "Honor." Mr. Bent had issued the first number of the "Hobart Town Gazette" on 1st June, 1816; but in 1824 he separated from all connection with the government and went into opposition. Before the press existed "PIPES" were used—that is, the offences of official men were hitched into rhyme, and either taught by repetition or circulated in manuscripts, like Beranger's songs and the squibs of the present day in France. These "pipes," by their satire, moderated the insolence of authority. Arthur established a rival "Gazette," and then the conflict commenced in earnest. Prosecutions of the press followed; and in 1827 a law was passed which made a licence from the Governor requisite, authorised a tax of threepence on each paper, and rendered sureties necessary. Bent was refused a license, but issued a monthly publication. The publishers were injured, and the Governor did not gain. The law was disallowed by Lord Goderich, and the press set free. Emigrants continued to flock in, and were located on free grants of land, until the country became too strait for their flocks. The richest soil was despised, because encumbered with trees from two to three hundred feet high, containing the finest timber; and open land, though otherwise inferior, was sought above all other for sheep. A wistful eye was turned to the continent. John Batman made a flying visit to Port Phillip, entered into a compact with the blacks for an immense territory, returned home and formed a company of Tasmanians who transported the stock that first cropped the natural herbage around the wide expanse of Port Phillip. This occurred towards the close of 1835. In 1836-7 and 8 large quantities of stock were shipped to South Australia, and that province may, in a certain sense, be also said to have been colonised from this island. The turmoil to obtain the rights of Englishmen continued, public meetings were held and petitions forwarded—libels were printed, and libellers prosecuted. A political association was formed, which worked in its own way without recognition by the Governor. Finally, in 1840, military juries were abolished, and the trial of crimes and misdemeanors committed to the inhabitants; and thus was reared in Tasmania that great bulwark of public and private freedom "trial by jury." But Governor Arthur's time came. He embarked on 19th Aug., 1836, and never were more joy and gladness expressed than on the occasion of his departure. Lieut.-Col. Snodgrass administered the government until Sir John Franklin took up the reins on 6th January, 1837. He summed up his own character in his reply to an address presented to him on his arrival, which deplored the absence and invoked the restoration of social peace. "With my whole heart I agree with you. Let us be divided then, if we cannot be united, in political sentiments, yet knit together as friends and neighbors in everything besides. Let us differ where honest men may differ; and let us agree, not in undervaluing the points of political dissent, but in respecting the motives which produce it; in cherishing domestic virtues which will be found to characterise individuals of every party; and in making the generous sacrifice of private feelings for the general good, rather than aggravating the importance of grievances which must render such forbearance impossible." Sir John Franklin was a contrast to Sir George Arthur in almost every point of view. When an unanimous petition was adopted in June, 1838, for the the concession of British institutions, he afforded it his friendly countenance, and in a despatch urged compliance with its prayer, but it proved unsuccessful. At the first sitting of the Council he threw open the doors to the public; and, as resignations fell in, and opportunity occurred, nominated to the Council or Commission those who had been rigorously excluded from both by his predecessor. The public breathed freer under the new *regime*. But Franklin, with rare injustice, was superseded before his time, and, as a compensation, was sent on an expedition to the North Pole, from which the noble-hearted man never returned. During his administration distillation was prohibited by law, and £7,431 were paid to distillers as compensation. A large body of emigrants was introduced under his auspices, most of whom and their children occupy independent and respectable spheres in life. Sir Eardley Wilmot succeeded to power on 21st August, 1843. His short and troubled administration presents few events of permanent interest. A question at once imperial, colonial, and social was discussed disastrously for him. He was also the victim of misrepresentation in private life. The colonists felt their power and exercised it. The liberty of the press had become an admitted fact, and the free expression of opinion in a council of crown nominees, but still colonists, brought affairs to a crisis. With the best disposition to promote the welfare of the colony, he was hampered by the authoritative instructions of the colonial office. The Secretary of State for the day or his subordinates were the virtual rulers of the destinies of a people removed to the distance of sixteen thousand miles, and existing in circumstances of which Englishmen could form no adequate conception. It took time to undeceive statesmen in England, but the Earl of Derby, Lord Grey, and Mr. Gladstone found their attempt to govern Australia from Downing-street a deplorable failure. The finances of the colony were embarrassed, and a "central committee" to aid the executive proffered its unconstitutional services, which were very properly rejected. The times were adverse, the price of produce was low, the labor market was overstocked, property had fallen in value, and all interests were in a state of confusion and distress. Imperial subsidies were withdrawn. In 1844 the duty on Sydney tobacco, rapidly improving in quality, was raised to that on American, and by way of retaliation a duty was placed on wheat—an example of mutual folly which may occur again unless the Australias be united in one general confederation. Additional taxation was determined on; the *ad valorem* duties raised to fifteen per cent. produced less than when at five, but other measures were objected to by the nominee council, of which the Governor was president. It will scarcely be credited that the sheriff refused to call a public meeting because one of the objects was to notice the appropriation of the revenue. On the 18th October, 1846, Mr. La Trobe superseded Sir Eardley Wilmot, who died at Hobart Town on the 3rd February, 1847. Sir William Denison arrived on 26th January, 1847, and Mr. La Trobe retreated again to his government at Port Phillip. The "patriotic six" nominees who had retired from the council in a body rather than register the edict of the Secretary of State for the colonies, were re-appointed, and the struggle became more intense. A dog tax was defeated on the ground of its illegality, a judge was arbitrarily removed for the alleged reason he did not pay his debts, and another appointed in equally necessitous circumstances. The Differential Duties Act was to be contested by the merchants, and the Governor to secure a bench on which he could rely, first proposed to suspend the Chief Justice: but that being disliked by the executive council, he requested Sir John Pedder to ask leave of absence. His reply was—"Were I to accept your Excellency's proposal I should, it appears to me, be for ever after degraded, and *ipso facto* render myself unworthy of holding the lowest office or employment which it is in Her Majesty's power to bestow on a subject." A Doubts bill was then passed, but it was not worth the paper it was printed on. Ultimately an indemnity for collecting illegal taxes was embodied in the Imperial Act, which conferred partial representation on the colony. The proceedings of Governor Denison were exceedingly unpopular. He lent himself to the mistaken policy of Downing-street; and, by the inadvertent publication of some secret despatches, came to be regarded as a wholesale slanderer of the colonists; and was consequently held in great dislike by some of the most respectable and opulent amongst them. He was accused of tampering with the purity and independence of the Bench; and of promoting land regulations with the avowed purpose of bribing a class to maintain an imperial policy repugnant alike to the moral feelings and material interests of the inhabitants. The Australian Colonies Government Bill was passed on 5th August, 1850, and under it, in 1851, a Legislative Council, consisting of sixteen elected members, four officials, and four non-officials, nominated by the Governor, was constituted. Among Governor Denison's last acts was the suspension of H. S. Chapman, Esq., then Colonial Secretary, but now Attorney-General of Victoria, because he did not vote, where a vote was useless, in opposition to a large majority in the Legislative Council. Mr. Chapman, like others, failed to obtain redress at the Colonial Office, and, in accordance with the rule of that establishment, the Governor was rewarded for his preference of imperial to local interests by his removal to the government of New South Wales, in which he seems to give much satisfaction. On 8th January, 1855, he was succeeded by Sir Henry Young, from South Australia, who had much to contend with in assuming the reins of Government, but being a man of great moral courage, fixed determination, and high principles, he is exercising an important influence over the colonists, and has already been the means of effecting much good to the community.

The act passed on 1st November, 1854, by the Tasmanian Legislature, received the Queen's assent in 1855; and in 1856 a Legislative Council and House of Assembly, both elective, were chosen. From that time the destinies of the island have been in the hands of the people themselves, as the semblance of interference from Downing-street does not remain. The Legislative Council consists of fifteen members. The electors must be twenty-one years of age, natural born, or naturalised subjects, with a freehold of the annual value of fifty pounds, or a graduate of any university in the British dominions, or barrister or solicitor on the roll of the Supreme Court, or legally qualified medical practitioner, an officiating minister of religion, or an officer or retired officer of Her Majesty's land or sea forces. The only qualification of members is that they shall be thirty years of age. Five members, or one-third of the council, retire every three years, but are eligible for reelection. The House of Assembly consists of thirty members —no judge of the Supreme Court, or minister of religion is eligible. The Assembly is elected for five years. The qualifications for an elector are - a freehold worth £100, being a £10 householder, or the holder of a £10 licence for depasturing stock on waste land, or having a leasehold of the value of £10 yearly, or having a salary of £100 per annum, and graduates, barristers, solicitors, doctors, and ministers, as in the case of the Legislative Council. Joint tenants and owners are permitted to vote, and contractors for the public service are disqualified as members. Absence for a session without leave, oath of allegiance to a foreign power, bankruptcy or insolvency, default to the public, attaint of treason, conviction of felony or infamous crime, and insanity, vacates a seat in either house. Both chambers are elected by the ballot, the success of which has been signal. The absurd practice of nomination-day movers and seconders at the hustings has been abolished, and the returning officer announces the names of the candidates, so that the noise and disturbance will in future be avoided. A free constitution and responsible government to its fullest extent are now enjoyed by the people of Tasmania. Some excellent laws have been passed transferring municipal authority to the districts and towns, which will be left to manage their local affairs by men chosen by the ratepayers. Perhaps the most important measures to those anxious to secure soil for a permanent home are the land acts.

STATISTICAL.

The reliable statistics commence with 1824. In that year the population was 12,643; the imports amounted to £62,000, and the exports to £14,500. In 1834 the population was 37,799; the imports, £467,617, and the exports, £208,522. In 1844 the population may be taken at 62,281, the census of 1842 giving 58,902, and that of 1847, 67,351; the imports being £442,988, and the exports, £408,799. In 1854 the population fell to 64,874; but the imports amounted to £2,604,680, and the exports to £1,433,021. Nothing could more completely refute the fallacy of an adverse balance of trade than the history of this colony. When the country was most rapidly increasing in wealth, the proportion of exports to imports was least. In the case of an individual, it is a necessary condition to a profitable trade that he should get more for an article in which he traffics than it costs him, and it is the same with communities. A very large proportion of imports are consignments, and cannot be placed to the debit of the country until purchased by a colonist. The imports increased pretty regularly by from fifty to one hundred thousand pounds a-year until 1840, when there was an increase of £241,471 (the imports that year being £988,356), the culminating point of our commerce prior to the discovery of gold in Australia. There was a rapid decline until 1844. Many will remember the trying times which commenced in 1840, and did not disappear till 1845, during which period houses of every character had to succumb. In 1844 the imports had fallen to £442,988, being less than they were in 1834 by £83,629. The exports increased progressively, and were largest in 1840, when they amounted to £867,000. While the exports of produce increased every year, the money worth was diminished during the disastrous times to which reference has been made. The export of imported articles fell off as a matter of course, and in 1844 the total exports fell to £408,799.

	Income.	Expenditure.
	£	£
1824	32,126	32,126
1834	142,701	117,865
1844	167,622	160,629
1854	387,784	366,331

From 1828 to 1835 were halycon days for a finance minister. The income and expenditure balanced to a penny, or was on the right side of the ledger, for every deficiency was made up by a loan from the commissariat. In 1836, the expense incurred for the penal management was cast on the colonial government, and the police first inserted on the estimates, and thus did the country become entangled in a mesh of difficulties, and oppressed by a heavy debt expended for imperial purposes, and which is now in process of liquidation. Instead of paying the commissariat, the English Government ought to contribute largely to the revenue of the island for years to come. Altogether, £162,669 had been borrowed and spent up to 1846. The revenue reached its culminating point in 1841, when it amounted to £242,432. The expenditure was highest in 1842, amounting to £185,071. That year the Registrar of the Supreme Court swelled the income by depositing £5,050, funds that had accumulated in his hands, but for which the Government is responsible to the rightful owners, as they establish their claims. The customs revenue has always been the mainstay of Tasmanian finance. In 1824, the different sources of revenue were not distinguished. In 1834, the customs revenue amounted to £65,722; in 1844, it had fallen to £63,464; in 1854, it reached £171,228. The largest sum received from the customs before the gold discovery was in 1840, when it reached £94,908, after which it fluctuated, falling to £63,464 in 1844, and rising to £88,370 in 1847.

	Vessels inwards.			Outwards.	
	No.	Tonnage.		No.	Tonnage.
1824	88	11,118	....	85	11,604
1834	150	33,441	....	143	32,192
1844	425	68,462	....	445	73,756
1854	1,057	198,612	....	1,028	200,398

These figures call for no particular remark.

The customs revenue for three decennial years stood as below, there being no separation of the customs from the general revenue till 1827, when it stood at £23,817.

1834	£65,722
1844	63,464
1854	182,489

In 1824, there was only one vessel of 42 tons that belonged to the colony. In 1834, there were 66 vessels, of 4,437 tons; in 1844, 152 vessels, of 10,727 tons. In 1854 there is no return.

The number of acres in crop is not given in an authentic form till 1828, when there were 34,033 acres in cultivation; in 1834 there wore 69,041 acres; in 1844 there were 121,938 acres; and in 1854, 127,782 acres. It is the same in reference to stock:—

	1828.	1834.	1844.	1854.
Horses	2,034	7,115	15,355	17,884
Horned cattle	84,476	74,075	85,302	108,752
Sheep	553,698	765,552	1,145,089	1,881,808
Goats	708	1,070	2,126	1,629

The produce for the following years is given below:—

	1829.	1834.	1844.	1854.
Wheat, bushels	318,641	218,348	807,924	790,588
Barley, ditto	60,664	89,487	174,405	125,835
Oats, ditto	34,166	120,247	221,105	526,547
Peas, ditto	8,776	11,488	8,658	6,665
Beans, ditto	235	545	1,072	653
Potatos, tons	5,192	7,114	18,349	23,256
Turnips, ditto	11,055	16,301	29,880	21,903
Hay, ditto	2,098	7,823	26,042	

The market price of wheat in 1829 was 7s. 6d. per bushel; barley, 5s.; oats, 5s. 6d.; potatos, £6 per ton; hay, £6. In 1834, wheat was 11s. 6d.; barley, 6s. 6d.; oats, 4s. 3d.; potatoes, £6; and hay, £5. In 1844, wheat is quoted at 8s. 3d. per bushĕl; barley, at 3s. 6d.; oats, at 2s. 6d.; potatoes, at £4; and hay, at £2 5s. In 1854, the average price of wheat, 12s. per bushel; oats, 9s.; potatoes, £20 per ton; hay, £22. The average price of meat in 1824 was 4½d. per lb.; in 1834, 3d. and 9-16ths per lb.; in 1844, 2½d. per lb.; in 1854, 6d. per lb. The population is given as subjoined:—

	1824.	1834.	1844.	1854.
Males	9,694	27,029	39,604	43,127
Females	2,949	10,770	*17,816	†25,482
	12,643	37,799	57,420	68,609

The rate of wages to bricklayers, carpenters, and masons, was, in 1826, 12s. a-day; in 1834, 7s. 6d. a-day; in 1844, 5s. a-day; and in 1854, 15s. a-day.

In 1824 there were 3 breweries, 1 distillery, 2 fellmongers 5 flour mills, 1 printing office, 1 ropemaker, 1 sailmaker, 1 saw mill, 1 soap manufactory, and 6 tanners. In 1834 there were

* Census for 1842. † Census for 1851.

8 agricultural implement makers, 13 breweries, 3 candle manufactories, 7 cooperages, 2 coachmakers, 3 distillers, 2 dyers, 3 engineers, 3 fellmongers, 2 foundries, 1 furrier, 1 mast and block manufactory, 1 steam mill, 40 water and wind mills, 1 pottery, 6 printing offices, 1 ropemaker, 3 sailmakers, 2 saw mills, 4 shipwrights, 1 snuff manufactory, 1 soap manufactory, 1 sugar boiler, 12 tanners, an l 2 wool staplers. In 1844 there were 71 agricultural implement makers, 40 brewers, 10 candle manufactories, 15 cooperages, 7 coach makers, 3 dyers, 13 engineers, 32 fellmongers, 5 foundries, 1 farrier, 2 mast and block makers, 15 steam mills, 53 wind and water mills, 2 potteries, 9 printing offices, 4 rope makers, 7 sail makers, 2 saw mills, 10 shipwrights, 1 soap maker, 30 tanners, 1 pianoforte maker, 3 woolstaplers. In 1854 there were 21 agricultural implement makers, 19 auctioneers, 102 bakers, 15 basket makers, 144 blacksmiths, 1 bone dust manufacturer, 6 brass founders, 42 brewers, 71 bricklayers, 43 builders, 151 butchers, 38 cabinet makers and joiners, 9 candle manufactories, 109 carpenters, 4 carvers and gilders, 22 chemists, 6 cider makers, 6 coach makers, 18 cooperages, 20 corn and ship chandlers, 1 dyer, 15 engineers, 28 fellmongers, 5 foundries, 9 furriers, 343 general dealers, 6 glue and size makers, 1 gold beater, 48 grocers, 7 gunsmiths, 21 ironmongers, 13 maltsters, 9 mast and block makers, 51 mills (wind and water,), 23 steam mills, 41 painters and glaziers, 31 pastry cooks, 2 pianoforte makers, 4 potteries, 13 printing offices, 378 publicans, 2 rope makers, 9 sail makers, 16 saw mills, 25 shipwrights and boatbuilders, 254 shoe makers, 4 soap boilers, 1 starch manufactory, 55 stonemasons, 84 tailors, 27 tanners, 31 tin workers, 16 tobacconists, 10 turners, 22 watchmakers, 72 wheelwrights, 30 wine merchants, 7 woolstaplers.

The post-office belonged to a private individual up to 1832.

	1834.	1844.	1854.
Number of Offices	27	43	65
Persons employed	60	71	95
Extent of Roads (miles)	434	674	679
Letters forwarded from Hobart	77.560	177,717	231,597
Newspapers	84,32	216,280	218,000
Letters received at Hobart	73,430	145,350	204,414

The following is the number of places of worship in the years named :—

	1824.	1834.	1844.	1854.
Episcopal	2	12	47	No return.
Presbyterian	1	2	10	
Roman Catholics	1	1	3	
Wesleyans		2	24	
Independents		1	12	
Baptists			2	
Totals	4	18	98	

The statistical returns for 1857 are not yet perfected, and it is necessary to fall back upon those for 1856, with the exception of the figures actually furnished by the census of 31st March, 1857, by which it appears the population consisted of 32,171 adult males, and 21,288 adult females, with 27,343 children under 14 years of age, and 690 military, including women and children; making a grand total of 81,492 souls. In 1856 only six male and ten female aborigines survived the scanty remnant of what was a large population fifty years ago. There were 6760 houses built of stone, brick, or iron; 8258 built of wood; one wooden and 14 iron steamers belonged to the Tasmanian ports; one coach runs daily between Hobart Town and Launceston, 121 miles, including the intermediate towns, and another six times a week. There is a daily coach from Hobart Town to each of the following places—Green Ponds, New Norfolk, Brighton and Brown's River; and from Launceston to Westbury and Deloraine, Perth, Longford, and Evandale, beside other conveyances. There were six lighthouses in 1856, yielding a revenue of £5515 The coin in the colony amounted to £507,914. Up to the end of the year 1856, 2,843,365 acres had been granted or sold, and 2,009,477 were held under depasturing licenses at a rent of £25,478 per annum. In 1856 there were 130,603, acres under crop; 18,019 horses, 88,608 horned cattle, 1,674,987 sheep, 2225 goats, 30,074 pigs, &c. There were 55 wind and water mills, and 28 steam mills, 13 printing offices, 400 publicans, and other trades in the same proportion. There were 71 public schools, 3717 scholars, maintained at an expense of £11,857 17s. 4d. The price of bread was 2¼ per lb., fresh butter 2s. 3d., coffee 2s. 3d., tea 2s. 9d., moist sugar 4½d., loaf sugar 7½d., tobacco 5s. per lb., beef and mutton 7d. per lb. The revenue of Hobart Town Municipality for the year was £18,210, the expenditure £15,945—Launceston: revenue, £6649; expenditure, £5777. There were 221 boys and 176 girls in the Queen's Orphan School.

In order to place the trade of the island of Tasmania before the reader, at one glance, the figures commencing with the year after gold was discovered in Australia are tabulated :—

Yrs.	Vessels inwds.		Vessels outwd.		Imports.	Exports.	Revenue.	Expenditure.
	No.	Tonnage	No.	Tonnage				
1852	791	135,470	824	135,989	860,488	1,509,883	£181,079	£177,462
1853	1024	192,420	999	188,279	2,278,397	1,757,596	348,503	191,443
1854	1057	198,612	1028	200,398	2,604,680	1,438,021	387,784	336,331
1855	885	161,212	871	159,256	1,559,797	1,428,629	405,352	506,973
1856	934	157,826	945	156,396	1,442,106	1,207,202	398,218	424,074
1857	1021	164,008	1031	167,058	1,271,087	1,354,655	423,973	395,633

The Custom House records of the port of Launceston do not extend farther back than 1829, in which year 36 vessels 3571 tons entered inwards; 40 vessels 3863 tons cleared outwards; the imports were valued at £61,174, the exports at £54,982; and the revenue was £10,326 7s. 4d. In 1834 there were 42 vessels 6887 tons inwards, and 45 vessels 6490 tons outwards. The value of the imports that year was £115,942, and the exports £85,909, the revenue £21,046 2s. 6d. In 1844 179 vessels 22,146 tons entered inwards, 187 vessels 24,801 tons cleared outwards. The imports amounted to £152,464, and the exports to £217,571, the revenue that year being £24,932 11s. 8d. In 1854 413 vessels 70,020 tons entered inwards, and 393 vessels 70,492 tons cleared outwards; the imports being £780,744, and the exports £714,546, while the revenue amounted to £66,491 8s. 1d. We subjoin in a tabular form the trade of the ports of Hobart Town and Launceston for the ast six years, which covers the field over which the gold discoveries spread.

PORT OF LAUNCESTON.

Years.	Vessels inwards.		Vessels outwds.		Imports.	Exports.
	No.	Tonnage	No.	Tonnage.		
1852	336	49,233	352	49,914	£224,266	£482,370
1853	354	70,098	375	69,726	686,057	639,747
1854	413	70,020	393	70,492	780,744	714,546
1855	375	58,515	366	59,056	492,628	690,379
1856	403	54,647	413	53,579	467,580	532,567
1857	474	58,480	478	59,687	458,921	694,185

PORT OF HOBART TOWN.

Years.	No.	Tonnage	No.	Tonnage.	Imports.	Exports.
1852	455	86,237	472	86,075	636,222	1,022,513
1853	640	122,827	624	118,553	1,587,340	1,117,849
1854	644	128,592	635	129,906	1,823,936	718.475
1855	510	102,702	505	100,200	1,067,169	738,250
1856	531	108,179	532	102,817	974,526	675,235
1857	547	105,528	551	107,371	812,166	660,470

The estimates of the expenditure for the year 1858, are as follows:—general expenditure, £143,529 15s. 1d.; local expenditure, £62,342 3s. 2d.; land fund, £50,929 4s. 2d. Total, £256,801 2s. 5d.

LAND REGULATIONS.

Population only is required to develop the resources of this island, and the recent land acts are calculated to attract small capitalists, who also themselves possess laboring capabilities or have them within the family circle. The Waste Land of the Crown is divided into three classes—1st. Town Lands situate within the limits of any town or township, or within five miles of the boundaries of either Hobart Town or Launceston; the upset price not to be less than one pound per acre, and the town land to be sold by auction only, and not otherwise.

The second class is called Agricultural Land, and may be

said to comprise all the other unalienated soil within the settled districts, and liable to be increased by fresh proclamations of suitable land for the plough, in any direction where it may be discovered. The lowest upset price is one pound per acre, and the land will be put up for sale by auction in lots not exceeding 160 acres: if not sold by auction they may be privately purchased at the upset price. Until 1853 agricultural land was given in quantities not exceeding 640 acres to each person, at £1 per acre, payable in 10 years, a small charge being made for surveying and interest.

The third division comprises Pastoral Lands which will be put up for sale in lots not exceeding 1280 acres each. The lowest upset price is ten shillings per acre. If not disposed of at auction they may be purchased privately at the upset price. Both agricultural and pastoral lands may be sold by private contract. Any person, upon payment of the expense of survey, has a right to purchase, at a fixed price of one pound per acre, one section containing not more than 320 acres of agricultural land and 640 of pastoral land. This arrangement completely obviates the delay, uncertainty, competition, and injustice of the auction system, and enables the *bonâ fide* colonist to select his site and enter upon it at once. But this is not all: lands purchased at public auction or private contract may be paid for in cash or a credit obtained. For town lands a tenth is added to the price as premium: one-fourth is the deposit and one-fourth payable annually thereafter, so that the credit would spread over three years. Upon the price of agricultural and pastoral lands one-fifth is added as premium,—the deposit is a fifth, and the annual payments one-tenth, so that the credit is spread over eight years. But more than this: about one-third of the island is little known, being designated "Unsettled." Any one who lights upon a favorable spot, and is willing to plunge into the bush and live there, may have land for nothing. The conditions are that the plot applied for shall not be less than 50 nor more than 640 acres,—that the applicant shall possess one pound of capital for every acre of land applied for, either in money, live stock, machinery, implements of husbandry, and other articles applicable to agricultural purposes or to sawing timber,—he shall for five years actually reside on the spot, and clear, fence, and bring into cultivation five acres for every fifty, or erect buildings or machinery of the value of £250 for every such fifty acres, In the event of death the property will decend to the heirs. Upon the full performance of the conditions, a deed of grant in fee simple will be issued, and the holder may then do what he likes with the property. If he prefer he may at any time make the land absolutely his own by payment of ten shillings an acre, and thus cancel the conditions of occupation. Not more than ten thousand acres may be let for a term of ten years, at a peppercorn rent, on condition that the applicant place on the land within twelve months 100 sheep or 20 head of cattle for every one thousand acres. The pre-emptive right of purchase, to the extent of 640 acres, is secured at the rate of ten shillings an acre with compensation for improvements if the run be required for agricultural purposes before the expiry of the lease. The survey fee for 50 acres in the settled districts is £4,—if in heavily timbered country, £5; for 320 acres, £11 or £13 15s.; 640 acres, £13, or £16 5s.; and so on in proportion, according to size of section. This is by far the most liberal land system that exists in Australia at the present time.

The gross receipts of the land fund during the quarter ending 31st March, 1858, were £91,577 9s. 1d., and the expenditure, £54,275 3s, leaving a balance of £37,302 6s. 1d. The quarter just past shows an advance on the corresponding quarter of 1857 of £7695 15s. 2d.

The government are taking steps to facilitate the operation of the new land regulations. The island has been divided into districts, to each of which a surveyor is to be appointed, who will show the maps and give all necessary information. A considerable quantity of land has been taken up already.

CHARACTER AND PRODUCTIONS OF THE VARIOUS DISTRICTS.

Though throughout the colony the settlers are all engaged in agriculture, in sheep and cattle farming, or in cutting of timber, certain districts have a more marked character than others in the nature of their productions, and the occupation of their inhabitants. Thus on the north-western coast where dense forests are being cleared by numerous small settlers extending from the Mersey to Circular Head, large quantities of excellent timber, potatoes, and agricultural produce are shipped either direct to Melbourne or to Launceston. Along the coast to the eastward of the Tamar are some considerable sheep farms: southward and westward of Launceston, extending for many miles in both directions, lies the greatest agricultural district of the island, comprising Morven, Norfolk Plains, Westbury and Deloraine, which produce vast quantities of wheat, oats, barley, meat and dairy produce, which are carried to Launceston and shipped to the adjoining colonies. As the traveller proceeds southward along the main road to Hobart Town, into what are called the Midland Districts, he passes through large estates on which sheep-farming is carried on to a large extent, and with great success, as shewn by the large quantities and superior quality of the wool annually sent to the London market. As the traveller continues his journey he again enters an agricultural country Southward of Hobart Town lies the district known as the Huon, remarkable for the density of its forests, and for its potatoes, quantities of which are sent to the adjoining colonies. Its climate is moist and congenial to vegetation. On the eastern coast butter and cheese of the best quality are produced. There are several coal-fields in the island, viz., the Mersey and the Don, on the north coast, Fingal, New Town, Douglas River, Schouten Island, and Port Arthur. Of the fifteen or sixteen millions of acres which the island contains, about three millions are private property: the remainder is crown land, of which about two millions of acres are occupied by the settlers under grazing licenses. The area under cultivation at present is about 140,000 acres. The soil and climate are highly favorable to English fruits and vegetables of all kinds; and in the public gardens at Hobart Town and Launceston may be seen plants, both English and foreign, which at home require the shelter of the conservatory, flourishing with all their native luxuriance in the open air.

GENERAL APPEARANCE AND CONDITION OF THE TOWNS.

The person who comes to Tasmania arrives either at the port of Launceston, in the north, or Hobart Town, in the south, which are the chief outlets for the shipping and commerce of the island. If the immigrant arrives at Launceston, he passes up the Tamar, a beautiful river (navigable for vessels of the largest tonnage), or, rather, the estuary of two inland rivers, which empty themselves into it at Launceston, forty miles from its entrance. The town is situated in a valley, enclosed on the east and west by two hills, and, both from the river and the surrounding elevations, its appearance is highly picturesque. If the vessel which bears the passenger arrives at Hobart Town, he will be carried up the Derwent, a noble river, for about forty miles, until he reaches the city, where it is still three miles wide. The capital rises from the verge of the arm of the sea at Sullivan's Cove, gradually ascending up the slopes of seven moderately elevated hills, and is magnificently backed in its western aspect, at the distance of three or four miles, by the lofty mountain named after Wellington, which is 4,195 feet high. As the traveller extends his acquaintance with the interior of the country, he will often discover the same charms of natural scenery in the sites of towns and villages, and the homes of the colonists; and when he stops to examine the signs of social and commercial advancement, he will find ample evidence of the progress made by the people. In Hobart Town, in Launceston, and in the interior towns and villages, he will find clergymen, merchants, professional gentlemen, shopkeepers, master tradesmen, mechanics, and many Government officers, and others of character certainly equal to those in a similar position in other countries. Hobart Town and Launceston contain numerous places of worship of all denominations, and in every district of the interior there are one or more ministers. Schools of excellent character, under able conductors, are to be found throughout the colony. There are others, also, established with assistance from public funds, wherever a sufficient number of children is to be found, and much anxiety and liberality are manifested by the Government and the inhabitants in promoting religion and education. There are many institutions, which are noted in succeeding pages. The principal towns and the interior abound with excellent hotels and inns. Both Hobart Town and Launceston are well supplied with pure water. The former town is lighted with gas, and a company to effect the same object for Launceston is in course of formation. The local affairs of both towns are managed by a mayor and aldermen. In the general appearance of the towns, the stranger will trace a resemblance to some of corresponding size in the old country; the streets, which are of considerable and regular width, are drawn at right angles, and whilst many of them are built with regularity, and have some architectural pretensions, others display all the variety of style and material which mark the colonial town.

Some of the churches, banks, the High School at Hobart Town, and the principal shops, would do credit to any city. There are three daily, and one tri-weekly, newspapers, published in Hobart Town; and one daily, one tri-weekly, and one bi-weekly, published in Launceston. The shops are constantly supplied with English goods of all kinds, and the productions of our Eastern possessions.

FARMING.

The Tasmanian settlers are extensively employed in pastoral and agricultural pursuits; and wool and wheat form the two great staple productions. The adaptability of the climate and the soil to these important purposes has long been established, whilst the excellence of the products is known throughout the world. Sheep farming is carried on to a large extent on the estates of the principal landowners, who also lease from the crown large tracts of unalienated land. The pastoral territory presents either the alternate fall or rise of a smooth, undulating surface, sometimes running into flats, or one broken and riven, terminating in deep gullies or steep ridges. The *Eucalyptæ*, with its everlasting olive-green foliage, uniformly covers the surface, and the character of the forest prevents the vegetation of the grasses from being impeded. In some parts this vegetation is luxurious beyond description, and extends from the level of the sea to the highest altitudes. The abundance and excellence of the pasture, combined with the mildness of the climate, facilitate the operations of pastoral industry; and on the estates of many colonists these natural advantages have been further improved by the importation from England and

Germany of the best blood, and by the adoption of greater care in the breeding, rearing, and dressing of the sheep, and the preparation of the wool for the home market. The high price which the produce has realised of late has given a stimulus to this branch of industry.

AGRICULTURE.—The English plough and harrow are employed in cultivation, and the mode of working the land is that of England, and followed up to that model so far as local circumstances render it convenient or profitable; still the science which agriculture has become in Britain is as yet in its infancy here. Manuring, rotation of crops, fallowing, thorough or superficial draining, and irrigation, are as yet far from being common operations; they are confined to particular farms only; and although the experiments have been crowned with signal success, they have hitherto found few imitators. Many of the agricultural implements and machines in use at home have been introduced of late; and the price of labor has induced a desire to extend the use of these practical aids; but in theoretical or scientific farming—the analysis and classification of soils—little has been accomplished. The agricultural calendar which guides and regulates the farmer in the routine of annual labor and farm management is just the reverse of that to which he was accustomed in his native land. Thus, the month of January in Tasmania corresponds, as regards season, with the month of July in European latitudes, but as regards agricultural operations it corresponds with August.

As in New South Wales, the agricultural industry chiefly spreads over valleys, which are superior to those of the sister colony as regards their extent of available lands and the fertility of their soil. Though the agricultural progress of the colony has been great, its vast capabilities of soil and climate, and its great facilities for irrigation on the largest scale, must, when the very liberal system of disposal of the public lands comes into operation, and attracts a new population, and when the improvements introduced at home shall have commenced here, give a new stimulus to that progress, and raise still higher the reputation of this colony as an agricultural country. To his Excellency Sir Henry Young, the Governor, belongs the credit of having produced, at the last annual meeting of one of the Tasmanian agricultural associations, a valuable paper on various topics of interest to the farmer.

TRAVELLING.

The two chief towns are Launceston, in the north, covering an area of 1¼ square miles, with a population of about 8,000, and Hobart Town, the seat of Government, in the south, covering an area of over two square miles, and containing a population of about 20,000. The two towns, which are 121 miles apart, are joined by one of the best roads in the world, along which a four-horse coach runs day and night, performing the journey in fourteen hours. Starting on this road from Launceston, the traveller reaches Perth at the distance of 11 miles, next Cleveland 30 miles, then Campbell Town 42 miles, Ross 47 miles, Oatlands 70 miles, then Green Ponds and Brighton, and after 17 miles more, during which he crosses the Derwent at Bridgewater, he reaches Hobart Town. Leaving the southern suburb of Launceston, the traveller is conveyed by a daily four horse coach to what is termed the Western district. On this road, ten miles from Launceston, he passes through Carrick, Westbury 20 miles, and Deloraine 30 miles; and from thence, pursuing a track through the forest, he may reach the settlements from the Mersey to Circular Head, on the rivers which empty themselves into Bass's Straits on the north. Passing out of Launceston on its eastern side the traveller proceeds through the districts of Patterson's Plains, and the White Hills. At a point of the main line, 8 miles from town, a cross road branches off to the town of Evandale, 11 miles from Launceston, and further on the village of Lymington on the Nile, to both of which places a public conveyance runs daily. At Perth, above-mentioned, a branch road turns off to Longford (to which also a coach runs daily), Cressy, and Bishopsbourne, in the district of Norfolk Plains. From Campbell Town, on the main line of road, a cross-road, along which a conveyance passes twice a-week, starts to Avoca, 62 miles from Launceston, Fingal 70 miles, Cullenswood and Falmouth on the eastern coast, 104 miles from town. Branch roads in the same manner as the traveller proceeds southward carry him to the districts of Macquarie, Bothwell, Hamilton, and other places on either side of the great highway. Leaving Hobart Town, the traveller is conveyed by steamer to New Norfolk, at the distance of 21 miles, situated on the Derwent north of the capital. Leaving Hobart Town to proceed southwards, he comes to the settlement of Brown's River, at the distance of 10 miles, and to the settlements on the River Huon, to which he may go by land or be conveyed by steamer—a distance of 22 miles. Steamers run constantly from Launceston to the ports on the north-western coast, and from Hobart Town to places on the eastern course. One steamer weekly, starting every Tuesday from Launceston. Steamers also leave Launceston every two or three days for Melbourne, which is thirty hours sail. A powerful steamer runs between Hobart Town and Melbourne, between which the passage is double the length; and a steamer also runs from Hobart Town to Sydney, accomplishing the passage usually in three or four days. A line of telegraph runs from George Town, at the entrance of the Tamar, to Launceston, and thence along the main line of road to the capital; and in the course of twelve months a submarine cable across Bass's straits will connect Tasmania with the colonies of Victoria, New South Wales, and South Australia.

RATES OF WAGES.

The following are the current rates of wages:—joiners 10s. to 12s. per day; painters 10s. to 12s; carpenters 10s. to 12s; plasterers 10s. to 12s.; plasterers' laborers 6s. to 7s: bricklayers 12s. to 14s.: bricklayers' laborers 7s. to 8s.; masons 12s. to 14s. masons' laborers 7s. to 8s.; quarrymen 14s. to 16s.; blacksmiths 10s. to 12s.; shipwrights 10s. to 12s.; tailors 10s. to 12s.; wheelwrights 10s. to 14s.; compositors 14d. per thousand; pressmen 3*l*.3s. per week; bakers 2*l*. to 2*l*.10s.; cabinet-makers 2*l*.10s. to 3*l*.; male servants 30*l*. to 40*l*. per annum (found); cooks 30*l*. to 50.; coachmen 30*l*. to 50*l*.; grooms 30*l*. to 50*l*.; gardeners 50*l*. to 60*l*.; female cooks 30*l*. to 40*l*.; married couples 50*l*. to 60*l*; general female servants 20*l*. to 22*l*.; housemaids 18*l*. to 20*l*.; laundresses 26*l*. to 30*l*.; nursemaids 14*l*. to 16*l*.; farm laborers, per annum, with rations, 30*l*. to 40*l*.; ditto married couples, 50 to 60*l*.; bullock drivers 40*l*. to 45*l*.; ploughmen 40*l*. to 50*l*.; shepherds 25*l*. to 30*l*.; ditto with families 50*l*. to 55*l*. The following is the scale of rations for agricultural servants:—Flour, 12 lbs. to 14 lbs.; meat, 10 lbs. to 14 lbs.; sugar 2 lbs.; tea, ¼lb. weekly.

PRICES OF NECESSARIES OF LIFE.

The following are the prices of the common articles of domestic consumption:—beef, 4d. to 8d.; mutton, 5d. to 6d.; veal, 8d. to 10d.; pork, 10d. to 1s. per lb.; lamb, 3s. 6d. to 4s. per quarter; ham, 1s. 4d. to 1s. 6d. per lb.; bacon, 1s. 4d.; cheese, 1s. 6d.; butter, fresh, 2s. 6d.; potted ditto, 2s.; eggs, 3s. per dozen; candles, 8d. per lb.; soap, 5d.; bread, 9d. per 4-lb. loaf; potatoes, 6lbs. 1s.; tea, 2s. per lb.; sugar, 5d. Wearing apparel and cloth, being imported, are of course not so cheap as at home, but are reasonable in price. Cottages may be obtained at from 10s. to 20s. per week; ordinary lodgings 20s. to 25s. per week.

ARRANGEMENTS FOR THE RECEPTION OF IMMIGRANTS.

Satisfactory arrangements are made for the reception of immigrants coming to this colony by means of the bounty tickets issued by the colonial government. At Hobart Town and

Launceston officers are appointed and depôts for their reception are provided. The information published by the government, states, that "careful provision is made for the protection and advantageous settlement of female immigrants not under the charge of relatives. The ship is on arrival immediately inspected by the Immigration Officer, by whom the capabilities and wishes of each woman with regard to employment are ascertained. The women are then landed in govèrnment boats, and admitted to a large and commodious building, where beds, provisions, and other advantages are provided for them. Here they remain for some days to wash their clothes and make preparation for service, in charge of an experienced matron, under the direction of the Immigration Officer. Persons who wish to obtain their services are required to make written application; on which printed 'authorities' are transmitted to approved applicants, who on presenting them at the depôt are at liberty to make arrangements with the immigrants by mutual consent; the women receiving such advice and information as they may require. No person is permitted to hire any female from the depôt without the 'authority' above mentioned; and as this is sen only to those who are known to be suitable employers, no young woman can fall into improper hands on first arrival in this colony."

GOVERNMENT, LAW, &c.

GOVERNMENT.—Captain-General and Governor-in-Chief: His Excellency Sir Henry Edward Fox Young, K.C.B., Knt., Private Secretary and Aide-de-Camp: H. Maule, A. C. G.

THE MINISTRY.—Premier: The Hon. Francis Smith (Atterney General). Colonial Secretary: The Hon. William Henty. Colonial Treasurer: The Hon Frederick M. Innes; and (without office) the Hon. W. P. Weston, John Walker and R. Q. Kermode.

EXECUTIVE COUNCIL.—The Governor and the Ministry. Clerk: R. C. C. Eardley Wilmot.

PARLIAMENT.—LEGISLATIVE COUNCIL.—Composed of fifteen Members for twelve districts. President: The Hon. Thos. Horne, puisne judge. Chairman of Committees: The Hon. W. E. Nairn. Members: Jordan (1), Ed. Bisdee; Huon (1), Richd. Cleburne; Longford (1), W. P. Weston; Hobart (3), Jno. Walker, E. S. P. Bedford, Thos. Horne; Meander (1), W. E. Nairn; Cambridge (1), F. Burgess; North Esk (1), J. H. Wedge; Tamar (2), W. Henty, W. S. Button; Buckingham (1), T. Y. Lowes; South Esk (1), P. H. Gell; Derwent (1), W. Langdon; Pembroke (1), J. Whyte. Clerk of the Council: R. C. C. Eardley Wilmot. Usher of the Black Rod: Major Fraser.

HOUSE OF ASSEMBLY.—Composed of thirty Members for twenty-four districts. Speaker: The Hon. Captain Michael Fenton. Chairman of Committees: Robert Officer, Esq. Members: Hobart (5), M. Miller, T. D. Chapman, W. Boys, R. W. Nutt, J. Dunn; Clarence (1), E. Abbott; Franklin (1), J. D. Balfe; Kingboro' (1), A. Nicholas; Glenorchy (1), R. Officer; Queensboro' (1), D. McPherson; Richmond (1), T. G. Gregson; Sorell (1), A. Morrison; Brighton (1), H. Butler; Deloraine (1), A. F. Rooke Morven (1), F. M. Innes; Westbury (1), T. Field; Fingal (1), F. Smith;

George Town (1), C. S. Henty; New Norfolk (1), M. Fenton; Norfolk Plains (1), J. C. Gregson; Ringwood (1), K. Q. Kermode; Selby (1), R. C. Gunn; Campbelltown (1), W. R. Allison; Cumberland (1), T. L. Gellibrand; Devon (1), J. A. Gibson; Launceston (3), J. Crookes, J. Matthews, A. Clerke; Glamorgan (1), C. Meredith; Oatlands (1), H. F. Anstey. House Clerk: F. H. Henslowe. Sergeant-at-Arms: R. Power.

LAW.—Chief Justice: Sir Valentine Fleming, Knight. Puisne Judge The Hon. Thomas Horne. Attorney-General and Solicitor-General: F. Smith and T. J. Knight. Crown Solicitor and Clerk of the Peace: W. L. Dobson. Recorder and Commissioner of Court of Requests—Hobart Joseph Hone; ditto at Launceston: John Whitefoord. Master and Registrar of Supreme Court: William Sorell. Commissioners of Insolvent Courts:—Hobart: Fielding Brown; Launceston: W. G. Sams. Chairman of Caveat Board, F. H. Henslowe. Vice-Admiralty Court—Judge and Commissary, Sir V. Fleming, Knight, C.J.; Registrar, W. Sorell.; Marshal, J. Watkins. Clerk to Supreme Court, J. A. Watkins.

NOTARIES. — Notaries Public, Hobart—Messrs. Sutton, Nutt, Cartwright, Dobson, and Allport. Launceston—Messrs. Grubb, W. Henty, W. Douglas, R. Gleadow, Dawes, and Sams.

MILITARY.—Commander of the Forces: Major Hutchins, 12th foot. Assistant Adjutant-General, Lieutenant-Colonel Bradshawe. Commanding Royal Engineers: Lt.-Col. Robert G. Hamilton. Barrack Master: Captain MacKay. Deputy Military Storekeeper, R. Douglas.

COMMISSARIAT.—Assistant Commissary General in Charge: Stephen Owen. Deputy Assistant Commissary Generals: H. Maule and J. H. Sale. Cashier: T. Boot.

CORONERS.—Hobart: Algernon B. Jones; Launceston: W. Gunn.

CONSULS.—Consuls at Hobart—For United States, D. McPherson; for France, W. Lempriere; for Denmark and Portugal, L. Roope; for Hanover, E. Marwedel. At Launceston—For United States, J. Crookes; for Prussia, W. Henty.

MISCELLANEOUS. — GOVERNMENT DEPARTMENTS.—Surveyor-General; James Sprent, Director of Public Works: W. P. Kay. Secretary to the Board of Education: Murray Burgess. Inspector of Schools: Major Cotton. Colonial Auditor: E. J. Manley. Government Printer: James Barnard. Accountant of Stores: J. D. Loch. Assistant Colonial Secretary, T. B. Solly. Assistant Colonial Treasurer: T. V. Jean. Superintendent of Aborigines at Oyster Cove: J. Dandridge. Collector of Customs—Hobart: Henry D'Arch; Launceston: J. Burnett. Staff Officers of Pensioners—Hobart: Captain Russell; Launceston: Major Russell. Lloyds' Agents—Hobart: T. D. Chapman; Launceston, Du Croz and Co.

LIEUTENANT-GOVERNORS AND GOVERNORS-IN-CHIEF.—1804 to 1810, Lieut.-Governor Collins; 1810 to 1812, Acting Governors, Lord and Murray; 1812 to 1813, Acting Governor Geils; 1813 to 1817, Lieut.-Governor Davey; 1817 to 1824, Lieut.-Governor Sorell; 1824 to 1836. Lieut.-Governor Arthur (4 days in 1825, Governor-in-Chief Darling); 1836 to 1837, Acting Lieut.-Governor Snodgrass; 1837 to 1843, Lieut.-Governor Sir J. Franklin; 1843 to 1846, Lieut.-Governor Sir E. Wilmot; 1846 to 1847, Acting Governor Latrobe; 1847 to 1855, Lieut.-Governor Sir W. Denison; 1855 to date, Sir H. E. F. Young.

POPULATION.—On 31st March, 1857: males, 45,916; females, 34,886; total, 80,802; number of houses, 18,018. Also, 690 military, including women and children.

POLICE MAGISTRATES.—Hobart Town, William Tarleton, visiting Clarence Plains and Kingston; Franklin Edward Atkyns Walpole, visiting the district of Kingborough, with the exception of Kingston; Richmond and Sorell, Charles O. E. W. Wilmot, visiting Brighton; Campbell Town and Oatlands, Thomas Mason; Hamilton and Bothwell, A. McDowall. Launceston, W. Gunn; Longford and Morven, Charles Arthur; Port Sorell, W. T. Noyes; George Town, J. Whitefoord; Horton, H. T. A. Murray, visiting Emu Bay district; Westbury, J. P. Jones, visiting

Carrick; Glamorgan, E. C. Shaw, Visiting Magistrate; Spring Bay, H. J. Vicary, Visiting Magistrate. Inspector-General of Police, John Forster, J.P. Superintendents: Hobart, F. J. Weale; Launceston, J. O'Connor.

SHERIFFS.—Sheriff: The Hon. W. E. Nairn. Under Sheriffs: Hobart—T. J. Crouch. Launceston—W. G. Sams.

PENAL.—Comptroller-General: The Hon. W. E. Nairn. Chief Clerk: J. Kerr. Civil Commandant—Port Arthur: James Boyd. Superintendent—Impression Bay: R. T. Stuart. Superintendent of Prisoners Barracks, and Keeper of House of Correction for Males, Hobart: Thomas P. Reidy. Keeper of Cascade Factory, Hobart (for Females): R. Atkins. Officer in charge of Brickfields Nursery: J. C. Peel. Visiting Magistrate to Convict Establishments, Hobart: E. S. P. Bedford. Superintendent of Penal Establishments, Launceston: C. J. Irvine. Queen's Orphan School, New Town—Superintendent: Algernon Burdett Jones. Chaplain: Rev. T. J. Ewing. Medical Officer: E. S. P. Bedford.

GAOLS.—Hobart—Keeper of Males: Thos. P. Reidy. Females: R. Atkins. Launceston: C. J. Irvine. Oatlands: J. Pain. Campbelltown: J. Musslewhite. New Norfolk: J. Morey. Richmond: S. McNeilly. Longford: J. Gomley.

IMMIGRATION OFFICERS.—Hobart: J. D. Loch; Launceston: W. G. Sams. Emigration Officer and Shipping Master: Captain Henniker Launceston.

COMMISSIONERS OF IMMIGRATION.—The Colonial Secretary for the time being; the Colonial Treasurer for the time being; Henry Butler, Askin Morrison, and Thomas D. Chapman. Secretary, F. C. Tribe.

BOARD OF EDUCATION.—South—Hon. W. E. Nairne; Hon. E. S. P. Bedford; Henry Button; Robert Officer; and G. W. Walker. North—R. C. Gunn; James Aikenhead; J. W. Gleadow; C. A. W. Rocher; W. K. O'Keefe; and W. Cleveland.

EDUCATION.—In Southern Electoral Districts in 1856, there were forty-six Schools, with 2577 Scholars. In Northern Electoral Districts, twenty-four Schools, with 1140 Scholars. The expenses were £12,922 16s. 5d.; balance in excess of vote, £2636 7s. 1d. H. C. Cotton, Inspector of Schools. Murray Burgess, Secretary Southern Board of Education.

MARINE BOARD.—South—The Mayor of Hobart Town; the Collector of Customs; William Crosby, Crawford Mayne Maxwell, Henry Boate Tonkin, Wardens; C. M. Maxwell, Senior Warden. North—The Mayor of Launceston; the Collector of Customs; R. Green, G. Gilmore, A. Macnaughtan, Wardens; G. Gilmore, Senior Warden; G. Boothroyd, Esq., Clerk.

MUNICIPAL COUNCILS.—HOBART TOWN—Mayor: Osmond Henry Gilles. Town Clerk: J. K. Winterbottom. City Surveyor: Thomas Browne. LAUNCESTON—Mayor: Henry Dowling. Town Clerk: James Henry. Town Surveyor: George Babington.

MEDICAL.—Principal Medical Officer and Deputy Inspector of Hospitals: Thomas Atkinson, M.D., Hobart. Purveyor: J. T. Cox. Hobart Town. General Hospital: Doctors Eckford and Brock. Convict Establishments—Hobart, Prisoners' Barracks: F. G. Brock, C. S. Cascade Factory: W. Benson, C. S. (and for the Gaols, Hobart.) New Norfolk Lunatic Asylum, Surgeon Superintendent: G. F. Huston, M.D. Port Arthur: T. C. Brownell. Impression Bay Invalid Depot: W. Seccombe, C. S. Cornwall Hospital and Infirmary, Launceston—Surgeon Superintendent: Dr. Miller. St. Mary's Hospital, Hobart—House Surgeon, Jas. Jackson.

POST OFFICE.—Hobart Town—Postmaster-General: F. M. Innes, corner of Elizabeth and Collins-streets. Launceston—Postmaster, St. John E. Browne, George-street. All letters and packets (newspapers alone excepted) posted at any of the post-offices of this colony, must be prepaid by means of adhesive stamps, which may be procured at the various post-offices throughout the colony, and of the principal booksellers in Hobart Town and Launceston. Letters and packets to be forwarded from one part of the colony to another, and ship letters and packets to be transmitted beyond seas, to any of the Australian or other colonies and India, must bear a stamp to the value of sixpence, for every half-ounce or portion thereof in weight.

ESTIMATES.—GENERAL EXPENDITURE FOR 1858—His Excellency the Governor, 4000*l.*; The Establishment, 2500*l.*; Legislative Council, 1710*l.*; House of Assembly, 4966*l.*; Colonial Secretary's Department, 2953*l.*; Colonial Treasurer, 2953*l.*; Audit, 1758*l.*; Customs, 9252*l.*; Post Office, 23,631*l.*; Accountant of Stores, 736*l.*; Public Works, 9380*l.*; Government Printer, 4059*l.*; Registrar of Births, &c., 703*l.* 10s.; Electric Telegraph, 2335*l.*; Lunatic Asylum, 8797*l.*; Education, 1809*l.* 12s. 1d.; Judicial, 24,249*l.* 5s. Ecclesastical.—Church of England, 9810*l.*; Church of Scotland, 3070*l.*; Church of Rome, 1755*l.*; Grant for Wesleyan Missions, 600*l.*; ditto Jewish Church, 150*l.*; total, 15,000*l.* Pensions, 6330*l.* 1s. 8d.; Charitable Allowances, 14,000*l.*; Grants in aid of Public Institutes, 800*l.*; Convict Discipline, 8300*l.*; Miscellaneous, 4975*l.* Total, £146,224 1s. 8d. LOCAL EXPENDITURE FOR 1858.—Police in twenty-one districts, 37,532*l.* 12s. 2d.; Gaols, 9963*l.* 10s.; Inspector of Stock, 75*l.*; Charitable Allowanees, 1150*l.*; Grants in aid of Public Institutions, 1050*l.*; Coroners' Inquests, 983*l.*; Education, 12,000. Total, £62,754 2s. 2d. LAND FUND.—Various items in connection with the establishments, £50,049 4s. 2d.

ELECTRIC TELEGRAPH.—Open between Hobart Town and Launceston, 121 miles. Office hours, from 8 a.m. to 6 p.m. Inspector of Telegraphs and Superintendent at Hobart Town, W. H. Butcher. Superintendent at Launceston, G. Butcher. A station is now erected at George Town, in charge of Mr. J. Duigan, by which communication is extended to the Tamar Heads. No charge for date, address, or signature. Messages must be written with ink, in a clear and legible manner, and bear a proper date, address, and genuine signature. Messages delivered free of charge within one mile of the office; over that distance, porterage charged; or if delivered on shipboard, an extra charge to cover boat expenses. Messages transmitted in the order of reception; precedence for government despatches, police service, and cases of sickness or death. All messages strictly confidential. Payment in advance will be required, except for replies to interrogatory messages on which may have been written the words, "Reply paid for." It is desirable that figures should be avoided, and words substituted. From or to Hobart Town and Launceston, for not exceeding ten words, 3s.; for every additional word, 2d.

ECCLESIASTICAL.

CHURCH OF ENGLAND.—Bishop of Tasmania: The Rt. Rev. Francis Russell Nixon, D.D. Archdeacons—Hobart Town: Ven. R. R. Davies, A.M. Launceston: Ven. W. Tancred, M.A.; Senior Chaplain, St. John's, Rev. W. H. Browne, L.L.D.; Chaplain Trinity Church, Rev. F. Hales.

ROMAN CATHOLIC CHURCH.—Hobart Town: The Rev. R. W. Wilson, D.D., Bishop of Hobart Town. The Vicar-General: Very Rev. William Hall. Launceston: Revs. J. Butler, J. Lucas.

CHURCH OF SCOTLAND.—Moderator: Rev. A. Turnbull, D.D. M.D. Clerk: Rev. R. Russell, Revds. J. Lillie, D.D., and Rev. R. M'Lean, M.A. Launceston—Rev. R. K. Ewing.

WESLEYAN CHURCH.—Hobart Town: Rev. John Cope. Launceston: Rev. T. B. Harris. Horton College: Rev. J. A. Manton.

INDEPENDENT CHURCHES.—Hobart Town: Revds. F. Miller, G. Clarke, and J. Nisbet. Launceston: Revds. C. Price and W. Law.

FREE CHURCH.—Hobart Town — Moderator: Rev. W. Nicholson. Launceston—Rev. J. Lindsay. Oatlands: Rev. L. Campbell.

BAPTIST CHURCHES.—Hobart Town—(vacant). Launceston—Rev. Henry Dowling.

BETHEL.—Supplied by various Ministers.

JEWISH SYNAGOGUES.—Hobart Town—President: S. Moses. Treasurer: P. Levy. Secretary: P. Moss. Reader: H. Jones. Launceston—President: Ald. Cohen. Treasurer: B. Nathan. Reader: H. L. Harris.

BANKS AND PUBLIC COMPANIES.

THE BANKING ESTABLISHMENTS.—Hobart Town—Bank of Van Diemen's Land, T. Giblin, manager; discount days, Monday and Thursday at twelve. Commercial Bank, James Alfred Dunn, manager, discounts daily at twelve. Bank of Australasia, George Matson, manager; discount days, Monday, Wednesday, and Friday, at noon. Union Bank of Australia, N. Gresley, manager; discount days, Monday, Wednesday, and Friday. Savings' Bank, G. W. Walker, Actuary; deposits received daily from ten till three. On Saturdays, deposits received until nine. Launceston—Commercial Bank, George Dean, manager; discounts daily at twelve. Bank of Australasia, C. Thomson, manager; discount days, Monday and Friday at twelve. Union Bank of Australia, J. G. Jennings, manager; discount days, Monday and Friday at twelve. Bank of Tasmania, Francis Evans, manager; discount days, Monday and Thursday at twelve. Savings' Bank, H. Dowling, actuary; deposits daily.

INSURANCE COMPANIES.—Hobarton—Hobart Town and Launceston Marine, Thomas Macdowell, manager, discounts daily; Tasmania Fire and Life, Thomas Macdowell, discounts daily; Derwent and Tamar Fire, Life, and Marine, Thomas Hewitt, Manager, discount days, Tuesdays and Fridays at eleven; Cornwall Fire and Marine, W. S. Turner, agent; Liverpool and London Fire and Life, Allport, Roberts, and Allport, English company; Alliance Fire and Life, R. W. Nutt, agent, English company; Professional Life Assurance, A. Crombie, agent, English company; Imperial Fire, Kerr, Bogle, and Co., agents, English company, sub-agents, Westbrook and Butler. Launceston—Cornwall Fire and Marine, J. Aikenhead, secretary, discount day, Wednesday at twelve; Hobart Town and Launceston Marine, James Peters, agent; Derwent and Tamar, Fire, Life, and Marine, C. J. Weedon, agent; Launceston Fire and Marine, A. J. Marriott, secretary, discount daily: Liverpool and London Fire and Life, C. McArthur, secretary, English company; Imperial Fire, Francis Evans, agent, English company; Colonial Life Assurance Company, Jas. Gibson, agent; Australasian Life Assurance, C. McArthur, agent; Australian Mutual Provident Society, L. Sherwin, agent. Tasmanian Fire and Life, James Peters, agent.

PUBLIC INSTITUTIONS.—Royal Society, Hobart—Patron, the Queen; President, Sir H. Young; Secretary, Dr. Milligan. Launceston Branch, Secretary, Rev. H. Kane. Tasmanian Public Library—Patron, Sir H. Young; President, the Bishop of Tasmania; Secretary, A. Gardiner; Library, Barrack-street. Mechanics' Institutes—Launceston: President, Rev. R. K. Ewing; Secretary, A. J. Green—Hobart: Patron, Sir H. Young; President, the Bishop of Tasmania; Secretary, M. Burgess. Schools—Superintendent of Queen's Orphan Schools, A. B. Jones; Inspector of Schools, Major Cotton; Master of the Hutchins School, Rev. J. R. Buckland, B.A.; Master of the High School, Rev. J. Harris; Second Master, Rev. W. Quilter; Master of the Grammar School, Launceston, Rev. H. P. Kane. Horton College (Wesleyan), Ross—Head Master, Rev. J. A. Manton. New Norfolk Lunatic Asylum Commissioners—Thomas Atkinson, President; the Hon. E. S. P. Bedford, Henry Butler, the Hon. W. Henty, J. A. Moore, Robert Officer, W. S. Sharland, Henry Lloyd, Wm. Tarleton, James Turnbull; G. F. Huston, Surgeon Superintendent. Court of Medical Examiners—President, Dr. Officer; Members, Drs. Bedford. Seccombe, Agnew, Maddox, Brock, and Casey. Legal Examiners—Messrs, Hone, Pitcairn, Brewer, and Butler; Hobart.

CHAMBER OF COMMERCE at Hobart Town and Launceston. The Royal Exchange, at Hobart Town.

COMPANIES.—Steam—Tasmanian Steam Navigation Company: the "City of Hobart," plying between Hobart and Melbourne, and the "Tasmanian," Hobart and Sydney; Manager, C. Toby; Offices, Franklin Wharf, Hobart. Kangaroo Point and Hobart Company; the "Venus;" Secretary, R. Hawkins. The "Black Swan," and "Royal Shepherd," each three times a month from Launceston to Melbourne. The Huon Steam Company's steamer, "Culloden," plies between Hobart and the Huon twice a-week; Captain J. Gourlay. The steamer "Monarch," between Hobart and New Norfolk daily. Gas Company, Hobart: Capital, £60,000; Managing Director, G. Whitcomb; Engineer, R. Falkner; charge 20s. per 1,000 feet, cash,—25s. credit.

SOCIETIES, INSTITUTIONS, &c.

AGRICULTURE.—Agricultural Societies—Southern Tasmanian Agricultural Association: Patron, the Governor; Secretary, S. Hughes—Midland Agricultural Association, Ross; Secretary, J. Maclanachan—Van Diemen's Land Agricultural Company: Office and Directors in London; Agent in Tasmania, J. A. Gibson, M.L.A.—Northern Agricultural Society; Treasurer, Wm. Dodrey; Secrerary, H. B. Nickolls.

SOCIETIES.—*Temperance Societies*—Tasmanian Temperance Alliance, Hobart; Secretary, C. Abbott. Hobart Catholic Abstinence Society; President, Very Rev. W. Hall, St. Peter's Hall, Collins-street. Hobart Total Abstinence Society; President, W. C. D. Smith. St. Joseph's Teetotal Society, Launceston; President, Rev. T. Butler. Tasmanian Teetotal Society; President, Rev. C. Price; Sec. S. J. Sutton. *Benevolent Societies*—Maternal and Dorcas Society, Hobart; Patroness, Lady Young; President, Mrs. Nixon—St. Andrew's Benevolent Society, Carrick; President, Rev. T. Reiby. St. Andrew's Benevolent Society, Hobart; Sec., Miss McLoughlin. *Religious Societies*—Hobart Town City Mission; Secretary, Jno. Rothwell Jews' Benevolent Society, Hobart: Treasurer, S. Moses. Tasmanian Congregational Union; Secretary, Rev. J. Nisbett. Launceston Town Mission; Missionary, Jno. Whittaker. Tasmanian Colonial Missionary Society; Treasurers, B. Rout, Hobart, and W. S. Button, Launceston. Cornwall Auxiliary Bible Society, Launceston; President, Rev. H. W. Browne. Tasmanian Auxiliary Bible Society; President, His Excellency Sir Henry Young, Governor; Depot, 72, Liverpool-street, Hobart. Wesleyan Missionary Society, Hobart. Evangelical Unions of Hobart Town and Launceston.

BUILDING SOCIETIES.—Hobart—The Tasmanian Permanent Building and Investment Association: Chairman, the Hon. W. E. Nairn; Managing Director, R. Worley; shares, £50 each. Launceston—The Launceston Building and Investment Society; Secretary, G. Bushby. The Northern Permanent Building and Investment Society, Launceston: Secretary, J. H. Greville.

MASONIC LODGES.—Tasmanian Union Lodge; Tasmanian Masonic Benevolent Fund; Operative Lodge; Lodge of Hope; St. John's Lodge; St. John's Chapter,; Hope Chapter.

ODD FELLOWS' LODGES.—Grand Lodge of Tasmania; Tasmanian Primitive Lodge; United Brothers' Lodge; Royal Victoria Lodge; Albert Lodge; Loyal Southern Star Lodge; Loyal Rose of Tasmanian Lodge; Loyal Kingston Lodge; Loyal Cornwall Lodge; Loyal Somerset Lodge; Star of Tasmania Lodge; and Pride of the West Lodge.

INDEPENDENT ORDER OF RECHABITES. — Salford Unity — Tasmanian District, No. 79 (Launceston) Tents. Star of Tasmanian, No. 1 (Launceston); Hope of Tasmania, No. 2, and Victoria, No. 6 (Hobart Town).

LIBRARIES.—Hobart Town—Tasmanian Public Library, No. 1, Barrack-street; Mechanics' Institute, Melville-street; Wesleyan Subscripton, Melville-street; Lawrence's Circulating Library, Elizabeth-street; Westcott's

Circulating Library, Collins-street; Young Men's Association, Royal Exchange Rooms, Macquarie-street; Depot of the Sunday School Union, Messrs. Walsh and Sons, Wellington Bridge, Agents for Melbourne *Argus*, *Sydney Morning Herald*, *Bradshaw's Guide to Victoria*, &c. At Launceston—Launceston Public Library; Wesleyan Subscription; Mechanics' Institute.

MISCELLANEOUS.

BIRTHS.—Ten pounds penalty may be recovered on information against parents and occupiers of houses in the colony, for not giving notice of a death within ten days, and of a birth within six months, after which no births can be registered, unless they took place in the Colony prior to November, 1838, the date of the Registration Act. A fee of five shillings is payable if the registry of a birth is delayed beyond six weeks. When notices are sent, those of a birth should contain date of birth, name, trade or profession, and residence of father, maiden and surname of mother, and sex of child, whose christian name may be added to the entry at a subsequent date, after baptism. Notices of death should contain date of death, sex, age, name, rank or profession of deceased, and cause of death.

CAB FARES.—By Distance—Not exceeding one mile, 2s. 6d.; for every half-mile over a mile, and for every fractional part of a mile, 1s. By Time.—Not exceeding half-an-hour, 3s.; if exceeding half-an-hour, but not exceeding three quarters of an hour, 4s. 6d.; above three quarters of an hour, but not exceeeing one hour, 5s. 6d. For every fractional part of any subsequent hour in the same proportion. And one-half more shall be payable for any period between the hours of ten o'clock at night and six in the morning. Cab license, £3.

COACHES.—Coaches from Launceston—To Hobart Town, the Royal Mail, every day and night (Saturday and Sunday nights excepted); hour of departure, five o'clock. To Longford and Perth, two conveyances, daily (Sundays excepted), at three and five o'clock. To Patterson's Plains, Spearman's van, three times daily. Launceston to Carrick, Westbury, and Deloraine: from Union Hotel booking office, George-street daily, at 7 a.m. and 2 p.m. Deloraine to Launceston: from Poole's booking office, daily, 2-30 p.m. Launceston to Nile Bridge and Evandale: from Bull's Head booking office, daily at 3 p.m. (except Sundays), arriving at Evandale at 7 p.m. Evandale and Nile Bridge to Launceston, daily, at 6-45 a.m., arriving in Launceston at 10 a.m. Hobart Town to Launceston: from Ship Hotel booking office, per Lord's Mail, every morning and evening (Saturday and Sunday excepted) fares, inside, £4, outside, £3. Day coach: fares, inside, £3, outside, £2 5s. Launceston to Hobart Town: from Club Hotel booking office, at 5 morning and evening. (Saturday and Sunday excepted), passing through Brighton, Greenponds, Campbelltown, Oatland and Perth. Hobart and Green Ponds: Fisher's, daily. Hobart and New Norfolk: Lucas's, daily. Hobart and Richmond: Guy's, and Mail Cart, twice weekly. Hobart and Brown's River: Fisher's, daily. Hobart and North-West-Bay: Worley's Conveyance, twice a week.

DUTIES.—Brandy, per gal., 12s.; rum, and all other spirits and strong waters, per gal., 10s. Wines, per gal., in wood, 2s.; in bottle, per doz. quarts, 6s.; per doz. pints, 3s. Tobacco, 2s. 6d. per lb.; ditto, soaked, for sheep dressing, 3d. per lb.; cigars, 3s. per lb.; snuff, 3s. per lb. Tea, 3d. per lb. Coffee, 1½d. per lb. Refined Sugar, 6s. per cwt. Raw Sugar and Molasses, 3s. per cwt. Dried fruits, 1d. per lb. Hops, 2d. per lb. Malt, 1s. per bushel. Malt liquors, in wood, 3d. per gal.; in doz. quarts, 1s. 6d.; in doz. pints, 9d.

FIRE ENGINE STATIONS at Hobart Town.—Tasmanian, O. H. Hedburg's, Argyle-street; Derwent and Tamar, Brown (late Brown and Douglas), Bathurst-street; Cornwall, Davidsons, Liverpool-st. Engines are also stationed at the ordnance stores, colonial hospital, police-office yards, and military barracks.——Fire Engine Stations at Launceston.—Cornwall,

Mr. Cogdell's, next to the police-office; Tasmanian, Mr. Lonargan, York-street; Derwent and Tamar, Cimitiere-street; Launceston, at Fiddyment's foot of Sand-hill; Liverpool and London, rear of Mr. M'Arthuer's, St. John-street. Superintendent of Brigade, James Lonargan, York-street,—Volunteer Fire Brigade.—Engine station, rear of Mr. M'Arther's, St. John-street. Foreman—E. Whiting; assistant ditto, W. C. Crew; hon. sec., R. Edwards; treasurer, E. Blount. Cornwall Volunteer Fire Brigade: Foreman, Mr. W. H. Rawlings.

HARBOUR DUES.—One penny per ton inwards and outwards.

HOTELS.—At Hobart Town the Ship Inn in Elizabeth-street is a favorite resort for settlers and visitors. At Launceston, the Cornwall and Club Hotels are the most prominent.

LIGHT-HOUSES.—At the Iron Pot Island, Cape Brune, Low Head, Swan Island, Goose Island, and Kent's Group.

LIGHTHOUSE RATES.—Every coaster entering inwards, 4d. per ton; every other vessel, 9d.

MARKETS.—Hobart Town: The Old, New, and Fish Markets, at the Wharf and end of Collins-street: Clerk, F. J. Drake.

MARRIAGES.—All marriages solemnized in the colony since November, 1838, are registered in Hobart Town, from the officiating ministers; and deputy registrars may issue licenses for marriages.

OMNIBUSES.—Two Proprietors ply between Hobart and New Town, and one between Hobart and Sandy Bay, daily.

PILOTAGE RATES.—By the Port Act, 1855, the rates in no case are to exceed one shilling per ton for sailing vessels, and 8d. for steamers; and in no case, for any one act of pilotage, shall the charge exceed £30 nor less than £4. Vessels not exceeding 50 tons are free from pilotage, except the master actually employed one, when the pilot shall be entitled to £4. Vessels that enter the Low Heads in stress of weather, only half pilotage.

SEASONS IN TASMANIA.—The Summer quarter commences December 22nd, 6 h. 6 m. a.m. The Autumn quarter commences March 21st, 7 h. 21 m. a.m. The Winter quarter commences June 22nd, 4h. 2 m. a.m. The Spring quarter commences September 23, 6 h. 14 m. p.m.

SHIPPING MASTER'S OFFICE, Franklin Wharf, Hobart Town; established 1st March, 1856, under the provisions of Act of Council 19 Vict., No. 22.—Shipping Master, George Hawthorne. This office is for the purpose of regulating the shipping and discharge of seamen. Launceston Office, Queen's Wharf: Shipping Master and Immigration Officer, Capt. Henniker.

STEAMERS (see Companies).

THE COAST.—The steamer Titania leaves Launceston about 10th, 20th, and 30th of each month, for Port Sorell, Torquay, Emu Bay, and Circular Head. Communication with these places by small sailing craft is constant and regular.

TIME.—Hobart Town, lat., 42 deg. 53 m. S.; long., 147 deg. 25 m. E.; in time, 9 h. 49 m. 39 s. before London. Launceston, lat., 41 deg. 26 m. S.; long., 147 deg. 11 m. E.; in time, 9 h. 48 m. 43 s. before London. Diff. of lat. between Hobart Town and Launceston, 1 deg. 27 m. S.; long., 0 deg., 14 m. E.; in time, 56 s. The centre of Tasmania (nearly) is east of London 147 deg. 18 m.; in time, 9 h. 49 m. 11 s.; that is, when it is noon at London, it is 9 h. 49 m. 11 s. in the evening here. Hobart Town is west of Sydney 3 deg. 52 m. 20 s. S.; in time, 0 h. 15 m. 29 s. Launceston is west of Sydney 4 deg. 15 m. 10 s. S.; in time, 17 m. 1 s. Launceston is west of Hobart Town, 0 deg. 0 m. 14 s.; in time, 56 s. Melbourne is west of Hobart Town, in time, 10 m. 38 s. Adelaide is west of Hobart Town, in time, 34 m. 18 s. The longest day is 15 hours, the shortest day of winter, 8 hours.

SOUTH AUSTRALIA.

POSITION AND BOUNDARIES.

The boundaries of the colony of South Australia, are as follow:—On the north, the 26th degree of south latitude; on the east, the colony of Victoria; on the west, the 132nd degree of east longtitude; on the south, the Southern Ocean. The coast line of the southern boundary, owing to the irregularity of the shore, exceeds 1,600 miles in extent. In its course it traverses Spencer's Gulf and St. Vincent's Gulf, rounding Yorke's Peninsula and Cape Jervis, running eastward to the Murray mouth, and then south-east till it meets the boundary in lat. 38°. The western boundary is only about one-fourth of the extent of the southern line, the northern about one-third, and the eastern one-half. The province contains about 300,000 square miles, or nearly 200,000,000 acres. The progress of discovery during 1857 having led to the conviction that a tract of good pastoral country exists in the western portion of the province, and extends outside its western boundary into a sort of no-man's-land, lying between South and Western Australia, steps have been taken by the Government to annex that tract to South Australia. The district in question lies between the 129th and 132nd parallels of east longitude, and naturally belongs to this colony. From its geographical position, whatever use could be made of it by any one, all the commercial advantage of its occupation would necessarily fall to South Australia. As it is understood to belong politically to New South Wales, application has been made to the Government of that colony, as well as to the Home Government, for permission to include the district within the jurisdiction of the South Australian Government. A general revision of the boundaries of all the Australian colonies is much to be desired, and might well be considered in connection with the federation question.

ADELAIDE AND SUBURBS.

The metropolis lies nearly south-east of the Port, and consists of two portions, North and South Adelaide. South Adelaide is laid out in a series of streets at right angles, the principal north and south streets (from 99 to 132 feet wide) being nearly one mile in length; and the east and west streets (from 66 to 132 feet wide) from a mile and a quarter to a mile and three-quarters, and bounded by four terraces, facing the cardinal points of the compass, nearly corresponding with the streets in length. In the intersections of the main streets squares are introduced at measured intervals. South Adelaide contains all the Government Offices, and all the principal wholesale and retail marts and stores of the city. Between North and South Adelaide the River Torrens winds its course, and both the divisions of the city are surrounded by public reserves called "Park Lands," which the terraces face. The river is spanned by a massive iron bridge, which cost, with its approaches £22,000. The bridge is in a line with King William-street, the central thoroughfare of the city, thus connecting the hearts of North and South Adelaide. There are two other substantial bridges across the river, respectively at about a mile above and below this central one. The inhabitants of Adelaide are chiefly dependent on the Torrens for their domestic supply of water, which is furnished them by an army of water-carriers, who charge 2s. or 2s. 6d. per load for it. But very costly waterworks are now in course of construction, and will in a year or two quite supersede this irregular and insufficient mode of supply. At a distance of about four miles to the east of the city, the Mount Lofty range of hills takes its rise, extending north, south, and east for many miles; the highest peak being Mount Lofty, elevated 2,285 feet above the level of the sea, and forming a fine land-mark for vessels approaching the Port. The hills are crowned with forests of gum-trees, from which the citizens are supplied with their usual domestic fuel. Adelaide is under the management of a Mayor and Corporation, and is rapidly improving both in reference to the beauty and value of its structures. During the past year great progress has been made in planting the squares and public reserves, and in placing shade-trees along the principal lines of street.

Around the city of Adelaide are numerous suburbs. The most populous and important is that in the eastern vicinity, consisting of a cluster of townships, including Kensington, Norwood, Magill, Stepney, &c. The townships of Kensington and Norwood stand on a large area of land, which is fast being filled up. A Mayor and Corporation have been appointed. In the extreme south-eastern corner of the plains, or rather at the foot of the hills, is Glen Osmond, one of the most lovely spots in the colony, where the first mine (lead) was discovered and worked. Southward there are the districts of Mitcham, Unley, Edward's town, &c., and the Marine township of Glenelg, New Glenelg, and St. Leonard's, three miles to the south of which is Brighton. These townships are incorporated and governed by a Mayor and Corporation. To the immediate west of Adelaide are the populous suburbs of Thebarton, Hindmarsh, and Bowden; north-east and north are Walkerville, Payneham, Islington, and Enfield. The city of Adelaide being laid out in the centre of a vast plain, having a radius of several miles in every direction, ample scope is afforded for laying out suburban townships, which are, indeed, continually rising up.

COUNTRY TOWNSHIPS, PORTS, &c.

Some idea of the country townships will be gleaned from the list of Post-Offices, and the frequency of making up the mails. The most important northern towns are Gawler Town, about 27 miles from Adelaide; Angaston, about 50 miles; Kapunda, about 52 miles; and Kooringa, the locality of the far-famed Burra Burra mines, 102 miles distant. Gawler Town has now a Mayor and Corporation, and is connected with the metropolis by a railway, which was opened for traffic throughout on the 5th October, 1857. Surveys have been taken, and estimates prepared with a view to extend the Gawler Town Railway to Kapunda, and a Bill to authorise the scheme passed the Assembly, but was rejected by the Council, during the past year. Another Bill has been introduced with better success, which authorises the construction of a portion of the line, without borrowing more than £80,000—£50,000 being supplied out of the general revenue. It was originally contemplated that from Kapunda the railway should diverge into two lines—one to Blanche Town, on the Murray; the other to the Burra Burra Mines. It is, however, uncertain whether this project will be carried out, or whether tramways for horse traction may not be adopted in preference: but tramways for horse traction have been condemned by a select committee of the House of Assembly. The traffic from the northern districts is very great, both in wool and corn as well as in minerals.

The eastern, north-eastern, and south-eastern districts of the colony include a large extent of highly productive agricultural country. Mount Barker, Gumeracha, Strathalbyn, and Macclesfield are the centres of farming operations. In a southern direction, Morphett Vale, Willunga, Noarlunga, and Yankalilla are also eminently productive. The chief ports, besides Port Adelaide, are Port Lincoln, Port Augusta, Port Wakefield, Port Onkaparinga, Port Willunga, Port Elliot, Rivoli Bay, and Guichen Bay. Between Port Elliot and the Goolwa, or lower portion of the Murray, an excellent tramway, seven miles in length, worked by horses, is in successful operation. Along the southern coast-line are several jetties and wharves, but the principal jetty (as to length and cost, though not in importance) in the colony will be the new structure now being erected at Glenelg, stretching out into Holdfast Bay, and on account of which the sum of £29,000 has been voted by the Legislature.

On tracing the course of the Murray upwards from the sea mouth to the Great North-West Bend, the settled districts will be easily found, by drawing a line north-west from the Bend to the head of Spencer's Gulf. Within the limits bounded by the Gulf, the Murray, and the line drawn, the most important mercantile and agricultural districts will be found. To the north and north-west of the above line the country is either unexplored or occupied by squatters. To the east and south of the Murray extending to the Victorian coast-line is a large extent of valuable country, chiefly occupied by sheep-farmers and stockholders, geographically and commercially more in connection with the Portland Bay District of Victoria than with other portions of South Australia.

The principal port of the colony is Port Adelaide, sometimes confounded by strangers with Adelaide, the capital. The port and metropolis are, however, above seven miles apart, but are connected by the City and Port Railway. Port Adelaide is a creek perfectly sheltered from the sea, and is accessible to vessels of fifteen or sixteen feet draught of water. The Port Town was designed by Colonel Gawler, the second governor and land commissioner, on the shores of the central portion of the harbour, and adjacent waters of the North Arm, covering an area, exclusive of public quays, government and public reserves, streets, squares, &c., &c., of 1124 acres; but the only part as yet occupied and built upon is that which fell to the share of the South Australian Company, and at the back of their property towards the "Old Port," a first landing place used in the early days of the colony. The depth of the harbour at this part being insufficient for large vessels, measures are in progress for deepening it. At the North Arm the depth at low water spring tides is from eighteen to twenty-one feet; and we are informed that a company has recently been formed in London for the erection of wharves and warehouses at this port, to which a road has recently been made by the government. A steam dredge is also at work upon the bar, and when this work is completed vessels of any tonnage will be able to enter in safety, and to load and unload in perfectly still water, remaining afloat at all times of tide. Wharves, warehouses, a patent slip, and every convenience for shippers exist at the port, which is being continually improved under direction of a Trust appointed by the Legislature, and invested with ample funds for the purpose. Lines of rail are laid down from the principal wharves to the terminus of the City and Port Railway. The local affairs of the Port are managed by a Mayor and Corporation.

DISTRICTS, ROADS, &c.

South Australia, as far as the settled portion, is divided into counties, hundreds, and districts. The division of most political importance is the *district*, the ratepayers of which have the power of levying rates on land and buildings, of granting licences to public-houses and pounds, and also for slaughtering cattle, depasturing, and timber cutting on the Crown lands. The funds arising from these sources are applied to forming and keeping in repair the roads of the district. For all the great main trunk roads there is a board, called the Board of Main Roads; this is formed of chairmen of the District Councils. It is supplied with funds by grants of money from the Legislature. The hundreds and counties are divisions of minor importance, chiefly serving for electoral purposes and the convenient mapping out the large territory forming the province.

Of the main roads formed and thoroughly macadamized, there are from Adelaide the following;—Nine miles to Port Adelaide and the North Arm; nine to the Bay and Brighton; thirty south to Willunga; twenty-four east to Mount Barker; twenty-six north to Gawler Town; and thirty north-east to Gumeracha, by two routes. These lines, with the necessary culverts, drains, and bridges, have been formed at a very heavy expense. Of the district roads, few have been constructed of any durability, excepting those suburban to Adelaide, and streets of townships or villages. The long range of hills running from Willunga northward, for more than 100 miles, furnish excellent stone for metalling the roads; while the soft lime-stone crusting the plains, more or less near the surface, forms an excellent base for the harder metal. About twenty-three miles of streets and roads have been constructed within the bounds of the city.

RIVERS.

The River Murray is the great natural artery of southern and south-eastern Australia, draining portions of the three colonies of New South Wales, Victoria, and South Australia. Its outlet is within the limits of the latter province, and its stream, from the mouth to its point of intersection with the boundary, measures 493 miles. Before entering the South Australian territory the Murray flows through the colonies of Victoria and New South Wales for more than 1,500 miles. The sea-mouth of the Murray is dangerous, owing to the shifting sands and the heavy ocean surf, but of late many vessels have safely entered. The navigation of the Murray commenced in August, 1853, by the Lady Augusta steamer, under the command of Captain Cadell, who proceeded as far as Swan Hill. Scientific surveys and investigations have been made with a view of ascertaining the practicability of rendering the sea-mouth safe for navigation; and during the year 1857 the passage has been made with tolerable regularity. Many steamers and barges are now plying on its waters, and merchandise from Adelaide is regularly carried as far as Albury, a distance of 1,750 miles. It should be understood, however, that this merchandise is carried into the Murray, not only by its mouth, but by the Tramway from Port Elliot to the Goolwa hereinbefore mentioned. As the sea-mouth of the Murray is situated within the bounds of South Australia, this magnificent river, now proved to be navigable for nearly 2000 miles, is claimed by that colony as its own peculiar possession; and it should be recorded to the honor of the South Australians that, by their sole energy and enterprise the several fine steamboats and barges have been placed upon its waters, for the common benefit of all three colonies, whenever they become sufficiently alive to its importance. Great discontent having been expressed in Melbourne at the arrangement by which foreign produce, especially tobacco, was taken up the Murray after paying Customs dues according to the South Australian tariff, a new intercolonial agreement was entered into early in the year, by which the South Australian Custom-house officers collect duties on goods entering the river intended for consumption in New South Wales or Victoria in accordance with the scale of dues imposed in those colonies. The amount thus received is paid, in equal proportions, to the Treasuries of those two colonies. This arrangement seems to work well, and to have given satisfaction up to the present time, but is liable, at any moment, to disorganization.

A great peculiarity of most Australian rivers is their losing themselves in marshes or reed-beds; which is the case with two of the principal South Australian rivers, the Torrens and the Gawler. Both of these rivers also, in the dry season become in places strings of water-holes, connected by tiny rills of running water. As already stated, however, the River Torrens affords a never failing supply of pure water to the citizens of Adelaide; and although wells have been sunk all over South Adelaide especially, its water is preferred to that of the wells, which are more or less brackish. A full inquiry into the extent and capabilities of the River Murray has been made by the Legislature of New South Wales, during the present year, 1858.

MINES.

South Australia has been long celebrated for its numerous copper and lead mines. Among the former the unbounded wealth of the Burra Burra Mine, about 98 miles to the north of Adelaide, is of world-wide fame. It is particularly noted for its "chamber" of Malachite (green carbonate of copper), and its lodes of red and grey oxides of copper. It is in the hands of a company; the shares in which, originally £5 each, have attained the price of £225, and are now quoted at £150.

The lead mines of Glen Osmond, already mentioned as about 4 miles to the eastward of Adelaide, have yielded a large return of galena, one of the richest ores of lead.

There are also some excellent copper and smelting works established in the colony; about 20 miles south from the Burra mines, which have furnished a sensible item to the exports.

Gold mining to a small extent has also been carried on in the Hilly District, where the rivers Torrens and Onkaparinga take their rise; the gold diggings having first been opened at Echunga near Mitchell's Flat, on the tributaries of the latter river. But the far more abundant yield of the Victorian gold diggings disheartens this branch of enterprize in South Australia.

SOIL, CLIMATE, &c.

The climate of South Australia is considered by those colonists who have resided for a series of years there and in Victoria, to be warmer and drier than that of the latter colony. The soil varies considerably even in the same district. The generality of the soil in the wheat lands for miles around Adelaide and to the north of that city for a considerable distance, say 100 miles, is of a light sandy loam. For which reason, experienced agriculturalists begin to think seriously about the means of manuring their arable lands. To the providential circumstance of the plains in the neighbourhood of Adelaide especially being very lightly timbered, may in a great measure be attributed its early and rapid progress as an agricultural colony.

PUBLIC WORKS.

No better test of the progress of a country can be found than that supplied by the character of its Public Works, their magnitude, and the energy with which they are carried forward. In this respect the year 1857 has been signally distinguished. The year opened with the extension of the Northern Railway to Salisbury, and the omen thus exhibited on New year's Day has been amply verified since. On the first of June a further portion of the line was opened for traffic as far as Smithfield; and on the 5th of October the whole line to Gawler, about 25 miles from Adelaide, was completed. The telegraph had anticipated the railway, and has been in use between the metropolis and Gawler since the 13th of April, 1857. During the year rapid progress has been made in the construction of the intercolonial line of telegraph, to connect Adelaide with Melbourne, Sydney and Hobart Town. The first wire of that line was affixed by His Excellency Sir R. G. MacDonnell to the post in the centre of Adelaide, on the 9th of August, 1857; and on the 6th of November following, 60 miles of the line was opened for use. The present southern terminus of the line is Goolwa, near to the mouth of the Murray; but the contracts for the construction of the remainder of the line have been carried out with so much vigour that it is nearly completed. While the extension of telegraphic communication has thus been in course of accomplishment in a southerly direction, the extension of railways to the north has been a subject of constant consideration.

The conviction which is gaining ground, that our great lines of internal communication must be railroads, and not macadamised roads, has tended in some degree to restrict the operations of the Main Road Board. But several important works are in progress under the superintendence of that body; and during the year three substantial and elegant bridges have been completed and brought into use. They are the MacDonnell Bridge, which spans the Torrens, on the north-eastern road, about 6 miles from Adelaide; the Stanley Bridge, which is thrown over the Onkaparinga, at Grünthal, on a branch of the south-eastern road; and the bridge over the Angas, at Strathalbyn. Other bridges are in course of construction in various parts of the colony, and will soon be opened, very much to the facilitation of communication between the settled portions of the country. The most pleasing feature in connexion with these structures is, that they are built with an evident intention that they shall be permanent ornaments to the localities in which they stand. Profiting by the experience of the past, the engineers have provided against the contingencies which have proved fatal to so many Australian bridges, and in deference to the tastes of the present day pains have been taken to secure elegance and grace, as well as firmness and stability.

On the coast there are several important works in progress. Among these we may name the deepening of the harbor at Port Adelaide, and the approaches to it; the erection of light-houses at Cape Borda, on Kangaroo Island, and at Cape Northumberland; and the construction of a Jetty at Glenelg. All these works are in progress, and will be completed at an early date.

One of the most important public works now in progress is the scheme for supplying the city of Adelaide with water, for which £200,000 has been voted by the Legislature. The Waterworks are being constructed under the direction of Commissioners, consisting of the Mayor of Adelaide (Mr. Lazar), Mr. W. S. Maturin, and Mr. U. N. Bagot.

HISTORY.

The actual founder of the colony, so far at least as relates to the fundamental principle upon which it is constituted, was Mr. Edward Gibbon Wakefield, the cardinal point of whose theory was, that land without labor is valueless, and that to ensure a constant supply of labor, the land must be sold at a "sufficient price," the proceeds of the land sales being applied to the introduction of laborers. On this principle South Australia was founded, this being the first of Her Majesty's colonies to which the Wakefield principle was applied.

The discovery of Australia has been effected by numerous instalments, reckoning from the visits of the Dutch in the early part of the 17th century, down to the survey of St. Vincent's and Spencer's Gulfs in the beginning of the present century. The explorations of Sturt, who in the year 1830 descended the River Murray, gave a new impulse to the vague dreams of emigration which for some time previously had been rife in England. At length the South Australian Association obtained an Act authorising the settlement of the colony, but prohibiting the occupation of the land as a dependency of the British Crown until after £35,000 worth of land had been sold, and £20,000 had been invested in Government securities. The Commissioners appointed under the Act adopted the expedient of issuing preliminary land orders, 437 of which were issued at £81 each, the holder of each order being entitled to select 80 acres of country land and one acre of town land. So little faith, however, was reposed in the scheme, that the whole project would have failed had not two or three gentlemen agreed to take up the unsold shares at the reduced price of 12s. per acre. The diminution of price was effected by increasing the area of the preliminary sections from 80 acres to 134. In consequence of this increased inducement, the requisite amount of money was raised, and the Commissioners sent out Colonel Light to suggest the site for the capital. He arrived in August, 1836, and after examining Nepean Bay, Port Lincoln, and Encounter Bay, decided upon establishing the capital where it now stands. Captain Hindmarsh, the first Governor, arrived at the close of the same year, and proclaimed the colony on the 28th of December. On his departure he was succeeded by George Milner Stephen Esq. (colonial secretary), as acting-governor. His successor, Colonel Gawler, arrived on the 12th of October, 1838. Captain George Grey, the third Governor, arrived in the colony on the 10th of May, 1841; Major Robe on the 14th October, 1845; Sir Henry Young on the 1st of August, 1848; who was succeeded by B. T. Finniss, Esq., as acting-governor; and Sir Richard MacDonnell, the present Governor, on the 7th of June, 1855.

During the twenty-one years that have elapsed since the

establishment of the colony it has passed through many vicissitudes. The early files of the local papers are filled with humiliating disputes between the Executive officers of the Government, private squabbles, and melancholy narrations of official incapacity. The short career of office of the first two Governors was characterised by numerous inconveniences resulting from delayed surveys and wasted time and capital. Colonel Gawler, to obviate the evils that he saw advancing, launched out into a heavy expenditure, vastly augmenting the evils he had hoped to avert. To meet his liabilities he drew upon the British Treasury, and the Home Government dishonored his bills. The result was a fearful panic and an almost universal bankruptcy. Captain Grey found upon assuming the reins of Government, that whilst the revenue was only £30,000, the expenditure was £150,000, exclusive of a debt of £300,000. Adopting the most rigid measures of economy, he reduced the expenditure of the Government within the narrow limits of the revenue just mentioned, and notwithstanding the check thus given to everything before the close of his administration, the province had so far progressed in material prosperity and reputation, that the Home Government paid half the debt, and accepted colonial securities for the other half. The whole of this has since been liquidated. The discovery of the Burra mines toward the close of Captain Grey's administration opened up a new source of wealth to the colony, but the mining mania to which that discovery gave rise, resulted, on the other hand, in wide-spread embarrassment. Still more recently, the discovery of the precious metals in the adjacent colonies, and particularly in Victoria, exercised a marked influence upon the fortunes of South Australia. The gold-fields of Ballaarat and Mount Alexander drew away vast numbers of persons from the colony; shepherds, farmers, merchants, traders, professional men, and laborers going in ever increasing multitudes, some by ship, others by overland conveyances, and some on foot. The excitement of all classes amounted to a *furor*. The laboring classes in numerous instances sold everything they possessed, to raise the amount of their passage money to Victoria; for which purpose even cottage freeholds were conveyed to purchasers for the pitiful sum of £5! whilst others, unable to dispose of their humble possessions, nailed up boards against their windows and doors, and left their homes to the mercy of the elements; which, after the *exodus* of the thieves and housebreakers for the land of gold, was all the danger the owners had to dread. The industrial operations of the colony were brought to a standstill, the coin was leaving the colony, the bank reserves were rapidly disappearing. The urgency of the case became so imminent, that notwithstanding the almost superstitious disinclination of the Government to interfere with the currency, it was evident that some extraordinary step must be taken, and the Governor specially summoned the Legislative Council on the 28th of January, 1852. So great was the excitement that the Standing Orders of the House were suspended, and a Bill expressly framed to meet the emergency was hurriedly carried through all its stages, and received the assent of His Excellency, who prorogued the Council the same day on which he called it together. This extraordinary example of hasty legislation produced the well-known "Bullion Act," by which the Governor was empowered to establish an Assay Office, and to appoint an Assayer, who should cast the gold into ingots, the banks being at the same time authorised to issue notes against bullion, which might also be legally tendered instead of coined gold. Simultaneously with these prompt measures an overland escort was established, which brought over from the Victorian gold fields the fruits of the successful mining operations of the South Australian diggers to a very large amount, and the monetary system of the colony was thus preserved from utter ruin. The Bullion Act was loudly denounced at the time by some who imagined they saw in it the secret agency by which the credit of the colony would be overturned; but time verified the soundness of the principles upon which that Act was based. At length numerous emigrants to Victoria returned to the colony, the pursuits of copper and lead mining and agriculture were again taken up, and a steady career of prosperity has since been chronicled. Every year enlarges the area of land under cultivation; the wool exports are increasing in a most cheering manner, and the mineral resources show no signs of abatement. The passing of the New Constitution, by conferring upon the Parliament the entire control of the Land Fund, enables it at the same time to regulate the influx of immigration according to the state of the labor market, and places it in possession of ample means either for increasing the population or for supplying re-productive labor to the settlers already there.

The experience of the past encourages the hope that a long career of expanding prosperity is before them. The commercial vicissitudes that have afflicted the neighboring communities have scarcely affected that. The discovery of large tracts of good land, moderately well watered, in parts of the interior which had too hastily been assumed to be arid and sterile, has opened the prospect of an indefinite extension to their pastoral occupations. The agriculturists have, as a body, been enabled to secure that position of competence which results from the unencumbered possession of their farms and homesteads. Another bountiful harvest has added to their wealth, which from its abundance is gladdening the hearts of all with the promise of cheap food. Attention is now keenly directed to the means available for turning to profitable acment; the second seven of Official and non-Official, or Nominee

count those fruits of the earth with which the British farmer is unfamiliar; and the operations of drying fruit and especially of making wine, are being vigorously commenced in various parts of the colony. Some of these wines were sent to the Paris Exhibition, and were declared by the judges superior to any sample shown of Rhenish wine; and a demand for them has already arisen in the English market—but the wines on which the greatest hopes are founded, have more the character of the Spanish, than the French or German. These are already being produced to a considerable extent, and are displacing second-class foreign wines. So great an impetus has been given to this branch of industry, by the successes of the past three years, that the breadth of land occupied by the vine will doubtless be doubled during 1858. Mining, once the sheet anchor of the colony, has now many rivals in the work of contributing to the general prosperity; but the mining interests were never in a more sound and flourishing condition than at the present moment, and await only a more adequate supply of labor to develop wealth, as some sanguine colonists believe, not yet paralleled.

POLITICAL AFFAIRS.

The political administration of South Australia includes several phases. The province was at first governed exclusively by the Governor and the Council of Government. According to the Act by which the colony was founded, the province was to have had a Government embodying the representative principle as soon as the population numbered 50,000 souls. This was reached about the year 1849. But the disasters of the colony under Governors Hindmarsh and Gawler induced the Imperial authorities to devise a new form of Government prior to the announced period of representative institutions; and on the 10th of October, 1843, Governor Grey opened a new Legislative Council, consisting of three official members and four non-official members, with himself as President. None of the members were elected, but the change consisted in the addition of certain non-official members; the former Council, though styled the "Council of Government," having had and exercised ample powers of legislation, by passing, amongst other necessary laws, the Act constituting the Supreme Court of the colony. Seven years afterwards the representative system was inaugurated by Sir H. Young, who, on the 20th of August, 1851, opened the first South Australian Legislature in which the representative principle was admitted. That Legislature consisted of eight nominee and sixteen representative members, the proportion which was observed till the close of that régime. Thus there were three periods of about seven years each. The first seven years consisting of a purely Official Govern-

administration combined, but without the representative element; the third seven of Executive and Legislative Government, with the principle of popular representation included. They have now entered upon another phase of political development, the characteristic features of which are that the Legislature is entirely elected by the people, and that the Executive is responsible for its actions to the Legislature.

On the 24th of October, 1856, the Royal assent to the New Constitution framed by the Legislature of South Australia was received by the Governor, who proclaimed it the same day in the *Gazette*. The chief features of this Constitution are—two Chambers, one of 36 and the other of 18 members, all elective; five responsible Ministers requiring to be returned to Parliament as the condition of holding office. No property qualification for members of either house. Members of the Lower House returned by universal suffrage; members of the Upper House returned by persons possessing a small property in land, by leaseholders, and by all householders paying £25 per annum rent. The qualifications thus enumerated result in the enfranchisement of about two-thirds of the community as electors for the Upper House. The duration of the Lower House is limited to three years; the Upper House cannot be dissolved, but one-third of its members retire every four years. The manner of voting is by ballot. All money bills are originated in the Lower House. For the purposes of the Lower House the colony is divided into 17 constituences, but for the Upper House the whole province forms but one electoral district, each person qualified to vote being entitled to vote for the full number of 18 members.

The General Election took place on the 9th of March, and the first Parliament elected under the existing Constitution was convened on the 22nd of April, 1857. The Legislative Council elected Mr. J. H. Fisher as President of that body, and the House of Assembly chose Mr. G. S. Kingston as Speaker. Since that time there have been several changes in the *personnel* of the House of Assembly, new elections having taken place to supply vacancies which have occurred in the districts of Barossa, Yatala, East Torrens, and Onkaparinga. These frequent re-elections, although they keep alive a certain degree of political excitement, are generally regarded with disfavor, on account of the needless expense to which they put the country. With triennial Parliaments as the rule, it is thought that gentlemen should not seek the honor of a seat who are not able to retain it during the short term of the existence of the Parliament.

The principle of Ministerial responsibility, for the first time introduced into the Constitution, led to the overthrow of three successive administrations at a comparatively early period of the Session. At the inauguration of the New Constitution, the old occupants of the Treasury benches retained their seats and their offices, with Mr. B. T. Finniss as Premier. Early in August the Finniss Ministry were compelled to retire, having been defeated on almost every question of importance during their career as responsible Ministers. His Excellency then sent for Mr. John Baker, a member of the Legislative Council, who associated with himself Messrs. Gwynne, Bagot, Hart, Blyth, and Milne. Mr. Baker's Ministry was sworn in on the 21st of August. On the 25th of August, the new Ministry first appeared, as such, before the Legislature, and were met, within an hour of taking their seats by a no-confidence notice of motion, tabled by Mr. Torrens, the Treasurer in the preceding Government. The hostile motion came on the very next day, and was carried by a majority of 17. Within 24 hours the Baker Ministry was at an end, and Mr. Torrens, the mover of the fatal resolution, was empowered to form an Administration. On the 1st of September Mr. Torrens's new Government was sworn in, the gentlemen composing it being Messrs. Torrens, Andrews, Hughes, and MacDermott in the Lower House, and Mr. Davenport in the Upper house. Mr. Torrens made a more successful *debût* than did Mr. Baker, but he mismanaged his position, and was overthrown September 22, on a motion by Mr. Hanson, affirming that Mr. Torrens's Government, by repealing certain Crown lands regulations by proclamation, instead of by enactment, had acted in an "illegal and unwarrantable" manner. The assailed Ministers made a desperate defence, and as they contrived to make many believe that their act, if illegal, was justified on grounds of public necessity, their overthrow was only effected by a majority of three votes. A few days afterwards the now existing Ministry was gazetted, consisting of the following gentlemen:—Mr. Younghusband, Chief Secretary; Mr. Hanson, Attorney-General; Mr. Hart, Treasurer; Mr. Reynolds, Commissioner of Public Works; Mr. Dutton, Commissioner of Crown Lands and Immigration. Mr. Younghusband is a member of the Upper House; the other Ministers are in the Lower House. This Cabinet possesses elements of stability of which its predecessors were destitute, and has commanded a large majority in the House on all important occasions.

POPULATION AND STATISTICS.

No census of the population has been taken since the 31st of March, 1855, so that all attempts to estimate the number of the people made since that time, being founded on imperfect data, must necessarily be to some extent hypothetical. But as they have official statistics of the principal elements of increase we may calculate with a tolerable degree of accuracy the number of inhabitants in the province at any given time.

Starting from the last census, we find that the population

on the 31st of March, 1855, numbered 85,821. The excess of births over deaths during the nine months included between the 1st of April and the 31st of December, 1855, amounted to 1,711. The registered births in 1856 were 4,488, and deaths 1,147, leaving an excess of births of 3,341.

The population of the colony, in the early part of 1858, was supposed to amount to 109,917 souls, comprising 55,735 males, and 54,182 females. The births for the year 1857, amounted to 2,640 males, and 2,543 females, together 5,183; the marriages to 1,218; and the deaths to 1,304, namely, 728 males, and 576 females. The number of vessels arrived for the year was 414, of an aggregate burthen of 166,310 tons. By these were conveyed to the colony 5,385 male adults, 2,150 female adults, and 1,551 children, making a total of 9,086 souls. The vessels departing from the colony, for the year, were 404; conveying away 1,854 male adults, 1,018 female adults, 578 children, being a total of 3,440. The number of immigrants which arrived at the public expense during the year, was 3,965; of whom 2,422 were males, and 1,543 females. The estimated value of imports for the year, was £1,623,052 5s. Of these the re-exports amounted to £214,388, leaving a balance of imports consumed in the colony of £1,400,664 5s. The exports, the produce of the colony, amounted to £1,774,184, which added to the imports re-exported made the total estimated value of exports, £1,956,572. The revenue for the year amounted to £726,325 19s. 2d., consisting of—general revenue, £451,525 19s. 2d.; and loans for public works, £274,800. The expenditure amounted to £664,366 1s. 8d.—being £480,234 14s. for general purposes; and £184,131 7s. 8d. for public works. The gold licences for the year amounted to 272, for which the sum of £136 was received. The stock in the colony at the end of the year consisted of, 2,075,805 sheep and lambs, 310,400 cattle, 26,220 horses, 1,647 goats, and 38,199 pigs.

LAND SALES.

The land sold by auction and private contract during the year 1857, amounted to 177,818 acres, realising the sum of £215,076 8s. The auction sales amounted to 120,892 acres, which realised an average price of £1 6s. per acre; and the private sales, to 37,326 acres, averaging £1 0s. 4d. per acre. The quantity of land under cultivation was 235,966 acres, of which 175,865 acres were cultivated for wheat.

All Crown lands in the colony of South Australia, except such reserves as may be made by the Government for public purposes, are open to purchase at the upset price of £1 per acre for country sections. All Crown lands are submitted, in the first instance, by public auction, but lots that pass the hammer without a bidding may afterwards be selected privately at the upset price.

It may here be observed, that during the first two years after the establishment of the colony, the Land Sales were conducted on a different principle. The first purchasers of land, to whom the colony was indebted for its very existence, as already stated, were called "preliminary" land holders. And, as they had purchased in London, of course, before the first settlers had landed, or surveys had commenced, it became necessary to hit upon some expedient for determining the priority of choice of the land, or "preliminary section," as it was termed, of each purchaser. Those sections consisted of 134 acres of Country Lands; for which the purchaser paid only the sum of £80, being at the rate of about 12s. per acre; the difference in price having been allowed to them as a boon; with the addition of one acre in the City of Adelaide. As soon as a few thousand acres in excess of the demand had been surveyed and mapped out into sections of 134 acres and duly numbered, a general meeting of the "preliminary land-holders," or their agents, was officially called, to draw lots for the order of choice; and shortly afterwards another meeting was held for these "preliminary" purchasers to mark off upon the maps the sections they had selected.

The result of this priority of selection was to confer small fortunes upon the lucky possessors of the sections immediately surrounding the City of Adelaide; who eventually subdivided them into the suburban townships or villages already mentioned. After these preliminary purchasers had become satisfied, the sections were again marked off upon the ground, and on the maps, into blocks of 80 acres; which was the size (with few exceptions) of all future sections. "Land orders" were afterwards sold in London, authorising the holder to select 80 acres of land upon payment of £80; and being numbered consecutively, they took priority of choice accordingly, and formed, in consequence, a source of profit to those who retained them for any length of time; when they were eagerly bought by parties anxious to secure favourite spots, or localities valuable for their mineral prospects.

Several well-known copper and lead mines were in this manner purchased or selected by the fortunate proprietors. And it may be observed that the purchase of land orders in London operated as a valuable mode for transmitting capital to the colony, and at the same time became a fund in England immediately applicable to the purposes of emigration.

In the colony the system of applying for surveyed sections by tender was adopted; viz.: sending a written application for any specified section of land, at the same time paying into the treasury ten per cent. on the purchase money of £1 per acre, and the balance within a month after receiving the official notification of acceptance; which system was attended with the happiest results, as it had the effect of rapidly studding the face of the country with small thriving farms, cultivated by the working man, whose toil was sweetened by the reflection that he was laboring solely for the benefit of himself and his children.

To this cause is mainly attributable the present prosperity of South Australia, which as a wheat growing country has been able to hold its way, notwithstanding the allurements of gold-digging in the colonies immediately adjoining; and there can be little doubt but that the flour of Adelaide secures for that colony a larger share of Victorian gold dust than any other single natural production.

HORTICULTURE.

During the first few years of a colony, gardening must necessarily partake of a utilitarian character; thus fifteen years elapsed before South Australia had collected more than 1000 different species of plants, and these were chiefly such as are valuable in agriculture, for domestic use, or as fruit. But during the last seven years a great change has occurred; impo - tations from England and elsewhere have been numerous and costly, and these have furnished the country with all the best fruits adapted to the climate, many of which were wanting, and also some of the choicer shrubs, timber trees, and flowers. So that rapid progress is now being made in improving the towns, villas, and homesteads, by planting parks, public squares. streets, and gardens, with ornamental and useful trees and plants. This may be said to be especially the case in and around Adelaide, where the luxuriance of the soil is not to be surpassed, and rarely equalled, by that of any other part of Australia. There and in the gardens within four or five miles may be found, growing in vigor and beauty, most of the favorites of Europe, the climate of the southern portion of which resembles much that of Adelaide. It is true that the Spanish and horse chesnuts, walnut, the plane tree, and many others, here become stunted by the heat and drought of the long, rainless summer; nor, except in the hilly districts, do the succulent vegetables, or the bush fruit, thrive well; but no place in the world seems better adapted to the growth of stone-fruit, the apple tribe, roses, oleanders, pinks, geraniums, oranges, loquats, melons, and most of those highly ornamental productions called in England, green-house shrubs. This impetus to horticulture has been much assisted by the establishment, about three years ago, of a botanic garden, supported by Government, and conducted by Mr. G. W Francis, F.H.S., a well known botanist. This garden consists of about twenty acres of ground, situated close to the city; it is laid out with much taste upon a plan both scientific and ornamental. It has already been the means of introducing much that it was very desirable to procure; while from the public interest it has excited, and the number of persons who attend daily for amusement or instruction, it is evidently creating a taste for ornamental horticulture, and it is to be hoped will be the means of still more rapid advancement. The native vegetable productions are of a peculiar character: there are no succulent plants of the nature of the cactus or eupherbia; few ferns and few bulbous roots, nor is there much variety in the foliage of the trees. The ubiquitous gum-trees (*eucalyptus*), the curious grass-tree (*xanthorrhœa*), and the sombre she-oak (*casuarina*), abound here as in the other Australian colonies. Notwithstanding this sameness of the trees, yet the hills and valleys are in the season of winter and spring surpassingly beautiful, with the lovely heaths and shrubs. The different species of *epacris, pimelia, tetratheca, pultenœa, Daviesia, Dillwynia, callithrix*, and many others are of surprising richness of color and delicacy of form; while many varieties of the beautiful wattle or acacia add a rich sweetness of odor, and combined with the above and the graceful *callitris* (native pine), the no less graceful *exocarpus* (native cherry, which bears its stone outside the fruit), and the *tusanus* (or native peach), compensate for, and in a great degree conceal, the uniformity of the larger trees, without detracting from their grandeur and magnificent proportions. The native plants, in an industrial and commercial point of view, have scarcely been examined, yet it is well known that the bark of the common wattle or acacia is excellent for tanning, and is alone used in the colony for that purpose. Many of the wattles eject a strong clear gum like that produced by the cherry-tree. The gum-trees yield a resin like kino or lac, and the grass-tree is often abundantly covered with a similar material. A patent has, moreover, been lately taken out for the making of paper from a kind of rush, which is found in abundance.

EDUCATION.

The Government system of education now in operation was commenced in 1852, in pursuance of an Act of the Legislature passed during the previous year. It comprises a Central Board of Education, having seven members and a secretary, in connexion with which are two inspectors of schools.

The present members of the board are Messrs. W. C. Belt (chairman); Marshall McDermott, M.P.; William Gosse; J. C. Paisley, A.M.; Arthur Hardy; Samuel Davenport, M.P.; and R. B. Andrews, M.P.; Secretary, E. W. Wickes; Inspectors, William Wyatt and H. E. Smith.

Teachers, approved after examination or the production of

satisfactory testimonials, are licensed by the board to teach in specified localities, and the fees they receive from the parents or guardians of their pupils are supplemented by stipends, payable quarterly, varying from £40 to £100 per annum, according to the qualifications possessed, and the number of pupils taught; the schools being inspected at least three times during the year.

The course of instruction at present required from licensed teachers must, at the least, comprise reading, writing, arithmetic, with the rudiments of English grammar, and geography; but the board are earnestly desirous that the usual course, whenever possible, shall be made to include English grammar (thoroughly taught), English composition, geography (with exercises on maps and globes), mental arithmetic, lineal drawing and mensuration: singing also, when practicable, is recommended. In German schools the teaching of the English language is indispensable.

The Scriptures are read daily in the schools, but no instruction of a denominational character is allowed to be given during school hours.

In connexion with the Central Board of Education is a depôt, from which licensed teachers are supplied with school books at cost prices.

District Councils are authorised to act as District Boards of Education in subordination to the Central Board; and district school-houses, including teachers' residences, are erected on the approval of the project by the board, wherever the residents locally interested raise by subscription an amount equal to one half of the cost of the building, the board, being authorised by the Education Act, furnish the remaining half.

The number of schools in connexion with the Education Board, the pupils attending them, and their cost to the government have been as under:—

	No. of Schools.	No. of Pupils.	Cost. £	s.	d.
In 1852 ..	69	3,283	3,089	15	10
,, 1853 ..	111	5,273	6,718	6	8
,, 1854 ..	125	5,464	8,538	15	0
,, 1855 ..	138	6,039	9,616	2	10
,, 1856 ..	147	6,516	8,979	0	2
,, 1857 ..	167	7,480	10,538	18	0

The pupils at the schools in the province, not in connexion with the Education Board, are estimated at about two-fifths of the aggregate number under instruction, which gives an approximate total amount of about 12,500 at school, or 1 for every 8½ of the population.

The Collegiate School of St. Peter is under the mastership of the Rev. G. H. Fan, A.M., and three or four assistant masters: and there are several other establishments where the classics and mathematics and some of the modern languages are taught.

RELIGION.

Notwithstanding the number of religious denominations that exist in South Australia, each of which is actively engaged in diffusing its own views of doctrine and discipline, yet nowhere does there exist greater unanimity of feeling or more cordial co-operation in all that concerns the common weal and the best and highest interests of society.

Nowhere perhaps has the value of the voluntary system in religion been more thoroughly tested, or its efficiency in the promotion of "peace and goodwill" among rival sects been more completely demonstrated.

Return of the number of Places of Worship of each Denomination in South Australia, specifying the accommodation and average congregation of each during the years 1856-7.

Denomination.	Number of places of Worship		Adapted to contain.		Average Congregation	
	1856	1857	1856	1857	1856	1857
Church of England	28 9*	27 6*	6602	6483	4215	3900
Church of Rome	11 1*	18 2	3320	4590	2140	3280
Church of Scotland	4†	8	750	425	200	320
Free Presbyterians..	6	6	1760	1660	1205	1140
Congregationalists.. .. .. Independents and Baptists	29 9*	3* 12	5280	5418	3256	3573
Wesleyans..	38 24*	67 20	7729	14410	7056	12644
Bible Christians	23 4*	33* 1	2870	4022	1165	2290
Christians..	4	5	910	1150	510	555
Primitive Methodists	2	24* 3	550	3055	350	1280
Lutheran Church	13 6*	16 14*	3688	4785	2621	2606
Society of Friends	2	2	190	200	30	33
Jewish Congregations	1	1	140	100	60	25
Unitarians	3 1*	1	670	300	405	150
Moravians..	..	1	..	300	..	200
Total..	164 54*	235 58*	34459	46898	23713	31941

Total number of places of worship in 1856, 218; 1857, 293.

The information contained in this return has been obtained by the Chief Secretary of South Australia, from the ministers of the several denominations, specially for this work, and may, therefore, be considered correct.

* Rooms and buildings temporarily used as places of worship.
† Three of these churches were without a minister during 1856.

GOVERNMENT, LAW, &c.

GOVERNMENT.—Governor-in-Chief: His Excellency Sir Richard Graves MacDonnell, Knight, C.B. Private Secretary: John Claudius Paisley, M.A.

EXECUTIVE—Hon. W. Younghusband, Chief Secretary; Hon. R. D. Hanson, Attorney General; Hon. B. T. Finniss, Treasurer; Hon. A. Blyth, Commissioner of Public Works; Hon. Francis S. Dutton, Commissioner of Crown Lands; Hon. A. H. Freeling (not in the ministry) Surveyor-General; Clerk, A. Kinloch. Commissary-General, W. H. Maturin, A.D.C. to his Excellency the Governor.

LEGISLATIVE COUNCIL.—President: The Hon. James Hurtle Fisher; the Hon. Thomas S. O'Halloran, the Hon. John Baker, the Hon. William Younghusband, the Hon. John Morphett, the Hon. Edward C. Gwynne, the Hon. Anthony Forster, the Hon. Abraham Scott, the Hon. Edward Stirling, the Hon. William Scott, the Hon. George Hall, the Hon. Charles Harvey Bagot, the Hon. Henry Ayers, The Hon. Samuel Davenport, the Hon. Arthur H. Freeling, the Hon. Charles Davies, the Hon. George Fife Angas, the Hon. Charles George Everard. Clerk of Legislative Council—Francis C. Singleton. Assistant Clerk and Sergeant-at-Arms, J. G. A. Braithwaite.

HOUSE OF ASSEMBLY.—Speaker and Chairman of Committees—The Hon. George S. Kingston. Members:—City of Adelaide: Robert Richard Torrens, R. D. Hanson, Francis S. Dutton, Boyle Travers Finniss, J. Bentham Neales, Wm. Henville Burford. Port Adelaide: John Hart, John Bristowe Hughes. West Torrens: Luther Scammell, James Wm. Cole. Yatala: John Harvey, R. B. Andrews. Gumeracha: Arthur Blyth, Alexander Hay. East Torrens: L. Glyde, J. H. Barrow. Sturt: Thos. Reynolds, John Hallett. Noarlunga: Thomas Young, Henry Mildred. Mount Barker: F. E. H. Wulf Krichauff, J. Dunn. Onkaparinga: William Milne, William Townsend. Encounter Bay: H. B. Strangways, A. F. Lindsay. Barossa: Walter Duffield, William Bakewell: The Murray: David Wark. The Light: J. T. Bagot, W. H. Maturin, Victoria: George Charles Hawker. Burra and Clare: George S. Kingston, Morris Marks, Edward John Peake. Flinders: Marshall MacDermott. Clerk of House of Assembly: G. W. D. Beresford. Assistant Clerk and Sergeant-at-Arms: J. N. Blackmore.

MISCELLANEOUS.—Vice-Admiral, His Excellency the Governor, Sir Richard G. McDonnell. Auditor General, W. L. O'Halloran; Assistant Auditor-General, W. L. Haining. Registrar-General, R. R. Torrens; Deputy Registrar-General, W. B. T. Andrews. Commissioners of Insolvency, C. Mann and Matthew Smith. Official Assignee and Curator of Intestate Estates, L. W. Thrupp. Magistrate at Port Adelaide, R. F. Newland. Commissioner of Police, Major Egerton Warburton. Postmaster-General, John Watts. Secretary of Waterworks, C. N. Wornum. Secretary of Central Road Board, C. Thompson. Inspector of Schools, W. Wyatt. Colonial Architect, E. A. Hamilton. Colonial Storekeeper, William Reylin. Coroner, Dr. Woodforde. Government Printer, W. C. Cox. Gaol-keeper, L. Egan. Comptroller of Convicts, C. S. Hare. Registrar of Births, Deaths, &c., J. F. Cleland. Colonial Surgeon, and Superintendent of Lunatic Asylum: R. M. Moore. Health Officer and Colonial Surgeon at Port Adelaide: Dr. H. Duncan. Superintendent of Botanic Gardens, G. Francis.

LAW.—Chief Justice, His Honor Sir Charles Cooper; Second Judge, His Honor Benjamin Boothby; Master, Henry Jickling; Prothonotary and Registrar, C. A. Wilson; Clerk of Arraigns and Associate, W. Hinde. Sheriff, W. R. Boothby. Crown Solicitor, W. A. Wearing. Commissioner of Insolvency, C. Mann.

COURTS.—Supreme Court, Local Courts, Mayor's Court, Court of Insolvency, Court of Appeal, Vice Admiralty Court, and Police Courts. Stipendiary Magistrate, Adelaide, C. Mann. Police Magistrate, S. Beddome.

There are nearly 200 Justices of the Peace. SUPREME COURT.—Law Terms consist of twenty-seven days each, and commence—first term, last Monday in February; second term, last Monday in May; third term, last Monday in August; fourth term, last Monday in October. Civil Sittings—the third Monday in each of the four terms. Criminal Sittings—first sitting, second Monday in February; second sitting, second Monday in May; third sitting, second Monday in August; fourth sitting, Monday after termination of the fourth term. THE INSOLVENCY COURT is open at the Supreme Court Office. LOCAL COURTS.—These courts are now established at Adelaide, Port Adelaide, Kooringa, Gawler Town, Mount Barker, Strathalbyn, Woodside, Gumeracha, Clare, Kapunda, Angaston, Tanunda, Wellunga, Morphett Vale, Percola, Port Lincoln, Robe Town, Normanville, Port Elliott, Goolwa, Yankalilla, Magill, Auburn, and Salisbury.

CUSTOMS.—Port Adelaide—Collector of Customs, G. F. Dashwood; Naval Officer and Harbor Master, B. Douglas; Immigration Agent, Dr. Duncan.

MAGNETIC TELEGRAPH DEPARTMENT.—Director: Charles Todd. Charges for messages are as follows:—(names and addresses free): Between Adelaide and the Port, and the Port and LeFevre's Peninsula, not exceeding 20 words, including delivery within half a mile, 6d.; and 3d. for each ten words, or less, additional. Between Adelaide and the Peninsula, double the above rates. A line is opened between Gawler Town and Adelaide, also to Goolwa. The stations on the telegraph line to Melbourne are through Geelong, Ballaarat, Raglan, Warrnambool, Belfast, Portland, Mount Gambier, Guichen Bay, Goolwa, and Port Elliott.

POST OFFICE.—Mails are despatched as follow:—*Suburban:* Port Adelaide 8½ miles from Adelaide, Hindmarsh and Bowden 2¼, Woodville, Alberton 7, North Adelaide 1¼, Enfield 6, Walkerville 2¼, Norwood 2, Campbell Town 5, Payneham 3, Makill 4, Unley 3, Mitcham 4½, Edward's Town 4, Sturt 8, Brighton 8½, Plympton 3½, Glenelg 6, Glen Osmond 4¼, Thebarton 1½, Lefevre's Peninsula 9. *Northern Route:* Grand Junction 8 miles, Salisbury 16, Gawler Plains 20, Gawler 27, She-oak Log 37, Greenock 45, Kapunda 52, Hamilton 62, Apoinga 82, Kooringa 102, Lyndock Valley 37, Tanunda 45, Nuriootpa 48, Angaston 54, Truro 64, Templers 36, Stockport 46, Riverton 61, Auburn 70, Watervale 76, Penwortham 80, Clare 86, Mintaro 79, Penfield 22, Virginia 27, Port Wakefield 124, Charlton 152, Melrose 167, Port Augusta 212, Moorundee 89, Little Para 14, One-tree Hill 20. *North-Eastern Route:* Old Shepherd's Inn 10½, Houghton 14, Chain of Ponds 21, Gumeracha 25, Blumberg 27, Mount Pleasant 36. *Eastern Route:* Crafers 10 miles, Hahndorf 18, Balhannah 22, Woodside 26, Lobethal 32, Charleston 38, Mount Torrens 40, Echunga 24, Mount Barker 21, Nairne 25, Kanmantoo 37, Macclesfield 29, Strathalbyn 38, Langhorne's Creek 48, Wellington 69, Robe (Guichen Bay) 200, Mosquito Plains 220, Penola 250, Mount Gambier 280, Meadows 33, Milang 51, Tin Pot 33. *South-Eastern Route:* Coromandel Valley 9 miles, Cherry Gardens 12, Clarendon 17. *Southern Route:* O'Halloran Hill 12 miles, Reynella 13½, Morphett Vale 15, Noarlunga 20, McLaren Vale 25, Willunga 30, Port Eliot 58, Goolwa 65, Currency Creek 50, Aldinga 27, Myponga 40, Yankalilla 50, Normanville 53, Rapid Bay 62, Bald Hills 55, Inman Valley 60, Encounter Bay 69. *On the Coast:* Port Lincoln, 210 miles.—The rates of postage for inland letters is 2d. under half an ounce; over half an ounce and under one ounce, 4d. Book post, including pamphlets, &c., under four ounces, 2d. (The same charge to all the colonies.) Letters for the Australian Colonies and Great Britain, 6d. under half an ounce. Letters must be prepaid.

RAILWAY.—South Australian Railway. Board of Commissioners: W. Hanson, R. B. Colley, and John Brown. Engineer, W. Hanson; Assist. Engineer, W. G. Coulls. Secretary, R. Borrow. The City and Port Line extends for seven and a half miles from Adelaide, through Bowden, Woodville, and Albert Town to Port Adelaide. The North Line extends for twenty-five miles from Adelaide, through North Adelaide, Grand Junction, Dry Creek, Salisbury, and Smithfield, to Gawler.

REGISTRATION.—Births may be registered without charge for forty-two days, or after six weeks upon making a declaration, and paying a fee of 5s. Births, &c.; may be registered either at the office of the Registrar of the district in which the parents live, or at the General Registry Office. Information of Births, &c., by letter are not attended to.

ECCLESIASTICAL.

CHURCH OF ENGLAND.—Bishop of Adelaide, Right Rev. Augustus Short, D.D. (1847.) Dean, Very Rev. James Farrell. Archdeacon, the Venerable W. J. Woodcock. Andrews, W. B., Mount Barker. Coombs, W. H., Canon, St. George's, Gawler Town. Cooper, A., Christ-church, O'Halloran Hill, and St. Mary's, Sturt River. Evans, F., St. James's Woodville. Farr, G. H., Canon, St. Peter's Collegiate School. Farrell, Very Rev. James, Dean of Trinity Church, Adelaide. Hammond, O., Port Lincoln. Ibbetson, D. J. H., St. Mary's, Kooringa. Jenkins, E., St. Matthew's, Kensington. Marryat, C., Canon, St. Paul's, Port Adelaide. Miller, E. K., St. George's, Magill. Needham, R. W., St. Michael's, Mitcham. Neville, T. R., St. Philip and St. James's, Noarlunga, and St. Stephen's, Willunga. Packard, D., St. Andrew's, Walkerville. Platts, F., St. Saviour's, Glen Osmond. Pollitt, James, St. Luke's, Adelaide. Russell, A. R., Canon, St. John's, Adelaide. Boake, J. A., Salisbury. Sabine, J., Norwood. Schoales, I. C., All Saints, Hindmarsh. Sheldon, J., Mount Gambier. Titherington, J. B., St. Peter's, Glenelg, and St. Jude's, Brighton. Watson, J., Port Elliot and Goolwa. Wood, William, St. Barnabas, Carel, and St. Mark's, Penwortham.

CHURCH OF SCOTLAND.—Haining, R., Adelaide. Ross, W., Inverbrackie.

ROMAN CATHOLIC CHURCH.—Bishop, Right Rev. —— —— Vicar-General, Very Rev. M. Ryan. Smyth, John, Port Adelaide. Roe, John, Gawler. Lencioni, Maurice, Adelaide. Fallon, John, Kapunda. Tappeiner, Joseph, Clare. Palhuber, John, Clare. O'Brien, Michael, Mount Barker. Snell, Joseph, Morphett Vale. Hughes, Peter, Willunga. Woods, Julian E., Penola. Russell, Patrick; Reoden, J. J.; and Carew, J., Adelaide.

BAPTIST CHURCHES.—Abbott, Jacob, open communion, Pulteney-st. Buttfield, J. P., Uley. Daniel J., Rapid Bay. Dewhirst, Edward, Congregational, White's Room, Adelaide. Gurr, William, Particular Baptist, Salem Chapel, Kermode-street, North Adelaide. Hannay, J, open communion, Angaston. Kither, John, Chain of Ponds. Maddern, E. Verere, Chain of Ponds. Morton, R., Gumeracha. Playford, Thomas, open communion, Bentham-street. Prince, George, Particular Baptist, Ebenezer Chapel, Kermode-street, North Adeilade. Stonehouse, George, open communion. Bay Road. Tuck, H. L., Gumeracha. Squibb, W. R., Houghton.

CONGREGATIONAL CHURCHES.—Austin, J. B., Macclesfield. Ayling, J., Lyndoch Valley. Cox, F. W., Adelaide. Cheetham, H., Kensington. Evan, C. W., B.A., Adelaide. Hall, C., McLaren Vale. Harris, J. Macclesfield. Hodge, M., Port Adelaide. Hotham, J., Port Elliott. Kelsey, J., O'Halloran Hill. Leonard, J., B.A., Gawler. Mudie, G. Salisbury. Newland, R. W., Encounter Bay. Nicholls, W., Brighton. Oldham, W., Kapunda. Philps, A. R., Morphett Vale. Roberts, J., Middleton and Goolwa. Stow, T. Q., Adelaide. Watt, C. D., Norwood.

FREE PRESBYTERIAN CHURCH.—Gardner, John, Adelaide. Anderson, John, Strathalbyn. Moir, John Strachan, Gawler Town and Smithfield. Bennev, James, Morphett Vale. Mercer, Peter, Port Adelaide, McCalman, D., Mosquito Plains.

UNITED PRESBYTERIAN CHURCH.—Lyle, W., Adelaide. Coward, R. L., Truro.

WESLEYAN CHURCH.—William Butters, Chairman of the District, R. C. Flockhart, Charles Colwell (Clare), Kooringa; Jabez B. Waterhouse. Kapunda; Matthew Wilson, Clarendon; Spencer Williams, Peter R. C. Ussher (Nairne), Mount Barker and Nairne; William M. Bennett, North Clarendon; Harcourt, J., Adelaide; Hill, William, Yankalilla; supplies wanting for Goolwa, Strathalbyn, and Kersbrook. Number of members in the colony, 2,203.

GERMAN LUTHERAN.—Hensel, C. A., Blumberg. Kavel, A., Longmeill Kappler, A., Hope Valley. Meyer, H. A. E., Bethany. Mucke, C., Tanunda. Maschmidt, C., Kleinzig. Oster, P. J. Hoffnungsthal. Strempel, C. F. Hahndorf. Tirchelman, C. J., Salem, or Bremen.

PRIMITIVE METHODISTS.—Cole, Henry, Adelaide. Tear, E., Mount Barker. Wright, J. G., Kooringa. Whittaker, J. G., Adelaide. Whitefield, W., Nairne.

BIBLE CHRISTIANS.—Culver, James, Kapunda. Fursman, William, Mount Barker. Hillman, T., Kooringa. Kien, S., Gawler. Kien, T. E., Mount Torrens. Ridclift, J., Watervale. Roberts, J., Willunga. Rowe, J., Adelaide. Way, J., Adelaide.

SOCIETY OF FRIENDS.—May, J., Mount Barker.

MORAVIANS.—Schondorff, C. S. D., Bethel, near Kapunda.

JEWS.—Gollin, B., and Moratta, S., Adelaide.

UNITARIAN.—Woods, J. C., Adelaide.

BANKS AND INSURANCE COMPANIES.

BANKS IN ADELAIDE.—South Australian Banking Company, North Terrace: Manager, George Tinline. Union Bank of Australia, Pirie-street: Manager, Nathaniel Oldham. Bank of Australasia, King William-street: Manager, S. Tomkinson. Savings' Bank, Exchange Chambers, King William-street: Accountant, John Hector.

INSURANCE COMPANIES.—Albion Life Insurance Company, A. Scott. Alliance British and Foreign Fire and Life Assurance Company, Fox, Lloyd and Co. Adelaide Lloyds' Association of Underwriters, Cowie and Aspinwall. Cornwall Fire and Marine Insurance Company, Abraham Scott. Church of England Life Assurance Institution, F. S. Dutton. Derwent and Tamar Marine Assurance Company, Black and Wright. Hobart Town and Launceston Marine Insurance Company, F. J. Beck and Co. Imperial Fire Insurance Company, A. J. Wright. Melbourne Lloyds' Association of Underwriters, Fox, Lloyd and Co. Monarch Fire and Life Assurance Company, Jos. Stirling and Co. Northern Assurance Company, Elder, Stirling and Co. Professional Life Assurance Company, R. B. Colley. The Royal Insurance Company, Acraman, Main, Lindsay and Co. South Australian Insurance Company, R. E. Tapley, Secretary. Fire Brigade, Superintendent, Thomas Hills.

SOCIETIES, INSTITUTIONS, &c.

ADELAIDE HOSPITAL.—Colonial Surgeon, R. Wm. Moore. Assistant Colonial Surgeon, Morgan Thomas. Clerk of Hospital (also Clerk of Vaccine Board), William Johnson. Dispenser, Henry Briggs. Assistant ditto, Receiver and Issuer of Stores, William F. Wheeler. Matron, I. Briggs.

CHAMBER OF COMMERCE.—Offices, Green's Exchange. Committee of Management — S. Tomkinson, Chairman; M. B. Henriques, Deputy Chairman; George Hall; G. S. Young; Alfred Watts; J. R. Black; Abraham Scott; John Hector; Abraham Abrahams; R. B. Smith; J. H. Clark. Secretary, D. Melville. Committee meet every Thursday. General meetings, quarterly, and on special occasions.

DESTITUTE BOARD. — Office, Destitute Asylum, North Terrace. Members—the Hon. the Chief Secretary; the Colonial Chaplain; the Colonial Surgeon; the Immigration Agent; Very Rev. M. Ryan; Rev. John Gardiner; Rev. W. Ingram; Rev. R. Haining; W. Giles. Secretary, E. Holthouse. Relieving Officer (resident), J. W. Bee.

DISTRICT COUNCILS.—Chairman of Association, A. H. Davis; Secretary, J. K. Penney. District Councils are held at Alexandrina, Aldinga, Angaston, Barossa East, Barossa West, Bremer, Brighton, Burnside, Clare, Clarendon, Echunga, Encounter Bay, Highercombe, Hindmarsh, Kondoparinga, Macclesfield, Mitcham, Morphett Vale, Mount Barker, Mount Crawford, Mudla Wirra, Munno Para East, Munno Para West, Myponga, Nairne, Noarlunga, Onkaparinga, Para Wirra, Payneham, Port Elliott and Goolwa, Port Gawler, Rapid Bay, Strathalbyn, Talunga, Tanunda, Torrens East, Torrens West, Tungkillo, Walkerville, Willunga, Yankalillo, Yatala and Upper Wakefield.

FORESTERS.—Names of Courts: Perseverance, Happy Home, Homely Retreat, Australia's Pride, Pride of the Forest, Huntsmen's Pride, Forester's Retreat, Robin Hood, Rose of the Forest, Salisbury's Pride, Bushman's Pride, Mountain Glen, Mountainous, Industry, Concord, Old Oak of England, Court Kensington, and Adelaide.

INSTITUTIONS.—South Australian Institute: Secretary, Nathaniel Hailes. South Australian Agricultural and Horticultural Society: President, G. S. Kingston, M.P.; Secretary, F. S. Driffield. Botanic Gardens: G. Francis, Superintendent. Vaccine Institute: Drs. Gosse, Woodeford, and Bayer.

LUNATIC ASYLUM.—Superintendent, R. W. Moore. Head Keeper, John Cavanagh. Matron, I. Morris.

MASONIC LODGES.—Provincial Grand Lodge and the South Australian Royal Arch Chapter. The Craft Lodges: Friendship, Harmony, United Tradesmen's, Concord, Truth, Unity, Fidelity, Kooringa. Scotch Constitution: Adelaide St. John's Lodge. Irish Constitution: Duke of Leinster Lodge, Adelaide Lodge of Mark Master Masons, Leinster Chapter of Royal Arch Masons.

MEDICAL PROFESSION.—The Board meets quarterly, on the first Tuesday in January, April, July, and October of each year. Diplomas and certificates to be forwarded, under cover, to W. Wyatt, Secretary, at Adelaide Hospital, at least three days previous to each meeting.

MUNICIPAL CORPORATIONS.—Adelaide: John Lazar, Mayor; W. A. Hughes, Town Clerk. Port Adelaide: Edward French, Mayor; W. Boykett, Town Clerk. Kensington and Norwood: John Carlin, Mayor; J. E. Moulden, Town Clerk. Glenelg: S. P. H. Wright, Mayor; W. R. Wigley, Town Clerk. Gawler: R. J. Turner, Mayor; J. Rudall, Town Clerk.

ODD FELLOWS.—Names of Lodges: Adelaide, Hope, Albion, Stuart, Albert, Gawler, Flinders, Hindmarsh, Burra Burra, Noarlunga, Britannia, Sir John Franklin, Brighton, Onkaparinga, Norwood, Wellington, Newton, Angas, Park, M'Donnell, Rynella, Highercombe, Willunga, Gumeracha, Auburn, Mintaro, Temple of Peace, Macclesfield, and Loyal Woodville. There are several Friendly Societies.

SOCIETIES.—Sun Land, Building, and Investment Society. Atlas Land, Building, and Investment Society. Equitable Permanent Building and Investment Society. Permanent Land and Building Association. West Adelaide Building Society. Temperance Permanent Land and Building Society. Ancient Order Hibernian Society, St. Patrick's Lodge. Engineers' Mechanical Society. Independent Order of Rechabites, St. Patrick's Lodge.

MISCELLANEOUS.

CARRIAGES, &c.—Fares, from 3s. to 5s. per hour. The regulations, with Carters' Fares, &c., are issued in the local publications.

COACHES & CONVEYANCES.—To Angaston, Brighton and the Bay, Glenelg, Clare, Campbell Town, Glen Osmond, Kapunda and Koringa, Kensington, Magill, Mitcham, Mount Barker, Norwood, North Adelaide, Payneham, Port Adelaide, Port Elliot, Truro, Unley and Walkerville. Also to Willunga, Strathalbyn, and Yankalilla.

COUNTRY DISTRICTS.—GAWLER TOWN.—R. J. Turner, Mayor; H. D. Murray, Stipendiary Magistrate. (For Churches, &c., *see* Ecclesiastical.) Freemasons: Lodge Fidelity. I.O.O.F., M. U.: Lodge Gawler. South Australian Banking Company; Manager, Alexander Grace. Union Bank of Australia; Manager, E. C. Windsor. Professional Life Assurance, F. F. Turner, J. Rudall, Esq. South Australian Insurance Company (Fire) Duffield and Turner. Corporal Evans, in charge of Police. Five Hotels. KENSINGTON AND NORWOOD.—John Carlin, Mayor. Court Kensington, Forester's Lodge. Six hotels. GLENELG.—S. P. H. Wright, Mayor. Two hotels. PORT ELLIOTT AND GOOLWA.—Trains from Goolwa to Port Elliott. Port Elliott Institute; Secretary, William Small. Ferry boat to Hindmarsh Island. Special Magistrate, B. F. Laurie. Postmaster, J. P. Tripp. Deputy Harbor Master, F. Taylor. One hotel.

CROWN LANDS.—Leases without the hundreds, ten shillings per annum per square mile; Pasturage Leases within the hundreds, where the District Councils Act is not in force, £1 per square mile; Depasturing Licenses for commonage as above—16 head of great cattle for each 80-acre section—five of small equivalent to one of great cattle. Sales of Crown Lands, by public auction, take place every Thursday, at the Local Court House, at eleven o'clock; upset price 1*l.* per acre.

HARBOR DUES.—Scale of Harbor Dues leviable by the Harbor Trust upon all ships or Vessels entering Port Adelaide:—Vessels from Great Britain, Foreign Ports, Mauritius, Cape, and India, for every ton per register, 7s. 6d.; vessels from Australian Colonies, Van Diemen's Land, and New Zealand, for every ton per register, 2d.; vessels from ditto, ditto, ditto, if paid in advance, per quarter, for every ton per register, 6d.; vessels constantly engaged in coasting trade, payable in advance, per quarter, for every ton per register, 3d.; vessels occasionally engaged in coasting trade, per voyage, for every ton per register, 1d. On Vessels from Great Britain, Mauritius, the Cape, India, and Foreign Ports: For mooring vessels from 70 to 100 tons, 15s.; for unmooring ditto, 15s.; for removing ditto, 1*l.* 10s. And, in addition, for every 20 tons above 100 tons register: For mooring, 2s.; for unmooring, 2s.; for removing, 2s. The rate of Harbor Dues on Vessels entering Port Adelaide from Victoria, Van Diemen's Land, the other Australian Colonies, and coastwise: For mooring and unmooring vessels from 70 to 100 tons per voyage, 10s.; for each removal, 1*l.* And, in addition, for every 20 tons above 100 tons register, to be charged: For mooring and unmooring, 2s.; for removing, 2s.

LIGHT DUES.—The rate of light dues on vessels from Great Britain, Mauritius, the Cape, India, and Foreign Ports, 3d. in per ton and 3d. out per ton. The rate of light dues on vessels from Victoria, Van Diemen's Land, and the other Australian Colonies, 1½d. in per ton and 1½d. out per ton. And the rate of light dues on vessels coastwise: From 30 to 50 tons per voyage, 8s.; from 50 to 100 tons per voyage, 7s.; and above 100 tons, at the rate of 1d. in and 1d. out per ton.

NEWSPAPERS.—*South Australian Register*, daily; *Adelaide Observer*, weekly. A German paper is published weekly, and the *Government Gazette* every Thursday.

POPULATION.—Estimated population on 31st March, 1858:—males, 56,698; females, 54,823; total, 111,521.

RATES OF PILOTAGE.—For every vessel taking a pilot, 3*l.* 5s.; and, in addition, for every foot of draft above nine feet, 15s.

SAILING DIRECTIONS.—A full account of Sailing Directions for Harbors, Out-Ports, &c., are published in the *Royal South Australian Almanac for* 1858, issued by R. Douglas, Chief Harbor Master.

STEAMERS.—To Port Lincoln and Port Augusta, the steamer *Marion;* to Guichen Bay, the steamer *Ant;* to Melbourne, the *Havilah, Burra Burra* and the *Admella;* to the River Murray, by the Company's vessels, from Adelaide.

TARIFF.—All imported goods, with the following exceptions, are admitted at a duty of five per cent. ad valorum:—Beer, porter, ale, cider, and perry, 4d. per gall. Bricks, fire and bath, 5s. per 1000. Coffee, 6s. per cwt. Corn, meal, flour, viz: wheat, barley, oats, maize, and millett, peas, beans, and pulse, 6d. per quarter; malt, 3d. per quarter: flour, meal, bran, and pollard, 2d. per 100 lbs. Fruit (dried) of all sorts, 4s. per cwt. Hops, 2d. per lb. Iron, bar and rod, 10s. per ton; sheet and hoop, 14s. per ton; pig, 2s. per ton. Pitch and tar 1s. 6d. per barrel. Provisions and preserved meats, 8s. per cwt. Resin, 6s. per bar. Salt, 8s. per ton. Spirits or strong waters of all sorts, 9s per gall. Sugar, refined and candy, 4s. per cwt.; muscovado, 2s. per cwt.; Molasses, 1s. per cwt. Tea, 2d. per lb. Tobacco, manufactured, 1s. per lb.; unmanufactured, 6d. per lb.; cigars and cheroots, 2s. 6d. per lb.; snuff, 1s. per lb.; sulphered and tarred for sheepwash, 6d. per lb. Wine, 1s. per gall. Wood, posts and rails, handspikes, and poles, 1s. per 100; pailings, 6d. per 100; shingles and laths, 6d. per 1000; trenails and spokes, 2d. per 100. Oars, 2s. per 100 ft.; square timber, balks, deals, battens, quartering, planks, boards, and sawn, hewn, or split timber of all kinds, not otherwise enumerated or described, 2s. 6d. per 40 cubic ft. *Free List.*—Animals, living; baggage of passengers; books, printed; bullion and coin; coals, coke, and other fuel; plants and trees; seeds and roots, garden; specimens illustrative of natural history; pictures and prints; works of art; wool; tallow; skins and hides (raw); bark; gum; bales of wool; and ore bags.

TONNAGE DUES.—Vessels loading or discharging at the wharves are charged 3d. per ton register

TOWAGE RATES FOR STEAM-TUG.—For vessels of 200 tons, 8*l.*; for every additional ton, 7d.; or towing loaded lighters (100 tons), 8*l.*; for every additional ton, 7d.; for towing empty lighters, 4*l.*

NEW SOUTH WALES.

POSITION AND BOUNDARIES.

The colony of New South Wales (so named by Capt. Cook from its fancied resemblance to the South Wales of the mother country) occupies the eastern side of the continent of Australia. On the east it is bounded by the Pacific Ocean, from whence it stretches into the interior as far as the line of the 141st meridian, which divides it from South Australia. The line of the 26th parallel is its northern frontier, but it is proposed to form a separate colony of the northern portion, now known as the Moreton Bay District, with the 30th parallel as its southern limit. The southern boundary is a line drawn from Cape Howe to the River Murray, near Mount Kosciusko, which separates it from Victoria, and thence along the course of the river to the meridian of 141° E. The area embraced within its limits is upwards of 400,000 square miles, forming a compact mass of territory. Along its maritime frontier, between the 26th parallel and Cape Howe, a range of about 900 miles, there are many inlets forming safe and excellent harbors, the entrances to which are mostly narrow, and only visible when a vessel nears the land.

SEASONS AND CLIMATE.

The climate of New South Wales, particularly in the inland districts, is highly salubrious, although the heat in summer is sometimes excessive. The seasons are the opposite of those in England, January being the middle of summer, and July of winter. Spring and autumn are brief, but well defined, and the winter is of a bracing coolness. During the summer months hot winds occasionally blow from the north-west, and probably derive their heat from the immense tract of country which they traverse. They seldom continue more than twelve hours and are generally succeeded by a southerly gale, which seldom lasts longer than half an hour and is followed by heavy showers of rain. In the autumn months the weather is generally unsettled, and the month of March may be considered the rainy season. The land breezes at this time are usually from south to west, and somewhat feeble. During the winter months the mornings and evenings are chilly, and the nights cold; hoar frosts are frequent and are more severe in the interior. In the spring months the cold begins very sensibly to moderate, with occasional showers; but the weather upon the whole, is clear and pleasant.

HISTORY.

The settlements of the British on the eastern coast of New Holland must be traced to the separation of the North American Provinces from the mother country. In the reign of Elizabeth, it was decreed that banishment should be the punishment of rogues and vagabonds; and in 1619, during the reign of James I., the system of transportation was commenced, prisoners being allowed to transport themselves to America at their own expense. In the reign of George I., parliamentary enactment regulated the system, which was declared to have been beset with many abuses, defeating the ends of justice, and on the other hand, inflicting great cruelty on the convicts themselves. But, under the new law, far greater abuses sprang up. A practice of contract was adopted for disposing of the criminals, who were, in fact, sold as slaves at the average rate of £20 per head, the number transported being about two thousand per annum. On the separation of the United States from England, this inhuman system ceased; but, as the home prisons became crowded, transportation to the west coast of Africa was tried. It was soon, however, abandoned. Captain Cook returning about this time from his voyage in the southern hemisphere, and describing in glowing terms that part of Terra Australis which he had discovered and named New South Wales, it was resolved to form a penal settlement at Botany Bay.

On the 13th of May, 1787, a fleet of eleven sail, comprising H. M. frigate *Syrius*, an armed tender, three store ships and six transports, sailed from England; and, having touched for supplies and stock at Teneriffe, Rio de Janeiro and the Cape of Good Hope, anchored in Botany Bay, during the 18th, 19th, and 20th January, 1788. Captain Arthur Phillip, R. N., was the appointed Governor of the new colony, and he immediately found that Botany Bay was not suitable for the purposes designed. He accordingly proceeded on a boat expedition; and, examining an inlet marked as a boat harbor in Captain Cook's chart, and called Port Jackson, entered between the lofty heads, and discovered one of the finest harbors in the world. Thither the fleet was directly steered, and on the memorable 26th of January, 1788, the British ensign was hoisted on the silent and solitary shores of Sydney Cove, now the capital of a country whose wonderful natural products and industrial enterprise must, to use the expressive language of one of her chief historians and statesmen, William Charles Wentworth, "be speedily precipitated into a nation." The little colony so established consisted of 1,030 individuals: it now numbers 310,000 souls. Its stock consisted of one bull, four cows, one stallion, three mares, and three colts. According to the latest official returns, the live stock of the colony then numbered:—Horses, 168,929; horned cattle, 2,023,418; sheep, 7,736,323; pigs, 105,998.

During the first two years the progress of the colony was retarded by incredible difficulties, which nothing but extraordinary patience and perseverance on the part of the residents, and the moral and physical courage of Governor Phillip, could have withstood. In 1790, however, the arrival of the second fleet changed the aspect of affairs, and the colonists began to look forward with hope.

At the latter end of 1792, Governor Phillip embarked for England. The government was then successively administered by Captains Grose and Paterson until the 7th August, 1795, when Captain Hunter, R.N., arrived in Sydney, and assumed the administration of affairs. His government lasted five years; and the accession of a regiment for the colony, called the New South Wales Corps (afterwards the 102nd Regt.), and the arrival of capitalists and other free settlers from England, imparted new incentives to industry, and an improved tone to society. Captain Hunter was succeeded by Captain King, who had many vexatious difficulties and determined opponents to contend with. One anecdote, illustrative of the state of things under his rule, may be mentioned here. He had preferred charges against a gentleman in the colony, and prepared despatches to be forwarded to the Secretary of State. The officer who had charge of them incautiously mentioned the circumstance to some friends of the gentleman in question; and when he arrived in Downing-street, the despatch box was found to contain only a bundle of newspapers, the lock having been picked and the papers abstracted. Captain Bligh, who had acquired an unenviable notoriety by his treatment of Christian and his comrades in H.M.S. *Bounty*, when sent to convey the bread fruit from the South Sea Islands to the West Indies, succeeded Capt. King. Placed in arbitrary power, the iron rule of this officer was resisted by the colonists, and after a short reign of eighteen months, he was deposed by the officers and men of the New South Wales Corps; and the government was successively administered by Lieutenant-Colonels Johnstone and Foveaux, and Colonel Patterson, from the 26th January, 1808, to the 28th December, 1809, when Lieutenant-Colonel, afterwards Major-General, Macquarie arrived, and assumed the reins of government, the New South Wales Corps being ordered home. This Governor's sway was exercised for twelve years, during which period great progress was made. Population, both free and bond, increased; public buildings were erected at the expense of the British Government; roads were constructed by convict labor, and government farms established. One of the most valuable labors which the annals of the colony of this period present was the exploration of the Bathurst country. The principal mountain range in the colony, named the Blue Mountains, had never been passed by a white man. Of an elevation, nearly perpendicular, of from 3000 to 5000 feet, they seemed to defy all communication with the interior. Their summits were deemed inaccessible, and even the aborigines declared them to be impassable. However, in 1813, a severe drought compelled an arduous search for new pasturage; and a pass was at last found by Messrs. Wentworth, Blaxland, and Lawson, by following the course of the River Grose, and a road was soon commenced and completed.

Governor Macquarie was relieved in December, 1821, and was succeeded by Major-General Sir Thomas Brisbane, K.C.B., during whose administration the liberty of the press was established, the right to publish being previously prohibited except by direct license from the governor. He remained in office until the latter end of 1825, when he was succeeded by Lieutenant-General Darling, whose administration extended to October, 1831. It was surrounded with many serious difficulties and embarrassments; some, perhaps, attributable to the many unpopular proceedings of his own, and others to the violence of faction. His successor, Sir Richard Bourke, was a far more popular governor; but the vexed question of convict discipline, and the vehement opposition of the free colonists to the conferring political and social rights upon the emancipists, still embarrassed the proceedings of the government, and the fierceness of partizanship contrasted strongly with those beneficent and wise measures which are recorded on the pedestal of the statue of Sir Richard, which the grateful colonists erected in the Outer Domain, by subscription, after his departure.

Sir Richard Bourke, after six years' administration of the Government, embarked on the 5th of December, 1837, for England, and on the 23rd of February, 1838, Sir George Gipps arrived in Sydney and assumed the reins of Government. One of his first acts was to throw open the proceedings of the Legislative Council to the public and the press. The year 1838 was disastrous to the colony, whether as regarded in its commercial, agricultural or pastoral enterprise; and in November a day of general fasting and humiliation was appointed to be held throughout the territory, severely suffering from a long protracted drought.

On the 7th of January, 1839, the minimum price of Crown Land was raised from 5s. to 12s. per acre; and on the 22nd of March, 1839, an act for regulating the occupation of Crown Lands, known as the Squatting Act, was passed in an extraordinary session of the Nominee Legislature. Both measures materially affected the sales of lands. The amount realised in 1837, was £116,475; in 1839, £92,968; and a downward tendency of a more considerable character was evinced for some years. On the 20th of October, Sir George Gipps announced to the Legislative Council the determination of Her Majesty's Government to discontinue transportation to New South Wales; and on the 20th of November, 1839, His Excellency announced, that for all purposes connected with the disposal of Crown land the colony was to be divided into three districts, viz., the northern, the middle (or Sydney), and the southern (or Port Phillip). A new system of land sales was established, the price in the northern and middle districts remaining at 12s. per acre, and in the southern being fixed at one pound,

Early in 1841, a great public meeting was held in Sydney, for the purpose of adopting petitions to the Queen and British Parliament, praying for a concession to the colony of the boon of a Representative Legislature.

In July, 1841, the fifth census of the population was taken. The result was:—males, 87,298; females, 43,558; total, 130,856.

In 1842, two most important measures came into operation; the first was the incorporation of the cities of Sydney and Melbourne, in both of which the municipal elections were conducted with great spirit. The second was the Crown Land Sales Act, 5 and 6 Vict., c. 36, under which Mr. Gilbert Wakefield's system of Bounty Emigration was brought into force. The upset price of land was fixed at £1 per acre, and one half of the proceeds of all land sales was appropriated to immigration purposes.

The year 1843 marks an important era in the political history of New South Wales. On the first of January, Sir George Gipps received a despatch from the Colonial Minister, enclosing the Constitutional Act, 5 and 6 Vict., c. 76, by which further provision for the government of the Australian possessions was made. By this act a Legislative Council was constituted, partly elective, partly non-elective; electoral districts were constituted, and on the whole a liberal measure of self-government was conceded to the colonists. This act was proclaimed on the 5th, and took effect from that day; and the general election took place in June. In August the Council met for the despatch of business. Mr. Alexander McLeay was elected Speaker, and Sir George Gipps opened the session in person. The monetary confusion of the colony, arising from excessive speculations and other causes, was particularly adverted to in His Excellency's speech; and on the 23rd of the same month, Mr. Richard Windeyer moved the appointment of a select committee to consider the means of staying the further evil consequences to be apprehended from the monetary confusion lately and still prevalent in the colony. The financial and commercial position of New South Wales was a most critical one. A great depreciation in the value of every kind of property had taken place. The sudden cessation of transportation, and the consequent diminution of Government expenditure; the introduction, on a large scale, of the bounty system of immigration, to meet the expenses of which the local government drew out their deposits from the Sydney banks almost as rapidly as they had lodged them;

the consequent necessity on the part of the banks to restrict their discounts as suddenly; the fall in wool fifty per cent. below its former prices; the destruction of the crops by two years' drought—these were the most prominent among the causes of the embarrassment of the colony. Painful disclosures in respect to the mismanagement of the Bank of Australia, and certain malpractices on the part of some of the chief officers of the Sydney Banking Company, tended to increase the panic and monetary confusion. The value of cattle and sheep was so depressed, that the conversion of them into tallow was generally determined upon by the graziers; and "boiling down" operations were begun on a large scale.

This manufacture, begun in despair, was carried out to a great extent in succeeding years. The export of tallow, which in 1843 was 5,680 cwt., amounted, in 1850, to 128,000 cwt. The importation of tallow candles between those years, was at the rate of £20,000 per annum; but the establishment of extensive candle manufactories during the last few years, in all parts of the colony, has prevented the continuance of a large export of tallow, and during the past year no more than 22,298 cwt. was shipped.

The first session of the Legislative Council ended on the 28th of December. The panic that had overtaken the colony created much discussion and alarm. To the question, "To what do you attribute the present monetary embarrassment of the colony?" the reply of the gentlemen connected with the committee which had been appointed, may be summed up in a very few words: "The immense abstraction of the public moneys of the colony to pay for the transmission of labor for private purposes." Further discussions on this subject soon afterwards arose both in Sydney and in England, in reference to the abstraction of the colonial land funds for immigration purposes. The Under-Secretary of State for the colonies, Mr. Herman Merivale, when occupying the chair of Political Economy at Oxford, propounded his Land Preparation Theory, which, it must be remarked, had been frequently brought before the colonists, with equal ability, by Dr. Bland, in speeches made by him in the Legislative Council.

On the 2nd of April, 1844, Sir George Gipps issued a new code of regulations relative to the occupation of Crown lands beyond the boundaries of present location. The squatting interests took the alarm, and a strong agitation was raised throughout every district of the colony, both within and without the boundaries. The "Pastoral Association of New South Wales" was formed, and meetings held in various parts of the colony. Nineteen petitions, bearing 6,500 signatures, of gentlemen largely connected with the pastoral, commercial, and maritime interests, were presented to the Council, and transmitted to England for presentation to Her Majesty and Parliament.

On the 20th of June, the select committee presented their

report, together with a voluminous mass of evidence, to the Colonial Legislature. After an elaborate examination of each of the grievances to which the evidence referred, the committee prefaced their recommendations by advising that an address be presented to the Governor, requesting that the Pastoral Regulations of the 2nd of April be recalled, because they were in the opinion of every witness impracticable in principle, and oppressive and ruinous in detail.

At the commencement of 1845, the Bank of Australasia having entered an action against the Bank of Australia for the recovery of £160,000 borrowed money, the trial commenced before the Supreme Court, Sydney, and ended on the 8th of April, when the jury not agreeing, no verdict was returned. In June, the Court at the request of both parties, granted a trial at bar, which lasted 20 days. The jury found a special verdict, which still left the case in a doubtful position. The plaintiffs appealed to the Privy Council, and finally, judgment was given against the Bank of Australia. To the credit of New South Wales, it is to be recorded, that the whole of the debt, together with interest, costs, and various heavy expenses, was paid by the shareholders of the latter ill-fated institution, whose mismanagement had involved many of the oldest and most respectable colonists in ruin.

In July, Sir George Gipps issued a new code of Squatting Regulations, greatly modifying the unpopular code of 1844.

In December, His Excellency received a despatch from Lord Stanley, directing him, with the assistance of the Executive Council to take evidence and report upon:—1. The advantages and disadvantages of the proposed Separation of the Middle (Sydney) and Southern (Port Phillip) Districts of New South Wales. 2. The most eligible boundaries of the colony of Port Phillip in the event of Separation being conceded. 3. The form of Constitution for Port Phillip, which the Executive Council and the members for Port Phillip and Melbourne may recommend. The desired inquiry was accordingly begun, and Dr., now Sir Charles Nicholson, Mr. J. P. Robinson, Mr. Thomas Walker, the Rev. Dr. Lang, and other gentlemen interested in the question, were examined.

Separation having been conceded, it is now useless to trace the rise, progress, and ultimate success of one of the most important movements in the history of British colonisation, and which erected the dependent district of Port Phillip into a separate colony, honored by the Queen designating it Victoria. Sir George Gipps, who had firmly opposed the plan of "Financial Division" when that boon was prayed for by the Port Phillip colonists, found at last that they would accept of no terms but those of "Political Separation."

On the 26th January 1846, the anniversary of the foundation of New South Wales, a grand banquet was given to Mr. W. C.

Wentworth in the hall of the Sydney College, in testimony to his valuable services in the Legislative Council, and the pure and fervent feelings of respect in which he was held by the colonists. In the following month a banquet was given to Mr. Archibald Boyd, as a mark of gratitude for his zeal and exertions in advocating the squatting interests of the colony. In April, Mrs. Caroline Chisholm, the advocate of systematic colonisation, was presented with a valuable testimonial raised by public subscription.

In June, the protracted disagreements between Sir George Gipps and the Legislative Council reached their climax, His Excellency having proposed to the Council to renew the Crown Lands Occupation Act. The House refused to pass the measure, and voted an address explaining its reasons for refusing to renew the Act.

On the 11th of July, Sir Geo. Gipps, after an administration of eight years, embarked for England. He quitted the scene of his long government with impaired health, and died soon after his return home. Bright passages in his career will long be gratefully remembered by the colonists. His generous yielding to the protest of the Patriotic Association in regard to the proposed exclusive clauses of the Sydney Corporation Bill of 1840, and his cordial recognition of the principle of giving equal political rights to all classes of the community, will not be forgotten by those who pen the record of his reign. His assent to the local legislature's measure for the abolition of imprisonment for debt, and various other liberal acts of his administration, will be cited as favorable contrasts to those edicts in respect to the occupation of Crown lands, against which the colonists so loudly appealed. That this opposition aggravated the illness under which Sir George was suffering, there is no doubt, and he retired chagrined and offended with the colonists.

On the 2nd of August, 1846, Sir Charles Augustus Fitz Roy arrived at Sydney, as the successor of Sir George Gipps. A few months after his arrival, a despatch from Mr. Gladstone, notifying the wish of Her Majesty's Government that the Legislative Council of New South Wales should favorably consider the renewal of the system of transportation, threw the colonists into great excitement. Their indignant and universal remonstrances, and the agitation which ensued, will form prominent features in future records of this period.

The year 1847 gave promise of increasing prosperity, and in opening the session of the Legislative Council in May, Sir Charles offered his congratulations on the condition of the colony. The colonists were on the 6th December, 1847, plunged into grief by the death of Lady Mary Fitz Roy, through an accident caused by her being thrown from her carriage.

Sir Charles Fitz Roy, in the early part of the year 1849, acquired much unpopularity, in consequence of his having, when on a tour to Tasmania and Port Phillip, promised the colonists of the latter province that as they had protested against the landing of any convicts at Melbourne, an exile ship then expected should proceed to Sydney, and land the convicts there. Sir Charles returned to Sydney soon afterwards, when a deputation appointed at a public meeting, headed by Mr. James Norton, waited upon him, and explained to his Excellency the equally strong feelings existing in Sydney, as to the reception of the convicts.

On the 15th of May, the new Legislative Council assembled, and Dr. Nicholson was elected Speaker. In Sir Charles Fitz Roy's opening speech he dwelt upon the gratifying fact that since the resumption of immigration in 1848, fifty-four ships had arrived in the various ports of the colony, bringing no fewer than 13,161 immigrants at the public expense. This appeared to be a notification of a gratifying character, but on the 11th of June the ship *Hashemy* having arrived in Port Jackson with convicts, another great public meeting was held in Sydney on the Circular Quay, when a solemn protest against their landing was adopted; and Mr. Robert Campbell, Mr. Robert Lowe, and four other gentlemen proceeded to Government House, as a deputation from the meeting, to present the protest to the Governor. They were informed that it was contrary to official etiquette to receive a deputation without previous notice. On the following Monday, a second great meeting was held, when it was resolved to petition her Majesty to dismiss Earl Grey from the Colonial Office, and to grant to the colonists the boon of responsible Government. On the 5th of February, in the following year, 1850, Sir William Molesworth, amongst other petitions to Parliament in respect to colonial grievances, presented one from New South Wales, with 6000 signatures, complaining of the attempt to revive transportation. Other petitions were soon afterwards presented by Mr. F. Scott, on the same subject, from other towns and districts of New South Wales; and after several further demonstrations in the colony, an association was organised under the designation of "The New South Wales Association for Preventing the Revival of Transportation." On the 1st of January, 1851, however, this association was dissolved by union with the Australasian League, which, having been formed in Tasmania, was joined by the colonists of New South Wales, Victoria, and South Australia, and their league, solemn engagement, and ultimate success are now matters of history. The delegates who visited the colonies for the purpose of establishing the Australasian League, were the Rev. John West, Mr. Weston, and Mr. Westgarth.

On the 18th of the same month, Sir Charles Fitz Roy issued a proclamation, announcing the receipt of a copy of the Acts of the Imperial Parliamant, 13th and 14th Victoria, cap. 59, by which the district of Port Phillip was separated from New

South Wales, and erected into a separate colony, to be known and designated as Victoria; provision being made, otherwise, for the better government of Her Majesty's Australian possessions.

A new era in the history of New South Wales must now be dated. On the 12th of February, the existence of the extensive gold-field near the town of Bathurst was discovered; and on the 6th of May the discovery was officially announced at Bathurst. (Particulars in another page.) It is adverted to as another of the great features which Sir Charles Fitz Roy's reign presents, and as illustrative of his great tact in preserving order, by and with the advice of wise counsellors, when the excitement attendant upon the discovery of gold-fields in the two colonies, New South Wales and Victoria, might have led to incalculable confusion.

A most important point in respect to the gold discoveries, namely, the settlement of the *quæstio vexata* as to the management of the gold-fields, was raised by Mr. Wentworth on the re-assembling of the session in 1852; but by a happy coincidence, the Australian R. M. steamer arrived on the afternoon of Mr. Wentworth's motion, having on board despatches from Sir J. Pakington, announcing that Her Majesty's Government had determined to place at the disposal of the Governor and Legislature of New South Wales (and also of Victoria) the fund arising from license fees and royalty on gold, with the power of framing the necessary regulations. Thus this long contested point was satisfactorily adjusted, and the Executive and Legislative Councils were enabled to proceed together in harmony.

To other important features in the administration of Sir Charles Fitz Roy, we will now briefly refer. It was during this period that the uniform two-penny postage rate was introduced into the colony; a system which it must be admitted conferred great benefits on the public, and it is a source of just pride to say that New South Wales was the first British colony which introduced this system, and also that which admitted books, parcels and magazines for publication at a moderate rate of postage; and then followed the introduction of ocean steam communication with India and Europe.

We must next refer to the incorporation, endowment and inauguration of the University of Sydney with its affiliated Colleges and Grammar School. The turning the first sod of the Great Southern Railway, the laying the first stone of the site of the Fitz Roy Dry Dock, the first stone of the Sydney Exchange, and the establishment of the Sydney branch of the Royal Mint.

The great act of Sir Charles Fitz Roy's reign, however, was the passing of the Constitution Act of New South Wales, by which the great political principle of Responsible Government, was conceded to the colonists. The Royal assent to this measure did not arrive here until after the departure of Sir Charles, who retired amidst the approving plaudits of the people. His Excellency died in London, on the 19th of February, 1858.

The political features in the administration of his successor, Sir William Denison, have, as yet, been those necessarily attending the establishment and inauguration of the new form of government, which renders necessary the entire revision of the existing electoral system. The inauguration of the new Act was celebrated on the 17th July, 1856, by a National Banquet, to which the Governor-General, the Judges, the former Ministers and those of the day, the Foreign Consuls, and Mr. James Macarthur were invited to attend. The hon. Dr. Bland, the earliest champion in the cause of Responsible Government, presided.

Various changes in the ministry have taken place since that time; and at the date of writing this, the new electoral bill has not passed into a law. All other great questions, now lying in abeyance, must therefore be deferred until a new parliament assembles.

In other departments, religious, educational, scientific, literary and social, the administration of Sir William Denison has been one of marked progress; new churches, colleges, schools, and scientific institutions and societies have arisen and are rapidly advancing. His Excellency's lectures before the Philosophical, the Agricultural, and the Horticultural Societies of New South Wales, and the Young Men's Christian Association, together with his visit to Norfolk Island to inquire into the condition of the Pitcairn Islanders (recently transplanted from their less genial home) and confer on them a political constitution, give ample promise, that so soon as present political difficulties are adjusted, the administration of Sir William Denison will be one in every way illustrative of the "Poetry of Progress."

STATISTICS.

The Sydney branch of the Royal Mint was established on May 13th, 1855, During the year 1857 the coin issued consisted of 499,000 sovereigns, and 537,000 half sovereigns. The total value, £767,500. The quantity of gold dust received for the purpose of coinage, from January 1st to August 6th, 18 8, was 218,174 ounces, the total value of gold coined being 595,500 sovereigns, and 486,000 half sovereigns, the total being £838,500; which is an increase, during the seven months, of £71,000 over the entire amount coined during the previous year, 1857. The coin is declared a legal tender throughout the Australasian colonies.

The gold districts are described as the western, the southern, and the northern. The western comprises Stoney Creek, Bathurst, Sofala, Tambarura, Louisa Creek, Mudgee, and Orange; the southern embraces Braidwood, Tumut, Adelong, and the Goulburn; and the northern district the Hanging Rock and the Rocky River. The first gold found in Australia was discovered in the Bathurst district, in the year 1889, by a shepherd named McGregor, who, upon two or three occasions, brought small parcels of it to Sydney, but it excited no particular interest till after the discovery of gold in California, to which place a colonist named Edward Hammond Hargraves emigrated for the purpose of gold-digging, but being struck with the remarkable similarity of features the country presented to those of the Bathurst district, he became possessed of the idea that it also contained gold. When he returned he almost immediately made the discovery which has effected the great results now experienced in the Australian Colonies. In 1842 the Rev. W. B. Clarke also discovered it. Sir Roderick Murchison, in 1844, from the comparison of the maps of the mountain ranges and specimens of the Siberian gold regions and Australia, predicted the probability of gold being found. Other travellers, at several successive periods found traces of the precious metal, but it was reserved for Mr. Hargraves to open to the world the vast unexplored treasures of the continent, and even to be the instrument of its civilisation, in consequence of the attraction of population. New South Wales is less rich in gold than Victoria. Much interest has lately been manifested in quartz-crushing, and it is expected that a large amount of gold will be forthcoming as the result of the extensive works in progress. During the first seven months of the year 1858 the quantity of gold received by escort in Sydney was 127,963 ounces.

The importance of opening up the country by means of good roads has been kept in view, as may be gathered from the fact that the sum of £80,000 is to be expended during the year 1858 on the main trunk lines.

The bank returns in the following table gives a comparative statement of the transactions of the eight banks, namely, New South Wales, Commercial, Australasia, Union, Joint Stock, English Scottish and Australian, Oriental, and London Chartered, during the first six months of the years 1857 and 1858:—

	JUNE 1857.	JUNE 1858.
Capital paid up	£5,167,600	£5,169,700
Dividend	842,200	851,400
Reserve	1,150,400	1,211,800
Total liabilities	5,801,300	5,238,700
Total assets	7,609,900	7,354,600
Working capital	1,660,000	1,949,500
Discounts	4,597,600	4,865,600
Notes and deposits	5,371,100	4,930,000
Coin	1,724,900	1,593,800

This return exhibits for June 1858, compared with June 1857,—an increase of paid-up capital of £2,100; an increase of dividend of £9,200; an increase of reserve of £61,400; a decrease of liabilities of £567,600; a decrease of assets of £255,300; an increase of working capital of £289,500; an increase of discounts of £268,000; a decrease of notes and deposits of £441,000; a decrease of coin of £131,000.

The Inspector-General of Police has published a report of the state of crime during the year 1857, which shows a considerable decrease compared with that of 1856. During the year 1857 the number of prisoners (male and female) summarily dealt with was 5,695; committed for trial, 202; and 1,309 discharged. The amount of stolen property, in the Metropolitan district only, recovered during 1857, was £1,469 13s. 3½d., out of £10,038 18s. 9½d. stolen.

The number of schools connected with the Denominational Board, during the year 1857, was as follows:—Church of England, 104; Presbyterian, 18; Wesleyan, 11; Roman Catholic, 69. The number of children was 8,066 boys, and 6,947 girls; total, 15,013. In connexion with the National Board there were 62 schools, and the number of scholars was 3,181 boys, and 2795 girls; total, 5,976.

The letters and newspapers received from Europe by the E. and A. R. M. Company's steamships, during the first seven months of 1858, were:—Letters, 111,260; newspapers, 181,788 The number despatched from Sydney, per the same medium' was:—Letters, 128,508; newspapers, 143,073.

SYDNEY.

The city of Sydney, the capital of New South Wales, is situated in 33° 52′ S. lat., 151° 17′ E. long. It was so named, in honor of Viscount Sydney,* Secretary of State for the colonies in 1788, the year of the foundation of the colony. The early progress of the city was not very marked, as for nearly a quarter of a century after its original establishment, this now important city was little more than an insignificant village of bark huts and frail wooden buildings, scattered here and there among fields and gardens. Shortly after the arrival of Governor Macquarie in 1809, a survey of the locality was made, and the plan formed of the present town.

Sydney is built partly on a small promontory, and partly in a narrow valley, about seven miles from the heads of Port Jackson. The formation on which it stands is a freestone rock, which passes inland in undulating and nearly parallel ridges, and affords a beautiful and durable building material. The greater part of the city is enclosed on three sides by those portions of the harbor known as the Stream on the north, Woolloomooloo Bay on the east, and Darling Harbor on the west. At the entrance to Sydney Cove, on the eastern side, is Fort Macquarie; and on the west, Dawes' Battery. There has also been a battery lately constructed on the point at the western entrance to Woolloomooloo Bay, known as Lady Macquarie's Chair; and a splendid fort and martello tower on Pinchgut Island; together with a battery on Kirabili Point, on the north shore. The ranges from these batteries will completely command that part of the harbor by which the city is approached. The views from the higher part of the city are bold, varied and picturesque. To seaward the magnificent harbor of Port Jackson—capacious, convenient and equal to any in the world—with its numerous and romantic inlets, or coves, presents one of the grandest and most interesting features of natural beauty in Australasia. Inland, the diversity of hill and dale, of rock and woodland, of grassy slopes and brilliant parterres, with their orange groves and vineyards, interspersed with stately mansions, substantial homes, and neat cottages, combine in forming many interesting and pleasing prospects.

The harbor, which in some places is three miles broad, is completely land-locked; it possesses excellent anchorage, and is well sheltered from storms. Extensive and well arranged docks, for repairing ships and steamers of the largest tonnage, have been constructed. The Royal Mail steamers are placed in the dry dock, Waterview Bay, on their arrival. Along the water-side are wharves, stores, ship-yards, patent slips, mills, manufactories, &c.; behind these, terrace-like, rise the numerous public and private buildings of the metropolis. The streets are mostly laid out at right angles, are long and wide, well macadamized, and are lit with gas. George and Pitt-streets have a width of sixty feet for carriage way and a pathway of twelve feet. Lofty stone or brick edifices, with handsome shops, range along the principal streets.

Sydney has several extensive public parks, the principal of which are Hyde Park (between the city and the suburb of Woolloomooloo) and the Outer Domain—the Inner Domain being the enclosed ground around Government House. In the vicinity of the latter, and bounded on one side by the picturesque inlet known as Farm Cove, are situated the Botanical Gardens, in which there are specimens of almost every tropical plant. These gardens, to which the admission is free, form, in connection with the Outer Domain and the peninsula lying between Woolloomooloo Bay and Farm Cove and which is terminated by Lady Macquarie's Chair, one of the principal resorts of the citizens.

The public buildings of Sydney are numerous, and may fairly vie with those of a European capital. The Government House, situated in a demesne overlooking the harbor, is built of white freestone, in the Elizabethan style. The Legislative and Executive Council Chambers form an extensive range of buildings. The Australian Mint is a noble structure.

The public Banks are substantial and ornamental, almost unequalled for architectural beauty. The Exchange, Benevolent Asylum, Hospitals, Theatres, Temperance Hall, Court House, Custom House, Public Library, School of Arts, Post Office, the Markets, Herald Office, &c., are edifices well adapted to their several purposes.

Sydney is an Episcopal See, and the residence of the metropolitan of Australasia. The present boundaries of the city were defined by the first Municipal Act passed in 1842, and it is divided into eight wards.

The ecclesiastical edifices comprise many large and commodious churches; Episcopalian; Independent or Congregational; Presbyterian; Baptist; Roman Catholic; Wesleyan; Unitarian; a Friends' meeting house and a Jewish synagogue.

There are many educational establishments, the most important being the University of Sydney, which was established by an Act of the Legislature, introduced by Mr. W. C. Wentworth about 1847, and owes its existence mainly to the exertions of Dr. Bland. It was founded in 1830, with a fund of £10,000, subscribed in shares of £50 each. The building is commodious, the education unsectarian, and, by the Queen's Letters Patent, the Degrees conferred by this University are recognised in all similar institutions of the British Empire. The College of St. Paul, founded by members of the Church of England, under the Colleges Act of 1854, was opened in 1857, and several students of the University are resident there. An Act of Incorporation was passed for the College of St. John, founded by the members of the Roman Church, and vigorous movements have been made by the Presbyterians and Wesleyan Methodists towards the establishment of Colleges within the University for the members of their respective creeds. The Roman Catholics subscribed about £20,000 towards their college; the subscriptions of other denominations being equally munificent. The Australian College is intended for preparatory training of youth for the higher course of instruction. A normal school, for secular education only, and many excellent seminaries for both sexes, including the National and Denominational Schools and Sydney Grammar School, are well attended.

The Australian Museum was established in 1838, and Incorporated in 1853. Specimens of various minerals and valuable collections of natural and artificial products are in abundance. A new building, equal to the demands of the accumulated treasures, is in course of erection, adapted for the purposes of this institution.

The magnificent Episcopalian Cathedral of St. Andrew is nearly completed. Its dimensions are as follows:—external length, east to west, 178 feet; length transept, north to south, 116 feet; internally, length of nave, from western door to entrance of choir, 106 feet; from the latter to its eastern wall, 53 feet breadth of nave and adjoining aisles, 62 feet; and of the choir within the screens, 37 feet; height of the two western towers, 116 feet; the eastern tower, 84 feet; and the roof, 64 feet.

The new Town Hall, in the course of erection, is intended to accommodate five or six thousand persons, on occasions of public meetings, balls, concerts, &c. The offices connected with the business of the Corporation (see names elsewhere) will be on the basement story, and the whole arrangements of the building are very complete. The sewerage of the city has been well provided for.

The Great Southern Railway connects Sydney with Newtown, Petersham, Ashfield, Burwood, Homebush, Parramatta, Fairfield, Liverpool and Campbelltown—thirty-four miles. The line of the Great Northern Railway extends from Newcastle to Honeysuckle Point, Waratah, Hexham, East and West Maitland—twenty miles.

A line of electric telegraph is now nearly completed between Sydney and Albury, a border-town of New South Wales and Victoria. Albury is about 360 miles from Sydney, and when the telegraph is finished the communication will be complete between Sydney, Melbourne, and Adelaide, the capitals of the three colonies.

The Observatory is a great ornament to the town. The position is excellent, and it is situated so that a full view can be obtained of the harbor and the city. There are already ten Meteorological Observatories in full work, stationed severally at Cape Moreton, Armidale, Ettrick (Richmond River), Maitland, Bathurst, Parramatta, Deniliquin, Albury, and Cooma.

The recent enlargements and improvements of St. Philip's Church have been effected; also St. Mary's Cathedral; the Independent Church, and the United Presbyterian Church.

The Destitute Childrens' Asylum, at Randwick (near Coogee), is as far completed as it is intended to be at present, and occupied by 150 children, the old establishment at Paddington having been abandoned.

The great function that Sydney performs for the colony, is that of being the entrepôt of its commerce. It is also the political metropolis, and the resort of hundreds who, having made their fortunes, choose to reside where the conveniences of living are most multiplied, and who prefer the society and amusements of a city to rural pleasures. Commerce, however, is the great feature of Sydney. Extensive operations are carried on in connection with the South Sea whaling, and hither come the foreign imports and the Island produce of the Pacific, for re-distribution over the whole territory. Hither, too, comes the colonial produce that is ready for exportation,

Sydney has many populous suburbs, including Woolloomooloo, Surrey Hills, Paddington, the Glebe, Newtown, Redfern,

Balmain, Pyrmont, St Leonard's, North Shore, South Head Road, &c., all of which may be regarded as portions of the city, in consequence of the extensive building operations of the last few years.

From the directory of Sydney, published in 1858, we gather that there were 111 merchants, 31 importers, 8 custom house agents, 85 brokers, 40 auctioneers, 25 warehousemen, 68 corn factors and dealers in produce, 37 timber merchants, 12 wool-brokers, 8 potato and 11 coal and fuel merchants, 13 millers, 6 flour merchants, 32 wine and spirit merchants, 287 grocers, 193 butchers, 97 bakers, 84 greengrocers, 32 confectioners, 10 poulterers, 22 dairymen, 6 fishmongers (about 60 street salesmen), 487 publicans, 307 shoemakers, 193 tailors, 127 drapers, 15 hatters, 43 dressmakers, 38 milliners, 54 architects and engineers, 128 builders, 241 carpenters, 134 masons, 44 quarrymen, 8 brickmakers, 56 plasterers, 147 painters and glaziers, 108 upholsterers, 89 smiths, 18 brassfounders, 49 ironmongers, 27 earthenware dealers. There are other occupations enumerated in the work not mentioned in this list.

COUNTIES AND TOWNS PROCLAIMED BY LETTERS PATENT.

(The figures after the names of the towns, show the number of miles from Sydney).

Cumberland (Metropolitan County): Sydney (city); Parramatta, 15; Windsor, 35; Richmond, 39; Liverpool, 20; Cambelltown, 33; Castlereagh, 39; Appin, 45; St. Leonards, suburb; Pitt Town, 34; Penrith, 33; Longbottom, 7½.—Camden: Berrima, 86; Kiama, 88; Wollongong, 64; Wilton, 43; Picton, 52; Camden, 40; Murrumba. St Vincent: Braidwood, 164; Broulee, 190; Kioloa; Ulladulla, 165; Huskisson, 125.—Northumberland: Newcastle, 80; East and West Maitland, 127; Greta; Wolombi, 93; Gosford, 35; Singleton, 120.—Durham: Paterson, 130; Seaham; Clarence Town; Dungog, 125; Leamington; Merton, 180; Musswellbrook, 160; Aberdeen.—Hunter: Jerry's Plains, 190; St. Albans, 70.—Cook: Hartley, 78; Emu, 36; Bowenfells, 80; Rydal, 86.—Westmoreland: O'Connell, 115.—Argyle: Goulburn, 125; Marulan, 109; Bungonia, 117.—Murray: Yass, S., 186; Queanbeyan, 182; Bungendore, 160; Lasbert. King: Gunning, 131; Yass, N., 186.—Georgiana: Buckburridgee; Cook's Vale.—Bathurst: Bathurst, 121; Blaney, 136; Carcoar, 145.—Roxburgh: Kelso; Rylstone, 161; Rydal, W., 36.—Phillip: Cooyal, 150.—Brisbane: Scone, 191; Murrurundi, 196; Merriwa: Ailsa.—Bligh: Casilis, 245.—Wellington: Wellington, 231; Mudgee, 171; Orange, 157.—Gloucester: Raymond Terrace, 100; Stroud, 30.—Macquarie: Port Macquarie, 278; Wingham; Kempsey; Marraville.

Northern Counties.

STANLEY: Brisbane, 640; Ipswich.—CANNING: Toorbul.—MARCH: Maryborough.—LENNOX.—FITZ ROY.—CAVENDISH.—AUBIGNY: Drayton, 172.—CHURCHILL.—MERIVALE: Warwick, 582.— BENTINCK. — BULLER. — WARD.— ROUS. — RICHMOND — DRAKE.—CLIVE.—GOUGH.— HARDINGE.—GRESHAM.—RALEIGH. —CLARENCE: Grafton.—DUDLEY.— VERNON.—INGLIS: Tamworth, 275.—DARLING.— POTTINGER.— BUCKLAND.—PARRY.—HAWES.

Southern and Western Counties.

NAPIER.—GOWEN.—LINCOLN: Dubbo, 260.—GORDON: Kurea. —ASHBRUNHAM.—MONTEAGLE: Mulgan.—HARDEN: Binalong, 111; Munringo; Bookham; Bowning; Jugiong, 230,—CLARENDON, Gundagai, 255.—WYNYARD; Wogga Wogga.—GOULBURN: Albury, 360.—BUCCLEUCH: Tumut, 249.—COWLEY.—BERESFORD: Cooma, 254; Bunyan.—DAMPIER.—AUCKLAND: Eden, 350; Boyd, 240; Pambula, 236.—WELLESLEY: Bombalo, 290. WALLACE.

SHIPPING, HARBORS, &c.

About 1100 vessels entered the ports during 1857, with a gross burden of 351,413 tons, and with a marine population of 18,728 persons. Of these vessels, 770, or rather more than two-thirds, arrived with cargo, 330 in ballast; but of this latter number, all but 57 were bound to the port of Newcastle to take in coals, there being no return freight to that port.

The destination of the majority of the ships was port Jackson, the great focus of the marine trade of the colony, a preeminence it owes to its unrivalled facilities for shipping, both coastwise and by inland transit: nearly all the foreign trade converges to Sydney. With the exception of coals, very little native produce is shipped away from local ports, nearly all of it finds its way first to the great central emporium. This concentration of trade in the metropolis tends, undoubtedly, to aggrandise the chief city at the expense of the outports; but there is a mercantile compensation in the greater cheapness and convenience that is induced: the course of free trade shews that it is cheaper as well as, in other respects, more convenient for produce to be forwarded to a central depôt, where every commercial facility is to be obtained, rather than to foster the premature independence of outports. In this way, not only does wool come down from Port Curtis, but is even brought from New Zealand to be sold or shipped at Sydney.

The outports of New South Wales certainly have rather a limited foreign trade: thus, at Twofold Bay, a really convenient harbor, only two ships were entered. The district, however, which it is adapted to accommodate is, comparatively speaking, not of any very great extent, and a considerable portion of the local trade which might concentrate there is intercepted by the adjacent port of Broulee, situated a little more to the north, and, in some respects, more convenient for the back country.

Port Stephens, the second best harbor in New South Wales, makes no figure as a commercial *entrepôt*: its comparative desolation is in strange contrast with its capabilities. Newcastle, though far inferior as a port, has run away with the trade of the Hunter River, as well as that of the pastoral country beyond, and the railway will tend to confirm and consolidate that supremacy. Railways will in future be likely to alter greatly the present course of traffic, diverting it from existing routes into new channels.

The limited maritime business of Moreton Bay, is very remarkable, considering the quantity of pastoral produce raised in the northern districts; only twelve vessels were entered at that port in the course of the year, being at the rate of one a month: the main cause of this is, doubtless, the very inferior accommodation that exists there for vessels of a large class—a matter which will, doubtless, engage the attention of the first legislature of the new colony, for we can hardly imagine that after the separation, the northerners will be content to see their produce all carried away by coasting steamers, to the envied metropolis of the south, without an effort to retain it. The difficulty and expense that will be attendant on making a satisfactory port anywhere in Moreton Bay, may precipitate the development of some of the more northern ports. Wide Bay, Port Curtis, and Rockhampton, are said to possess natural advantages which could be turned to account at less comparative cost than would be necessary at Brisbane, but they are further removed from the present nucleus of population, though not less favorably situated as respects access to the interior.

The amount of shipping, taken as a whole, represents pretty nearly the extent of the inward and outward commerce of the colony; but some of it is independent, and is the consequence of the maritime facilities offered by the port of Sydney: Thus, thirty vessels from the South Sea whale fisheries during the year put into Port Jackson. Compared with the number of vessels cruising about in these seas, this cannot be considered a large number, seeing that no port in this hemisphere can offer such advantages for refitting as Port Jackson. During the past year the convenience afforded by this harbor to whalers has been illustrated in several instances, and its advantages only require to be more widely known, to be more generally used. Thirty nine vessels from various islands in the South Seas also entered the port during the year: a proof of its superiority as a commercial *entrepôt* for the scattered traffic of the South Pacific.

The number of vessels registered for the year ending 31st December, 1857, including steamers, was 500, the gross tonnage being 52,661 tons, employing about 3,757 men and boys.

IMPORTS.

The imports entered at the port of Sydney, during ten years ending 31st December, 1857 :—

1848, 1,182,874*l.*; 1849, 1,313,589*l.*; 1850, 1,333,413*l.*; 1851, 1,563,931*l.*; 1852, 1,900,436*l.*; 1853, 6,342,397*l.*; 1854, 5,981,063*l.*; 1855, 4,668,519*l.*; 1856, 5,460,971*l.*; 1857, 6,729,408*l.*; The imports of butter and cheese during 1857, were valued at 50,025*l.*; grain, &c., 392,131*l.*; hides and leather, 409,284*l.*

From January 1st to May 31st, 1858 :—value, 2,953,180*l.* During the corresponding period of 1857 :—1,995,923*l.*

EXPORTS.

From the port of Sydney during ten years ending 31st December, 1857 :—

1848, 1,155,009*l.*; 1849, 1,135,944*l.*; 1850, 1,357,784*l.*; 1851, 1,796,912*l.*; 1852, 4,604,034*l.*; 1853, 4,523,346*l.*; 1854, 4,05 ,126*l.*; 1855, 2,884,130*l.*; 1856, 3,430,870*l.*; 1857, 4,011,592*l.* The exports of wool during the year 1857, were 17,044,201 lbs., valued at 1,275,067*l.*; tallow, 37,574 cwt., valued at 82,132*l.*; oils, &c., valued at 32,306*l.*; hides and leather, 122,653*l.*; bark, 180*l.*; butter and cheese, 12,547*l.*; live stock, 28,185*l.*; grain, &c., 58,588*l.*

From January 1st to May 31st, 1858 :—value, 1,760,769*l.* During the corresponding period of 1857 :—966,379*l.*

Export of Gold.—Since the first discovery of gold in New South Wales, February, 1851 :—1851, 144,120 ozs. 17 dwts. 16 grs., 468,336*l.*; 1852, 818,751 ozs. 18 dwts. 17 grs., 2,660,946*l.*; 1853, 548,052 ozs. 19 dwts, 21 grs., 1,781,172*l.*; 1854, 237,910 ozs. 13 dwts. 23 grs., 773,209*l.*; 1855, 64,384 ozs, 14 dwts. 3 grs., 209,250*l.*; 1856, 42,463 ozs. 17 dwts. 1 gr., 138,007*l.*; 1857, 48,982 ozs. 6 dwts., 187,249*l.* This return includes a large portion of Gold brought from Victoria, Tasmania, and New Zealand, but the quantities cannot be accurately ascertained. The Imports of Gold during 1857, the first year that this item was recorded amongst the imported commodities at the Sydney Custom House, amounted to 93,318 ozs. 9 dwts. 10 grs., valued at 332,274*l.*

The total amount of exports during 1857, was 4,011,592*l.* and of imports 6,729,408*l.* Excess of imports over exports, 2,719,816*l.*

COAL.

Previous to the year 1845, *one* coal pit, and *one* coal shoot, at Newcastle, were sufficient for the supply of Sydney, and the few coasting steamers then running from Port Jackson.

In 1849, the item of coals was for the first time deemed of sufficient importance to have a table assigned to it in the annual statistics of the colony, which are compiled from official returns in the Colonial Secretary's office. In that year it was shewn that six coal mines had been worked, producing 48,416½ tons of the declared value of £14,647. From that date the coal-mining operations of the Hunter district exhibit a rapid increase. The Australian Agricultural Company had given up the monopoly of coal-mining (very irregularly granted to them by the Earl of Bathurst, when he held the Colonial Seals in 1824); and operations on the rich and extensive seams of Burwood Hills, a short distance from Newcastle, had begun.

During the year ending March 31, 1858, the quantity of coal raised from the three of the latter Company's pits which are now worked, was 90,634 tons, of which 39,397 were shipped at Newcastle for Melbourne. The quantity produced from two of the Burwood Hill tunnels was 91,950 tons —being an excess over the year's products of the Australian Agricultural Company's pits of 1,316 tons. The Newcastle Coal and Copper Company, also shipped largely to Melbourne and Geelong during the same period, but we are not in possession of the exact quantities. The country more immediately connected with Newcastle in which workable coal seams exist, may be considered as occupying an area of at least 200 square miles,in which there is a known series of four or five seams, making an average of from 19 to 20 feet of coal. The Rev. W. B. Clarke has prepared some valuable documents in reference to the progress of the mines, and the prospects of the colony in reference to the production of coal.

At Morpeth and Hexham, on the Hunter; at Wollongong to the south, and Brisbane to the north, and in other *locales*, valuable coal seams were opened, and seventeen pits and tunnels are now reported to have been worked, the yield from fifteen of which, during the year ending 31st December, 1857, was 210,434 tons, of the declared value of £148,158.

But whilst the export trade during the last nine years rapidly increased, from the causes we have already adverted to, *imports* of coal have made no mean item in our Statistics of Customs, since the commencement of steam communication between England and Australia in 1852. The following are the official returns during the last five years; the imported coal having been brought, with fractional exceptions, from Cardiff, in *Old* South Wales, for coaling the ocean steamships:—

	Exports.		Imports.	
	Quantity. Tons.	Value. £	Quantity. Tons.	Value. £
1853	55,501	81,078	8,389	18,697
1854	59,297	101,752	10,956	21,952
1855	61,484	58,893	2,577	4,358
1856	84,086	65,730	1,083	2,355
1857	96,457	46,120	11,568	16,031
Totals	356,825	353,573	34,573	63,393

Captain J. Lort Stokes, R.N., whose discoveries in Australia have so richly contributed to the stores of geographical knowledge, visited Newcastle in 1851, and carefully inspected the coal mines. In a letter to the then Colonial Secretary, the Honorable E. Deas Thomson, Esq., dated the 20th June, he says:—"At Newcastle we tried a seam of coal belonging to the Australian Agricultural Company, *and found it to raise steam twenty-five minutes sooner than is effected by English coal.*"

Mr. John Anderson, inspector of machinery at the Royal Arsenal, Woolwich, reports, that upon the return to England of the E. and A.R.M.S. Company's steamship *Oneida*, under sail (her machinery having broken down during her voyage to Suez), six bags of the coal with which she had been furnished in Sydney, by the Australian Agricultural Company, with a view to subject the coal during the voyage, to various severe tests, was forwarded under the sanction of the Home authorities, to the chemical department in the Royal Arsenal, in order to make trial of its *time value* for steam-engine purposes; and the relative merits of New South Wales, Whitworth, Welch, and Hartley coals. Having described the mode by which he combined the four descriptions of coals with eight successive experiments, he pronounces his opinion, "that for steam purposes, the coals received from the *Oneida* were about equal to the Newcastle coal termed Whitworth, which correspond with a considerable variety known as Wallsend, Lambton, Peland, Primrose, &c., but that it is slightly inferior to the Hartley and Welch variety of coals." Mr. Anderson adds, that the three kinds of English and Welch coals were selected at random, from the bulk used in the furnaces of the Royal Arsenal; and we may also observe, that the coals supplied to the *Oneida* were taken from the A. A. Company's D. and E. pits, near Newcastle, and that no further care was taken in screening them than is always observed in supplying our colonial steam marine.

The following return shews the quantity and value of coal obtained in the years specified:—

YEAR.	NO. OF MINES.	QUANTITY.	VALUE.		
		Tons.	£	s.	d.
1849	6	48,516¼	14,647	4	3
1850	9	71,216¼	23,375	15	6
1851	10	67,610	25,546	8	6
1852	10	67,404	36,885	2	0
1853	13	96,809	78,059	0	0
1854	12	116,642	119,380	8	0
1855	14	137,076	89,082	18	0
1856	14	189,960	117,906	17	7
1857	17	210,434	148,158	5	6

IRON.

Among the mineral products of New South Wales the article of iron may fairly be expected to take a principal place in a few years, when the difficulties of communication between Sydney and the Fitz Roy iron works (about 70 miles distant from the capital) have been overcome by the extension of the Great Southern Railway. The fields, or rather rocks, of ironstone surrounding the Company's works, spread over a large area. The ore is of such extraordinary richness that it can at once be manufactured at the forge. Specimens of the ore wrought in this way were exhibited at the Great Exhibition in London, in 1851.

AGRICULTURE.

From the 1st January, 1857, to 31st January, 1858, total number of acres in crop, 185,007. The produce consisted of wheat, maize, barley, oats, rye, millet, potatoes, tobacco, and sown grasses.

VINEYARDS.

The number of acres of land planted with the vine, and of the quantity of wine and brandy made from the produce thereof, in the colony of New South Wales, during the year ended 31st March, 1858, within the settled districts, consisting of Bathurst, Brisbane, Bligh, Camden, Cook, Cumberland, Durham, Gloucester, Hunter, King, Macquarie, Murray, Northumberland, Phillip, Roxburgh, Stanley, and Wellington, were 1,072 acres, 103,216 galls. wine, 1,414 galls. brandy. The returns from the vineyards beyond the settled districts have not been received. It is, however, estimated that the wine made from the produce of the districts of the Clarence, Gwydir, Liverpool Plains, Macleay, Maneroo, Murrumbidgee, and Wellington, may be taken at 35,000 gallons. This would make a total of 138,216 gallons; being an increase on 1856 of 42,568 gallons.

RETURN OF THE NUMBER OF BIRTHS, MARRIAGES, AND DEATHS, REGISTERED DURING THE YEAR 1857.

Births.—Male, 6,266; female, 6,235; total, 12,501; being an increase on 1856 of 2,404.

Marriages.—Church of England, 1,045; Church of Rome, 853; Wesleyan Methodists, 153; Primitive Methodists, 4; Independents, 43; Baptists, 22; Unitarians, 4; Lutheran, 4; Hebrews, 7; Christian Israelites, 2; Latter-Day Saints, 1; Registrar's and Deputy-Registrar's Offices, 96. Total, 2,234, being an increase on 1856 of 544.

Deaths.—Males, 2,390; females, 2,456; total, 4,846, being an increase in 1856 of 643 The distinction of men, women, and children has not been made up at this date.

POPULATION.

Return of the increase and decrease of the Population of New South Wales from the 1st March to December, 1857, and of the total number on the latter date:—

Increase by immigration (including military), male, 11,125; female, 6,397; total, 17,532. Increase by births, male, 6,266; female, 6,235; total, 12,501. Total increase, male, 17,401; female, 12,632; general total, 30,033.

Decrease by departure, male, 4,612; female, 1848; (No account of immigration to or from Victoria *viâ* Albury, &c.) Decrease by deaths, male, 2,998; female, 1,961; total, 4,959. Total decrease, male, 7,610; female, 3,809; general total, 11,419.

Net increase, male, 9,791; female, 8,823; total, 18,614.

Population on 31st December, 1856:—male, 161,882; female, 124,991; total, 286,873. Population on 31st December, 1857:—male, 171,673; female, 133,814; total, 305,487.

TALLOW AND LARD.

The returns from the slaughtering and boiling establishments are not yet completed; several not being yet furnished to the Government. The following may be taken as a near approximation, in round numbers:—

Sheep slaughtered, 280,000; horned cattle, 50,000; tallow produced, 100,000 cwt.; pigs slaughtered, 1000; lard produced, 35,000 lbs.

GOVERNMENT, LAW, &c.

GOVERNMENT.—His Excellency Sir William Thomas Denison, Knight-Commander of the Most Honorable Order of the Bath, Governor-General in and over all Her Majesty's Colonies of New South Wales, Van Diemen's Land, Victoria, South Australia, and Western Australia; and Captain-General and Governor-in-Chief of the Territory of New South Wales and its Dependencies, and Vice-Admiral of the same. Private Secretary: Alfred Denison. Aide-de-Camp: Laurence H. Scott, Captain 11th Regiment.

EXECUTIVE COUNCIL.—President: the Governor. Colonial Secretary: Hon. Charles Cowper, Esq. Attorney-General: Hon. James Martin, Esq. Solicitor-General: Hon. A. J. P. Lutwyche, Esq. Colonial Treasurer: Hon. Robert Campbell, Esq. Secretary for Lands and Public Works: Hon. John Robertson, Esq. Clerk of Executive Council: E. C. Merewether. Under Secretary: W. Elyard. Secretary to Treasurer: H. Lane. Under-Secretary to Board of Crown Lands and Public Works: M. Fitzpatrick.

PARLIAMENT.—LEGISLATIVE COUNCIL.—Consists of forty-three Members. The following are their names:—A. A'Beckett, J. Alexander, G. Allen, A. Berry, J. W. Bligh, E. Broadhurst, Sir W. W. Burton (president), A. Bushby, J. Comrie, J. Dickson, J. Docker, H. G. Douglass, W. P. Faithfull, R. Fitzgerald, G. Hill, G. K. Holden, T. Hood. R. M. Isaacs, R. P. Jenkins, R. Johnson, D. Jones, E. Knox, Capt. J, Lamb, Capt. R. Lethbridge, F. Lord, A. J. P. Lutwyche, J. Macnamara. F. L. S. Merewether, J. Mitchell, J. L. Montefiore, J. Norton, C. Riley, H.

G. Smith, W. Spain, Sir A. Stephen, C.J., Justice Therry, E. D. Thomson, C. B., R. Towns, R. J. Want, A. Warren, E. Wise, H. Hunt, and R. M. Robey. Clerk of Council, Mr. Macpherson.

LEGISLATIVE ASSEMBLY.—Consists of fifty-four Members, elected for the undermentioned districts:—Argyle: D. H. Deniehy. County of Bathurst: W. H. Suttor. Brisbane, Phillip, and Bligh: J. Robertson. East Camden: J. Marks, R. Owen. West Camden: J. Macarthur, W. V. Wild. Clarence and Darling Downs: A. Hodgson. Cook and Westmoreland: R. T. Jamison, J. Martin. Cumberland Boroughs: W. B. Dalley. Cumberland, North Riding: T. W. Smith, G. Hills. Cumberland, South Riding: E. Flood, S. A. Donaldson. Durham: W. M. Arnold, S. D. Gordon, R. Jones. Gloucester and Macquarie: J. Williamson. King and Georgiana: P. Faucett. Lachlan and Lower Darling: J. Paterson, W. Macleay. Liverpool Plains and Gwydir: R. L. Jenkins, E. H. Lloyd. Maneroo: D. Egan. Murray: W. Forster. Murrumbidgee: J. Hay, G. Macleay. New England and M'Leay: W. Taylor, A. O. Moriarty. North-Eastern Boroughs: R R. S. Bowker. Northumberland Boroughs: E. C. Weekes, J. Dickson. Northumberland and Hunter: G. B. White, A. W. Scott, W. R. Piddington. Parramatta: G. Oakes, J. Byrnes. Roxburgh: W. Lee. Stanley County: H. Buckley. tanley Boroughs: B. Cribb, J. Richardson. St. Vincent: A. Aldcorne. Southern Boroughs: T. A. Murray. Sydney: R. Campbell, C. Cowper. R. Tooth, G. Thornton. Sydney Hamlets: J. Campbell, Sir D. Cooper. Wellington County: G. H. Cox. Wellington and Bligh: G. W. Lord. Western Boroughs: H. Rotton. Wide Bay, Burnett, and Maranoa: W. B. Tooth. Speaker: Sir Daniel Cooper. Clerk of Committees: W. M. Arnold. Clerk of Assembly: R. O'Connor. Shorthand Writer: J. H. Palmer. Parliamentary Draftsmen: C. W. Murray and F. Meymott.

MISCELLANEOUS. — GOVERNMENT DEPARTMENTS. — Auditor-General: W. C. Mayne. Collector of Customs: Lieutenant-Colonel J. G. N. Gibbes. Landing Surveyor: F. Garling. Surveyor-General: G. Barney, Postmaster-General: W. H. Christie,. Deputy Master of Mint: Captain E. W. Ward, R.E. Denominational School Secretary: H. C. Wills, Inspector of National Schools: W. Wilkins. Port Master: J. Crook. Medical Adviser to Government: Dr. Greenup. Health Officer: Dr. Alleyne. President Medical Board: J. Mitchell. Immigration Agent: H. H. Browne. Colonial Architect: A. Dawson. Colonial Storekeeper: J. Buchanan. Government Printer and Inspector of Postage Stamps: William Hanson. Director Botanic Gardens: C. Moore. Dry Dock Civil Engineer: C. K. Mann. Coroner for Sydney: J. S. Parker. Police Magistrate for Sydney: D. Forbes. Inspector-General of Police: John M'Lerie, P.M. Water Police Magistrate: S. North, P.M. Surgeon, Police Force and Vaccine Institute, J. Y. Rutter. Superintendent Lunatic Asylum, Tarban: Dr. Campbell. Registrar-General: Christopher Rolleston. Gaoler, Darlinghurst: H. C. Beverley. Chief Inspecter of Distilleries: J. Stirling. Superintendent of Light and Pilot Board: R. F. Pockley. Shipping Master, Sydney: T. H. B. Venour. Steam Navigation Board: H. H. Browne, Chairman. President Medical Board: James Mitchell. Colonial Astronomer: Rev. W. Scott.

LAW.—Chief Justice: His Honor Sir Alfred Stephen, Knight. Puisne Judges: Their Honors J. N. Dickinson, Roger Therry, and S. F. Milford. Chairman of Quarter Sessions: T. Callaghan. Crown Prosecutor: J. S. Dowling. Crown Solicitors: J. M. Dillon, and W. W. Billyard. Chief Commissioner of Insolvent Estates: W. H. Purefoy. Sheriff: J. O'Neil Brenan. Under-Sheriff: George Uhr. Master in Equity: G. H. Deffell, Prothonotary and Curator of Intestate Estates: S. Raymond. Commissioner of the Court of Requests: A. Cheeke.

MILITARY.—Captain-General and Governor-in-Chief: Lieut.-Colonel Sir W. T. Denison, K.C.B. Commander of the Forces: Lieut.-Colonel Percival. Brigade Major, Captain Lovenn, R.A.

ECCLESIASTICAL.

CHURCH OF ENGLAND.—Bishop of Sydney and Metropolitan of Australasia: The Right Rev. Frederick Barker D.D. Dean of Sydney.

Rev. W. Cowper, A.M. Bishop of Newcastle: The Right Rev. William Tyrrell, D.D. Chaplains: Rev. R. Allwood, B.A., Edward Synge, M.A., W. M. Cowper, M.A., G. W. Richardson, W. H. Walsh, M.A., W. Stack, B.A., C. C. Kemp, W. F. Gore, B.A., R. L. King, B.A., G. King, A.M., A. H. Stephen, B.A., F. Ashmin, B.A., G. Gurney, B.A., T. Hayden, B.A., H. Sking, B.A., &c. Registrar of the Diocese: James Norton. Secretary to the Bishop and Deputy-Registrar: H. K. James.

ROMAN CATHOLIC CHURCH.—Archbishop: The Most Rev. John Bede Polding, O.S.B. Clergy of the Archdiocese—Sydney: Very Rev. H. G. Gregory, D.D., O.S.B. Vicar-General; the Venerable J. M'Encroe, Archdeacon. Churches in Sydney: St. Mary's, St. Patrick's, St. Benedict's, Sacred Heart. Also, at Balmain, North Shore, Petersham, Ryde, &c. Clergy: Revs. D. M. O'Connell, J. Gourbellion, S. A. Sheehy, J. Keating, P. Newman, M. M. Corish, W. Donovan, J. Sheridan, P. Kenyon, J. J. Therry, P. Powell, P. Birch, J. L. Rocher, &c.

WESLEYAN CHURCH.—The New South Wales District is one of the Nine Districts into which the entire connexion is subdivided. The Chapels in Sydney are York-street, Princes-street, Surrey Hills, Paddington, Chippendale, Hay-street, Newtown, Toxteth, and Sussex-street. The Conference of Australasia meets annually, when the ministers are appointed to their various spheres. Chairman of the New South Wales District: Rev. S. Rabone. General Secretary of Missions: Rev. J. Eggleston.

CONGREGATIONAL CHURCHES.—Rev. W. Cuthbertson, B.A. (late Rev. Dr. Ross's), Sydney; J. Beazley, Redfern; W. Slatyer, Bourke-street, Surrey Hills; Balmain, J. Arnold; S. C. Kent, Newtown; South Head, (vacant); J. Gibson, Newcastle; T. J. Waraker, Ipswich; E. Griffith, Maitland; G. Charter, Wollongong.

BAPTISTS.—Rev. J. Voller, Bathurst-street; Rev. George Whiteford, Goulburn-street. Rev. Philip Lane, Hinton. Rev. B. G. Wilson, Brisbane.

SYNOD OF AUSTRALIA.—Moderator: The Very Rev. Matthew Adam, Windsor. Presbytery of Sydney—Sydney: St. Andrew's, John Dougall; Pitt-street, James Fullerton, L.L.D.; Woolloomooloo, J. M'Gibbon. Paddington: James Milne. St. Leonard's: vacant. Parramatta; J. Coutts. Campbelltown: W. Mackee. Wollongong: C. Atchison. Shoalhaven: J. H. Garven. Windsor: M. Adam. Portland Head, George M'Fie. Ipswich, Moreton Bay: Dr. W. L. Nelson. Port Macquarie: E. Holland.

PRESBYTERIAN CHURCH OF EASTERN AUSTRALIA.—Moderator of Synod: Rev. Dr. Mackay, Sydney. Clerk: Rev. Arthur M. Sheriff. Sydney, Scot's Church, John Dunmore Lang, D.D.; Balmain, James Collins, Moderator; Tumut, P. Fitzgerald; Lower Hunter, W. Chaucer; Murrurundi, A. Black; Warwick, Darling Downs, T. Kingsford; Brisbane, T. Bell; Mission to the Aborigines, W. Ridley, B.A.; Itinerant Minister, Moreton Bay, G. Wagner; also, Revs. A. Salmon, W. Lumsdaine, C. Stewart, W. Grant, A.M., J. Cameron, H. M'Kael, W. M'Intyre, A. M'Intyre, J. M'Culloch, A. Cameron and C. Ogg.

UNITED PRESBYTERIAN CHURCH.—Rev. Hugh Darling.

BETHEL UNION.—Chaplain of Mariners' Church: Rev. L. E. Threlkeld. Secretary: Lieut. Sadlier, R.N.

UNITARIAN CHURCH.—Rev. G. H. Stanley.

PRIMITIVE METHODIST.—Rev. Jabez Langford, Sydney.

SYDNEY SYNAGOGUE.—President: Samuel Cohens. Treasurer: J. G. Raphael.: Secretary: Alfred de Lissa. Minister to Hebrew community: Rev. H. Hoelzel.

INSTITUTIONS, COMPANIES, SOCIETIES, &c.

BANKS.—Bank of New South Wales, George-street; Union Bank of Australia, corner of Pitt and Hunter-streets; Bank of Australasia, George-street; Commercial Banking Company, George-street and Brickfield Hill; Australian Joint Stock Bank, 282, George-street; English, Scottish and Australian Chartered Bank, George-street; London Chartered Bank of Australia, George-street; Oriental Bank Corporation, New Pitt-street; and Savings' Bank, Barrack-street. Branches of the Savings' Bank are established at Parramatta, Windsor, Maitland, Bathurst, Goulburn, Singleton, Newcastle, Wollongong, and Sofala.

CHAMBER OF COMMERCE, SYDNEY.—Chairman: Mr. Willis. Deputy Chairman: G. Thorne. Secretary: A. Thomson. Newcastle Chamber of Commerce—Secretary: P. M'Auliffe.

CONSULS OR REGULAR CONSULAR OFFICERS.—America (United States of): R. D. Merrill, Consul. Belgium: M. Cloquet, Consul-General Hugo Von der Nahmer, Acting Consul. Bremen and Lubeck: Louis Chapalay, Acting-Consul. Chili: W. H. Eldred, Consul. Denmark: G. Were, Vice-Consul. France: L. F. Sentis, Consul. Hamburgh: R. Waterson, Acting-Consul, Sydney; G. Appel, Vice-Consul at South Brisbane, Moreton Bay. Hanover: J. Dhanis, Consul. Hawaiian Islands: C. St. Julian, Consul-General. Naples and Sicily: L. F. Sentis, Consular Agent. Netherlands: G. Kohler, Consul; F. C. Prost, Vice-Consul. Portugal: M. J. Soares, Consul. Prussia: — Kischner, Consul. Russia: E. M. Paul, Vice-Consul. Sardinia: P. A. Detruc, Consul-General. Spain: ———— Consul. Sweden and Norway: G. Were, Consul. Switzerland: L. Chapalay, Consul.

COMPANIES.—Sydney Exchange; Australian Trust; Colonial Sugar Refining; Ophir Copper Mining; Australian Gas Light; Bathurst Copper Mining; Carangara Copper; Wentworth Gold Field; FitzRoy Iron and Coal Mining; Pyrmont Bridge; Australian Agricultural; Newcastle Colliery; Peel River Land and Mineral; Australian Freemasons's Hall; Church of England Cemetery.

CUSTOMS.—Collector of Customs at Sydney: Colonel J. G. N. Gibbes. The Out-ports are Newcastle, Brisbane, Eden, Botany Bay, and Broken Bay.

EDUCATION.—Secretary of National Board: W. C. Wills. Schools—Denominational: King's (Parramatta), Protestant Orphan (Parramatta), Roman Catholic Orphan (Parramatta), St Phillip's, St. James's, and Female School of Industry. Also, Sydney Grammar School; Sydney College; Lyndhurst College; Moore College, Liverpool; Denominational Model Schools, Sydney; and a large number of private schools.

INSURANCE.—Sydney Insurance Company: Australian General Assurance; Sydney Marine Assurance; New South Wales Marine Assurance; Australian Mutual Provident Society; Derwent and Tamar Fire, Life, and Marine Insurance; Launceston Fire and Marine Insurance. *Branch Offices*:—Liverpool and London Fire and Life Insurance; Royal Insurance; Waterloo Life Assurance; Alliance Life and Fire Insurance; Imperial Fire Insurance; Profesional Life Assurance; People's Provident Assurance Society; Monarch Fire and Life Assurance; Northern Assurance of London; London and Oriental Steam Transit Insurance. Several of the offices in Sydney for insurance against fire grant policies on houses in the country.

INSTITUTIONS.—Mechanics' School of Arts; Tarban Creek Asylum; Sydney Ophthalmic; Australian Library; Australian Museum; Australian Club; St. Vincent's Hospital; Union Club; Sydney Club.

MUNICIPAL.—Mayor: John Williams. Sixteen Aldermen for eight wards. Town Clerk, C. H. Woolcott. City Treasurer, E. Lord. City Engineer: Edward Bell. City Surveyor: T. R. Roe. Health Officer: Isaac Aaron, M.D.

MINT.—Importation of gold dust or gold bullion for coinage, from twelve ounces upwards, received at the Mint daily. Deputy Master of Mint: Capt. E. W. Ward, R.E. (See article elsewhere.)

SOCIETIES.—*Religious Societies*—Diocesan Board of Missions; the Church Society; Newcastle ditto; Young Men's Christian Association; Bible Society; Tract and Book ditto; London Missionary Dorcas Society; Congregational Union, Church Building, and Missions Societies; Bethel Union. New South Wales Alliance for the Suppression of Intemperance. *Miscellaneous*—Hebrew Benefit; Jewish Philanthropic Society for Relief of Destitute Children; Female Refuge; Infirmary and Dispensary; Benevolent Society; Metropolitan and Counties Permanent Building and Investment Society; Philosophical Society; Sydney Land and Benefit Building Society; Celtic Association; Guarantee Society; Horticultural and Agricultural Society.

STEAM BOAT COMPANIES.—Kiama Steam Navigation; North Shore Ferry; Australasian Steam Navigation Company; Phœnix Wharf Steamers; European and Australian Royal Mail Steam Ships; Shoalhaven Steam Navigation; Hunter River ditto.

SYDNEY EXCHANGE COMPANY.—Chairman: T. C. Breillat Deputy Chairman: T. W. Smith. Secretary: Alex. Thomson.

UNIVERSITY.—Provost: Sir Charles Nicholson. Vice-Provost: Hon. Frederick Lewis Merewether, B.A. Professors: Rev. J. Woolley, D.C.L.; M. B. Pell, Esq., M.A.; J. Smith, Esq., M.D.; Mons. P. Dutruc; J. H. Scott, Esq. Secretary: H. Kennedy, Esq. St. Paul's College is in connexion with the Sydney University, for the tuition of students belonging to the Church of England. Professor of Medicine: Dr. Smith. St. John's (R.C.) College is also in connection with the Sydney University, for students belonging to the Roman Catholic Church. Rector, the Very Rev. Dean, D. V. M. O'Connell.

MISCELLANEOUS.

COACHES run regularly from various Booking Offices to the different Townships in the interior, to and from Sydney, including Camden, Campbelltown, Liverpool, Picton, Penrith, Parramatta, Narrellan, Mudgee, Hartley, Windsor, Bathurst, Sofala, Louisa Creek, Meroo, Tambaroura, Goulburn, Yass, Gundagai, Myrtle Creek, Bargo, Iron Mines, Berrima, Puddy's River, Memlau, &c.

ELECTRIC TELEGRAPH.—Communications by telegrams with South Head, Port Phillip, Liverpool, Campbelltown, and Goulburn. Line in course of construction to connect Melbourne, Adelaide, &c., with Sydney.

HACKNEY CARRIAGE FARES.—Fares by Distance:—Not exceeding half a mile, Ninepence; for every half mile or part of half mile over and above any number of miles or half miles completed, Ninepence. Fares by Time:—Not exceeding half an hour, Two Shillings and Threepence; for every half hour or part of half hour after any number of half hours completed, Two Shillings and Threepence. One-horse Vehicles:—For every car or vehicle drawn by one-horse, two-thirds only of the above fares to be charged.

IMMIGRATION.—Board consisting of several gentlemen, with staff of officers. Institution for Female Servants attached. Branches of Immigration Department at Moreton Bay. Full and detailed particulars of the Regulations for Immigrants' Passages, &c., are issued in *Cox and Co.'s Australian Almanac*, published in Sydney.

NEWSPAPERS.—"Armidale Express," weekly; "Bell's Life in Sydney," weekly; "Bathurst Free Press," and "Times," weekly; "Church Chronicle," weekly; "Era," weekly; "Freeman's Journal," Wednesdays and Saturdays; "Goulburn Chronicle," twice a week; "Goulburn Herald," weekly; "Illawarra Mercury," twice a week; "Maitland Mercury," Tuesdays, Thursdays, and Saturdays; "Maitland Northern Times," twice a week; "Moreton Bay Courier," twice a week; "Moreton Bay Free Press," weekly; "Darling Downs Gazette," weekly; "Braidwood Dispatch," weekly; "Mudgee Times," weekly; "North Australian," Moreton Bay, weekly; "Sydney Morning Herald," daily; "Shipping Gazette," weekly; "Sydney Mercantile Journal," fortnightly; "Yass Courier," weekly.

OMNIBUSES leave Sydney, at intervals during each day, for Surrey Hills, Woolloomooloo, Paddington, Glebe, Waverley, Newtown, Strawberry Hill, Camperdown, Cook's River, Darling Point, Redfern, Chippendale, Parramatta, South Head Lighthouse, &c.

POST OFFICE, SYDNEY.—Postmaster-General: W. H. Christie. Secretary: T. K. Abbott. TOWN LETTERS—Not exceeding half oz., 1d.;

exceeding half oz. but not exceeding 1 oz., 2d.; exceeding 1 oz., but not exceeding 2 oz., 4d.; and so on increasing 2d. for every additional ounce or fraction of an ounce. COUNTRY LETTERS—Letters not exceeding half oz., 2d.; exceeding half oz., but not exceeding 1 oz., 4d.; exceeding 1 oz., but not exceeding 2 ozs., 8d.; and so on increasing 4d. for every additional ounce or fraction of an ounce. NEWSPAPERS—to go by the morning mails must be posted before 8 a.m.; and for the afternoon mails before 3 p.m. at the General Post Office, and if posted within 7 days from the date of publication, nil; if posted later, 1d. each. BOOK PARCELS—OPENED BOTH ENDS—Not exceeding 4 oz., 2d.; and 1d. extra for every additional 2 oz. or fraction of 2 ozs. INTER-COLONIAL POSTAGE.—Letters not exceeding half oz., 6d.; exceeding half oz., but not exceeding 1 oz., 1s.; and so on increasing 6d. for every additional half ounce or fraction of a half ounce. Letters overland to or from Victoria are charged the same rates as when sent by sea. INTER-COLONIAL BOOK PACKETS—Not exceeding half-pound, 6d.; exceeding half-pound but not exceeding 1 pound, 1s.; and so on, increasing 8d. for every additional half-pound or portion of a half-pound. Iron Letter Receivers in various parts of the city.

RAILWAYS.—Chief Commissioners: Capt. B. H. Martindale, R.E., and Capt. E. W. Ward, R.E. Secretary: John Rae. Engineer-in-chief: J. Whitton. The lines now open are the Great Southern, from Sydney to Campbelltown, 34 miles; and the Great Northern, from Newcastle to East Maitland, 16½ miles.

SAILING DIRECTIONS for the Harbor of Port Jackson are issued by the New South Wales Government, containing particulars under the following heads:—Aproach and Entrance, Western Channel, Eastern Channel, Entering in the night, Anchorage within the Heads, and Tides. These have been rendered necessary for Master Mariners, in consequence of the erection of a new Lighthouse, and several additional Obelisks or Beacons.

STEAM FERRIES cross the Harbor every few minutes to Balmain, Pyrmont, North Shore, &c.

STEAMERS leave Sydney—(see daily papers and railway guide)—for Melbourne, New Hobart Town, Wollongong, Parramatta, Brisbane, Broulee, Clarence River, Kiama, Grafton, Cundle Town, Eden, Morpeth, Newcastle, Raymond Terrace, Moreton Bay, Wide Bay, Manly Beach, Shoalhaven, &c.

TARIFFS.—Import Duties: Spirits—Brandy and gin, per gal., 10s.; whiskey, rum, and all other spirits, per gal., 7s.; spirits, cordials, liqueurs, or strong waters, sweetened or mixed with any article, so that the degree of strength cannot be ascertained by Sykes' Hydrometer, per gal., 10s.: perfumed, spirits, 7s.; wine containing more than 25 per cent. of alcohol, of a specific gravity of ·825, at the temperature of 60 degrees of Fahrenheit's thermometer, for every gallon, in proportion to strength, 10s. Wine not containing more than 25 per cent. of alcohol, of a specific gravity of ·825, at the temperature of 60 degrees of Fahrenheit's thermometer, per gal., 2s.; Ale, porter, and beer, of all sorts, in wood, per gal., 1d.; in bottle, per doz., 2d. Tea, per lb., 3d. Sugar: refined and candy, per cwt., 6s. 8d.; unrefined, per cwt., 5s. Treacle and molasses, per cwt., 3s. 4d. Coffee and chicory, per lb., 2d. Cigars, per lb., 3s. Tobacco and snuff, per lb., 2s. Opium, 10s. per lb. Export Duty: gold, per oz., 2s. 6d.

COUNTRY DISTRICTS.*

ALBURY.—Albury is situated on the right bank of the Murray where the river is crossed by the great Southern Road; it is 378 miles from Sydney, and 200 miles from Melbourne. Other distances are 140 miles from Deniliquin, 120 from Gundagai, 80 from Wagga

* A large proportion of this information is copied from Waugh's Australian Almanac for 1858.

Wagga, and 28 from Beechworth. By the course of the Murray it is about 300 miles from its source, and about 1800 miles from its debouchure in Lake Alexandrina; the respective travelling distances being 140 and 700. The first settlement was made here about eighteen years since, but the place made no progress until within the last nine years. The district is scarcely exceeded in fertility and beauty by any tract of country in Australia. The production of wheat and other cereals is rapidly increasing, and now amounts to about 50,000 bushels. There are many flourishing vineyards and beautiful gardens, where, owing to the great mildness of the climate, many tropical plants can be cultivated, Albury being about 700 feet above the sea level. Of the geology of the district but little can be said, it being but little different from the neighboring districts. The rocks are all of the old formations, granite, and the varous kinds of slate, the latter intersected with immense dykes of quartz. The country is everywhere more or less auriferous. Population, 2,015. Persons travelling from Victoria to the Adelong diggings take coach to Beechworth, thence to Albury.

ARMIDALE.—The town is situated on the squatting district of New England, County Sandon, and embraces the southern portion of that county, and the western portions of the counties of Vernon and Hawes. Post Offices in the district, at Armidale, Walcha, Clerkness, Falconer, Bendemeer, Uralla, and Rocky River. Population, 3895.

BALRANALD.—Police district of the Lower Darling, on the Murray River. Population, 694.

BATHURST.—This Police district is situated in the county of the same name. Since the discovery of gold in the neighborhood it has risen rapidly in importance. The district includes Avisford, Sofala and western gold-fields, Stoney Creek, and Tambaroora. There are three churches: Episcopalian, Rev. Wm Coombes; Roman Catholic, Rev. D. McGuire; and Presbyterian, Rev. Alexander McEwan. Population, 12,005. About 100 miles from Sydney.

BERRIMA.—This district embraces the south western portion of the county of Cook, being bounded on the north by Bargo; south, Wingelo Creek; west, Wollondilly River; east, Coast range; and contains about 2,300 square miles, of which the average cultivation is 3,500 acres. Population, 2,227.

BINALONG.—This police district, as amended, embraces the north eastern portion of the Lachlan squatting district, and a south west portion of the county of King. Population, 1884.

BOMBALA.—This police district embraces parts of the counties of Wellesley and Wallace. Population, 1,273.

BRAIDWOOD.—This police district embraces the south western portion of the county of St. Vincent, and the eastern portion of the county of Murray. The Araluen gold fields are included within its limits. In extent it embraces an area of 1,400 square miles or 90,000 acres, of which 2,227 by the last report were under cultivation. The five gold-fields of this district, viz.: Araluen. Little River, or Mongarlow, Bell's Creek, Bell's Paddock, and Major's Creek, are comprehended in the police district of Braidwood. Population, 3,045.

BRISBANE.—One of the townships in Moreton Bay, called North and South Brisbanes, fourteen miles from the mouth of the Brisbane River, and thirty-five miles from Ipswich. Population, 5,844.

BROULEE.—This police district is situated in the county of St. Vincent. The township of Moruya, where the Court is held, is situated about three miles from the mouth of the Moruya River. It was first located in 1852, and already gives constant employment to 5 or 6 coasting vessels, between there and Sydney. A good deal of gold has been found near Mogo Creek, very coarse, and so scattered that it has not hitherto yielded sufficient to remunerate the digger. It is thought the true lode will yet be struck. Population, 1,207.

CAMPBELLTOWN.—This police district embraces the south eastern portion of the county of Cumberland. The town itself is one of the oldest in the colony, and though the great south road passes through it, like many others, it has been rather in a declining state for some years. It is about 34 miles distant from Sydney, and is united by the Great Southern Railway. Courts of Petty Sessions are also held at Picton and Camden; to the latter of which Narellan is annexed. The district includes Liverpool, Camden and Narellan, and Picton. Population, 7,827.

CAMDEN.—Seat of James Macarthur, Esq., a good agricultural and extensive wine producing district.

CARCOAR.—Population, 2,943.

CASINO is in the squatting district of Clarence, and embraces the county of Rous, and part of the county of Richmond, it is bounded on the north by the range dividing the waters of the Logan and other rivers from those of the Clarence, Richmond, and Tweed. The soil along the banks of the river is a rich alluvium well adapted for cultivation, but at any distance from it, it consists of stiff clay only adapted for pastoral purposes. The amount of cultivated land in the district is only about 1,000 acres. Population, 1,283.

CASSILIS.—This district embraces the eastern portion of the county of Brisbane, and the whole of the county of Bligh; in length about 60 miles from S.E. to N.W. There is very little cultivation carried on in this district, perhaps not more than 300 acres altogether. Population, 761.

CLARENCE RIVER.—See "Grafton.

COOMA.—This police district extends from Micalago, on the north, to the McLaughlan River, on the south, and from the Coast range in the east, to the Snowy Mountains on the west; and comprises about 6,000 square miles, of which there are about 1,000 acres generally under cultivation. Population, 2,006.

DALBY.—This police district is situated in the Darling Downs. Population, 678.

DENILIQUIN.—Deniliquin was established in 1852, and, at present, the population of the town approximates to 300. It is entirely a pastoral district—an extensive and opulent one. There is no agriculture. Moama, a rapidly rising town on the Murray River, is in the Deniliquin Police district. At Deniliquin there are four public houses and three stores. At Moama, two of each. There is also another public house in the district, being that occupied by W. Carter, at Red Bank, where the Government intend to lay out a village. Population, 725.

DRAYTON.—This police district extends from the dividing range westerly to the river Barwan, a distance of about 250 miles, with an irregular width exceeding 50 miles. It contains the townships of Drayton and Toowoomba, the latter, though it has only been settled about three years, promises to excel the older township from which it is only about three miles distant, in its buildings and number of inhabitants. There is a Benevolent Society established at Drayton, of which the Rev. William W. Dove is Treasurer. Population, 1,457.

Dubbo is the squatting district of Wellington and Bligh; the land under cultivation is estimated at 800 acres. Population, 1,626.

Dungog.—Dungog, Port Stephens, and Clarence are united in one district. The Magistrates, however, seldom sit out of their respective portions of the district, as a Court is held in each place. The district is mountainous, valley very fruitful, with abundance of good water. Plenty of cedar exported from the Chichester River. Clarence Town, as the head of the Navigation of the William River and the Shipping Port of an extensive agricultural district, is rapidly increasing in importance, and is in regular communication weekly by steamer with Sydney and Maitland. Population, 2,582. Port Stephens,—Population, 1,222.

Eden.—In the police district of Maneroo, which though almost exclusively of a pastoral character, is computed in this portion of it. The land generally under cultivation is about 1,500 acres. Population, 1,251.

Gayndah.—In the northern districts, viz.: bounded by Port Curtis and Wide Bay. There is little or no cultivation. Population, 1,309.

Gosford.—This district embraces the south east portion of the county of Northumberland; bounded on the north by Lake Macquarie, and south by the Hawkesbury and Broken Bay Road. Population,

Goulburn.—This district embraces the southern portion of the county of Georgiana and the whole of Argyle. Notwithstanding its pastoral character, the returns of land under cultivation in March, 1856, were 9,104. Population, 7,028.

Grafton.—The Clarence River, in which district Grafton is situated, was discovered 1838. It is the largest river known on the eastern coast, with 12 feet water on bar, and navigable for 60 miles, by vessels of 300 tons. There are large quantities of rich alluvial plains, cedar brushes, and swamps on the river and its tributaries; interspersed with sandstone and ironstone ridges, in the lower part of the district; and sandstone, clay, slate, and granite, in the upper portion. Copper has been found in several places; also coal of good quality; and gold has been found in barely payable quantities, upon all the waters of the Clarence, and other minerals which are not so well known. Towns—North and South Grafton, first opened for sale in 1851. Trade steamship, "Grafton," 300 tons, every fortnight to Sydney. Population, 1,069.

Gundagai.—This district is bounded on the N.E.N., and N.W., by the Binalong district; on the W., S.W., and S., by Wagga Wagga; and on the S.E., E. and N.E., by Tumut. It contains about 2,208 square miles, and the land generally under cultivation is stated at 3,000 acres. Jugiong is the second town of the district. Gundagai and the country for five miles round are considered highly auriferous,—every indication that can lead to such a belief is presented in its geological features. A spur of Mount Parnassus, in the town, is a valuable quartzridge. Gold has for the last three years been obtained on a part of Jones's bush, about five miles from town (in one instance as much as an ounce and a half was got in one dish), but the fact has not excited any desire on the part of the inhabitants for search, and has consequently not led to the discovery of a payable gold-field. Population, 966.

HARTLEY.—The police district of Hartley contains an area of about 2,050 square miles, of which upwards of 3,000 acres are generally under cultivation. Population, 2,273.

HUNTER RIVER.—Commences at Newcastle and extends beyond Maitland, and is one of the oldest and finest agricultural districts, also for vine cultivation.

ILLAWARA.—Between Botany Bay and Shoalhaven. A fertile and beautiful district, supplying fruit and agricultural produce to Sydney. The traffic is carried on *viâ* Wollongong.

IPSWICH.—In the Moreton Bay district, embracing parts of the counties of Canning, Stanley, and Ward. Population, 4,558.

KIAMA.—This district forms a portion of the counties of East Camden, bounded on the north by the Macquarie or Terry's River, south by the Crooked River, east by the sea, and west by the Illawarra Range. Population, 3,883.

LEICHHARDT.—Population, 828.

M'DONALD RIVER.—This district comprises the south-west portion of the county of Northumberland, and part of the south portion of the Hunter. Its extent in square miles cannot well be ascertained, but the land generally under cultivation may be estimated at 2,000 acres. There are no resident magistrates in the district, but James Wrigg Dalyell, P.M., Wollombi, attends on the second Tuesday of every alternate month. Population, 723.

M'LEAY RIVER.—This district is bounded on the north by the range of mountains south of the Clarence River, and on the south by the range that divides the waters of the M'Leay and Hastings. Its area cannot well be determined, but there are about 2,000 acres generally under cultivation. Population, 962.

MAITLAND.—This important township is situate on the Hunter River, about three miles from Morpoth and six from Raymond Terrace, consisting of East and West Maitland. It is approached by steam-boats up the Hunter, and is connected with Newcastle by the Great Northern Railway, distant 20 miles. The Paterson River is in the immediate neighbourhood and the country around is picturesque, the land being in a high state of cultivation. Population, 15,290.

MARYBOROUGH.—Situated on the Mary River, Wide Bay. Population, 669.

MOLONG.—This is an extensive district, situated in the county of Wellington, the area of which is not sufficiently known, nor yet the land under cultivation, though in the immediate vicinity of the township, it may be stated at 350 acres. Population, 1,446.

MORETON BAY.—See page 193.

MOULAMEIN. In the Murrumbidgee squatting district, bounded by the Merribal Creeks, Edwards, and Murray Rivers. Population, 299.

MUDGEE.—Population, 4,208.

MURRURUNDI.—Population, 921.

MUSCLEBROOK (amalgamated with Merton).—Population, 1,028.

NEWCASTLE.—This town owes its name of importance to the coal-fields by which it is surrounded. Coal is supplied from the Newcastle pits to the various colonies. About 90 miles to the north of Sydney. Population, 4,580.

ORANGE.—This district is in the county of Wellington, and contains about 600 square miles. The township of Orange was first opened about 1848, and now contains a large number of valuable buildings. The district is known to be full of valuable minerals, particularly copper, and much gold; and is also a fine agricultural district. Population, 2,041.

PARRAMATTA.—Connected with Sydney by the Great Southern Railway, distant about 14 miles. Is considered the second town in New South Wales, but possesses no advantages to make it important, the land being low and barren. Visitors from Sydney, per sailing or steam-boat on the Parramatta River, constantly avail themselves of a trip to this neighbourhood. Population, 15,758.

PATERSON.—Paterson is the principal town of the county of Durham. The police district embraces the midland and northern portion of the county, and contains a population of 1,227 males, 1,153 females. The land generally under cultivation is somewhere about 4,700 acres. Population, 2,399.

PENRITH.—Population, 4,804.

PORT CURTIS.—This police district extends from the Wide Bay and Burnett district on the south, northward along the sea coast, about 200 miles to Broad Sound, and is bounded on the west by the Leichardt district, at a distance from the sea varying from 50 to 100 miles. Port Curtis was first located in March, 1854. Population at last census, 287; but the new gold-fields have greatly augmented the numbers since July, 1858.

PORT MACQUARIE.—The police district of Port Macquarie embraces nearly the whole of the county of Macquarie, and the N.E. portion of the county of Gloucester, extending over an area of nearly 10,350 square miles, of which from 2 to 3,000 acres are generally under cultivation, especially in the Manning River, a place rapidly advancing as an agricultural district. Townships:—Wingham, Government township; Tarree, private township; Tinonee, Government township; Chaltham, private township; Cundletown, private township; a township has also been laid out on the Upper Manning, named George Town, the property of Isabella Mary Kelly. Population, 2,652.

PORT STEPHENS.—A large estuary 15 miles in length, and contracted to about a mile in breadth in the centre, into which the Rivers Karnah and Myall flow.

PATRICK'S PLAINS.—See Singleton.

QUEANBEYAN.—This police district includes the greater portion of the county of Murray, and part of the counties of Cowley and Buccleugh, in the Murrumbidgee squatting district. It comprises an area of about 3,000 square miles. The cultivation is represented at 3,600 acres. Population, 2,622.

RICHMOND.—A quiet township near Windsor, about 36 miles from Sydney. A beautiful country around, and undulating towards the Blue Mountains.

RAYMOND TERRACE.—This district comprises the southern portion of the county of Gloucester, north eastern portion of the county of Durham, and south eastern portion of the county of Northumberland. In March, 1857, the number of acres under cultivation is reported as 9,427. Population, 4,007.

RYLSTONE.—The geological character of the district indicates that gold is to be obtained in greater or less quantities throughout its whole extent; at one spot a party have been working with tolerable success for nearly 12 months. Agriculture.—Until of late years, this was almost wholly a pastoral district; the last returns of live stock which were completed on the 31st March, 1857, showed a total, including horses, cattle, sheep, and pigs, of 92,703; and a return of agriculture completed at the same time, showed that there were 1,237 acres of land in cultivation. Population, 997.

SCONE.—Embraces the north west portion of the county of Durham and eastern portion of the county of Brisbane. It is estimated to contain 1,000 square miles. Population, 1,100.

SHOALHAVEN.—Population, 3,322.

SINGLETON.—The Singleton or Patrick's Plains police district, is bounded by the Wollombi on the south, and Muswellbrook and Paterson Ranges on the north; Black Creek on the east, Jerry's Plains on the west; and, in round numbers, contains an area of 900 square miles, of which there are about 7,000 acres generally under cultivation. Population, 3,419.

SURAT.—This police district is situated in the pastoral district of Maranoa, and part of the district of Darling Downs, and extends from Chinchilla, in Darling Downs district, to River Warrego, the western boundary of the Maranoa district. Population, 415.

TAMWORTH.—This police district is bounded on the north-east by Moonbi, Bell's Mountain on the north-west, Liverpool Range on the south, and Narribie on the west. Population, 2,985.

TENTERFIELD.—The amount of cultivation in this district is about 500 acres. Population, 675.

TUMUT.—This district is very large. There are computed to be upwards of 2,000 acres under cultivation. District very far behind in every thing useful and ornamental;—bad bridges, worse roads, and no public spirit. No schools, no public societies, nor charitable institutions—only one town in the district, and the progress very slow. Geologically, very auriferous; diggings going a-head, and very rich, but there is a great want of people to develop them. Population, 1,467.

WAGGA WAGGA.—The geological features of the country present no auriferous indications. There is much fine gold deposited in the river sand, but this is brought down by the waters of the Tarcutta and Adelong Creeks. It would not pay for washing. Population, 1,416.

WARIALDA.—In the pastoral districts of Gwydir and Darling Downs, bounded on the north by the range dividing the waters of the Macintyre Brook from those of the Dumaresq River, known also as the Severn, to the confluence of those streams, and by the rivers Dumaresq and Barwan, also there known as the Karawla or Macintyre; west by the River Warrego, downwards to where the 29th parallel meets it; on the south by the 29th parallel to where it is cut by Mr. Kennedy's return track from the River Warrego, thence by the range dividing the waters of the River Gwydir from those of the Namoi or Peel to the western boundary of the pastoral district of New England; and on the east by that boundary. Bingara is a township, situated on the banks of the Gwydir or Big River, distant from the Bingara gold-fields about 10 miles. It is likely to become from its position a place of some importance. The land in the township as well as in its immediate vicinity, is of an auriferous character. The land is also well adapted for agricultural purposes. Population, 1,040.

WARWICK.—This police district extends from Dividing Ridges, Pilton and Dalrymple Creeks, on the north, to Quartz Pot Creek, on the south, the McIntyre brook ranges on the west, and main range east. Population, 1,862.

WEE WAA—(Namoi River).—The police district extends from Narrabry on the east, to the junction of the Narraw and Barnwan Rivers on the west, a distance of about 180 miles; and from the Warrabangle Range on the south, to the Mehi Creek on the north, the average distance in this direction being about 150 miles. The district is purely a squatting one. The whole of the country comprised within it is a dead level, as flat as Holland. The aborigines who sometimes accompany stockmen on their trips to Maitland are struck with amazement when they see for the first time the ranges of hills on the upper Namoi. The finest cattle which enter the Maitland market are sent from this district. Wee Waa is 260 miles and Walgett 360 miles from Maitland. Population, 374.

WELLINGROVE.—This squatting district is bounded by the Bolivia Range on the north; on the south by the Bundarra River and Benlomond Range; and east and west by the New England squatting district boundaries; it comprises an area of about 3,000 square miles. The town of Wellingrove is 70 miles north of Armidale and 320 miles from Maitland. By the last returns in March last, 397 acres were reported as under cultivation, but from recent purchases of land at government sales, the extent is greatly on the increase. There are three townships in the district, Wellingrove, Glen Innes, and Stonehenge. Population, 1,091.

WELLINGTON.—Embracing the north-western and midland portions of the county of Wellington. By the last returns there were 180 acres under cultivation and 10 acres of vineyards. Population, 1,993.

WIDE BAY.—Beyond Moreton Bay and the boundary of the county of Stanley, and is the last port of the colony of New South Wales; it receives the waters of the Mary Fitzroy River.

WINDSOR.—Embraces the north-western portion of the county of Northumberland, and the north-eastern portion of the county of Cook, and the southern portion of the county of Hunter. It contains an area of about 2,500 square miles. There are about 13,915 acres under cultivation, not including vineyards and gardens. Population, 8,431.

WOLLOMBI.—Embracing the midland portions of the county of Northumberland. The cultivation of this district is generally about 4,500 acres. Population, 1,519.

WOLLONGONG.—This district embraces the south-east portion of the county of Cumberland, and the north-east portion of the county of Camden, and may probably contain about 120 square miles. By the return in March, 1856, there were upwards of 4,300 acres under cultivation. Population, 4,506.

YASS.—The police district of Yass embraces a southern portion of the county of King, and a northern portion of the county of Murray, and portions of the counties of Buccleuch, Wynyard, and Harden. It contains an area of about 2,000 square miles. In March, 1856, the number of acres under cultivation was stated to be 5,855, and on the increase. Population, 4,099.

MORETON BAY.

This district was discovered during an exploring expedition in December, 1823. It is about 500 miles to the northward of Sydney. Moreton Island is about nineteen miles in length, and four and a half in breadth. The bay is forty-five miles in length and twenty in breadth. The River Brisbane flows into the bay about the middle of its western side.

Steam communication is maintained between Brisbane and Ipswich, daily, and between Moreton Bay and Sydney, weekly.

The climate of this district is hot during the summer months, and is never subject to extreme cold or hot winds. During the winter months it is adapted for invalids, especially those afflicted with consumption and other diseases of a wasting character. Fruits of various kinds grow luxuriantly, also maize, wheat, &c. Darling Downs are behind Moreton Bay over the mountain range, a magnificent sheep country, also accessible from the Clarence River. From Moreton Bay to Macquarie is 270 miles of coast; there are nine rivers with bar harbors, which can be entered by coasting vessels and small steamers, namely, the Brisbane, Tweed, Richmond, Clarence, Bellinger, Macleay, Hastings, Camden Haven, and the Manning.

The country around Moreton Bay is an extensive squatting district, occupied by some of the first and now most wealthy settlers. The returns of sheep and cattle sold in the Sydney and other markets, from the neighborhood of Moreton Bay, have been very extensive.

The principal towns in the Moreton Bay territory are, Brisbane, Ipswich, Drayton, Warwick, Dalby, Maryborough, Gayndah, Grafton, and Gladstone. (Some particulars of many of these will be found in the alphabetical arrangement of districts.)

The population of Moreton Bay to the north of the intended boundary between Moreton Bay and New South Wales is about 22,000.

It is in contemplation to make the district of country of which Moreton Bay is the centre, a separate colony, with Brisbane as its capital, but the measure has not yet been carried into effect.

There is a well-appointed staff of Government officials, and departments consisting of Board of Works, Custom House, Supreme Court, Immigration Board, Survey and Land Offices, &c., under the superintendence of the Government Resident, Captain J. C. Wickham, R.N.

At Brisbane there are banks connected with the Bank of New South Wales, Union Bank of Australia, Australian Joint Stock Bank and the Moreton Bay Savings Bank. At Ipswich the Bank of Australasia and Bank of New South Wales have branches.

WESTERN AUSTRALIA.

This colony comprises the western portion of Australia from the 129° east longitude to the Indian Ocean, and extends between the parallels of 13° 44′ and 35° south latitude. The Swan River Settlement embraces, however, only the south-western corner, or that portion which is to the southward of the 30th parallel, and westward of the 120th meridian. The extent of the territory is 1,280 miles long, from north to south; and 800 miles broad, from east to west. Three distinct parallel ranges of mountains form the most distinguishing features, the highest and most easterly having its termination near King George's Sound; the second passing behind the Swan river, and extending to Cape Leuwin. Several rivers rise on these dividing ranges, on the banks of which settlements have been formed. The town of Freemantle is at the entrance to Swan River, the seat of Government being at Perth, about nine miles inland to the north. Guildford is about seven miles, and York fifty miles further east. King George's Sound, with the town of Albany, is attached to this colony.

The history of this colony up to the year 1850 contains little of interest, for it is but the account of a settlement struggling for bare existence, as up to that period it presented the aspect of a colony without sufficient capital to render available its natural resources, and with a scanty population. Up to the year 1850 the position of Western Australia was an anomaly in the history of colonisation, as never had a colony been so thoroughly impoverished and yet lingered on; this arose from the want of a market and the high rate of the small amount of available labor. Immigration had ceased, and the only capital introduced was a small amount of Imperial expenditure, and the equally small returns for exports. Under such an unpromising aspect the colonists naturally looked for some means to enable them to throw off the burthen of their long endured adversity, and but one presented itself, and that was to request the Home Government to make the colony a penal settlement. In 1850 the request was granted, and since then the colony has progressed year by year, exports have greatly increased, the settlers have a market for their stock and produce, public works are progressing, and although all this arises from the introduction of convicts, the statistics of crime show an immunity from transgression against peace and propriety that never could have been anticipated.

The principal townships in this colony are Freemantle, Perth, Guildford, Albany, Augusta, Kelmscott, York, Peel Town, Busselton, Kingstown, &c.,; the best districts for settlement being the Avon, the Hotham, the Williams, Arthur, Beaufort, and South East rivers, with part of the country adjacent to the Swan, the Harvey, Brunswick, Preston, Capel, and Yasse.

The population of the colony is 9,028 males, and 4,573 females; there are 7,214 horses, 26,297 cattle, 198,386 sheep, 8,651 pigs, and 1,532 goats. 18,000 acres of land were cultivated in 1857. The colony possesses large tracts of land suited for agriculture, and if, as is expected, land be reduced to 5s. an acre, grain to a considerable amount will be produced.

The colony is particularly adapted for horse breeding, and produces valuable timber, now being largely exported.

VICTORIA, OR PORT GREGORY DISTRICT.

This district, situated between the River Murchison and the Irwin, was first discovered by Capt. Grey, but was not settled until after the discovery of the Geraldine Mine by the Messrs. Gregory. The whole of this district contains minerals which are now being exported. Coal has also been discovered in one locality, and there is every indication of its existence in several others. The number of mines actually known to possess ores are twelve; of these four are lead and eight copper; several of these, as yet, have not been worked. Generally they have a most promising appearance, good ore being on the surface; besides these the whole of the district contains a vast number of lodes, some of which are easily traced for five or six miles, and it is the confident opinion of numbers well versed in mining, that it will one day prove to be one of the richest mineral districts in the world.

In addition to the minerals and the grazing of sheep and cattle, this district contains large flats of most superior agricultural land At present much of it is shut up in the squatting leases, yet sufficient is open for the present wants of the district. On the Lower Greenough one flat contains 10,000 acres of very rich land, giving with very slight cultivation 80 bushels to the acre, it is situated about 7 miles from Champion Bay, and is sold in blocks from 30 to 100 acres at £1 per acre, or leased at £10 per 100 acres, with right of preemption. This flat has the great advantage for new beginners of being nearly free from timber, and is open for sale. A considerable quantity has this season been taken up for tillage.

Western Australia possesses one of the finest climates in the world, and has been found particularly beneficial to Indian invalids.

DUTIES.—The ports of Western Australia are open for

ships of all nations, with moderate harbor and pilotage dues; imported articles are subject to custom duties. The imports from 1st October, 1856, to 30th September, 1857, were £108,703 14s. 11d. Duty free, £16,784 0s. 7d. The exports, £44,198 18s. King George's Sound is not included in this return. The receipts and expenditure of Government were as follow:—Receipts, £89,079 19s. 8d.; expenditure, £90,190 12s. 10d. The number of births and deaths during the same period were:—Births, 507; deaths, 158. The tariff, with rates of agency, tonnage, &c., are published in the *Western Australian Almanac* for 1858.

GOVERNMENT, LAW, &c.

GOVERNMENT.—Governor and Commander-in-Chief: His Excellency Arthur Edward Kennedy. Private Secretary: H. Wakeford.

EXECUTIVE COUNCIL: His Excellency the Governor, the Hon. the Commandant, Colonial Secretary, Comptroller-General, Surveyor-General, Advocate-General, Collector of Revenue.

LEGISLATIVE COUNCIL.—The members of the Executive Council, the Hon. W. H. Mackie, M. W. Clifton, J. W. Hardey, S. P. Phillips, E. Hamersley. Clerk of Councils: H. Wakeford,

DEPARTMENT OF GOVERNMENT.—Colonial Secretary, Hon. F. P. Barlee; Chief Clerk, Charles Sholl; Surveyor-General, Hon. J. S. Roe, Lieut. R.N.; Assistant Surveyors, A. Hillman, F. Gregory, and R. Austin; Treasurer and Collector of Revenue, Hon. A. O'G. Lefroy; Deputy-Treasurer, Albany, H. Camfield; Collector of Customs, R. M'B. Broun; 1st Clerk and Shipping Master, W. Gale; Auditor-General, W. Knight; Clerk, E. L. Courthope

LAW.—Commissioner of Civil Court and Chairman of Quarter Sessions, His Honor A. MacFarland; Advocate-General, Hon. Richard Birnie; Crown Solicitor, G. F. Stone; Clerk to ditto, J. Stone; Sheriff, F. D. Wittenoom; Bailiff, John Chipper; Clerk of the Peace, Commissioner of Court of Requests, and Official Assignee of Insolvent Estates, A. H. Stone. RESIDENT MAGISTRATES:—Albany, H. Camfield; Vasse, Captain J. Molloy; York, R. G. Meares; Bunbury, G. Eliot; Swan, S. W. Viveash; Toodyay, J. Harris; Champion Bay, W. Burges; Murray, D. S. Murray; Canning, Thomas Hester. Police Magistrates:—At Perth, T. N. Yule; a Freemantle, T. Brown; and at York, W. Cowan.

MEDICAL.—Colonial Surgeon, J. Ferguson; Ass. Col. Surgeon, Freemantle, and Health Officer, J. Shipton; Medical Attendant at Albany, — Baesjoux; ditto York, Robert Viveash; ditto Bunbury, J. Sampson.

POST OFFICE.—Postmaster-General, A. Helmich. Post Offices also at Freemantle, Guildford. Mandurah, Northam, York, Toodyay, Vasse, Bunbury, Australind, Albany, Upper Swan, Canning, Port Gregory.

HARBOR MASTER, J. Harding: Pilot, Rottnest, W. D. Jackson; Pilot, Albany. W. Pretious.

REGISTRAR-GENERAL, C. Sholl; Acting ditto, and Immigration Officer, A. Durlacher. Gaoler at Perth, T. Farrelly; do. at Albany, W. Burrill. Superintendent of Rottnest Penal Establishment, H. Vincent.

MILITARY.—Commandant Garrison Staff, Lieut. Colonel John Bruce; Staff Surgeon, G. T. Galbraith, M.D.; Captain Palmer, commanding 12th Regiment. Deputy Commissary-General, W. F. Mends.

CONVICT ESTABLISHMENT.—Comptroller-General, Hon. E. Y. W. Henderson, Capt. R.E.; Chief Clerk, J. E. Henderson; Superintendent of Establishment, T. H. Dixon; Chaplain, Rev. Mr. Alderson; Roman Catholic

Chaplain, Rev. T. Donovon; Principal Medical Officer, G. T. Galbraith, M.D.; Surgeon, G. Atfield, M.D. Visiting Magistrate, Freemantle, T. Brown; branches at North Freemantle, Fresh Water Bay, Mount Eliza, Guildford, Toodyay, York, Champion Bay, Bunbury, and Albany.

POLICE ESTABLISHMENTS.—Stations at Perth, Freemantle, Guildford, York, Toodyay, Northam, Beverly, Dundaragan, Champion Bay, Mandurah, Bunbury, Vasse, Australind, Albany, and Beaufort river. Superintendent of Water Police, G. Clifton.

ECCLESIASTICAL.

EPISCOPALIAN.—Right Rev. M. B. Hale, D.D., Lord Bishop of Perth, Revs. G. P. Pownall, Z. Barry, — Alderson, W. Mitchell, J. Brown, W. D. Williams, C. Harper, and H. Brown.

WESLEYAN CHURCH.—Rev. S. Hardey, Superintendent, at Perth, Rev. W. Lowe, at York.

CONGREGATIONAL CHURCH.—Rev. J. Johnston, at Freemantle; Rev. A. Jones, at Guildford.

ROMAN CATHOLIC CHURCH.—Right Rev. J. M. Benedict Serra, D.D.; Right Rev. Rozendo Salvado, D.D., Bishop of Port Victoria; the Chaplains are, Revs. M. Griver, Thomas Lynch, T. Donovan, Canon R. Martelli, V. Garrido, Y. Bertram. Convent of the Immaculate Conception, Perth, Lady Superioress and eight Sisters of Mercy. Convent of St. Joseph, Freemantle, Lady Superioress and five Sisters of St. Joseph, Branch Convent of St Teresa, Guildford, of the Sisters of Mercy.

EDUCATIONAL.—Secretary of General Board of Education, E. L. Courthope. Government Schools at Perth, Freemantle, Guildford. Upper Swan, York, Toodyay, Bunbury, Port Gregory, and Albany. Master of Vasse Mixed School, L. T. Cook. There are several private schools.

PUBLIC INSTITUTIONS, SOCIETIES, &c.—Swan River Mechanics' Institute: Patron, His Excellency the Governor; President, J. S. Roe, Esq., R.N., F.L.S., Surveyor-General. York Agricultural Society: C. Wittenoom, Hon. Sec. Agricultural and Horticultural Society: J. Sinclair, Sec. and Treas. Western Australian Bank: established 23rd June. 1831, Capital £20,000, in 2000 shares of £10; Cashier, Francis Lochee. Wanerenooka, Mining Company: F. D. Wittencom, Hon. Sec. White Peak, Geraldine, and Yanganooka Mining Companies. Perth Horticultural Society: H. Wakeford, Hon. Sec. London and Liverpool Fire and Life Assurance Company: Capital £1,500,000, A. H. Stone, Agent.

FRIENDLY SOCIETIES.—Lodge of St. John's, Western Australia, No. 712. Perth Lodge of Unity, No. 753. Sons of Australia Benefit Society: W. Graves, Secretary Independent Order of Odd Fellows, Manchester Unity, New Swan Lodge, No. 4,406.

SHIPPING.—Upwards of eighty vessels entered inwards and outwards at the Port of Freemantle from 1st October, 1856, to 30th September, 1857. Eighteen vessels belong to the port.

CONVICT SHIPS.—Twenty convict vessels arrived, w t 4,476 prisoners between 1st June, 1850, and 30th September, 1857.

NEW ZEALAND.

POSITION.

New Zealand is situated between 34 and 47 degrees south latitude, and between 166 and 179 degrees east longitude. This country lies in the immense Austral Ocean, between New Holland and Cape Horn. On the east that ocean rolls to South America, on the south to the pole, on the west to Van Diemen's Land, and, on the north, it stretches boundlessly away to the arctic circle. New Zealand consists of two large islands the north and the middle, otherwise New Ulster and New Munster, with a lesser one called Stewarts or New Leinster, and several scattered islets. The extreme length, from North to South Cape, exceeds 1100 miles, its breadth varies from 1 to 200 miles, though 100 is the average. The Northern and Middle Islands are separated by Cook's Straits, and Stewart's is divided from the middle island by Fourneaux's Straits. The north island contains, it has been computed, about 31,174,400 acres of area; the middle, 46,126,080; and Stewart's 1,000,000. The country is divided into six provinces namely, Auckland, Wellington and Taranaki, or New Plymouth, in the northern island; and Nelson, Canterbury, and Otago, in the middle island. A Governor is appointed by the Queen, and the provinces are governed by superintendents and a provincial council, elected by the local residents. Each province contributes its proportionate share of members to the House of Representatives, which, with a second Chamber, constitutes the General Assembly, and legislates for the entire colony. The second or upper chamber of the General Assembly is nominated by the Governor. The various Superintendents (who do not sit in Parliament) have their Executive Councils, consisting of Private Secretaries, Treasurers, and Law Advisers.

The distance from Auckland to Taranaki is about 130 miles; Taranaki to Nelson, 160 miles; Nelson to Wellington, 120 miles; Wellington to Canterbury, 160 miles; Canterbury to Otago, 170 miles; Otago to the Bluff, 120 miles.

New Zealand is most nearly of all countries the antipodes of Great Britain, and lies 1500 miles east of the island of New Holland.

DESCRIPTION.

The country is of volcanic origin, and presents many indications of mineral wealth. The soil, generally, is rich and fertile. The harbors are numerous and excellent. Rivers are numerous, being supplied by running streams from the high mountains, principally fed by melted snow.

The climate is pronounced as genial and healthy as any other part of the southern hemisphere and is frequently visited by persons suffering from delicate constitutions. The variations of temperature are not so common as in many of the Australasian group, and the weather being milder on the whole, consequently persons may promote health by frequent exposure to the open air. Altogether, the country is a remarkably healthy one. The climate varies with the latitude, and may be compared with the south of France in the north and the south of England in the sôuth.

There are no railways constructed in New Zealand for the present, but the country is by no means unfavorable to their formation. The fine rivers and water frontages go far to supply the want of railways, and the former might not present any engineering difficulties. It is impossible, however, to predict what may result from the gold discoveries in Auckland, Nelson, and still more recently in Dunedin, Otago. Canterbury is extremely well adapted for railways, and a line is contemplated to connect Lyttleton (the port) with the plains.

Roads are being constructed in many parts of the country; in the province of Wellington alone there are 150 miles of metalled road, and persons may ride on horseback from one part of the country to the other. From Dunedin to Christ Church the journey has been performed in eight days. There is a fortnightly post from Dunedin to the Writaki, and from Christ Church to Timarn; it is in contemplation for the post to go through from Christ Church to Dunedin, as the rivers and creeks do not render progress through the country at all difficult. During the summer months the road from Christ Church to Nelson is considered good.

Many persons have supposed that New Zealand is a slow sort of place, inhabited by a rather intelligent race of savages, together with a moderate number of Europeans, who can, without much difficulty, raise an abundance of food for their own use, but with no prospect of ever becoming more than well-conditioned farmers, living in a state of rude plenty. And though it has been stated that the Southern or Middle Island contains a wide extent of open, well-grassed land, capable of feeding some millions of sheep and cattle, and that English grasses are gradually superseding the all-pervading fern in the Northern Island, and yield a pasturage richer, and able to sustain more stock to the acre, than that of the mother country itself, yet on these points many who have not been the spot are still incredulous.

HISTORY.

Captain Hobson was the first governor of New Zealand (appointed in 1841), and had great difficulty in obtaining the same by treaty from the natives. He acted in several capacities, as Consul, Lieutenant-Governor, and Governor, during the periods extending from January, 1840, and September, 1842. The native inhabitants were a wild and lawless race, and the European occupants, generally, consisted of whalers and runaway sailors. After New Zealand became a dependency of the British Crown, the natives yielded a willing obedience to law, and abandoned the barbarous purposes of their race to a great extent. Captain Hobson, whilst acting as Governor of New Zealand, died on 10th September, 1842, worn out by bodily fatigue and harass of mind, generally respected for his assiduity and good conduct.

Most of the early settlers in the northern part of the North Island, were from New South Wales, and with Sydney have all their associations been preserved and their intercourse maintained. Sheep have been taken to New Zealand from Victoria by a few of the old squatters and stockowners retreating from the advancing wave of population, which in some parts of that colony has so interfered with pastoral pursuits.

THE NATIVES.

As a proof that the British, both imperial and colonial, were in no little awe of the Maori (or natives), it may be stated that although the whole number now surviving is only estimated at about 70,000, they have been paid the compliment of commanding the undivided attention of two entire regiments of European soldiers; this force has, however, been reduced to to one regiment. One of these was usually quartered at Auckland, and the other at Wellington; but they were held in constant readiness to be forwarded into any neighborhood where the native attitude may become so far threatening as to appear to require a demonstration. In his heart, the Maori utterly despises the soldier; he does not approve of his style of fighting. They own large numbers of livestock of all kinds, but especially of horses, of which they are very fond, and in many districts of the Northern Island they have lands in cultivation exceeding in extent and value those of the settlers. Apart from the deference to the Maories implied in the large physical force retained for the purpose of controlling them, every acre of land acquired by the British is bought and paid for, instead of being deliberately stolen, as is the case with other colonies. Each tract is made the subject of a special treaty; the claims, however remote, of each several native are hunted up and provided for, and a regular deed is prepared, signed, and witnessed, as formally as if involving a transaction between one white and another. The prices often given are very high indeed; for the New Zealander is singularly tenacious on the subject of land, and so astute and keen-witted is he, that he readily enough appreciates the peculiar features which constitute attractiveness in the land of which the "pakeha" seeks to get possession. The Maories are recognised as British subjects, and held to be amenable to the laws, and yet allowed to carry on war with one another without interference. Only when their quarrels seem likely to embroil the whites does the Government step in. Energetic remonstrances are indeed made, and the moral influence of the Government is alone brought to bear to bring about an amicable settlement of their differences. But the feuds are not interfered with by anything like physical force; and the Government seems usually greatly inclined to preserve a perfectly neutral position. The New Zealander adopts the bush style of fighting, hiding amongst the fern and behind trees, and digging rifle pits around his pahs. They thus often spend whole days over a battle without any very sanguinary results. The worst form of the Maori savagery—cannibalism—has long been at an end, the last case known having occurred in 1842, in the Bay of Plenty.

The traveller can now proceed through New Zealand as safely as through any country in the world. The natives so far from being likely to molest him, act rather as a police to protect him from harm.

Physically, the Maori is a fine fellow. Generally well grown, and with his muscular system fully developed, he is capable of great labor, and if not too hardly pressed, does not show much disposition to shrink from it. When well dressed and clean, he looks more like a Spaniard or Italian than a savage, and occasionally very handsome men indeed are found amongst them. They differ much in appearance, which has led to the belief that they consist of more than one race, and vary in color from almost black to delicate olive, their hair is sometimes quite straight, sometimes very curly, and sometimes as thoroughly woolly as that of any negro. The old system of tattooing is now being dispensed with by the young people. It would be a great pity if so fine a race were to pass altogether away, and some very good suggestions have been made to avert the natural consequences of their present ignorance and mismanagement, and to arrest, if possible, the rapid diminution of their numbers, which is at present unquestionably going on.

LAND.

The total quantity of land under cultivation in the six provinces amounted in 1856 to 114,570 acres. More than half of this was in Auckland. Wellington and Nelson had each about 14,000 acres under crop; New Plymouth, 9000; Canterbury,

8000; and Otago, 5000. The greater portion of cultivated land—to the extent of 80,000 acres—is occupied with sown grass, and this is especially the case in Auckland. Wheat is the crop next in favor, and potatoes and oats come next. The quantity of fenced land is not fully stated, but it would not seem to be double the cultivated area, except in Canterbury. The minimum price of land in the Province of Canterbury is £2 per acre, in the other provinces, 10s. per acre. The evils of six different land systems, of six sets of land regulations, in a couple of little islands barely large enough to form one good colony, will be apparent to any one who has ever studied the science of colonisation. Each province has made its own regulations both as to the lease and the sale of land, and the Canterbury government has set the highest price on its land and pasturage. But then, as compensation, very secure and equitable conditions of tenure are granted to the squatters. Under these regulations the waste lands are being rapidly occupied with sheep, thus showing that even a high rental is no discouragement to squatting, provided that arbitrary taxation is renounced, and a fixity of tenure is granted that will enable the settler to calculate his probable outlay and returns.

The revenue of the colony for the year 1853 was £149,820; in 1854, £292,040; in 1855, £175,895; and in 1856, £188,828. The revenue for 1857 was considerably larger than 1856, for 1858 it amounted to nearly £400,000. The great increase in the second of these years was owing to a sudden expansion of the territorial revenue in consequence of the reduction in the price of land. The land sales yielded that year more than double the usual amount. But speculation having gorged itself, the land revenue fell off again in the two succeeding years to about the same amount as prior to the disturbance in price. In the year of speculation the land sales yielded £180,000. At ten shillings an acre this will represent 360,000 acres as having been then alienated from the Crown. (Further particulars are noted under the heads of the respective provinces.)

CATTLE, SHEEP, &c.

It is presumed that the settlements on the Middle Island are increasing most rapidly in population; and so with regard to live stock. In 1856, Auckland had only 2,894 horses, 24,555 head of horned cattle, and 36,749 sheep. Wellington had in the same year 2,000 horses, 20,000 head of cattle, and 250,000 sheep. Nelson: 1,637 horses 13,893 head of cattle, and 285,100 sheep. Canterbury: 1,307 horses, 15,355 head of cattle, and 276,089 sheep. Otago: 1,076 horses, 15,600 head of cattle, and 129,902 sheep. And New Plymouth, 329 horses, 2,525 head of cattle, and 18,148 sheep. These figures only represent the quantity of stock belonging to Europeans, no returns having been made of those in the possession of aboriginal natives. The number of pigs in New Zealand is considerable. Sheep farming has prospered greatly of late in the southern provinces, and there is plenty of room yet for its definite increase The total number of sheep at present in the four provinces of Wellington, Nelson, Canterbury, and Otago, is not less than 1,200,000.

IMPORTS AND EXPORTS.

No very late returns have been published. The total exports from the colony during four years amounted to £1,808,472, the province of Auckland itself having furnished £617,046. This province has as many as seven shipping ports, but almost the entire trade, with the exception of about a fourth of that in exports, centres in Auckland itself. The imports to Wellington during 1856 amounted to £179,028, and the exports to £80,417, of which but a small portion was shipped to or from the second port in the province, Wanganui. Nelson only imported goods to the value of £81,172, and exported produce, and a few other trifling articles to the value of £29,775. In the list of exports from this province, the two principal items are—wool, £15,679; and gold, £40,000. Canterbury had, in 1856, a trade in imports of £90,446, and in exports of £47,831, which was mainly from the Port of Lyttelton. The imports to Otago were valued at £60,810, and the exports at £25,737, of which a small portion was to and from the port of Bluff, the remainder belonging to Otago itself. Into New Plymouth were imported goods worth £27,215, while the exports from there only amounted to £8,868.

The value of the imports at the several ports from various countries, during first quarter of 1857, amounted to £218,489 15s. 8d., while the second quarter ending 30th June, was £238,016 5s. 11d.

The value of the exports from the several ports of New Zealand, during first quarter of 1857, amounted to £120,811 4s. 6d.; while the second quarter ending 30th June was £87,586 5s. 0d.

Much of the wool and other produce of New Zealand is taken to Sydney and Melbourne for sale or shipment, and in return a large quantity of imported goods is supplied to the various settlements from these ports. A large proportion of the trade of Auckland is done with Sydney, but Wellington, Canterbury, and Otago principally trade with Melbourne. If the proposal of the Melbourne Chamber of Commerce to establish direct steam communication with Wellington is carried out, it is said the whole trade of the four Southern Provinces will be directed from Sydney to Melbourne.

The increase in the total amount of exports from Canterbury and Otago is very marked, and is mainly attributable to the development of sheep-farming in those two provinces.

In 1853 the clip (estimated at between £8000 and £9000) from Canterbury was sent coastwise to Wellington for final shipment: the first wool shipment to England from Lyttelton direct sailed in 1856. Nelson also appears at a disadvantage, as compared with Wellington, from a similar circumstance; since, while the amount of wool sent from Nelson in 1856 was estimated at 800,000 lbs., and valued at £45,000, the return only credits the province for £15,000 worth shipped from the port of Nelson, "excluding considerable quantities shipped at other outlets of the province, and cleared at other ports of the colony"—we believe Wellington chiefly, but some at Canterbury.

The totals of vessels entered inwards for Auckland, New Plymouth, Wellington, Nelson, Canterbury, Otago, and the Chatham Islands, were in 1853, 238; 1854, 293; 1855, 378; 1856, 326; or an aggregate total for the four years of 1,235 vessels.

The returns of tonnage for the same period show the following general totals, viz.: in 1853, 65,504; 1854, 74,831; 1855, 88,614; 1856, 85,748; or for the four years, a total tonnage for the colony of 313,697, of which the Auckland total amounts to 186,261, or 58,825 tons, more than half the total tonnage of the entire colonies for these four years.

The customs revenue at the several ports during the first quarter of 1857, amounted to £31,531 11s. 8d.; while the second quarter, ending June 30, was £34,203 16s. 1d. We much regret that later returns were not obtainable by us for this work.

POPULATION.

Compared with its area, or compared with the other colonies on the main land, New Zealand has but a handful of people. At the close of 1856 the total European population was as follows:—Auckland, 15,335; New Plymouth, 2,488; Wellington, 10,252; Nelson, 7,509; Canterbury, 6,160; and Otago, 3,796. This number, exclusive of the military and their families, was only 45,540, the males being in excess of the females by about 5000, which is less than half the population of Tasmania or South Australia, and only about one-tenth of that of Victoria. It is scattered, too, over six separate provinces, the provinces being again subdivided into little settlements; for there are no fewer altogether than sixteen ports of entry, or an average of one port for less than every three thousand souls. This want of concentration has hitherto been a great drawback to the prosperity of New Zealand, both politically and commercially, and has been one of the aggravations of its early struggles. But, in years to come, as each province grows in independent strength, the vigorous assertion of local and municipal rights may be found to have wrought out social results sufficiently valuable to compensate for the inconvenience of earlier days. The political development of New Zealand, determined as it must be to some extent by its geographical peculiarities, will assuredly differ from that of the colonies on the mainland, where there is such an enormous and unhealthy aggregation of population and wealth in the chief seats of Government and trade.

The several provinces rank as follows in the order of their populousness:—Auckland, Wellington, Nelson, Canterbury, Otago and New Plymouth, the first two having between them rather more than half of the whole number. The population has shown a steady increase, and a balance in its favor from Australia, notwithstanding the strong attractions of the gold-fields in Victoria, which drew away many who were not attached to the soil. A slight return current was caused by the reduction which was effected in the price of land. This tempting bait enticed away a few from the colonies where land was sold by auction at a pound an acre, to that where it could be had for five or ten shillings. But the attraction proved less powerful and less permanent than had been anticipated. Fewer emigrants were decoyed over than had been hoped for, and even of those, many returned again. The result of the experiment on the whole, has been to show that the effect of cheapening the land has rather been to stimulate speculation, and an investment of capital unproductive for the present, than to promote extensively actual occupation and tillage. A more reliable source of supply of population will be the direct immigration from Great Britain, which is still being carried out. Immigrants from the mother country, who can obtain good wages from the time of their landing, and who can easily secure little freeholds in which to invest their savings, seldom roam. And New Zealand possesses many special attractions well adapted to retain the industrious settler in his own homestead, notwithstanding the golden rumours that may come from other places.

MISCELLANEOUS.

To the north of the East Cape, the sea-breeze is invariably from the north, and sets in about ten o'clock, preceded by a calm, the sky being clear, with every indication of heat. It gradually dies away towards sunset. Should this breeze continue with strength after sunset, and the sky become cloudy, a smart gale may be expected, accompanied with heavy rain, for ten or fifteen hours, when the wind will suddenly shift to the westward, and the weather become fine. The wind at north, weather cloudy, will usually terminate in a gale, accompanied with rain, though of short duration. The wind at north-west generally strong, with heavy rain, seldom exceeding a day. The wind at west, weather unsettled, squally, with showers. The wind from north-north east to south south-east invariably terminates in a smart gale, with rain continuing three or four days. The general shift of wind follows the course of the sun. There is a south-east wind, exceedingly cold, with a clear sky and settled fine weather, which frequently continues for several days, terminating in a calm, or shifting to south-west. The westerly gales always die away at sunset, within a short distance of the sun.

The Newspapers are:—The "Southern Cross," "New Zealander," "Examiner," and "Register," at Auckland. The "Independent" and the "Spectator," at Wellington. The "Examiner" and the "Colonist," at Nelson. The "Herald" and the "News," at Taranaki. The "Lyttelton Times" and the "Canterbury Standard," at Canterbury. The "Witness" and the "Colonist," at Otago. The "Chronicle," at Wanganui. "Hawke's Bay Herald," at Ahuriri.

Young and Co.'s line of packets, between New Zealand and London, consist of first-class ships. Agents: Bain, Grahame and Co., Auckland. Also, Arthur Willis, Gaun and Co.'s line, between New Zealand and London, are first-class regular traders. Agents: Brown and Campbell, Auckland, and Mr. Lutter in Lyttleton.

Some details in reference to steam communication between England and New Zealand, also between Melbourne and Wellington will be found at the end of particulars respecting Otago.

The following is a sketch of the various Provinces of New Zealand:—

AUCKLAND.

This town is built on the northern side of the Isthmus which divides the Waitemata from the Manukau, and is bounded on the north by the shores of the former harbor. The site of the town, as laid down on the official plan, has a frontage to the water of about a mile and a half, and extends inland to the distance of about a mile. Most of the houses are built near the water, in the bays and on the headlands. The lower parts of the town being separated, the roads, generally, are inconveniently steep. The harbor has the appearance of a lake, viewed from several positions in the town. The villages of Onehunga and Newmarket are near Auckland, on either side. The land for several miles around the town is in a high state of cultivation, and is extremely valuable.

Generally speaking, the suburbs of Auckland present very indifferent scenery, being comparatively bare of trees, and distinguished only by the number of its volcanic hills. The surrounding country is open, undulating, intersected in all directions by the numerous creeks of the Waitemata and Manukau, and easily available for agricultural purposes; but it presents few of the characteristics of a New Zealand landscape, and it has nothing to mark it as a foreign country. The natural scenery, however, of the country, taken altogether, will bear comparison with England in mountain, river, coast, and harbor.

There are no port charges, harbor dues, or taxes, levied on shipping; and the harbor is open to all the world, to enter and depart free of charge.

The population of the province of Auckland is about 16,000, the township having about 8000 inhabitants.

The exports and revenue of the port have very much increased during the last five years. Auckland exports Kauri gum, flax, copper ore, gold, timber, wheat and potatoes. The country is independent of foreign supply in the principal articles of food. Within a radius of fourteen miles of Auckland there are upwards of 22,000 acres of land fenced in, of which more than 18,000 acres are in crop. Fruits and vegetables thrive well, though less highly flavored than in the mother country; the flowers, also, are abundant, but the native flowers have no scent. The nature of the soil is excellent, the land being well watered; and at all seasons of the year flowers and vegetables abound. Agricultural pursuits are strenuously followed, but as the yield of wheat, &c., has been more than what was required by the inhabitants for their consumption, and the cost of export considerable, many farmers have suffered much loss.

In the neighborhood of Auckland proof of volcanic agency everywhere appears. The whole surface is covered with scoriæ, blocks of burned stone ejected by subterranean fires abound, and crateriform hills are seen in every direction. At Wellington, the southern extremity of the Northern Island, shocks of earthquake of greater or less intensity are not uncommon, but Auckland has been free from these visitations since its settlemeht, while right through the centre of the same island, from the Bay of Plenty on the north-east to the boundary of the New Plymouth Province on the south-west, there runs a belt of country in which mighty subterranean forces are still at work. The hills in the immediate neighborhood of Auckland, consisting entirely of extinct volcanoes, and usually presenting their respective craters in very perfect form, run from about 400 to 600 feet in height.

GENERAL GOVERNMENT.—Governor and Commander-in-Chief, His Excellency Colonel Thomas Gore Browne, C.B. Private Secretary and Clerk of Executive Council: Captain F. G. Steward. Aide-de-Camp: Ensign H. J. Wynyard, 58th regt. Assistant Private Secretary: James Holt. CABINET MINISTERS:—Colonial Secretary: Hon. E. W. Stafford. Colonial Treasurer: Hon. C. W. Richmond. Attorney-General: Hon. F. Whitaker. Without office: Hon. H. Sewell. Clerk of Council: F. G. Steward. Commissioner of Waste Lands: C. P. O'Rafferty. Auditor-General: Charles Knight. Lands Claims Commissioner: F. D. Bell. Registrar: T. Outhwaite. Registrar-General: J. B. Bennett. Sheriff: L. O'Brien.

GENERAL ASSEMBLY.—LEGISLATIVE COUNCIL: The Honorables G. A. Arney (Chief Justice), R. H. Wynyard, C. B. (Commander of the Forces), T. H.

Bartley, J. A. Gilfillan, John Salmon, W. Swainson, and F. Whitaker, for Auckland. Charles R. Blakiston and H. J. Tancred, for Canterbury John Johnston and Henry Petre, for Wellington. J. Curling, for Napier. Sir S. O. Gibbes, Bart., for Wangarei. W. H. Kenny, for Ouchunga. John H. Harris and James Menzies, for Otago. G. Cutfield, for New Plymouth. M. Richmond and H. Seymour, for Nelson. Speaker: T. H. Bartley. Clerk: J. J. Piercy.

HOUSE OF REPRESENTATIVES.—AUCKLAND.—His Honor John Williamson, T. M. Haultain, W. Brodie, H. Carleton, T. Beckham, J. J. Symonds, T. S. Forsaith, W. C. Daldy, T. Henderson, W. Lee, R. Graham, and F. W. Merriman. WELLINGTON—W. Fox, S. Clifford, J. E. Featherstone, W. B. Rhodes, W. Fitzherbert, A. Renell, A. M. B. Brandon, J. Ferguson. NEW PLYMOUTH—The Hon. C. W. Richmond, C. Brown, A. W. East. NELSON—A. Domett, F. A. Weld, J. Curtis, W. T. L. Travers, Dr. Monro. CANTERBURY—His Honor J. S. Moorhouse, J. S. Ollivier, Crosbie Ward, J. Hall, R. Packer. OTAGO—H s Honor Captain Cargill, J. Macandrew; one vacant. Speaker: Charles Clifford. Chairman of Committees: Hugh Carleton. Clerk: F. E. Campbell.

LAW.—Chief Justice; His Honor George Alfred Arney. Acting Puisne Judge, southern district: H. B. Gresson. There are seven acting Barristers and fifteen Attorneys in Auckland.

CUSTOMS.—Collector and Comptroller of Customs and Navigation Laws and Registrar of Shipping: William Young. Sub-Collectors: T. Bateman, Russell; W. B. White, Mongonui; H. R. Aubrey, Wangarei and Kaipara; G. M. Mitford, Kawhia.

RESIDENT MAGISTRATES.—Auckland: Thomas Beckham. Howick: T. M. Haultain. Onehunga: J. J. Symonds. Russell: James Reddy Clendon. Mongonui: W. B. White. Wangarei and Kaipara: H. R. Aubrey. Whaingaroa: W. Harsant. Waikato; F. D. Fenton. Turanga: H. S. Wardell.

MILITARY.—Colonel commanding: Colonel C. E. Gold, C. B. Major of Brigade: Captain F. R. Stack, 65th Regt. Acting Aide-de-Camp: Capt. G. Wynyard, 58th Regt. Captain W. M. King, commanding Royal Artillery, Auckland. Lieut.-Col. Mould, commanding Royal Engineers, Auckland. Major William H. Kenny, commanding N.Z. Fencibles, Onehunga. Staff Officers: Captain T. M. Haultain, Panmure; Lieutenant J. A. Hickson, Otahuhu; Lieutenant J. J. Symonds, Onehunga. Medical Officer: Staff Surgeon, J. T. W. Bacot, Howick.

COMMISSARIAT.—Ass. Com-Gen.: H. Stanley Jones; ditto, J. C. R. Wood. Storekeeper and Barrack Master: W. Plummer.

MILITIA.—New Zealand Militia: Lieutenant Colonel: Major Henry Matson.

TARIFF.—Ale, beer, cider, and perry, in wood, the gallon, 6d.; ale, beer, cider, and perry, in bottle, the gallon, 1s.; cigars, and snuffs, the lb., 3s.; coffee, chicory, and chocolate, the lb., 2d.; iron, rod, bolt, bar, hoop, and sheet, not otherwise manufactured, per cwt., 1s.; salt, per cwt., 1s.; spirits and strong waters, sweetened or otherwise, strength not exceeding the strength of proof by Sykes's hydrometer, and so on in proportion for any greater strength than the strength of proof, the gallon, 8s.; sugar, raw and refined, of all kinds, and treacle and molasses, the lb., 0½d.; tea, the lb., 3d.; tobacco, the lb., 1s. 3d.; wine, in wood and bottle, containing less than 25 per cent. of alcohol of a specific gravity of ·825 at the temperature of 60 degrees, Fahrenheit's thermometer, the gallon, 3s.; wood, of all kinds, not manufactured into furniture, the cubic foot, 2d.; boots and shoes, hats, apparel of all kinds, and all material for making apparel, jewellery, cutlery, clocks, watches, and plated ware, and all silk, woollen cotton, and linen manufactures (except corn and gunny bags, and wool packs), sperm, stearine, and wax candles (measuring outside packages), the cubic foot, 3s.; all other goods, wares, and merchandise (measuring outside packages, the cubic foot, 1s; or at the option of the principal officer of Customs at the port of entry at which the same shall be imported, the cwt.,2s.

DUTY FREE.—All articles for the supply of Her Majesty's land and sea forces; animals, living; bricks, slates, and stones, for building purposes, and mill stones; boats; books, printed, not being account books; bottles full of an article subject to duty; bullion and coin; casks, empty; coal; corn, grain, meal, flour bread, and biscuit; gunpowder, fit only for blasting purposes; iron, pig; machinery, viz., brick and tile making, draining, flax, hay and wool pressing, straw and turnip cutting, reaping, thrashing, and winnowing machines, steam engines and appartus for ditto, and machinery for mills, including hand flour mills; manure; oil, blubber, and bone, being the produce of fish or marine animals; plants, bulbs, trees, and seeds; passengers' personal baggage; ploughs and harrows; specimens illustrative of natural history; tobacco for sheep wash, subject to its being rendered unfit for human consumption, and to such regulations as the Governor shall from time to time prescribe in that behalf.

AUCKLAND PROVINCIAL GOVERNMENT.—SUPERINTENDENT: John Williamson. EXECUTIVE COUNCIL.—F. W. Merriman, J. Brennan, Henry Matson, and Daniel Pollen. Chief Clerk and Treasurer: Daniel Pollen. The Auckland Provincial Council consists of twenty-four members, representing six districts, with a Speaker, W. Powditch. Land Surveyor: C. P. O'Rafferty. Road Surveyor: Allan O'Neil. Inspector: Thomas Russell. Law Officer: F. W. Merriman. Harbor Master and Pilot at Auckland: I. J. Burgess. Harbor Master at Russell: E. Bolger. Harbor Master and Pilot at Manukau: T. Wing. Pilot at Hokianga: J. Martin. Pilot at Kaipara: J. Stanaway. Registrar of Deeds: Robert Kelly. Surgeon and Health Officer: W. McGauran. Coroners: Auckland—H. J. Andrews; Wangarei—T. B. Kinderdine. Inspector of Armed Police: James Naughten. Sergeant Major: Charles Brown. Guard-room: Old Post Office, High-street.

INSTITUTIONS AND SOCIETIES AT AUCKLAND.—Mechanics' Institute; Choral Society; Chamber of Commerce; Auxiliary of British and Foreign Bible Society; Young Men's Christian Association; Auckland Museum; Auckland Farmers' Club; St. Andrew's Society; Hibernian Benevolent Society; Independent Order of Odd Fellows. M.U.: Fountain of Friendship Lodge, Good Intent Lodge; Order of Free and Accepted Masons: Lodge Ara, 348, under the constitution of the Grand Lodge of Ireland; Waitemata Lodge, under the English Constitution; Land Association, No. 2.; New Zealand Presbyterian Home Mission; United Society of St. George and St. Patrick; Union Bank of Australia; Oriental Bank; Savings Bank; Australian Mutual Provident Society; Imperial Fire Insurance Company; London and Liverpool Fire and Life Assurance Company; Unity Fire and Life Insurance Company; Northern Assurance Company; Lloyd's Agency.

CHURCHES.—St. Paul's Church, Rev. J. F. Lloyd. St. Matthew's Church, Rev. D. Jones. St. Barnabas' Church, Rev. G. A. Kissling. Church of England.—Lord Bishop: G. A. Selwyn, D.D. Archdeacon: Ven. William Williams, B.A. Canterbury.—Bishop: H. C. Harper, D.D. Archdeacon: Ven. O. Matthias, M.A. Roman Catholic Church.—Auckland.—Bishop: J. F. Pompaliar, D.D. Vicar-Gen.: Very Rev. J. M'Donald. St. Patrick's Church (Roman Catholic). Presbyterian Church, Rev. D. Bruce. Wesleyan Chapels. Primitive Methodist Chapel, Rev. R. Ward. Independent Chapel, Rev. A. Macdonald, Second Independent ditto, Rev. T. Hamer. Baptist Congregation, Rev. James Thornton. Jewish Synagogue.

PUBLIC SEMINARIES AND SCHOOLS.—St. John's College, Bishop's Auckland. Wesleyan College and Seminary. Church of England Grammar School. Episcopalian Day School (St. Paul's). Episcopalian Day School. Episcopalian Infant School. Roman Catholic Day School. Wesleyan Day School. Auckland Academy. Presbyterian School. There are five Ladies' Schools.

NATIVE INSTITUTIONS.—St. Stephen's, Judge's Bay. Three King's Wesleyans). St. Mary's College (Roman Catholic).

POST OFFICE.—Auckland.—Postmaster W. Corbett. Mails are despatched to the following places:—Onehunga, Otahuhu, Papakura, Wairoa, Drury, Mauku Creek, Waiuku, St. John's College, Panmure, Howick, Turanga Creek, Waingaroa, Kawhia, New Plymouth, Waikato, Rangiawhia, Taupo, Napier, Poverty Bay, Coromandel, Mahurangi, Wangarei, Bay of Islands, and Mongonui. Between the Bay of Islands, Waimate, and Hokianga, Wangaroa and Monganui, mails are conveyed overland. RATES OF POSTAGE.—Inland and Intercolonial Letters,—Not exceeding ½ oz., 2d.; not exceeding 1 oz., 4d.; not exceeding 1½ oz., 6d.; and so on, 2d. for every ½ oz. Letters to the United Kingdom.—Not exceeding ½ oz., 6d.; not exceeding 1 oz., 1s.; not exceeding 2 oz., 2s.; and so on, 1s. for every oz. Letters for transmission through the United Kingdom to British Colonies and Foreign Countries, are liable to various additional Rates, tables of which may be seen at every Post Office: thus, on a letter for Canada or the United States of America, not exceeding ½ an ounce, the extra rate is 8d., and the total pre-payment here must be 1s. 2d. In addition to all the foregoing rates Letters posted at any Country Office in the Province are liable to pre-payment of the local post rate at 2d. per ½ oz. Registration of Letters,—Fee 1s. The Letters must be presented one hour before the closing of the mail.

PRINCIPAL PLACES IN NEW ZEALAND.—Auckland; Aotea; Akaroa; Bay of Islands, Motu Mea Islet; Bream Head; Banks Peninsula, East Head; Bluff Harbor; Cape Maria Van Diemen, Cape Islet; Cape Brett; Cape Colville; Cape Egmont; Cape Palliser; Cape Foulwind; Cape Farewell; Cape Campbell; Coromandel Harbor; East Cape, Islet; Great Barrier, Nagle Cove; Hokianga, Flagstaff; Kaipara, North Head; Kawhia; Kapiti, Mahew Islet; Kaikora Peninsular, East Head; Lyttleton, Port Cooper; Mount Egmont (8,270 feet); Mongonui, White's Point; Mount Cook (13,200 feet); Mercury Bay; Manukau Harbor, North Head; Massacre Bay, Motupipi; Molyneux Bay, Landing Place; North Cape, Cape Islet; New Plymouth; Nelson; Otago, Tairoa Head; Poverty Bay; Point Rodney; Pigeon Bay; Port Napier; Port Hardy; Port Gore; Port Underwood; Port Pegasus; Queen Charlotte's Sound, Motuera Island; South Cape; Three Kings, N. E. extreme; Tauranga, Bay of Plenty; Tory Channel, White Rocks; Wangaroa, Peach Island; Waikato Heads; Wangarei Harbor, Lord's Point; Whaingaroa, West Coast; Wanganui; Wellington, Pipitea Point.

WELLINGTON.

Wellington is in latitude 41° 16′ 40″ south, longitude 174° 47′ 53″ east. High-water full and change, 10 hours 20 minutes; rise, 8 feet at springs.

The province of Wellington comprises all that portion of the Northern Island of New Zealand which extends from the 39th degree of south latitude; bounded on the north by the province of Auckland, on the south by the sea, on the east by the sea, and on the west by the province of New Plymouth to the mouth of the river Patea; contains 9,728,000 acres, 2,446,000 of which were on the 13th November, 1857, declared open for selection and purchase.

This was the first settlement in New Zealand, having been founded in January, 1840. The harbor of Port Nicholson is very fine, and the most central in New Zealand. Its advantageous position in reference to the other settlements of the colony is apparent on a glance at the map. The subsidiary settlements of Wanganui and Ahuriri are within this province.

The population of Europeans is about 11,000, and the township of Wellington has about 3,700 inhabitants.

Slight shocks of earthquake are felt more or less throughout the whole of the southern and eastern part of the north island of New Zealand; they are generally scarcely perceptible, but there have been two experienced in Wellington in a greater degree than elsewhere.

Wellington is perhaps more generally known as having been the principal seat of the late New Zealand Company's operations in their colonizing efforts; it now constitutes one of the six provinces into which the New Zealand Islands are divided. Its geographical position and other natural advantages mark its commercial and political importance, which viewed in connexion with the increasing population of the southern provinces, the development of their vast resources, and the accumulating wealth and influence of the settlers, leave no reasonable doubt as to the place which Wellington must eventually occupy in relation to the islands generally.

The prospects of the province are now defined; with an extensive back country, gradually advancing in importance by the location of enterprising settlers, all that would appear to be required to shew its capabilities is a steady influx of population, accompanied by a due proportion of capital. The colonists are in the enjoyment of institutions which enable them to manage their own public affairs. The extremities of the province are brought together by regular steam and other communication, and a considerable coasting trade has been established.

Farms and sheep stations are studding the country; inland towns are now being formed; three have already been established in the valley of the Wairarapa, others on the east coast, and arrangements are being made in available situations in other directions, to concentrate and locate a portion of the population.

Inland communication has been so far provided for by means of admirably constructed roads, as to enable vehicles of all descriptions to traverse at least seventy miles towards and through the Wairarapa Valley; and on the Great North-Western-road, no impediment exists between Wellington and Wanganui, a distance of 120 miles, passing through the fertile districts of Manawatu, Rangitikei, and Turakina. Wool and other productions are frequently forwarded by these lines. The importance of these public improvements is besides materially felt in their influence upon trade, not only by opening up the country and offering inducements to settlement, but by the increased demand for articles of daily consumption.

Many circumstances contributed in the infancy of this settlement to aid the fluctuations both in the import and export trade of the Port of Wellington, arising principally from the undecided occupations of the inhabitants, and the uncertain state of the land question, which operated powerfully in retarding the development of the resources of the country, by obstructing the tide of immigration, and otherwise checking the employment of capital and labor; and it was only by the removal of this difficulty that a feeling of confidence sprang up, the foundation of a permanent and increasing demand for British manufactures was established, and the real productive power of the province began to exhibit itself.

The varied nature of the exports is an encouraging feature in the progress of the trade of Wellington. The fisheries once so productive, and constituted, in the first years of the colonisation of this part of New Zealand, the chief source of wealth, realizing in 1844 and 1846 an export valued at £18,000 and £17,000 respectively, have been almost abandoned.

The timber trade is a source from which much should be expected, as it only requires an extended application of machinery to establish itself. These, with the staple article of wool, amounting in value as an export in 1857 to £70,000, and rapidly increasing in quantity, together with the general provision trade, valued in 1854, at £28,463, will no doubt for some years constitute the chief exports of themselves sufficient to make Wellington a commercial depôt in these islands.

Nearly 5,000,000 acres of land have been purchased from the natives in this province, of which, in round numbers, 4,000,000 acres are open for sale. The sales of land for 1857 amounted to £63,734. It is expected that the Manawatu district, which contains several hundred thousand acres of the richest agricultural land, will be thrown open for settlement in the course of a few months.

The Committee of the Chamber of Commerce at Wellington, at the annual meeting, held July 28, 1858, issued a report (from which some of the above facts have been taken), containing statements under the following heads:—Steam Postal Service, Customs, Tariffs, Light-houses, Insolvency Laws, Joint Stock Companies, Arbitration, Post Office, Supreme Court, Banking Establishments, Finances, Statistical Returns, &c. The subjects are each treated at length, and give evident proof of the progress of this province.

A Lighthouse is in course of erection at the entrance of Wellington Harbor; the light will be visible at a distance of twenty-five miles, and will render the harbor accessible at all hours.

Vessels going down to Wanganui will find a good anchorage under the Island Kapiti, S.S.W.55 miles from Wanganui, and should lay there with S.W. or westerly weather, as it is only a few hours run from Kapiti, with easterly winds, which are fair for taking the bar.

PROVINCIAL GOVERNMENT.—Superintendent: J. E. Featherstone. Provincial Sec.: W. Fitzherbert. Treasurer: J. Woodward. Solicitor: Ade

Batte Brandon. Executive consists of: Secretary, Treasurer and Solicitor, and two unofficial members, W. Fox, and Hon, John Johnston. Speaker of Provincial Council: A. Ludlam. Harbor Master: W. Leslie. Pilot (Wellington): J. Davis. Wanganui: W. Abernethy. Napier: W. Murray. Resident Magistrate (Wellington): H. S. Hill, Wanganui, D. S. Durie; Napi.er, John Curling. Principal Postmaster: J. F. Hoggard. Collector: S. Carkeek. Judge of the Supreme Court: W. Johnston. Chief Commissioner of Waste Land: W. Fox. Principal Surveyor: R. Park.

CHURCHES.—Church of England: Bishop Designate: The Ven. Archdeacon C. J. Abraham, D.D. Archdeacons: The Ven. O. Hadfield and W. Williams. Bishop's Commissary for the Province: Rev. J. A. Baker, M.A. Clergymen: Revs. W. Coleuso, J. Hamlin, T. B. Hutton, H. W. St. Hill, C. H. S. Nicholls, W. Ronaldson, A. Stock, R. Taylor, Riwai Te Atu (native), E. Wheeler, S. Williams. Roman Catholic: Right Rev, Bishop Viard. Very Revs. J. I. P. O'Reilly and J. Forest, V.G. Revs. J. B. Pititjean, J. Lampilla, S. Pezant, E. Reigner and J. Seon. Church of Scotland: Rev. W. Korton. Free Church of Scotland: Revs. John Moir and J. Thom. Presbyterian Church: Rev. D. Hogg and James Duncan. Wesleyan: Revs. James Buller, J. Innis, W. Kirk, W. Woon. Independent: Rev. J. Woodward. Primitve Methodist: Rev. J. Sunth. Hebrew Congregation: Rev. J. E. Myers.

MILITARY.—Major of Brigade: Major N. J. Coote. Lieutenant-Colonel Patience in command at Wanganui, and Lieutenant-Colonel Wyatt in command at Napier (Ahuriri). Dep-Assistant Com-General: A. F. Adams. Dep.-Storekeeper War Department: J. O. Namley. Resident Engineer, Royal Engineer Department: Capt. V. T. Mairis.

TARANAKI OR NEW PLYMOUTH.

The district of Taranaki, which occupies the country around Mount Egmont, has been highly spoken of for the fertility of its soil, the serenity of its climate, or the extent of land available for agricultural purposes. The produce of this part of New Zealand has been very extensive, considering that the European population does not reach 3,500. The anchorage for vessels is indifferent, which is a great drawback to the progress of the district. Considerable quantities of produce have been forwarded to other parts of New Zealand, showing that New Plymouth possesses larger productive powers than any of her neighbors, and was the first to feed itself. When the native and land questions are settled, and the country really opened for settlement, this province will be highly attractive.

The distance from Auckland is about 130 miles

NELSON.

This province comprises all that part of the Middle Island which lies between Cook's Strait on the North, and the Mawera or Grey, in latitude 43 degrees 21 minutes south, and Huranui rivers on the south, and contains 18,000,000 acres of land. Along the western portion of the northern boundary of the province formed by Cook's Straits, is Massacre Bay, containing about 60,000 acres of fertile alluvial land. Rivers and creeks abound. The population of Nelson amounts to about 7,000.

The climate of Nelson is universally admitted to be excellent. One peculiarity of the climate has been stated, namely, that there are only two seasons—summer and winter. Nearly all the indigeneous trees being evergreen, there is no periodical fall or renewal of the leaf. Flowers bloom during the winter months. The scenery generally is beautiful, and travellers have ever spoken highly of the hospitality of the inhabitants.

Nelson is considered by many the most genial climate in New Zealand, and, not like Wellington or Auckland, subject to boisterous winds or continuous rains. The town, though small, is set out square, and surrounded by most picturesque scenery. The inhabitants number about 2000. There appears no doubt from its close proximity to Massacre Bay, to which place a steam vessel is continually plying, as also numerous small craft, that it will become one of the most flourishing towns in the southern province.

Situated in Massacre Bay is Collingwood, recently constituted a port of entry. At this place the River Aouriri empties itself, having received its waters from its tributaries, the Slate and Boulder rivers, besides numerous streams and creeks, whose waters are of unrivalled purity and crystalline appearance; they resemble in many instances streams of molten silver, one in particular, about 16 miles from the port, which the natives have named the Silver Stream. The country in this district is wild and rugged, covered alternately by dense manuka scrub and pine forest. A considerable amount of gold is distributed through this locality, but it is said it will never become a good paying gold field, although much of the precious metal is obtained in the rivers in the dry seasons; at least £100,000 of gold has been exported during the last twelve months. No definite leads are found, as in Victoria, fromthe fact that since the period of gold being displaced from its native sphere, and deposited on the surface of the globe, a continual course of convulsions of a recent date has entirely distorted the features of the country. Yet the amount of gold that will no doubt be permanently obtained will so far enrich this province as to keep the price of labor at a proper and remunerative standard. The natives here are of a very intellectual and crafty class; they obtain a tolerable amount of gold.

Other minerals, such as coal, copper ore, limestone, &c., are found in various parts, but want of labor has hitherto prevented a systematic prosecution of the works. Farming operations are extensive throughout the province. The export of gold during the quarter ending 31st December, 1857, was 6,747, ounces.

NELSON GOVERNMENT.—Superintendent: John Perry Robinson. Executive Council: Provincial Secretary and Commissioner of Crown Lands, Alfred Domett; Provincial Solicitor, Henry Adams; Provincial

Treasurer and Resident Magistrate, John Poynter. Speaker of the Provincial Council: John Wallis Barnicoat. Sheriff and Postmaster: Benjamin Walmsley. Resident Magistrate, Collingwood: H. G. Gouland. Resident Magistrate, Wairau: S. L. Muller. Chief Surveyor: T. Brunner. Collector of Customs, Nelson: D. Rough. Sub-Collector, Collingwood: D. Johnston. Coroner: Jos. F. Wilson. Clerk to Provisional Council: George White. Registrar of Supreme Court: John Sharp. Harbor Master and Pilot: J. S. Cross. Judge of Supreme Court: R. B. Gregson.

CHURCHES.—Church of England: Revs. R. B. Paul (archdeacon), H. F. Butt, J. C Bagshaw (Head Master of Nelson College), T. L. Tudor, R. J. Lloyd, and T. Bowden. Presbyterian: Revs. T. D. Nicholson and P. Calder. Wesleyan: Revs. J. Warren and J. Watkin. Baptist: Revs. D. Dolomore and E. Thomas. Roman Catholic: Revs. A. M. Garin and D. Moreau.

SOCIETIES.—Literary, Nelson School, Horticultural, Musical, and Total Abstinence Societies, Chamber of Commerce. Chess, Turf, and Jockey Clubs. Cook's Straits Mining and Nelson Mining Companies. Nelson Coast Steam Navigation Company. Odd Fellows, M.U., four lodges; and Freemasons, one lodge.

MISCELLANEOUS.—There are several flour mills, saw mills, malthouses, and breweries. The *Nelson Examiner* is published twice a week. The *Colonist* is also published twice a week Hotels are numerous in Nelson, also in Motueka, Waimea, Richmond, Wakapuwaka, and Stoke.

CANTERBURY.

The province of Canterbury occupies the centre of the middle island; it is bounded on the north by the province of Nelson, and on the south by that of Otago; and lies between the parallels 43° and 45° of south latitude. It contains about 12,000,000 acres, of which about 3,000,000, on the east side of a dividing range of snowy mountains, are known to be available land. The country on the west side of the Snowy Mountains has not yet been explored. Of the district on the east side of the mountains, about two-thirds are level, and the remainder, hills of moderate elevation. The whole is admirably adapted for grazing sheep and cattle, being mostly covered with good native grasses; and there is a margin of fine arable land along its seaboard. Banks' Peninsula, which juts out from the middle of the east coast, is a volcanic mountainous district, in a great measure covered with wood. There are four good ship harbors in Banks' Peninsula—Port Victoria, Akaroa, Pigeon Bay and Port Levi.

The climate is healthy, and well suited to Englishmen. The prevailing wind is the sea-breeze from the north-east; a fine cool, wholesome wind. In the spring and summer, there are sometimes strong winds from the north-west, which resemble, on a small scale, the hot winds of Australia. The winter extends from the middle of May to the middle of August

The natives in the province consist of a scattered remnant of former tribes, in number about 300 souls, who live for the most part in villages near the coast.

There are no native wild animals, or noxious reptiles of any kind. The dogs, cats, rats and pigs, which are found in a wild state, were left there by Captain Cook, or have escaped from the settlements. The only objects of sport are wild duck of various kinds, wood pigeons, and quail, of which there are great numbers.

Canterbury was originally promoted by members of the Church of England, and organised under the patronage of the Society for the Propagation of the Gospel in Foreign Parts, for the purpose of making the experiment of founding a Church of England settlement. Only members of that church were invited to join the enterprise, and all the arrangements were made upon strict Church principles. It was, however, found impracticable, and the province is now governed upon the same principle as the colony at large. The first body of colonists arrived in December, 1850. With the exception of a survey of the country, some barracks for the immigrants, and a few houses at Lyttelton, they found that but little preparation had been made for them. Owing, however, to the natural advantages of the country, and the stream of emigration, the colony steadily advanced. Capital, accompanied by a proportion of labor, poured in; and, simultaneously large importations of sheep, cattle and horses, arrived from Australia and Tasmania. A few roads were made to open the country around Christchurch, and the settlers set to work to build, fence and plough.

The population in 1857 was about 6000, of whom about 2000 live in the towns of Christchurch, Lyttelton, Kaiapoi, and Akaroa; upwards of 3000 in the agricultural districts; and about 700 at the sheep and cattle stations. It is covered with natural grass, and is almost entirely occupied by sheep farmers. The export of wool for the year 1858 is expected to reach two millions of pounds. The minimum price of land in this province is £2 per acre; yet it has advanced more rapidly than any other part of New Zealand. In the other provinces the minimum price of land is 10s. per acre.

Lyttelton is the principal post town, and is situated on the north side of Port Victoria. There is good anchorage in five fathoms water, about five miles from the heads, and the harbor is perfectly easy of access. Lyttelton is a town of about 800 inhabitants, and contains the custom house, bank (Union Bank of Australia), principal post office, resident magistrate's court, town hall, hospital, gaol, merchants' offices, and warehouses, and retail stores and shops. The sittings of the Supreme Court are also held there. Its population is chiefly engaged in supplying the shipping, and in carrying on the commerce of a place which pays about £20,000 a-year in customs duties, and has an export trade rapidly increasing, and already amounting to £80,000 in value. The trade between Lyttelton and the inland country is carried on by small sailing craft. The land communication is confined to horse-roads over the hills, which separate Port Victoria from the plains. The "Lyttelton Times" is published twice a week.

Christchurch, the capital, is on the banks of the river Avon, about seven miles from the sea, eight from Lyttelton, and two from the river Heathcote, where steamers and small craft take in and discharge their cargoes It is a dry, healthy site, and is in the centre of the agricultural districts. Its inhabitants number nearly 1000; and the superintendent's office, provincial government offices, council chamber, office of the land and survey departments, registration of deeds office, post-office, bank (Union Bank of Australia), library, college, bishop's residence and principal schools are established there. It has a weekly newspaper, the "Canterbury Standard;" and a produce market is held every Saturday.

Kaiapoi is about ten miles from Christchurch, on the banks and near the mouth of the river Wai Makariri (or Courtenay), up which vessels, drawing five or six feet of water, can go up as high as the town. It is the centre of a very rich agricultural district, and the shipping port of a large pastoral tract. There are upwards of 20,000 acres of fine land in its immediate neighbourhood yet unselected.

Akaroa is a small town on the harbor of the same name, in Banks' Peninsula. It is rather isolated from the rest of the province, but is the resort of the whaling ships that fish off the coast. It was founded in 1840 by the French, who, however, only planted a few settlers there. The district is richly timbered, and the climate is milder than that of the plains; the vine flourishes here, and the gardens are abundantly stocked with all sorts of garden fruit.

Timaru is a town situated on a roadstead near the southern end of the province, and is the outlet for a large pastoral district.

Roads have been constructed through the agricultural districts, but elsewhere, generally speaking, the country is so dry and sound that it was unnecessary to form any road whatever. The road from the wharves, where the boats discharge and take in their cargoes to Christchurch, is an excellent metalled road. The great north road from Christchurch is now completely drained, and all the requisite ferries, bridges and culverts completed. The great south road has few natural obstructions, and drays can traverse the country in almost all directions. Several other roads are made from the capital to open up the land through the farming districts. There is an abundant supply of metal in all directions.

One cause of the steady advance of the settlement has been the export of wool. There are now about three hundred thousand sheep in the province. The sheep runs average from about 10,000 to 30,000 acres in extent. The price of sheep may be quoted at about 25s. to 30s. There are about 15,000 head of cattle, and abundance of rich pastures in the neighbourhood of the great swamps which lie along the coast. A considerable amount of butter and cheese is made for the home and Australian markets, and oxen are chiefly used for draught purposes. Heifers may be quoted at from £5 to £7. A good milch cow brings a high price; and as much as £20 is sometimes given. Good bulls fetch their full value.

Horses are still too scarce to be kept for the purposes of breeding only; and the increase in this stock is derived mainly from mares in use for draught or riding; but the climate and the country seem particularly favorable for horse breeding.

There are about 25,000 acres fenced, and 500 acres bearing grain and potatoes. Most of the farming is still rough, but there are some very highly and carefully cultivated estates. A good deal of the best machinery has been imported from England, and much of the threshing is now done by steam power. The soil in the agricultural districts is of good quality, and varies from light loam on a gravelly subsoil to a strong loam on a subsoil of marl or stiff clay. The clover pastures are very rich. The price of farm produce is very fluctuating; and wheat has varied from 4s. to 10s., or even 12s. per bushel. Attention is being now paid to the rearing of trees, especially English forest trees.

Coal exists along the eastern base of the Snowy Mountains; and one seam is being successfully worked at the Malvern hills, about 30 miles from Christchurch. Limestone is found in the northern part of the province. There is also a good building stone on the hills of Banks' Peninsula. There are plenty of fish off the coast. The mountain range in which gold is now found in Nelson extends all through the province of Canterbury. Timber is scarce, there being only a few woods in the neighbourhood of the towns and agricultural districts. The large forests lie at the base of the mountains and on Banks' Peninsula.

The resident Magistrate holds a Court at the towns of Lyttelton, Christchurch and Kaiapoi, weekly, for hearing petty criminal cases, and civil cases where not more than £20 is at issue. He also holds a quarterly session at Lyttelton and Christchurch, for the hearing of civil cases, in which sums up to £100 are involved. In this court a jury of four may be called in by either party to the suits. A Criminal Court of quarter sessions is held at Lyttelton every three months, for the trial of all but capital felonies; and the Supreme Court is held at Lyttelton, as occasion may require, by the Judge who resides at Wellington.

The religious bodies are unsupported by the Government, and each denomination provides its own establishment, but the Government, in devoting sums for educational purposes, appropriated the amount proportionately. The

Canterbury Association set apart a certain amount of the proceeds of the land sales to form an endowment for the support of clergymen of the Church of England: a bishop, an archdeacon, and ten clergymen form its staff; but the Wesleyans and the Presbyterians have erected churches, and provided funds for the maintenance of their respective ministers. A college for the education of youth has been founded at Christchurch; it possesses endowments in land. There are besides many schools, both public and private. By a recent ordinance, the sum of £2500 a year for five years, has been appropriated out of the public revenues to purposes of education.

In a colony so recently founded, there are, of course, but few amusements. A choral-class has been established both at Lyttelton and Christchurch. There is an annual cattle-show held at Christchurch, where there is also an annual ploughing match and horse races. Horticultural exhibitions are held both at Lyttelton and at Christchurch, and there is a public regatta at Lyttelton annually on the Queen's Birthday. The 16th of December is kept as a public holiday throughout the province, to commemorate the landing of the first settlers. Cricket is a favorite amusement among all classes.

There is a regular daily mail between Christchurch and Lyttelton, and delivery of the letters in those towns. A mail also runs once a week from Lyttelton to Akaroa, and twice a week from Christchurch to Kaiapoi.

Part of the province of Canterbury was originally called the Canterbury Block, and was placed at the disposal of the Canterbury Association under Act of Parliament. The rest of the province was subject to land regulations made by Sir George Grey. By the Constitution Act, the power of making laws respecting the land, was originally reserved to the General Assembly; but this has been since altered, and the waste lands are now entirely at the disposal of the provincial governments.

The provincial legislature of Canterbury has cancelled all the old regulations, and has established one set of regulations to apply to the whole province.

The lands are divided into public reserves, town lands, rural lands and pastoral lands. Town lands are sold by auction at an upset price, to be fixed by the legislature. All the lands in Lyttelton and Christchurch have been sold. There is a small quantity of town land in Akaroa, and Timuru is but just brought into the market; in the latter the upset price is £12 for the quarter acre section. Rural land is sold at a fixed price of £2 per acre. There is a limit as to the form of the section, to prevent undue monopoly of a frontage, but none as to size, from twenty acres upwards. A trigonometric and topographical survey of the country extends for several miles beyond the purchased land. There are certain old pre-emptive rights overhanging a limited extent of land, principally in the neighbourhood of Christchurch; but these rights are rapidly dying out, and only a very small portion of the available land is affected by them.

Until applied for to be purchased, all land is open for pastoral purposes. There are three classes of runs; those under 1000 acres, those above 1000 and under 5000 acres, and those of greater extent. The government has power to give waste land in payment for two objects: 1. As compensation for private lands taken for public roads, by consent of the owner. 2. In payment for public work done under contract for the government. Thus a man can undertake to construct a road or build a bridge to his own farm, and can receive payment by selecting a piece of land to the extent of one acre for every £2 worth of work done. There are a few runs in the district, outside the Canterbury Block, still held under old leases, issued by Sir George Grey; these were leases for fourteen years. The Provincial Council of Canterbury, in altering the regulations, made it optional for all squatters to exchange their licenses and leases for licenses under the new regulations. All those within the Canterbury Block exchanged, but those outside the block mostly retained their old leases.

The maps deposited at the office of Miles, Kington & Co., Melbourne; and Gilchrist, Watt & Co., Sydney, the agents of the Provincial Government in these towns, respectively show the lands open for purchase.

PROVINCIAL GOVERNMENT.—Superintendent: His Honor W. S. Moorhouse. Speaker: Charles Bowen. Executive Council: R. Packer and W. J. W. Hamilton, Members of Council for Christchurch, Lyttelton, Christchurch Country District, and Akaroa. Clerk to Council: G. A. E. Ross. President of Executive Council, Resident Magistrate, Commissioner of Police, and Sheriff: H. Tancred. Harbor Master, &c.: J. Parsons. Collector of Customs: W. J. W. Hamilton. Postmaster at Lyttelton: W. L. Howard. Magistrate, &c., at Akaroa: J. Watson. Postmaster at Akaroa: J. Watson.

CHURCHES.—Bishop of the Diocese: Henry J. Chitty Harper, D.D. Archdeacon: Ven. O. Matthias, M.A. Clergymen: Rev. C. Mackie, W. W. Willock, J. Wilson, G. Cotterill, B. W. Dudley, W. Aylmer, and H. Jacobs. Wesleyan Minister: Rev. John Aldred.

SOCIETIES, &c.—Agricultural and Botanical and Lyttelton Horticultural Societies; Lyttelton Colonists, Christchurch Colonists, Lyttleton Loan, Lyttelton Choral, and Christchurch Harmonic Societies. Cricket, Jockey, and Chess Clubs. Freemasons, several Lodges. Lyttelton Savings' Bank.

MISCELLANEOUS.—There are several first-class hotels and boarding houses, and a considerable number of professional and tradespeople in Lyttelton and Christchurch. The *Canterbury Standard* is published weekly.

OTAGO.

This is the most southerly settlement in New Zealand, and includes more land than any other province in the colony, having a surface of 16,000,000 acres. Its inhabitants, principally, are Scotch, being founded by them in 1848, in connexion with the New Zealand Company. The province is governed by a Superintendent and Provincial Council, all elected by the people. The climate is temperate, though colder than the other settlements The town of Dunedin, the capital of the province, is nine miles from the port. The European population is about 6,000; while there are about 500 natives scattered on their own lands in various parts.

There is an excellent harbor at the Bluff, a large district in the province, and another at Invercargill, which is about 120 miles south of Port Chalmers and the chief town of Dunedin.

The province of Otago lies at the extreme south of the Middle Island, and is washed on three sides by the waters of the Pacific Ocean, while it is bounded on the north by the province of Canterbury. It extends from Foveaux Strait to the Wiatangi River, in S. lat. 44° 50′, and from 166° 30′ to 171° E. long., and has thus an area of about 30,000 square miles. The whole of the Middle Island is traversed by a chain of lofty mountains, varying in altitude from 4000 to 13,200 feet, and covered with perpetual snow. There are three large lakes in the interior of the province, but their existence and position on the map rest solely on native testimony. Otago is a country abounding in streams of the purest water; seven of the largest rivers in New Zealand flow through its plains. Near Dunedin, on the south, there are three plains, where the early settlers have purchased 40,000 acres of fine level land; while on the north, there are extensive tracts of arable land, which have been let as sheep-runs for a period of fourteen years. The southern plains are the largest in the province, and contain land of every description. Men of capital have been attracted to this district, and the surveyors are at present laying off a block of 600,000 acres to meet this class of purchasers.

Otago was founded in 1848 by the New Zealand Company in London and the Otago Association in Edinburgh. The company sent a competent surveyor, Mr. Tuckett, accompanied by Colonel Wakefield, to that part of the Middle Island lying south of Nelson, to select the finest harbor and district they could find for the colony. 400,000 acres were attached to the towns of Port Chalmers* and Dunedin, and the sale and colonisation of them handed over to the Otago Association. The company appointed Captain Cargill to be their resident agent,

* Port Chalmers was named after the illustrious Dr. Chalmers, and Dunedin is the Gaelic name of Edinburgh.

a man well qualified to lead his countrymen in any enterprise; and so universally has he been esteemed by the colonists, that they have twice conferred upon him the highest civic honors which it is in their power to bestow. Emigration is now carried on by the Provincial Council through their agents in Great Britain.

The grand feature of the climate of Otago is its mild and uniform temperature. The summers are as far removed from the heat of Australia as the winters are from the cold of Canada. Three causes combine to produce this uniformity, viz., the latitude, prevailing winds, length and breadth of the Middle Island, and its mountains. The latitude and longitude of New Zealand correspond to that of France and Spain, and the inhabitants of Otago are the antipodes of those who live in the south of France. The town of Dunedin is three degrees nearer the equator than Paris, yet the mean temperature of both places is nearly the same. The absence of the extremes of heat and cold appears to depend upon the size of the island, and the prevailing winds. The Middle Island is 500 miles long by 150 broad; and lying, as it does, in a slanting direction across eight degrees of longitude and six degrees of latitude, the easterly and westerly gales are intercepted, and are bent to the shape of the coast, and hence north-east and south-west winds are those which prevail, and communicate to the land the equable temperature of the Pacific Ocean. It is a remarkable phenomenon, that when the wind blows from the snowy mountains (N.W.), it is always warm, and is the sure forerunner of a south-wester. The N.W. wind blows on an average one day in each month, and is sometimes accompanied by lightning. The mildness of the winter is such, that the farmer would prefer more frost to destroy the weeds; but this, again, is counterbalanced by other advantages, such as breaking up new land when the ground is moist, and carrying on all kinds of out-door work as in summer.

The provinces of Otago and Auckland being furthest removed from Cook's Strait, which divides the North and Middle Islands, were not affected by the earthquake that took place on the 23rd of January, 1855. These periodic shocks occur but once every seven years, and are not attended with danger to life. For the last twenty years their influence has been chiefly confined to the east corner of Cook's Strait, so that the inhabitants of Otago (who are 400 miles S.W. of this point) are no more affected by an earthquake in that quarter than the people of Great Britain are by an eruption of Vesuvius.

There are three harbors on the east coast of the province, named respectively the Otago, the New River, and Bluff harbors. The first of these, which is the principal one for commerce, is that from which the province derives its name, and is about 200 miles from Canterbury. This loch or arm of the sea is fourteen miles long, and is a picture of such uncommon beauty that the eye never wearies of looking on it. The hills that surround it are of every shape, densely wooded; and so luxuriant is the vegetation, that the trees never cease growing till they have dipped their branches two or three feet into the salt water. The Otago Harbor is divided by two islands into an upper and lower harbor, with sand-banks in each of them. The channel in the lower harbor resembles the letter ∞ made the wrong way, as on its side. The tide rises six feet, and covers an area of twenty-six square miles. The tidal flow of this volume of water is through a narrow entrance a quarter of a mile broad. The current is equal to three miles an hour, which is of great service to small vessels working up against the south-west wind. The west coast and its harbors present an aspect altogether different from the eastern. There are twelve magnificent harbors on the west of the province, fit for the largest vessels in the world; indeed, it is impossible to imagine a coast line better provided with places of refuge. Beautiful as these harbors are to the eye, they are almost useless to the province from two causes. First, their great depth. Many of them are so deep that no ship's cable could reach to the bottom. The other objection is the greater of the two: the range of mountains which skirts the head of the western harbors prevents all access to the interior of the country, so far as is yet known. Mount Cook, named after one of Britain's most distinguished navigators, almost rivals the Alps of Europe in height, attaining, as it does, nearly 13,000 feet of elevation above the sea. Mount Aspiring forms a magnificent spectacle, not only owing to its great altitude, viz., 9,135 feet above the sea, but owing to its bold and symmetrical shape of a steep cone or spire. The mountains in the vicinity of the Wanaka and Hawea Lakes are Black Peak, 7,328 feet; Pesa, 6,426 feet; and Grandview, 4,703 feet above the sea. The Wanaka Lake is 1036 feet above the same level. The Eyre Mountains rise 6,084 feet, and the Dome 4,505 feet above the sea level; Takituna, 4,998 feet; Hamilton, 4,674 feet; Lingwood, 2,602 feet; Ida, 5,498 feet; Kyeburn, 5,129 feet; Rock and Pillaux, 4,675 feet; Benmore, 6,111 feet; Totara Peak, 5,876; St. Cuthbert, 4,962 feet; Mount Cargill is 2,297 feet, and Mihinaka 1,895 feet above the level of the sea.

The Provincial Council of Otago consists of nineteen members, elected by persons twenty-one years of age, who have been six months resident in the colony. The Executive Government is vested in the Superintendent and three members of Council.

In the early days of the settlement, all denominations worshipped under the same roof. The Church of Otago was composed of members of the Free Church of Scotland; members of the Church of England; the Established Church of Scotland; the Lutheran Church of Sweden; English and Irish Presbyterians; Methodists; Baptists; United Presbyterians;

and Independents,—all worshipped together for five years; and if they had certificates of membership from clergymen, they were, *and still are*, admitted to the same privileges as members of the Free Church of Scotland. In 1853, those in communion with the Church of England were joined by one of their own clergymen, the Rev. J. A. Fenton, and they have sent for another clergyman. There is a Presbytery in Otago, which meets twice a year. The members are, the Rev. T. Burns, the Rev. W. Will, the Rev W. Bannerman, and the Rev. W. Hood.

Denominational Schools are established at Dunedin, Port Chalmers, and their vicinities, Taieri East, Taieri West, Native Village and Waihola, Tokomairiro, South of Tokomairiro, Waikouaiti, Goodwood, Moeraki, and Waitaki. The total number of scholars is 2,750. The Local Government have established a system of provincial education.

Of Minerals, gold has been detected in the Maturna, and very generally on the Waiopai plains, also in the Tuapeka and Lindis, but its existence in remunerative quantities has not yet been made apparent. Coal is very generally distributed, and is found frequently of very fair quality, notwithstanding that surface coal only has as yet been taken out. Coal and lignite are formed on either slope of the Kurai and Kakanui Mountains, and the Horse Range; these are exposed to view in various river beds. The districts of the lower Taieri, Tokomairiro, Clutha, Pomahawk, and Mataura also possess these stores of subterannean fuel. Limestone is met with abundantly on the Maruwhenna, Waireka, Awamoko, Kakanui, and Shag rivers. It is also found near Dunedin, at the Waihola Lake, in the Waiau, Oraisea, Aparima, and Mataura rivers. Flagstones and roofing slate are found in the Maruwhenna and Kakanui. Such is a very superficial view of the formations and mineral fields of the province hitherto discovered.

The extent of the Province and its natural divisions must be considered. The surveys executed during 1856 and 1857, have extended over 15,407 square miles, and there remain to be surveyed 11,233; the whole area of the province being 26,640 square miles, or 17,049,600 acres. In the surveyed districts the natural divisions consist of forest, 1,329 square miles; pasture, 12,516; swamp, 144; barren, 1,309; and lakes, 109. In the unsurveyed districts the natural divisions can only be approximated to; and it is believed that about 2,500 square miles of natural pasture will yet be found in them; while the remaining 8,733 consist of barren snowy mountains and wooded valleys.

New Zealand has never been cursed with convict labor. When Earl Grey, some years ago, asked the provinces if any of them would accept of this moral blight, the universal voice of all the provinces was, Away with them! we will not enrich ourselves to the ruin of posterity and our adopted land.

Otago, like all other British colonies, is peopled from every quarter of the globe, but its pith and stamina is British blood. Foreigners are not entitled to a vote in public affairs; but if they renounce their own country, and apply to the Sheriff to be naturalised, they are admitted to all the privileges of British subjects.

The province of Otago has but recently been adapted to people of agricultural and pastoral pursuits. Of this there are many evidences, the most wonderful of which is the sudden decrease of the aborigines during the last half century. Though once numerous, they have destroyed themselves by the scourge of war. The settler of the Middle Island has nothing to fear from man, beast, or reptile. The native population in Otago amount to 500, and, as there are very few births amongst them, it is to be feared that the race will be extinct before the close of the present century. 16,000 acres were reserved for them when they sold the province to the Crown.

The town of Dunedin is situate at the head of the Otago harbor, from the opposite side of which, although the houses are not numerous, it has even now a fine appearance. In front of the town lies the Dunedin Bay, with its boats sailing about, the small craft at anchor. On the other side is seen the dark blue of the Pacific Ocean; and, in the background, Mount Flagstaff is seen towering far above the town and surrounding country, giving it such a picturesque and beautiful appearance that it is looked upon as one of the finest landscapes in New Zealand. The built part of the town has a fine cool brook running through the centre of it, and the surveyed town is bounded on the N.W. by a clear stream, flowing from Mount Flagstaff, yielding a supply of pure water sufficient for the largest city in Britain.

The land is naturally divided into agricultural and pastoral. That most suitable for agricultural purposes can be purchased, in any part of the province, at the low price of ten shillings per acre. Flax and grass land can be got in any quantity, and is the only kind cultivated now; it is cleared at a much less outlay than bush land. Flax land is prepared for the plough at from twenty-five to thirty shillings per acre; grass land at fifteen shillings. The cost of fencing for the last five years has varied according to the vicinity of a wood and the supply of labor, and may be reckoned at from 12s. to 21s. per chain of sixty-six feet. The most common fencing in Otago is a ditch four feet wide, a turf dike two and a half feet high, and two rails on the top. In the town, split paling only is used. Wire-fencing has also been introduced.

The soil of the province of Otago is excellent, and well adapted to the cultivation of grain of all kinds. Its depth, however, cannot be judged of by the height of the crops grown, as flax has been found growing ten feet high upon a soil not more than six inches in depth; and luxuriant crops of wheat have been raised from soil five inches deep. The climate of Otago is the real source of its fertility, and when the soil is exposed to its influence for six months it yields a much greater crop. Inch Clutha, Waikouaiti, and other localities, have rich soil from two to three feet deep, which yields forty-six bushels per acre, and has a growth of such strength that it is cut three feet above the ground, in order to save the threshing-mill. The heaviest timber in the colony grows upon Inch Clutha, an Island seven miles long, in the centre of the Clutha River, with fine natural scenery.

The colony is suitable as well for the man of substance as for the man of small means. Estates of from 2,000 to 100,000 acres of land, rich, level, and dry, may be purchased, either for pastoral or agricultural purposes; or, if capital be invested in sheep, a depasturing license may be obtained for any number of sheep not exceeding 25,000, on payment of a deposit of £20. The applications for Runs have been far in excess of the extent of country at present available; but as fresh country is opened up, and first applicants fail to stock within the time limited, parties on the spot are likely to get suited.

The Merino is the only breed of sheep that is yet reared in Otago. They are usually imported from Sydney or Twofold Bay, and have for some years been landed at Port Chalmers. In 1856 there were 333,314 lbs. wool exported to Britain and elsewhere, the estimated value of which was £19,316. The advantages of sheep-farming are so apparent to persons of small means, that many of them invest in sheep. In 1855, there were seventy-six thousand sheep, and in 1856, one hundred and thirty thousand.

For the last few years, emigration to Otago has been chiefly carried on by residents in the colony sending for their friends, but the supply has not been equal to the demand, or even to fill up the vacancies for tradesmen, shepherds, and laborers, who have become their own employers.

Large sums have been spent in taking laborers from Melbourne, but along with them went purchasers of land to the extent of 10,000 acres, so that the demand for laborers, instead of being lessened, was rather increased. To remedy this state of things, the Provincial Council have voted the sum of £20,000 as a permanent fund for emigration; those availing themselves of this fund having to repay the amount of assistance they may receive from it, within a period to be agreed upon - either one, two, or three years.

Five hundred persons in Great Britain have been applied for by their friends in Otago, who have given a guarantee to the Provincial Government to repay their passage-money, which is £8,000. This is one of the strongest proofs of their prosperity, for it is unreasonable to suppose that they would invite their friends to leave home and certainty in Britain, for an uncertainty in Otago. Every man without means must, at the outset, be prepared for an extra effort; if he be unwilling for this, he is unfit for any province in New Zealand.

The class of emigrants who apply for passages must produce unexceptionable certificates of moral character, and their skill must be of the kind that the settlement requires, viz., shepherds; ploughmen; agricultural laborers, who can ditch, and fence, reap; female domestic servants and dairywomen; sawyers, and country mechanics.

The area of the province is 16,000,000 acres; land sold 70,000 acres; depasture runs taken up 81 acres; extent of runs 1,000,000 acres.

The population on the 31st December, 1857, according to Government returns, was as follows:—Dunedin, 890; Port Chalmers, 89; Eastern District, 592; Western District, 604; Central District, 632; Tokomairiro, 518; Clutha, 174; Murihiku, 147; Nathna District, 464; total, 4,631. The natives in the seven districts numbered 481.

Births, Marriages and Deaths.—Number of births during 1857: males, 88; females, 91—total, 179. Marriages, 38. Deaths: males, 11; females, 10—total, 21. These returns do not include the Maories, or native population.

Revenue and Expenditure.—The revenue from Crown lands for the year ending 31st December, 1857, amounted to £15,200 7s. 9d. The expenditure, £21,363 7s. 9d.

Immigration and Emigration.—During the year 1857, the number of immigrants who arrived in Otago was 589; emigrants, 220. For quarter ending March 31, 1858:—Immigrants, 884; emigrants, 112. From November, 1857, to May, 1858, the total number of immigrants was 1419, from Great Britain, in several vessels.

Shipping.—Vessels inwards and outwards of ports out of New Zealand:—Inwards, 14; outwards, 14. Ports in New Zealand:—Inwards, 39; outwards, 32.

PROVINCIAL GOVERNMENT.—Superintendent: W. Cargill. Clerk: J. Logan. Executive Council: J. McGlashan, W. H. Cutten, and W. C. Young. Provincial Treasurer and Solicitor: J. McGlashan. Clerk: J. A. Cheyne. Provincial Council.—Town of Dunedin: J. Kilgour, A. Rennie, W. H. Cutten, J. H. Harris, W. H. Reynolds. Eastern District: W. Martin, W. C. Young, W. Lambert. Western District: G. Hepburn, J. Glashan, W. Prudie. Central District: J. Macandrew, A. J. Burns, W. Stevenson. Tokomairiro District: J. Cargill. Southern District: J. Shaw, J. Anderson. Northern District: R. Williams. Town of Port Chalmers: vacant. Speaker: J. Macandrew. Clerk: R. Chapman. Collector and Comptroller of Customs and Navigation Laws: C. Logie. Sub-Collector and Deputy Postmaster, Bluff Harbor: A. J. Elles. Sub-Treasury and Postmaster: C. Logie. Deputy Postmaster at Port Chalmers: J. Monson. Registrar of Supreme Court, of Births, Marriages and Deaths, and Official Administrator of Intestate Estates: R. Chapman.

BOARD OF ROAD TRUSTEES.—This Board is composed of the Superintendent and Executive Council, and two representatives from the following districts:—North-east Valley, Wakari, Town, Anderson's Bay, Green

Island, North Taieri, East Taieri, West Taieri, Tokomairiro, Port Chalmers, and Invercargill.

MISCELLANEOUS.—Secretary of General Board of Education, J. M'Glashan. Chief Commissioner of Waste Land Board: W. H. Cutten. Chief Surveyor and Civil Engineer: J. T. Thomson. Harbor Master: C. Logie. Pilot into the Heads: R. Driver. Pilot of the Upper Harbor: W. Stewart. President Mechanics' Institute: James Macarthur. Secretary: W. Langlands. Town Board of Dunedin: A. Rennie, J. Kilgour, G. Smith, G. Duncan, W. H. Cutten, W. Langlands, William Lambert, Dr. Purdie, R. Chapman. Chairman of Flour Company: James Macandrew. Presbytery of Otago.—Dunedin: The Rev. T. Burns. Taiori: The Rev. W. Will. Tokomairiro: The Rev. W. Bannerman. Elders.—Dunedin: Mr. James Macandrew. Taieri: Mr. Richard Runciman. Tokomairiro: Mr. George Brown.

INTERCOLONIAL AND INTERPROVINCIAL STEAM COMMUNICATION.

The New Zealand Royal Mail Steam Packet Company has commenced operations, supported by a subsidy of £14,000 per annum from the British Government and £10,000 from the New Zealand General Government. It is expected that one steamer will run once a month between Auckland and Sydney and another between Cook's Straits (Nelson) and Sydney; an arrangement the more probable as the Victorian Government has, by its arrangement with the Provincial Government of Wellington, forestalled the operations of the company in the direction of Melbourne. Sydney will thus be secured in the undisturbed possession of the trade of the Nelson gold-fields, as well as the whole native trade of the north. The competition may possibly lead to a steamer being placed between Melbourne and Auckland direct, as the N. Z. R. M. Co. will otherwise have two boats unemployed. Their fleet consists of the "Prince Alfred," 1000 tons, 300-horse power; the "Lord Ashley," 600 tons, 100-horse power; the "Lord Worsley," 600 tons, 100-horse power, and the "Arridale," 300 tons, 80-horse power. The "White Swan," s.s. is engaged in the interprovincial service, and the "Queen," s.s. has been purchased by an Otago merchant jointly with a Melbourne firm and is intended for the Otago and Canterbury local trade, with occasional trips to Melbourne. The "Wonga Wonga," s.s. and the "Tasmanian Maid," s.s. are engaged in the Cook's Straits trade.

In addition to the above steamers sailing vessels ply twice a month, or oftener, between Sydney, Auckland and Nelson, having first class accommodation for passengers.

The Government of Victoria and the Provincial Government of Wellington have recently made arrangements with the Australasian Steam Navigation Company to run a steamer between Melbourne and Wellington. It is understood that the steamer will leave Melbourne on the 15th, and Wellington on the first of each month. As several steamers already ply between Wellington and the other ports of New Zealand, passengers from Melbourne will experience no delay in proceeding to the other provinces. The fares between Melbourne and Wellington are:—for cabin passengers, £16 16s., for steerage, £9.

LIST OF WORKS ON AUSTRALIA.

The following Catalogue was prepared at the Public Library, Melbourne, and it is thought its insertion in this HANDBOOK *may prove useful.*

Aborigines' Protection Society, Reports and Extracts.
Angas (G. F.), Savage Life and Scenes in Australia. 2 vols.
——— Views of the Australian Gold Fields.
Anley, The Prisoners of Australia. A Narrative.
Aristides, on Britain, Australia and Africa.
——— Crisis, a Glance at the Forerunners of.
Arthur (Col. G.), Defence of Transportation.
Australia, Impartial Examination of all Authors on.
——— Friend of, Plan for Exploring.
——— How to Farm and Settle in.
——— The Commerce and Finance of.
——— The Draper in.
——— A Voice from the far Interior of, by a Bushman.
——— Its Scenery, Natural History, &c. Religious Tract Society.
——— Hints on Emigration to. 1830.
——— and her Treasures.
——— A Month in the Bush.
——— Emigrants' Guide to ; with Memoir of Mrs. Chisholm.
——— and the Gold Regions, Guide to. By a Liverpool Merchant.
——— Van Diemen's Land and New Zealand. New Liby. U. K.
——— New Zealand, and Tasmania, their Rivers, &c. By an Englishman.
——— and Canada, Emigrants' Guide to. 1844.
——— Western, Journal of Expeditions to. 1829-32.
——— and America, Information for Emigrants to.
Australasian, The.
Australasia, Journal of.
Australiad, The, A Poem.
Australasian League and Conference. Sessional Papers.
Australasian Quarterly Report.
Austral-Asiatic Review, The.
Australian Magazine, The Illustrated.
Australian Question, The. Letters published in South Australian Register.
——— Year Book of Facts.
——— Keepsake. Scenery in New South Wales, &c.
——— The, Practical Hints to Intending Emigrants.
——— Royal Mail Steam Navigation Company. Reports, &c.
——— Settler's, An, Diary of Travels. 2 vols.
B** (M. de), Histoire de l'Expedition de 3 vaisseaux envoyé aux Terres, Australes. Hague, 1739.
Backhouse (J.), Visit to Australia.
——— Extracts from the Letters of.
Bannister (S.), on Abolishing Transportation.
——— (Thos.), Britain and her Colonial Dependencies.
Bartlett (T.), Colonisation and Resources of New Holland,
Bennet (H. G.), Letter to Lord Sidmouth on the Transportation Laws.
Bogue (A.), Steam to Australia.
Bonwick (J.), Geography of Australia and New Zealand.
——— Geography for Young Australians.
Boyd (H. V.), Voice from Australia.
Bright (J.), History of New Zealand and Australia.
British Dependencies open to Colonization, Short description of.
——— Colonial Electric Telegraph Company, Prospectus, &c.

Browning (C. A.), The Convict Ship.
Buckton (T. J.), Western Australia.
Bunce (D.), Australasiatic Reminiscences.
Burdwood (J. R. N.), Australian Directory, 1853. Hydrographic Office.
Butler (S.), Handbook for Australian Emigrants.
——— Emigrant's Handbook of Facts.
Byrne (J. C.), Emigrants' Guide to New South Wales, Australia Felix, and South Australia.
——— 12 Years wanderings in the British Colonies. 2 vols.
C. (W.), Practical Hints for an intending Emigrant.
Campbell (W. E.), on the Crown Lands of Australia.
Capper (J.), Australia as a field of Capital, Skill and Labor.
——— Our Gold Colonies.
——— Emigrants' Guide to Australia.
Carron (W.), Exploration between Rocky Bay and Cape York.
Cassel's (J.) Emigrants' Handbook.
Castilla (F.), Postal Charges considered.
Caswall (H.), Hints from the Journal of an Australian Squatter.
Chambers' Emigrant's Manual. Australia and the Gold Diggings.
Chapman (H. S.), Parliamentary Government for the Australian Colonies.
Church—Bill proposed to be introduced into Legislative Council for enabling the Bishop, &c., to provide for the affairs of the Church.
Clacy (Mrs.), Visits to the Gold Diggings of Australia.
——— Lights and Shadows of Australian Life.
Clarke (W.), Statement respecting Discovery of Gold in Australia.
Cobbold (R.), History of Margaret Catchpole.
Colonial Advocate, The.
——— Land and Emigration Commissioners' Report.
Colonist, The, published by Society for the Promotion of Colonisation.
Colonisation, Society for the Promotion of. Report.
Cooley (W. D.), History of Maritime and Inland Discovery. 3 vols.
Cooper (F.), Adventures in Australia.
Croker (T. C.), Memoirs of J. T. Colt. 2 vols.
Cunningham, (P.), Hints for Australian Emigrants.
Dawson (R.), Present State of Australia.
Delessert, (E.), Voyages dans la Nouvelle Hollande. 1847.
D'Ewes (J.), Sporting in both Hemispheres.
——— China, Australia, and Islands of the Pacific. 1855-6.
Dobson (T.), Australasian Cyclonology.
Earl (G. W.), Capabilities of the North Coast of New Holland.
——— Enterprise in Tropical Australia.
——— Eastern Seas. 1832-4.
Earp (G. B.), What we did in Australia.
Eden (Hon. W.), History of New Holland.
Edwards (W.), What shall we do with our Criminals?
Emigrant and Colonial Gazette—a Weekly Newspaper.
Emigrants' Letters—from Settlers in the British Colonies.
Emigrant Family, The, or Story of an Australian Settler. 3 vols.
Emigration, Hints on.
Erskine (J. E.), on Discoveries of Gold in Australia.
Eyre (E. J.), Journal of Discovery in Central Australia. 1840-1. 2 vols.
Far off Asia and Australia, by author of "Near Home."
Fauchery, Le Mineur en Australie.
Female Emigration Fund, Statement of
Flinders (M.), Voyage to Terra Australis. 1801-2-3. 3 vols.
Frome, Exploratory Journal to Lake Torrens.
Gold Fields, Gleanings from, by an Australian Journalist.
Gowen (J. R.), on Emigration to the Swan and Canning Rivers.
Grey (G.), Expedition of Discovery in N. W. and W. Australia. 1837-9. 2 vols.
Hale (M.B.), Transportation Question: or Why W. Australia should be made a Reformatory Colony.
Hargraves (G.), Australia, its Gold Fields described.
Hayes (Cath.) Sketch of, including her Tour in the Australian Colonies.

Haygarth (H. W.), Bush Life in Australia.
Henty, Claim on the Colonial Government.
Hervey (T. K.), Poetical Sketch Book—Australia.
Hodgkinson (C.), Central Australia—Port Macquarie to Moreton Bay.
Hodgson (C. P.), Reminiscences of Australia.
——— (A.) Emigration to the Australian Settlements.
Hood (J.), Australia and the East in 1841-2.
Howitt (R.), Australia, Historical and Statistic.
——— (W.), Boy's Adventures in the Wilds of Australia.
Hughes (W.), Origin and Condition of the Australian Colonies.
Irwin (F. C.), State of Western Australia. 1835.
Jackson (J. A.), National Emigration to the Australian Colonies.
James (T. H.), Six Months in Australia, Port Phillip, &c.
Johnson (J. P.), Plain Truths regarding Australia, and New Zealand.
Jones (H. B.), Adventures in Australia. 1852-3.
Jorgenson (J.), Narrative of his own Life.
Kerguelen, Relation de ses Deux Voyages dans les Mers Australes.
King (Capt.), Sailing Directions. Inner Route, Torres Straits.
——— Survey of the Inter-tropical and Western Coasts of Australia. 1818-22. 2 vols.
——— Voyage to Torres Straits in search of ship *C. Eaton*.
——— (J., of Irrawang), Australia a Wine growing Country.
King George's Sound, Description of.
Knight (Charles), Settlers and Convicts. 2 vols.
Lancelott (F.), Australia as it is. 1852. 2 vols.
Land and Labour in Australia, by a Port Phillip Squatter.
Land of Promise, or my Impressions of Australia.
Landor (E. W.), The Bushman, or Life in a New Country.
Lang (Dr. J. D.), Account of Cook's Land.
——— Emigrants' Manual for Australia.
——— Origin of the Polynesian Nation.
——— Free om and Independence for the Lands of Australia.
——— Transportation and Colonisation.
Leichhardt (L.), Expedition from Moreton Bay to Port Essington. 1844-5.
Leigh (W. H.), Emigrant, a Tale of Australia.
M'Combie (T.), Essays on Colonisation.
——— Australian Waste Lands Bill considered.
——— Australian Sketches.
MacGregor (J.), Commercial Statistics of all Nations. 5 vols.
MacKay (A.), Tour in the Great Gold Field of Australia.
Mackenzie (D.), Emigrant's Guide with Australian Vocabulary.
——— Ten Years' Practical Experience in Australia.
——— Visit to the Gold Fields of Australia.
Maconochie (A.), Views regarding Convict Management.
——— Australiana; or Convict Management.
——— on the Management of Prisoners in the Australian Colonies.
Malone (R. E.), Account of the state of the Australian Colonies.
Mann (W.), Residence in the Australian Provinces.
Martin (M.), Australian Sketch Book.
——— British Colonial Library 8 vols.
Meinicke (C. E.), Das Festland Australien.
Melville (H.), Present State of Australasia, including New South Wales.
——— Western Australia, South Australia, and New Zealand.
——— Australasia and Prison Discipline.
Merewether (F. L. S.), Reports on Emigration.
Merivale (H.), Lectures on Colonisation and Colonies. 2 vols.
Milligan (Dr.), Memoir on Western Australia (Madras Journal, Oct. 1837).
Mitchell (Major T. L.), Three Expeditions into the Interior of Eastern Australia. 2 vols.
——— Journal of an Expedition into the Interior of Tropical Australia.
——— (now Sir T. L.), Australian Geography.
Month, The.
Moore (G. F.), Letters from the Swan River.

Moore (Hon. G. F.), Evidences of an Inland Sea collected from the Natives of Swan River Settlement.
Morgan (G. O.), Settlers in Australia—a Prize Poem.
Morrison (J. R.), What should the Government do for Australia?
Mossman (S.), Account of the Gold Regions of Australia.
——— and Banister, Travels in Australia.
Mudie (R.) Picture of Australia.
Mundy (Col. G. C.), Our Antipodes, or Rambles in the Australasian Colonies.
Nixon (Bp.), Cruise of the Beacon in Bass's Straits.
Norton, Australian Essays.
Ogle (N.), Emigrants' Manual for Western Australia.
Parker (E. S.), The Aborigines of Australia—a Lecture, May, 10, 1854.
Payne's Patent Process for the Preservation of Wood, Memoir on.
Pearson (L.), Emigrants' Guide to Port Curtis.
Perils, Pastimes, and Pleasures of an Emigrant in Australia.
Phillips (J. A.), Gold-mining; a Scientific Guide for Australian Emigrants.
Perry (R.), Australian Sketches.
Powell (J. G.), Voyage to the Swan River.
Power (W. T.), Three Years in China, Australia, &c. 2 vols.
Pridden (W.), History and Condition of Australia.
Puseley (Dr.), Rise, Progress, and Present Condition of Australia, Tasmania, and New Zealand.
Recollections of Sixteen Years' Sojourn in Australia.
Read what I Heard, Saw, and Did at the Gold Fields.
Remarks on the Maintenance of Macadamised Roads.
Report of Proceedings for Establishment of Steam Communication between the Australian Colonies and New Zealand. 1850.
Rienzi, Mélanésie et Australie.
——— L'Oceanie. 3 vols. 1836-8.
Ritchie (L.), History of Oriental Nations. Australia, &c. 2 vols.
Roberts (J.), Voyage to Swan River and Van Diemen's Land.
Roggevin, Voyage en Australie. 2 vols. Hague, 1739.
Rovings in the Pacific. 1837-49. By a Merchant. 2 vols.
Rowecroft (C.), Tales of the Colonies. 2 series.
Russell (A. A.), Tour through the Australian Colonies. 1839.
Rutter (G. S.), Hints to Gold Hunters.
Shaw (J.), Tramp to the Diggings of Australia. 1852.
Settlers and Convicts, or Australian Backwoods.
Sidney (S.), The Emigrants' Journal.
——— Gallops and Gossips in the Bush.
——— The three Colonies of Australia, New South Wales, Victoria, and South Australia.
——— Australian Handbook.
——— Female Immigration as it is, and as it may be.
Sinclair (J.), Australian Lyre.
Smith (S.), Whether to go and Whither, or the Cape and the Great South Land.
——— The Settler's New Home.
Speeches delivered at the Australian Dinner in London. 1858.
Steam to Australia: the Rival Routes, by X. X. X.
Steam to Australia and New Zealand.
Stewart (R.), Geographical Description of the Australian Countries.
Stirling (P. J.), Australian and Californian Gold Discoveries and their Consequences.
——— (Sir J.), State and Condition of Western Australia.
Stokes (Commander J. L.), Discoveries in Australia. 1837-43. 2 vols.
Strzelecki (P. E. de), Discovery of Gold and Silver in Australia.
Stuchbury, Travels in Australia.
Sturt (Capt. C.), Expedition into Central Australia. 1844-6. 2 vols.
——— Two Expeditions into the Interior of South Australia. 1828-31. 2 vols.
Swan River and King George's Sound, Journals of Expeditions to. 129-382.

Tagart, (E.), Life of Capt. P. Heywood.
Tegoborski, Conséquences éventuelles de la Decouverte des Gîtes Aurifères en Californie et en Australie.
Train (G. F.), American Merchant in Europe, Asia, and Australia.
Ungewitter (Dr. L. H.), der Welttheil Australien.
Vines (F.), The Cue to Prosperity, or Our Lands and How to get at them.
——— A Glorious Future for Australia.
Visit to the Antipodes, with Reminiscences of Australia.
Visit to Australia and the Gold Regions. Ch. K. Society.
Voyage aux Terres Australes. 187-16. 6 vols. 4to.
Waghorn, on Emigration to Australia on the broadest principles.
Wakefield (E. G.), View of the Art of Colonisation.
Warfield, Australia.
Waithen (E.), Viage a las Tierras Australes. Madrid, 1778. 4 vols.
Wells (W. H.), Gazetteer of Australia.
West Australian Association Reports.
Western Australia, Report on Present State of the Colony. Perth.
Western Australia, Journals of several Expeditions to. 1829-32.
Western Australia, with a map.
Westgarth (W.), Report on the Condition, Capabilities, and Prospects of the Australian Aborigines.
What should Government do for Australia?
Wheeler (D.), Letters and Journal; Australasia.
Witsen, on New Guinea, &c., *in Dutch.*
——— Migration of Mankind. ,, Amst. 17.
Young (R.), Wesleyan Religious Deputation to Australia.

VICTORIA.

A'Beckett, (Sir W.), Judgments of the Supreme Court of New South Wales, Melbourne, 1847.
——— Magistrate's Manual. Melbourne, 1852.
——— Out of Harness.
A'Beckett (T. T.), The Gold and the Government.
——— Defence of State Aid to Religion.
Aboriginal Inhabitants of Victoria, Plea on behalf of.
Adamson (T.), Acts and Ordinances in Force in Victoria.
Akhurst (W. M.), Mirror of Beauty—a Burlesque Extravaganza.
Aldwell (J. A.), Prize Essay of the Melbourne Labor League.
Allan (J.), Contractor for Castlemaine, Letter to Legislative Council.
Am Fur Ghaidical, a Gaelic Periodical.
Amsinck (Lieut.), Docks and Harbor Accommodation.
——— a Backwoodsman's Essays on Internal Communication.
Archer (W. H.), Statistical Register of Victoria.
Argus Libel case, Queen *v.* Wilson and Mackinnon.
——— The Editor of—a Sketch reprinted from the Express.
——— Anatomy of the Argus, by Caustic.
——— ——— ——— Examined.
——— Enquiry into the Principles of Representation.
Aristides, Correspondence with Lieut. Governor respecting Aborigines.
Arm Chair, The.
Australia Felix, Monthly Magazine.
Ballingall (J.), Shipwrecks, their Causes and Means of Prevention.
Bank, The People's, Prospectus of.
Becker (L.), The Men of Victoria.
Best (A. T.), Essay on the Eight Hours' Question.
Blandowski (W. von), Personal Observations in Victoria.
Bounty Immigration, Letter to the Legislative Council, &c.
Bonwick (J.), Discovery of Port Phillip.

Bonwick (J.), Notes of a Gold Digger.
——— W. Buckley and his Port Phillip Black Friends.
——— Early Days of Melbourne.
Brough (Rev. G. M.), Address to Members of the Church of England.
Cairns (Dr. A.), Dangers and Duties of Young Men of Victoria.
——— New Year's Sermon. Death of Sir Charles Hotham.
——— Inauguration of Political Independence of Victoria.
——— Church and State.
Campbell (C.), Remarks on National Education.
Carr (J. E.), Lecture on the New Constitution.
Chinese Question, The, Analysed. By one who knows them.
Church of England Record. Diocese of Melbourne.
Civil Engineers, Victorian Institution of—Proposed Bye Laws.
Clarke (A.), Raw Gold and Sovereigns—Free Trade in Money.
Clutterbuck (J. B.), Port Phillip in 1849.
Collingwood East, Reports of Municipal Council of.
Colonial Gems, or the Ninety. By a Gumleaf.
Colonial Reform Association, Rules, &c., of the.
Co-operative Freehold Land Investment Society, Rules and Report.
Corbett (F. A.), Railway Economy in Victoria.
Coster (F.), Land System for Victoria.
Council, Legislative, Catalogue of Library of the.
County Courts Act.
Davitt (A.), Origin and Progress of the National System of Education.
Dobie (W.) Visit to Port Phillip.
Electors, Handbook for.
Electors of Victoria, Letter to, on State Education. By a Schoolmaster.
Exhibition, Melbourne, 1854. Paris, 1855. Instructions for Committee.
Farm Society, Evangelistic. Temperance and Educational.
Fawkner (J. P.), Proposed Marriage Act. 1857.
Fellows (T. H.), Common Law Practice Act. Melbourne, 1856.
Fellows (T. H.), The New Constitution of Victoria.
Financial System. Addressed to the People of Victoria.
Foster (J. F. L.), The New Colony of Victoria.
——— Speech on Immigration.
——— Three Letters to Hon. J. F. Palmer.
——— Fourth Letter to do.
Free Church, The. Narrative.
Geelong, Water Supply to.
——— Report of Committee of Harbor Trust.
——— Historic Sketch of Christ Church, Geelong.
Gipps Land, Progress of Discovery in.
Glass (C. E.), Miner's Companion.
——— Road Guide to the Gold Fields.
Gold Digger's Magazine.
Gold in Victoria, by Colonus.
Gold Era of Victoria, by a Melbourne Merchant.
Gregory (J. H.), Letter on Church Music.
Griffith (C.), Present State of Port Phillip District.
——— on Water Supply of Melbourne.
Hamon (A.), Can all the Gold be extracted from the Quartz ?
Harris (H.), The Chinese in Victoria.
Haydon (G. H.), Five Years' Experience in Australia Felix.
——— The Australian Emigrant.
Hearn, (Prof.), The Primary School.
Hellicar (V.), Coin and Currency.
Hippocrates at Abdera, dedicated to C. J. Latrobe.
Hovell and Humes' Statement of Facts connected with Overland Expedition to Port Phillip. 1824-5. Edited by Rev. W. Ross.
How the Money goes, or the State Aid Question examined.
Howitt, (W.), Land, Labor, and Gold, or Two Years in Victoria. 2 vols.
——— Tallangetta, the Squatter's Home. 2 vols.
Hughes Wharf, Correspondence between Government and W. Hughes.
Hughes (D. A.), Statement of Facts respecting Wharf Premises.

Just (P.), Employment of Painting and Sculpture.
Kentish (N. L.), Proposals for establishing, in Melbourne, a Victoria Sheep and Cattle Assurance Company.
—— Question of Questions. Making Food Cheap, &c.
—— Treatise on Penal Discipline.
—— Valedictory Letter on leaving Melbourne.
Kerr's Melbourne Almanack and Port Phillip Directory.
Land and Labor in Victoria, by an old Colonist.
Land Question, a new Idea on. A Letter to C. J. LaTrobe.
Lang (J. D.), Condition and Prospects of Port Phillip.
—— (G. D.) and F. L. Drake, Abstract of Evidence in Trial of.
Laughing a Crime, or £20 no Comedy. By a Gold Digger.
Law Reform, Report of Meeting at Geelong on.
Lindsay (H. L.), Industrial Resources of Victoria.
Lucas (H.), Journal of a Voyage from London to Port Phillip.
McCombie (T.), History of Victoria.
Macardy (J.), Money, Where shall I Deposit it ?
MacEachern, (J.), The Dynasty of La Trobe and Foster Illustrated.
—— Manifesto of the Democratic League.
Madison (J. W.), Victorian Prophecy of the End of the World.
Martin (J.) and G. Milsted, Correct Report of the Case of the Trustees of Hodge *v.* Jamieson.
Melbourne Directory, The.
—— Bradshaw.
—— Benevolent Asylum Annual Reports.
—— Chamber of Commerce, Reports of.
—— Report on Promotion of Agriculture.
—— Hospital, Annual Report.
—— Ladies' Benevolent Society, Reports.
—— Union Benefit Society, Articles, &c.
—— Public Library, Catalogue of.
—— Mechanics' Institution, Reports.
—— and East Bourke, Horse and Cattle Stealing Prevention Society, Rules, &c.
—— Letter to the Citizens of, by a Fellow Citizen.
—— Orphan Asylum, Reports.
—— Exhibition in connexion with Paris Exhibition, Catalogue.
—— Monthly Magazine.
—— and Collingwood City Mission Reports.
—— Gas and Coke Company, Deed of Settlement of.
—— Young Men's Mutual Improvement Association, Rules, &c.
—— —— Church of England Society, Reports.
Morgan, Life and Adventures of W. Buckley in Victoria.
Mossman (S.), Railways in Victoria.
Murray (R. D.), Summer at Port Phillip.
Nixon (F. H.), The Chinese Puzzle Adjusted.
Oldham (T.) and T. E. Rawlinson, Treatise on Railways and Harbor Accommodation for Victoria.
Parker (G. E. S.), The Aborigines of Victoria—a Lecture.
Pastoral Tenants of the Crown in Victoria, Statement of the case of.
—— —— Opinions of the Council on the Right of.
Perry (C., Bp. of Melbourne), Sermon preached upon Landing at Port Phillip.
Petitions of the District of Port Phillip for Separation from the Territory of New South Wales.
Pollard (N. W.), Prize Essay on Internal Communication.
Port Phillip, Report, Commercial, General, and Statistical of.
—— Farmers' Society, Transactions.
—— and Colonial Gold Mining Campany, Reports.
—— Supreme Court, General Rules. 1844.
Prahran Mechanics Institution, Rules of.
Price (John), Biographical Memoir of.
Raffaelo (C.) The Eureka Stockade.
Registrar General's Report on the Statistics of Victoria. 1851-8.

Richmond Volunteer Fire Brigade, Report.
Rusden (G. W.), The Old Road to Responsible Govertment.
Shillinglaw (J. J.), Australian Shipmasters' Guide.
Skinner (C. B.), Acts, Rules, &c., in Insolvency for Victoria.
Snowball (J.), Correspondence of the Government of Victoria, &c.
Squatting Orders, Locking up the Lands, &c.,
State-Aid Question, The, by a Scotch Catholic.
Stephen (Sir G.), Systems of English Bankruptcy and Colonial compared.
Stoney (Capt. H.B.), Victoria, including an account of the Ballaarat Disturbances.
Talbot (Susan), Poems.
Tracts for Electors at Stirring Times.
Tuckey (J. H.), Voyage to Establish a Colony at Port Phillip.
Verdon (G. F.), The Present and Future of Municipal Government in Victoria.
Victoria Illustrated, a Series of Views.
——— as she is and as she may be.
——— Guide to the Gold Fields of.
——— How to settle in.
——— Supreme Court of, Catalogue of Library of.
——— Bible Society, Reports.
——— Convention, Resolutions and Proceedings of.
——— Exhibition of Art, Dec., 1856, Catalogue of.
——— Industrial Society, Catalogues of Annual Exhibitions.
——— Philosophical Institute, Transactions.
——— Institute for Advancement of Science, Transactions.
——— National Education Commissioners, Reports.
——— Religious Tract Society. Reports.
——— Total Abstinence Convention, Proceedings of.
——— Turf Club, Rules and Regulations of.
——— Tent and Cottage Sermons.
——— Commercial and Nautical Almanack.
——— Mining Institute, Transactions of.
——— Acts and Ordinances.
——— Government Gazette, 1854 to 1858.
——— Votes and Proceedings of the Legislature. 1851-57.
Victorian Hansard.
——— Electors' Guide, or the Black and White List.
Waifs and Strays of Sea Life, or Adventures between Liverpool and Melbourne.
Wathen (G. H.), Victoria in 1854.
Wealth, the Way to. Dedicated to all true Victorians. By Junius.
Wekey (S.) The Land, with reference to the Cultivation of the Vine.
Wesleyan Schools, Statement, &c., with Government respecting.
Westgarth (W.), Australia Felix, or Historical Account of Port Phillip.
——— ——— Victoria—late Australia Felix.
——— Victoria and the Australian Gold Mines in 1857.
——— Reports on the Condition of Victoria since the Discovery of Gold.
——— Commerce and Statistics of Victoria since the commencement.
Wilkie (Dr.), Failure of the Yan Yean Reservoir.
Willis (Judge), Charge on opening the Criminal Session for Port Phillip, 1842.
Wood (J. D.), The Gold Fields Act, a Practical Explanation.
Woolley (R.), Four Letters to Legislative Council on Railways.
——— Letter to the Speaker and Legislative Assembly.

NEW SOUTH WALES.

Aboriginal Natives of New South Wales, Remarks on Origin, &c., of, by a Magistrate.
Arden's Sydney Magazine.
Acts and Ordinances.
Atkinson (J.), The Agriculture of New South Wales.
Baker (C. J.), Visit to Sydney and Melbourne.
Balfour (J. F.), Sketch of New South Wales.
Bannister (Saxe), New South Wales.
Barrington (G.), Voyage to New South Wales, with a Detail of his Life &c., 2 vols.
Bennett (G.), Wanderings in New South Wales. 1832-4. 2 vols.
Boyd (B.), on Transferring the unemployed Labor in Van Diemen's Land to New South Wales.
Braim (T.H.), History of New South Wales. 2 vols.
Breton (Lieut.), Excursions in New South Wales, Western Australia, and Van Diemen's Land.
Burton (W. W.), State of Religion and Education in New South Wales.
Busby (J.), Authentic Information relative to New South Wales.
Callaghan (T.), Acts and Ordinances of the Governor and Council of New South Wales.
Collins (D.), The English Colony in New South Wales, from 1788 to 1801 2 vols. 4to.
——— Second Edition Abridged. 1 vol. 4to.
Cunningham (P.), Two Years in New South Wales. 2 vols.
Dangart (H.), Index Directory of Hunter River, New South Wales.
Debate in the Legislative Council of New South Wales on Immigration to the Colony. Sydney, 1840.
Dixon (S.), Voyage to New South Wales.
Dredge (J.), Brief Notices of the Aborigines of New South Wales, including Port Phillip.
Field (B.). Geographical Memoir of New South Wales.
Government Gazette.
Grant (J.), Voyage of Discovery to New South Wales. 4to. 1803.
Harris (A.), Guide to Port Stephens, the Colony of the Australia Agri-u cultural Company.
Hall (E. S.), State of New South Wales, Dec., 1830.
Heads of the People, New South Wales.
Henderson (J.). Excursions in New South Wales. 2 vols.
——— Observations on New South Wales and Van Diemen's Land.
Hunter (Capt. J.), Historical Journal at Port Jackson. 1787-92. 4to.
King, the Settlement of Port Jackson. London. 1789.
Lang (Dr.), Letter to Lord Stanley occasioned by Observations of Sir. G. Gipps.
Lang (Dr. J.D.), History of New South Wales. 2 vols.
Legislative Council Votes and Proceedings.
Letter from Sydney. Edited by Gouger.
Letters, Collection of, for a History of New South Wales. 2 vols.
Lhotskey (Dr. J.), Journey from Sydney to the Australian Alps.
McCombie (T.), Arabin, Adventures of a Colonist in New South Wales.
Macarthur (J.), State of Prospects of New South Wales. 1837.
Maclehose, Picture of Sydney, and New South Wales Guide.
Munn (D. D.), Present State of New South Wales, 1811.
——— Emigrants' Guide to Port Stephen's.
Mansfield (R.), Analytical View of the Census of New South Wales, for 1841, and for 1846.
Majoribanks (A.), Travels in New South Wales.
Meredith (Mrs.), Residence in New South Wales. 1839-44.
Mudie (J.) Felonry of New South Wales, Life in Botany Bay, &c.

New South Wales. Its Condition by a Twelve Years' Resident.
——— and its dependent Settlement in Van Diemen's Land.
——— its Present and Future Prospects submitted to his Majesty and Parliament.
——— its Past, Present, and Future Condition.
——— by the Hermit in Australia.
——— and its dependent Settlements, historical account of—in illustration of twelve engravings by W. Preston, a Convict, from drawings by Capt. Wallis. 1821 folio.
O'Harra, History of New South Wales.
Osborne (A.), Notes on New South Wales.
Oxley (J.), Journals of Two Expeditions into the Interior of New South Wales. 1817-18.
——— Historical Account of the Colony of New South Wales, and its Dependencies.
Pack (B. C.), Recollections of Sydney.
Phillip (Governor), Voyage to Botany Bay, with an Account of the Establishment of the Colonies at Port Jackson and Norfolk Island.
——— Letters to Lord Sydney.
Postscript to the Tract for the Times, addressed to the Laity of New South Wales.
Reid (T.), Voyages to New South Wales.
Southampton to Sydney.
Strzelecki (P. E. de), Physical Description of New South Wales and Van Diemen's Land.
Sydney, Magazine of Science and Art.
Sydney, Letter from, edited by Gouger.
Teggs Magazine.
Tench (Capt. W.), Account of the Settlement of Port Jackson.
——— Narrative of the Expedition to Botany Bay.
Thompson (E. D.), Speeches on first and second reading of Bill for Dividing the Colony into Electoral Districts. 1851.
Townsend (J. P.), Rambles in New South Wales.
Trevelyan (W. C.), Description of New South Wales.
Tuckey (J.), Voyage to establish a Colony at Port Phillip.
Waghorn (Lieut. T.), Steam Navigation from Singapore to Port Jackson.
Wild's (R.), Life of Sir J. Franklyn. 2 vols.
Wentworth (W. C.) Description of New South Wales. 2. vols.
Westgarth, (W.) Remarks on Royal Mint at Sydney.
White (J.), Journal of a Voyage to New South Wales.
Witte (J.), Voyage to New South Wales. 1787-8-9.
Wreck of the Dunbar, Narrative of the.

SOUTH AUSTRALIA.

Acts and Ordinances.
Allen (J.), South Australian Almanac.
——— Journal of an Experimental Trip by the "Lady Augusta" up the Murray.
Angas (G. F.), Illustrations of South Australia. Folio.
Bennett (J. F.), Historical and Descriptive Account of South Australia.
Capper, (H.), South Australia.
Chauncey (W. S.), Guide to South Australia.
Clara Morrison, or South Australia during the Gold Fever. 2 vols.
Correspondence relative to the Dismissal of the Original South Australian Commissioners.
Duncan (Dr. H.), Account of the Colony of South Australia.
Dutton (F.), Account of South Australia and its Mines.
Finance, Minute and Estimate of Expenditure. 1844. Adelaide.
Gouger (R.), South Australia. 1837-8.

Government Gazette.
James (F. H.), Residence in South Australia.
Lee (F.), Sailing Directions for South Australia.
Legislative Council, Votes and Proceedings of.
Leigh (W. H.), Voyages and Travels in South Australia. 1836-8.
Napier (C. J.), Colonisation in South Austra'ia.
Reminiscences of a Sojourn in South Australia.
Reports of the Colonisation Commissioners for South Australia.
Scottt (T.), Description of South Australia.
South Australia, How to Settle and succeed in. By a Bushman.
——— ——— a Description of. C. Knight.
——— ——— in 1844-5.
——— ——— The Great South Land, or four papers on Emigration.
South Australian, Milunga, and North Arm Company, Prospectus.
——— ——— Record.
South Australia, Letter to the small Farmers and Peasantry of the United Kingdom, on the Advantages of Emigration to South Australia.
Stephens (J.), History of the Rise and Progress of South Australia.
——— Sanitary Reforms, delivered at Adelaide. 1849.
——— Exposure of T. H. James' South Australia.
Statistical Returns of South Australia, 1845-54.
Torrens (R.), Colonisation of South Australia.
Watson (H.), South Australia, a Lecture delivered at Chichester.
Wilkinson, (G. B), Working Man's Handbook to South Australia.
——— South Australia, its Advantages and its Resources.

NEW ZEALAND.

Acts of Assembly.
Adams (C. W.), Spring in the Canterbury Settlement.
Angas, (G. F.), Illustrations of New Zealand. Folio.
Bidwell (J.), Rambles in New Zealand.
Brees (S. C.), Illustrations of New Zealand.
Bridges (W.), New Zealand and Ireland.
Bright (J.), History of New Zealand, for Emigrants.
British Colonisation of New Zealand. 1837. Parker.
Brodie (W.), Past and Present State of New Zealand. 1845.
Brown, (W.) New Zealand and its Aborigines.
Campbell (E. T.), New Zealand.
Canterbury, Brief Account of the Province of.
Canterbury Papers. Parker.
Canterbury Settlement. Four Illustrative Views.
Chambers' Emigrants' Manual. New Zealand.
Chamerovzow (L. A.), New Zealand; Rights of the Aborigines.
Cholmondeley, (T.), Ultima Thule, or Thoughts on New Zealand.
Constable's Miscellany, Vol. 4. Destruction of a British Vessel on Coast of New Zealand.
Cooper (J. R.), New Zealand Settler's Guide.
Cruise (R.), Journal of a Residence in New Zealand.
Dieffenbach (E.), Travels in New Zealand. 2 vols.
——— New Zealand and the New Zealanders.
Earle (A.), Residence in New Zealand, 1827.
Earp, (G. B.), Handbook for Emigrants to New Zealand.
Fitton (E. B.), New Zealand Emigrants' Guide.
Fitzroy (Capt. R.), Remarks on New Zealand. 1846.
Fox (W.), Six Colonies of New Zealand.
Government Gazette.
Grimstone (S. E.), The Southern Settlements of New Zealand.
Heapy (C.), Narrative of a Residence in New Zealand.
Hinds (S.), Official Documents relating to New Zealand.
Hursthouse (C.), New Zealand. 2 vols.
——— Account of New Plymouth.

Jameson (R. G.) Travels in New Zealand, South Australia, &c.
Lang (J. D.), New Zealand in 1839.
Legislative Council, Votes and Proceedings of.
Letters from Wanganui, New Zealand.
Letters to Settlers and Laboring Emigrants in New Zealand.
Macdonnell (T.), Observations on New Zealand.
Mackillop (H. F.), Twelve months' Service in New Zealand.
Majoribanks (A.), Travels in New Zealand.
Marshall (W. B.), Two Visits to New Zealand. 1834.
Martin (S.M.), Letters on the State of New Zealand.
Matthew (P.), Emigration Fields.
Morrell (B.), Four Voyages to the Pacific. 1822-31.
——— (Mrs.), Narrative of a Voyage to the Pacific.
New Plymouth, Information respecting Settlement of.
New Zealand Handbook for, by a Magistrate.
——— Portfolio, Edited by H. S. Chapman.
——— a Summer's Excursion in.
——— British Colonisation of. Aborigines Protection Society.
——— Association Reports.
——— Company's Reports.
——— and its People.
——— a Poem.
New Zealanders, The, addressed to Earl Grey.
——— Library of Entertaining Knowledge.
Nicholas (J. L.), Voyage to New Zealand. 1814-15. 2 vols.
Paul (R. B.), Account of Canterbury Settlement.
Petre (H. W.), Settlements of the New Zealand Company.
Polack (J. S.), New Zealand, Travels in that Country. 1831-7. 2 vols.
——— Manners and Customs of the New Zealanders. 2 vols.
Power, (W. T.), Sketches in New Zealand, with Pen and Pencil.
Representatives, House of, Votes and Proceedings of.
Ritter (C.), Colonization of New Zealand. From the German.
Rochfort (J.), Surveyor in New Zealand.
Savage (J.), Account of New Zealand, 1807.
Shortland (E.), Southern Districts of New Zealand described.
——— Traditions and Superstitions of the New Zealanders.
Supreme Court of New Zealand, Rules of.
——— Procedure Commission, Reports.
Swainson (W.), Lectures on the New Zealanders.
——— Account of Auckland.
——— on the Climate of New Zealand.
Terry (C.), New Zealand, its Advantages and Prospects as a British Colony.
Tucker, Southern Cross, or Gospel in New Zealand.
Wade (W. R.), Journey to the Northern Island of New Zealand.
Wakefield (E. J.), Adventure in New Zealand, 1839-44. 2 vols.
——— Illustrations to ditto. Folio.
Ward (J.), Information relative to New Zealand.
Webb (Mrs.), New Zealand Pilgrims.
Wilson (Mrs. R.), New Zealand and other Poems.
Wood (Lieut. J.), New Zealand and its Claimants.
——— Twelve months in New Zealand.
Yate (W.), Account of New Zealand.

TASMANIA.

Acts of Council.
Bent (A.), Michael Howe, the last and worst of the Bushrangers.
——— Appeal to Australasian Public for Relief for A. Bent.
Bischoff (Jas.), Sketch of History of Van Diemen's Land.
Bonwick (J.), The Bushrangers, illustrating the Early Days of V. D. Land.

Curr (E.), Account of Van Diemen's Land.
Declaration of Minister of Church of England in Van Diemen's Land.
Dixon (J.), Van Diemen's Land as place of Emigration.
Denison (Sir W.), Information regarding the Colony of Van Diemen's Land.
——— Drainage and Sewerage of Towns.
Derwent Star and Van Diemen's Land Intelligencer.
Evans (G. W.), Description of Van Diemen's Land.
Frankland (G.), Van Diemen's Land Survey to the end of Colonel Arthur's Government.
Fry (H. P.), Penal Discipline, with Report on Treatment of Prisoners in Van Diemen's Land.
Franklin (Sir J.), Narrative of some Passages in the History of Van Diemen's Land.
Godwin, Guide to Van Diemen's Land.
Goodrige (C. M.), Voyage to South Seas, and Eighteen Years' Residence in Van Diemen's Land.
Hermit in Van Diemen's Land.
Jeffreys (C. H.), Delineations of Van Diemen's Land.
Hull (H. M.), Guide to Tasmania.
Kemp (E), a Voice from Tasmania.
Knox (J.), Poetic Trifles.
Leakey (C.), Lyra Australis; Poems written in Tasmania.
Lhotsky (Dr. J.), Sketches of Tasman's Peninsula.
Gellibrand (J. T.), Proceedings in the case of.
Loch, on the System of Education pursued in Van Diemen's Land.
Melville (H.), Van Diemen's Land Almanack.
Meredith (Mrs.), Nine Years in Tasmania. 2 vols.
Morgan, Municipal Act of Van Diemen's Land, 1852, with Observations.
Murray (R. L.), Appeal to the British Nation.
Parker (H. W.), Rise, Progress and State of Van Diemen's Land.
Prinsep (A.), Journal of a Voyage from Calcutta to Van Diemen's Land.
Royal Society of Van Diemen's Land, Papers and Proceedings of.
——— ——— Rules of, as altered, Feb. 9, 1854.
Smith (W. S.), Van Diemen's Land, Past, Present and Future, a Lecture.
Savory, Quintus Servinton, a tale. 3 vols.
Statistics of Van Diemen's Land, 1828-49. 6 vols., folio.
Stoney (Capt. H. B.), Residence in Tasmania.
Tasmanian Society for Diffusion of Useful Knowledge, Rules, &c.
Van Diemen's Land, Observations on, London 1801.
——— Emigrants' Guide to.
——— History of, 1824-35.
——— Annual. Edited by Dr. Ross.
——— Rise, Progress and Present of.
West (J.), History of Tasmania. 2 vols.
Widowson (H.), State of Van Diemen's Land.
Year in Tasmania.

VOYAGES ROUND THE WORLD.

(Containing matter relative to Australia.)

Arago (J.), Narrative of a Voyage round the World in the Uranie and Physicienne Corvettes, commanded by Capt. Freycinet, 1817-20.
Bligh (W.), Voyage to the South Seas.
Bougainville, Navigation autour du Globe de la Frégate Thétis et de la Corvette l'Esperance, 1824-6. 3 vols.
——— Album Pittoresque, par Vicomte de la Touanne. Folio.
Cook (Capt. James), Voyages. 8 vols.
D'Entrecasteaux (B.), Voyage à la Recherches de la Perouse.
Delapert (E.), Voyages dans les deux Oceans, Atlantique et Pacifique, 1844-7.
Dupersey, Voyage de la Coquille, 1822-5. 6 vols.

D'Urville (D.), Voyage de la Corvette Astrolabe, 1826-9. 19 vols.
Fitzroy (Capt. R.), Narrative of the Surveying Voyages of H. M. S. Adventure and Beagle, 1826-36. 4 vols.
Forster (G.), Voyage round the World, 1772-75. 2 vols.
Freycinet (L. de), Voyage autour du Monde, sous le commandement du Capt. Baudin.
Gerstaecker (F.), Journey round the World. 3 vols.
Hamilton (G.), Voyage round the World in the ship Pandora, 1791.
Holman (J.), Voyage round the World, 1827-32. 4 vols.
Jukes (J. B.), Voyage of H. M. S. Fly in Torres Straits. New Guinea, &c., 1842-6. 2 vols.
Labillardiere's Voyage in search of La Pérouse, 1791-4.
Perouse (J. F. G. de la), Voyage round the World, 1785-8. 2 vols., with atlas, folio.
Peyron, Voyage de Deconvertes aux Terres Australes, 1800-4.
Rochon, Voyages aux Indes Orientales, &c.
Ross (Sir J. C.) Voyage in the Southern and Antartic Regions, 1839-43.
Schouten (W. C.), Voyage through the Great South Sea. From the Dutch.
Turnbull, Voyage in which he visited Botany Bay and Norfolk Island.
Vancouver (Capt. G.), Voyage of Discovery to the North Pacific Ocean. 6 vols.
Wilkes (C.), Narrative of the United States Exploring Expedition, 1838-42. 5 vols.
Wilson (T. B.), Narrative of a Voyage round the World, 1828.

COLLECTIONS OF VOYAGES.

(Containing matter relative to Australia.)

Account of several late Voyages towards the Straits of Magellan, New Holland, &c., by J. Narborough, J. Tasman, &c.
Burney (Capt. J.), Chronological History of the Discoveries in the South Seas. 5 vols., 4to.
Callander (J.), Terra Australis Cognita, or Voyages to Terra Australis during 16th, 17th and 18th centuries. 3 vols.
Dalrymple (A.), Collection concerning Papua, &c.
Dalrymple (A.), Historical Collection of Voyages in South Pacific, being chiefly a literal translation from the Spanish and Dutch writers. 2 vols., 4to.
Dampier (Capt. W.), Voyages and Descriptions.
Dutch E. I. Company, Voyages undertaken by. London, 1703.
Edinburgh Cabinet Library. 38 vols.
Geographical Society, Journal of the Royal.
Hakluyt Society, the Publications of the.
Harris (J.), Collection of Voyages and Travels. 2 vols, folio.
Histoire des Navigations aux Terres Australis. Paris, 1756. 2 vols., 4to.
Kerr's General History and Collection of Voyages. 18 vols.
Pinkerton (John), General Collection of the best and most interesting Voyages and Travels. 17 vols.
Prévost (Abbé), Histoire Generale des Voyages. 20 vols.
Purchas (Samuel), His Pilgrims. 5 vols, folio.
Rochon (A. M.), Voyages aux Indes Orientales, &c.
Shipwrecks and Disasters at Sea. 3 vols.
Spitbergen et Le Maire Miroir Oost and West Indical. Amst., 4to. 1621,
Struyck (N.), Miscellaneous Tracts. Amst., 1753.
Thevenot (M.), Relation de Divers Voyages curieux.
Tuckey (J. H.), Maritime Geography and Statistics.
Valentyn (F.), Beschryving van Oude and Niewe Oost Indieu. Amst., 1726. 8 vols., folio.

NATURAL HISTORY, &c., OF AUSTRALIA.

Brown (R.), Prodromus Floræ N. Hollandiæ et Insulæ Van Diemen.
——— Supplementum Prodromi Novæ Hollandiæ.
Bunce (D.), Australian Manual of Horticulture.
Busby (J.), Visit to Vineyards of Spain and France, forming a Guide to the Culture of the Vine in Australia.
Catalogue of the Natural and Industrial Products of New South Wales.
Darwin (C.), Voyage of a Naturalist.
Donovan (E,), Natural History of the Insects of New Holland, &c.
Earl (G. W.), Native Races of the Indian Archipelago.
Forster (G.), Florulæ Insularum Australium Prodromus.
Fitton (W. H.) Geological Specimens from the Coast of Australia.
Forster (J. and G.), Characteres Plantarum quas ad Insulas Maris Australis collegerunt, 1772-5.
Geological Society, Transactions of.
——— Quarterly Journal of the.
Endlicher (Dr.), Novarum Stirpium Decades.
——— Stirpium Australasicarum herbarii Hugel. Dec. III.
Gould (J.), The Birds of Australia and Supplement.
——— The Mammals of Australia.
——— Introduction to the Birds of Australia.
Guillemin Icones Plantarum Australasiæ Rariorum.
Hannaford, Jottings in Australia.
Harvey (W. H.), Sea Weeds of the Southern Ocean.
Hobbs (W.), Elaiopathy: Administration of the Oil of the Dugong, a lecture.
Hooker (J. D.), Flora of Tasmania.
——— ——— New Zealand.
Hooker (W. J.), Botanical Miscellany.
Hugel (Baro de), Enumeratio Plantarum quas in N. Hollandiæ orâ Austro-occidentali ad fluvium Cygnorum Collegit.
Johnson (A. K.), Physical Atlas.
Jukes (J. B.), Sketch of the Physical Structure of Australia.
Kilgour (J.), Effect of the Climate of Australia on Foreign Constitutions.
King (Captain P. P.), Abstract from a Meteorological Journal kept at Port Stephens, New South Wales, 1843-7.
Labillardiere (J. J.), N. Hollandiæ Plantarum Specimen. 2 vols.
Latham (R. G.), Ethnology of the British Colonies and Dependencies.
Lewin (J. W.), Natural History of the Birds of New South Wales.
——— ——— Lepidopterous Insects of New South Wales.
Lindley (J.), Sketch of the Vegetation of the Swan River. (Bot. Reg., vol. 23.)
M'Coy (F.), On the Formation of Museums in Victoria.
Meston (R.), Prize Essay on the Catarrh in Australian Sheep.
Meteorology, Observations made at the Observatory, Hobarton, and by the Antartic Expedition, 1841, with Abstracts of the Observations 1841-48.
Mackenna (J. W.), Mortality of Children in Victoria.
Meteorological Observers in Victoria, Instructions for.
Magnetic Observations—are they as useful as necessary? By a Civil Engineer.
Mueller (Dr. F.), Fragmenta Phytographiæ Australiæ.
Nicol (W.), On Fossil Woods from Newcastle, New South Wales.
Notes on the Distribution of Gold throughout the World.
Priess (L.), Enumeratio Plantarum quas in Australasiâ Annis 1838-41, collegit. 2 vols.
Pritchard (H.), Researches into the Physical History of Man. 5 vols.
Sabine (Col.), Astronomical Observations at Hobarton.
Shaw (G.), Zoology of New Holland.
Sinclair (J.), Gardeners' Magazine.
Smith (Sir J. E.), Correspondence of Linnæus and other Naturalists. 2 vols.
——— Specimen of the Botany of New Holland.
Smith and Adamson, the Australian Gardener.
Southey (T.), Treatise on Sheep, addressed to the Flockmasters of Australia.

Suttor (G.), Culture of the Vine and Orange in Australia.
Sweet (R.), Flora Australasica.
Tasmanian Journal of Natural Science, &c. 3 vols.
Van Diemen's Land, Transactions of the Royal Society of.
Victorian Agricultural and Horticultural Gazette.

WORKS ON ETHNOLOGY, LANGUAGES, &c., OF AUSTRALIA.

Australia, Aborigines of. Swan River, 1836.
Bunce (D.), Language of the Aborigines of Victoria and other Australian Districts.
Coates (D.), Rev. W. Beecham and Rev. W. Ellis, Evidence on Aborigines.
D'Eichthal (G.), Etudes sur l'Histoire des Races Océaniennes.
——— sur l'Histoire Primitive des Races Océaniennes.
Ellis (Rev. W.), Polynesian Researches.
Grey (G.), Vocabulary of the Dialect of South-west Australia.
——— Mythology of the New Zealanders.
——— Poetry of the New Zealanders.
——— Proverbial and Popular Sayings of the Ancestors of New Zealanders.
——— Library of Philology, vol. 2, part 1. Languages of Australia.
Hale (W.), Ethnography and Philology of U. S. Expedition, 1838-42.
Kednall (T.), New Zealand Grammar and Vocabulary.
Logan (J. R.), Journal of the Indian Archipelago and Eastern Asia.
Meyer (H.), Vocabulary of the Aborigines of South Australia.
Meinicke (C. E.), das Festland Australien.
Milligan (J.), Vocabulary of the Dialects of Aboriginal Tribes of Tasmania.
Mitchell (Sir T.), History of the Boomerang.
Moore (G. F.), Vocabulary of Western Australia.
New Zealand Grammar and Vocabulary, 1820.
Nind (S.), Vocabulary of St. George's Sound.
Schurmann (C. H.), Vocabulary of Pamkalla Language.
Spruner (Dr. C.), Historisch Geographischer Hand Atlas. 3 vols.
Threlkeld (L. E.), Key to the Aboriginal Language.
Tiechelman (C. T.) and C. W. Schürman, Outline of a Grammar and Vocabulary of the Aboriginal Language of South Australia.
Williams (W.), Vocabulary of the Adelaide Aborigines.
——— New Zealand Grammar and Vocabulary.

COLONIAL PUBLICATIONS

Printed and Published at the office of this HANDBOOK, 78, *Collins-street East, Melbourne:—*

CRICKETERS' GUIDE FOR AUSTRALASIA. Compiled by W. Fairfax. Demy 12mo, 2s. 6d., annually. With Frontispiece.
BRADSHAW'S GUIDE TO VICTORIA, with Map of Melbourne and Suburbs. Compiled by W. Fairfax. Demy 12mo, monthly, 6d.
VICTORIAN HANSARD.—The Debates and Proceedings of both Houses of Legislature.—Sessions I and II. Octavo, two volumes, half bound, now ready.
SOUTHERN SPECTATOR MAGAZINE, monthly. BAPTIST MAGAZINE, monthly.
FACTS AND FIGURES, monthly. VICTORIAN PRICES CURRENT, monthly.

CPSIA information can be obtained
at www.ICGtesting.com
Printed in the USA
LVHW101943050123
736480LV00003B/100

9 783375 128852